TRANSCENDENT

EDITED BY

ANTHONY S. BUONI & ALISHA COSTANZO

TRANSCENDENT
Transmundane Press, LLC | www.transmundanepress.com
Editor-in-Chief & Co-Publisher: Alisha Chambers
Content Editor & Co-Publisher: Anthony S. Buoni

ISBN-13: 978-1-948309-91-2
ISBN-10: 1-948309-91-2
Worldwide Rights
Created in the United States of America

Editors: Anthony S. Buoni & Alisha Costanzo
Cover Design: Dean Samed
Interior Layout: Alisha Chambers

DEDICATION

For Jason. You continuously inspire my creativity and keep me moving in the right direction. ~Alisha

To my mentors, Lynn Wallace and Michael Lister, for daring me to follow my dreams. ~Anthony

Dear Gill
Thankyou
for all thy
management

Kes AW
'19

CONTENTS

TABLE OF CONTENTS

TABLE OF CONTENTS

TABLE OF CONTENTS

ACKNOWLEDGMENTS

First, thank you to all of our wonderful contributors. This collection was an amazing project to work on, and you made the process fun. We hope you are as proud of this collection as we are.

Also, discovering more about you and your stories through the progression of guest writing and interviews produced some serious cosmic connections.

Second, thank you to Dean Samed for creating this stunning cover and so completely nailing the themes in the book.

Third, thank you to Will Jacques for the custom border for our cover page and wonderful artwork. Their tales fit in perfectly.

Finally, thank you to all of our Kickstarter backers. A new goal achieved. A new dream reached.

THE ASTRONAUT'S GHOST
Ken McGrath

I was nine when I saw the astronaut's ghost out by Purcell's farm, near the hay barn where my brother Jack died. But it wasn't him I saw that night.

I was grounded at the time because of some trouble I'd gotten into at school. Basically, I'd unspooled all the bog roll I could find right into one of the toilet bowls and flushed. I don't even remember why I did it. Probably boredom.

Funny thing is though, I'll never forget the shock of seeing it backing up and flooding the place. Water just kept rising and rising, pouring over the edge. It just kept coming, splashing all over my shiny new Clarkes, and me thinking, *Mam is going to kill me for getting my shoes wet.*

You know that feeling you've probably only gotten as a kid? When you're in real, proper trouble, where your stomach just knots, your fingers go tingly, and you're about to pee fire? That was exactly how I felt standing there, unable to stop what I'd started.

Mam double-barreled as me as soon as she got me out of Mr. Hickey's office. She didn't even wait to get me home first. Just started, right there in the school car park, with all the kids in Miss Dunne's junior infants class gawping out the window at us. Mam roaring her head off, me stood there pure embarrassed, telling me how mortified she was and that I, Elizabeth Margaret Shaw, had let her down so badly. What was I thinking? Didn't I know she played bridge with Eileen McNamara, the vice-principal? How was she supposed to show her face next week, and so on? And on.

And on.

I was only ever Elizabeth Margaret Shaw when I was in serious trouble. Otherwise, it was plain old Lizzie to the parentals and Beth to everyone else.

So, anyway, there I was, the night I saw the astronaut's ghost, having been under house arrest for more than a week with no T.V., no Internet, no nothing. You better believe, I was going mad.

And worst of all? Amy Purcell from up the road was having a sleep-over I just *had* to be at. I pure flipped out. I mean how much more trouble could I get in? That's what I thought. I climbed out the bedroom window, hopped the wall so the folks wouldn't hear the gate creaking and took off up the road to Purcell's farm as bold as brass. All nine-year-old brazen swagger on a dark country lane with not even the cows watching.

A pitch, black night in October, before the new houses were built, back when ours was actually in the countryside. And just before I came up to the Purcell's, it appeared, cutting through the darkness like a slice of white static. A ghost. It glowed but didn't cast any light, only lit itself up. Tilted its helmet to look at me, then started flashing in and out of existence, moving in these weird jerky twitches, like the girl from *The Ring* films. No noise, just a constant epileptic appearing and disappearing, the whole time pointing at its chest, at the letters above its heart. WBSIRE.

It's only now, seven years later, that I've figured out what that means. Too late, out of time.

Apparently, Amy's da found me standing in the lane by their barn, screaming my lungs out. Screaming about this ghost.

The parentals thought I'd been attacked or something much, much worse had happened. Obviously, everything checked out okay, and I think in the end, they figured I got spooked by a cow or some other animal moving about beyond in the fields, in the dark.

Back then, I used to watch a lot of old BBC shows online; *Doctor Who*, *Day of The Triffids*, *Quatermass*, loads of *Hammer Horror* movies. *Twilight Zone*, *Tales of The Unexpected*, that sort of thing; stuff I was probably far too young for. I was always drawing pictures of the monsters from them, so I reckon they thought my imagination went into overdrive, that I'd scared myself. Maybe if it was just a regular ghost I'd seen, they'd have thought it was Jack instead and believed me.

For ages after, when I'd get upset about it, Dad used to calm me down, saying it couldn't have been an astronaut's ghost. He said to become an astronaut you'd have to be a scientist like my brother Finn, who was off in America, and science doesn't believe in ghosts, only logic. That's what he'd say, and Mam'd always laugh. I tried to understand but didn't find it funny. Now that I understand things, I actually find it scary.

My parents weren't bad, not at all. They really tried, bless them, but I was a bit wild, and they were old when they had me. More often than not, I was left to my own devices. I wasn't an only child, but I may as well have been. The other three were all either dead or moved out before I even understood what brothers and sisters were.

Was I an accident? Well, Finn was seventeen when I was born, so maybe a little, but it's a bit on the harsh-side to say that, and there's no denying I was loved. Maybe, it's because of what happened to Jack that my parents were trying to work things through, to fill that void. Then, I ended up coming along.

Every now and then, some kid in school would say how I was an accident, but after I punched Michael Russell in the mouth and knocked out his two front teeth when I was seven and he was ten, no one ever repeated it. Not to my face anyway. I haven't had to throw a punch since, so it must have been a good one. Honestly, we were so young; I don't think I even understood what he was saying; I just knew it was bad and I'd had enough.

Would you believe Michael Russell actually tried to shift me last weekend when I bumped into him out in The County? Ha, no chance, fella. *Morto.*

So, maybe I was a late blessing then? Well, that's how Mam always put it. Man, she can be such a dote sometimes. Life hasn't been easy for her. When I was born, she and Dad should have been thinking more about retirement and having the house to themselves, what with Susan already moved out, Finn preparing to leave for college in America, and Jack gone. Then: surprise. All of a sudden, *slap, bang,* new daughter, and you're back buying nappies and waking up for mid-night feeds. I love them for it, but you won't catch me doing that when I'm pushing fifty. Not a hope.

Our little miracle, that's how Dad put it years later when I asked him. I was visiting him in the home. He'd gone senile by that stage. The Alzheimer's came on quickly and wiped everything out fast. He lasted just under four years once it got its claws into him. I was fifteen a week when we buried him, and I still miss him every day.

It was the year before he died when dad told me that I was his little miracle. The sentiment's nice, but the details grossed me out. Who wants to think of their parents like that? And my parents were old when they had me, don't forget. I suppose it's nice that they still fancied each other, that the love was still there, but yeah, yuck.

I bet he didn't know who he was talking to. It was one of those odd days, where he was talking fine but speaking like it was years ago, like he was out of time somehow. He sat there in his old, worn-out body, but his mind had jumped back to escape where he was now. Dad never looked at his hands when he was like that, as if he knew that seeing his old, wrinkled fingers and palms would break the spell, bring him crashing forward in time to where he didn't want to be.

I'd taken a scissors to my hair two weeks before. Cut it all off, then took dad's old beard-trimmer from the press under the sink and shaved it almost to the scalp.

"Her hair. Sweet Jesus, she looks like Sinead O'Connor." Mam actually cried when she saw it. She owned a hairdressers' inside in town, so it properly broke her heart, called me a Hair-Butcher. After a couple of weeks though, she came around to it. Used to sit beside me on the couch, running her fingers over the soft fuzz while we watched the talent shows on Sky One after dinner.

Said she enjoyed the feel of it. Then, she started complimenting my face and my high cheek bones, so of course, I had to grow it back. There's no point in rebelling if your parents give you a thumbs up for it.

I still looked a lot more boy than girl that day in the home when Dad told this story about how he had a vasectomy after the twins were born, but somehow, something must have grown back. Or there was a just a little guy in reserve waiting for a chance to get through. Personally, I didn't want to picture any of that, but it's too late to be squeamish. Either way, whatever happened, all those years and nine months later little Elizabeth Margaret Shaw arrived kicking into the world. Technically, it was eight months, and I was born by C Section, but you get where I'm going with this.

Anyway, Susan's the eldest. We never got along. I think because Mam got pregnant just after Susan left, a lot of people in town didn't believe it and thought it was Susan had gotten herself into a spot of trouble. I questioned them about it, and it's not true, thank God. Susan's own kids, Emily and Jacqueline, are right stuck-up cows. She's an accountant in Wexford. Got a beautiful house, Adrian, her awesome husband who has a business making all these jams and craft products, but she's just...we just don't get each other.

After the funeral, they were all up at the house, E and J either too stupid or selfish to care about what was going on, sighing and acting bored. Susan had the nerve to turn around and say to me to bring them outside to play.

Oh, I lost it with her. Roared about he was my dad, too, about how she wasn't the one going up to visit him in Padre Pio's every evening. Poor Mam, having to listen to that, but Susan deserved it.

Since Dad died, Susan and Mam have been getting on better, which is nice. Nothing like a funeral to bring a softness back between people. I still can't stand her though.

Then, there were the twins, my brothers, William Butler and Jack Butler. Named for the Yeats boys, the famous Irish poet and his brother, the painter. I think my parents must have been romantics. Hard to imagine them, her a hairdresser and him a Garda sergeant inside in Thurles, naming their boys so fanciful, but there you have it.

Finn's nice, more like an uncle than an older brother. Always had art supplies for me when he visited. I never met Jack. He's only ever been a headstone in the graveyard to me. He died at fifteen, two years before I was born. Fell through the hay in that shed out by Purcell's farm where I saw the astronaut's ghost. He'd climbed up the bales to near the roof when it all shifted, and poor Jack fell, went right down through the hay and broke his neck. Finn was the only one there at the time. Stayed holding his brother, his dead twin, afraid to let him go. I can't imagine what it'd be like to lose someone that's such a part of you.

Dad used to say that after that, after Jack died, all Finn wanted to do was run away. That the moon itself wouldn't be far enough for him, so America had to do. You could tell there was a hurt beneath the joking when he said that. Dad's gone nearly two years now, so he'll never know just how close he was to being right.

Finn is William. No-one ever called him Liam or Bill or Willie or any of the others. Not around here anyway; maybe when he moved to the States, people called him by his real name. Or maybe they just called him Doctor Shaw.

I was eight before I even learned his name was William. I'd grown up calling him Finn, and why would I have thought any different? One day, Mam cut an article out of the paper where he was mentioned, some award for achievements in science or whatever he was working on. She'd a scrapbook for all of those clippings. It was this big, thick, book, and it needed to be, Finn was a smart one.

"They've got his name wrong," I said pointing to the caption, *'William Shaw (right) being presented with a medal for...,'* and Mam burst out laughing. Turns out, when Susan was a toddler, she couldn't say William, so she took to calling him Fing. That turned into Finn, and Finn was what stuck. He'd been Finn for so long by the time I came along, no one even thought to tell me his real name.

I was fair mad at Mam for a while over that, but she reckoned it was hilarious. Dad was kinder about it, brought me into town and bought me sweets, told me it wasn't right that Mam had laughed, but that it was kind of funny. I didn't mind; it's easier to forgive these things when you've a big bag of Dolly Mix and Cola Bottles in hand.

I've only thought of it because I found that scrapbook in the attic the other day and had a flip through it. Man, Finn had done a lot by then and lot more since, like getting to meet the American President and going up to the International Space Station. It's always the same though; you go searching for one thing and get distracted after finding something unrelated. I'd never have imagined it was a sign, until now. And now, it's too late.

You see, after I saw the ghost, I must have done about a million drawings of it. I'd completely forgotten about them until I went looking for art things: sketches, drawings, stuff I could use for this portfolio I've to put together for a college course I wanted to do after the Leaving.

I'd spread them out on the living room floor and tried taking half-decent photos with my phone when Mam came in, proper shocked at the sight of them. Said she was sure she'd thrown them all away years ago, but no, there they were: copy books, A4 pages, the backs of strips of wallpaper, white chalk on black paper, absolutely anything I could get my hands on. All full of pictures, all weird and beautiful and haunting in their way.

The letters WBSIRE scratched on every single one.

Looking at those pictures was like crashing back to that night, like looking at the astronaut's ghost through static, where everything was scratchy. I remembered it being there and not there all at once. And it was another warning from outside of time that I missed, and now, it's too late.

We were watching the launch on TV, Mam and myself, watching Finn. Sitting there, feeling so proud of him. The camera zoomed in on Finn standing there in his flight suit. He waved and tapped his chest just above his heart, where the nameplate was. WBSIRE. William Butler Shaw, Ireland.

My fingers went tingly, my stomach knotted, and I don't even remember screaming.

Apparently, the launch was fine, but when they left the atmosphere, the shuttle was hit by solar flares, or cosmic winds, or a gamma ray burst. Something. I don't know. My entire science knowledge comes from a stack of *Fantastic Four* graphic novels Finn left behind when he moved out. I think he always wanted to be Reed Richards, but I've no idea why. Reed was a dick.

I've watched it over and over online. Listened to the commentary as they're hit by the storm, as they disintegrated and disappeared. Atoms smashed to smithereens, thrown to infinity, lost. And Finn somehow flung back to that night.

Maybe, he wasn't even coming back to me; maybe, it was because that was the place where he lost his brother, where he stopped being whole. But he went back to the wrong time, and I was the only one there. I had seven years to figure it out, but I didn't, and, now, it's too late.

The problem with ghosts is everyone thinks they're something from the past. No one once thought it was a message from the future that the astronaut's ghost delivered.

It was a warning, one I didn't understand until now, and now, it's too late.

Now, I'm out of time.

FINDING GALATEA
Ali Abbas

When I burst in, her hair looked auburn. Must have been some trick of the low, reddish light. There weren't enough layers of make-up to hide the haunted look in her eyes.

"What do you want darling?" she asked, not meaning a word of it.

"You." I showed her the picture on my phone. "You're Yulia, right?"

"You have to leave." She scampered backwards on the bed.

A footstep on the stairs three floors below. Heavy. That meant finding another way out. I flung open the curtains to the watery afternoon sun. The building pressed close to its neighbour, the flat roof a short jump away. In daylight, she was slighter, just the shoes made her seem tall.

"Yevgeny sent me. We have to go." I pulled, but she was reluctant, disbelieving.

"You don't understand. Yev…"

"*Now.*" I yanked her to her feet. Her sweat lay underneath a miasma of lubricants and cleaning wipes. Under all the men. Part of me wanted to lay on reassurance, to tell her I was here to save her, that she would be safe. I couldn't get the words out for gagging. She wasn't heavy, and the window wasn't latched. She could have jumped herself if not for the heels.

This was my third find with the Diamond DreamGirls Escort agency. She looked nothing like her picture on the website. The punters would start turning away before the police took an interest in the illegals.

I left her in a bedsit on the Caledonian road. The landlady knew my handler cum colleague Rowley. I didn't know the client, Yevgeny, but I guessed he wasn't another pimp. A boyfriend, or a brother maybe. He wasn't my problem. I called Rowley, and the job was done.

Careless of my neighbours, I took off every stitch of clothing outside my flat and left them in a pile with the smells they absorbed. The laundry knew to wash and rinse them over and over. I sank into a bath of plain, cool water and let my head drop below the surface.

Another day, another job. Another body to find, preferably living, amongst eight million.

London was killing me. Humanity, in all its heaving diversity, pressed together without the space to stretch its arms out and breathe. My senses faced a constant assault of detail. I dared not fill my lungs.

I don't drive unless I have no other choice. I need to get where I am going, not sit in traffic. That means taking the tube, where in winter, the base notes are damp wool. An injudicious sniff outside the high wall of my scarf would douse my synapses with myriad layers: bodies spanning the spectrum of hygiene, wet Ugg boots, hair sprays, and nose-tickling perfumes. All this littered with breakfasts and the assorted brands of toothpaste.

The tunnels amplify the train's rattle. The silence of Londoners is a fable. Headphones grind white noise like a radio in another room. Old ladies raise their voices, unaware or uncaring of the commuters trying to shut them out. Colleagues hide their disappointment at ending up in the same carriage with voices pitched to carry. Beneath it all, the susurrus of breathing. The heartbeat of a single organism made up of individuals packed in a steel cylinder.

In this mass of compressed flesh, I could not help but see everything. The dapper South Asian guy with the neatly trimmed beard, his grey slacks picked out with a subtle maroon check, confident in brown shoes. The sad-faced school girl in pop socks and flats despite the weather, weighed down by a rucksack more than half her size. The stout man balancing a tablet and coffee, my eye drawn back to the imminence of an accident. The pretty woman with the perfect nails who got on three stops after me, when all the seats were gone, for four days in a row.

The last morning, late in January, I saw her drop onto a still warm, just vacated spot and break out her make-up. Stifled, I could not say, "You are so beautiful, every swipe of brush and line of pen only mars the delicate perfection." I watched, all other senses dampened by the growing well of defeat. No words would come, and I had no way of knowing what misguided aesthetic, or what pain made her slap on this mask.

I called Rowley, the only person who would care if I was alive, and that only for his commission. He plied me with platitudes and offers of time away. Then, he swore at me for leaving a job unfinished.

The next day, I landed in Seville.

Sunlight burns scents from the air, a natural disinfectant. It throws up sharp contrasts to erase detail. Living in Seville's golden glow, through a mild, dry winter, drove home what an assault the moist grey of London had been. My shoulders edged into a new, easy alignment and my gait loosened.

I ate my paper-wrapped lunch in the garden of the Mezquita, under the shade of the orange trees. My senses weighed only by the razor edge of *membrillo* over smooth *Arzúa*, and the memory of citrus. Time relaxed around me, pliant and accommodating. I don't know how many days or weeks she waited before I discovered that I did not eat alone.

A young woman sat on the other side of the tree in a green pool of her broad skirt, white blouse filled with convex shadows. A lily in a pond of algae. Her foot poked out into the dappled sunshine on the flagstones. Leaning forward, face intent, she wrote on her ankle with a biro. I blocked her light.

"Please." She handed me the pen, squinting up.

I dropped to my haunches.

She had only drawn a single line.

Birds trilled overhead accompanied by the timpani of our hearts.

"May I?"

She nodded, allowing me to take her Achilles tendon between my fingers. With deliberate strokes, I traced out a treble clef around her line. I fell in love with that ankle first, and the promise held in the arch of her foot, dipping shyly into her dusty flat shoes.

"Perfect." She smiled, eyes wide now that I was in the tree's cool shade. "I've seen you every day, looking so contented in your loneliness. I didn't want to interrupt."

It was only then that I realised she had no determinable scent, and to lose her would be to lose all hope.

She breezed into my life like a cool pillar of air, a freshness and respite. Make-up found her face inhospitable, lipstick receded from the edges of her lips, swallowed in an instant. Her skin accepted no masks, each tiny mark was the flourish that proved perfection.

In the blushing, touching, tentative phase of love, all fingertips and butterfly kisses, we swayed in clubs thronged with kohl-tipped eyes, and featureless, ill-defined faces. Among the flailing arms and throbbing beats, her dance was one of stillness, an eye of calm within a raging sea. The twisting of her hand, the flutter of her lashes held back the mannequin hordes, hungry for sensation. Her motionless movement was the narrative of self-possession, a melody that echoed every tune that ever played. Discs spun in the shells of textile mills and distilleries, the decayed remains of industry. Blinking lights burned from gantries, sweat dripped from girders. She was icy and immune, cotton silk in this land of flesh and leather.

Her dirty laugh proved she was no angel. The throaty chuckle beggared every iota of written erotica. Her eyes sparkled with the mischief of upturned apple carts, her pursed-lipped smile pulled first down, then up; its energy irrepressible beneath her cool demeanour.

She was wholly European, eyes Scandi grey, slight Mediterranean stature and complexion, a Slavic angle to her cheek. Raven hair fell to her waist like a druid from the valleys of South Wales, but Englishly particular about how she took her tea. Exquisite, she did not intimidate. Some women make you turn away from their beauty for fear of falling. Her attraction was accessible, it invited the eye, and promised a life of unending fascination.

Each morning after that chance meeting in the Mezquita, I asked myself what the hell she was doing with me.

"We have no word for the sadness," she said in a flat white moment one afternoon, "Of knowing the perfect moment for an action has now passed."

She moved in the next day.

The way she dressed held no pattern. Some days socks came before her bra. She randomly selected which leg first dipped into her trousers. If she wore a billowing skirt her knickers might go last. The vantage of her self-awareness shifted, inside to out, outside to in.

When I asked, she laughed then sobered as if this insight was new.

"You are my only anchor. You are the lantern light by which I see myself. You notice everything about me, which means I do not blow away in the breeze or fade from memory. You are my touchstone, my certainty. Everything else should be stochastic. Why chain it with routine?"

I loved to watch. Her skin, pale salted caramel, betrayed the faintest blemishes. The subtle variations played hide and seek in her body's rise and flow, reassured me she was human, convinced me she was real.

Physically, we lived in the same space, a small apartment from which the glint of Guadalquivir sparked between the neighbouring buildings. But she inhabited a place inside me. Somewhere close to where my legs meet my belly, or the sanctum where my heart converses with my kidneys, the chain through which my mind tells my diaphragm to flex. How did I know, in the time before she came into my life, the way my blood should run, the physics of oxygenation? The absence of an imposition on my senses was a freedom that let me lower my guard. That let me let her in. We, Beatriz and Cyrus, made sense.

Except, of course, nothing is quite so simple. Picking at a salad one evening, without looking up she said, "You find people."

I watched her toying with a cherry tomato, the absence of her frank gaze made me uneasy. "That's my job."

"How?"

"I don't know. I see things, details. I smell things, hear inflexions. Somehow, it comes together in a picture, a belief, and I know where to look." This was a departure. Thus far, our conversations were tours of concepts and abstractions.

"Can you find someone for me?" She diminished, a smaller, less vibrant version of herself. My body ached to reach out and offer reassurance.

"Of course. Who?"

"My sister."

Doubts bordered my thoughts for the first time. I had been certain that some hand of fate brought us together, not that she might know of the underground that sourced my work. What if it was not fate that brought her to the Mezquita? What if she had come looking for me?

She took me to a library, in an ancient Moorish building set around a courtyard with a tiny fountain. Shelves stretched to the high ceilings with no ladders to reach the topmost books. Light fittings hung from chains interspersed with wind chimes, in this place where the wind did not intrude. It was empty but for us.

I let the familiarity of the space seep in. Libraries have always been kind to me, light softened by the presence of words. They thicken the air, slow the passage of time. A dry, syrupy dust compresses scents until all I can smell is books.

"I'm not like you," she said as if I did not know. She pressed her ever-present diamond studs into my palm. In a shimmer of heat haze, her clothes fell, empty and lifeless.

I could never smell her, but now, the density of the air and the pervasive hush was missing her presence. As far as I could tell, she had vanished, not only from the library but from the face of the earth.

Panic spiked its fingers through my ribs. My own heartbeat thundered, my pulse throbbed in my ears. I couldn't breathe. Without her, my body forgot the discipline of its most basic functions. How easy it had become to end me; her absence, my asphyxiation.

Overhead, the wind chimes giggled, a crystalline collision of laughter. I looked up. The sunlight was a little brighter, the motes of dust picked out with greater clarity. I blinked to see a shape, a ghost, something and nothing. I resonated with the shimmer of a chord, a triad of distant tocsins.

She was behind me, forehead pressed between my shoulder blades. Her laughter shook me. I turned to hold her naked form, sucked in a long, life-affirming breath, and pressed my lips to her clavicle. The salt of her skin blending with the salt of my tears.

"I'm sorry, Cyrus." She bit her lip, hard. A single bubble of blood oozed out. Her tongue pressed it to mine, sealing her oath. "Even if you cannot sense me, I will never leave you."

She took back her earrings and slipped them on but ignored her clothes.

"My people are not like your people. The minds of a select few can solidify and identify us." She leaned in, the desire written over every inch of her flesh given a stellar gravity. "You give me form. Your ferocious attention to detail completes me. Without you, I am only an idea, a spirit."

Perhaps her absence robbed her of her mind. What she said made no sense. Surely, she existed before I met her under the shade of the orange trees. She never talked of a past, and I never probed. Only her present had meaning, her time with me, and the aching hours when we were both about our work.

"These record our lives." She held a book. "Only someone who is present on a page can read it." The book was hers, marked by a treble clef inscribed on the maroon leather cover. A thousand pages of the book were closed to me, but from our meeting in the garden of the Mezquita, they flicked through my fingers. New words dragged across the last written page describing me as I read them. She closed it and replaced it with another.

"This is my sister's book. Read it."

"I've never met her."

"You must have." She pressed the new tome into my hands. The pages felt like an impenetrable mass. She put her palms on the cover. "I had a dream of my sister in London. She had been given a form, and she had chosen not to bind herself to it with diamonds. There are so few who have the power to see us, to make us corporeal. If not you then who?"

Her small hands had narrow fingers, the skin smooth. Fingernails perfect. I had seen those hands before.

I lost my grip on the book; it fell, open, to a page. The rattle of a tube train, a vacated seat, still warm.

"This is our glamour. I am exactly as you want me to be. These hands, eyes, lips, belly, feet. Your design, from your desire." She recovered the book, pushed it into my chest. "You made me be what you need."

"What of your need?"

"I wanted to live and to find the one who would see me as I want to be seen." She laughed, that throaty sound so misplaced in a library, better suited to a brothel. "Well, I'd have liked to have been a little taller."

"What of love?"

"I am what you need. You are what I need. Love is what we nurture between."

"And your sister?"

"I guess Joanna found you. A man so meticulous in his attention to detail he could make her whole. Without binding, she could hold that shape for hours." The book between us did nothing to deaden her heartbeat. It hammered at me, insistent. "You can find out why she wanted to be human."

She did not bother to dress as I hauled blocks of pages to find the moments I appeared in Joanna's book. Her hand was a reassurance on my elbow. Her breath a moist billow of strength. We flipped through frustrating descriptions and half understood references. We discovered little more than that Joanna burned with a desire for justice, to right a wrong and that danger stalked her.

All the while, my strength and certainty grew. Need defines love. We love only that which fulfils our needs, be they abstract, spiritual, or bound up in the myth of altruism. I needed Beatriz as my respite and my sanctuary, and now, I understood why she needed me. It gave my presence in her life a purpose, a solidity.

I hated my skills since the day I became aware of them and all through the gruelling years of training. That night, she whispered to me the secrets of her family. As her breasts rose and fell against my chest, I felt as though those skills gave me a chance to be worthy of her love.

While she slept, I pieced together all the women from whom I had composed the symphony of her body. Some deeply loved, some only seen in passing. Some parts, I could not reclaim from memory. Did my desires really impose themselves on her being, or did my senses only perceive her to be as I wanted? Sleep overcame me as I pondered this insanity, the arrogance that could infuse my ability to create my own Galatea.

Flying leaves my skin covered with a skim of kerosene. I left my clothes outside the door of my apartment, unwilling to bring the smell inside. The boiler would not fire. Beatriz scrubbed me with cold water and unscented soap until I felt my skin was once again my own.

We shivered that first night together in my hometown, underneath all the blankets.

The next day, I took her to the Elephant to try and pick up Joanna's trail, working with hints and tips from her written life.

We found nothing in the shadows of the shopping centre or the reflections in the vinyl sprayed windows. No mote nor beam of light that remembered the passing of the beauty my imagination had imposed upon her form.

Sometimes, between the grease smoke of the restaurants and the muted lights of massage parlours, I thought I saw the heat haze shimmer or heard the echo of a tocsin chord, but every time I turned my head, it vanished.

I would have to call Rowley.

"You got the bug, Cy. Can't keep away," he said, weary rather than amused.

"Maybe. What's the news?"

"Same old. You looking for a job?"

"Looking for a person."

"You're not going freelance on me?"

"Nothing like that. I'm looking for a girl."

"Word is you found a girl. Cute one. Bit short for my taste."

Of course he knew. Rowley made his money by knowing things, knowing who was lost, who could do the finding, and just how much the client could pay.

"She's looking for her sister."

"If they look anything alike, she'll have turned some heads."

I gave him a description, and that the trail started around the Elephant and Castle, or maybe down as far as Kennington.

"A bit far south and east for me son, but I'll keep my ear to the ground. Tell them randy teenage boys to break out the Kleenex." He hung up with a snigger. We did a lot of work with Eastern European girls. They were usually found through prostitution sites, kept drunk and high in tiny studio apartments. Trawling the websites looking for a face was unskilled labour we contracted out.

Beatriz saw a different side of me then. Purposeful and direct. I had a quarry to track down, my focus narrowed on the task of finding. We spread the search west towards Waterloo, and I caught glimpses. Reflections of reflections that could not bring themselves to forget Joanna. There were absences and spaces in the flow of people.

Through it all, Beatriz clung to my hand, peering, sniffing, listening for some sign of her sister.

It wasn't enough. The vague signs led back to the West End, where a hundred thousand of the desperate and the deviant thronged the streets and alleys, filled the walk ups and the loft spaces. London's sensory overload condensed and distilled into a potent poison. Rowley usually handled it himself.

"You coming onto my manor, Cy?" he asked when I called.

"You know it's not business." We were on genial terms, but that would not last a tussle over money. For all the years of training together, the years of working, Rowley was particular about money.

"Personal will get you killed, son."

"Something always will."

"Start on Poland St. Some new tarts there taking a lot of business."

Beatriz walked hip to hip, my arm wrapped around her waist. We got stares from the tourists because she was out of my league, and from the villains because if she was being paid, they weren't getting a cut.

It rained. A small mercy. It dampened the pervasive odours of marijuana and crushed dreams. It hid the pretty youths that came to this town to do something and wound up getting done. Through those bleak thoughts, I caught the shimmer in an open doorway.

Stairs led straight up. A list of girls' names in neat, fat-tip-marker handwriting was tacked to the bare wall, each with a single number beside it. Six rooms up the narrow stairs, six girls. London at its finest.

We walked onwards to Piccadilly where I sat Beatriz down in a cafe with a flat white. She was no innocent, but some latent sense of decency made me keep her away. She promised to stay put until I knew what we were dealing with.

Worn wooden stair treads led up to windowless gloom. Paint flaked off the bannisters, and a line of grime trailed along the wall at hand height. I went straight to the top and worked my way down. The first room was empty except for a menu of services pasted to the wall, proving no business is recession proof. In the second, a Slovenian girl pretended to be Italian. She was unremarkable, disappointed not to get her first customer of the day. The stench of irregular hygiene and unchanged sheets pushed me away faster than the broad smile and bed-patting welcome. I almost stumbled into the next room.

"Personal will get you killed Cy. I did tell you." Rowley stood waiting. He held a handkerchief to his nose, and I caught a cleansing whiff of citronella as he waved me into the room with a gun. The uneven floorboards creaked under my steps. My mind raced through the permutations. The edges of his cheeks flexed as he grinned behind the hankie. "You'll get there in a minute lad."

The light shifted. A diamond winked on his finger.

"The thing with you, Cy, is that your heart was never in the job. Me? I didn't like finding people. I liked finding out stuff. Rerum Cognoscere Causas. You had a thing for the international girls at the LSE, didn't you? You could have learned from the motto." He was buying time for something. Footsteps on the stairs. Two sets, one heavy one light. One of them unwilling. The thunder of analysis in my head slowed to a crawl, replaced by a single truth. He had Beatriz.

He put the hankie down for a moment. Even against the residual stink in the room, too much citronella became sickening.

"Good boy. Figure out the rest for me because I ain't done with you yet."

"Diamond DreamGirls." I spat it out against the swelling tide in my throat. Red hair turned to brown, tall to short. "They found a way to trap spirits. Every girl is exactly the girl you want."

"Twenty-first century, Cy. Guy, girl, neither, both. You want it. They have it. Old school gangsters are running that show out of Ireland. No one left to sell guns to. Gotta hand it to 'em. They know their fae creatures, how to trap 'em, how to hold 'em. And they play a long game."

"And you're just here to kill the geese that lay the diamonds." I got it. He never had been patient about money.

"They're closing in. Tired of losing the merchandise. I need a finder to pin it on, and I get one more payday for my trouble."

The footsteps stopped outside. The door swung open. I turned. Beatriz struggled in the arms of a brawny man with a buzz cut. I picked out the two-day stubble on his cheeks and the claret of a football shirt under his jacket as I lunged for him. Rowley would not fire. Not here, with the busy street outside. He needed a clear route out of the building.

I wrenched Beatriz away.

Pain exploded through the back of my head.

Beatriz cried my name once as a haze descended over my senses.

My face hit the floorboards.

The floorboards were old oak. High heel divots pocked the smooth grain, the surface worn by years of grinding misery. I felt this through my cheek. It provided an alternative to the pounding in the back of my head. At least there was no sensation of blood. No sensation of Beatriz, either. My diaphragm stalled.

You're a complete liability.

The voice pierced my brain, battering against the red glow of pain. *Breathe.*

Something hit me between the shoulder blades. Twice. Hard. Air and dust filled my lungs in a choking whirl.

Are you able to get up?

I groaned, it was easier than trying to shake my head.

The light around me changed. A glow hit my closed eyelids before I sensed a shadow. Small hands wormed under my armpits. A light, floral scent replaced the antiseptic wipes and cheap perfume that lay over the room.

"You really have a thing for short women."

I opened my eyes a crack, wincing in advance against the expectation of a new wave of agony. Dark hair framed symmetrical features. Joanna.

She steered me onto the bed as my legs gave way.

"You're a hard woman to find."

"It's your fault I look so distinctive," she waved a hand in front of her face. "I've been tracking spirit disappearances for months. Your ability to fix me with a shape turned out to be a mixed blessing."

"So, the make-up on the tube was to make you less conspicuous?"

She blushed, a heightening of colour under peaches and cream skin. "No, I'd never done make up before. I was out of my depth."

I managed to cough out a laugh before dropping my head between my knees.

"What's this?" She plucked at something under the lapel of my coat. Earrings.

"Beatriz."

"Clever sis. This buys us a bit of time. Come on." She hauled me to my feet.

"I don't understand."

"The diamonds are part of her. They're how she's bound to the mortal plane. If she's not wearing them part of her essence will go into making new ones. It goes on until there is nothing left but a pile of gems."

"She's dying now?" I lurched to the door.

"She's been dying since the day she met you." Joanna wedged her narrow shoulder under me to help me down the stairs. "I don't know what she sees in you. The point is that with these diamonds, your friend can control how quickly she transforms. Without them, he has to wait for nature to take its course."

"What about you?"

"There's no way I'm giving up my immortality. I can use the shape you gave me for a couple of hours at a time before I have to rest. Which is why we have to get moving."

"I'm no fighter. We need some kind of plan."

"I know. I saw. I was in my spirit form behind the door. He had no idea I was there. That's all the advantage we've got, so we use it."

The rain had eased off. Under the rising petrichor, I tasted leaded fuel and an engine running too rich. Rowley had his affectations, a MkII Jag among them. Only one place he would go from here.

And he was in a car in London.

We could make up time.

He kept two floors of a tall town house in Highbury. The ground floor was for living, and the basement had his sound system and a dentist's chair. Bach was his escape from his own heightened senses.

The bonnet of the Jag was still warm. My footsteps in the hall were enough to alert him. He waited in the basement with the door open. Beatriz was strapped to the chair, her delicate features pinched in an unconscious agony. Loops of copper wire connected to a car battery marred the perfect crescent of her toes.

"I'm glad the Irish didn't get you. They love tradition. They'd have done your knee caps with a drill." Unthreatened, he stood with his back to me, weighing diamonds into soft bags. "Coffee's on if you fancy some." He pointed into the kitchenette. The movement of his body revealed the gun lying in easy reach. He wasn't worried because he knew I didn't use a gun.

"It's over. The Irish aren't going to be far behind me. Let me leave with the girl." I tried to keep my voice even, and my body still. I wanted to snatch Beatriz off the table, to take her in my arms and try and squeeze life back into her. My voice was still thick from the blow to my head, and a light buzzing in the room that added to my throbbing headache. How hadn't it driven Rowley mad?

"She's done for. I don't need the diamonds she left with you. I've found adding a little pain speeds up the process very nicely."

I watched as another pair of earrings emerged. Beatriz seemed to shrink, her body less present, more ephemeral.

"They all do it differently, earrings, pendants, regular rings. Each one has a thing." He picked up the gun and waved me back before removing the new earrings. Putting the gun down again he plucked off the gold cups and posts with a twist of his pliers. Discarded gold chains and blank rings piled on the corner of the table. "It's not even a crime. They're not people, Cy. There's no body, just a pile of transportable wealth."

"You know I'm not into violence. Let me take her. Please. For old time's sake. I'll lead the Irish off. You'll get away clean." The buzzing grew worse, and I was going to throw up.

"That was always your problem. No commitment. Now, the Irish, they know how to stick to a task. If they didn't find you before, they'll find you now. I'll do you a favour and make it quick. Unlike the walk-up in Poland Street, this basement is sound proof."

He turned to me, holding the gun. An old service revolver, another affectation.

"I'll have those other diamonds since you're here." He gestured with his free hand. I closed my eyes and dug into my pocket, trying to focus my mind. I looked him squarely in the eye. He would do it. Despite the years of association, he was willing to kill me for money.

"Okay."

"Good boy, no need to make this hard."

"I wasn't talking to you."

The buzzing wasn't mechanical; it was the collision of chords, layers upon layers of them. Rowley couldn't hear it because he didn't have the same ability as I did. The plan rested on just how good my abilities were compared to his.

Joanna appeared in a glittery shower beside him. She chopped down hard on his forearm.

The gun went off, burying a bullet into the cork floor.

I kept my attention firmly on her arms, seeing the muscles tense with a wiry strength.

She jabbed him in the throat. Choking, he fired twice.

The bullets passed through the hazy area where her midriff would have been, had I not been trying desperately to ignore it.

She slapped the gun from his limp hand as I made my way around the dentist's chair.

He fell, scattering an incalculable fortune in diamonds over the floor.

Joanna held the gun in uncertain hands as I unhooked the copper wires, tied Rowley up and shoved him into the kitchenette.

"How does this work? Do I pull the lever?"

"The Irish will want him alive, for a while." Rowley struggled against his bonds, whimpering into the kitchen towel I had shoved in his mouth.

"So?" Joanna shrugged. "I'm going after them next. For my people. For my sister."

Her sister. My lover. I'd been trying not to look at the dentist's chair, and the frail, faint image of its occupant. Beatriz was barely there. Her hand was little more than a haze. What gave my life meaning was lost in a litter of meaningless wealth.

I wrapped both hands around the remains of hers. Desperate to squeeze, terrified of squeezing. My tears fell on the chair and dripped onto the floor to join the pieces of Beatriz and who knew how many others.

The Mezquita seemed like a lifetime ago. I could see the image with perfect clarity. Her lithe form limned in cool winter sunshine, the turn of her ankle and the promise in the arch of her foot.

Joanna gasped. The diamonds rustled at my feet. The memory a mere note within the background noise that nagged at me. Now silenced.

"Whatever you are doing, keep doing it."

Her back to me on the bed. The faint blemishes on her skin. The tremble of black hair as she danced without moving. The memories flooded through me as her hand solidified. The noise dimmed. She choked, then spasmed off the chair and into my arms.

"I knew you would come."

Fewer diamonds littered the floor. Somehow, between her magic and my attention to detail, the transformation reversed. With time and information, I could save them all. For now, I had to save one. I still had the original diamonds wedged in my palm. I peeled away just far enough to give them to her.

"Let me finish it," I said, trying to keep my voice level.

She picked them out and put them back in her ears. "I'm already just as I want to be. Exactly the way you found me."

GREY MAN WALKING PAST
David Kotok

The clouds drum. The sky spits fire. The night is a cauldron of flame, turning the world to a cackling dance. A demented god snaps a celestial switch, laughing like a jackal as the heavens' rip, hurling shrieks of thunder to suck wind from my lungs. The fiercest of the Tiangou dogs devour the moon as the clouds clench into tight, black fists.

I ready myself for the next climatic roar, but fear still thumps as surprise in my chest. I clutch the sheets and curl around my knees. The air is viscous, a jelly of noise slapping the doors and squeezing my bones. Rain batters the roof. The palms toss like maracas. I cannot sleep for the storm. Cannot sleep for the fiend stalking outside, cast as smoke in the jangling night.

I seek comfort away from the window, but my bed is a spread of distortion. The body that lies close to me, breathing calm in the chaos, is a dusky deception. Strands of her hair fan on the pillow, but I grasp the empty creases of her departure. I search across the sheets for a bruise in the cotton, a remnant of her, but there is nothing. I smell my fingers for her trace but detect only the taint of stale tobacco. She's a whisper and a memory and an ache. She is a wound.

But I am not alone. I have company. I'm followed. I'm pursued. Out on the balcony, pressed against the glass, demons coalesce.

The Grey Man is out in the howling, pacing from left to right, trailing sugarcane arms, marching quick-step to spurts of barking light. Large and looming, he slides across the curtain, shrinking until he vanishes, and scurries back to the jig. Tall and thin, his shadow fills the drapes and slithers away, waving tangled dreadlocks, strutting a circle, around and around, timing his path against the monsoon rhythms.

He's a bamboo clump. Or a wired pole blurred by rain. Or a potted plant, twisted and shaking. He just looks like a man is all, a tall man, thin as sticks. The husk of a man who has no business on my balcony, twirling knives and stamping his feet.

The applicant is dressed in an ill-fitting suit and plays with the collar of his shirt like it's a noose. The cuffs hang over his hands, nails ingrained with volcanic mud. His bravado is studied, and he sits down before being asked. I catch his eye and hold it, and I ask if he's okay. He squints confusion, his head sinks into his shoulders and he fingers his collar. He doesn't speak.

"Never mind." I point at the interpreter. "She will ask my questions and tell me what you say."

He smiles vacuously. Sweat beads on his eyebrows, in the creases above his nose.

"She has no questions of her own. She has only my questions and your answers."

The interpreter falls into routine and asks if the man is feeling well. His chipped teeth grind as he nods and clicks his knuckles. He opens his bag, a new laptop satchel, empty of laptop, and takes out a faxed letter from a crewing agent. It's written in shoddy English: This crew staffs must onside vessel inside 2 day.

"The port authorities say the ship sailed yesterday. Please explain."

The applicant's smile drops. His face tilts to the interpreter. His hands cup like a beggar.

The bedsheet wrapped over me is little comfort. I lie blind as the typhoon evokes its ghosts. I can't face the appalling carnival outside, yet I'm driven to look. Is he out there, baring hollow fangs, flicking a yellow tongue, sharpening claws? Ticks and moans filter through the sheet. Has he slipped the door? Are berserker eyes inches from mine, incisors bared to bite and suck the aspic from my sockets? I tug off the cover and flinch, but there's no slashing blade at my throat, no depravity thrusting at my face.

The room is empty of menace, but for lines of shade clinging to the cupboards and chairs like a shroud.

A flare bursts the sky, and a piercing crack raps the doors and shudders in my ribs. I hold my breath, poised to count the miles between my bed and the spitting clouds as another retort bleaches the room. There's no distance, just the tightening space between my shivering morsel of flesh and the snarling gods throwing pitchers at the roof, fuelling the Grey Man on his circular parade. He's out there, crowned with tentacles, shivering like a peacock, serpentine fingers beckoning as he skims from left to right across the curtain, shrinks, dissolves, and displays again. Left to right.

"The wet season is always like this," I say to the pillow, holding it close, kissing the cloth, imagining her mouth, her illusory essence.

If she were here, monsoon nights would not be so busy with ghouls and assassins. We'd smile at the bluster and lock arms as branches cast their patterns like a shadow play on canvas. We'd point as the pictures shifted, as ballerinas became fat clowns and distorted into people we knew. Trees and bushes shook puppets back into twigs, not like they do now. The sketches evolve and solidify, like the limbs of the mango, laced with prongs of frangipani stitched into the form of the Grey Man. He snakes like a celestial dancer weaving ancient milk, bends his spine and giggles as the heavens boil.

My mind wanders to the childhood comfort of a soft toy, a fox-cub, always close when dreams fattened with fear. When I was an atom crushed against the immensity of the world, the dark brimmed with the smallest of articles, swimming around like a soup, as rain lashed the house and shook the trees. I was a feather to be whisked away on a breeze, just the ceiling to save me from vanishing into the stars. My frailty is a constant, from child to adult. I am a molecule of irrelevance spinning in the monstrous enormity.

"The wet season is always like this." I shout and switch on the lamp, and the thin man disappears, too feeble to fight the glow.

I take out the battered toy, but he's eyeless and vulnerable, one arm tagged to matted fur by a safety-pin. I tuck him under my chin, but he's a memento of my insignificance, of tears and helplessness against the drift of time. Of creaks on the stairs and doors slamming, of my mother's shrill cries and my father's passive sigh. The hard rev of an engine, and the screech of tyres spinning a tense silence up the stairs and across the landing.

History crawls indifferent in the chug of the air-conditioning. Neither past nor present will let me sleep.

The weather splutters, the light bulb pops, and night soaks the room in a cloying blackness. I count to three and rapid spears of flame propel the Grey Man past the window. His limbs trail across the glass with the slightest touch.

"The wet season is always like this, and you are nothing but a fiction of the wind."

A resounding thwack rents the room, and blue sparks define my tormentor in a twist of silhouettes. The fox-cub gasps under my grip, and I'm choking on air, flaying at the peril dancing in the storm, the Grey Man animated by a lick of electricity. He raises a hand in cheery wave as the AC clunks to a halt, the power supply severed. He's cranking up tension, tempting me to open the door, to draw me into the cool air and his realm of fire and flood.

Clasping the water jug like a club, I yank the screen back. The tiles are empty, the marble splashed with rain. A plastic chair lies on its side, the Fiji palm flutters, the hibiscus is delirious in its terracotta pot. The clock is stuck on 2:33, and the room is clammy and hot. Sweat soaks the mattress, the sheets, my scalp, my skin. Somewhere, my stalker is sucking his teeth in anticipation.

The squall swings south and is soon a distant rumble.

"Thunder is the friction of clouds," I say, but it was ever the clump of giants.

A scarf is tucked tight on her brow. She wears no make-up and has a faint moustache. Her nails are painted blue, the varnish chipped. A scarlet blouse with a glitter heart shines on her chest, and her jeans are tight. She's a contradiction. Pious from the throat up but tainted by pop idols.

She won't look at me, but she's not nervous. She's following instruction, but if honesty could be extracted like a tooth, she'd rather walk the paths of her village than foreign streets of gold. She's a prisoner watching sunlight glide across the cell floor, the passing of space and time of minimal interest to her passive acquiescence. The expectations of family and the chains of obligation are too strong for dissent. She will only say what she's been told to say.

A jaw-busting yawn births a lump under my tongue, a muscle forced under the bone by the depth of my tiredness.

"It is truth." She lowers her head.

I spin my pen around my fingers. It spirals off and smacks into the security pane that separates us. "What truth? Whose truth?"

I don't own a truth myself.

Plastic bangles turn under the mantra-like click of her nails. Whatever falls from her lips is truth. She's subdued by religious directives, lurking mysticism, and the demands of duty. Spirits blow bubbles in rice fields, birds are the souls of relatives telling her to soar, serpents are the incarnation of evil neighbours telling her to defy. Malevolent imps bear the camouflage of authority and cast barriers she must climb. And overseeing all is the One True God who would deny such fanciful existence but is merciful enough not to extinguish it.

Is that the truth? Is that where truth lies?

I'm thirsty, but the jug's empty. I'm fully clothed but shoeless. Guess I was too croaked on Filipino rum to undress. My watch is loose on my wrist, and my wedding ring bites my finger. I don't remember getting home.

I struggle with my jeans, and there's a scratch by the wall, near the balcony.

It repeats and stops, repeats and stops. There's no bad weather to frame the Grey Man, only the flicker of a streetlamp to give a blush to his canvas, not strong enough to cast an outline. He's never prowled a quiet night before. He prefers the dramatic, arriving under cover of forked flames, announced by a crazed *gamelan* of timpani and gongs. So why is he here, scraping and tapping in the silence? Is he plotting some new trick?

A bruise on the curtain fades and rebuilds. Spindles slide on the window. Not the hoax of a potted plant or a thicket of rustling bamboo, but a man dressed in a mantle of deceit. He lacks solidity; he's ether and shade, skeletal thin, too weak to break glass, only able to stroke its brittle fragility, but bristling with intent. He shivers against the dimmest of dawns, casting a silhouette to let me know he's there.

The clock blinks 2:58. The glow of the city lies even, its bustle a murmur. No shadow stains the curtain, no elongated nails scrape against brick. The Grey Man has slithered to his hidey-hole. Waiting for the bitter gods to unleash him once more.

2:59, 3:00, 3:00, 3:00.

I run cartoons over and over to coax slumber, but Jerry slices Tom clean in half, and the blood smells of ink. A girl in a shower blows a kiss under a waterfall, rubs soap over her ample bosom. Her buttocks wobble as mosquitoes settle on my arms, my waist, my legs, stabbing poison saliva into my wet hands. Blood runs on her legs, down her back, pools in my palms, mixing with the poison, smelling of iron. A fog of insects bury their beaks. I sit up and rub my repulsive head.

I'm unfaithful, even in nightmares.

5:59, 5:59, 6:00.

The clock's wake-up call whoops like a police car. No longer funny.

The last applicant sits in the booth. I'm too tired to think straight. I tried to swap her for a bundle of papers and a stack of data-input, but my colleagues just opened files or picked up phones. I said that I'd had no sleep, the AC had broken, the ceiling had caved in. They blinked in unison.

She smiles sweetly and looks at me under her fringe. Her lips are pink, her skin chocolate-smooth. She's pretty, and she knows it. She pushes a lock of hair behind her ear and fiddles with an earring, a line of chipped turquoise threaded by wire. Eyelashes blink mascara thick. She flirts, but the booth is bomb proof. A film covers the screen, made to bind and drop in a solid lump, and not a burst of shards. It looks heavy.

"I'll ask again, how did you meet him? 'He met me' is not an answer."

The interpreter translates, dry and without emotion. The girl says something. I pick up my pen and swivel it around my thumb. The pen switches back and forth easily, like a rotor. I'm impressed, but my skills are ignored.

"She doesn't understand," says the interpreter. "She says it's not so simple."

The alarm button by the desk has my attention. I fight the urge to press it. The interpreter coughs. The girl pouts, ever so gently.

"Why are you prepared to...," my question remains poised, the ending lost.

"What do you know about…" My words have an echo, a gargle about them, like water slipping down a drain.

There are voices. An exchange takes place. My hands tremble. The desk, the girl, the world is out of focus. I may have nodded off. Tails of mist swirl at the edge of my vision.

"Him," I say. "What do you know about *him*?"

"He is a kind and generous person."

A bell, maybe a siren, rings. A haze seeps through the walls. Feet clatter on a corrugated roof. A fizz cuts the air from behind, overtaking and thumping into my brow. I fend off another blow. The girl stares at the interpreter, who stares at a spot on the ceiling. If banshees are in song, if imps cling to my back, they do not notice.

"How much money does he give you?" My question, but I don't know the voice.

The girl bows her head like I'm the Judge of Turmoil. A web of sulphur tightens around my neck and rakes in my nose. I need this to end, but the girl's shoulders shake. She clings to the counter. She may be nailed to the chair.

"Tell me his name."

Forceful. Urgent.

"Don't you know? Can't you remember?"

She looks up. Her eyes glisten.

"What's his *fucking* name?"

The interpreter leaves and slams the door.

The girl snivels. Tears run on her cheeks in swabs of coal.

I press the big red button.

Klaxons wail and spin around the office.

The hammer is hard under the pillow. I sacrifice the cushion at my chest for the comfort of my cheek. The wooden handle is reassuring somehow, the cold metal lump of the head more so. It wasn't my idea. The waitress at the Eastern Promise, the new girl with dyed tresses and ribbons, talked about protecting herself from a Devil in Green Underpants. The Devil's an urban folk-tale, a city-wide scandal about a hog-like beast clad in emerald knickers, ravishing women as they snore in their beds. Perfect for the scoffs of ex-pats pegged to polished teak bars. Not that I scoffed. I have my own demons, and a weapon seemed a good idea, for the rest it might bring.

I said that it was sensible, and she beamed and touched my arm, letting it linger. Long enough to let me know.

"Looks like your wallet is there for the taking," said someone with a wink.

I sank my beer and left. I see too many forfeit liaisons during the day. My wife may have walked, but really, it was only a minor indiscretion, and I've begged her back. She needs to come home. I'm a ghost stuck in aimless repetition, lost and wandering in circles.

She hasn't replied, but I act as if celibacy will be a talisman for forgiveness. I will decline temptation, for ever and ever. Amen.

03:45. 03:46. 03:46.

I don't know who took the photo. I wish I hadn't been wherever I was, hadn't been so wrecked and easily compromised. Wish I'd kept my hands in my pockets. As regrets roll over belly-up for dissection, as *what-for* becomes *what-if*, my ears are tuned beyond the apartment. No storm, but a scratch in the wall like the nibble of teeth, gnaws the plaster and tramps the dido towards my bed.

Rats chewing cables? Termites dining? Surely, I can't hear these things. But the scrape of a ravenous phantom, tapping his nails along brickwork, searching for whatever it is he eats? Dust and light are not enough for him. He needs sinew and marrow. He needs to shatter the barriers keeping us apart, so he can feast. His talons feel for the weakest point to prise open and snag the prey, to reach through the mortar and nip the meat beyond. And with a body snared, he will slip within to flush the juices of the host into his own slender frame.

I am the Grey Man's larder. He will consume my fleshy being, swallow my essence as my skin contracts to a tighter fit and my muscles move to his command. He will leech on my fester, ignoring the pain of our bonding as my innards fill and become his gut. I am a bespoke coat, tailored to provide his relish. Inside me will live the Grey Man. A hermit crab. A parasitic maggot.

I will be sucked to parchment and brittle bone. A thin man haunting the night, seeking a fresh cadaver as my own host. This is the Grey Man's torturous transformation of corruption and rebirth, on and on, a myriad of hosts trapped in a cycle of pain and perversion.

He is closer now, slurping on the cement, breaching the divide between us. His vile spit softens the masonry, decaying my sanctuary, crumbling all substance. I grab the hammer and smack the wall to warn the toothy worm that I am armed. Cement flakes into my mouth and nose like hard snow until I drop defeated, coughing and hacking. Orange shapes flit on my eyelids.

Dragons.

Stars.

Fire-balls and snakes and flesh.

A girl licks my ear. I can't see her face, but her left tit swings free, and my tongue hangs like a thirsty dog.

Sin captured in a camera flash.

The photo was propped on the dining table against the farewell note. I don't remember the bar, don't remember the girl. I do remember a rubbery teat rolling under my thumb. She's never called, nor has her accomplice with the camera. No demands have been made. No offers, no threats, no promises. Maybe the plotters aren't driven by money. Maybe they've no desire to wring out a steady stream of positive decisions.

Their silence suggests revenge. Malice is what makes them smile. An act of spite for the ruination of false dreams. Such motivation is insatiable, so I can't know if the game is over. I suspect not. There'd be no sport in letting it go. They can pick their moment. There's more fun in taking time, in re-opening scars as they heal.

Well, I have news for my persecutors. There's a more efficient torment on my veranda. If you have more games to come, you're too late. I have no more to take. My life is lacerated already. I'm a husk waiting to be filled by the Grey Man. I am no more than a whisper in the rain.

The window creaks.

I turn off the lamp, and the thin man floats beyond the curtains, swords dragging from his waist as he shrinks under the passing glimmer of a car. The curtain wavers as he levers the hem. He's outside, by the wall, in front of the pots. He's inside, behind the curtain. He's fucking everywhere.

My bowels are alive with beetles. My blood fuelled by stress and alcohol. If I hadn't been downing the sauce, I wouldn't have tweaked a strange breast in a strange bar. I wouldn't be alone with a mallet as company. And I wouldn't be hunted as fodder by a starved ghoul.

I kick the drape apart with my foot. The chair is still on its side. The hibiscus is in its pot.

Sunrise is a pollutant orange.

I'm shattered. I'm crushed, but the applicants don't care. They're merciless. More than a hundred of them spill from wooden trays and march in a line through the door. Each has been shrunk to a white form with a photo and a ream of papers in a plastic folder sealed with a helpful sticker. Green, amber, or red.

I've been taken off interviews. My work's been inconsistent. Half-finished notes, leading questions, meandering rejection notices, low productivity, setting off alarms. My minutes are garbled, focused on irrelevancy.

"Like what?"

"Like the smell of drains by the office and the size of rats on Antasari."

Grit clogs my tear ducts.

There have been complaints. Accusations of coarse language, of threatening behaviour, of throwing things. There'll be an investigation. I'm too emotionally bled to argue, and my customers don't give a shit. They don't ponder these things, they are unsighted of each other, they believe they act alone, that I exist for their personal demands. They have no concept of the flocking drove they form a part of, the hateful horde they have become. They are ruthless in their combined calls for immediacy and service, ferocious in their incredulous denials and artless posing. They order my attention, exploit my fatigue, smiling cynically for the camera as they badger and fawn. A thousand hopeful souls crammed into boxes and placed in orderly queues.

Hidden in the throng will be a fistful of fakers. Take this first red faking entrepreneurial flair in a letter with a clip-art logo. She's tried it before; different name, different blouse, different wig, with glasses, without glasses. Or the next. A marketing manager last year, today a consultant with a new bank account and a fresh operating license issued yesterday. His startled face is trapped in a photo-booth image under a greased quiff; different name, same flamboyant hair. Here, a teacher with a letter laden with bad grammar; here, a student in a bogus college; here, director of a non-existent import-export business, and of course, a flock of fiancées dependent on myopic middle-aged men.

If I put a match to their paper identities, the fake and the genuine, the job would be done. There'd be no criticism, just a bin brimming with crisp ash and a shocked hush. If I had a match. If I had the courage.

As I dither, the paper mob clamours, demanding a decision whilst the telephone buzzes relentless. A favourable decision, yes sir, please sir, embossed with the stamp of the Crown. A decision and another and yet one more still. Decisions to turn data, to run scanners, to power printers and charge desk-tops. Decisions, decisions, decisions are what we need.

This is a decision factory. We are decision machines. Decisions are us.

The only sleep I capture is booze-induced. It's not sleep. It's collapse. It doesn't refresh the wreckage, it doesn't make the day easier to drift through, but it's better than no rest at all. I don't need much convincing.

The Promise draws the same old soaks whose names I forget but whose idle banter is enough for me to feel like I'm not drinking alone. One says I've got a thirst on, and he's right. I'm knocking them back.

"It's a form of sleep therapy," I say.

"I can't take pills, might not wake up," I explain.

"I'm on chasers already," I boast.

The waitress slides into the bar and cruises the tables, laughing and flicking her peroxide bangs. She sees me and waves. I wave back. She shouts an order at the barman and looks at me. Her almond eyes blink, toying with her ribbons.

She asks how I am, and I say I'm better by the slug, and she laughs as though I said something naughty. She looks familiar, but I can't place her. I ask if we've met, and she tells me we meet at the bar, and her hand rests on my arm. She takes my drink, and plops ice cubes and sprinkles crystals into it and says sugar to keep me sweet, rum to keep me happy.

The barman points impatiently at the tray, and she rubs my elbow before skipping to a table. I can't stop myself. I watch her walk. She swings her bum, a pendulum in white cotton stretched to snapping point. I wonder what will happen when she bends over to set down the drinks. I see the seams split, and her buttocks spill free, at first neat and rounded and then expanding into their new freedom, filling the Promise and suffocating the bar flies. As if to test the theory, she exaggerates a bow and points those deadly cheeks in my direction. The flies are unaware of the danger.

"Jupiter rising," comments one.

"No panty line," says another.

I feel sick. I pay my bill and stagger through the doors and throw up in the street. Heads lean out of cars and jeer. A cab waits, and I fall into the back before the driver can smell the ruins of my shirt. He snarls, but I'm in, and I whimper my address. He's wearing white gloves, like a Wonderland rabbit. I lean out the window and gulp on the hot, fetid air. The door opens; the driver argues. There's someone next to him, wrapped in a halo of shimmering gold.

"It's my cab," I say to the angelic intruder as trees spin and waves of dark water wash around and around, but my words dribble unformed into shuddering sobs.

The driver wakes me by the apartment block and gives me my wallet. The cash has gone, however little it was. He doesn't care what I make of it, and I can't speak to protest. He wants me out of his car. He wants my stench clear of his torn and greasy upholstery. I can't find my keys, and I lean on him, and he growls and splutters. He smells thickly of tobacco and clove. His hair is unkempt, a nest of thorns dripping from his brow and into my teeth. I retch down his jacket.

Flickering lamplight twists his appalled face, eyes like black pebbles, nose a hawk's beak rearing to bite. A girl whispers and cool, thin fingers pull me. I look up, but coconut palms sway, and house lights are brilliant white pearls.

The building jolts and clangs like a bell. The interview screen fragments and falls as deadly spikes in a defiance of the maker's guarantee. A bomb blast rises from the east, bragging a muffled clout and belching a mushroom cloud. I sink to the floor, under the door frame, earthquake aware but confused by explosions. The room twirls, pitches left and lurches right. A thousand lives, ten thousand, stamp up the stairs and down the corridors, filling the lifts. They plod on, advancing as a legion, demanding a decision, demanding a right. The tower judders and leans to topple. The herd force their way into reception and stomp in unison, moving the earth.

I ask them to stop, but they won't listen. They lumber from side-to-side, and the floors groan under their feet. They are ashen and grim and reach for my arms and legs, pulling my shirt, my trousers, stroking my cheeks, slapping, punching, pinching, biting. I pull free, but they slump forward, arms outstretched, gawping like frantic cattle.

The foundations shatter, and the tower rears; I am on a ledge in the sun, on the nineteenth floor, looking down as the building sways. A pall of smoke spreads over the Central Business District. A spiral of bats coils from the Bogor volcano. The structure folds, and I bound down the outer shell as it collapses, leaping across snapping sheets of crystal and tumbling concrete as girders split from the walls. The pack chase in a billow of dust. Marble and steel implode, lanterns rupture onto the disintegrating facade as I race towards the ever-distant pavement.

I call her name as the stars blink and the moon shuts an eye. The cosmic void rocks like a calm and silent sea.

Detritus settles.

Steps on distant stairs pad a gentle tattoo. A door snaps, feet pace the landing, in the hall, in the kitchen. A toilet flushes, a tap runs, light flickers under my door. It's comforting, curiously mundane.

Did I go to work? Was I comatose all day or just an hour? Maybe only a few minutes of sleep to catch a bagful of hallucination. Where have I been? Where am I going?

Questions with no answers, just a fug moulding around a lumpen swarm, hobbling from my flat into the leafy avenues of Cipete. Destroyed lives shuffling out of my dreams, shunting down Antasari like a picture show, a morose collage dull with loathing, all hope shredded in leaves of paper. Maybe I worked through them, a million or more, without bias or favour, wielding my touch across the keyboard, breaking performance targets, inciting anarchy with my astonishing progress, burning up the hard drive, fusing the keyboard, incinerating promise with the curse of my invested authority. Faith boiled to vapour.

The clock blinks 1:37.

My bedroom looks strange, the walls smeared with unfamiliar shadows, dappled by a curious light. I'm exposed. The curtains are open but should be drawn. Monsters live on my balcony.

The chair is over-turned, the hibiscus dead in its pot. My watch is not on my wrist. My wedding ring has cut into my knuckle, a crust of blood around the gold, a throb of muted pain.

Has the Grey Man scalped the last vestiges of my marriage? How can that be?

He's a silhouette, as frail as a seed on the wind. He doesn't have the strength to prise a ring and peel a finger, but then again, he has no use of worldly goods, precious metals and polished stones. His violence is cunning, his cruelty insidious, his spite invasive. He creeps.

An itch at my heel, a tickle. I clutch the wooden handle under my pillow. A feeling of being rolled and mauled courses over me, a sense of being pulled apart, of silence popping with static, the hum of electricity down the wires, sparks erupting across the ceiling. Taps and hisses and blinding bursts of light spin around the room stirred by the turn of wheels, like the click of a camera. There's dread in the sticky, humid air wafting from the fan. It's so hot that I can't bear my own skin. My groin aches, my buttocks sting, my spine prickles, my stomach is bruised.

Something twitches in the bed. I wait for a rustle, a slither, the scuttle of cockroaches, the mewing of cats. I lie still, gripping tight on the hammer. I'm perspiring alcohol, there's bile in my throat, my heart pounds and spit freezes on my tongue, expectant and charged. There's breath behind me, or is it my own turning in the echoes of a spent nightmare?

Cars pass on the street, their lights casting a picture onto the window pane. The Grey Man sniffs the air, hair a shock of seaweed, chest swollen with globes of fat, ribs like piano keys clasping a bloated belly, hips framing a nest of wire. An androgynous beast, staring from sockets smeared with ash and set in a blank mask with a ripe mouth pouting like a flounder, calling to me, puckering for a kiss.

The demon smoulders as the car beams shine through his guts. His hide is soft and putrid, straining over fragile bones, hung with black-tipped udders. He's translucent, the legs of the over-turned chair poke from his thighs. His fingers stretch and beckon, nails painted silver, flexing like tapered blades. He wants to touch me, but he's trapped in the glazing and vibrates in frustration. His outline is blurred like engraving on a mirror, shuddering to break free. He shakes and shimmies in the gloom and sighs in ecstasy as he finally slips free of the glass to emerge as a physical presence knelt behind me, bent over, offering a nipple.

I will not turn to face the reflection. I will not embrace the image hung naked and hungry over my cowering body.

The car swings away, the patio returns, the intruder pales. The thin man doesn't have much longer. In moments, he'll wither to a scatter of filth and be no more, unless he finds that warm carcass on which to feed. He must act or be condemned to wander the monsoons.

The mattress shifts as he shuffles closer, and the room is a collision of flares, crashing across the walls, chased by the grind of gears and the snap of cogs. A muttering shadow with white hands waits in the doorway to applaud the vampire as he dissects and suckles and emerges from darkness cloaked in my raw flesh. The bedsprings creak, and my tormentor lies down and scratches my back and rubs my feet. He moans and fondles between my legs, reaching for my balls, to pluck my fruit, to devour me, to regain the form that evaporates from his porous tissue. I swing the cold metal.

The Grey Man shrieks as the hammer arcs. His features are blanched by shock, eyeballs jet discs under clumps of straw tethered by ribbons. The hammer descends, and his head explodes like a puff-ball in a cloud of spores. He thrashes about and pushes the ruins of his face around the heavy claw, trying to mend the damage. His manicured hands seep a deep red, almost pitch, which spreads like oil down a slender neck and over trembling, perfect breasts. My watch swings loose around a thin and quivering wrist.

A bulb flashes in the door as a shutter whirrs. The white gloves dance and vanish. There's a clatter on the stairs. The Grey Man shivers and lies still. He is not so thin and his hair is not so wild, though woolly.

And he is not so grey.

THE VISITOR
John Paul Davies

Dead leaves and newspapers blustered about the hospital entrance. Nothing else made itself known on the monitor, but the visitor was out there.

The security guard's fingers trembled as he reached for the desk drawer containing the bottle of Bell's. The whiskey would have to wait, however, as the visitor manifested himself on the screen, staring into the camera unwaveringly, as though he could see George through the lens.

George's chair rocked back, a flailing boot upsetting his tea flask, the contents of which soaked into his splayed pornography. Bastard nerves; the spilt tea insinuated mysterious patterns across his spread-eagled, stapled beauties.

Only wind-hurried litter came through the activated doors at first—leaves, fast food wrappers, dross—collecting in a heap at George's feet. No other discernible movement as he squinted out into the quickening sleet. Had the visitor lost patience after all and turned tail? The hum of distant traffic may as well have come from a different world.

Murdering George's hopes, the visitor detached himself from amorphous shadow, stepping forward into the harsh light of the lobby.

"Come in then, if you're coming," George said, feigning bravado as his pulse rate doubled, unable to meet the visitor's eyes.

"Much appreciated, George. You're all heart."

In overcoat, unbuttoned collar and loosened tie, the visitor resembled an after-hours businessman, dutifully calling on a sick grandparent.

"No change with our friend, then."

Not a question. The guard worked his jaw slowly as the visitor headed for the stairs, the moment to respond already passed. What he wanted with Billy Flood was anyone's guess.

An insistent tattoo from the stairwell soon pervaded, his footsteps resounding until it seemed the visitor were one of many climbers trudging steadily upwards.

Repositioned at his security station, little more than an alcove afforded by Reception, George followed the visitor's progress on his monitor. As expected, the visitor exited the stairwell at the sixth floor, disappearing momentarily between the coverage of the CCTV cameras.

George soon located him again, passing faded signs for operating theatres, maternity wards, the mortuary. The irregular jut of the visitor's hipbone did little to hinder his progress towards Ward Eighteen.

Life-supporting machines thrummed beyond curtained-off wards, the barely born and the nearly dead demanding a minimum level of privacy. The visitor noted the familiar scent of decay, the bladder failing along with the will. Certain lingerings that could not be scrubbed away.

Whatever you do, don't stop here. The duty nurse at Ward Eighteen willed the visitor to pass, his loathsome shadow spreading across her desk. Annmarie pretended to study the notice board, its outdated patient details colour-coded beyond comprehension. The visitor lingered to spite her, noting the swell of the nurse's stomach beneath her uniform.

Wasn't that how you killed your own Mother, Annie? Drank her dry from the womb?

Annmarie flinched at the words—mere fragments of her frenzied, night-shift mind. *Wake up now, Billy. Will you wake up and end this nightmare?*

The visitor, meanwhile, materialised at the patient's bed, dabbing the sleeping man's forehead with a damp cloth. Billy Flood's eyes fluttered in motor response behind their lids.

The surrounding beds had long given up the incurable or the cured. Final ward moments replayed, unfailingly dank and tedious. Impotent anger gave way to acceptance; realisation dawning only as the eye lost focus on the visitor, and each skittering pupil retracted into extinction.

Others, refusing to wake, were afforded a considerate death. Death stealing in without fanfare, gently closing the door behind it.

Stifling a yawn, the visitor carefully set down a small jewellery box, as though to surprise the patient with a gift on waking.

How many nights were given over to this?

The visitor stiffened as the ward's wall-clock flipped over to midnight: 00:00

"Wake up now, Billy."

No change in heart rate or blood pressure, the patient reduced to these oscillating vital signs. A regular artificial beep declared the comatose man's existence, that his was life still to be preserved.

Billy Flood: Nil By Mouth.

The visitor looked down at the patient despondently, pitifully prone in his sickbed and hospital-issued smock with a slit for the arse. So much for the legendary gambler.

The drip bubbled, and an amber liquid crept along the tube taped to Flood's forearm, bound for the perforated vein. Tracing the fluid's languid movement with his index finger, the visitor applied slight pressure to the tubing to provoke a response from the submerged man.

None forthcoming, the visitor abandoned his vigil, crossing the ward to look out its windows. His face a shrivelled ashen wick behind the pane, a soulless avatar yet to be assigned identity.

Across the hospital grounds, the chimneystack of the crematorium rose like some temple to forsaken gods—dark amongst the dark, its height could not be ascertained. The visitor watched ash fill the sky like an ill sleet of snow, imagining outcast angels descending at last.

In that maudlin light, the visitor's face appeared decimated by some wasting disease; recently recreated, the rejected flesh padded back to the bone and papered over. Turning from the window, he shook his head sadly once again at Flood before pocketing the small box from the table. Life was never easy.

"Time is all I have, Billy Boy. Tomorrow, then?"

The shadow of his visitor permeated the borders of Billy's consciousness; memory and dream collided inside his fractured skull as he floated through without past or future.

The familiar footage continued: a racehorse nearing the winning post. Billy watched from the white running rail while the visitor moved across his drawn lids, summoning storm clouds to gather over Flood's racetrack.

The horse's pursuers closed in, destroying the daylight between them, and Billy knew in these agonising moments that it was over. Blind Man's Buff was floundering, the twelve-to-one shot that would have rescued Flood from his latest degenerate spiral.

Through the turning fog of its breath, the horse's eye strained to look at him; the turf, and Flood's hopes, turning to quicksand beneath its hooves.

Devil's Daughter had been the one. Even the greenest punter could see that now as the winning horse loomed menacingly behind Flood's pick, eating into the lead with every stride. Flood was forced to endure the final furlong of the race, replaying in a cruel, constant loop.

The monitor registered the increase in Flood's pulse as he willed his horse on again, the visitor tracking this development with renewed interest.

"Still flogging that dead horse, Billy Boy?"

The *Racing Post* fell from George's lap, its pages scattering as the intercom disturbed his dreamless doze. The usual routine played out: five minutes to midnight, the constant visitor striding towards the stairwell.

"Bracing out there, George. Catch your death."

The security guard grimaced as he drank tea from his flask, remembering the first time he met the visitor. It began as a small loan, a tide-over, but small problems untended became big problems.

The front page of his strewn racing guide showed Devil's Daughter crossing the winning line. At the rail, Billy Flood could just be made out, impossible to tell in his expression whether he had backed the horse or not.

Wake up now, Billy. Blood still flowed on its blind course beneath the skin, pulsing her lips as she kissed his cheek and gently touched his closed eyes, wishing she could follow him through to that other realm. Annmarie uselessly held his heavy hand against her stomach, urging him to feel the rhythm of his own burgeoning flesh through her, as if this should rouse him.

Hearing the visitor's approach, Annmarie hurriedly left Billy's bed and returned to her desk, each reverberating footstep sounding a death knell inside her head.

The baby kicked before she could reach her sanctuary, and pain ran like a lit fuse, trilling her entire nervous system. Blind panic followed; Annmarie grit her teeth as the floor threatened to lurch away.

You don't have to be afraid, Annie. This one won't hurt you, you know.

Even at the extreme of her agony, she refused to submit against her own rebelling body, trying to blank out the visitor's words. As he eventually reached the ward, Annmarie drew a ragged breath again.

"Brought you some fruit, Billy Boy," the visitor said breezily. The searing pain slowly subsided as the baby withdrew its protestations.

"Grapes are very dear nowadays."

An insect thrummed inside the overhead light's casing, amplified in Billy's sensitised state. Testing the dimensions of its casket drowsily, the creature dreamt of escape in each illuminated moment.

The intermittent light created a strobing effect across the jaundiced glow of the ward. Annmarie's baby gurgled, surprising itself with the sound, laughing until its father was compelled to join in.

Billy blinked, distrusting his senses. How many times had he dreamt of waking like this? Impossible to tell, coma-drifting between the abandoned islands of his remembered life. How long since he had stood up, even? Billy drew back the thin sheet and walked towards his new family, praying his legs would carry him such a short distance.

"Beautiful, Annmarie. Look at him. Beautiful, isn't he?" His own voice seemed unfamiliar, dredged from the dry gulch of his throat. "Can I hold him?"

"You better had. Thought he'd be shaving before you woke up."

Billy reached out to take his newborn son into his arms. "Everything's going to be okay now, Annmarie."

Holding his boy tentatively, afraid he might shatter to pieces, his son beamed with recognition.

"No more gambling. No more wasted time. Promise."

The baby ceased his gurgling, meeting Billy's gaze as though to test the sincerity of his father's pledge.

"Will you take us home now, Billy?"

00:00

After the next strobe, they were gone. The light finally giving up the ghost, leaving the ward in a pallid near-dark. And Billy alone in it, eyes burning, the cradle of his arms empty.

"Annmarie?"

Their bed abandoned, Flood stumbled over to the faint glow of the window, lifting up the blinds. Snow gently fell outside, wavering his reflection, and the weight of the boy imprinted in Billy's arms with the smell of talcum powder, the rawness of new skin.

Signalled by a low, artificial hum, sullen light eventually restored. Billy turned from the window, hoping to see Annmarie and their baby again.

Others now occupied the beds, the ward seemingly back in business. Thin discoloured sheets drawn over the newcomers' writhing bodies like second skins, their faces almost apparent, as though the sheets were liquid, filling the moulds of skulls beneath. Sallow flesh showed in torn places, and Flood was bound once again in the tomb of his bed, almost gagged by his own sheet.

The howling began then, a unison of agony rising from the trembling shrouds; the cacophony filling Flood's ears and mind as he tried to hold on to the fragmenting image of Annmarie and his son.

Where Billy slept, the unseen dead of the ward stepped closer.

The visitor studied the monitor as Flood's heart rate rose majestically. What would he feel when the heart burst, yielding to the unrepentant pulse? Survivors talked of euphoria at the moment of attack, of even seeing lost loved ones again. The heart tricking the mind into thinking paradise beckoned.

That Flood came knocking on his door was inevitable. Riddled with the gambler's sickness, he was only one race away from ending the unforgiving streak.

"Should have come to me first, Billy. We could have settled this more pleasantly. Have you brought what was asked for?"

Billy slowly retrieved the requested items, placing them on the desk for inspection.

"Very good, Billy. Now, we can do business together."

The visitor still regretted not keeping closer order on his client. Finding it difficult to decide who had been the most retched in the situation—Flood's mugger or the mugged himself. On rifling through Flood's pockets, the thief of limited ambitions would have discovered nothing but IOU's and losing betting slips.

Selecting poor quarry for his fruitless debut, the shivering addict was unaware of whose skull he had caved in. The candles scattered about the mugger's squat flared wildly at the visitor's entrance; the motionless humps of other bodies in dingy sleeping bags bore no witness, cocooned in their own grubby ecstasies.

"What is it you see?" the visitor had asked, crouching down, an eager ear to the mugger's frothing mouth. No revelation forthcoming as vessels erupted, the white of the unfortunate's eyes filling with blood. The loaded syringe fell from his twitching hand, splintering on the squalid floor.

Though removed from the scene, some kind of wrench was used in the mugging: short in length, easy to swing. The detective speculated to Annmarie that Billy must have flinched back suddenly; had he moved the other way, he wouldn't be lying in Ward Eighteen. Billy's attacker overdosed shortly afterwards, along with a number of other homeless addicts. Drugs cut with a variety of household detergents had been circulating recently, the detective explained.

From the darkness beyond the ward, the baby's screams could no longer be denied: a declamation of the life it had been forced into. The newborn howls traipsed along the corridor, seeking out Annmarie at her desk as she vainly tried not to listen.

The harried cries from the unseen woman followed, rising with the infant's in a horrendous commentary to the brief overlap of their lives.

"Oh, do be quiet, Mother." Annmarie almost giggled insanely, fearing she would never stop if she allowed the laughter to escape her lips.

"Mother." Just a word, formed from second-hand memories, pieced together from photographs. Not a woman who had ever walked, breathed, or loved.

She suffered for hours, Annie. I should know. I was there.

The visitor fed on her solitude, cajoling the thirty-year-old screams from forsaken wards.

The visitor looked up suddenly from Billy's bedside, setting down the jewellery box as though listening in to Annmarie's thoughts.

"Better hope Billy wakes up sharpish," he said, lips sliding apart in a slight approximation of a smile; a wound unstitching. His eyes settled on Annmarie's stomach. "Wipe the slate clean, and you can still play at happy families."

The visitor's slender fingers traipsed the jewellery box. "Unless Billy defaults, that is."

Take us home now, Billy? Annmarie asked, far off, her voice straining as she spoke his name.

Billy failed to stir. On the bedside table sat the small box the visitor had left behind. Although reticent to touch anything he had, Annmarie picked it up for closer examination. Its sides pulsed in her hand, as though whatever the box contained tested its bounds. Resisting the urge to throw the infernal thing out of the window, she unfastened its silver clasp, looking around all the while, fearful of the visitor's return.

Strangely detached on first glimpsing its contents, as though she hovered over herself from a high corner of the ward. Annmarie opened the box and discovered what the visitor had been harbouring all along.

"No, not *this*."

The box fell from her numb fingers, Billy's unaffected face doubling, trebling through her fierce tears.

"Not this, *Billy*."

The scan of their unborn boy seemed tarnished now, no longer theirs. The copy Billy once proudly kept in his wallet fluttered to the floor. The thought was almost too much; the idea that that *thing* had been carrying their child around, not Billy.

She shook her husband, demanding Billy wake to answer her. Exhausted, she let his head fall back to the pillow.

A lock of hair lay on the tiled floor, disinterred from the box—individual red strands that she instinctively knew were hers. Annmarie touched the back of her head as though the violation continued.

Annmarie shook Flood's unresponsive body on the screen, and George enjoyed this development in his evening's viewing. But any amusement he derived was short-lived as the screen switched back to the main entrance, settling on the visitor waiting patiently in the sleet.

The visitor stepped forward swiftly on this occasion as the doors opened.

"It's time, George." The visitor's pale, thin hand disappeared into a coat pocket.

The monitor at George's desk showed Annmarie slumped in a flickering corridor. Shielding her stomach with one arm, she howled mutely, her face straining towards the camera.

"Just give me one more chance." George staggered back towards the poor protection of his desk. "You've got to give me more time, that's all."

The visitor studied a stain on his shirt cuff, as if the blight might possess some deeper meaning.

"That's debatable," the visitor said.

If such thing as a soul existed, George's was flung wide open as the visitor moved nearer still: a soul laden with value and price.

The visitor came closer.

George sank into his chair heavily, as though anaesthesia diluted the blood. His heart accelerating to its end, all breath escaped him. In his final expression, George contemplated the stashed bottle of whiskey he never got to drink.

The visitor retreated in the security guard's eye.

The monitor tracked the visitor moving along the hospital's corridors, its desolate arteries; the dark figure an insidious chemical streak infiltrating a developing photograph.

The visitor entered Ward Eighteen, where Billy Flood woke and slowly sat upright.

EXACTLY AS WE ARE MEANT TO BE
J.A.W. McCarthy

It starts the same as it did last time and all of the times before: I'm lying on my stomach, eyes open, covers half-off, one arm dangling over the edge of the bed like a dead girl in a movie, fully believing that I am about to become one of those dead girls.

Footsteps weigh in the hall, then in my room just out of my line of sight, the floorboards chattering wooden teeth under uncertain feet. I wiggle my fingers towards the baseball bat I keep tucked between the nightstand and the wall, but my fingers don't move. All of the joints in my hand strain, but it does nothing more than dangle at the end of my dead-girl arm. This is when the other hands come.

Fingertips drag over the top of my back, bare where the collar of my stretched-out t-shirt dips down between my shoulder blades. Hands pull the sheets down to my ankles, and cold pricks every inch of my legs but doesn't last long; once the fingernails dig into my skin, there is only the hot sear of pain.

Of course, I can't scream. I can't really see her either, not with all this hair over my eyes. There's just a small, shadowy form—crouched, maybe—creeping along the end of my bed, pulling up strips of my skin with her soft, smooth fingertips. For some reason, even though I have never really seen her, I know she is female.

In the morning, after everything finally goes black again and the sun forces its way between the curtains, I roll onto my back and draw my right leg up to my chest. From mid-thigh almost to my knee is a bright pink stripe of raw flesh where my skin used to be. I keep my nails short and neat, so I can show that I am not harming myself, and as expected, my fresh coat of polish—Galaxy, my favorite shimmering black—is un-chipped and my nails are clean: no blood, no skin, no proof of what was done to me in the night.

"It's sleep paralysis," Jim insists every time, until I stop telling him all together. "Your mind wakes up, but your body is still asleep. That's why you can't move."

Then, she's real, and she's there, and she's really touching me, taking from me.

"Well, Ella, I mean, your mind is still half-asleep. It's a hallucination."

I used to show him the bruises, my skinned knees, the long scratches up and down my forearms.

He said I was doing it in my sleep, whether I was in his bed or my own. "Maybe you sleepwalk?"

When it got worse—the times when I saw her, when I woke up to a dime-sized chunk taken out of my thigh or a slender strip of skin peeled from my upper arm like a curl of orange rind—I called the police, told them someone had broken into my house and attacked me.

"No sign of forced entry," the officer said after a cursory glance around my house. Like Jim, he suggested seeing a doctor, a sleep study, laying off the weed before bed.

Jim leaves for Portland tomorrow. He heads back to his apartment early so he can pack, leaving me alone for the next three nights. As I'm kissing him goodbye, his body presses hard into mine, his thigh swiping across the raw wound on my own. It leaves a sticky smear of blood on the hem of my long t-shirt. When I cry out, he chuckles and makes a joke about how the aliens won't leave me alone. I tell him that I hope he doesn't crash and die on the way to Portland.

Right now, it's easy because I can make myself small enough. Mother complains that people secure their doggy doors these days, but I don't need to use those yet; I can still slip in through a crack in the window frame, or between misaligned floorboards, or a gap under the kitchen door. I know I am supposed to hate being like this, but I love creeping around Ella's house, slipping into her life, touching her books and trying on her lipstick and tasting the roasted meats she stores in the refrigerator after she's eaten all she can, fingers sticky-sweet and dripping with grease as she stands over the kitchen sink. I'm practicing, shadowing, and I'm getting good: now, I lick my fingers just like she does, and I press my lips together to spread the lipstick to the edges just like she does, and I fold down the corner of the page to mark my place in a book just like she does. Mother says that when I am bigger, when I am almost done, it will become more difficult for us both.

Sometimes, I take things, more than just a bite of meat or a cookie from the box in the pantry. With the food, it's no big deal—she just blames her boyfriend—but if I were to take the shiny onyx earrings or the delicate gold chain she always wears, she would know too much about me, and people might start listening. Like when the policeman came, and he walked around her house, and he stood in her bedroom. He even flipped open the lid of her little mother of pearl jewelry box, and I was so afraid she would see that I had tried on her rings, but she was busy trying to show him her arms. So far, I have taken a grocery list (*tampons, soy sauce, apples, string cheese*—she really likes string cheese), three earring backs, and a couple of twist-ties from her bread bags. Green and orange, like pumpkins, like Halloween. I tried to clip them to my earlobes, but they just scraped the shiny skin there, making me bleed.

Mother says I'm lucky to find my match right here in the city; when she was small like me, she had to travel three states over and live in an old Volkswagen bus with her own mother until they found the right one. She hated taking from the woman at first, but she was glad she did because she ended up so beautiful with her long, wavy, dark hair and brown eyes. She learned to walk in delicate heels and make her gauzy skirts swish against her legs, and she painted the nails she took so that they would grow in pale pink on her own hands. It took months to take everything—"You can't give up now. I didn't sacrifice so you could be incomplete," Grandmother said— chipping teeth and peeling up ribbons of skin so that the woman couldn't even bear to have the bed sheets touch her open flesh. There were so many times that the woman begged the police and the doctors for help. Near the end, her family did as they were told and put sedatives in her wine and tied her to the bed at night. Though it seemed cruel to my mother, Grandmother taught her to untie just one hand before she took more. Once my mother was big enough, after she was finally able to dig down to the bone, she went to visit the woman one last time and found her dead. This made my mother sad, so when she had me, she told me this story, and she called me after the woman: Rose.

When I have my own daughter, I will name her Ella, and I will teach her what I know so that she doesn't have to be lucky like me, or go far to find the perfect one.

I used to be scared to sleep alone, but now, I'm almost relieved when Jim is gone. For three nights, I can push the kitchen chairs up under the doorknobs and leave the dowels in the window tracks and lock the bedroom door, all without judgment and the condescending comments of a man who thinks he is protecting me.

Every night he says, "I'll hear them. When they break in, they'll see me here, and they won't hurt you. They'll have to go through me first."

Yet every morning, he surveys me with bleary eyes, talking about his crazy dreams, not a scratch on him. He grabs my hands and suggests mittens at bedtime. He thinks he's protecting me from myself.

On the first night, I take extra precautions. Before the sun sets, I pry the nailed boards from the crawlspace entry in the backyard. Down on my belly beneath my small, straight rambler, I run my flashlight over pipes with cobwebs in their elbows and bricks that look like they're sweating thick icing. My hands and feet scramble along the ground and against the walls, so I can turn over and see the bottom of the flooring above me, the light from inside identifying the gaps in the pink insulation that let the cold air into my bedroom.

When I spot small handprints in the dirt, I'm frightened for a moment, but my knees rub them away before I can hold my own hand to the indents. It's at once reassuring and disappointing that there is nothing down here besides spiders and other strange insects, and the familiar scent of my perfume as if years of it in the air above has leeched through the floorboards. On my way back outside, something small and sharp scrapes against my palm. I think it's a tiny nail or a screw until I hold it up to the light and see that it's an earring back.

I check every room, every closet, every cupboard or corner a person could hide. My fingers find locks and turn them as far as they will go into door and window frames. I put the chairs in place and settle in front of the TV with leftover chicken wings straight from the fridge, wiping my greasy fingers on my bare legs, careful to avoid the open wound that is too big and sore to bandage.

My mother had a sister—long dead before I was born—who would wake after terrible night terrors to find claw marks up and down her legs and arms. Her sheets would be streaked with blood as bright and sudden as the pain that made her scream. She swore she wasn't harming herself in her sleep, but who would be able to do this to her after she locked herself in her room and nailed boards over her windows? Their father stayed in her apartment with her, until she accused him of cutting off her hair and pulling out her teeth. The police were no help, and the doctors started talking about involuntary commitment.

It wasn't long before she was found dead in her bed, bled out from over a hundred little punctures, a pair of manicure scissors still clenched in her fist. Though it appeared to be as everyone thought—the strange suicide of a mentally-ill woman—the police arrested an ex-boyfriend without an alibi. He still had the keys to her apartment.

My mother got the chicken recipe from her. She told me all about my aunt as she was showing me how to glaze the wings. Though the nighttime injuries hadn't started yet, I remember vowing that I would never tell her if they did.

I go to bed thinking about my aunt, still tasting her chicken along the back of my teeth as my tongue pokes around for gaps and my fingers dig into the roots of my hair against the pillow. It's not likely that I will wake to a new wound tomorrow, not this close to the last one that still throbs hot and liquid on my thigh. There will not be a new nick or scrape until after Jim spends the night again, a bruise across my cheek or a split down my lip so that Tamara at work will look at me with her wet, droopy eyes and ask if everything is okay at home: *How's the relationship? Does Jim get angry sometimes?* I just wish that *she*—the woman with the smooth fingertips who crouches at the end of my bed—would leave my face alone.

I'm not supposed to go out tonight—"Don't be greedy," Mother chides me—but it's all I can think about. *She's* all I can think about. It's because I'm getting close. Mother says we are overachievers, each generation of us more accomplished than the one before, so I can believe I am almost done even though I am still small.

I practice saying her name: *Ella, Ella, Ella,* rolling around inside the velvet parts of my mouth, bouncing off stunted teeth and nesting in the back of my throat, *Ella.* It's like a song, and I wonder how she sounds when she says her own name. Does it lilt and tumble like satin unfurling across a wooden floor?

Even when I am angry, I will enjoy calling for my future daughter, my Ella.

In Ella's house, I perch on her windowsill as I watch her sleep. She is strangely peaceful, more so than when she is with him, and I have a feeling I would not have to make her still this time, even though I will take nothing tonight.

Still, I can't resist running my finger over her lips until they part, her breath clutching warm against my skin. I can't stop myself from curling a lock of her burnt-red hair around my thumb.

In the bathroom, I dip my fingers into all of the little jars and rub the pearlescent creams into my skin so that I can be as soft and beautiful as she is. I spray her perfume into my hair like I saw her do once, careful not to spill it again.

I need to know what she knows, to do these things as easily and naturally as she does.

Before I leave, I go into her closet. I am still too small to wear her things, but that doesn't stop me. I am glad she likes green and soft fabrics and black faded like old leather—things that I like immediately, things that I don't have to learn to like. Mother often says that she sacrifices for me just as her own mother did for her.

I don't think this is a sacrifice, though; I can't imagine my mother didn't enjoy doing these same things that I now do.

Curled on my side in bed, I think about what my life was like before this started happening, back when I could blame the occasional scratch on my face on dream-restless hands or a simple itch in my sleep. I had friends over for movies and drinks; I slept with the window open in the summer; I didn't crawl around under my house, looking for gaps that would allow a person entry; I didn't change the locks every three months. I wasn't constantly mired in a strange mix of fear and numbness.

That's why, as I'm sliding out of bed, what I see makes we wish for one little cut instead, something that I can understand.

Six outfits are laid out across my bedroom floor, shirts inside cardigans over skirts and pants ending in shoes, like a string of inverted paper dolls. Most of it is not quite right, though: a purple t-shirt with a red skirt; my interview blazer over the moth-chewed sweater I only wear at home; last year's office Christmas party dress with wool socks tucked into sandals. I would check my doors and windows again, but I already know they are exactly as I left them.

My bathroom reeks of a perfume that used to be my favorite but now makes me vomit bile into the sink. I would have preferred another chunk of flesh or a clipping of my hair taken—at least that seems to have a purpose, unlike this bizarre, labored violation.

I thought I knew what she wanted. I thought there wasn't anything worse that she could do.

My mother used to see a woman who looked exactly like her sister shortly after her death. She would see her blended into a crowd downtown or getting off a bus near the university, always hurrying and keeping her head down so that my mother was never quite sure. At first, my mother agreed with the worried loved ones who told her these sightings were just a physical manifestation of her grief, this woman another pretty, dark-eyed brunette whose features could be molded into the lines my mother knew. Then, on the day that she was packing up her car to move from the family home, my mother saw the woman standing at the far end of the block, watching her. She even wore my aunt's favorite dress, the green lace one their parents had wanted to bury her in. When my mother ran to her, the woman seemed to shrink, becoming lost between houses and behind fences she couldn't possibly scale. That was the last time my mother saw her.

Sometimes, I wonder if I am walking in the same loop as my aunt. If I am doing things differently enough. At what point will we cross? Before I throw all of my clothes in the laundry, I check the closet. My favorite dress is still in there.

This is the life that I want: my own bed in my own home full of my own things that I picked out myself and don't have to share with anyone. I want to work in a nice office where I have my own desk with blue and black and red pens and flowers that I buy on my way in. I want to linger in record stores on the weekends and drink the fancy coffees that I smell on her breath even under the toothpaste. I want a boyfriend who likes the same TV shows and makes me make those noises, the ones that she makes when her legs go stiff under the sheets.

Mother says I will know I am almost done when Ella becomes weak. Once I have a piece of every part of her, I will be complete, and she will start to unravel until she dies in her bed or falls drunk down the stairs or her family sends her away. She will be no more, and I will exist in her place, finally what I was always supposed to become.

I don't want Ella to end up like the other Rose. I don't want to be sad like my mother, reminded of what I have done every time I say my future daughter's name. Because of this, I am careful, and I keep my hands clean, and I try to pace myself despite my eagerness. Sometimes, the urges are so strong that I can't stop myself from visiting, but it is only to observe and learn: wine with dinner, coffee before shower, a jacket with a hood when the smoky clouds start to suffocate the sky. Pen in my right hand, paper under my left, reminders to boyfriends end with a heart or *love*. Fingers on every lock on every window and door before bed each night. Chairs under doorknobs when no one else is around.

Tonight, on the last night before her boyfriend returns, I settle next to her in bed and take a piece of her tooth. Just a chip, a crumb of bone that I immediately press into my own mouth. Her eyes race behind her closed lids as I do this, but she makes no other movements. I can hear the pounding of her heart, the fear I cause illustrated beneath her t-shirt. I say her name as I take one fingernail and one toenail. "Ella, I am sorry. Ella, I am almost done."

I don't leave until she can roll over again, her finger tapping a bloody cadence on the blanket as she dreams. Before I go, I press my ear to her mouth and am reassured by the roar of her lungs and a pulse returned to its relaxed jog against my cheek.

This is what I will look like when I sleep. This is what I will sound like.

I know how to put on her perfume and arrange her clothes, and I have watched her cook enough to know what goes in the pan first. I know how to wash my body and talk to a man and make him come back even when I don't want him around. When I have my own home, I will know where everything goes. I know how to cocoon myself and drive away the people who love me and make sure it is just me, exactly as I am meant to be.

47

I've been documenting what she does to me. There are Polaroids in my dresser drawer, tucked out of sight under lingerie from boyfriends past: the naked patch where my eyelashes used to be; a hole in my forearm dug deep by fingernails so gnarled and filthy that I could feel the infection setting in; the bare patch on my scalp behind my ear; the raw crevasse that looks like it's splitting my thigh in two. This morning, I add to the collection close-ups of my bloody finger and toe where my nails used to be. I have to snarl to get a good picture of my chipped tooth.

Back from Portland, Jim calls and asks if he can come over, but I tell him that I'm not feeling well and I don't want to get him sick. I know he will show up tonight anyway with chicken soup from the deli by his apartment, so I'll answer the door in my robe and show him the bedtime gloves on my hands, taking the soup with a closed-lip smile so that he'll believe he has done everything he can. Next weekend, when he asks what happened to my tooth, I'll have prepared a story about too much whisky and a clumsy bite into a chicken bone.

It's exhausting, but these small arms-length lies to boyfriends and mothers are better than more elaborate stories to doctors and police. My aunt told the truth, and she ended up dead, her memory tarnished by pity head shakes and prayers for her troubled soul. I can tolerate the missing ribbons of skin and fingernails if that is what she must take from me. Everything will heal and grow back. What scares me most, though, is the piece of paper I find under my pillow as I am settling into bed tonight. It's my stationary and my handwriting but not my words.

Dear Ella. I am sorry. Love.

I am getting too big. I can't slip between the floorboards anymore, so I thread my arm through the gap beneath the kitchen door, reaching far enough to turn the deadbolt so the rest of me can come in. Her boyfriend took the chairs from the doors after she went to bed.

For four weeks, I have left Ella alone, instead biding my time watching my teeth straighten, and the freckles bloom across my cheeks, and my hair grow in long and shiny and burnt red. Tonight, though, I am here because I cannot wait any longer. This is the last thing I will do to her. Because I am almost done, Mother says I must hurry; I can't stop now.

Lying on her side, knees pulled to her chest, she looks like she is trying to hold everything in, trying to keep me out. As I roll her onto her back and make her still, her eyes fly open so that she will be watching me the whole time. Her boyfriend snores next to her, his back to us, but I whisper anyway: "This is the last time, Ella. I promise."

I do it fast—Mother assures me it is a small mercy. I peel up her left eyelid and plunge my short, neat Galaxy-colored nails into her eye socket. The panic—a new kind, fresher than the usual plod through her limbs every time I take—surges outward from the center of her chest, seizing against my thighs as I sit astride her. I thought it would be like plucking a grape from the stem, but the muscles cling as strong as her fear, and as I tug—listening to her boyfriend's snoring, trying not to shake the bed, Mother's *now! now! now!* bouncing around inside my head—I see my reflection go dull in the gaping black pupil of her green eye.

One of the first things she took was a piece of my tongue. I remember shortly before that accidentally cutting my tongue as I was licking melted chocolate from its foil wrapper. The sweetness was marred by the blood, but the blood was as rich as the chocolate, dampening the sting of what was nothing more than a quickly forgotten paper cut. Though I was afraid to taste after what she did to me, once I allowed myself, everything was brighter, richer, deeper.

I wish I could say it's like that now.

What little I can eat is unidentifiable after my hospitalization. My favorite satin robe is no better than an over-bleached hospital gown after I told Jim it's over. Everything I see with my remaining eye is flat and hazy, no edges or corners or unbroken colors after my mother ensconced herself in my guest room. I am missing a piece from every part of myself, but compared to my aunt, I am lucky.

She is a very lucky one, though. *She* is half me and all herself, a person-and-a-half who can exist outside of me and also be me. She's my child in a way. That's why when she comes to my bed again, I know she's not here to finally kill me.

"You won't scream?" she asks, perching on the edge of the mattress, pressed up against me even though the other side of my bed is empty.

I shake my head, surprised that I can move.

She looks down at her hands braced on her thighs, small and tensed and ready to spring her out the nearby window.

"I am so sorry, Ella." Her voice is strangely stilted—practiced, even—her only mistake being how she drags out the *L*s in my name.

I tap the note I keep on my nightstand, the one that I know better than to show my mother or the doctors or the therapist I now have to see twice a week. "I know."

"You want to know why I do this."

I have walked the same loop as my aunt, but now, I know we will not cross. Everyone in my family says I look like her, and I can see it in the way my mother looks at me, the worry in her eyes as they trace the same bones and the same empty spaces that make me more like that long-dead woman every day. I know she believes me when I say that Jim didn't do this to me, and that may be partly because she never really believed that an ex-boyfriend killed her sister either. If I call for my mother, wake her up to see this strange creature that somehow looks like me, things won't be any different. My aunt will still be dead, and I will still be as I am, and this creature will still be all of me.

"What's your name?" I ask.

Her whole face lifts in surprise, and I think this is what others saw when they looked at me, before the hole in my face. "Rose."

"My clothes, my perfume—you've been watching me for a long time, haven't you? You were learning how to be like me?"

Rose nods.

Sitting up, I lean towards her so that our faces are just inches apart. She smells like me—not like my perfume or my soap, but like my fingers smell after I rub my scalp. If I touch her, she will feel like me, too—same fuzz on her earlobes, same rough patch on the back of her wrist—and if I let my tongue brush against her lips, I know what I will taste. Looking into the mirror of her eyes, I even know we are thinking the same thing.

As she moves her hands onto my thighs, Rose smiles the same tight-lipped smile I recognize from school pictures and graduation programs and birthday party scrapbooks. She doesn't move, doesn't make a sound as I pull the eye patch from my face and place it over her—*our*—left eye. Her right eye closes automatically under my lingering fingers, her body loosening so that pulling her down is easy, sliding her into the warm crater I left in the mattress is easy, tucking the blankets around her is easy. The smile remains on her face as I dress, as I grab the cash from my purse, as I open the window.

"Goodbye, Rose," I say.

"Goodbye, Rose," she echoes.

EMRY, THE ONE WHO REMEMBERED
J.N. Powell

She wrapped the powder-blue sash around her waist four times to honor those who had died. She paused and carefully layered the silk garment a fifth time.

After today, there would be five souls to mourn.

The silver-plated mirror on the wall reflected her image as she wrapped the sash, yet she did not recognize the oval face, the high cheekbones, the almond eyes that stared back. Though she did not know herself, the wooden frame made of rosewood and stained a deep mahogany seemed familiar. A wedding gift, wasn't it? And the jade comb on the dresser, the same soft green of the hot springs in winter, had been passed down for generations.

A stranger to herself, wisps of knowledge still remained.

Wisps that told her today would be another Joining ceremony. The fifth one. Her memories became more fractured and fleeting with each Joining, but she always tried to remember those who had been sacrificed in the ceremonies. What were their names?

Emry turned away from the mirror, the comb, and concentrated on getting dressed, but the sight of her new hands brought on distracting hints of recollection. They were so lovely, with long fingers and delicate skin; which of the chosen had they belonged to? She'd thought the disfigurement would be the most trying part of the Joining, but her new body parts were hauntingly beautiful. She looked at her hands again and smiled, forgetting for a moment the gruesome manner in which they were obtained.

No, do not forget.

Her smile faded as she searched for the memory of the first who Joined with her. It had been a woman. A mother. The name came, softly, as ripples upon a lake: *Wren, the one with beautiful hands.*

She finished tying the traditional knot of mourning in her blue sash, and a loud knocking resounded on the door. It was Lord Alaric with the ceremonial headdress, but as soon as she realized it, the knowledge danced away, replaced with images of a parade for warriors marching to battle, of blood-soaked weapons, and of empty beds.

"Come in," she said with another's intonation: *Vance, the one with melodious voice.*

The door opened, and a man entered, dressed in fine silks and jeweled rings. His hair curled slightly at the ends, just behind his ears and beneath the silver crown.

"Emry?" he said.

Emry-Neve-Wren-Chandra-Vance. The collective names of the chosen flowed through her mind, almost devouring it, but she mustn't speak the names. Not yet.

"How are you feeling?" he asked.

His expression strained, stance fidgeted, and Emry understood that he loved her. Lord Alaric loved his queen. He had pleaded for her not to go through with the Joining, hadn't he? And what had she replied?

"I am tired, but I will be fine," she said in Vance's voice.

He stepped toward her, perhaps to embrace her, but she turned to the mahogany mirror and watched her painted lips. "What did the mystics say?"

Her heart no longer ached for Lord Alaric. Not since the moment she received a new heart from Neve, the one with courageous spirit.

He lowered his eyes and stepped back. "They believe today is very auspicious for the final Joining."

A calming clarity brightened inside her, like a sunrise chasing away the mist.

"I am the final host," she said, childlike, as if the fact had never occurred to her before.

"Yes." He bowed slightly and presented the headdress, but a deep sadness dwelled in his tone. "None of the other hosts made it to the fifth day."

Emry studied its engraved runes of fortune, the tiny bells of silver, and the charcoal feathers half-painted red, positioned like a peacock's. She took it with Wren's lovely hands, placed it on her head, and raised her chin to look at Lord Alaric.

When the little bells jingled, a new wave of memories rushed through her. Chaotic images of a corpse-filled battlefield, chained and starved survivors, burned out homes, and scorched crops. Were the memories hers or theirs? Her eyes rolled back. Lord Alaric caught her in his arms before she hit the ground.

He carried her to a chair, hand-carved with dragons and stormy seas. "Don't listen to them. Stay with me, Emry."

Emry-Neve-Wren-Chandra-Vance. It took all her strength not to say it aloud. Each were the names of the chosen, each lived within her, but she mustn't say it until the name was complete.

She shut her eyes and breathed in deeply. Lord Alaric stood so close; she could smell the amber incense in his clothes. As his queen, she must've loved him once, but Neve's heart made him a stranger.

Emry sat up, smoothed out her silken robes, and gave him a weak smile. "The chosen are impatient. I feel like I am being pushed out."

"You don't have to be an oracle. We could win this war with soldiers and strategy, like we always have before." In his eyes was hope, the boyish hope of saving the one he loved. "You don't have to die for the kingdom."

Emry froze. She did not remember having to die, but something stirred inside her with affirmation: *for the kingdom*. She nodded to herself and to the spirits dwelling inside her. They would never stop echoing those words.

"I am Joined to the chosen. I can never escape them."

"You could learn to bury them." He begged her to release him from a terrible decision, but it had been her decision, too.

"They are the ones who will bury me," she said.

Emry could not even remember her own voice, only the musical quality of Vance's. She could not remember her own hands, her own feet. All she could do now was offer what remained of herself to the gods—and pray it was enough to become the oracle her kingdom needed.

Lord Alaric closed his eyes. He cleared his throat, stood, and offered his arm.

She took it, and walked with Chandra's steady feet out of the room. In silence, they followed the king's guard through the vacant palace and into a large hall of soaring ceilings and echoing walls. Emry tried to recall the specific events from yesterday, or any of the days before, but the details slipped away like fish in a stream. If she pressed too strongly to find her own memories, she was swarmed with the spirits of the chosen.

Hundreds of people, both regal and poor, quietly murmured in the ceremony hall. When Lord Alaric and Lady Emry entered, they shushed and divided to form a walkway. As the people watched with captivated attention, she secretly thanked Chandra. Her own feet would have faltered.

Emry focused on the platform ahead and the two silver thrones studded with rubies. Lord Alaric led her to one, then seated himself in the other. Between the thrones and the enraptured crowd was a stone altar rimmed with grim reliefs: leaping tongues of fire, gaping skulls, and piles of bones. A hundred half-melted candles were clustered at its base, burning blood-red flames.

"You faithful gathered here, we bless you," said a mystic to the watching flock. She wore a white mask, carved into a frown and furrowed brow, as did three others standing at the edge of the dais. They each held ornate, toothed daggers in their hands.

"On this fifth Day of Joining, we act as both gift and witness to the birth of our oracle. With your sacrifice, this kingdom's favor with the gods is ensured. And with such divine guidance, we shall win this war. We shall have peace once again. Kneel and know this: only the most ardent and holy may be chosen among you."

The four mystics walked into the kneeling crowd and held their knives aloft as they searched, hunted, for the one the blades were drawn to. The people pressed closer when they approached, then slumped down when they continued past.

"Emry," said Lord Alaric.

Emry-Neve-Wren-Chandra-Vance. The names overwhelmed her mind like a flooding riverbed, but she forced her lips silent.

"Do you not remember me? Is that why you refuse to stop this?"

She felt Wren's hands tighten on the arms of the throne. Neve's heart raced to near bursting. The chosen were adamant; they urged her to say the words, the names. She struggled to stay herself and in control. It was still her body, wasn't it? It was still her soul. The other hosts who had failed to complete the Joining had spoken the incantation too soon, and the gods would not come. Without aid from the divine, the joined parts had decayed, and the hosts had died.

"No, I do not remember you," she finally said.

Lord Alaric met her gaze. The torment there, the guilt. He reached out and touched Wren's hand, but she pulled it away.

A part of her wished she had her old heart back, the one that longed for the love of Lord Alaric. He seemed a good man. But that heart, Emry's heart, wouldn't have been strong enough to survive the Joining. It wouldn't be strong enough to do what must be done.

She looked into the kneeling crowd, the hopefuls, the ones willing to die to make her an oracle. "The kingdom needs an oracle, and I am she."

A voice from the masses shouted: "The chosen has been found."

The crowd parted until a path was formed from the ceremonial altar to the back of the hall. A young woman stood, singled out and surrounded by the four mystics. She approached the stage as the unchosen stretched their arms, hoping to touch the worthiest of their number. The woman's green eyes were alight with pride.

"I am honored to offer my eyes," the young woman said.

Lord Alaric quietly recited the response. "With your eyes, the final piece, the kingdom shall see what the gods see."

The woman smiled at his words and bowed deeply before taking her place upon the altar. She lay back and clasped her hands as the four mystics positioned themselves on either side of the altar, daggers at the ready.

Emry faced Lord Alaric. He offered his arm one last time, and she smelled the familiar traces of incense. She wished she remembered what his love was like, what it was to love at all. She kissed him on the hand. Isn't that what Lady Emry would have done? A heartbroken smile, a nod, stepping away. He

54

understood.

Emry took her place by the altar. "Chosen, what is your name?"

"Leigh."

Emry-Neve-Wren-Chandra-Vance-Leigh.

Yes, that was it. Leigh, the one with all-seeing eyes. The incantation was complete, and all the parts of her quieted. She knew what she had to do. "Give me her eyes."

Two of the mystics held Leigh down on the altar while the other two cut away the flesh with their knives. The blades hummed and glowed crimson at the taste of her blood. Leigh screamed and strained against the mystics, but her face was mutilated until bone was bare and the green eyes stared up. Her arms and legs went limp as the blood streamed down and pooled beneath her. The crowd murmured in reverence as they watched.

Emry took the exposed offering with Wren's lovely hands. Only the divine, if the chosen was true, could allow such a bond. The emerald eyes brightened for a moment, and she imagined them watching her. They saw straight through her. They looked into her very soul. Then, the eyes of Leigh, so wise, so discerning, dissolved into her skin, and Emry's own vision went black as the Joining began.

And she remembered: when she received her new heart, new hands, new feet, and new tongue, the Joining had been painless at first. The old parts fell away, to be saved and preserved as relics, and the new pieces grew from the stumps. It was not until later in the night, when the veins and the bones and the tendons stretched inside her, connecting to the adopted parts, that the pain came. She was put in separate quarters to rage and wail alone. By morning, the agony of Joining had passed. By morning, she had never seen such perfect hands, such perfect feet. The memories of the night before faded away as the memories of the chosen nestled deeper inside her.

But now, with the final Joining, Emry felt the pain. It consumed her. She could not breathe; she could not scream. The gods needed room inside her. They needed the chosen to be forgotten and erased.

No, do not forget.

Emry willed her new eyes to open. A searing light as fierce and burning as the sun greeted her. She wanted to run from the light, to hide, but the steadfastness in Chandra's feet kept her still.

For the kingdom.

She listened to the slow, strong pulse of Neve's courageous heart. Each beat filled her with strength, and she raised Wren's blood-drenched hands to the gods. She stood firmly upon Chandra's feet and saw the future with Leigh's green, piercing eyes.

The kingdom needs an oracle, and I am she.

Emry spoke the incantation with Vance's melodic voice:

Emry-Neve-Wren-Chandra-Vance-Leigh.

The mystics had said she and the chosen would be burned away by the fires of the divine within her. Nothing would be left. The last of her memories, her being, would rush out, and she would be replaced to overflowing with visions and terrible truths.

So be it, but she would never forget the chosen. Emry spoke their names again and again into the abyss, into the universe, until the gods came like fire, and she could speak no more.

"Emry?"

Her eyes were open. She saw beyond the light.

"Emry?"

The fires within her simmered. Could they stay tamed? She was back in her room and in her bed. Lord Alaric sat in the chair, hand-carved with dragons and stormy seas.

"I'm here," she said. Was it the voice of Vance or her own? She no longer knew what parts belonged to her and what belonged to the chosen, whether she was brave or graceful or both. Whatever she was now was who she was— Emry, Neve, Wren, Chandra, Vance, Leigh. Their spirits whispered as one. No more chaos. No more madness.

"We will win the war," she said, seeing in her mind every soldier's sword, every battle won, every life saved. The prophetic fires inside her crackled in agreement.

Lord Alaric came to her side, the scent of amber incense in his clothes. He could barely speak through the tears: "You are alive."

Emry pulled herself to standing and carefully unwound the powder-blue sash, wrapped around her waist five times to honor the dead. There were no more souls to mourn.

THE TAPPING
Anthony S. Buoni

A honey candle's flames singed a wayward thread from the front panel of Eze's azure ceremonial robe, furling the blue rogue until the strand vanished. She pulled a simple hemp belt through a lapis lazuli clasp, tightening the gown around her hips. A matching beaded choker dug into her neck.

She could barely swallow, but pulling at the collar offered no relief.

Too ornate for both the weather and her tastes, the elaborate outfit's thick material didn't breathe in the humid spring air—sweat already beaded on the small of her back.

Of course, spectacular presentation comes at my great discomfort.

Although useless, she again pulled at the unyielding collar.

Maybe it'll kill me. Perhaps then, they'd feel bad about all this ridiculous pomp and circumstance. Why can't I wear normal, comfortable clothes to the ritual? Or, at least, something light and airy, such as my solstice misrule costume.

She scratched at the bobbing twig protruding from her hair, knocking the beaded stick free. Crashing on the vanity, beads scattered across an oval mirror set in a luxurious silver frame.

Three times a year isn't enough to call down the solstice moon. Where does time go?

On the last misrule eve, the loose-fitting, silken dress flowed like dragonfly wings on the wind as she and the other children ran door-to-door, begging for slow-baked meat pies and fizzy fishwine. Like always, her three best friends at her side, hooting and hollering and singing to the darkness between residences, ignorant to the sharp teeth and jagged claws lurking in both the darkness and adulthood.

But those customs were reserved for younger tribe members who had not yet taken the Oath of Four Moons, a stuffy confirmation recognizing the broadening responsibilities of growing up.

Eze sighed. *It can't be over. I don't feel like I've outgrown that innocent silliness.*

She picked up the little wooden effigy Eustis had carved for her last frost-melting day and ran her thumb over his intricate whittles. *Such talent for a pretty boy. Shame how hard Za picks on him.* Eustis couldn't help his naivety. His family had descended from the Falcon Forest tribes, far from hectic village life.

"You're daydreaming again." Yenni blew out the honey candle, taking the figurine from Eze's hands and returning it beside a nosegay of melody blossoms on the vanity. Something about those bright red petals re-invoked the misrule dress...

"Mom, please."

"Please what, let my only daughter miss what could be the single most defining gala of her life because she's left her powers of reason and accountability somewhere in the cascading falls of Mount Morgue?" She snorted. "Not even the frivolous fairies of the high planes would let that happen to their children, and they eat their accursed young."

"Mom, I—"

"Don't 'mom' me. You've been moping around for the better part of a month, and I'm sick of it. When you took your Oath, you accepted accountability and obligation. You're a woman now. It's time you start acting the part."

At the time of her pact, she had regarded herself as grown, mature. But as the heavy, tapping ceremony robes and gaudy jewelry swallowed her whole, she wanted nothing more than a mouthful of sickly-sweet carbonation and the kiss of the gentle material against her pale flesh.

She couldn't protest.

Mom wouldn't allow it.

Duty, after all, was duty, a fact often repeated by her father, the Anoki mayor.

Today her duty and destiny awaited on Wishing Hill, in the sap of the crooked woem tree.

Already, tribal drums beat in that hallowed spot, the hypnotic drone promising sacred knowledge and a secure, indefinite spot for her family in the tribe. She had not heard the moment that the rhythm had begun, but something in the cycling, shifting measures seemed as old as time. Their music wafted through the village streets, growing faint in the distance separating the family home from the endangered tree, but still arriving as an uninvited, yet ever-present phantom creeping into the window overlooking her turnip and pepper garden.

Who first whispered my name to that maddening cadence, alerted my existence to their endless tempo?

Yenni straightened the beige sash draped across Eze's chest, patting the sparkling government insignia fastened over her daughter's heart before collecting up the beads from the vanity and reassembling the bobbing barrette. "Stay still. This is your father's big day, and we must properly represent this clan. I don't want you looking like we belong in the Deep Dregs with the dirty beggars or those awful Wasteland savages. Shame how those lowlifes can't get their act together long enough to taste civilization. I suppose not everyone can be blessed with good sense."

"Mom, you're overreacting." Eze readjusted the sash in the mirror in defiance. "No one cares what we look like. All they want is what's stored inside that stupid tree."

Yenni placed a hand on her daughter's shoulder and squeezed as she slid the beaded twig back into place. "That stupid tree is the last woem standing in our city. It could be the last one in the entire world. When the council blessed your father with the honor of the final Tapping, it elevated this family. Think about the future, and don't mock good fortune."

"The only mockery is that we are destroying the tree in the first place." Eze pulled away from Yenni and straightened a loose tuff of feral brown hair that had wandered in front of her left eye in spite of the barrette. Thick and unruly, her locks always needed attention, a genetic blessing from her father. "How can you stand by Dad as he ends the last of something? It's wrong."

"You don't understand because you're young. When you're married and have more worldly experience, things that didn't make sense before become clear. Our people have participated in this revered rite since the three tribes unified forces and founded this place. It's tradition."

"It won't be after today."

"Enough of that speak. Your venomous tongue will bring the wrath of the gods upon us." Yenni again tugged the sash, covering the white skin of Eze's neck between the choker and robe. "There. Now, you're presentable. Remember to stand straight and smile during the service. And try not to cross your arms; it'll look like you're hiding something. We want you to appear open, honest, and confident. Who knows how many potential suitors will be in the crowd."

Eze's cheeks grew hot. "Mom, you're out of control. I'm nowhere near ready for that."

"But everyone will be watching. We're playing an integral part in history. Take the stage with dignity."

"There's nothing dignified in extinction. And for what—a cheap thrill?"

"You'll understand when you drink the sap, Eze. It'll pull aside your preconceived notions about life and show you truth. Pure truth."

"How do you know that? It's not like you've ever tasted the tree's blood before."

Yenni cleared her throat. "I don't need prior experience to understand the impact resulting from taking part in the Great Mysteries. The visions spawned from the holy milk have ushered our civilization into the modern era, leading our greatest thinkers and social planners to the very ideas that form the cornerstone to our society. We are fortunate that your father and this family have been inducted above all of our tribe to be included among the ranks of the chosen."

"Yeah, I must be the luckiest maiden in town."

Yenni stepped back and frowned. "Not perfect, but it'll do."

"Gee, thanks, Mom."

"I wish you could see yourself the way I see you."

"You've already told me how you see me: not perfect."

"That's not what I meant. You've always had this wild streak, this…relentless determination. It scares your father, but what I see is a leader. The future."

"Mom, please."

"Let me have my moment." Her eyes watered. "You're my only child, and you're growing up so fast. It's hard, you know, letting go."

Yenni hugged her. "Get your melody blossoms so we can hurry down to the tree. We keep on sitting around, acting all foolish and sentimental, we're going to be late."

"Really, Mom? You're foolish. I'm ready."

Yenni hugged her again, leaving the room as Eze grabbed the wispy, bright red flowers from the ceramic vase and followed.

Drums echoed in the empty streets.

The robes stuck to sweat pouring down Eze's back as she trailed Yenni through the Anoki village's oldest section, struggling to match her mother's pace.

Why must that crone move so fast?

Her sandals kept catching the bottom of the robe's sweep. As they cut through the normally bustling business sector, she stumbled twice on the uneven path underfoot, nearly dropping the vibrant flowers into sunken cobblestones filled with muck from recent rains mixing with the feces of the sad-eyed beasts that pulled wobbling wooden carriages and creaking vegetable carts.

Any normal day, she would insist that I wear better shoes through this area, that this part of town was filthy, diseased. Curse the cold winds of winter's first snow.

Yenni moved faster and faster toward the ceremony.

An eerie desolation replaced the usual throng of merchants toting portable kiosks lined with clothes, produce, and needful trinkets for local shoppers and curious tourists. Shutters hid the windows of most of the small shops; the doors on the two- and three- story residential buildings lining the perfectly squared blocks pulled shut and bolted so that the village elite could watch the last tapping.

Gone were the random Deep Dregs hobos beseeching the wealthy for leftovers and loose change. The occasional untouchable Wastelander sleeping under tattered blankets in hidden nooks of the oldest edifices could not be found. Even the gentle, warm south winds common to the season held their breath, leaving Eze and Yenni's footsteps free reign to tumble down the deserted street and bounce off the tightly-packed homes.

"Mom, slow down."

"We can't be late. Your father is waiting."

"We have plenty of time."

"What I wouldn't give to see the world with young eyes again. If I knew at your age what I now know…"

She always reminisces with longing, as if she'd traded some part of her soul to marry into a comfortable life. Was the union with Dad so loveless, so contrived, that true happiness eludes her even with their social status and opulent possessions? "I don't think you would like what you see."

"Are you certain about that?"

"I just think things could be a little different."

"How so? Haven't we provided you with the best this world has to offer?"

"I mean, I guess. If you say so."

"If I say so? You don't know how lucky you have it, how things really are out there beyond the toxic dunes and the scorched deserts. You'll figure it out. When you have little ones of your own, you'll see."

I refuse to follow suit. No matter where life leads me, I will never end up like you.

Turning on Kron Street, a whistle pierced the drums. Two of Eze's friends, Eustis and Ulotta, sat on a bench sharing elderberry wine from a wooden tankard.

"Mind if I have a moment, Mom?"

"We really need to hurry. Being a little late is mysterious, but take too much time, and it becomes rude."

"Please, Mom?"

Yenni's brow furrowed. "Make it quick."

Eze pecked her on the cheek and dashed over to her friends, to Eustis.

Sitting cross-legged, the beautiful boy brightened when he saw them, holding up the drink. "Hey, Eze. Want a sip?"

Eze avoided his gaze, those dreamy blue eyes so much like the end of the sea and the start of the sky. "Sorry, Eustis. I'd love to, but I have to be at the Tapping."

"Aw, I know. I thought it might loosen you up, help settle any last minute nerves you may have."

"I'm fine, thanks. I see Za is nowhere to be found again."

"Yeah. You know how he is. I bet he's terrorizing some farmer's cattle on the west bank, scaring them until their milk sours."

"Probably. At least if he gets into any trouble, his parents can bail him out."

"They always do."

"Must be nice having enough money to pay for your own stupidity." Ice dripped from Ulotta's words. "My parents would let me rot in a cell if I got caught doing half of the stuff that moron does."

There is that attitude again. She's not been herself lately. It must be the moon. Everyone goes nuts when the fragments realign and smile in the night sky.

"I really like those earrings," Eze said. Ulotta always like talking about style. "Are they new?"

Ulotta tossed her hair, the sparkling hoops glinted. "I've had them forever. Not my fault you didn't notice."

The words stung. The jewelry was new. "What?"

"Come on. Don't play dumb. You're too busy peacocking around and admiring yourself in the mirror lately."

"I don't know what you mean."

"Just look at yourself. Those fancy digs are better than anything in my home. What a waste." Ulotta turned her back to Eze. Giggling, she took the wine from Eustis, locking eyes and brushing her fingers against his during the exchange.

She knows, yet she is making a move. Why him? She could be with someone so much more worthwhile and interesting, someone much better suited for her.

Eze forced a laugh. "It's funny that you think that this gaudy getup looks nice, but it's really nothing special. I feel like a sack of bitter potatoes that's been trampled by a heard of seven-toed brag bangers. And this pointy thing around my neck—don't even get me started."

"It doesn't matter what you're wearing. We weren't invited to the big brew-ha-ha." Ulotta took a deep swill. "Not much use in us attending the shindig anyway, huh? I'm not stupid. It's an exclusive club, and we're not welcome. Unlike some other people I know."

"Hey, that's not fair. We should be happy for her. Za, too. They are our friends." Eustis stood and opened his arms for a hug. "You look great."

Eze stepped forward to return the embrace, but Yenni called out, "Eze, quit messing around. We have to go."

Ulotta crossed her arms. "See? Already too good for us."

I didn't realize her capacity for cruelty. Such a drag. "It's not like that. I just—"

"Come one, Eze."

The drums beat on, filling the void the trio once filled with laughter.

Eze's shoulders slumped. "I'm sorry, but I have to go, you guys. I'll catch you two later. Maybe tonight afterwards."

"Yeah right." Ulotta took another drink from the wine. "See ya around, I guess."

"You'll be great today." Eustis winked. "I know that you'll make everyone proud. Especially your dad."

"Thanks. Means a lot."

Yenni approached, and Eze stole a quick hug from Eustis. *You even smell good, too. Like lavender and burning leaves.*

She rushed to her mom's side, glancing over her shoulder at her friends. Ulotta had leaned into Eustis, her elbows on her knees, her right hand on his shoulder. She whispered into his ear, and he laughed. *What was she telling that beautiful boy?*

Eze quickened her pace, matching her mother's wide, confident strides. *I will not stumble again.*

In Saints' Square, underneath the shadow of the lofty church, Yenni paused at the town's well, sat at its rim, and drew up the wooden basket. The oldest building in the village, ravens huddled in the temple's bell tower, cackling and cawing at the two women below. *They're mocking us with their subsong. Worse, they are probably happier than we'll ever be.*

Splashing water over her knuckles, Yenni stabilized the container on her lap. "This should only burn a few minutes."

"I thought we were in a rush."

"We are. I'm hot, though. No good to look thirsty at the service." She cupped her hands and drank, offering the basket to her daughter. "It isn't becoming. Plus, you have to always arrive at these things late—fashionably, but not obnoxious tardy."

Oh, now you want to be best buddies?

Eze took a drink and looked down the well. *How deep was it, anyways?*

Yenni took another drink. "I used to be so scared when you kids would play in this square. My silly, overactive imagination had you tumbling down, down, down, maybe never even reaching the bottom."

Eze crossed her arms. "How come we have time for this, but not for my friends?"

"Friends, huh?"

"Mom, they were just wishing me goodwill."

"They aren't your friends, sweetie."

She lowered the rope. The basket disappeared into the darkness.

"I've known them for years. Since I was little."

"Sure you have. Some of my favorite memories are of you playing at the retrograde campsites in the Falcon Forest, spending the entire weekend at the Crescent River's edge, skipping those flat prayer stones that you painted together across the water and laughing like crazy people. Birthday feasts, school dances, the market trips—all that is about to change. I don't think you realize how much."

"But I don't want things to be different."

"You know the changes began the moment your father got elected into office."

"Sure, there were changes, but it didn't alter my friendships until he was appointed for this final tapping."

Eze dragged her sandal across the wellhead's side. *Damn, I've said too much.*

The last thing I need is to add fuel to her arrogance. If she thinks that she is right, I'll never hear the end of it.

The changes were undeniable: subtle conflicting opinions on where to hang out, petty squabbles over who would pay for meals, and unusual periods of silence among company whose conversation was known to never miss a beat. Eustis, always sweet, now carried an air of indifference. Za, always instigating adventure and some wayward trouble for them, had not shown his face in weeks. But the most drastic change had stemmed from Ulotta. Once Eze's best friend, the only person who knew her deepest hopes and secrets, her feelings for that pretty, dumb boy, and her worries about the ceremony, Ulotta's warm smile had mutated into a judgmental scowl, her conversation shifting from laughter to cold resentment.

It wasn't fair.

"So, you've already noticed the difference."

"Not so much with Eustis. Ulotta is a different story."

"Well, her design and interests differ from the boy's. She sees you as competition, and he sees you as a prize."

"Mom, you don't know what you're talking about. He is a sweetheart."

"No." Yenni's tone had changed. She cleared her throat. "What I mean is that your interpersonal relationships are changing. It would kill me to see you settle for someone beneath you."

"Settle? Beneath me? Mom, that's a long ways away. Right now, I only want to get the tapping over and done with."

Yenni smiled and stood. "Then, let's get on with it."

Outside the village, a wide plain extended from the final open air market to the great Crescent River. Once dense with woem, rotting stumps and overgrown sawgrass littered the landscape. The duo followed a well-worn trail, swatting at the occasional blood sucking insects that swarmed by the river.

The terrain sloped upward. In the far corner of the deforested land, where the plain gave way to the steep high grounds and the swaying sycamores, pines, and magnolias that encompassed the immense Falcon Forest, the final remaining woem towered over a crowd of pulsing, high-ranking Anoki huddled together at Wishing Hill. Although a smaller, sickly specimen, the woem stood with an air of dignity.

The drums, louder since mother and daughter had cleared the city's walls, had shifted from steady, restrained measures to an uncontrolled cacophony, wild rhythms ferocious with ravenous passion.

A tribe poised and eager to heal with intoxicants.

When they reached the assembly, the crowd parted so that Eze and Yenni could enter the inner circle where the Anoki mayor stood beside the wisest of the twelve tribes, those entrusted with the sap's visions.

Hoods cloaked the sages' faces, though their identities were well known. The cadre consisted of the Anoki elite, a secret society assigned responsibility with the village's most precious resource. Their linage traced back to the original settlers, warring Wasteland tribes who peacefully settled the fertile oasis.

Her father, dressed in the same white robes as the sages, would receive his own hood after the ceremony, and their family would stand among the village vanguard, alongside the wealthiest Anoki such as Za's family.

Here we go.

Smile.

Stand straight.

The mayor extended his arms in greeting. "And now that the circle of my family is complete, we can commence with the festivities."

The drumming ceased, the loud silence revealing the river's gentle current and a light breeze sweeping through the Falcon Forest, tickling what remained of the woem's triangular leaves.

Normally deep green with neon yellow ribs, the vegetation turned rusty brown before dropping in the spring, heralding the saps' return from exile during the coldest months of the year. With warmer weather, the sap rose from its deep, complex root system, allowing new growth to sprout from flimsy, brittle branches.

The fallen foliage crunched with each step as Eze and Yenni took their place beside the gnarled trunk, an intricate knot of twisting, serpentine veins that split overhead into thin, fragile limbs that offered little shade and no nutritional value. Too weak for construction, the tree's only asset coursed through the circuitous channels, waiting for release.

The mayor kissed Yenni on the cheek and squeezed Eze's hand. *That's right, Dad. Make a great show of it.*

He faced the crowd, smiling. "This is a bittersweet day for our village, our people. Anoki have always existed beside the woem. Whereas our barley and wheat fields, orchards, fruit trees, and vegetable gardens have nourished and provided for our physical bodies, the mystical woem has cultivated our intellect, our consciousness. Its bounty has allowed us to peer into the other side, offered answers to our deepest concerns, and heightened our appreciation to the gods.

"Our species has endured. When the moon shattered and the old world collapsed, the subsequent plagues, mutations, and resource wars nearly wiped humans off the face of the planet. Technology failed us, forcing our hand to search for better solutions before the nomadic tribes destroyed themselves.

"Our forefathers discovered the secrets of the woem amid societal and political anarchy, and because they decided to share its knowledge with one and other instead of forwarding the devastation, the Anoki culture was able to take root and thrive."

The crowd applauded.

I can't believe they are eating everything he says up like this. Every school kid knows our history.

The mayor waved his hand, silencing the crowd. "We have used this resource sparingly. Although the ichor has taught us many things, its deepest riddle—how the tree propagates—has eluded us. Never once during our long history together has an Anoki discovered a seed to replant or managed to clone a woem. Two generations ago, futile attempts at replication almost eradicated this magnificent gift from the gods.

"I have been tasked with the heavy burden of tapping this final woem. The divine sap we imbibe today will heal our tribe. When we cross over into the ethereal realm, we will commune with the spirit guides, using the visions to weigh in on the problems facing the modern Anoki so that we can fortify our future, pass down our way of life for years to come."

The crowd cheered.

Drums thundered.

"And what of the questions that future Anoki will pose?"

The question silenced the assembly, the voice of protest stemming from an unmistakable source.

Za.

Troublesome and reckless.

Free and mischievous.

The prodigal son of the village's most prominent family.

No surprise he crashed this party. Eze couldn't hold back a smile. *Finally, some action. This should be interesting.*

Wild-eyed, Za stood in the center of the throng, a dromedary bag fashioned from the spotted hide of a seven-toed brag banger slung over his shoulder, his tattered olive traveling coat and black slacks caked with purple mud found only in the radioactive Wasteland dunes far from the Anoki village. His right hand clenched a bouquet of melody blossoms. Dark rings circled his bloodshot eyes.

My stars, he's been to hell and back.

The mayor cleared his throat. "Za, my boy. What is this query that you've brought to our venerated ceremony?"

"This ceremony is an injustice. Knowingly participating in the extermination of an entire species is a sin unforgivable by the gods." Za pointed to the crowd. "How can you stand and watch this? Have you no compassion, no souls? Did you not learn from our ancestors' mistakes? Their greed mined the moon for ore until it collapsed. Wanton production obliterated fragile resources, nearly driving our race to extinction. And here you sit idly, applauding as what remains of our hope is uprooted to entertain the addictions of the rich. You are not even permitted to partake in the mysteries, and yet you stand by and encourage these so-called wise ones."

Who knew Za could sing such elegant words? Maybe he was paying attention in school all along.

The mayor crossed his arms. "Listen here, son."

"No, you listen. All of you. This rite is a crime, and I won't stand by while you destroy the last gift that the gods have bestowed upon us. There are some things that are better left alone." Za directed a threatening gaze at Eze. "You ought to be ashamed of yourselves."

"This ceremony is legal by decree," the mayor said.

Za spit, the saliva hitting the leather shoe of a nearby Anoki. "Yeah, your decree. But just because you say something is all right, that doesn't make it so."

Eze licked her lips. *No one has ever spoken to my father like that. Amazing.*

"That's enough," the mayor shouted, arms flailing. "Get him out of here. He's bringing negative energy to this holy day, and I don't wish to listen to these false, empty words anymore."

Two large men surrounded Za, reaching for him as the boy slowly backed away, both palms out.

"You can toss from me from your little tea party, but your crime will not go unpunished. The gods will rain down their wrath when your judgements come to pass."

Za threw the red flowers into the crowd and ran, the two men fast on his heels.

That crazy kid. His father probably won't let him out of the house for three or four cycles after a stunt like that. Such an idiot. What did he think he was going to accomplish?

Uneasy murmurs rippled through the Anoki.

A single leaf dropped from the woem and spiraled down, landing on top of Eze's right foot.

"My humble friends." The mayor silenced the crowd with a wave of his hand. "Pay no attention to our interrupting guest. In the folly of his youth, he fails to understand the benefits of our actions here. Tonight, I shall focus my visions on our youth. I pray to the gods that this tree's sacrifice will provide clear and concise answers that we can offer our children about the future. May I please have the extractor?"

A hooded sage held up a narrow wooden tube that split into three sharpened prongs.

The crowd cheered as the sage presented the tap to the mayor. "Do you accept the charge, Mayor? Will you take the sap and bond your soul with the energy of the woem until the end of time?"

That's Za's mother giving my dad the tap. I'd recognize that voice anywhere.

"I do, my sage. My family and I do not enter into this pact lightly. We accept the mysteries with pure intention and light hearts."

"Then be it so, Mayor. I give to thee answers to questions unknown, second sight beyond this world, and a warm welcome into the infinite. May you and yours prosper and help guide this village into the future with steady, objective hands."

Za's mother passed the tap to the mayor, and they exchanged a bow before she took her place at the side of the other sages.

So this is how something special winks out of existence forever, with nobility and self-importance.

The mayor held up the tap over his head, reciting the words that Eze had heard him practicing since he was first allotted with the tapping: "And with the combined blessings of the gods and the Anoki who walked before me, I consecrate this woem. I offer my awareness, my soul in exchange for realization, wisdom, and guidance. May we gain insight, find peace, and heal ourselves with your blood, sacrosanct and pure."

The mayor plunged the spile into the center of the woem's trunk, each prong sinking deep into the soft wooden flesh with ease.

Were there something as precious locked within my heart, would they not hesitate to pierce and drain it, too?

The crowd gasped.

Above, a crow circled in ever tightening spirals.

Soft chanting from the sages, a pious plainsong reserved for the highest of holy days.

Time froze. Everyone waited for the ocher sap to drip.

"Well, mayor," Za's mother said. "Are we flowing?"

"Not a drop." He ran a finger along the spout and scratched his head. "Nothing, nothing at all."

"Let me see." Za's mother broke rank and leaned over the tap, poking and prodding the prongs. She pulled off her hood. "It's properly inserted. I don't understand."

The other sages gathered around, each taking turns fiddling with the tap.

Whispers in the crowd escalated into a grumble; the tight circle of Anoki lost form as the witnesses broke off into smaller groups. Some wandered off, conversing in low, angry voices.

They don't know how to handle this. They've waited for this moment only to have their hopes dashed.

"What now?" asked the mayor.

Za's mother orbited the tree and removed her hood. "I've discovered the problem."

The mayor and the other sages congregated around her.

"What is it?" one hooded male asked.

"This woem has already been tapped. Someone has come before us and drained out the sublime."

"What do we do?" The mayor wiped off the sweat pouring from his brow with a white handkerchief.

"There is nothing we can do. The tree will shrivel and die in the next few days. The woem's legacy is finished."

The mayor embraced his wife. "What about my family? We are to be inducted into the mysteries."

Za's mother placed a hand on the mayor's shoulder. "I'm sorry, but fate has dealt a contradictory hand. Without the sap, we'll be unable to sanctify your place among the initiates."

A tear streaked Yenni's face.

I guess our days of high society are finished. Good riddance. I hate most of those people anyway.

Incensed grumbles rose from the Anoki, the anger growing into shouts of vengeance:

"Who would steal the sap?"

"The fiend."

"Answers. Who has the answers?"

"Justice, we need retribution for this crime."

"Kill the thief. Strap them to remorse rock with barbwire, and let the lizards peck out their eyes."

The mayor stood tall and faced the crowd. "There, there, citizens. This day has been touched with tragedy and sadness, but fear not."

"You don't seek revenge?" someone in the crowd called out.

"No. Our people are resilient, much more than this nonrenewable resource we've knelt before for far too long. We should be grateful for all that we've learned while we had the chance. Maybe the sap was a crutch holding us back. Now that this chapter in the Anoki storybook is closed, it's time that we turn inward, find which way that works best for ourselves on our own. Let us return to our village and take the night to relax with our families. Tomorrow, we begin a new page in history."

Uncertain mumbling.

Pockets of Anoki drifted from the dying tree and headed for the village.

The shadow cast by the woem stretched beyond the rallying Anoki. Already the largest fragments of the moon appeared in the darkening sky, pale jagged jewels stretching from one end of the horizon to the next.

The mayor placed an arm around Yenni. "Let's go home, dear. Are you coming with us, Eze?"

"I'll be home soon, Dad. I want some time to reflect."

Yenni hugged her daughter. "I'm sorry things didn't pan out the way we planned."

Sorry for you or for me? Eze swallowed her sarcasm. "It's okay. Maybe this is the best thing that could have happened."

"What do you mean?" he father asked.

"Well, now we aren't responsible for destroying the line and ending the tradition. Now, we can rebuild with clean conscious."

The mayor smiled. "We will make a fine leader of you yet. See you at the house."

As Eze knelt and placed the melody blossoms at the base of the woem's trunk, her parents walked arm in arm toward the village as stars winked to life in the murky heavens.

❦

Eze took her time returning home, leaving the last woem when the insect attacks shifted from annoying to unbearable. Already, her skin burned from the poisonous saliva the swamp flies secreted when extracting blood. By morning, the bites would welt, requiring a salve of virgin goat fat to remedy the incessant itching. Mother always kept a tin in the medicine cabinet with the other elixirs and tonics, a personal pharmacy on hand "just in case."

She's prepared for everything except for what happened today. Will she ever be the same after this?

The trail winding past the woem graveyard seemed shorter, narrower than before. Thorny vines nipped at her ankles and toes along the way.

I'll never come out here without proper shoes again.

When she reached the village, her footsteps echoed in the empty streets.

Not a soul in sight. The word must have spread. This is a day for mourning, but I couldn't be happier.

When she reached Saints' Square, familiar laughter and voices danced in the darkness. Eze huddled beside a statue of a lion outside the chapel and listened.

"You should have seen them. Those snobs never saw it coming."

Za—he hasn't gone home yet.

"I wish I could have been there. They would have never let Eustis and me get close."

Ulotta, and she actually sounds happy.

"I still think that it was a bad idea. We could get in serious trouble."

Eustis. Beautiful Eustis. What did they do that has him so worried?

Her three friends sat on the well, passing around another bottle of fizzy fishwine.

"Look here, idiot," Za said. "You keep your big dumb trap shut, and we'll have nothing to worry about."

"Yeah, don't make us have to hurt you."

That's enough.

She stepped into the center of the square. "Hey, what's up?"

Her friends tensed.

"Hey, Eze." Za tightened his grip on the dromedary bag at his feet. "A total mess down by the river today, huh?"

"You could say that."

"What are you doing out so late? Didn't your dad tell everyone that we should all be home with family?"

"Yeah, why don't you go home to your loved ones?" Ulotta pulled a bright green apple from her jacket pocket and took a large bite. "Where you belong."

"You all are still out. Besides, I needed some time with myself."

"I can walk you home if you'd like," Eustis said, standing.

Ulotta grabbed his shirt and pulled him back down. "You aren't going anywhere. Eze is a big girl. She can get herself home just fine."

"I wouldn't mind hanging out for a bit," Eze said. "That is, if I'm invited."

Ulotta tossed the half-eaten apple into the well. "You aren't invited. We don't want you here."

Eustis pulled away from her and stood by Eze. "I want her here."

At least someone is on my side. "Thanks, Eustis."

Eustis took Eze's hand. "There is something that you need to know."

Ulotta sprung up. "Shut up, Eustis."

"Do it, and it's your funeral." Za pulled a large knife from his tattered coat; the blade gleamed in the moon light.

Bad news... "For real. What's going on? Why is everyone acting like hungry slime carp during drought season?"

Eustis squeezed her hand. "Za stole the woem sap."

"He did what?"

"He drained it last night before the drummers got there to cast the circle and draw down the ancients."

Za relaxed his hold on the knife. "You can't tell anyone."

Eze's heart pounded in her chest. "This is crazy, even for you. The sages will kill you if they find out. Your mother will be the first one to slit your throat and leave you to bleed out on remorse rock."

Za lowered his head. "I know. But I couldn't take it anymore. That stupid tree has held back our village since it began. I grew up having my parents remind me daily about our station in life, drilling the importance of our participation in the visions. Those artificial dreams don't help anyone. There are no answers in the sap. The sages are addicted to the drug. I've heard my parents talk about their withdraws after taking it, how they can't wait for another fix. Worse, they don't want to share with anyone else even though they go on and on about unity and peace. The blood of the woem stands for hypocrisy, and I had to tear the false ideal to shreds."

"He's a hero, Eze." Ulotta stood by his side. "Not a spineless follower like you."

Eze slapped her, hard. "The only reason I showed up to the ceremony was because it mattered to my mom. My parents feel they have a great duty to the community. Taking a place beside your family is an honor to them. Improving their standing offers a greater chance of helping the village. They were following tradition."

Za snorted. "Tradition."

Fire burned inside Eze. *I'll slap him, too, if he doesn't watch that tongue.*

Eustis stepped between them. "Everyone relax. We're friends. We don't need to fight over this."

Za sheathed the blade. Remorse crossed his face. "You've always been smart. Grounded. When they announced that your dad would oversee the tapping, I saw what it did our friendships. The fallout wasn't pretty, and I thought that if I destroyed the sap first, it would level the playing field and save this group. I didn't want to lose my best friends."

"Where is it?" Eze asked. "What did you do with the sap?"

Za patted the dromedary bag. "There is never much vital juice. That tree wasn't in the best shape, either. I drained every last drop within minutes."

The power to end wars and alter minds casually slung around his shoulder. "That's a whole lot of trouble in there. What are you going to do with it?"

"I don't know." Za unhooked the bag and offered it to her. "You're always the voice of reason. Since you're also in on the conspiracy, I think that you should decide. After all, it is your turn to join the ranks of the chosen."

"Looks like we have some new traditions to start," Eustis said.

"I say we drink it." Ulotta reached for the bag, but Za pulled back.

"Eze gets to choose." Za handed her the reserve. "We can trust her decision."

She traced her fingers against the cork.

Too dangerous to hide, yet too valuable to throw away.

"Za, what happens when you dilute the sap?" she asked.

"What do you mean?"

"Will it still grant visions if it's mixed with something, like red berry tea or thorn juice?"

"Yeah. It's potent. What the sages don't drink at the tapping ceremony, they cut with fishwine, stretching it out over the wheel of two years, sipping it on each of the six solstices and equinoxes."

"That well extends into the aquifer, right? Something pollutes it, the whole town gets sick?"

A slow smile crossed Za's lips. "Yeah. That's the first well on the grid. Might take a few days, but with the way the river flows, a contaminate would spread out to every household."

"Do you really want to level the playing field?"

Za nodded.

Eze unstopped the cork and tipped the spout toward the well's infinite darkness.

Even in the dark, the thick sap glowed yellow-brown as it poured like cold syrup from the container. Eze squeezed the vessel, forcing out the viscous sap in gelatinous globs.

When the last drop was extracted, the friends set fire to the empty container, taking in the blue and orange flames as the desolate, broken satellite chased twinkling stars.

Will Jensen 11/13/18 Beginning At The End

74

JOIN THE MOB
Daniel Loring Keating

I wake to the sort of acrid bright sunlight that hangovers are made from, entering my bedroom through the window that overlooks C Street. Outside, people are whooping and hollering and laughing. The road is flooded with humanity, all of them with pure happiness on their faces. My calendar shows that it is a regular day, no public celebration scheduled. I throw my coat on over my nightclothes and descend to the street and ask the first person I see, an older man with long white hair and a bushy beard, what is happening, and he clasps my hands, tears in his eyes, and says, "Trevor Joyner is dead!"

We stand there like that, silent, hands together, a few droplets of moisture leaking out of his eyes and onto his face.

"Who?"

The man peels away rather than answer, swallowed up by the rollicking, rejoicing crowd. I think to ask someone else, but every seemingly amenable person turns away. After a few minutes of watching aimless cheering, I give up.

Back inside, I switch on the TV, an old tube job I rescued from a dumpster a few months ago. The screen hums and comes to life.

"Reporting to you from Washington," the pretty brunette on the screen says, a large, ornate, white building behind her. The capitol building. "Again, we have confirmations that Trevor Joyner, the infamous man responsible for six counts of *parishev*, is dead. A raid on his compound last night by United States Marines killed Joyner and six of his followers. More on the story as it develops."

I dial the first person who comes to mind. My brother Peter picks up on the third ring. "Jake?"

"No, it's Nicholas." The TV runs images of people dancing in the streets outside the White House. "I've just seen on the news this man that was killed, and there are people celebrating in front of my building."

75

"Yeah, isn't it great?" I can barely hear him over the voices and moving bodies in the background. Little firecrackers go off outside my window, and people cheer through the grimy glass.

"Who is this man? I've never heard of him before. And what is *'parishev'*? That's what the news said he did, but I've never heard the word before."

"Are you kidding?" A woman's voice, whooping in delight, fills the phone, and I jerk it away, my ears ringing from the sudden, unexpected sound. Gingerly, I replace the phone against my ear. "—about that, Betty and her friends and I are all celebrating the news. You can't be serious, right, Jake? Everyone knows Trevor Joyner."

"I don't." I cover my other ear in hopes that it'll make Peter easier to understand. "And I told you, it's Nicholas calling. What is *'parishev'*? I've never heard of it before."

"*Parishev* is *parishev*, little brother." His voice gets quieter. Whistling air rushes by the phone on his end. He is no longer hushed or solemn. "Sorry, tripped. But yeah, that's what's going on. You should get over here. We're all celebrating. This has been ten years in the making, man."

"What has been?" I ask.

The dead phone in my hand beeps at me, struggling to be heard over the cheerful voices outside. Part of me wants to just go back to bed, to sleep this off, to let the world do its own thing, but I dress and prepare myself to push through the crowds that await me outside.

Fifteen minutes later, I knock on Peter's door. He has a nice job, something in corporate training, and the lack of dents and dings in the door and the absence of aroma proves it's a nicer building than mine.

The door opens. Rather than my brother, I'm greeted by his girlfriend, Betty, a short young woman, three years older than me, one older than Peter, with hair dyed an unnaturally bright shade of red. Her hips start at a small, skinny waist and flare out into what Peter describes as "porn-star proportions."

"Oh, Johnny." She looks me up and down. I can never tell if she's sizing me up as a threat or like she wants to jump me. "I'm glad you could make it. Peter wasn't sure you could."

"It's Nicholas. And yeah, of course I made it. I don't have any idea what's going on out there."

"What do you mean?" She steps back and grabs me roughly by the collar. "Get in here and party. This is a holiday, my man."

I stumble into Peter's apartment. Betty shuts the door, her mouth open and her eyes huge; she struts over to a couple of her friends, all of whom are raising drinks. "Isn't it still a little early for that?"

"You've always been such a party-pooper, Jake." Peter sidles up next to me, offering me a beer. I shake my head, declining, and he shrugs, pouring back the contents of the bottle he'd just offered me. "'Sides, work's canceled for today. They're expecting the president will declare it a national holiday later, but Betty and Katie and I already found out from our bosses that business is closed for the day to celebrate. If you had a job, you'd probably have the day off, too. Guess it's not so different from a normal day for you, is it?"

I glance desperately around Peter's apartment. It really is nice, all stylishly off-white walls and small, rectangular paintings of splatters and lines and other modernist stuff. Two couches shaped like crescent moons cup a table in between them. "What's going on?"

Peter shrugs his massive, six-foot-seven shoulders. His voice isn't as deep as you'd think from a guy his size. "I told you. Trevor Joyner's dead. No more *parishev* for that asshole. Isn't that right, everyone?"

Betty and her friends cheer lightly, raising their glasses. He raises one of his bottles in return and takes a big swig out of it.

"I don't know what that *means*." I grab Peter by the shoulders and force him to look at me.

"What do you mean, you don't know what that means?" Peter's forehead wrinkles. His voice is low again, but none of them are paying attention to us.

"It's like the world is playing the biggest prank ever on me." I can see how cold the bottle in his hands is, his skin is sticking lightly to it and the brown glass is fogged enough to be noticeable. "I've never heard of Trevor Joyner and the word '*parishev*' sounds like nonsense. I don't have any idea what's going on."

"Listen, Jake." Peter covers one of my hands with one of his own. "It's okay. I don't know what you took last night, or this morning for that matter, but I'm sure it'll all come back to you. Trevor Joyner is the biggest *parishevist* in the world. He committed his first act of *parishev* ten years ago, and we've been looking for him ever since. And now, we got him. The fucker's dead, deader than a fucking doornail."

"I get that he's *dead*."

Betty's friends cheer again, but it strangles in their throats at frustration on my face. One of them, an unusually tall woman, clears her throat as she and Betty resume chattering, albeit at a greatly reduced volume.

"I get that he's dead. I don't know who he *was*. And you keep using that word like it's means something to me. I've *never heard it before*."

"Right." Peter's brow wrinkles further. This is what he does. The more worried he gets, the more he resembles an old mop. "Look, like I said, I don't know what you took last night—"

"I didn't take anything. I haven't been on anything in months."

"Of course." Peter takes another swig of his beer. There's a slight *clink* as the small amount of liquid that is left in the bottle rushes back to the bottom. "That's why you don't understand something so basic that a kindergartner would get it. Everyone knows *parishev*, Jake, it's like the most evil thing in the world."

"Why do you keep calling me Jake?"

One of Betty's friends, the tall one, points at Peter's TV. "More coverage on. Look, they're going to release photos."

Peter and I drift over, not that it's necessary. He has an enormous big-screen television that probably wouldn't fit in my room.

"New details in the death of notorious *parishevist*, Trevor Joyner," the reporter says. "Allegations, stemming from the release of the photos of Joyner's death, have been raised that the Marines who located and surrounded Joyner's location executed the man in cold blood rather than apprehending him. We must warn viewers at home that the following images are extremely graphic and not meant for children."

The screen changes to a still, blurred image of a man, limp against a wall, a neat circle in his forehead above his right eye, a splatter of red on the wall behind him, which seems to otherwise be made of unfinished stucco. He's an utterly normal guy in his mid-forties, maybe a little gray in his hair unless that was dust on the camera, a little stubble on his chin, wearing a blue plaid shirt and jeans.

The reporter reappears, sitting behind her shiny desk, neon digital graphics swirling behind her head. "Experts have pointed out that from the way the body collapsed and the angle of entry of the wound suggest that Joyner was shot on his knees from close range, which heavily suggests an execution-style killing. So far, the military and White House have refused to comment on these allegations. More on the story as it develops."

"Turn it off." Peter sets his empty bottle on a nearby table with another *clink*. "We don't need to listen to this garbage anymore. So what if they executed the guy? He's dead. That's what counts."

My worries don't register with him at all. "What are you talking about? They're saying he may have been murdered in cold blood."

"He's a *parishevist*." Betty finally looks at me from her small circle of friends. "He deserves worse."

"What about due process? What about a trial?"

"Fuck trials," Betty says. Her friends all nod. "Did all the people that were affected while he was committing *parishev* get trials? Did they get due process? Did they get anything other than *parishev*?"

"What the hell are you people talking about? What the hell is *parishev*?"

Peter's gone to Betty, and she and her friends no longer pay me any attention.

"I think they should have blown out his kneecaps first," a short redhead says. Her name's Dinah. She works for the subway, collecting fares; I saw her down there once, and she smiled at me. "If all they did was shoot him, they let him off easy."

"Kneecaps," Betty roars. "Don't stop there, they should have skinned the little cunt alive and poured salt all over him."

A couple of Betty's other friends chime in, trying to outdo Betty's suggestion, and before I can say anything or make up my mind to go, my brother holds up his hand.

"No, no, everyone," he says. "My brother's got a point. They shouldn't have killed him. They should have caught him and shipped him back here and sent him to prison so he could have enjoyed all the benefits of getting bent over again and again in the prison shower."

Betty and her friends cheer, raising their bottles, and Peter cheers, too, and for a second, I'm not sure that it's blood flowing through my veins or ice water, the kind that drips off a roof and freezes at night. "So that's it, then? Now people deserve to get raped?"

"What the fuck, Jake?" Peter asks. Is this even him?

"It's Nicholas." The room spins.

"Jake, man, I think you need to leave. You need to get your priorities in order."

"Clearly." I stand. They back away, and I sway and almost fall. No one tries to catch me, and I push my way out of Peter's plush apartment and back into the street.

The sun is directly overhead, and the street is still full of people. Dolls in little plaid shirts are hung from a lamppost. Cackling, a man in a leather jacket with a thin mustache stands up on a car under a doll, strikes a match, and lights it on fire.

The crowd cheers.

A cop wades through and climbs on the car, too, saying something to the man, who gestures one more time to the crowd, which cheers him again as he jumps down off the car. The cop beats at the burning doll, putting out the flames.

"What the fuck is going on?" My voice doesn't sound right, it sounds like a glass train that's gone off the rails and is shattering into a million pieces slower than I can think. I stumble into someone, like hitting a marble pillar. I'm instantly bruised and practically bounce off.

The image on my brother's television looks down at me, and I've completely lost my mind. I'm looking at a dead man.

But I'm not looking at a dead man at all. A t-shirt emblazoned with the picture of Trevor Joyner with a hole in his head and "*Parishev* This" below it.

"You all right, kid?" the man wearing the t-shirt asks.

"Where'd you get that shirt?" The man's face is hidden in the forest of legs and arms as the crowd closes around my prone body; the sky overhead, so blindingly bright, pinpoints my vision on the t-shirt.

"Guy down on the corner of Y and W is selling them." The man clutches at the edges of the t-shirt and pulls them so that the graphic is flat. "Pretty neat, huh?"

I shake my head.

"Please," I say, quietly. "Please tell me what *parishev* is. I feel like I'm losing my mind, and I don't know what this guy's done. What the hell is *parishev*?"

"What's *parishev*?" The man straightens and lets his t-shirt fall. He's got a gut; it makes the words jump out, like the words push toward me. "*Parishev* is *parishev*, my boy, no other way to put it. Tryin' to explain *parishev*'d be like trying to explain blue to a man who can't see. You can see, can't you?"

"Yeah." I try to push myself to my feet. "I just—I don't understand what's happening. This is so barbaric. Why is everyone acting like this?"

"Because he's dead, my boy." The man claps me on the back as I rise, and I still can't face him. It's easier to think of him without one. "Trevor Joyner is dead, that fucking scum, and he'll never be able to trouble another person with his *parishev*."

"I just told you I don't know what that *is*." I shove the man, and he stumbles into the crowd. A couple of people keep him from falling.

"What's your problem?" another man in the crowd asks.

"Yeah, what gives, why are you pushing?"

"You got an issue, son?"

"He's got fucking sympathies," the man I'd pushed says, pointing at me, his finger straighter than a spear. "He said we're *barbaric*."

I don't think anyone in the crowd knows who to blame. It's all about line of sight, I figure. From where Person A is standing, the man is pointing at Person B, not me. From where Person B is standing, he can't tell who is being pointed at because I'm behind him. From where Person C is standing, the man is pointing at Person A.

And so forth.

The first punch lands on someone else, as does the second.

I get hit in the stomach, although I'm not sure by who or what, and I go down again.

After that he crowd closes, I'm kicked and kneed, and at one point, someone falls on top of me and pushes himself up by pressing down on my ear. I scream and, years later, someone pulls at my collar and drags me, still screaming, out of the mass.

A police officer deposits me against the side of a building before pulling out a club and wading back into the giant fight, swinging the club, knocking people's heads and arms and hands in all different directions.

I close my eyes and cover my head with my hands.

Where did the blood covering me come from? Is it mine or someone else's? How badly am I hurt?

The police officer is back, and the street is nearly deserted, a few people milling around, nursing their arms and their heads, a few limping.

"You okay, kid? Looks like it got pretty rough in there."

I shake my head.

"Can you tell me your name? Is there anyone who can come and pick you up."

"My name?" I glance around, as though answers might suddenly become evident, and wince. I think my ribs are broken. "No. I don't know."

The cop shakes his head, kneels beside me. "Hey, it's not worth taking you in, but I saw the whole thing that started this."

I try to push myself up, but I feel another bone break in my leg and sink back down, panting.

"You have to get your shit sorted out, son."

"Why are people acting like this?" My voice is now definitely not my own, a vocalization of the end of the world.

"Sometimes, people just need to die," the cop says. "You get that, son?"

RETURNAL
Connor Phillips

When they bring their blame to your doorstep, you are still asleep. Only the beat of their fists and the stamp of their boots, the shrill of their voices and their torches' heat are enough to disrupt your oblivious dream. When the window splinters in its frame and the latch forsakes the door, you're awake.

The light flicks on, and they are already in the room while you are still tucked between your covers. You haven't a moment to think, to wonder or guess or even remember.

They don't bother with questions. They have all sorts of answers.

The ones at your bedside dip their torches and spread the flames first, stroking the corners of your sheets, the bangs of your hair, and your sweating cheeks. The rest of them watch before tossing in theirs.

Now, you are wide awake. You lurch out of bed to the window and see their blame, see them marching it down the street. They yell and taunt. They scream. They call you evil things.

They set fire to your hedges at the edge of the drive. Then the old oak that grows in the yard.

They light up the boughs that bundle and drape. Then the bark, then the roots.

Then the house, the only home you knew.

They exchange fire for stones. They use water. They use tools.

Ropes.

Just words. But these words are more than enough.

You notice their faces. Ones you recognize. The faces of all the people you ever knew.

Pinched and twisted, warped and wrung out, wrenched wide under the weight of the blame they carry. They bring it to your bedside and pile it upon your chest one-brick-at-a-time.

The faces you knew, or thought you knew, will say, *no*—we thought we knew *you*.

You learn to recognize their blame. You learn its face. It's just like your own. Denying, pleading, fossilized in fear.

They hold this face against yours, so you can breathe its last breath before they cave it in with a pipe.

Still, you don't understand. You don't understand. You don't understand.

The trauma of these trials takes your mind again and again. It delivers compensation without explanation—simply serving upon you the sentence for something you don't remember.

You try to testify, you keep trying, but the judgment's been passed.

You scream for your innocence, but these words are your last.

They laugh as they drag you out the back door to bury you alive.

Each time they come for you, the memories of your life before loosen and unwind, until all the unraveling ribbons are shredded, pulped, and processed through the supreme authority of the blame, until the blame is all you remember, until the blame is all that you know.

Eventually, you learn there is nothing else.

Eventually, you learn that death is no escape. Death is a memorial to their blame.

You learn to wake and leap from your bed. This moment is the last moment you wouldn't rather be dead.

All that is left for you in this house, in this home, in this terrible town is their blame, and it's coming for you. The only chance for you is outside of everything you once thought was your life.

You learn to fling off the covers you keep hiding under, to stop waiting for their shouts to smash through the walls, for their conviction to fold you over, do you in.

You learn to *run*.

You have fifteen seconds.

Five seconds for you to wake up and burst into the hall, to find out they are already here.

Four more seconds before the first window scatters and slices your feet.

Three seconds until the first is inside.

Another two seconds until you are fighting him off.

You only have one more second before you are surrounded, dragged to the floor.

It takes you a long time to learn that after fifteen seconds, your only chance of escape is surrendered.

In fifteen seconds, you dive through the panel of the kitchen window.

You fall to the ground and crawl through the weeds.

The only way of evading them is vaulting over the stone wall and into the slender space between the neighbor's fences.

You drop down and dodge through the shadows, the blame of your neighbors pressing in at your sides. The sour shouts that cut into your back are never far away. The light from their torches always seems to know where you're going, searing every surface, prodding and steering you back out of the dark. Street after street and block after block, you sneak in search of a safe haven.

In the windows, lamps snap on with the spiteful shine of searchlights. Dogs howl until hoarse, catching your scent, and someone will yell—suddenly spying you, and the blame descends in upon you once more.

Already fleeing this blame for so long, you've tried every direction, every turn and corner, but their blame is always there, always waiting, an ambush at the end of every outcome.

Your mind becomes a map of tragic trajectories through streets, paths and alleyways that have betrayed you.

Every sidewalk, every storm drain, every dumpster, every doorway, every shed, every stable, every swimming pool, every parking garage, every picnic table, every baseball field dugout, every playground slide, every bus stop, every space beneath every car and every porch, every inch of this town that has given you up is nothing more than a reminder of just how much you have lost from their blame.

A world of ever-sustained blame cycles through you, cutting its tunnel deeper every time. Clustered in its catacombs, you find yourself sinking from one second to the next, pretending again you can find a way out. This time, you skid down under the lip of a culvert you think you've never tried before.

Then, you see by the patterns stitched into the blackened grass how you already have.

You hunch still in the dust, unsure of why you always believe the next chance will be the one to change you. You feel it now, the lesson setting in. Maybe they always wanted you to get away, get a little bit further.

Why not sit and wait now, just this once?

Catch your breath.

Forfeit their hunt.

Try submission for a change.

You get up and climb over into the road. You hold your branded hands out to them; show them what you know now. Maybe they will let it be a little easier.

They aren't here for you.

Not yet.

For once in forever, you find yourself still ahead. Still unknown for the moment. You see their lights sundering the section of streets out of which you just came, and you sprint.

Maybe this one is it.

You make it to the outskirts of town.

Here, reduced into the center of your empty skin, you find your way to the edge of the woods. Past the reams of trees, you limp into some new nothingness that has always sat upon the barrier of your world. You surrender yourself to it: to the leaves, to the needles, to the brambles and thorns, to the thick desolate wilderness that seems to go on and on. You plead to the pulse of its silence. You ask for mercy, just mercy.

Beyond the humiliation, beyond the pain, you crumple forward on all fours in search of some sort of calm, some sort of end, if you could even imagine it.

And somehow, in this place, they begin to lose ground on you. The snarling dogs whimper when they lose your trail. The torchlight at your back grows dimmer, scorches slimmer, and the shouts turn to whispers.

Soon, nothing is at your back, except for the dirt and the damp and the darkness, into which you collapse.

The blame doesn't find you, but it doesn't disappear either. It sits instead as a heavy, spoiled scar on your body, a toxic knob encircling you, refusing to heal.

But it is no longer the night, which you thought was unending. You lie on your back for hours, staring up at the sun, at its quiet globe grazing on the tops of the trees, until your pupils threaten to blister.

Until you see nothing but motes.

You sleep for as long as you possibly can, dreaming you are something small and short-lived, perhaps just a blade of grass.

How long before you move again. How long you try to silence every synapse, sink the thoughts into the depths of the dirt beneath your cheek. How long it takes you to learn that the cost of snuffing out the bad thoughts only lets the worst ones sneak up on you.

The thought of the blame being able to find you here becomes a thought so inescapable it spurs your wrecked body upward, upon your feet into the air where the whole of you threatens to become untethered. The burden of your offended flesh, the strange weight of branded meat, holds you to the cobbled mud, across coils of roots and stone and covered valleys.

Back into the thickest snags of the wood, across unsought acres rendered forward forever, you continue deeper and dimmer into chambers of trees wreathed in immaculate shadows. The thought takes you further still, through bearings least pertaining to path—paths only of indeterminable route, marked only by the want of any sort of way, paths only of the most resistance.

The forest draws itself open for you, this new world made for your new skin. Its frozen floors and rasping walls, its ceiling that shivers and wails with the wind—it was here for you all along—it lets you in. You roam the rooms of this new home and settle into its bed of wet and moldy leaves. You just try to sleep, just try to dream. You try to stop twitching. You try to stop twitching.

The dreams, when they do come, are full of their faces, waiting and watching at the edge of the woods. You can hear the sneaking mutter of their schemes to trick you and trap you back into their blame. You don't feel afraid though, just buried in anger.

You spit and seethe, you belch and seize and sprint through the trees. The clatter of your teeth as they sink into things. The tremor of your changing frame. The blows of something budging its way out from your brain. Your muscles wrack in spasms with your smoldering gut, spilling open inside by the strength of your hate.

These dreams wander through you, weaving in and ever thicker, until some unknown toll is staked away for you to awake.

When you wake, you walk. You travel and map every withered bit of your world, tracing your tracks in order to forget. To untether the trials that have become your mind, to purge all the dead ends that did you in.

Your stomach is a knot you may never find a way to untie, and though you have no appetite, you take note of your ribs reaching through your torso, sharp against your taut gray skin. Your search for sustenance bares little beyond brittle nuts from the pines and the white roots of the trampled grass. Riding the resolution of your perpetual motion, you manage to tread forward, seeking only moments lost in always passing, seeking only to never stop.

Days or weeks or any number of suns gliding over the forest in slumping arcs and still you wander, still you walk. You walk until you could rewrite yourself into the land through your steps, step into the discovery of an entry, or better—an exit. You walk with the thought of never stopping until your bones splinter, turn to dust. Until you could be blown apart across the earth and air by a single breath, certain in some way to never arrive.

Your endless trail feeds and fills up the woods; until one day, you stagger right out of its side. Then, you see it, the *town*—right there—and your flesh burns as you look, feeling tight and ready to burst with fresh blood. But this isn't your town; it's a whole other town sitting on a different side of the same woods as yours. Beneath you, it sits still and silent and waiting.

The houses against the hills glaze the air with flickered window light. Pillars of chimney smoke quake out across town into the blue haze of spent day, shading your vision and what you might find there.

Streetlamps rouse on across the blocks at random, empty and spread with the presence of night closing in. Empty—but also heavy with humming notion, unspoken promise of warmth and light and the life to be lived behind the planks and plaster of a wall.

Beyond the dirt and the damp and the darkness. Beyond the woods.

Beyond a latch on a window or a lock on a door.

You can't stop your feet from stealing down through the hills, down the slopes to the fields to a trail to a fence, then you find yourself right there in the yard. You stand in between pinned-up linens drying fresh in the breeze. They skim slowly across the bare flesh of your back, and you lean into them, unable to understand how anything could feel so soft. For a second, it's enough to make you forget, enough to make you stop counting the course of your failures.

It's enough to make you not notice how, in some other yard, a dog barks.

When you surface again to sense your setting, you hear the shouting, how it has already started.

Sickness stirs in you because it is children this time, their shrieks getting louder in serration as they run toward the yard.

When you try to swallow, you taste your blistered insides flooding up in your throat.

More shouts even nearer, just down the trail.

The dog starts howling, just like the rest.

You notice, now, the true test of the blame—children screaming, sentencing death to your name. The sheets catch across you and wrap you in. The familiar well of lead brims up through your chest and pools through your limbs. Your muscles surrender into sponges, and your knees jimmy inward. The terror lumps up in your neck, keeping you fixed through the seconds for them to come across the fence and find you here.

It stabs you, a knotted clod of recognition. You nod your heavy head. This time, you face it. This time, you let them find you. And every time after. At least you know that all there is, anywhere, no matter what, is the blame, always waiting for you. You close your eyes and wait for it to find you.

You wait.

And wait.

You unfasten your eyelids and look around. Just the light of the windows, the stars and the night. Just the smeared clicking of crickets, the breeze sweeping the trees. No sounds, no sight, no singed scent of the blame. Still. You stay still. You wait for a hot hand to land on your ankle, for something to tell you this is just another trick of the blame.

You wait a long time. Night peels its first layers, each folding over you unnoticed. You think about moving an inch, in any direction. Even when you know the waiting is over, further inertia is the only notion you have left.

You wait until someone is behind the window facing the yard.

A woman. Standing there in the bedroom. Staring through the window.

Staring at you.

No—staring into space.

Her finger and thumb pinching her lip. Her eyes softer than sheets. Stolen deep in her thought, a smug smile hidden that never floats to her face.

All that there is, and still, there is more. Every other potential could pass away. Even this one, arresting your stead.

Your curdled skin shivers. How much longer will you wander, lost of all entry until your every shred of substance fades away—what sort of presence will remain?

She could be looking right into it, if only she knew.

The hallway lights flick on. She flinches away from you, from the window. Someone further inside speaks to her. And when she responds—you see it in her face—not the smallest, single trace of the blame. Without warning, she moves out of frame. You strangle the tremor sprouting open inside you; when a moment later, the room pitches off in the darkness.

The slow unsheathing of your fingernails as you claw through the earth.

The scabbing flaps of blood upon the palms of your hands.

Under mounds of frozen dirt, you disappear, the fever of your fingers gasping in handfuls, through detritus, through rot. Through the splinters of your stick shovels, through the snarl of numb muck. Through all that there is and still, you'll keep digging. Until the digging is done. Until all that there is is this hole. This foundation. In which to fill with all the things that you lost. In which to bury what it was you once had. No—build.

No—reclaim.

In the new town, you steal a shovel. You patch the hole, refine the foundation. You lever stones from the soil, chink the blade as you render them into the promise of a wall. With every short rest, you grip the handle and scalp the edge with stolen file, determined to sustain it far sharper than you found it.

In the new town, you steal pants, a shirt, a stain-spattered coat and boots. You claim these items in the dawnless hours of the town, choosing only garbs lost to any host, of any further use.

In the new town, you steal an axe. You fell only the thin trees of the wood unfit for future growth, their snagged limbs cracking open as death wedges in. You lever them to the floor and unworm the work of mulch burrowing into the grain, then rut the axe's edge into the tip of each log and lug them off and away, over and again until the dark pins you down.

Each time you slip into the new town and wander another unborn day, you find something new. A trowel, a chisel, a wool pair of socks—relics from the present past off to omission. You marvel at what remains in the space under stoops, behind the gap of a worktable and a wall, in the recessed dust shadows of a shed. Some small promise of what can be found fallen beyond the barrier of a life. It is so easy for you to gather each thing almost gleaming in a crack, in a crevice, in a place void of all thought.

Somehow, these items suggest they are already yours.

You scrub everything you claim in the guts of a stream. You scour every surface in the bite of the current until your fingers keep clenched. Then, you fist a rock rounded off by the water and scrape your skin until the cold bumps smooth into flat flesh and pinprick wells of red rise from your pores and drop into silent rush upon the banks of your ankles. You stand there and stay there and wonder how long you will have to remain before the water will finally round you off as well.

Will the woods permit your new state of creation? This suffered space so unmarred of its rawness, how could it ever grant you a peaceful place to remain?

After days at your labor, the dirt begins to yield like sand to your digging. The stones almost haul themselves out of the earth when you pry them, always in the right shape for the next bit of wall. The trees, once you fell them, pull across the ground like a sled; they pare down so easily into log after log. The work bellows its will through your hands, through your arms, through your chest and your head. A fugue takes over, filling in. A will folding out from within you but formed below and away from any true place involving you.

Thin scrim of starlight bands strip across the thatched limbs to the piled and plastered stone to the dirt. You sit fixed in the bent count of their hours as they slip in shifting blots through the coat of the forest, and when they pan across your dark body, you hardly notice how they snuff out, lost into some substance, or nothingness, passed along through your veins, or deeper beneath. You often fail to feel the wind anymore, despite it blowing through these nights as if sucked out of some ageless era of ice.

Despite your new possession of clothing, you sometimes forget to wear much of anything. On these nights, you just sit on the same stump and witness the same stars spend their light to wonder at nothing beyond how long it has been since you have seen any single sliver of the moon.

Snow gathers in mute creation throughout the woods and compels you into your house. Flurries trundle over your doorway, and you cover the opening with thick bundles of sticks and hay. You steep in the dim light of this house, its walls all around you, now full in its form. This is the first time you've ventured inside. It has been awhile now since you first noticed this house is everything different from how you believed it should be.

The snow slowly ceases to stop until the pines past the window slits can no longer be found. You lay in the center of the room with your back to the sloping stones. At first, you had felt it was just the being too big; the ceiling reaching too high, the floor stooping too low. The wall rounding around back into itself, containing a shape neither circle nor square. The obvious exceptions of so many things in this house that one day might permit the emergence of a home. You wonder what mistake coded within you could have determined the design of this place. You look about this dead shell so severed from sense. At what stage in your burst of creation had you forgotten to put in a fireplace, or a chimney, or a level bit of floor for a bed in which to sleep, dream, and safely remain?

You start to see something there, enclosed in the cold room's lack of corners. It hangs down in the space where the wall slopes in to meet the ceiling at no discernible point. The shape of this chamber—amassing in your mind. The berm of snow creeps up over the highest window slit and the gloaming gray seals you in. When the groaning of the weighted roof is finally choked off in the silence, you begin to remember.

You remember this kernel recalled from some hidden slot in your body, pulled out by the certainty of this fade sinking in. The part of you that waited away to build this house, to place you inside and have you linger into the death of the light, the exhaustion of the air. The blame presses around you, catches up to you here, finds you; it never once left. Within the shape of this place, another presence remains, waiting to be sprung out. You just needed to find its entrance.

Already, the bolt of your body slides open. The tremor of something rushing in and reaching out. Unsealing the passage for your return. It presses up along the walls, races against the ceiling. Filling your form in flooding luster. Within the change, the kind of light that can birth in bottomless murk.

So endless and red. So complete in its rage. It takes shine upon your ignited mind.

Within this change, the knowledge that there is no change at all.

Returned to your hide, the strength to snarl in the face of their blame.

Your stone house splinters against the strain.

And you remember. You remember why they blame you.

SIGHTSEEING
Alistair Rey

As a general rule, speech is a commodity in Morocco. Conversations and friendly greetings quickly transform into veiled sales pitches at a moment's notice. Merchants in the medina hawk their wares. They call out in multiple languages, beckon you to their stalls, and aggressively place unwanted objects in your hand for consideration. In Fes, I purchased a small lamp after enduring a prolonged lecture on artisanal craftsmanship. I had no desire to own the object, but in the end, it proved more expedient to pay the hundred dirhams for the lamp than waste the afternoon explaining myself to an insistent storeowner. Those volunteering restaurant recommendations will typically lead you to the establishment of a business partner. If you are lost, pedestrians offering to show you to your destination will strategically steer you in the direction of their uncle's workshop where you can sip tea and examine Arabian carpets. Not that these types of encounters are without their charm. It was simply something to which I was unaccustomed. After a few days in Fes, however, I acclimated to the street culture of the bazaars and even came to enjoy it in a strange way.

I was traveling to Marrakesh—the second leg of my journey—when I met the man who would tell me about the Wādī. He was unassuming at first glance: slightly past middle-age, well-dressed, and clean-cut. He introduced himself as Abbas and inquired about my trip, where I was from, and whether I was enjoying Morocco. It was the type of polite chatter you might expect on a long train ride in which two strangers know they will be spending a significant amount of time together and try to make the best of the situation. When I told him I would be spending a week in Marrakesh, he made a face and asked whether I would be taking any excursions. I hadn't considered it, I told him.

"There are many places to visit in the area," he said. "Most people tend to spend a few days in Marrakesh and take day trips outside the city. Tour companies run regular service to these destinations."

When I said I didn't much care for the company of tourists, Abbas laughed and nodded approvingly.

"You could consider Wādī al-Dimā then. Not many people go there."

Four hours south-east of Marrakesh was a city that had been uninhabited since at least the turn of twentieth century. It had originally been a Berber settlement prior to the Roman invasion. In the early Christian era, the site had served briefly as an Augustine monastery before being overrun by Arab conquers. Abbas seemed well-informed on the locality. I sat listening to him discuss its history, trying to form an image of the place in my mind. I stared out the window at the passing landscape, imaging what such a city might look like with its mix of Roman, Christian, and Islamic architecture.

"And now, it's completely abandoned?" I asked when he finished.

He nodded sadly. "No money. It's located in the valleys of the Atlas Mountains. They don't get much business that way. People have left. It's a sad thing. Inevitable, but still sad."

Abbas dug into his wallet and pulled out a card. I felt stupid for letting myself be disarmed by his congeniality and expected a well-rehearsed sales pitch recommending a restaurant in town or offering some type of local service. But he didn't launch into a polished sales pitch. Instead, he simply held out the card, indicating for me to take it. He knew a person who could take me to Wādī al-Dimā if I was interested. There was no obligation, he assured. Tour companies didn't usually run buses out to that part of the countryside, and I would need a private guide.

I tucked the card into my rucksack and told him I would consider it. Abbas nodded and changed the subject. For the rest of the trip, we discussed North African politics, the Arab Spring and his impression of British tourists—which, to be honest, was quite amusing. Arriving in Marrakesh, he wished me a nice trip, hopped into a cab, and left me to haggle with the cab drivers milling about the station entrance. I never saw him again.

I enjoyed Marrakesh with its mosques, large squares, and winding streets. Each morning, I awoke to the *adzhan*, listening to it drift across the morning like a strange and enchanting music that summoned the faithful to prayer. Other tourists in the hotel were not as enamored with its resonant beauty and complained about the noise.

"Can't you do anything about it?" asked one man who had been woken at sunrise by the muezzin's call. The manager at the hotel desk stared at him helplessly.

His expression reminded me why I despised tourists. Aversion for one's own kind is a peculiar type of loathing.

I recalled the card that Abbas gave me. The idea of an isolated village seemed appealing. By my fourth day, I had already managed to visit all the major attractions in Marrakesh. My afternoons increasingly degenerated into wandering from café to café, trying to occupy my time and avoid the sightseers congregating at Jemma el-Fnaa.

Why not head further afield and explore the environs?

I called the number on the card, and a man answered in French. As I worked through some clumsy greetings recalled from my A-level French classes, the man fluidly switched to perfect English.

"I know Abbas," I said. "I want to go to Wādī al-Dimā."

I was instructed to meet at a nearby café in an hour, an austere building made of dirty stucco and flaking plaster. Once inside, however, the courtyard opened onto an impressive restaurant with a rooftop terrace overlooking the city skyline, where I sat drinking a glass of wine, always a rare find in Moroccan cities.

As I waited, I watched the sky slowly fill with soft evening light and listened to the *adzhan* resonate across the city. I became transfixed by its low, rolling utterances and must have momentarily closed my eyes because when I opened them again a young man was seated across from me at the table, smiling. He introduced himself as Ayman.

We chatted for a few minutes as I gave him a brief summary of my trip. Ayman took it all in, listening attentively and interjecting when appropriate.

"And you are traveling *alone*?" he finally asked, a bit taken aback by this revelation.

I nodded, smiling at his disbelief. A young Irish girl was not the stereotypical lone traveler, I agreed, although I was quite capable of handling myself when necessary.

"My father had reservations about me traveling alone," I said. "He advised Spain as an alternative, but everyone goes there."

Ayman scoffed. "No, not Spain. Morocco is better."

Why I wanted to go to Wādī al-Dimā puzzled him. Not many people knew about the place, and it was not listed in the travel books.

"There is nothing there. It's a ghost town." He mulled over this phrase and asked if he had used the proper English expression.

"If you mean it is completely abandoned, then yes."

"*Abandoned.* That's the word I was thinking," he said, more to himself. "Well, it is. Nobody has lived there for a hundred years."

"And why is that?"

Ayman shrugged. "Economy dried up. Lack of water. No infrastructure. Take your pick. There have been some other theories, too. In the 1950s, a French entrepreneur had plans to turn it into a retreat for artists. I'm not so knowledgeable in the details, but something went wrong. Mainly, it's just a sad place that doesn't attract tourists."

"Perfect," I said. "Will you take me?"

We negotiated a price and planned to leave the next morning.

Ayman arrived at my hotel at daybreak in a pristine SUV. The ride into the mountains was pleasant. An hour into the trip, Ayman turned off the main highway and navigated along the local roads. We passed towns and villages, many of them poor and decrepit-looking. You could tell the places leased to European contractors by the modern apartment complexes and swimming pools. The unequal distribution of wealth was evident everywhere. At one point, we passed an old man sitting on the side of the road selling vegetables from a cart. At another location, a child directed a herd of goats across the road. The craggy mountains gradually came into view, towering over the shrubs and Argania trees. For most of the trip, I snapped pictures of the people and scenery as Ayman educated me on local points of interests.

"You might be the first person to visit the Wādī in a long time," Ayman said as we cruised along. "Nobody has ever asked me to take them out there."

"That so?"

"Yes. I am curious."

"So, you've *never been?*"

He shook his head. "No, not many people go there. Setti Fatma, Tidssi, yes. But not to the Wādī. Once the people left, it was forgotten."

He cast a look in my direction. His eyes concealed behind dark sunglasses made it difficult to read his expression, but I imagined he was trying to instill confidence in me. "I know where I'm going. It's difficult to get lost out here."

I just nodded and returned to snapping photos of the countryside.

As the afternoon progressed, the terrain became more mountainous and barren. The craggy formations took on strange shapes as though hewn from an alien substance. The peculiar way they reflected the light caught my eye, making them appear to shimmer in the distance. I chalked it up to the rising heat, although this reasoning hardly explained the odd effects of the mountains, which cast long shadows across the earth despite the high declination of the noon sun. It was almost as if they defied nature and obeyed laws known only to them.

The walls of the city came into view as we turned onto a stretch of rutted dirt roads leading into the valley. Unremarkable on first inspection: flat sallow plaster mottled with water stains and scabby paint. Judging from the length of the walls, the city was not large. The gates that had once protected the settlement were in a state of complete disrepair and jutted from the earth like teetering giants. Outside the walls, wild and barren fields extended upward along the sloping mountains. The city had sprouted up in the sterile wilderness like a mushroom clinging to the craggy incline of the valley. I could not help feeling slightly disappointed as the car came to a halt.

A small row of crumbling buildings was visible through the gate's entrance. The worn brick and arches suggested that they were Roman, although this was simply an inference on my part. I snapped a few pictures of the exterior as Ayman laced up his hiking boots. What would my friends back home think when they saw them? They were not the typical photos of tourist attractions or people lounging around the pool.

"Crazy Laura," they would say in that playful way meant to conceal their envy. "Always has to be different."

"Ready?" Ayman asked as I adjusted my camera settings.

We entered through the gates, passing the old crumbling structures. Behind these, a network of deserted streets fanned out before us, snaking in odd directions with little sense of structure or design. Dust littered each avenue, and debris crunched under our feet as we advanced further into the medina.

The height of the surrounding buildings seized me with a sensation of vertigo. The buildings pitched and weaved at peculiar angles, seeming to take the shape of the winding streets with their curved and convex facades.

The tan-colored stone glistened faintly in the afternoon light, reminding me of the rocks we had seen coming into the valley. Despite the afternoon heat, they were cool to the touch.

Further along, the buildings became noticeably more modern with windows, doorframes, and decorative features. Some of the ornamentation was quite beautiful. The engravings along the walls resembled a fine stone filigree reminiscent of the gothic stucco calligraphy and girih-like panels in Fes. A surreal silence permeated the streets with no tourists elbowing you for a view and no chattering voices intruding on the stillness. The isolation was complete.

It was paradise.

"Have you noticed the streets?" Ayman said, as though he whispered this in my ear, but when I turned around, he was crouched in the debris a good five meters behind me, examining an engraving running along the base of a building.

I shook my head, and he made a spiral shape in the air with his finger. "Not straight."

A shadowy outline in the window of the building opposite me looked like a person slumped against the wall, although the shape didn't stir when I called out.

Inside, we found a bare, cavernous room. Bits of broken rock covered the floor. A mannequin made of dusty rags and twigs was propped against the windowsill. The face was blank except for two crudely formed eye sockets and a stitched mouth. The angle of the body, however, gave the dummy an unnatural life-like quality—an idle spectator casually gazing out to the empty street.

"What is it?" I asked Ayman, prodding at the bundle of rags and sticks, half expecting it to leap at me.

Ayman stared at the thing in silence and shook his head.

I took a few photos of the mannequin, and we continued down the empty avenue.

On the next street, we discovered a second mannequin huddled in the corner of a gutted building.

A third and fourth turned up in the following two constructions we explored.

In each room or building we entered, the same grotesque sculptures greeted us. Although each was made of rags and sticks, none were identical. Evident care had been taken in positioning these objects in such a way as to give a semblance of life and movement. Limbs made of branches and husks bent at just the right angles; matted cloth bundled together to create the illusion of contrapedal balance and poise.

Wandering in and out of the demolished buildings, we were surrounded by these mute, inert creatures. We had entered their world. We were the strangers among them.

"This is creepy," I told Ayman candidly after mulling over our latest discovery. "I think we should leave."

Ayman agreed, and we marched back along the street leading towards the gates. I had not taken particular note of the buildings we passed upon entering. Many of them looked similar, and their fluid, curving design often made it difficult to detect where one building ended and the next began. An impression of warped and towering walls surrounded me on all sides.

On our second tour, I gave greater consideration to the particularities of each building, scrutinizing them for familiar markings or distinctive features that might indicate we were headed in the right direction. However, this proved impossible. None of the buildings jogged my memory. The streets turned and coiled with greater frequency as we walked, and I remembered the way Ayman had made a spiraling gesture in the air with his finger.

Not straight, he had said.

When we came to a plaza with a building I was certain we had never passed, I paused. A soaring gothic construction had statues running along the expanse of the entire facade. The carvings were a mix of human and animal forms arranged in an intricate arabesque pattern. In the pale afternoon light, the adornments looked like petrified bodies.

Every structure in the city had an unusual organic quality as though having been turned to stone rather than carved from it.

"I think we went the wrong way," I said after studying the plaza and adjacent arcades.

Ayman looked up at the carvings and nodded.

We followed the winding street back the way we came. The quiet, which I had found so pleasant earlier in the afternoon, unnerved me as we trekked along the vacant streets. Everything around us hinted at life, yet nothing stirred—the only noises were our footsteps and the wind. Not even the call of birds or the slithering sounds of lizards through the rocks punctuated the silence.

"I feel like those things are watching us," I said with a light laugh. I offered the comment simply for the sake of conversation. I wanted to concentrate on something other than the crunching of stone and brick under our shoes. Not that it wasn't true. I couldn't help thinking about the mannequins concealed behind each wall and enclosure, how they silently observed us meandering back and forth.

Ayman cast an unsettling look around. "No, not them. Someone else."

"What do you mean?"

He only shook his head.

Ayman seemed to be losing command of his English, his responses terse, often abrupt. Whereas earlier that morning he communicated with the fluidity of a native speaker, he now seemed to search for the proper words and become frustrated when he couldn't find them. Of course, it could have been that he simply preferred not to talk. Our current circumstances hardly encouraged gratuitous conversation.

Despite our change of direction, the streets grew shorter and wended at sharper angles. Every time I thought we were about to come upon a street or building we had passed before, I was mistaken. Street after street, new buildings, squares, and courtyards appeared, like walking in a maze.

At each intersection, I paused to consider which direction looked most promising. After a while, they all looked the same. We wandered aimlessly, hoping to stumble across a recognizable landmark that would direct us back to the gates.

The afternoon shadows elongated. By my calculation, we had been lost for a few hours, although the light in the sky suggested it was considerably later. The flat blue rapidly diminished to a burnt orange. I could not spot the sun or tell in which direction it was setting, but it clearly advanced towards evening. The sky didn't appear to drain of daylight like a normal sunset. Rather, it seemed to absorb color, ingesting tints of azure, umber, and vermillion like a canvas stretched tight above us.

"What time is it?" I asked, looking up at the sky.

If he heard me, he paid me no mind. His gaze fixed on the far end of the street where a succession of minarets stood silhouetted against the sky, their tapering outlines stark and imposing in the dusk.

Ayman placed a finger to his lips.

"*Shhhhhhh.*" He gestured to his ear.

I listened. The wind echoed through the empty buildings and passages, a desolate sound, reminiscent of barren desert landscapes and inhospitable terrain. Yet, something else—a low, sonorous reverberation just above the wind—lifted. Difficult to discern at first, I soon recognized the *adzhan*. It bled out into the evening, growing from a murmur into a resonant chant that progressively filled the air.

We stood there for a long time, listening. In the distance, shadows moved along the horizon without definite cause.

The sky turned a deep crimson, bathing everything in blood-red light.

The shadows flickered and moved in spastic gestures.

Squinting into the twilight, I was certain they were people, scuttling along the streets in single file.

Ayman's panic lined his face. Before I could utter a word, he bellowed something in Arabic and ran headlong in the opposite direction.

I followed him but could not see how he managed to dart across the rock and debris with such agility.

I called after him as he vanished into the darkness but only heard his retreating footsteps.

I called out louder, trying to project my voice over the incantatory *adzhan* pealing through the night, but he had fled.

The figures in the distance continued to writhe and gyrate, although they were now receding into the scarlet light. The file moved along, heeding the summons as the people disappeared one by one over the horizon.

Once the *adzhan* trailed off, emptiness surrounded me. Darkness completely veiled the streets and buildings. A faint red afterglow lingered, but it scarcely illuminated the area. I whispered Ayman's name but silence was my only reply.

Certain that Ayman would not return, I shuffled through the debris and rubble with my hands extended in front of me. With each step, I expected my fingers to graze rough stone or make contact with a wall, but I encountered nothing. I inched along, uncertain of the direction I traveled. The absolute darkness wasn't the most unsettling thing. The *feel* of the darkness was. Something lurked there with me, something silent and just out of reach.

After a while, my imagination conjured up a variety of monstrosities culled from old folk tales I had heard as a child. It was silly, but the more fantastical the beast I imagined, the more at ease I felt. I just about managed to calm myself and concentrate on finding my way through the dark when I heard the quiet sound of labored breathing.

"Ayman?" I kept my voice low.

The breaths grew hoarse and asthmatic, like somebody gasping for air. I stopped moving and listened.

"What do you want?" I asked the darkness.

I had not expected an answer, but a soft voice came through the blackness.

"Nothing which you can offer," it said.

Irregular footsteps scuffled through the debris ahead as Ayman staggered out of the dark, his movements rigid and jerky. Two flaccid arms dangled at his side, hanging there like bits of wet cloth. Although I knew it was Ayman from his clothing, I barely recognized him. His face deflated and shrank as though someone wore a mask of Ayman's face. Even the skin on his body looked loose-fitting and shapeless, like a garment pinned to an armature. His mouth dropped opened in a mechanical gesture and emitted a choked squawking sound as he lurched towards me. He tried to speak, like he was saying "dispossession" over and over in a garbled language.

I closed my eyes, awaiting the feel of his limp hands on me, but it never came. The hand that touched me was firm and warm.

A voice spoke in French, and I opened my eyes.

"*Ça va, madame? Ça va?*"

I lay in the dirt. The officer's hand gently nudged my back as he repeated the question. I blinked into the sunlight and sat up just outside the gates of the medina. The police officer handed me a bottle of water, speaking in French. When it was evident I didn't understand, he simply pointed to the gates and I nodded.

A second officer exited from a nearby car and approached.

The two spokes among themselves for a moment as I looked about for Ayman.

"Ayman?" I asked. "*L'autre homme?*"

The two puzzled men offered to help me to my feet.

The SUV was parked where we had left it, its pristine white now covered in a thin layer of dust. I shielded my eyes from the sun and cast a long look around the valley with its sloping hills and sparse Argania trees.

No Ayman, although one of the officers stood around a single chair near the entrance of the gate. From my vantage point, it looked as though a person sat in it, their face turned toward the city gates.

The chair had not been there when we arrived, and I moved closer. It was not a person at all. It was one of the mannequins made of sticks and rags, its posture oddly human and slumped in the chair like a dozing spectator. The face was plain with crudely molded eyes and a sewn mouth like the others.

However, the mannequin wore Ayman's clothes.

The officer murmured something in French and prodded the dummy. It made a dry sound like cornhusks rubbing together.

I shook my head slowly.

The officer assumed I was responding to his inquiry and left it at that.

They escorted me to their vehicle and helped me into the backseat. Making a U-turn sent up a trail of dust into the afternoon.

I nodded when I felt they were asking me a question, although I had little idea of what they actually said. I still felt numb as the city receded from view behind us and the car glided along the roads winding through the valley.

The officer in the passenger seat unhooked the handset of a two-way radio, and I made out the phrase "found a tourist" during the communiqué.

I hugged myself closer and passed the remainder of the trip in a rueful silence.

In Marrakesh, I went to a police station where an official recorded my statement. He patiently scribbled down my account with an incredulous expression. After the interview, I was given the contact information for the Irish consulate in Casablanca and told that I could follow up on the report there. I arrived at my hotel late and fell asleep quickly that night.

I thought I might still be dreaming when I woke at dawn to the tolling cry of the muezzin. I sat up in bed, listening to the *adzhan* with a shudder. It seemed to extend indefinitely, summoning God knew what at this hour.

After what felt like a long time, I got dressed and made my way to the hotel lobby, empty save for a lone man at the desk working the nightshift. His gaze shifted from me to the pages of the paperback he read.

I shuffled over to the ice machine in the corner and filled a bucket.

The *adzhan* resonated, pervading the lobby and rooms of the hotel.

The deskman remained oblivious, his eyes fixed on his book.

"Is there any way to make it stop?" I asked him in a weak voice. "Can't you do anything about it?"

The helpless look he gave filled me with shame, an all too identifiable and familiar kind of shame.

DARK MOON
Kathryn Hore

The Villagers

She walks.

Afternoon sets into evening, and the last yellow-red of sunset loses its hold across the farmlands, the winding country roads, the clutch of buildings and gathering spaces and communal halls that make up the village. On top the hill overlooking it all sits the big manor, casting a shadow across everything below. Beyond is the road leading away, and beyond that, the darkening woods. She walks through these woods each morning as the sun rises and each night after it falls. The darkness doesn't seem to bother her.

It should. And the villagers know it.

Still, she is not actually one of them. She comes from over the other side of those woods, so they bite their tongues and shuffle their feet and glance away, faces flushed with guilt, each evening as she closes her market stall in the square. Packing up her herbs and plants, whatever remains after the day's sales. Usually, not much does. What she brings from there to here is rare and sells well, her stall a busy one most days, her clients regular. She speaks to them with a soft, shy voice, chewing at her lip and rarely meeting their eyes. Even the most regular struggle to engage her in conversation. Perhaps this, too, is a distance that helps them keep their silence.

She is young. Sixteen, perhaps. Maybe seventeen. With black hair hanging long around her face and eyes half-hidden behind its strands, her countenance is timid. She startles easily. Her plants and her isolation are all she has. If only others looked out for her, the villagers think, family or guardians she returned to through the woods. If only she could comprehend that the dark amid the trees should be treated with caution. There are dangers that lurk in the woods at night. Wolves that prowl. And other things besides.

The villagers watch her walk away from their town each evening and know better than she, but still, they say nothing. Not a single word of warning.

And all the while, he waits.

That big manor house is his. This village understands that they owe him. He watches her with eyes sharper than most, his expression distinctly predatory. In the dregs of the day, he saunters to the edge of town as she leaves, leaning against a wall facing west to catch those last long rays, the warmth of them. A power in them. Drinking it in, he slouches back, thick yellow-blonde hair and an insouciant air, tracking her movements until she disappears down the road, beyond view.

He turns back to the town, slipping in before night, and they avoid him, the villagers; they keep out of his way. He smiles when they scatter, when they cross themselves as he comes, their superstitious signs and clutched talismans. Their eyes shift away from his, and he laughs, strolling through the main street and returning to the big house on the hill. The girl may be an outsider, come in from elsewhere, but he is one of them, and he has brought prosperity to their village. Industry and influence, investment that filters down to the villagers' increasingly comfortable lives. They owe him everything.

So, if there is a price for it…well.

If his desires stray and his dark eyes seduce. If yet another pretty young daughter of some outlying farmer catches his eye, or else some wayward son slipped away and disappeared. Youth, who turn their backs on all they have been raised to believe, will be mourned. The villagers pretend not to notice to whom they go. They only dip their heads in respect as he passes, even as they ward off his evil.

Once, not even a month past, the old midwife decided it had gone on too long. Somebody needed to speak up, to stand for those who fell to his spell. Too many of their young had gone. And now, the herb girl, with her shy mumbles and innocent eyes and no-one to protect her, had caught his notice, and it was too much. It needed to stop.

The midwife dared not confront him directly, but she did go to the girl. Taking her aside one late afternoon as the shadows lengthened, hiding in them from the sun.

Be warned, she tried to tell the girl. *He watches. His power must draw strength from somewhere; it must be renewed year on year. Great as it is, it must still be fed the innocent. Be afraid when he watches.*

People say that the girl did not understand. And they found the midwife in a ditch along the road beyond the village, neck broken, on the night of the summer festival.

The villagers keep their silence and give him their dues. While the girl walks, a regular, everyday pattern. Back down the darkening road leading to the woods, with the village at her back and his eyes hungry upon her. And the silent villagers know that if it were only the wolves in the wood she had to worry about, she might've had a chance.

The Girl

By the time the path twists into the forest, the sunlight has gone, leaving no more than the pale light of the waning quarter moon. She is more comfortable with that, with the trees stretching overhead and the darkness buffeted around her. When there is light and space, an open stretch of ground, she can see what length of road is ahead, what lies behind. How far she has come from the village at her back and how far she has still yet to go. There is a vulnerability in that. Better to be cosseted by darkness, cocooned by night. Cosy on the road winding through the trees with only her own steps, *tap, tap, tap, tap*, in breach of the weighted still.

It's a darker night than usual; it always is under the waning moon, so she draws out her small lamp and lights the wick. A dim circle of yellow pushing the darkness away, her held in its middle. It serves to do little more than force the shadows in the thickening wood into greater relief, but she knows every rise and fall of this road home from memory. She does not need the lamp. But she lights it anyway, with match and a scent of kerosene, because she supposes she should, because those in the village have tried to tell her more than once. It is dangerous to travel alone in the dark. It is dangerous in the forest at night. There are…wolves, they say. Yes, wolves. Then, they hesitate and say no more.

She is not worried about wolves. They are animals that will only attack if desperate and hungry, and the mild winter left the summer too bountiful. The wolves are content. She does not believe the villagers when they tell her the old midwife was chased into the ditch to her death by such creatures. The villagers don't look like they believe that either, though they tell her such, a story they cling to with something bordering on desperation.

In midsummer, it takes a long time for the skies to properly darken. Tomorrow is the longest of all days, and the strong sun reaches out until late, making the night warm. She prefers it cooler; the heat wears her out, but the wind picks up as she walks, which she likes, and the trees rustle and close in around her.

Tap. Tap. Tap. Tap.

Her footsteps, even and regular in the night.

Tap. Tap. Tap.

Tap-ap.

She frowns, a hesitation. The echo of her own footsteps travels back to her, bouncing off the trees, off the thick black all around. She glances over her shoulder but finds nothing. Even with her small lamp, she can see only a few feet behind; a full moon would grant her light, but this last quarter moon only brings more dark.

She shrugs it off. Turns and walks on, shaking out any concern like she shakes out her hair, which the wind picks up and blows back.

Tap. Tap. Tap.

Tap-ap.

She stops.

The sound stops, too.

It is only her own steps, a double-echo she tells herself with firm intent. Even if she has never before caught a hint of her own echo as she walks, nor ever before has she heard an echo sounding quite so like a half-hidden step of another somewhere in the dark behind.

The trees rustle. She is conscious of them. Of the whipping of the wind, the shifting of the woods. Her own breath filling her lungs and pushing out again, her heart thudding in her chest. She is alone. She likes to be alone. This walk home through the woods gives her solitude after a day spent on the stall, a respite after all those hours speaking with customers, facing the villagers' curiosity and interest. These others who exhaust her so. She does not want to let their fear infect her and spoil what little time she has to herself. Their confused warnings of the dead midwife or talk of wolves or cautious concern they will not otherwise name.

Her steps resume. Facing forward, moving on.

Tap-ap.

She does not stop this time. Nothing nor nobody will spoil her reprieve, not noises in the forest, not the echoes of her own steps. She points the lantern forward, keeping the darkness at bay for a few feet at least, what little distance the light manages to penetrate, and continues on.

Tap-ap. Tap-ap.

And if perhaps her steps quicken just a little, and if the warm breeze begins to seem like hot breath down the back of her neck, and if the rustling of the trees obscures other noises, dangerous approaching noises, then she will not acknowledge it.

She walks on. Determined not to hear. Not even as that double-echo of her own footsteps seems to be getting closer.

Tap-ap.

The Other

Renewal is required. Such is the way of things in nature.

He prefers to do such by day, in the light. With the sun's full strength behind him. But there are ways and means, and sometimes, even for him, the cloak of darkness offered by the night remains the most effective choice. Day may be his time, but night provides cover.

He is strong right now. He has waited until he is at his peak, until the last possible moment, light flowing from under his fingers, pulsing hard beneath his skin. The long hours of daylight create a fission across his surface, and he revels in it, the warmth of it, the sheer force of it. The heat. The potency. He can be no stronger than he is at this moment, and at times like this, he forgets what it was to be truly human, mundanely so, back like he once was.

He made his bargains many years gone, and he paid the price for them once, and he has learnt, since, how to appease that which he follows. Year on year, like the seasons, the cycle must be followed. Nature can be a harsh master.

They all owe someone; they all owe something. Even the likes of him, rambling alone in his big manor house.

He watches her, the dark-haired girl from the other side of the woods. Heat radiates from the baked earth, and he leans against his wall soaking up the flickering orange-red sunset, storing the energy that drives him. His addictions. That which he's given himself over to, to the gods of it, for they like to be called gods, and he doesn't dare say otherwise. Shades conceal his eyes, not for their protection but to mask their whiteness, and his hands rest in his pockets as he slouches. The girl does not notice him. Few can conceal themselves in broad daylight like he can, and she is too consumed with her own isolation and solitary needs.

As she disappears down the forest road, he pulls himself off his wall, but this time he does not turn back to the village. This time, he walks after her. Tomorrow is the day of the longest sun, and this must be done tonight.

Villagers scatter out of his way, with their grubby charms grasped in sweaty fingers, making their warding signs against evil. Not that it ever stops them sidling close enough to beg the benefits of what he can offer, his intervention in this petty squabble or his goodwill for that new enterprise. As if their rivalries and desperations were even worth his time. Now, he gestures for them to be gone, and they are. He follows at a distance out of the town and down the forest road, the last flickering light fading, so he pulls off his shades. White eyes tracking the girl ahead.

She is worn, no doubt, from dull villagers poking around her stall with their awkward conversations and mindless pleasantries. He understands her need to escape the crowding of the days, for there is something in her isolation and separateness with which he feels almost akin. Living in his high mansion and set apart by the marks traced on his body by masters that will claim him if he cannot offer up a sacrifice of real worth. He knows what it is to be alone.

The darkness grows, long shadows stretching, blending, shifting into night. He moves closer. Careful still, for he does not trust darkness. Ahead, she pauses. He sees a flare.

A lamp. She is lighting a lamp.

He grins. A wolfish expression, all teeth and need. And he thought she might be difficult to follow on a night so dark as this.

He stalks the yellow circle of lamplight dancing ahead. Keeping to the centre of the road, away from the deep ditches lining either side and the trees growing beyond. The midwife met her end in one of these ditches, and he knows this because the villagers told him, just as he knows they blame him for it. Fear is a useful thing, when carefully propagated. He encourages the blame sent his way. Yet, the fate of the old woman was not his doing; he would not have left her to rot in a ditch; he does not deal in death. Death in nature is too commonplace; it happens, regular and meaningless and of little interest to those he serves.

Pain is what he requires, that ultimate sign of life. Only the living can scream. Only the living cling to their physical presence with such desperation that they cry when it is damaged.

And if not by some offering, his body will pay such a price, and he has been through that before.

Never again.

Never. Again.

They are well into the woods before he makes his move. Shifting through the darkness with a renewed focus on his prey. To their sides, the trees thicken, branches tangle and rustle as the wind picks up, dies down. A natural rise and fall, a peak and renewal, seasons of strength, seasons to hide, rejuvenate.

She is almost within his reach. Her footsteps tap back to him, a regular rhythm, a kind of heartbeat.

Tap. Tap. Tap.

He releases a little of the stored energy running rampant beneath his skin and allows his own steps to make a sound.

Tap-ap.

An echo in the night, a hint of him to nag at her consciousness.

Tap-ap.

She hesitates, shivers.

Good. The uses of fear. Terror to make the mind freeze, panic to drive the screams. Such screams, such signs of life.

A little more energy released.

Tap-ap.

What girl wouldn't be scared, walking alone in the dark of night, along a deserted forest road?

Up ahead, she stops and glances back. She sees nothing, of course. He pulls all light into him, allowing none to escape; it is easy to create the effect of only blackness when you control the light. She turns forward again. *Tap. Tap. Tap.* Faster now, a quickening pace. His lips twist in satisfaction. He pushes on, matching her step. He knows how to stalk a prey better than any beast of the woods, better than any wolf.

Tap-ap.

Faster, he moves closer. Gaining on her now. A crackling energy through his limbs, sparks pushing to jump from his skin. Her shoulders hunch in tight, perhaps the fear of being alone. He moves so close that he can hear the breath catching in her throat. Feel the brushing ends of her blown-back hair scratch across his face. If she turns now, she will see him at her shoulder. Thick alight hair, pale skin glowing from far more than the light of her lamp.

The lamp. He wonders, in this last moment, at her use of it. Such has made it so easy for him to track her, he has not questioned it, yet he has watched her for a long time now, and never before has she seen the need for one.

But he is so close. Breathing down her neck. The thought is fleeting, for he needs this too much. Had it been day, his day, she would have seen his shadow, should he have chosen to cast one. Even now, she might see the glow of him. Hear his breathing in her ear.

So close, he can reach out…

He raises his hand, glowing with its own light, igniting through his limbs. He focuses it, controls it, channeling it through his fingers and bringing them down hard upon her shoulder.

And is flung, backwards, through the air.

He cries out. A strangled sound. The force of the blow drags his whole body away, an instant impact, and he hits dirt, ground, a hard distance behind. With a shocked whimper, a new pain flares through his fingers, a desperate burning across his palm.

His hand, where he has touched her, where he clutched her shoulder, is an agony.

He rolls to his knees but can get no further, panting too hard with the white-hot hurt of it. Gripping at his damaged wrist with his good hand, he gulps the pain down. His hand shakes. His hand no longer glows, burnt black.

An unwitting whine escapes from between his teeth as he lifts his gaze.

She stands on the path, watching him.

"Finally. I've been waiting for you."

Her voice sounds almost amused. She places the lamp on the ground by her feet and looks down, all shadows and relief, like the night, like the woods around them. Where is the sweetness, where is the innocence now? Her youthful mask shows no naivety there.

"You are certainly more patient than I, my friend of sun and light," she says, stepping closer, and despite the haze of pain, he knows to shy away. "I was starting to think I should've knocked off that old midwife much earlier."

He jerks his head up, and she smiles. "Didn't know that, did you? Ah, well. If I hadn't, you would've. It's not like our kind let interference slide for long."

He bares clenched teeth, trying to manage the pain. For all the energy in him, he cannot move, the agony in his fingers is too much, and the best he can do is kneel there, gripping his wrist and struggling not to cry out.

She drops to a crouch, until they are eye to eye, and if his are white, hers are only black.

"You took a risk, not coming for me sooner," she says. "Maybe you got complacent, alone in that big old house on the hill. Forgetting you're not the only one who has ever been offered a bargain. Or maybe you just got desperate to save yourself the wrath of your masters."

The light seeps from him at her close proximity, though he pulls it in fast and fights to contain it. She reaches out as if to caress his cheek. He flinches back on instinct, and she smiles at his fear.

"But my own demand their prices, too, my friend. And the Dark Moon, her wrath can be greater than any."

She stands. Stretches. Glances down and holds out a hand to him, as if to do no more than help him up. An invitation. A command. He shakes his head, words beyond him as he fights to marshal some kind of power, anything. But if the light belongs to him, the darkness is all hers, and they are surrounded by it, engulfed by it.

There is movement beside her in the night, something padding to her side. A wolf, looming and black, eyes shining. She caresses the beast's head, and the animal looks up, tongue lolling from between blood-stained teeth, death on its breath. Gazing at his mistress, adoration in his eyes. Waiting for a command.

Her hand once more held out to him, he is not being given a choice here.

"I'm not here to destroy you."

He hears her only from a distance.

"I'm thinking we can help each other, you and me. Together, we could be strong enough to conquer territory neither of us could contemplate alone. Can you imagine it? The power of it? The whole world would cower."

The wolf whines. He tries not to look at its dripping saliva or the brute strength of its jaw. He tries not to see the dark moon rising above all their heads. He is fond of the world. Perhaps, he is also fond of turning his small corner of it to his own desires, but he has never held ambition to conquer so much. He does not wish to revel in the suffering of so many without purpose.

Yet, the power she describes, the force…

"Yes. Once tasted, it is hard to give up, no?" She laughs low. "And if I'm not wrong, you're out of time. Longest day and all that. So, let us help each other, you and me, and we can appease all our demons."

His breath catches, and he can't help but nod. Appease all our demons.

Yes. *Yes.*

Her hand reaches out to him again.

"It won't hurt for long. I promise." Her smile stretches, something hungry, anticipatory. "You may even find you start to enjoy it, after a while."

His shoulders drop, and he closes his eyes and tries to draw breath. To summon energy, light. To face this one above him with dignity and pride. Out of time. The longest day. An offering must be made, and what else can it be?

When he raises his good hand, leaving the other lying useless and burnt in his lap, it shakes.

He reaches without looking, feels for her hand in the dark. Her offer, her promises. Fingers grasping for the possibilities of which she speaks, even when understanding the darker realities that lay beneath. They will help each other. They will conquer worlds.

They will appease their demons.

It won't hurt for long. It won't...

When the pain comes, he screams.

Oh, how he screams.

BECKONED
Melissa A. Winton

The room is dressed in timeless linens and beautiful collectibles from all over the world—tribal masks and weapons from Africa and South America, small figurines from France, Russia, and Italy, and trinkets from China and Australia. All places, she has only ever dreamed of visiting. The room is still uncomfortable. With her ankles crossed tight, her leg still jumps, vibrating the heel of her pump against the hardwood floor. The drumming of her foot clashes with the lazy horn crooning from the speaker of the radio. Beneath the long beige coat, doubled over on her lap, her fingers fidget and pick at imagined imperfections along her cuticles.

When the mahogany door swings open, a pleasant-looking woman steps from behind, her shiny blonde waves framing her face. The semi-fancy bordered dress flatters her small frame.

"Mrs. Montgomery?" she asks with a gentle smile.

"Yes."

"The doctor is ready for you."

With a deep breath, Mary Montgomery collects herself and her belongings and takes that deciding step she never thought she'd have to take.

The home-based office of the man, who introduced himself to her as Dr. Maxwell Ruebel, is decorated in rich woods, fine artwork, and international flare, just like the rest of his house—not that she saw much of it, having been brought in through the back door. A lonely tune is piping through the radio on the desk, next to it lays his tie. The somber melody does nothing to calm her nerves.

Although he had come highly recommended, the nonchalance and hastiness of their meeting doesn't sit well with her. He leads her into a hidden room beyond a bookcase.

Oh Mary, this is a mistake. She panics at the sight of the chair.

Come on, Mary.

113

He takes her arm, leading her across the room, and helps her into it. Her teeth clinch and her breath hastens, as she settles into the torn leather.

"Sarah, you're collected the payment, yes?"

"Yes, Doctor."

"Good."

But…

You wanted it.

He straps her in. Arms tight to the armrest. Legs secured within metal. Her stomach clinches, and she closes her eyes as she is reclined.

Please, don't do this.

I will take care of you.

A tear runs down her cheek. Instinctively, she reaches to wipe it, but the leather cuffs around her wrist stops her. Her racing heart falls into her stomach with the realization that there is no escape.

"Okay, Mary. Are you comfortable?" Dr. Ruebal asks, a ring of cigarette smoke circling his head, reminding her of one of those ciggy ads in the McClure's magazine. The doctor's unkempt appearance is nothing like those dapper gentlemen. His hair is greasy and disheveled from his tar-stained fingers combing through it every few minutes.

She masks her doubt with a meek smile and settles into the leather chair.

His scruff-covered cheeks rise up into a grin.

"Swell. Let us begin, shall we?" he says through the cigarette wedged between his yellowed teeth. After scribbling some notes onto a pad, he hands it off to his pretty assistant.

Dr. Reubel gives a brief explanation of the procedure and a few instructions. Mary inhales through her nose, filling her lungs to capacity. The assistant faces her, her kind eyes and that gentle smile giving some amount of comfort. As the air slips through her parted lips, Mary closes her eyes.

100…

99…

98…

9-…

"Night, night, Mary."

Drifting into a shadowed oblivion, every muscle gives in to the alluring emptiness. A calm cold engulfs her. Her mind hushes. A frosty breeze drifts across her face, carrying a peculiar smell that burns the inside of her nostrils. She turns her head away, but the odor is resilient and is uncomfortable. Fear embraces her in chills, crowning her head in tingles.

Someone is walking over my grave.

You are.

She jerks her head toward the whisper, searching the darkness. "Who said that?"

"Mary?"

"Who said that?"

"Mary? It's me."

In this black world, she spins around and around, searching for the other speaker. "Who else is out there?"

"Mary, it's just me, Dr. Ruebel. And Sarah, my assistant. I'm going to start asking you some questions, okay?"

She recognizes his voice calling to her through the black chasm he has placed her in. He needs to keep her consciousness alert, but she's not interested in him or his questions. She's only concerned about who else might be here with her. In *her* mind.

"Mary, I need you to let me know if you can hear me." His tone is firmer this time, edging on agitated. "Mary? Are you ready?"

She answers a breathless, "Yes."

"Good, good. Then, we can get started."

His voice muffles beneath some kind of rustling she can't identify. It sounds so far away, like another world, another dimension. A cold courses through her, triggering a spastic jerk in her muscles, and the need to cover herself consumes her. All of those insecurities she once felt as a young virgin, being admired by a lustful man for the first time, burn in her cheeks and between her breasts.

I see you.

In the darkness, she wraps her arms around her chest that grows heavy with every breath. She scans the blackness again, "Where are you?"

"I'm right here, Mary," he says. "I haven't gone anywhere. I apologize for that brief delay. I'll continue."

Please, wait...

"Now, where was I?"

No. Stop...

"Yes, here we go."

Don't...

"Do you know where you are, Mary?"

No...

"Mary, I said, do you know where you are?"

After a moment's hesitation, she takes a step. Then another. And another. There's an unpleasing aroma, like the paint thinner her father would use on the house where she grew up. The wind picks up, twirling her hair in its airy tendrils.

"No," she says.

"Can you tell me what it's like?"

"It's cold," she says with a shiver.

"All right."

"And, dark."

"Take your time, Mary. What do you see?"

She turns her face away from the penetrating current and tall, slender shapes come into view. With each stride, they become more visible, as though a shadowed fog lifts. Her breath catches at the sight of naked human trunks, sprouting from a decaying earth that seems to breathe with the ebb and flow of the wind.

"I'm in…"

Branches sway and reach for her, beckoning her to come closer.

"You're in…?"

She steps closer. "A forest."

"Okay, then. Now, describe to me what this forest looks like." He probes.

She swallows hard at the sharp pressure within and utters, "I'm scared."

"I assure you, you are perfectly safe."

Mary's eyes widen as she catches her breath.. "They're awful."

"Awful, how? Please, be more specific, Mary."

"The trees."

"What about the trees?"

"They aren't trees."

"How do you mean?"

"They're…people. But twisted."

"Twisted?" he asks in an almost absentminded tone.

Intermittent moans and grunts escape the forms, as they bend and melt into each other.

"They're…"

Heavy breaths ride the errant wind and encase her in the memory of that night. His words echo within her like fiendish teases, carrying the trace of his touch over her skin. Her stomach tightens in reprised anger and a small amount of ashamed pleasure. Her muscles constrict, as she bites her lip and holds her breath as the pressure within eases. Her heart drums a dizzying beat of desire and confusion, shame and guilt.

You know you want to…

"I really should be getting home." She blushes, reaching for her coat hanging on the rack next to his desk. He blocks her, cupping her hand in his, intertwining his fingers between hers, and massaging her shoulder. His eyes pierce into her and heat flushes within her cheeks.

"Come on, Mary. Have one drink with me." He beckons with a smile. *"To celebrate our big win."*

The burning in her cheeks move to breasts, as she takes in a deep breath, and settles between her thighs. *"All right, Mr. Daniels. But, just one."*

"Excellent." He rushes to the mini bar and gathers two tumblers and a bottle. She sits back down on the leather couch in his office.

Mary has only been working for Attorney Jacob Daniels a few months, but even in her interview, she knew how important this case was to him and the firm. She could never imagine quitting in the middle of it the way her predecessor did. Mary could never do something so unprofessional. How could someone just up and leave without notice like that?

He hands her a crystal tumbler filled with two fingers of a caramel liquid, and toasts, "To the two of us. We make a great team."

After tapping his glass to hers, he slams the drink down with a, "Woo."

She toasts back with a giggle and more blood warms her cheeks. "To us."

And sips the whiskey. It burns deep within her chest and forces up a small cough.

He laughs and points out that she had done it all wrong. He pours himself another. "Like this, sweetheart." And shoots the drink.

Wanting to impress, she mimics him, but with a forced smile and much more coughing. "I'll make a shooter out of you yet, Mrs. Montgomery." He pours her another.

"Oh, no. I said just one."

"Yes, that's true, but that was before I had to drink one more than you. If we're to be a team, we have to do things together."

And with that, she relents to another.

And eventually, another.

"Mary? What do you see?" the doctor asks, trying to get her attention again.

"I... I..."

I'll take care of you...

"Don't worry. I'll take care of you." He sits down next to her on the couch. "You can trust me, Mary. You do trust me."

She nods, throwing the room into a violent spin and pushing her off balance. "Oh, Mr. Daniels. I don't feel so good."

"That's all right, sweetheart. It would appear that you are a bit of a lightweight." He brushes the hair out of her face and holds her chin in his palm.

He gazes into her eyes, stopping her breath. She clears her throat and looks away, pressing her hands into the couch to stand. "I'm sorry, but I really need to..."

"Shhh..." He presses his lips to hers, forcing her to lie down, and places all of his weight onto her. She grabs at his shoulders to push, but the whiskey has drained her of strength. She moans for him to stop. He moans in response, forcing his hand up her skirt and between her thighs.

"Isn't this what you want?" He rips at her panties.

"No." She struggles against him.

"Oh, yes it is. I see the way you blush." He unbuttons his pants, pulling himself out and rubbing against her. *"You want me."*

"Mr. Daniels, please." She cries.

"And I want you."

"Don't." She whimpers.

"Let go, Mary." He forces into her warmth. *"I'm taking care of you, sweetheart."*

Tears stream down her face. She knows she cannot win, so she lets him.

"Fuck, you feel good." He thrusts.

A small noise escapes her, and he thrusts harder.

She knows no one will believe her because she had blushed. A lot.

He thrusts faster.

She had been attracted to him.

He thrusts harder and with a grunt.

She had wanted him.

He thrusts harder and faster, his breath heavy is sticky in her ear.

But, she hadn't wanted this.

He thrusts one final time, with all of his might, letting out a moan and, "Goddamn. We're one hell of a team."

Or had she?

"Go on, Mary."

Through a sudden tightness in her throat, she chokes out, "My husband…"

The sting of her teeth biting into her lip sends her stomach into convulsions.

"What about him?"

"He doesn't know."

"You love your husband dearly, don't you?"

She nods through the lump lodged in her throat. "So much."

"Then, this is for the best."

The writhing forms stop their grinding. They focus on her. Twisted arms with long, gnarly fingers reach out and point at her.

You wanted it.

"No. I didn't want it. Honest, I didn't. I tried to stop him. But, oh God. I'm so sorry." A sour tang floods her mouth, and a sharp aching rolls through her belly. Although she is paralyzed with guilt, her heart still runs like a coward.

"Now. Listen to me, dear. I need you to calm down and breathe. I understand. No one is judging you. I'm surely not judging you. Now, forget about all that hubbub you hear on the news. You're perfectly safe here. Free from all that hot air and judgment. You understand that, don't you?"

As she nods, tears spill from her eyes, blurring the humanoid timbers before her.

"That's right. Breathe. Who do you think is judging you?"

The words push through her lips, though it is not her speaking.

"Me." *Me.*

The fluttering feeling turns icy and tight. Panic grips her throat and stiffens her muscles.

"Oh, Mary." His voice is airy with astonishment, barely audible over the wafting breeze. "Don't blame yourself. That wasn't your fault. You were out of your wits. He took advantage of you. I see this all the time. Soon, this will all be over. But, what I want you to do is tell yourself that this was a tragic mistake, and that none of this is your fault. Can you do that for me, Mary?"

Along with the doctor, she waits for another involuntary response.

Only the wind blows.

"Mary? Remember, I'm here to help you. But, I can't bring you out of this darkness and into the light without your help. All right?" As the doctor's voice strains for a reaction, a strange force pulls her attention away from him.

"Mary?"

Through the limbs that point with arthritic fingers is an iridescent glow.

"Mary, are you still with me?"

A curious awe leaves his questions unanswered.

"Perhaps, we should stop. Mary?"

She hears metal clang and grumbles in the distance.

"Dear, I'm going to stop and wake you up, now."

"No." *No.*

"Are you sure you want me to continue?

"Yes." *Yes.*

"All right then. Let's move on, shall we?"

The wind whips around her, pushing her from behind, encouraging her to go to the luminescence bursting through the oily black like a red star.

She nods.

"Swell. Mary, you're going to forget all about that awful night. Move on with your life. A brand-new beginning. Now, where do you see yourself moving on to?"

"To the rose." *To the rose.*

"That's good. Very good. Wait. Did you say, the rose?"

"Yes." *Yes.*

"What is the rose?"

"The light." *The light.*

"Oh. That's good. Go to the rose, then. Go to the rose. Forget that awful night."

It burns red amidst swirling night, drawing her to it.

Closer.

And closer.

And closer.

Warm, lambent light touches her pale skin. "Something doesn't feel right anymore."

"What do you mean?"

She sets her foot down on the flaccid surface, its clotted mass squeezing between her toes.

"I-I don't know."

"Nothing bad is happening to you, Mary. It's normal." He sounds so sure of himself. "What do you see?"

A hint of formaldehyde tickles her nose. Her thoughts race with unnerving images of what could be under her feet. The doctor drones, but she pushes his voice aside and focuses on the rose. She doesn't want to break sight with it. She doesn't want to turn away from its light and return to the shadows.

But she must.

A tremble in her finger runs up the length of her arms, strengthening to an irrepressible quaking that settles in the clinch of her jaw.

"N-no, no, no, n-no, no, n-no, no..."

"What is it?"

"It... It..."

    ...can't be real.

"It's... al..."

    ...all over me.

"Oh God..."

    ... save me.

                                  You feel good.

A severe pinch low in her abdomen stabs through her fragile nerves.

"What is it-"

    "-I don't feel so good."

"It's all righ-"

    "-I'm sorry, Doctor."

"Shhh-"

    "-Stop."

"It's too late-"

    "Something's wrong."

"Everything's fine-"

    "-Please, stop."

"You wanted my help."

                                You wanted me.

    "-No."

"Calm down, Mary."

                                Let go, Mary.

    "Dr. Reubel, please..."

"We need to be a team."   *We're one hell of a team.*

   "Don't…"

"I'm taking care of you, sweetheart."   *I'm taking care of you, sweetheart.*

Betrayal's sharp edge slices deep into her trust. Again.

"Mary, the only way I can help you through this trauma you've experienced is if you trust me."

She grinds her teeth and nods through the pain.

"Now, tell me what you see."

She spits out through ragged breaths, "Body parts. Little f-fingers and t-toes. They look like they've been…ripped away. Oh, God, there's clumps of b-bloody skin and b-b-bone."

The salty taste of her own tears spill into her mouth. In the dark, she wipes her cheeks. "They're *everywhere.*"

"Listen to me, Mary. It's not real. This is simply a manifestation of your own guilt. Now, I want you to hear me. Quiet your sobs and listen to my voice."

She nods with a sniffle.

"Good. Do you still see the rose?"

Her gaze drifts back to where the rose shines through the grim; and again, she nods.

"Excellent. Imagine you're on a beach. That's warm, wet sand under your feet and in between your toes."

She wiggles her toes.

"Now, go to the rose, it beckons you."

She obeys.

Its glow is brighter, more vibrant than before. Like a prismatic ruby, its fragile petals refract the light into hundreds of tiny rainbows that dance over her ivory skin and gown. A hint of its perfume rides the breeze and overpowers the putrid alcohol smell that had lingered in the darkness.

Delicate. Precious. How could something so perfect live in a world so ugly?

"Touch it," the doctor says.

"I shouldn't."

"What are you afraid of?"

                    …
                    …
                    …

"I'm killing it."   *You're killing it.*

His voice thrums on, but she's stopped listening again. Instead, her eager fingers stretch toward the rose, inching closer and closer, until they're cupping the ethereal flower. She inhales its intoxicating fumes. Her head swims with all the effects of ether, weighing down her eyelids. They close without a fight.

It sets her free. No need for the doctor. No need to forget. Pain has relinquished hold of her broken heart, and she is no longer afraid. A timid curve breaks the hard line of her lips.

Shh…

She opens her eyes to blood.

It's all over her hands. The rose is bleeding. Crimson pools in the cups of her palms and oozes through her fingers, dripping onto the patchwork of skin and wisps of fine hair beneath her feet. As red gore pours, the bloom writhes, shriveling into a tiny, gray, newborn baby's skull, cradled in her bloodstained hands.

"Something's not right, doctor." Her voice is nothing more than a whisper, forced past a sudden pressure collapsing onto her chest.

The wind grows angry. Its icy currents slice at her cheeks, stealing the tears from her eyes.

Mary…

"Everything's fine, Mary."

Her skin jumps as a barrage of metal clinks and clanks sounding off around her.

"Just focus on the light."

Oh, Mary…   *Mary…*   **Come on, Mary…**

"Doctor? There's too much blood," his assistant says.

"I know, just hold this."

Mary.   *Mary?*   *I will take care of you.*

"They're calling me, doctor."

"No. No, Mary. Remember, it's not real."

Violent gusts of wind whip her hair in and around her face, slashing at her arms and neck. The acrid smell of alcohol fills the turbulent air once again, inducing ragged coughs.

You know you want to.   *Mary…*

"Give her some more."

"But, Doctor?"

"Don't question me. Give her more."

Oh, Mary…   **Come on, Mary.**

The toxic fumes choke her breath.

Shhh…   *Mary?*   *Mary.*

"Clamp."

Mary…   **Mary?**   *We're a team.*

A sharp piercing throb radiates from her core, and she doubles over with a wail. She tries to breathe through the vice-like grip, but her lungs are frozen with pain.

"Mary, can you hear me?"

Oh, Mary…   **What have you done?**   *Mary…*

"Mary, I need you to wake up."

Mary…   *Shhh…*   **It's all right.**

"Wake up, Mary."

          Relax, Mary.   *Mary…*

Just beyond the seizing heat emanating within her, past the clatter, the bangs, the rustling linens, and murmured voices of panic, an infant cries for her. An infant that now will only exist in her mind. A blanket of cold washes over her and pulls her under. Its frigid embrace comforts her.

          Come on, Mary…   *Let go…*   *We'll take care of you…*

"Mary. *Wake up.*"

You wanted it.   *Mary?*   **It's too late.**   *Mary*

She accepts the decision she was forced to make. Her shoulders slump. A sigh escapes her lips.

                              Shhh…

SKRIK
Bekki Pate

The sky is a blood-red swirl. The wind whips at my face. The bridge I stand on is rough against my bare feet, and the vortex of water that runs underneath it mesmerises me. It looks so inviting.

The urge to jump over the side and into the water is almost unbearable. I don't want to jump, but a part of me is so curious to try. To my left, two men walk towards me on the bridge. Or are they walking away? They are little more than a duo of black smudges against the shocking sky.

Boats glisten on the water. But the sky twists and turns, and panic rises. The water seems to bubble up, endless. I bring my hands to my face, and feel the sweat sticking to my skin. I feel faint. Something is building inside.

My hair is gone, my mouth is wide, toothless, and the sun beating down on me burns.

I lift my head to the sky.

I scream.

"George. George, get up. We'll be late."

My mother's voice breaks the terror of the dream. I open my eyes and am met with the blue-painted ceiling of my bedroom.

"George." She darts in, throwing the door open.

I grimace at her.

"Get up."

"Yeah." A high, annoying voice chimes in. "Mum says get up, or we're going without you."

Shit. I'd forgotten. We're seeing my dad this weekend, down where he lives now by the coast.

124

Emily's little face pops up from behind the door. She sticks her tongue out at me. I do the same to her, and she flounces off.

"All right. I'm up. I'm up," I say and wait until my mother has closed the door before I throw back the covers. I used to be in bed with my mother in the room all the time. She used to tuck me in and kiss me goodnight; she used to help me get dressed when I was tired on school-day mornings. But since I'd turned twelve and suddenly all I seem to think about are girls at school and whether or not I can see their growing breasts underneath their uniforms, I'd rather not have my mother in the room in the morning in case I get what John at school calls *morning wood*.

I reluctantly get up, get dressed, then try and brush my teeth with my eight-year-old sister hovering around me, asking stupid questions. My mother has packed our things, so all we need to do is get in the car. Emily is in the back—she still needs to sit in one of those stupid seats, but I ride in front, where Dad used to sit. Mainly because I don't want my mother looking over and feeling that emptiness there. I want to fill it, make sure she doesn't get sad again.

The car journey is long…

You can skip that part, George.

Okay.

Tell me about the beach. The day it happened.

Okay, so me, Dad, and Emily are on the beach. I am building sandcastles, and Emily is fussing around me as usual. Dad takes her to the pier; there's a bridge or something, people walking around, and they go for a walk together. Emily is wearing her Minnie Mouse costume. I continue to build sandcastles…I think…There's a man.

What does the man look like?

He's distressed, in pain or something. His face…he looks like he's screaming, but no sound comes out. He's almost not there.

Where is he?

On the bridge. He's pointing at something in the water.

What's in the water, George?

I can't. I can't look.

You can. What can you see?

Oh God…

Tell me what you see, George.

The water—it's so cold, but I don't feel it. Panic—I'd never truly felt that emotion before, never fully understood the word, until now. She's struggling; she's so far out, and I'm trying to reach her. Where's Dad? Dad. Help us. Help.

Calm down, George. It's okay.

Dad. *Dad.*

Okay, George, so you're going to start feeling more alert now, more conscious of my voice. It's time to come back to the room, George, gently, let yourself slowly come back to the room, back to alertness, back to being fully awake.

"George?"

George opened his eyes, and they rested on the silhouette of Mandy, his hypnotherapist. She was in shadow, a little unfocused, but as he sat up, his eyes adjusted to the room, then to her. He regarded again how pretty she was, and blushed when he remembered that he mentioned something about getting an erection.

"Are you okay?"

"Yes, I think so."

"Do you remember much of our conversation? What happened?"

"Yes, I get to that part, the part with the man on the bridge, pointing. And, I feel this overwhelming sense of panic, and I'm in the water, trying to grasp for my sister. Then, it all goes blank again, and the next thing I remember are the crowds on the beach, the strangers trying to comfort me. Them asking me for my mother's phone number. I had no idea what that was. I was just a kid. I remember Emily's calm, blue face, eyes closed. What could she have been doing out there? I try so hard to remember..."

"We'll get there."

George nodded, although he needed a bit more convincing. He'd been to three sessions now—Mandy was referred to him by someone his girlfriend worked with. He thought he'd give her a go, anything to stop those awful nightmares, the gaps in time, the contorted face of the man on the bridge. He needed to know what happened. His father and sister had died in the water that day, and although George was there, he had no idea how exactly it had happened. But after these sessions, he didn't feel anything other than more confused.

But as his girlfriend told him—it could take months, or even years, to get to the bottom of it all. There weren't any witnesses that day that could help him fill in the gaps; they just saw all three of them struggling in the water, and George carrying out the body of his dead sister. His father's body was recovered three days later, half-eaten by sea creatures. They'd never been able to find the man on the bridge—no one ever came forward, but George had an idea that he saw it all. He knew everything.

And he didn't want to tell.

It had been twenty years since this all happened, and going home sisterless to his mother was too much for her to bear. As soon as George was legally old enough to get a job and fend for himself, she moved away, and he only really saw her at Christmas now. He knew he was a painful reminder to her of all she had lost.

"Well, thank you for today," Mandy said. "Shall I see you next week? Same time?"

"Sure thing."

George shook Mandy's pale, cold hand and let himself out of the office. He passed the waiting area and went through the front door. He wrapped his coat around him against the cold and walked to the bus stop. He'd managed to swap his shifts around at work, so he could go to these weekly sessions with Mandy, but it meant he'd finish work later than usual. He didn't mind. If it helped.

He reached work and took his coat off at his desk, waving hello to his co-workers who were already taking calls.

He sat down, fired up his computer, and pulled out his flask of water. He allowed himself to think of Emily just once more, her little face, blonde hair, how she'd never had the chance to grow up, then he put it all away. Tidied it away in a box in his mind.

He put his headset on. The calls soon came flooding in.

"Emergency," he said as the call connected. "Which service do you require?"

Laura was waiting for him when he got home at ten pm. He was tired but not overly so. She greeted him with a warm smile and a can of beer.

"Sit down," she said. "How was your day?"

"It was fine. Same."

"How was Mandy?"

"Nothing much to tell." He managed a half-smile, and she looked at him strangely, as though she wanted to know more but didn't want to pry. She wanted him to tell her everything that had happened without her having to ask for it. But he wouldn't tell, and she wouldn't ask, so the subject was dropped.

George made them both a bacon sandwich that they ate together in a comfortable silence whilst watching TV, and George could no longer keep his eyes open.

They went to bed, and although George was tired, Laura's smooth skin and wet mouth was enough to make him want her. In the back of his mind, whilst they kissed and he slipped his hands underneath her shirt to touch her breasts, he was thinking about a girl he used to like at school. He could no longer remember her name, but the thought of how her school uniform looked as it hugged her small, round breasts, turned him on in a strange way he'd not felt since he was a teenager.

George and Laura fell asleep together, the bed-covers tangled around them.

The dream he had that night was terrifying.

He was on the beach again, building sandcastles. His father and sister were gone, which didn't bother him at first. But, then, he remembered.

The man on the bridge.

He looked up, and saw the man, pencilled into George's dream as though with paint or pastels. He held his face, his mouth open in a strange, almost uncomfortable-looking way, and they locked eyes. The man jumped up and down, glad to have got George's attention, then he pointed to the sea.

Don't look, George. Don't you look, young man.

But George couldn't help it, and he looked over at the sea.

His sister was floating face down in the water.

He ran to her.

Where was his father?

He lifted her up and out of the water, cradling her in his arms. It reminded him of when she was a baby, and his heart broke. He laid her down in the sand, only realising then that she was no longer wearing her swimming costume. His heart beat against his ribcage, and he looked around for something to cover her up with. He didn't want all these strangers looking at her, exposed. But it was too late. A crowd had formed. And when he looked up again, the man on the bridge smiled at him.

George's knees suddenly went weak. The breath went out of him.

The man on the bridge was wearing Emily's Minnie Mouse swimming costume.

"*Jesus Christ.*"

George woke up in a pool of sweat, and he couldn't breathe. He grasped the covers, and Laura was soon at his side, stroking his clammy head.

"You okay?" she asked.

He nodded.

"You want to talk about it?"

He shook his head.

"Okay."

The week passed in a blur, and when George got to Mandy's office again, he realised he couldn't wait to go under again. It was getting worse. If anything, the sessions were bringing everything up to the surface, and he knew this time that he couldn't bury it all down. It was going to come out, and he needed to understand it all as he did.

"Good morning, George," Mandy said.

"Morning."

"How have you been?"

George told her about the dream he had, and she nodded.

She gets paid an awful lot to sit there and nod. I'm in the wrong career.

Mandy put him under, and once again, there were the red swirls in the sky, the man on the bridge, his face contorted so horribly. His mother waking him up, the long car journey, them being dropped off at their father's new house. He remembered his mother kissing him goodbye, kissing Emily goodbye. A lump formed in his throat, and he tried to swallow it down.

The beach. Sandcastles. The tide. The water was choppy that day, as is usual for the coast of England. The waves were high, frothy. Emily was getting fussy, so his dad took her to collect seashells.

Then, they were gone. The man on the bridge appeared again.

George waded through the rough waters to get to his sister.

"What do you feel around you?" Mandy asked.

"The water. It's so cold. It's pulling me around," George said. "My...my hand hurts."

"Why does your hand hurt?"

"I don't know."

"Look at it."

George, his eyes still closed, looked down at his left hand.

"I'm bleeding."

"Where from?"

"Two of my fingers, and the palm of my hand."

"Do you remember how that happened?"

"No."

"What were you doing just before you got into the water? Was there something in the sand maybe that you cut your hand on?"

He paused. It hurt his head to try and remember the details. They just weren't there.

"I don't think so."

"Where else did you go, before you got into the water? There was something else."

George turned his head.

"The pier...there's someone underneath the pier."

"Is it the man? The man from the bridge? Did he come down?"

"I don't..."

Don't look, George. Don't you look, young man.

"Fuck."

"George."

"I can't look. I don't want to look, please."

"What can you see?"

"The man...the man with the face, he's there, he's..."

George stopped. A calmness suddenly washed over him. A relief.

"I'm in the water. I've got Emily. I can feel her weight in my arms. At least, I've got her. I've saved her in that way. She didn't get eaten by the fishes like my Dad did."

"Okay. You're going to feel more alert now, more conscious of my voice. It's time to come back to the room George, gently, let yourself slowly come back to the room, back to alertness, back to being fully awake."

George woke and sat up.

"Fuck..."

"Do you remember something more?"

"I think I'm beginning to," he said. "I think maybe I'm beginning to remember something."

That evening at work, George took his last call.

"Emergency, which service do you require?" A thousand times he'd said these words. To a thousand different people.

"There's a man on the bridge."

George's heart pounded.

"Pardon?"

"There's a man on the bridge."

George looked around, at all the normal things on his desk, at his colleagues.

I am awake, aren't I? This isn't a dream, right?

His finger hovered on the drop call button. It was the man, haunting him. It wasn't real.

Hang up, George.

"Hello? Please, I need help. There's a man here. He's going to jump off the bridge on the motorway. He's going to kill himself, please send someone."

Holy fucking Christ, George, you idiot. Pull yourself together.

"Can you tell me which bridge it is? The approximate location?"

The man told him.

"Okay, I'm requesting this now, someone will be with you soon."

"What should I do in the meantime?"

"Keep him calm, don't crowd him. Are you in a safe place?"

"Yes. Yes, I'm fine."

"Okay. Can I just get your full name and phone number?"

The man provided the details.

"Someone is on their way." George dispatched the police and paramedics to the scene.

"Thank you. Thank you so much."

"Thank you."

George hung up and exhaled sharply. He'd barely dared to breathe. George caught the tail-end of what his colleague, Alex, was saying.

"Yes, I believe my colleague has already got someone on their way to help. Yes, okay, thank you. Bye." Alex hung up the call. "Jumper?"

"Yep."

"On the bridge?"

"Yep."

"That was someone in their car, who happened to see him dangling over the side. I hope they get to him in time."

"Me, too."

"What could possess a person like that, so they felt that they had no choice other than to kill themselves? I don't get it."

George hadn't stopped shaking. He'd almost cut the call because he thought it was *his* man on the bridge. He thought he was being haunted. *Idiot.* He'd come so close to letting someone die. He felt sick. How could he trust his own judgement? How could he tell what was real?

He said bye to Alex and the rest of the night team and left.

"I've been thinking," Mandy said.

"Oh, right?"

"Your man on the bridge. The more you describe him, the more I feel like I know who he is."

"Okay?" Tired and irritable, he didn't really want to be there. Sick of his past plaguing his every-day life, he wanted it over and done with.

Mandy scrolled through her phone.

Rude. If she's had enough of me, then it's hopeless.

"Is this him?"

Mandy passed her phone over, and he almost dropped it and ran out of the office. There was his man, his hideous, screaming man on the bridge. He looked like an alien. He looked dead. The sky a bloody swirl of reds and oranges, and the dangerous waters below opened their jaws wide to swallow him whole. Two men on the bridge mocked him, mocking the screaming man, with their blank, vague stares.

"How? What *is* this?"

"Have you ever heard of Edvard Munch?"

"Err..."

Mandy almost smirked. He could tell she struggled with her professionalism, that she had deduced that he was an idiot who knew nothing. He wasn't traumatised; he was just stupid.

"He was a painter. He drew this picture. It's called *The Scream.*"

"But that's the man on the bridge."

"Yes, but he's also the man in the picture—this is a really famous picture. You sure you've never seen it before?"

George handed back her phone. He didn't like the way she was talking to him now; she was patronising him.

"Well, I'm not really into art all that much."

Mandy bit her lip.

"The question becomes now—what does this picture have to do with what happened that day on the beach?"

"Maybe...I don't know. I really don't know. Everything's so confused."

"Maybe, we could try another session? See if it brings anything to light?"

"Sure. Why not."

Mandy put George under, and he was back on the beach. This time he was reading a book, but the pages were all blank.

He saw the man on the bridge again, but this time, he wasn't scared. He felt ridiculous. This man was nothing more than George's imagination mixing up with reality. But the man still pointed towards the water. No, wait...he pointed to the side of the pier, underneath it, where the monster lurked.

Where George wasn't allowed to go.

"Call for your sister, George. Where is she?"

"Emily. Emily, where are you?"

A flash of blonde hair under the pier, and she turned to look at him. She waved. But something was there with her, something grotesque, something so *wrong* that his mind actively blocked it out. George's palm hurt, and already, it bled, and he was in the water.

Would a twelve-year-old really be building sandcastles?

But the memory was too much at that moment, and Mandy brought him out of it.

"Same time next week?" she asked.

"Sure."

He left dejected, not really wanting to ever come back.

That weekend, he visited his mother. He hadn't seen her since Christmas, and although it was a three-hour-drive, he felt like he couldn't *not* see her.

She holds the answers.

But the thought was false. She wasn't there that day; she didn't know what happened; she didn't have any answers.

He felt ridiculous, emasculated, that his horror-man was a stupid picture, that after searching for it online, it turned out to be one of the most famous pieces of art in history. He *must* have seen it before, he couldn't believe he'd have gone his whole life not knowing about this picture, yet it haunted him.

He pulled into his mother's drive. Her husband Clive watered plants in the front garden.

"George, how are you?" They shook hands.

He liked that Clive treated him like an adult. Even when he was a boy, he'd always shaken his hand, spoken to him like a friend. Clive would never replace his father, but he knew his mother would be taken care of. And she was happy, which was all George wanted.

George let himself into the house, his mother in the middle of making tea.

"My baby." She threw her arms around him. "How are you?"

"Good, Mum, great. How are you?"

"Good, good. Come and sit down. Do you want some tea?"

"Yes, please."

"Where's Laura today?"

"She had to work," he said.

She could have easily took it off if she knew, but the truth was that he hadn't told her. He hoped to be back before she got in from work. He wasn't sure why he would do that.

"Oh, that's a shame. Go to the living room. I'll bring this through."

George sat in his mother's neat, little living room. He almost sank into the sofa. Comforting and warm, he could easily fall asleep there. Part of him wanted to, so he walked around the room, admiring the new ornaments. There wasn't a lot of his childhood in this room, but he would never expect there to be. Just a few photos of him, a few of Emily. None of his dad. He picked one up of Emily when she must have only been three or four. She was beautiful.

She didn't deserve to die in such a way, at such a young age.

He put the photo down. He and his mother had a mutual unspoken agreement to keep their tears private.

He perused the books on fishing, politics, a few battered Catherine Cookson's, a few James Herbert. And another. His eyes gravitated towards it almost painfully.

A History of Art.

He picked it up with trembling fingers, just as his mother came in with the tea.

"You can take that home with you if you like. I don't know why I still have it," she said.

"What?"

Maybe she really *did* hold all the answers.

"Are you okay? You've gone white."

"I'm fine."

No, George, you *hold all the answers. You hold them in your hands. Right now. Turn the page.*

He flicked through the book, photos and paintings springing to life. They'd long been forgotten. Page 88. *The Scream*, by Edvard Munch. Also known as *Der Schrei der Natur* in German. Also known as *Skrik* in Munch's native Norwegian tongue.

"That was your father's book," his mother said. "You were fascinated by it."

"I was?"

"Don't you remember?"

Yes. Oh God, yes, I do remember.

The beach. The choppy waves. George sat, reading his father's book on art, flicking through the pages, landing on *The Scream*. The haunted man, screaming from out of the page.

His father and Emily had been a while, so he went to find them and help collect shells.

He left their belongings, the book, and walked towards the pier. He could see two figures underneath it, hidden in shadow. Hidden by the large beams. His heart pounded.

Something's not right. Stay away from it. Stay away.

"Dad?"

His father hunched over Emily, one hand twisted into her hair. The other hand had pulled aside her Minnie Mouse costume, and...

"Dad! What the *fuck* are you doing?"

His father jumped away as if electrocuted.

"Don't look, George. Don't you look, young man. Get away from here." His father said behind menacingly gritted teeth, conscious that other people might hear if he spoke too loudly.

"What's wrong, George?" Emily asked.

She's too young to know. Too young to know what's just happened to her.

George grabbed his sister, but she pulled away. The tide was coming in, lapping at his knees. Growing in force.

"Nothing's happening, George, just go. We'll be back in a minute," his father said.

"No. I'm going to tell Mum. I'm going to tell everyone. You'll be put in jail."

His father darted for him, a man that he loved so much, a man that he thought he knew, unrecognisable. Thunder on his face, he grabbed George by the shoulders and shoved him away. He tripped on a sharp stone hidden beneath the waves, and fell back, landing in the water. His father pushed him back again.

He couldn't breathe.

George picked up the stone, dislodged by his foot. The jagged edges cut into his palm. His father was about to throw him into the sea for a third time, but George put all his might behind the stone and thrust it into his father's temple. Blood poured, and his father's gaze dazed. He stumbled and fell into the water.

The tide heaved them all away from the pier, and Emily shrieked at the sight of her father floating in the water.

"Daddy. Why did you do that? *Why*? You've hurt him. He was just *loving* me, like he always does. He loves me more than he loves you."

"Emily, come here." George shook with rage, fear, and disgust. He didn't fully understand what he'd just seen, but he knew it was bad, knew it wasn't something a man should be doing with his daughter.

But all Emily knew was that her daddy loved her, and he was in trouble.

So, she went to him.

George tried to catch up, but the current took Emily and their father away too quickly, and soon, they both struggled to stay afloat.

Their father's body went under.

"Leave him, Emily, leave him. Come back to the shore."

"No, I can't. He needs me." She turned away from George and swim towards the spot where their father had disappeared.

"No, please." Sea water entered his mouth, and he coughed as it went up his nose. "*Emily.*"

Her head bobbed about for a few seconds before she went under. George's heart stopped, but she came up again. Went under again.

She's trying to find him. Under the water.

She was so far away—came up, went down. George did his best front-crawl to where she had gone under, the strands of her hair bobbing around just below the surface. He grabbed them and yanked her up.

"Emily?"

He dragged her back towards the shore. People were diving into the sea in a frantic effort to help, so thankfully he didn't have to carry her the whole way. They laid her down on the sand.

But that was it.

She was gone.

George looked over the sea, hoping that they would never find his father's body, that he would disappear forever.

A little boy built sandcastles in the distance. His mother worrying at the crowd of people, a hand to her face. She knew.

That little girl has just died.

But her son, too young to know or care about such things, just built sandcastles.

I wish that were me. I wish I were the one building sandcastles.
I'd give anything right now for that to be real.

A FAMILY FILM
Rachel DiMaggio

The more you try to remember, the murkier things get. There was popcorn, of course, and tucked around your feet, a crocheted blanket with granny squares of hunter green and brown. Your brother hugged a couch pillow, peeking over it. At first, you're thrilled by the figure, standing outside the townhouse window, a monolith on the grass. Mom and Dad really should have turned it off as soon as those black-tipped fingers reached out to turn the doorknob. And why, why hadn't they stopped the tape once the knife began its work? Every new apartment you enter, the first thing you check is the walls for overlooked specks of tell-tale blood.

Even twenty years later, you believe that's the tipping point where everything went bad.

"Don't bring that up again, Alice," Mitch says, almost first thing when you arrive for Thanksgiving.

You shrug and give him a confused frown. Of course, you weren't going to mention the movie.

"Dad was looking to move out before the summer started," Mitch goes on. He needs to make the point, really prove to you that it's nonsense. "How could a movie make him jump into bed with Faye Prine? Even if I granted there *was* a movie. Tell me again how many Blockbuster employees you've pestered about that thing?"

Not just Blockbuster. Try Library of Congress.

Your internet search history is littered with the name; every few months you try again, log into the film geek message boards and send your little ship in a bottle across the virtual sea.

"Looking for a movie from 1995 called *Blood is Thicker*. Vampire-themed slasher. Dark red slipcase, ransom-note title cards."

Finally, you ventured to the dark web chatrooms, where it seemed half of the avatars were stills from exploitation and snuff movies. You've seen that impaled woman from the cannibal movie so often it no longer shocks. Even there, no luck.

If it was truly an underground movie, how had Dad even gotten his hands on it? He'd never been a cinephile, more of a sports nut. He watched kung-fu movies during the football off-season. Mitch might be right. Dad must have been in a strange state of mind to pop a horror film into the VCR, much less let it keep playing once they started crying.

"Just let it rest."

"Honestly, I hadn't even thought of it since last year," you say. "I've had more important things on my mind since I started at the hospital."

"How's that going?"

"Getting to be routine. I drive one of those golf carts around all night. I got an emergency call once, but it was just a raccoon hiding underneath a car. I put some peanuts on the ground, and he came out."

"What are you going to do during the winter? You'll freeze."

"It's enclosed—kind of a plastic wrap thing. I get to read a lot."

Most people didn't think of women when they pictured a security guard, but you know this is a good fit, and you'll probably be working there until you retire. You're not at ease with chit-chat. Even this conversation with your brother feels like a chore. Driving in a huge circuit around the hospital building gives you plenty of time to think, to try to remember.

1995. The year Dad split on the family with no warning. The year Mom started having night terrors. If you'd ever needed Rhiannon around, that was the year. Of course, you'd outgrown imaginary friends by then. You tried writing to her in the journal, but it wasn't the same as sitting together in that knotted oak tree, sharing secrets. Down on the ground, too frightened to climb the branches, Mitch had gone red with frustration. *Climb up and we'll tell you*, Rhiannon said. *Don't be a baby.* Even now, you can't hear a Fleetwood Mac song without a pang for that lost little girl who had looked so much like you—a better version of you, a reflection that always had fun ideas, and liked the same foods you liked, and hated homework just as much as you did.

Then again, Rhiannon would have spoiled your time at school—a nine-year-old with an imaginary friend, one she actually spoke to? A freak, for sure.

Mitch's girlfriend has broken up with him, you realize. He's avoided talking about her, and his hair is much longer than she liked it.

"I'm sorry about Chelsea," you offer.

He nods and takes one of the spinach puffs from the platter, eats it in a single bite like a hungry kid. "Well, we wanted different things."

Just like that you are back in a strange conversation that feels blanched of all meaning. Half of you keeps on talking, making your face concerned and humorous as needed, while the other part is crafting an email to the rare films collector you met online last week. Rarity, not gore or bare flesh or snuff, was what turned him on.

"This is the rarest of the rare," he'd said in his reply to your initial email. "If the Library of Congress can't confirm its existence, it must not have been sold commercially. Are you sure your father didn't get somebody's weird home movie?"

"No. Quality was too high. It's like *Nosferatu* but frightening."

"I'll see what I can dig up. But you've already done a lot of your own research if you've stumbled onto my blog."

Years ago, you also thought *Nosferatu* might have been the forgotten film. The vampire's long-fingers and the deep shadows were familiar. But five minutes into the movie, you'd known it wasn't right. Your movie had been in vivid color; the red became your personal standard by which all reds were measured. *Nosferatu* was filmed in masterful black and white.

You have enough knowledge of underground film to write a book, but you never will. It's not that fascinating for its own sake. You'd trade a thousand remastered copies of *Burnt Lotus*—which you've seen only once at a basement screening, a nauseating experience—to find your cheesy vampire film on a library shelf. Among your own kind you are an imposter. You pretend appreciation for images, but they only dissipate when compared to the first movie, the only movie, that ever got inside you.

"Time for dinner." Aunt Susan sets the steaming platter of turkey on the table. "Everybody get while the getting's good."

Mom finishes her first glass of red, her movements chipper as she rearranges the fall foliage centerpiece, the cast iron trivets, the serving spoons. You make a mental note that you're not going to spoil her holiday with your own concerns. You sit down next to Mitch. The dinner is almost unbelievable in its variety and color. You think back to the last time you ate off a plate and not out of a paper bag or a plastic TV dinner shell.

"You've outdone yourself, Suze," Mom says after the first bite of turkey. "I'm never bringing food over again, it can't compare."

"Says the woman who brought three kinds of pie."

It's the same dance from every year since Dad left; the compliments are stale, the good cheer congealing on top of something murky. If Aunt Susan had her wish, all three of you would have packed up and moved in with her immediately. No point in Mom struggling to pay for the house by herself. You still hear the bitter arguments over the phone.

"I've got Alice and Mitch, and that's all I need." Mom had said, too many times to count.

That hadn't been precisely true; she had developed an unusual sleeping disorder complete with night terrors. Waking up to piercing screams once a week or so became almost normal. You and Mitch took turns going to wake her. The thought bubbles up that maybe this is why you always look for jobs that keep you out of your apartment at night; you're awake and out in the world where things are sane and safe. When you're indoors at night, you feel crushed with the weight of expectation, listening for those sounds of distress even though you live an hour away from your childhood home.

"And how is the new position?" Aunt Susan asks. "Staying busy, I hope?"

She wants to know you're too busy to pursue your fixation. That will never happen, but it won't hurt to let her believe it. Just as you start to respond, the phone in your pocket rings.

"Sorry." You silence the phone. The name Lawrence Carr flashes on the screen and excitement begins to whir in your head. He found it. Why else would he call on Thanksgiving Day? But you have to put it off. Already you can feel them watching. They're wondering, is this a normal phone call, maybe a wrong number, or is it related to the *obsession*? That utterly terrible screaming match between you and Mitch last year. Your reality pitted against his, then against everyone else.

"It doesn't exist," Mom yelled finally. "I don't remember it, Mitch doesn't remember it, and Dad always said the same. Every time you bring this up, I hope it's the last time because it really makes me wonder if you've lost your mind. Are you going to tell me Rhiannon was real, too?"

In the end, Mitch insisted you leave. "You can't help it if you remember something one way and we remember it another. But you can't keep on talking about this *delusion*, it's just going to upset Mom. It's upsetting me. You got fired because of this, you have to get a grip on it."

Technically, you'd been fired for performance reasons—they didn't know you were spending half of your workday looking online for the tape, only that your work was slipping.

The phone beeps for voicemail, and the year clicks back into place. They're waiting for an explanation. You've hesitated a moment too long.

"Wrong number," you say, and nobody challenges this.

The waiting message fills your head with possibilities. Around the table, conversation happens, and you participate. Yes, you're staying busy. No, nobody special, it's hard to date when you work nights. The benefits are just fine, and vacation days are generous. No, there isn't a new cockatiel yet; it was too soon after Cecil's passing. You loved that little bird, scratchy feet on your shoulder as you ate dinner and watched primetime TV. He'd started to know the theme songs to *Jeopardy* and *Wheel of Fortune*. When you were out at work, he had only the TV for company. For a while, you'd bought cable just so he could learn something besides late night infomercials. Then, he started copying your phone calls, saying, "VHS tape. Blood is thicker." And "1995." And after that, you'd been afraid to let Mom or Mitch come over to the house even for holidays. Nobody had complained much. Your apartments always looked uncomfortably cluttered and nest-like, nearly as soon as you moved in. It was obvious how seldom you left their confines.

Mitch is explaining again about the things he wanted, the things Chelsea wanted. Mom and Aunt Susan nod, agreeing that it's better things ended now.

Nobody wants a repeat of the disappearing spouse act. When Mom starts to stack up the plates, you slip away from the table and go upstairs. You lock yourself in the bathroom, and it feels just like it always did: your shoulders can relax, your face can stop looking so pleasant all the time. Susan isn't there to see and feel worried for poor Alice, poor Mitch, poor Mom. Nobody is here to eavesdrop on the message left on your phone.

"Lawrence Carr here, just had a few follow up questions on the film. I might have found it, but I have some questions, just to be sure. Call me when you can."

Lawrence Carr either has no Thanksgiving ritual to attend or has exiled himself. You can't say the idea didn't cross your mind. Let Mom apologize 'til her face turned blue, let Mitch take back all the little frustrated glances that accused you of being this way on purpose, being *sick* about this make-believe movie. His slight limp seems to get worse in those moments, when he's mad at you. Because the movie you've created in your head is about a family destroyed, and it reminds him of the way Dad left.

Six years later, when Mitch was in junior high, Mom took a few too many pills. Then she got in the car and tried to drive Mitch to the football tryouts. The car smashed into a guardrail and rolled over. The accident broke his leg in three places.

You owe it to all of them to show up, to make normalcy exist again as much as possible. But you need this other thing, too.

You call back, but Lawrence doesn't pick up. You leave the message, sounding a touch desperate. He won't mind; this is the way people get when they're so close to having their hands on that one film, that director's cut, that lost edit that finally provides an answer for the narrative.

You open the door, and Mitch is standing halfway up the stairs, hand on the rail, head down. Gripping his knee with the other hand.

"You okay?" The distress on his face is more real than anything you've seen in a while, and your worry is sincere.

"Just acting up again. I swear it's like the joints remember this place."

"Can I get you anything? Tylenol with codeine? I have leftovers from my dental work."

He hesitates and puts a little more weight on the leg. "Maybe so. Yeah."

You're staying in the guest room adjacent to the bathroom, and you get the Tylenol from your overnight bag. It's still got the tags on from last Christmas. Mom thought you might travel more if you had a fun bag.

As you give him the meds, the doorbell rings, and you look at each other in surprise. I didn't invite a plus one, your expressions say. What about you?

"Does Aunt Susan have a boyfriend?" you ask.

"I doubt it. She would've had him here for dinner, right? Not after."

You hurry downstairs while Mitch retreats to his room to swallow the pills. He looks exhausted, and you know it's not just the strain of your past behavior—it's being in this house, remembering the time he'd spent on Susan's couch while his leg healed. The endless soaps and game shows on the TV while she cleaned and her kids went to school, poor Mitch soaking it in just like Cecil had done. His mind chattering away at night about being a millionaire and not being the weakest link and all the rest of those old shows. That was better than remembering all the things Aunt Susan had to say about Dad.

Mom is at the door, puzzled, holding a tan package. A rectangular lump creases the outer paper.

"It's for you, Alice," she says. "They don't deliver on holidays…"

As you take it, heaviness drags at your stomach There's no return address on the package, and the writing is smooth and full of strange curlicues. When you open the envelope, a swoon begins in your head, the sensation of unexpectedly locking eyes with your high school crush. A black VHS tape. A peeling paper label that instantly takes you back to the moment when Dad put the movie on. The font familiar as your own face. *Blood is Thicker.*

You try to explain about how Carr must have found it, this must be from him, but they don't care about that. They're angry. Finally, you convince them to just watch for five minutes. You promise never to mention it again if they will just do this. You deserve the chance to prove it wasn't a dream, it wasn't something your mind created, a weird thought that fastened to you like a leech.

You're still trying to figure out how this found you. You must have mentioned that you were going to your aunt's house for Thanksgiving. He obviously sent it by messenger and not post office. But he'd called at dinner and the tape had arrived within an hour. You choose to ignore this; an explanation will present itself. For now, you have the precious evidence in your hands.

Your fingers are trembling as you connect Susan's ancient VHS player to the TV.

In the end, you all sit down to watch the tape. Mom has her glass of wine—her third? fourth?—and Aunt Susan reeks softly of some oil that she thinks will relieve anxiety. Mitch silently takes a seat on the couch next to Mom, his face taut with anger

"Five minutes. That's it," he says.

They are so stingy with their trust of you. Their skepticism stings. Rhiannon would have believed you. A stupid thought, because Rhiannon *was* you, the happy, carefree part. You sit down cross-legged in front of the VCR to push the play button. The remote control was thrown away long ago.

The opening credits splash luridly. Black text saying first, *Blood is Thicker,* then in smaller text, *The second cut is the deepest.* A sequel? You don't remember that part.

And the movie that plays seems a little off, too. There's the same house, with the windows shining bright and vulnerable in the darkness. The killer is the same. But the music doesn't sound right, and the hunted family looks different. You turn to see if your family is noticing this; they didn't recall the original, so will this spark their memory? Will they insist even later that tonight was the first time they saw this film?

You feel a glow of vindication as the first victim, the father, falls beneath the slashing blade. His strength bleeds out in gushes across the concrete basement floor.

There are more victims. At one point, the man with the knife crouches to lick blood from the kitchen tile. A little girl is chased from the ground floor of the house to the attic. You don't remember this, you don't want to see it at all. Her hair is like Rhiannon's used to be, at least until she falls out of the tiny attic window and all her beautiful little features smash against the roots of a giant oak tree. You turn in disgust and triumph. See? It was real. We did see this, in 1995. It was a real film.

Aunt Susan looks wrong; her eyes are glassy. Mom looks the same. You see Mitch staring back at you, and his face is afraid, not of the images onscreen, but of *you*. Your eyes must be doing that same gray-white trick. Mitch's eyes look the same as ever. All three of you are gazing at him, and he's saying words that can't penetrate. Something huge has its hands pressed tight over your ears, another over your mouth. You are nothing but hands to this thing, and you get up and follow your mother and aunt as Mitch gets up shakily and turns to run.

Of course, he doesn't get far, not with his knee.

Aunt Susan catches him first. She's got a heavy iron lamp in her hands, and it comes down on the back of his head.

You have a kitchen knife, and you are the one to slash at his arm and lay it raw to the tendons.

His other hand comes at you as a fist, but although your nose bleeds, you don't feel pain.

There's a strange rhythm to this act, as he gets away for a few moments, grabs at improvised weapons, but always gets knocked down again. His weapons aren't even close to a match for the blind power flowing into your mind.

Killing is a taste in your mouth, the sensual warmth of slippery fingertips.

Mom's wine glass is a broken-off spike, and when everything else is done, she stabs it into his left leg.

You leave him collapsed halfway up the stairs.

The movie is ending. The vampire extends its clawed hand to the screen, filling the visual field with darkness as a curious sting numbs your mind. The movie credits roll. You see a flash of deeper black when the last of the credits are gone, and your eyes smart. The pounding in your ears ebbs away. You turn to look at your family on the couch. When you press the eject button, there's nothing in the VCR. Mom laughs and sips from the glass again. Aunt Susan stands up and stretches.

"Help me clean up the kitchen, Alice?"

You go with her to the kitchen. The turkey's sharp bones look like a wrecked ship, strings of meat clinging like seaweed, flotsam of congealed fat in the leftover basting liquid. Aunt Susan hunches over an open drawer where shiny metal and chipped plastics are jostled together. Her hand disappears to the wrist as she gropes for something. There seems to be a knife missing, and she says there used to be eight wine glasses, not seven. But things get lost when you only use them occasionally.

After the holiday, you return to your apartment. It's cozy, and for once, you don't feel like anything is missing. There are strange people emailing you all the time. You don't get why they think you're interested in all this strange cinema news. One man named Carr tries to tell you that he made a mistake, and you may as well give up looking. You don't reply because you don't know what he's talking about. He emails a few more times over the next months, trying to start some kind of relationship, but you just don't have the energy.

In summer, you buy another cockatiel. Cecilia, you name her, because it is the first thing to come to mind. This bird learns a little quicker than its predecessor, and it likes to hop around the card table where you sit for dinner.

Fall arrives, and you provide Cecilia with a harvest bounty of extra bird food—and some berries for a treat—before you drive out to Aunt Susan's house. They are pleased to see you; everyone is so happy now. This job has lasted longer than any of your previous careers. Aunt Susan is seeing a new man, and he has a boat. They've been on the lake all summer, and her face is tanned and flushed at the same time. You help Mom set the table. For a minute you stand, leaning on a chair, trying to figure out what is wrong with the scene.

Without warning, it sweeps over you, the unaccountable sorrow and loneliness, the formless guilt. Something has gotten lost, someone has been forgotten.

Finally, you realize there are too many place settings.

You put the extra plate back in the cupboard.

Then, it is time for dinner.

THE LITTLE LANTERN
Nicholas Stella

Egbert walked the cracked sidewalk beside a road choked with idling cars and motor scooters that honked their frustration and belched fumes. Buses sat among them, their destinations displayed in foreign text.

He turned off the main road and down a narrow lane, a small artery in a city of industry that vomited by-products into the sky and birthed plastic offspring onto rotating belts and into waiting trucks.

Thunder rumbled, and the slice of sky between the buildings bordering the lane darkened with rolling clouds. Egbert adjusted his satchel, peeling it away from his perspiration-soaked shirt.

A green neon sign flashed BAR further along, and as the first fat drops fell, he darted into the doorway of the establishment.

He descended a flight of stairs, each creaking in complaint, making his way down under the dim light of a single dangling globe and into the bar proper.

"Hey, Egg-man," the barkeep said, throwing a bottle of bright green liquor into the air and catching it by the neck. "You come late."

He poured the liquid into a shot glass, downed the drink and slammed it on the bar top—*aah*—the universal noise to express quenched thirst.

"My students, Thet. They thirst for English just like I'm thirsting for a Starrenberg." Egbert planted himself on a stool, removed a book from his satchel entitled *English for Busy People*, and placed it on the bar.

"How about a Khlong-Dao, Man?"

"You won't give up 'til I try the beetle brew, will you?" Egg flicked through the book and found Chapter Twelve.

"It's the beer of my country." Thet reached under the bar and produced a black cap with silver lettering that read PIMP. "You like my new hat?"

"You know what a pimp is?" Egbert asked, biting his lip.

"A lucky man with many girlfriends."

"Close enough. Now, Chapter Twelve. At the bank," Egbert said, turning the book around for Thet to read. "Where's my Starrenberg?"

"I can get you a Starrenberg, but then, you can try a Khlong-Dao later. I'll put it on top of the house."

"On the house."

Thet placed the bottle on the bar, and Egbert grabbed it by the neck, took a long swallow and pushed the book towards the bartender. "Okay. You're at the bank. What do you say?"

"Yo, pimp. Where the cash at?"

"You really are my worst student."

"And you are my worst customer. You don't try the drink I say is the best. You can't live here and not try the beetle brew."

"Fine. Let's do Chapter Twelve, and I'll have your nation's favourite beverage."

"And the beetles."

"And the bloody beetles. Start reading."

By the time Egbert had finished teaching his barkeep-come-student how to open a bank account in English and question interest rates, a dozen patrons littered the bar. Egbert's beer was no more than suds.

Thet placed an open bottle of Khlong-Dao on the bar in front of Egbert along with a blue, plastic packet with the picture of a smiling beetle standing on two legs wearing a top hat and sporting a dancing cane.

"So, this is them?" Egbert asked, shaking the pack.

"The honey flavour," Thet said, "is nice to eat when you drink the Khlong-Dao."

Egbert took a healthy swig of beer, opened the pack and tipped the contents into a bowl Thet had placed on the bar.

The assortment of cockroaches, millipedes, centipedes and other various insects were a golden brown, carapaces smooth and flat, antennae long and delicate.

"Start with a little one." Thet grabbed a large, roasted beetle from the pile, popped it into his mouth and smiled.

Egbert prodded a millipede at the edge of the pile.

"It is death," Thet said.

"It is dead," Egbert corrected and picked up insect, its fine legs tickling his fingers.

"It's a potato chip," he said, putting it in his mouth and chewing its crunchy body.

"A potato chip with one hundred legs."

"You're no help," Egbert said. "It does taste good, though. Like honey."

"I did tell you that. Now, drink some Khlong Dao."

The cold beer washed the crunched remains of the millipede down, and Egbert once more reached for the pile of chitin and antennae.

146

"Good." Thet prepared drinks for another patron. "Have a bigger one this time."

He steered clear of the cockroaches and took something that looked like a Christmas beetle, putting it in his mouth as if it were nothing more than a Cheesy Puff.

"Nun ta," a patron at the bar said.

Egbert knew the word meant *good*. He smiled and took a mouthful of beer, the malty flavour combining with the honeyed bug to produce a taste agreeable to his palate.

"Do not have too much on the first time," Thet said as he passed by with a tray laden with drinks. "It can make you feel strange."

Egbert popped another millipede into his mouth as his tongue developed a tingle. He crunched through the delicate body and washed it down with the rest of his beer.

"One Khlong Dao, Thet, my friend," he said to the barkeep serving drinks in the corner of the room. He swivelled on his stool as Thet made his way back to the bar.

The young bartender was stopped by a group standing in the doorway. Thet spoke to the man in the middle, the shortest and smallest of the trio. His left hand was missing, and the right rested on a walking stick. He gestured with the stump of his left hand in Egbert's direction, and Thet looked over.

The one-handed man pushed past, followed by his two larger associates, and took a table in the rear of the room.

Egbert's fingers and toes tingled and he felt light-headed when Thet hurried behind the bar, removed three Khlong Dao beers from the fridge, and placed them on the bar top.

"You should go." Thet popped the tops.

"But I ordered another beer."

Thet's face blurred, and the neon lights behind the bar were a smear of pink, yellow, and green.

"Please." Thet picked up the beers and grabbed a few packets of beetles.

He turned on his chair and followed Thet's progress, but his clouded vision and the dimness of the room were in cahoots. He squinted when he heard raised voices and stepped off the stool, his legs wobbling.

Thet came into view, took Egbert by the elbow, and guided him upstairs and out onto the street.

"Go home, Egg," Thet said and disappeared back inside.

He was alone on the street, the asphalt wet from the drizzling rain, the streetlights flickering and buzzing.

He withdrew a packet of cigarettes from his pocket. One left. He lit up and pulled deeply. Dizzy, he spat the cigarette out and fell to his hands and knees, vomiting a soup of beer and insects into bushes by the side of the lane.

He lay on the ground with his head in the plants while he caught his breath, the slight rain dampening his clothes and skin. He rose with a groan, his mouth still tingling, hands and feet obeying reluctantly.

Moving down the alley, he passed closed doors and dark windows until he came to a machine with dancing lights recessed into the wall.

He squinted focus to his vision. It was as tall as he was with a rectangular face and rows of dark square buttons.

"Cigarettes." He needed a fresh pack, fished a two-hundred pang coin from his pocket. He leaned in close, found the slot and pressed the coin into the aperture.

"*Damn*." Something sharp sliced the soft pad of his thumb. He stepped away and sucked the wounded digit, tasting blood.

A button on the lower-half of the machine illuminated, revealing an illustration of a young man dancing a frozen jig. He was smiling, dressed in white robes with his hair in a top knot.

Egbert stooped and pressed the lit button, looking around in the dim lights for where to retrieve his smokes. He examined the entire machine but could not find where to get them. He gave the plastic face a thump with the palm of his hand.

"*Hei!*"

A young man stood in the rain wearing white robes, his hair in a top knot.

"Ser-Dan," the man said, placing a palm against his chest. He moved down the lane in the direction of the bar. He stopped about halfway along and squatted, pointing underneath a rubbish bin.

"What is it?" Egbert asked.

The man in white gestured for Egbert to join him.

He stumbled over, shivering from the cool rain soaking his clothes and stopped a few paces away.

The man seemed untouched by the rain, his appearance suggesting no evidence of the downpour. He pointed under the bin with more urgency and stood.

Egbert got down on his haunches. A five-pang coin lay in the gloom. Picking it up, he turned, but the man in white was further down the lane, outside the doorway to the bar.

He hurried over, his legs slow as if he waded through water.

The man smiled and pointed into the bushes where Egbert had been sick earlier.

"Wasn't feeling so great. Here." He offered the coin to him.

The man shook his head and continued to point at the bushes.

Egbert wrinkled his nose at the tang of vomit and looked under the bushes.

His wallet lay there under the foliage. He scooped it up, wiping the wet leather on his pants. "How did you know it was there?"

The man stepped to Egbert, face mere inches away. His dark irises filled with swirling flecks like fireworks in a night sky.

Egbert flinched when he grabbed his arm. The grip burned, like ice, like fire, and he collapsed to his knees.

The man dropped to the same height and turned his arm, enabling Egbert to see his own palm and his cut thumb. The small wound glowed golden as if light burned within.

Grip released, and the pain stopped.

Egbert inspected his arm for signs of injury, but his skin was clear.

Still dry and pristine in presentation, the man skipped off down the alley, beckoning for Egbert to follow.

"Wait—*Terng*," he said, as he entered the doorway. He had picked up more words than he realised during his time here.

The thump of music reverberated from downstairs, the bass causing a tingle in his ears and nausea in his stomach. He descended, a palm bracing each wall to the side as he went.

Patrons occupied every table, but there was room for him at the bar. Thet came over and placed Egbert's satchel on the counter.

"You must leave," he said, glancing at the back of the room.

"I need to talk to you."

"Take your bag." Thet came out from behind the bar and headed towards the stairs. "Come on."

Egbert stepped out into the alley.

Thet waited, hands on hips. "Those men are not good. They do not like foreign people."

"I needed my books."

"You have your books. Go home."

"I want to ask a question."

"One question, then you go home. The bar is very busy."

"Who is Ser-Dan?"

Thet took his hands from his hips and smiled a little. "He is a god. He finds lost things. His name means Little Lantern."

"What does he look like?"

"A young man. He wears the *tem*, the white robes of our people. And his hair is tied on top of his head. Why?"

"Because he is standing beside you."

Thet laughed. "Now, I know. You have had too much Khlong Dao and too much of the beetles."

"No," Egbert said. "Well, yes. Probably. My head is spinning, and my eyes aren't focussing that well, but I know what I see. He is still beside you, smiling."

"Go home to sleep. Tomorrow, I will serve you a Starrenberg."

"What does he do?" he asked, stepping towards Thet.

The bartender sighed. "We call him the Little Lantern because he shines light on things, sometimes things you don't know you have lost."

"Like my wallet. It was in the bushes."

"Mainly, he helps you find your way."

Ser-Dan walked to the far side of the lane, beckoning for Egbert to follow. "He's over there, now," he said, pointing to the white robed man.

"Follow him." Thet walked back towards the bar. "Maybe, he will take you to the airport."

Egbert grabbed Thet by the arm. "I live here. I have been for six months."

Thet shook his arm free. "No. You have *been* here. You have not *lived* here. You drink the beer of other countries, eat at the sausage restaurant, and speak English to me all the time. I am learning your language, but you never want to know about mine."

"But I had the Khlong Dao and the honey beetles."

"One beer in six months…" Thet said, as he entered the doorway of the bar and disappeared downstairs.

Egg looked up at the sky, at the breaking clouds and the pocked face of the moon peering from in between.

Under the moonlight and, over the wet streets, they went, Egbert developing a spring in his step, following the nimble god down the alley. They crossed the main road, dodging the traffic, Egbert feeling more grounded as he went, his head clearing.

"Where are you taking me?" he asked, but the Little Lantern simply turned and without a word, beckoned him on.

They turned off the main thoroughfare and into a smaller street that he knew well. His favourite Sausage King franchise was a few doors down, its flashing neon sign, bright interior lights, and small-goods dominated menu that drew him daily, a little oasis of familiarity in a city still foreign after so many months.

He slowed, his shoulders slouching as he stood in the glow of the restaurant.

"*Hei.*" Ser-Dan was a little further down the street, standing in front of a small stand with a tarpaulin cover.

Egg approached, and an old woman stood up from behind the stand, wielding a pair of long chopsticks.

"Tan Gor Sat?" she asked, raising a grey eyebrow.

Egbert removed the five-pang coin from his pocket and placed it on the counter.

"Tan Gor Sat," he said, ordering a bowl of noodles.

The old woman dropped a bundle of the noodles into a vat of boiling water recessed into the stand, stirring them with the chopsticks. She chopped a leafy, green vegetable into strands, then brushed them along with a half-dozen unidentified spices and ingredients into the bubbling water.

Egg looked up from the old woman's labours.
The Little Lantern was gone.

TABULA RASA
William Curnow

The courier brought it shortly after midday.

Jack had waited in an agony of expectation all morning, frequently checking the tracking information to make sure that it was still in transit, that he hadn't missed it. That had happened before, and it made him jittery and unsettled. He went from room to room, starting one task, then moving on to the next, leaving plates dripping but still dirty on the draining board, hardly noticing.

He sat on the sofa, so he had a view of the street outside, thought better of it, and got up to rearrange his tools. He checked the website again.

Don't look, and it'll come.

Of course, he couldn't help himself.

Every passing car or van sent him back to the window, the sounds of an engine slowing an exquisite agony of hope and disappointment, and he lived on a busy road.

Finally, a van stopped opposite, the courier's logo on the side. Jack waited long minutes in the hall, imagining the man finding the package, coming to the front door, each step an eternity.

A terrible thought struck him. What if it arrived damaged? To have come so far, only to have been dropped by some careless individual in the delivery chain? No, that would really be too much. But now that he had the thought, he could not let it go.

The bell rang.

"Hello?" Jack said, even as he was opening the door, as though he didn't already know who it was.

"Delivery here for Mr—" the courier read the name on the package "—Lubaszenko."

The man stumbled over his surname.

"That's me." Jack's gaze flicked to the large package wrapped in thick, bubbled polythene. It did not look as though it came to any harm.

"Heavy." The man adjusted his grip.

"Yes," Jack said.

He wanted to take it, to avoid any last-minute mishap. But first, the business of signing needed to be done with. More agony of waiting as the man put the package down on the doorstep and fumbled with a handheld terminal. He tapped in a few things with the stylus and passed it to Jack.

"Sign here," he said.

And Jack was left alone with his package.

He carried it into the house and put it on the kitchen table. Now that it was here, he was almost afraid to do anything with it. It hadn't been cheap. When he unwrapped it, would it prove to be a disappointment? Would he find that he wasted his money?

Doubt overwhelmed him. He left the package where it was, finished washing up, and tidied away the dishes, as though delaying the act of revelation might guarantee that what lay inside would be exactly as he imagined it.

Of course, he could only delay for so long before he had to see, had to touch it.

Working carefully from one corner with a sharp knife, Jack eased apart the tape that bound the package, the process taking on the aspect of ritual as he stripped off the layers.

A rectangular block of hardwood a couple of feet long, unlike any he had ever seen before. He didn't know what kind of tree it came from. The seller listed no information when he ordered it. But it was beautiful: the deep, rich colours, seeming to shimmer through the dark grain, were everything he had hoped for and more.

Already, he pictured what it would look like polished up.

How could he have worried? It hadn't been a mistake.

He made himself exhale as he ran his hand over the tight, dense grain.

He would enjoy working with it.

As he collected the plastic wrapping, a folded piece of paper fell out.

Strange. Not an invoice. No figures on it. Nothing to say how much he'd paid. And what language was it in?

Russian? No.

Not Arabic either. Some alphabet he didn't recognise. The wood had obviously come further than he had thought.

Well, it was here and in one piece, that was the main thing. What did it matter how it had got here or who had sold it?

Jack looked at the little clay maquette—the latest in a long line of experiments, each one a refinement, an improvement over the last, made and remade until he had the design fixed in his mind. Several practice versions of the sculpture in different woods stood on the windowsill, each closer to his vision than the last, but each lacking something; each a failure in its own way.

He turned the maquette over in his hands, looking for any last-minute changes he might want to make. There were none. This was the shape he had been looking for: a satisfying curve across the middle, which contrasted well with the sharp angles of the base. It would be technically challenging, but what would the point be of making anything too easy, too commonplace from such magnificent wood?

He would produce his masterwork in the old sense of the word. All those courses he'd attended, all the hours he'd put in learning new techniques, making mistakes, trying again, failing again, had led to this moment. Finally, he would create something of worth.

He began by drawing out the shape on the wood with a pencil. It fitted the block perfectly, as though it had been made for it; although he began the model long before he had any idea what size or kind of wood he would use, there would be little waste.

Jack took the measurements again anyhow. He liked to be thorough, and this was a piece worth being thorough about.

When he was certain, he put the block in the vice and tightened the screw, making sure it held securely. He picked up the gouge and mallet, almost overwhelmed, reluctant to make the first cut, savouring that moment when all the possibilities in the wood remained open.

Taking a deep breath, Jack rested the gouge lightly on the surface, testing it. He'd sharpened all his chisels for the occasion, but even so, it went through like a knife through butter, the curl of wood coming away in one clean piece.

He inspected the block. The cut had gone with the grain. He'd anticipated this being hard, physically demanding work, but if anything, he would have to be careful not to exert too much force in the roughing-out stage.

The second stroke was as smooth as the first, and he grew in confidence as he worked. He'd never found a piece that responded so well. Even when he made mistakes, it seemed that the wood knew, and when he put too much of his weight behind the blow as he cut against the grain, it did not splinter or shear away as he had expected it to, but only came away in the same smooth curl, a warning to be a little less heavy-handed next time.

He'd be the first to admit that he was an enthusiastic amateur, but carving this block of wood made him feel like a master, in control of every action, seeing his ideas being turned into reality with each stroke.

Quickly, the little failures of the week slipped away. There was just the wood and him. And then, only the wood. He concentrated first on thinning out the middle, which he had thought would be an awkward section. But it seemed no problem now.

Jack made progress, working steadily, understanding, adjusting in the moment. If he overworked one side, he would stop without consciously thinking about it and begin on another, never ceasing, always appraising.

The colours and patterns he revealed were wondrous. Where the outside of the wood was dark, reds and yellows came through, strange autumnal colours, wholly unexpected. Even the shavings were beautiful, perfect shards. He collected them, would he find a use for them, too?

Satisfied with his work on the middle, Jack repositioned the wood in the vice. The top didn't need much removed, and he was in too good a rhythm to stop: he would get it done then take a break.

Whether the mallet slipped in his hand, or whether there was some hitherto undiscovered weakness in the wood, he did not know. The blow seemed no different to any other, but the gouge cut a long, ugly scar through the centre of the block, much deeper than he'd intended.

He shook his head, brushed away the dust.

Shit, he'd split it.

That was what overconfidence did. He could hardly bear to look.

Stupid.

How bad? Perhaps, it was better than he thought.

He compared it to the maquette. The split went right across the central section of the block.

Stupid, stupid, stupid.

What could he do? Nothing precipitous, nothing stupid. He would take that break, make himself a coffee. Give himself time to think. The worst thing would be to make a rash decision, one that he would only regret later. He'd done that before, God knew.

As the kettle boiled, he turned on the radio to calm himself. It was the middle of the afternoon play. Someone walked through a forest, just the tread of the man's feet, the rustle of leaves, the calls of birds. Some experimental piece.

A whisper and a clacking of jaws seemed to come from behind him. With the kettle in his hand, he almost scalded himself as he turned, sending an arc of boiling water across the kitchen.

No one was there. Must have been in the play. A production trick.

He listened for it again, but the man was out of the wood, talking to an acquaintance. After a little while, a familiar situation played out: a marriage thwarted, two lovers parted; it seemed unlikely that the voice would return. Maybe it hadn't been part of the play at all but some curious interference.

Jack thought again of the block of wood as he drank his coffee. Perhaps, something *could* be saved.

When he returned to it, he worked at the area around the split, exposing it, cleaning it, so that he could see just how bad it was.

He was jumpy, unable to settle. The wood resisted him now, every moment threatening a mistake; he checked and rechecked his measurements against the maquette, reassuring himself that it was correct. But gradually, his breathing slowed, and his mind settled as he focussed on the work at hand, clearing away the splintered wood from around the gash. He would have to make alterations, yes, but not as extensive as he had initially feared.

He marked the area to be removed, set to work, and tried to picture the new design in his mind's eye, tried to fix it there.

For a while, he was back on track. But the moment he thought that, the chisel again went awry. This time, he was sure that it was nothing he had done. The blade caught on some hidden imperfection in the wood, shearing off the corner of his new design.

It was almost a relief to know that the wood was wrong, that there was nothing he could have done about it. Almost. It was scant consolation, even so.

He could not afford another block like this, and even had he been able to, it was not merely a matter of the money. This took him a long time to find: a rarity, a one-off.

When he checked the website in the hope that they might have another, the browser only returned a 404 error.

He must have gotten the address wrong, but when he tried again, a fatalism settled over him. Everything was ruined.

For the rest of the day, he avoided the workbench. He attended to bills, tried to read a few pages of a novel, watched TV. Anything to occupy himself. When nothing worked, he got a can of beer from the fridge, then another and another, and didn't stop until it was time for bed.

That night, he dreamed of a forest.

Like nowhere he had known, this was a primeval, pristine forest, but where he had always thought of pristine in terms of something clean, something healthy, he understood now that untouched could have another meaning and it imbued him with fear.

Ancestors watched him from the canopy. Wizened and envious of the living, they hung from the branches, loose-limbed, sagging flesh, their wicked sharp teeth clacking together as they whispered to him.

They were quieted by a sound deep in the forest. It called to them. The wood canopy let in no light, the forest floor bare but for the fungi that favoured the damp cool dark; this was a sacred place, a place where men did not venture.

Two men were with Jack: the young one, the bravest of the tribe; the old one, the wisest. In that way of dreams, where identity is mutable and boundaries permeable, Jack knew the warrior's thoughts.

He did not look at the terrible shrunken thing he held, the thing he had been chosen to take back, to return to the place it had come from. The rites had been performed. He would enter the forest alone.

The sticky woad still drying on his face, his skin sore and itching from the protections they had dyed into his skin, the warrior walked, and Jack went, too, sometimes with him, sometimes as him, the chattering growing louder all the while.

A hollow log sits deep in the forest, the old man had said. Take it there, place it just so.

Words needed saying, and the young man repeated them under his breath. Over and over. He didn't understand what they meant. A series of syllables, nothing more. Something necessary. An apology for the action, the old man had said. He was wise, knew all.

Still, the young man was afraid, despite his bravery.

The ancestors argued amongst themselves, were amused, feigned indifference. They would allow him passage; they respected the markings on his body, the words of introduction he had spoken. They would let him pass, but they did not like it.

Take it back, they urged him. Take it back, dead man, take it to the world of the living. It wants to live, to be one of you. It is our gift to you.

They grew angry when he ignored them, showed him his death. The further he ventured, the worse these visions became.

We cannot protect you there, young one, they said.

You don't want to die like this, they said.

He did not. He went on.

Come join us, they whispered. But it was not for the likes of him to live with the ancestors. They were only the guardians of the outer dark, and worse things lived in the wood than them.

Even they dared not follow him.

Come back to us, they called, their voices fading behind him. Come back to those who love you.

In he went, alone.

When he came back to the edge of the wood, the old man waited for him.

Is it done? the old man asked.

It is done.

The bravest of all the tribe did not tell of what had happened in the heart of the forest: the failure of nerve, flinging the thing blindly into the dark, and the forgotten words. It had been returned to whence it came. Surely, that was enough. His people would prosper again.

The next day was a work day. Jack sweated through the train journey, a couple of paracetamols doing nothing to take the edge off his hangover. Even so, he was glad to forget the disappointments of the weekend by occupying himself with the daily grind.

The plan quickly went awry. In conversation with a colleague, he couldn't stop replaying the moment his hand had slipped, and lost track of what he was saying.

When he returned to his desk, Jack sketched idly on a piece of paper. He drew the design he had planned, the design he had lived with for all those months, the design he could no longer complete. It was good, he knew that, but now that he looked at it again he saw how much it resembled its influences, how conventional it still was.

He crumpled the paper and threw it in the bin.

Then, without really paying attention, he doodled his way through a phone conference.

Only as the call wrapped up, he became aware of what he'd drawn. The new design utterly unlike the previous one.

An excitement grew in him. Something alien and distinct from anything he had carved before. Was it even possible?

The more he looked at it, the more it seemed that he'd been too rigid, too blinkered.

Yes, it might be possible.

He laughed at himself as he tore out the paper. This wasn't going to be the disaster that he had imagined. If anything, he'd needed something like this to shake him out of the rut he'd fallen into without knowing it.

The first thing Jack did when he got home was to go to the workbench and examine the block, comparing it to the sketch.

He traced the scar that crossed the surface. If he cut here and here...

Yes, that might work.

He drew the new design onto the block. Almost. A change to that section—yes, there was enough wood left—and it was right.

When he finished, Jack picked up mallet and gouge for the first time since the seeming disaster.

Again, the chisel cut like a dream.

How could he have made such a stupid mistake?

He should have given himself a break earlier, that was it. He would be more careful this time.

Jack worked for an hour, reminded himself of his own rule and took a break, even though he felt like he could go on and on.

But however careful he tried to be, he made another mistake immediately on his return, leaning too heavily into the stroke. Another split. He thought, at first, that he could work round it, keep the error to a minimum, but whatever he did only seemed to make things worse, until at last, his new design had been rendered impossible, too.

He swore. Nothing could rectify it.

In frustration, he put the chisel loosely against the block, hit it without purpose, wanting only to destroy, to obliterate.

A second blow, then a third. More wood split off. If he continued like this, he would end with a pile of shavings.

The thought made him hesitate, but his hands moved again, almost of their own volition. Not under his guidance, certainly.

The blow was harder this time. The movement purposeful. A large chunk of wood fell to the floor.

He told himself that he should stop, that he would regret this in the morning, but his hands kept going. There was something in there. Not his original design, nor the new one, but something else that lay within the wood. Something that wanted out.

He gave himself up to it.

How many hours passed? Three? Four? The whole night? Time slipped by as he carved.

This was his best work, possessed of a weird sinuousness, shapes and angles he had never thought of before, yet in some way subtly wrong.

Was this inspiration? If so, where did it come from?

It felt effortless, but he was not the one making decisions. His hands quicker than his brain, he remained a mere spectator in this act of uncovering, of unveiling.

If he tried to work against the wood, his fingers went numb and the chisel fell from his hands. He could only pick it up again when he relinquished his will.

He always knew what he had to do next, but could never see the shape of the whole he worked towards, as if it was being held from him, as if the form that waited inside the wood was too terrible for him to behold, as if, were he to see it now, the spell would break.

Another part of him, that dimly rational part pushed down deep inside, rejected this wholly: wood held no memories. But he could do nothing; the shape of it was no longer his to decide, if it ever had been.

Briefly, he came to in the early hours of morning. Something on the edge of consciousness kept disturbing him, buzzing like a fly. He waved it away.

Only later did he remember its similarity to his own voice and wonder whether it hadn't been a warning, but by then, it was too late.

Mid-afternoon and he was hours late for work. But he didn't care, barely even noticed.

The smashed maquette was dust ground into the carpet. The block had been roughed out, no details yet, but there was a definite shape to it, profane and suggestive, not of his own devising.

How many years had it waited there inside the wood?

Well, it would have to wait a little longer. He was done in, drenched in sweat, arms aching, drained.

Birdsong accompanied him to bed, the mocking chatter of the forest canopy. He threw open the window and collapsed on top of the sheets, dozing uneasily as sunlight poured into the room, half-listening to the traffic outside, half-aware of a phone ringing somewhere nearby.

He woke, or thought he woke, several times, to people talking in his room. In a daze, he found no one there, no one he could see anyway.

Jack woke back at the bench, still exhausted, but dressed, gouge in hand.

He couldn't bring himself to inspect the thing; blindly, he picked up the mallet and began to work.

This became the pattern of his days: when he worked, he wasn't tired— as though the work gave him energy, else blocked the exhaustion, for when he downed tools in the small hours, it was all he could do to crawl into bed, spent.

But he found no respite in dreams. Each night, a different man walked the forest: a hunter in the dead of winter, searching for game; a man running for his life from the soldiers who had made the men of his village dig a trench and lined them up in front of it; a man who had pretended to be dead for hours, lying under his neighbour, trying not to shiver, trying not to sneeze.

They all ended up in the same place, here, where the warrior had thrown the thing, where the tree had grown up around it. Even as the forest was tamed and where before there had been only a scattering of houses a town now stood, this place remained untouched. You did not have to know the local legends to know not to come here. The only ones to do so were the unfortunate and the lost. And each night, Jack accompanied them.

The ancestors had retreated into their trees. No longer did they drop down on their long limbs like ancient spiders to watch his passing, but he still heard them, their voices in the rustle of leaves, in the disturbances on the forest floor.

Back again, little brother? they whispered mockingly on the breeze. Back so soon? You must like it here.

On through the dark wood, they walked, Jack and his companions. On, on, on to the dark grove where the warrior's nerve had failed all those years ago.

There was only one way into it, a steep descent, followed by a scramble; a ring of sentinels had grown up at its edge, protecting what lay inside from prying eyes.

Always Jack kept his eyes down, even as his companion looked around in terror. Always the companion went in, driven by some compulsion Jack felt, too, but always Jack was stopped, unable to go on.

Not yet, the ancestors told him. You're not ready to see him yet.

Jack could only watch, could offer no help as his companions entered the grove. Sometimes, they came back; sometimes, they were never seen again. But when he saw the state of those who returned, he wondered who were the lucky ones.

Convinced that it was a real place he dreamed of, he scoured the internet, trying every search term he could think of.

Careful, the ancestors warned him in dreams. We know what you're doing. You wouldn't want to find us. We're so hungry, and there are things in this wood that would gobble you up.

They twittered amongst themselves like bad little children.

One night, Jack followed a woodcutter into the forest, and this time, he was not stopped when they reached the grove. The great tree's ancient limbs reached for him in this terrible, sacred place.

The ring of the man's axe broke the silence as he hacked at a branch. Later, the man wrapped his prize, surfed the internet, sent off the package.

See, the ancestors told him delightedly. You are part of a lineage.

A face emerged from the wood, roughhewn, rudimentary, but he could no longer deny it for what it was, no longer look away as his body worked to free it.

The ancestors spoke to him all the time now.

Show him to us, show us our king, they crooned. Soon, he will be with us. Such a long time we have waited. Soon, you'll show him to us.

Jack knew that when he did, when he revealed its features, he would wholly lose his power to resist.

He fought against them.

What are you doing? they asked as he laid down his tools.

It took all of his energy, a tremendous effort of will to ignore them as he fumbled with the vice and freed the wood.

Each step like lead, he dragged himself away from the work bench, desperation driving him on; he knew he would not have another chance.

Somehow, he managed to keep going, the strain incredible, as if the thing in the wood fought him, attempting to prevent him from this course of action.

But once he locked it away in a cupboard, the ancestors quieted down, their howls of betrayal dwindling away, the pressure released.

He should take the thing outside and burn it, but a strange apathy overtook him, and whenever he approached the cupboard, he found some other chore that urgently needed doing. It was not that he was afraid, he told himself, but that he was being silly, overwrought even, and the task was one that could be left for another day.

Jack dreamed that he destroyed the statue.

He sawed until the teeth blunted. It hardly left a mark.

He hammered it until the chisel broke.

The voices of the ancestors surrounded around him, making it hard to think as they shouted their disapproval, warning him of the consequences, screaming at him when he wouldn't stop.

He stood in front of the cupboard, open and empty.

Was he dreaming? It hardly seemed to matter.

He looked round, knowing where the block would be.

And there it sat, waiting on the bench, ready for him to put into the vice, ready to begin work again.

What had he been so worried about? He picked it up, no longer ugly as he turned it over in his hands, running his fingers over the grain; the unfinished nature of it, the beauty half-hidden in the wood demanded to be revealed.

He didn't have the strength to resist again.

That's it, the ancestors whispered as he tightened the screw, that's it.

Jack didn't remember finishing it, didn't remember a time when that wicked, grinning face hadn't been there to watch him.

But it let him go, and he slumped to the floor, tools dropping from his hands as the ancestors paid it homage.

There was an emptiness in his belly. When had he last eaten? His eyes wanted to close, let sleep come, but the need to eat was too great. He crawled to the kitchen, but the cupboards were empty, the contents of the fridge spoiled and furred.

Time off for good behaviour, they said, as he stumbled out of the flat, blinking in the daylight.

Don't be long. You're not finished yet. There's such a lot still to do.

Their laughter followed him.

The man in the corner shop watched him warily, but Jack didn't care as he gathered packets at random, ripping them open, flinging money down onto the counter as he crammed handfuls into his mouth, barely chewing, almost choking, leaving a trail of wrappers down the street.

Who knew when he would be released again.

The delivery note waited for him on the doormat. The package had been left with his neighbour. He didn't even think about not collecting it.

"Heavy," the woman said as she handed it over.

"Yes."

"Have you heard people hanging about outside?" She looked over his shoulder.

"No," Jack said. "Children, probably."

She locked her door behind her.

We've sent you a present, they whispered, tittering amongst themselves as he opened his own door. Such a lovely present for a growing boy. Why don't you unwrap it?

He didn't bother to take off his shoes, throwing down his bags and going straight to the table where he sharpened his tools, though he needn't have bothered; they would cut true so long as he did what they wanted.

When satisfied, he slipped the apron over his head, placed the wood in the vice and began, overseen by the king and mocking ancestors.

And as he worked, Jack tried to remember how many limbs the tree had.

THE EYES OF FIRE
Michael Edgerton

"And it grew both day and night,
Until it bore an apple bright,"- William Blake, A Poison Tree

I

If you're reading this, I assume you've heard of me: Jacob Foster, notorious journalist for the *Metro Telegram*. My side hustle, however, is as a horror and thriller author. Three days have passed since that insidious night in the Devil's Halo where I bore witness to the seraphic hideousness that sent me into a fervor of trembling inspiration. What I write is the true narrative of that night, as I saw it. If it were a hallucination brought on by something in the woods, or the supernatural, it is uncertain. I will doubtlessly integrate this into my works for years to come, and I write this to capture the terror awakened within me. Terror originating in some latent place in my mind that I may never feel again. A malevolence festers in that abhorrent place, a curse to we connoisseurs of darkness, that I fear is now lost to me.

II

Ghoulmans was always busy on Tuesdays. Perhaps that should have struck me as odd, but that was just one of the peculiarly refreshing aspects of the pub. The splendid oddity made it stand out amongst the countless bars scattered around Elm Street in Greensboro. Ghoulmans, with its Edison bulbs, grandiose Victorian bar, and a radio playing modern music, largely felt like an anachronism, but it worked. It smelled of exotic liquor and wood fire, a homogeny reminiscent of cigars I can't afford.

Across the pub sat some college students. Behind them, a table of octogenarians who looked older than the Ark. Next to the elderly was a collection of bearded men painted in tattoos, whose leather jackets and boots marked them as bikers. Sitting at the bar, a young man read from a collection of H.P. Lovecraft stories. The folio at the top of the page displayed the title: *Pickman's Model.*

I approved of his choice.

No character ever haunted me with more familiarity than Richard Upton Pickman.

Perhaps, the variety of music or the live jazz on Friday nights appealed to everyone, but Ghoulmans welcomed even the strangest of men—I should know, I'm normally the weirdest guy in the room.

I sat in one of the booths across from the bar, relaxed in the familiar red velvet cushions where I had spent many nights in jubilant stupor. I held the menu to indulge my vanity, but I always ordered the same drink.

Right below the Ghoulmans Martini read The Foster, printed in a typewriter font: Black coffee with two fingers of Simcoe Maple Whisky. The favorite drink of one of our favorite customers, Jacob Foster, brought to our menu in honor of the best-seller status of his first novel *The Ripper of Banecroft.*

My book published last December, a year since Morgan put my signature drink on the menu, but every time I saw it, my sense of achievement returned. That sublime feeling reminding me that my writing is not the pipe dream of a haunted man.

The ornate bar called attention to itself, that altar of the happy sinner's cathedral, a place of worship for some, the priest standing jovially behind the stained wood, pouring toxic manna from colorful bottles. Time for communion. Holy Spirits catalyzed the congregation to speak in fiery tongues, much to the shock of the less devout. Lust hung in the air, but for what? Nothing lecherous but far more intoxicating than any drug.

I waited for Dominic Javell, one of my oldest friends and occasional partner on my esoteric hunts that my Editor in Chief, William J. Wellwalker, sponsored. I suppose I have an appetite for the sinisterly spooky and the scent of the paranormal. A love that takes me to the morose cases when working the crime beat. About half way into my second year at the *Telegram,* and after several successful articles, I asked Wellwalker if he might indulge my love of the peculiar with an article about an allegedly-haunted Greensboro house. Wellwalker ultimately consented, with nervous eyes over my shoulder as I worked. His anxiety shifted to a stoic appreciation when my article garnered positive reviews. Wellwalker often permits my pulp pieces now.

That's what brought Dominic and I to that unhallowed forest, where eldritch nightmares cavort beneath the bloodied Heavens, and God hides his horrified eyes from the resentful rejects of his kingdom. Only an hour's drive from Greensboro was a woodland area reserved for recreation known as the Devil's Halo. Locals in Chatham County would frequent the outskirts of the woods, but the leash of superstition kept them from going any deeper. Naturally, the paranormal aura would draw folks like myself to the legend shaded canopy of gnarled trees. In the center of those woods, is the phenomena that gives the Devil's Halo its name. A barren clearing in the form of a perfect circle, ten feet in diameter, the heart of which hosted the most unsettling feature of the Halo—a seven-pointed stone table, like a primitive altar in a druidic sanctum.

The most famous and widely accepted superstitions were that in the night, Lucifer would leave Hell and trot in a circle, contemplating new ways to bring discord to humanity. The hellfire beneath his feet would then scorch the earth. A cabal of demons would accompany the Devil, roaming the forests and harming all who didn't bow to His Infernal Majesty. Local explanation for the stone altar was less paranormal but by no means *normal*. Any resident near the Devil's Halo will tell you that an obscure cult brought the table to commit sacrifices for their vile god.

Dominic walked through the door as the waiter brought my drink. I thanked him and took a swig. Coffee and maple whisky—my second greatest vice. In dark jeans and cream shawl-collared sweater that complimented his ebony skin, Dominic possessed a certain precision in his face mixed with a positive inquisitiveness that betrayed his profession as a photo journalist. A look that exudes the essence of personality and history.

"Getting drunk on the job, Foster?" Dominic sat across from me.

"I figured I'd drink like a responsible adult tonight instead of like we did in college." I took another swig.

"We were a dry fraternity." Dominic's sarcasm faintly accented his words.

"And that sorority house across the street was a pious convent."

We looked at one another sternly, but the façade dropped, and we erupted into laughter.

Dominic ordered a glass of water. He would be driving.

"I'm dying to get out there in the Halo—to stand amongst the dimensions of terror that we can't conceive of without first looking at the warped genesis of nightmares."

Dominic smiled slyly. His taut cheeks were spread just enough for those pearls in his mouth to steal the firelight. The fox-grin begged for adventure, but the arch in his brows betrayed his concern. According to his husband, it's what makes Dom such a bad liar.

"And what exactly do you expect us to see out there?"

"If we're lucky, we'll see Satan shitting on the ashes of a saint."

"You're a real bastard, you know that?" Dom mocked me. He was always the more moral one.

As if that's a bad thing.

"Who knows, at the very least, you'll get some eerie shots…probably something to make that prick Lin kill herself with jealousy."

Dominic's calm caution, his humble humanitarianism cracked open just for a moment, letting a malnourished gluttony rear its head. The physical sign of pride and desire one can only wear when dealing with art or addiction.

Possibilities seem to manifest themselves in the air, glowing like the treacherous lure of the angler fish.

"I suppose I can't complain about getting photos that could make Lin eat her heart out."

"And choke on the pretension," I added.

Dom's expression grew more familiar, fitting to the benevolent personality of Dominic Javell.

III

The outskirts of the Devil's Halo were thick with oaks, abundant in life. Squirrels played jovially in the underbrush, birds sang some sweet freedom, while the great branching veins of the oaks absorbed Heaven's warmth. As the horizon engulfed the sun into shades of soft orange like autumn leaves, it became hard to imagine that evil could exist in this idyllic garden. Dom's shutter fluttered like a hummingbird's wings, immortalizing the natural elegance of the forest.

Beauty, no matter how bright, couldn't penetrate the shadows of my mind that retold the curious legends of the Devil's Halo. Stories about incidents and atrocities, all happening within the confines of the woods before us: whispers in the winds or unnatural creatures shambling along the forest floor; campers bold enough to sleep in the Halo would wake up in another part of the woods, the tracks in the foliage and the bruises on their bodies suggesting that something dragged them; people finding the fleshless skulls of exotic animals—and sometimes human ones—sitting on the Altar, bare but unpolished.

Dominic and I walked in parallel, the crunch of leaves beneath our boots echoing like little bones, crushed in the maw of atrocity. We navigated with a small map as last light grew dim. It was eerie but not terrifying. I must admit disappointment in the mundanity of it all.

A root caught my foot, and I fell flat on my face. Rolling over, I looked to the sky, where detritus angels encircled the Halo. I've never liked vultures.

"Walk much?" He jeered as he helped me up.

"New hobby. Can't say I like it."

"I worry about you sometimes, Foster." Like always, his face betrayed the faux-casualness with which he spoke.

"Because of my ambulatory grace?" Dom's a big-hearted man, sometimes annoyingly so.

"You know why," Dom held a severity in his voice: faint but present.

"We can speak candidly about my methods. If coming here bothers you, you don't have to join me." I hoped for equanimity in my voice. I settled for defensiveness. "But you know, I enjoy your company on these stints."

"Stuff like this doesn't concern me. You've always been creepy, in a good way. The morbid side worries me. You can only see so much blood before it saturates your sanity and numbs you to the taste of violence."

Reporting on grisly crimes as research for my writing was part of the job. I've been exposed to the aftermath of a lot of violence, mostly by choice. How was I supposed to lay the full gamut of my vice before him? I have a problem, I'm addicted to the brutality, hooked on darkness—dependent on what it does to my writing. Any half-wit author can write about the monsters that lurk on the surface, but only someone who has stood before pure depravity can conjure the demons which fester in exile from human awareness. I inundate myself with evil, drink the viscous blood of inhumanity—all for the sake of my craft.

"Dom, the day I stop writing is the day you should start worrying. Cause that's when all this," I motioned to our surroundings, "Stops being my pleasure, and starts being my disease."

"All right." He switched lenses on his camera. "You remember when you told Lawrence and I that if you ever met a girl at a party who suggest the two of you 'Leave the party and go grab four to eight pints of Guinness,' you'd drop down on one knee and propose?"

"How could I forget? The next party we were at you told Sally Jensom to go up and say that to me."

"And you dropped on one knee but never told Lawrence and I what you told her."

"I said, 'I see you've met Javell and Heide, now let's grab a pint.'"

The conversation became quite pleasant then died. I'm not sure when. I suppose he felt as silenced as I at the peculiarity around us. I was anxious to arrive at the Halo. Impatient even. My gut lindy hopped in double time with my spleen. Last time my organs were swing-dancing I was having a staring contest with a 9mm.

The farther we went down the insidious trail, the more I wished I had brought my gun—not that bullets would have cut a clearer path in the grass or ceased the howling of wolves. The underbrush grew sparser, trees abandoned their straight posture—contorting in the shroud of darkness to where you might mistake one for some tentacled leviathan. By this hour, the starless night devoured the sun. The canopy of damned branches permitted the passage of moonlight, but only slivers. A mile or so from the Halo, the welcoming foliage of kindness was exchanged for ghastly organisms from a botanist's Halloween decorations.

The plants weren't native to North Carolina. Corpse flowers rose up from the ground, hideous natural obelisks, saturating the air with the stench of death. I read once how they evolved to give off the smell of rot. Perhaps that's why the vultures perpetually circled the caliginous horizon of the Devil's Halo.

Along the prickly, black-leaved bushes sprouted those tiny white and black plants, Doll's Eye, watching us, staring. Jackal's Food Plants, those odd desert parasites, grew here and there, but nothing disturbed me as the Devil's Fingers fungus. They were long, red tendrils that erupted from the ground in a starfish shape, adding to the necrotic pungency of the air. I dated a botanist for a few months who specialized in fungi—at least *something* lasting came out of that relationship.

Finally, the perfection in Halo's symmetry, the barrenness of the gray adamantine soil seemed a natural blasphemy to the laws of nature. The soil denied growth, it denied life, defied the will of God. Even the grasses and flowers in the clearing around the Halo bowed their heads in withering supplication to whatever deity crafted the unhallowed sanctum. It felt as if the place should not—rather could not—exist. A phenomenon humanity is unable to attribute name and categorization to. Or, perhaps something far worse, something that petrified me—*a knowledge I could not possess but that could possess me.*

My dirty boots treaded on hallowed grounds. Each movement—were they my own?—brought me closer to the Altar sitting in the inner Halo. How peculiar it was. A rough, rigid stone work cut to have seven distinct sides. A trembling left hand—my own hand—reached towards the Altar, smooth as marble. A jumpstart of surprise that I was alone, Dominic no longer there with me, but before I could react, before I could devote thought to panic, I blacked out.

IV

Flesh has a smell. Not skin, I mean flesh—the crimson meat that oozes an abhorrent miasma and combusts a steamy moisture into the air, far more repugnant than the stale odor of a corpse. That's what woke me to the benighted forest.

The façade of the Devil's Halo rotted, leaving no trace of its old carapace. Above the Heavens hemorrhaged a lascivious carmine, framing a black, gibbous moon that omnisciently spectated those palace Gardens of Pandemonium. Gray clouds flitted across the blood sky, but nothing was permanent enough to obstruct the view of that tenebrous moon, shooting glacial blue light upon my pallid skin.

The earth quaked—no—I did. I shook on the ground, overcome by some new terror I could not explain or reason. Steadily, and not without pain in my legs, I grabbed onto a low-hanging tree branch and pulled myself up. Clearly, I no longer lay inside the Halo where I passed out, so I walked down the trail that had been cut before me.

My brain commanded my eyes to take note of my surroundings, so that it may feast on my heart's abject terror. Grass and vines writhed sinuously, and the canopy of trees—now at a behemoth's height with knotted branches—were the homes of the abominations with membranous wings that croaked mad omens. Their imperceptible shapes shot down, picking at carrion scattered across the ground, which was neither distinctly human nor animal.

Congealed blood like viscous slugs plopped onto my head, sticking in my hair, stopping my gait. Hesitantly, I looked up to find a great spike that rose from the ground, and the alabaster body suspended on perilous point. The forest fringes, between the trees and rising up into the fog, were impalement barbs like fortress gates.

To my left, a bipedal creature with sallow scales and a mouth of needles dragged along a body. With little effort, it javelined its prey upon a branch, so that the still living body hung above him. Fingers tipped with raptors claws disemboweled its catch, and as the gore rained down, the creature opened up its horrible maw, catching whatever it could in a shower of death.

Harsh syllables of sonorous screams carried on the wind into a mosaic of dread, pouring in my ears and prickling my flesh. The gale brought along with it a terrible chanting, combined with screams and groans to form an echoing a sermon.

But what was the message? Where was the Priest?

I wish I could say it was the death, so abundant in that place, that had petrified me. But I didn't know true *horror* until I came upon a clearing. When the trail ended, I stood back at the namesake of this infernal place, though that, too, had changed. A malevolent cabal of the fallen inhabited the space, each their own sort of terror. An imposing Lord of Flies chanted out incantations—a benign anathema to honor the Prince of Darkness. The insectoid priest raised a prayer in Latin, and in response, the demons chanted back.

My mind could only comprehend fear, my heart ceased pumping blood, and in its place circulated terror. It coursed through my veins, accelerating with every second, a rhapsody of fear. The horror that marked me, was the *same* intense desire I had when Dominic and I discussed what we *might* see.

Something compelled me towards the inner Halo, as if a voice said, "Come and see," and there, I beheld the only thing to have ever grown inside the Devil's Halo: a Poison Tree watered in the tears of suffering and fertilized in the flesh of sacrifice. For years, it must have been nurtured with fears, envy and deceit, for the bark shone a sickly green, and the branches were stripped of any leaves like bones.

Why should it need them? There was no sunlight in this place.

Though it lacked leaves, each of the willow branches had a shining, black apple. In a fervor, a voracious desire replaced my fear. I craved to bite into the flesh of the apple. I yearned for the bitterness of that impious fruit. The urge for revenge, lust for your lover, the itch of withdrawal—all had been made inconsequential by appetite for fruit of the Poison Tree. I didn't just *want* the acrid apple. I *needed* it the way the junkie needs a fix. I would blast my sanity for the apple, just to have the blood of the Muses trickle down my chin.

After all, isn't that why I came to the Devil's Halo? To be possessed by some esoteric knowledge?

The longing in my eyes glinted off the shining dusky skin of the apple. I hadn't even taken it into my burning hands, yet it devoured my resolve.

I fell to my knees, the trembling of my desire failing my legs. The chanting grew louder, more insidious in a dissonance of malign reverence, to honor the arrival of His Infernal Majesty.

He stood before me, and though I did not intend to kneel, I thought it better I not stand, if my legs would even permit it. What had once been seraphic beauty had been scorched repulsively pale with small black horns rising from His forehead. His features were morose, full of malice and resentment, but I still dared not look him in the eye. The Devil, clothed in crimson and black, plucked an apple from the Poison Tree and held it as an offering for me.

"*Cape morsum mi filli*," commanded the Apostate Messiah.

I lifted my head. His gaze, like nothing I had seen before, formed of pride that destroyed any punishment allotted to him. Lucifer's eyes were an eclipsing moon over a spectral blue sun. They were eyes of fire, a frigid cobalt flame glowing ominously behind the consuming black disks. Surrounding the blaze was more darkness, contrasting with the ghastly white skin of Satan. They overflowed with purgative malignance, and if I had the power to divert my gaze, perhaps I would—but *alas*, I was too weak. Evil is too soft a word to describe what is in those eyes, so too, would malevolent not even begin to define the rapturous depravity that cavorts inside. It was a holocaust of wickedness, a stunning vision of perpetual sin, so that eons would serve insufficient to know all of its parts.

In my weakness, I reached for the apple, and the Devil smiled.

The chanting roared above the screams of the tormented.

My fingers grazed the surface of the forbidden fruit, when my eyes closed, and I blacked out once more.

V

Dominic found me passed out by the Altar in the Devil's Halo. How we got separated in the woods, he didn't know. He spent roughly an hour or two looking for me, and says that he even passed by the Halo once or twice, before coming back to it. He carried me from those woods to the car and drove me to the nearest hospital.

When I woke, I told Dom about what all I had seen. He said that he had no clue whether my trek through the woods and encounter with the Devil was true or not, but that he was glad he had found me before anything happened. The place frightened him severely, and he swore he'd never return to the Devil's Halo, in spite of the stunning photography.

The doctors say that I probably had some reaction to the plants or fungi, which caused the hallucination or my passing out. They offered no explanation for the marks in the dirt Dominic photographed by me, which made it look as if I had been dragged.

Of course, neither do I, except for what I saw.

Whatever truly happened in those woods, I might never know. What I do know, however, is that as soon as they let me alone with pen and paper, I wrote page after page, lest it become some obscure memory. If I can ever manage to replicate on paper the feelings that overcame me in the Devil's Halo, I would like to think it would satisfy my fascination with all this wickedness. But I am not like Tartini. It isn't enough, and after looking upon the eyes of fire, I know there is far more of the sinisterly peculiar to satisfy the appetite of my work.

Could these tremors in my hands be quivers of withdrawal?

This craving for darkness is my greatest vice, crowned even above my taste for coffee with maple whisky. Even still, I cannot make mention of it without speaking about my art. Writing may purge atrocities from my soul, but so, too, does it spur my desire to gorge upon monstrosity. They are married—and I dare not divorce the two.

I cannot remember if it was my craft that first implored me to look into the abyss, or if it was the abyss returning my gaze that compelled me to write. Perhaps I will never know if my art preceded my addiction to horror, but the eyes of fire have shown me that it does not matter. Perhaps I shall never be able to absolve my soul of the beguiling stains of my work, but that is a problem for my final judgement.

For now, there is work to be done, stories to write, *malevolence to discover.*

A FEW EXTRA POUNDS
Errick Nunnally

Bill hated the guy he saw every morning in the bathroom.

A potent mix of regret and mourning with a slathering of, yes, abhorrence. The lean, outdoorsy person who used to look back from the mirror was gone. The new guy placed one hand on the thick, pale flesh at his waist and hefted it, easily pinching five inches of slop, knowing he could grab more. Disgusted by his flabby chest, he noted every blemish, every errant hair and detail. He didn't dare cup his sagging breasts, or he'd start crying.

Anne left seven months ago. Seven months alone in the apartment they used to share. They'd been an active couple—cyclocross, rock climbing, 5K obstacle courses, half-marathons—and he never realized how much their physical activities meant to the relationship. Their entire network of friends had been built around competitive or recreational events. None of them had even bothered to call Bill in the last few months. He had nothing to offer, no excuses he could fill the space with, and they wanted nothing more than to get on with their lives without him weighing them down, or standing on the sidelines, watching life speed by.

Weighing people down. Primo choice of words, Bill, you fat pile of shit.

He didn't even understand how he'd gotten so heavy. A healthy diet, no alcohol, never smoked. Regular exercise remained a steady feature in his life until he couldn't take hauling the extra weight. It just wouldn't go away. Anne hung in there for the first few extra pounds, but they kept coming. He began craving high-fat meats and fried foods—tons of calories. The disgusting fast food meals he regularly ingested tweaked every pleasure center he had left— nothing else worked while he spiraled into depression.

Bill wandered into the bedroom he used to share with Anne. One of his favorite photos of them together perched on the dresser. They'd just completed a half-marathon in Colorado—their first as a couple.

That had been a great summer.

174

In the photo, they were both tanned and trim. Bill's black hair provided a fine contrast to Anne's dusky blond locks peeking out from underneath her headscarf. She sported a wide smile, her arm draped over Bill's shoulders, her other hand affectionately across his stomach.

He couldn't bear the thought of her hands on his stomach now; he knew the disgust she'd feel. He felt it every day. The framed photo thudded into the trash bin next to the door.

Is it because I'm so fat that I'm so hungry now? After all these years of eating healthy— food didn't make me this way. Is my body in some kind of rebellion? I don't deserve this.

On his way to the living room, he dragged his hand across all their event photos hanging on the walls. Some of the glass frames dropped and cracked when they hit the carpeted floor, bits of glass bounced. Bill paused by the last, the most recent. Their final trip together, before he'd begun putting on fresh new pounds every day. They'd done a night of mountain biking, and in the photo, Bill had visible scrapes and bandages.

It had been a particularly memorable trip because of a bad spill Bill had taken when a coyote—they'd all decided it was a coyote, it'd happened so fast—had been pinned in the glare of his headlamp on the way down the mountain. He'd jerked the bike's handlebars, succeeding only in tumbling over the beast.

As near as he could tell, the animal swore and grunted as vehemently as he did while they rolled down the rocky path. The thing nipped and scratched him several times before running off into the dark. It culminated in a good story and laugh back at the cabin while Anne patched him up.

Again, Bill hustled to the bathroom, struck by the sudden sensation of a full bladder. He'd been urinating more frequently these last few weeks. Despite ignoring the breasts stretched under his arms and onto his back, he sobbed anyway.

He couldn't see his penis anymore.

On the way back to the living room, yet another segment on the news burbled about the obesity epidemic. An alarming amount of people the world over were putting on a dangerous amount of weight.

Welcome to my world. Bill slapped the television off.

His doctor had no idea why he was putting on so much weight. The slim, young Indian woman had suggested phentermine to suppress his appetite, but he assured her he wasn't overeating. At the time, it was true. He had cravings, sure, but still resisted stuffing his face with junk. Subsequent physical tests, food diaries, and other programs did nothing; the weight kept coming. His doctor thought he was fortunate in that he wasn't demonstrating any conditions related to obesity.

"Other than being obese," he'd said.

When he wondered aloud if he'd been cursed by an angry gypsy woman, the doctor handed him a set of pamphlets describing surgical procedures to aid in weight loss. He'd crumpled the pamphlets in his swollen fists and dropped them in the trash, vowing never to enter Dr. Petra's office again.

How few options, and he had as he ran his hands over the tremendous leaden weight grafted to his abdomen, a bulbous, round pustule he wished would pop and drain. His stomach felt like he'd swallowed a bowling ball, it hurt his knees to heave himself out of a chair.

Later that night, when he lay down to sleep, Bill felt the first tremble.

His instinct was to sit up, but the fat around his middle prevented it. He rolled to his side, sliding his legs out of bed and using them to lever himself up. He was sure he'd felt a tremor. Like something pushing at him from the inside.

Gas, maybe. I shouldn't be surprised with the shit I've been eating lately.

He reconsidered his vow to never return to the doctor when a searing pain lanced across his abdomen, causing him to nearly black out. He looked down at his naked gut and could see a thin red line from his sternum leading down beyond the horizon. Reminiscent of the seam a gravid woman's stomach displayed, like a bean pod ready to release its vine. This was a cleaner line, however, and not the stressed skin of a perfectly normal human. Another shock of burning pain brought a body wide sweat and spittle dribbled from his lips. When he brought himself to look down again, nausea gripped the back of his throat, muscles seized, the contents of his stomach wobbled.

Red blossomed across the expanse of his skin, and he opened like a zipper, the flesh of his body uncoupling itself. Fat and veins, muscle tissue, bone—all of it parted with a sucking crack. Effluvium sloshed and blossomed in his nose as the gap widened. He gaped, unable to speak, unable to move, his body taking on a wholly unnatural rigor.

The pain stopped, lethargy gripped his limbs, and he slumped to his side in a pool of moonlight. For a moment, he happily greeted death, to never experience this again. Instead, he lay paralyzed, a beached whale, slopped onto the floor of his bedroom, an electric fear shocking his brain. He expected a river of blood and internal organs to spill across the carpet.

Where's the blood? He fought furiously to remain calm and think the situation through as the edges of his vision darkened.

Time took on a muddy quality with no clocks in his vision, only the gloom of a darkened apartment. When his sightline shifted like he'd been pushed, he felt a new sense of disorientation as if fifty pounds were being lifted out of him.

Another jerk, and a hand flopped onto the carpet in front of his nose. *Hand* was the best he could come up with to comprehend the bony, clawed fingers slowly digging into the carpet and pulling against his weight. An inky shoulder slick with his life's fluids appeared: hirsute, black skin, greased slick from being inside his belly. As the last of the creature pulled out of him, long feet and claws to match. A stubby tail passed in his vision.

The thing crawled a short distance and stopped, sniffing the air before pressing itself to its hind legs, stretching to its full height, and standing to roll its shoulders. Its joints popped and crackled.

The squatter stiffened, then looked over its shoulder, directly into the eyes of its former home. It turned. Multiple teats led up to a malformed chimp head, but its ears were pointed, too high on its head, and they swiveled like a dog's. The nightmare of a face had hollow eyes, milky globes devoid of pupils under a thick brow. She grinned at Bill, needle-teeth like crystal shards crammed into a mouth too large for her head. When she turned and stalked from the room, he wanted to sigh with relief, but remained glued to the floor.

It rummaged around, pawing through the broken frames in the hallway. When it passed back in front of the bedroom, it paused, a photo of Anne in hand, and again grinned in his direction. Then it disappeared into the living room. A drawer opened and closed, keys jingled. The front door unlocked, opened, and shut again. The rasp of a key in the lock and the final click told him he was alone with his thoughts.

Lost in time, Bill struggled to marshal his mind. He wanted to cry, but even that denied him. The building around him went on clicking and hissing, refrigerator pinging and clocks elsewhere in the house ticking. The barest hint of light creeping into the room told him dawn approached when the key jangled in the lock again.

After shutting the door, the monstrosity entered his bedroom. It hissed in his face and poked his nose. Bright red nipples stood erect through dry fur. It turned its attention to Bill's open abdomen, worrying at the space before crawling back in. His field of vision shook as the world adjusted itself, and seconds later, a shocking cold wormed its way through him. At first, a tingle in his fingers and toes, then a creeping chill up his legs and arms. He gasped as his entire body plunged into ice.

Except for the red line up his belly.

He looked down at the former opening, which still burned, despite the icy pinpricks spreading across his skin. He staggered to his feet and rushed for the bathroom. Glass from his earlier tantrum cut his feet before he got his flabby arms around the porcelain to void what was left of his last meal. His head hung limp on his neck as he tried to process. Had it been a nightmare? He pushed away from the toilet and looked back into his bedroom.

I woke up on the floor. Maybe I fell out of bed? It felt so real.

Bill prodded his distended belly, full of tension and…what else?

Nothing. Empty is what it is, you fat bastard.

Bill's hunger—what had been driving him to eat more often and at greater volumes—doubled. He scooted along his ass to the cabinet beneath the sink and pulled out some antiseptic and bandages. He cleaned the cuts on his feet as best he could before hauling himself erect and brushing his teeth. He felt mostly human when he finished—human enough to go and get something to eat, at least.

With nothing classier open on Sunday morning at this hour, he sidled across the street, determined to make the one block walk to McDonald's on his sore knees. He and Anne used to look down their noses at people who ate at such places. All of his former friends had done the same. They were healthy and fit, after all, and assumed that people who ate at fast-food restaurants loathed themselves.

Bill hated himself. When he stopped to reconsider what he was doing with his life, feeling a resolve he hadn't felt since he started gaining weight, his stomach trembled and did a flip as if it had been struck. He rubbed both palms on his belly, failing to sooth the flood of self-pity.

When next he looked up, aware again, he was sitting at the kitchen table with enough fast food to feed two people.

He chewed mechanically, lost in the flavor-saturated fat, salt, and sugar of the processed meal. Pleasure filled him as the snack settled in his belly. Not long afterwards, he tilted the large red box up to his lips, savoring the last bits and salty punch of the French-fried crumbs. The melancholy swept over him. A smothering blanket dipped in tar and cast over his heart, it dragged anything good he'd ever experienced into a pit where nothing productive ever returned.

With stiff fingers and clenched jaw, Bill dialed the number for Dr. Petra's office.

Bill sat in the waiting room, his leg twitching like a jackhammer, nails dug into the rubber armrests. It took humiliating begging to persuade them to book an appointment for the following morning. He didn't sleep. Dr. Petra knew him already, had all his records. He was fat and depressed and at last willing to consider her suggestions.

They booked his appointment between a 9:00 and a 9:15. An old woman shuffled out of the door leading to the examination rooms. Bill glanced at the clock on the wall. 9:02 A.M. The receptionist waved him over.

"Mr. Irvin?"

"Yes?" Bill grunted, heaving himself out of the wooden-armed chair. It leapt off the floor, wedged to his wide hips before falling free with a thump.

"Dr. Petra will see you now. This way."

He lumbered after the nurse, stumbling too close to her as she sat him in an examination room. He fiddled with a tongue depressor as he waited.

When the doctor entered the room, Bill discarded any pleasantries. "Dr. Petra. Thank God. Listen: I'm sorry I didn't listen to you before—"

"Bill, hold on—"

"I had a horrible nightmare last night, I can't stand this anymore, you have to help me—"

"Mr. Irvin."

"—something about this fat, it just keeps coming no matter what I do, and now, I've started having pains, then this—"

"Bill. Hold on, calm down. What pain is this, where?"

He swallowed hard, fingers absentmindedly working at the tongue depressor in his hand. His eyes stung, and he wiped away tears forming. "In my stomach. There's been—I dunno—tremors and sharp pains."

"And you're not sleeping well?"

He shook his head.

"You're paler than before, your eyes look terrible. Have you been taking any medication? What've you been eating?"

This tiny Indian woman looked older than he remembered. Perhaps, her small size had made him think she were younger. She had some streaks of gray in her hair and a long nose. Perfectly slim, with thin lips and a pointed chin, she reminded him of a little ugly bird.

A little ugly bird obsessed with what Bill ate.

Still. Obsessed. With what. Bill. Ate.

Squawk.

She always wanted to know what he was eating, how he was destroying himself.

Squawk.

What had *he* been doing to cause this? Like it was his fault, as if he'd been sneaking off in those first several months and eating buckets of fried chicken and potatoes. No, he had been exercising hard and eating right. And this was how she treated him; this was how a woman who was effectively his employee treated him.

Squawk.

She needed to learn more respect, needed to know he was her employer, he was in charge, she served at his whim, that he was not to blame for his condition.

The snap of wood broke the silence in the small room, the thin medical instrument broke between his thick fingers. Bill's large hands wrapped easily around Dr. Petra's throat before she could react. Her eyes bulged, and she made little wheezing sounds while clawing at his meaty fingers. She was stronger than she looked, healthy for her age.

Healthy.

Bill leaned in, using his weight to drive her backward, pinning her across the visitor's chair in the room. With little fanfare, the light left her eyes, and her limbs relaxed.

Easier than he'd thought.

Sweating, his heart raced as he leaned back against the examination bed to stare at the lifeless form. She hung backwards across the chair, broken, like an empty, manufactured thing. A cheap puppet made in India. His stomach trembled, and he felt hungry, not sick.

Hungry.

He now had two things to do: get rid of the doctor's body and get something to eat. The angry release had felt good; he'd felt no fear, didn't get caught up in what to do next. A warm calm flooded his body, flowed into his brain.

Bill peeked into the hallway. He opened the nearby linen closet, pulled out some sheets and a small cart, then returned to the room. He wrapped the body tightly in two sheets and dropped her into the cart. Everything prepared, he ducked into the bathroom, wadded up a couple of handfuls of toilet paper around paper towels, dropped them into the toilet and flushed. The commode performed as expected. He flushed again.

At the exit door, he leaned out. "Excuse me? The toilet's clogged and overflowing, I don't know what to do."

The receptionist eyed him with a knowing, icy stare.

That's right, bitch, fat people have huge asses and leave bigger dumps. Go fix it.

She slid by him, ignoring the cart and looked into the bathroom. Cursing under her breath, she grabbed a plunger and went to work. In the doctor's lobby, two old women sat in opposite corners of the office. They never looked up as Bill slid the cart out of the office. He retrieved a large box from the dumpster, slid the bundle of Dr. Petra into it, put the box in his trunk, and went for a drive.

Two blocks from the office park, he blacked out.

When Bill next came to, he sat at a cheap linoleum table with the corpse of a steak bomb in front of him, the last greasy onion ring poised to enter his mouth. The countertop was the color of bile, curled at the edges, and flecked with yellow highlights. It made what passed for food in Bill's life look even more disgusting. A few other particularly heavy men sat in other booths, mechanically consuming their meals, echoing the glassy-eyed eating that Bill was certain he'd been doing moments before.

In the corner, bolted above the din of cheap paper being crumpled and fatty foods being chewed, a grease coated television droned. It was set to the news and the lead-up to the tease about multiple murders was yet another segment on the obesity epidemic. The clip featured the usual scenes of tremulous wastes thundering down a city sidewalk as a talking head railed against the skyrocketing health costs of caring for the fatties.

As he slipped the last, soggy, fried bit into his mouth, he noticed his fingernails had dirt under them and the cracks on his fingers were darkened with filth. His stomach felt fuller than it had ever been, and the memory of what he'd done rammed against the back of his eyes.

When his gorge rose in panic, he clenched his teeth and tried to sit on his trembling hands. He couldn't reach beneath his thighs, so he stumbled to his feet, barely aware of the people staring at him or of the strangled noises coming from the back of his throat. Pain shot through his knees and back as he threw himself out of the sub shop and regained his bearings.

When he reached into his voluminous stretch-waisted pants to pull out his mobile phone, his fist got stuck in the pocket. Frustrated, he forced patience and slipped the phone out using just his fingers. Bill dialed Anne's number for the first time in several months. The phone's ringtone buzzed in his ear, each repetition a desperate reminder she hadn't picked up yet. The sudden click to voice mail, and Anne's recorded message made him hang up.

She works from home. She knows it's me.

Their phone numbers hadn't changed. He dialed again, tumbling into voicemail and repeated the process. This time, she answered.

"Bill, stop it. Just stop. Don't call me—"

"Anne, wait, please, don't hang up, *please*." A long, tense moment followed, Bill's desperation crackled across the line.

"What—what is it, what's wrong?" She held her voice steady, in a monotone.

He took a quivering breath and exhaled his words. "I need your help. I need...I need someone to help me. I can't do this on my own. I can't—the doctor, she—"

"Bill, if you're sick, you need to go to the hospital. *I can't help you.*"

He soaked up every molecule of sympathy in her voice.

"It's more than that, Anne. There's something serious. Something really strange happened the other night, and I'm scared. I'm really scared. Can I come by, can we talk?"

"Bill..."

"Please, Anne, please. I don't have anyone else to talk to. I swear, if you can't help, you'll never hear from me again—I swear."

She sighed and Bill imagined he could hear her teeth grinding, but her response was soft. "Fine."

She gave him the address.

When he stood outside of her new apartment building, he had second thoughts. A wave of trepidation swamped him, and he checked his impulse to flee. Anne would help; she could make sense of this. His tremendous girth jiggled as he took hesitating steps into the lobby. Bill's guts twisted and shot through with pain when he pushed the button on the elevator. A piercing lance of nerve-burning ache shot through his hips and nearly dropped him to his knees. He wrapped his hands around his belly and squeezed, trying to contain the wave of nausea that followed.

He forced himself to continue despite the overwhelming urge to turn and flee.

Anne…

Get Anne to help.

The elevator doors slid open, and walking through what seemed a dream, he stood in front of his ex-girlfriend's open door.

"Bill, you look awful. Oh my God, why aren't you at the hospital?"

A beautiful sanctuary, an oasis in the middle of his nightmare. Her dirty blonde hair was still streaked with sun-bleached strands. A slight sunburn painted her strong cheeks, and under an angular brow, piercing green eyes punctuated her strong face. Her lean lips parted in shock.

"Anne." He breathed low in the back of his throat. "It's not a medical problem. It's not."

She took a step back, a touch of fear around her eyes. He knew what she was thinking. They had lived together for five years.

"I'm not crazy. Just—please—let me explain."

She relented, stepped aside, and waved him in. "Would you like some water?"

A new living room set: two chairs and a love seat surrounding a glass coffee table. He dropped himself into a plush green chair. Anne looked good—no, she looked *incredible*. Even more fit, if that were possible. Slim, strong, the perfect weight. Bill's jaw clenched, and his thick hands curled into fists.

She's doing better without me. Like I was some kind of anchor slowing her down, a thing to be jettisoned. All for a few extra pounds. A creeping, deadly fat he had no control over, that wasn't his fault. And *she* left *him*.

"Bill?"

"Uh, yes. Please." The feelings and thoughts had swum into his brain, seemingly unbidden, connecting dots he didn't even know were there. Anne didn't deserve his scorn, their breakup had made sense at the time. If their roles had been reversed, he'd have made the same decision. As she poured him a glass of water, he gathered his resolve, tried to think clearly.

She glided back across the carpeted floor, her bare feet strong, and handed him the glass. He took it, and she stood waiting, arms crossed. Judging, a gaze spiced with regret.

What does she have to regret? I'm the one suffering. Our five years together were some of the best of her—our lives.

He took a gulp of water, taking her in as he swallowed.

"Why are you standing like that? Sit down."

"I'll stand, thanks. What is going on, Bill?"

"Why the attitude?"

"*Bill.*" She rubbed her eyes with one hand, keeping her arms crossed. Her phone rang, and she glanced at it sighing resignedly before answering. "Hello, unknown caller."

She had a compulsive habit of answering the phone when the caller I.D. had no answers for her. She needed to know who was behind the digital mask.

"Yes, this is she. Who is this? De——? Oh. Yes. Uh, yes. I don't—okay." She glanced at Bill and nibbled on one of her fingernails. "As quickly as possible. Right? You have my address? Okay, that's good. Right, goodbye."

"That didn't sound like a wrong number."

Anne cast about, hesitating before answering. "Delivery. A client needs to send me a thumb drive, trouble with uploads."

He lumbered up out of the seat.

She took a half step backward. "Hey, tell me what you need to tell me and—"

"You're not the one with this, this—problem." He waved vaguely at his abdomen. "You don't have this thing inside you, this God damned monster driving you like a sock puppet."

Anne held her hands up. "Bill. Calm down. You're not—"

"I'm not what? Not fat? Yes, I *am* fat."

Worry tugged at her eyes.

"What else? Huh? Not a monster? Yes, Anne, I *am*; I killed Dr. Petra today. Or yesterday—I don't know. But I strangled her with my bare hands. Okay?"

She took another step back.

No, I will not hurt Anne. I will not.

He pinched his eyes shut, listening to the wail of sirens in the distance, and when he opened them, he was in motion, arms up as she shuffled backwards, stumbling on the corner of the coffee table. Bill struggled to control himself as his arm flopped awkwardly across her shoulder like a sad bag of meat. She panicked and pitched backward, his weight taking them both down.

The glass table top shattered in a bright counterpoint to the dull impact of Anne's back on the edge of the metal frame. Her grunt shifted to a hoarse cry of pain as Bill came down on top of her, crushing the frame of the table with their combined weight.

Her trembling scream was strangled into an involuntary hiss of air.

Her legs twitched, and she managed to wheeze, "Bill get off me."

He tried—he did—but he couldn't. The line of heat up his belly spread to paralysis throughout his body with the crackling speed of an oxygen-fueled fire. Anne redoubled her efforts, her wild eyes locked on his deadened and jaundiced orbs.

He pitched slightly to the side, and his shirt hid the initial opening in his torso. The faint parting of flesh buried beneath Anne's strangled cries. When the shirt tore and the gore slathered arm of the thing living inside Bill slid through, Anne gulped breath, trying to scream.

It pulled itself from him, callously pushing against its host body, clawing at whatever handholds it could until it slithered out onto the carpet and gained footing. The milky white, dead eyes focused on Anne, and it crept towards her as she issued shrill, stifled screams.

The thing opened its misshapen mouth full of glass shards and snapped them shut over Anne's jaw and throat, worrying at the flesh. Squishy, warm blood saturated the carpet and Bill's face. Beneath them, a pool spread as the thing perched on Bill's arm, still tearing at Anne. Her whimpers ceased, but the monster continued to tear at her until finally it pulled free and licked its lips with a tongue as warped as its face.

It set to Bill's abdomen, meticulously closing the obscene gap at his core before stooping low, still carefully avoiding Anne's blood, and staring into his eyes.

"Warned you." Its voice was a hiss of crushed glass only hinting at the horror of the mouth it issued from. It held up long, clawed fingers before grinning and poking Bill in the nose. A hammering at the door caused it to glance over its shoulder. It skittered through the kitchen to the rear of the apartment, leaving no trace behind other than the lacerated remains of Anne. Voices could be heard through the door.

"Ms. Holmes? Anne Holmes? This is the police, answer the door please. If you don't answer the door, we will break it down. Is Mr. Irvin with you? Last chance, open up."

A chill seeped through Bill's brain as the first prickles of feeling came back to his fingers and toes. His future became clear.

The police crashed through the door as he regained enough control over his body to sob. His bulk jiggled on the corpse of his former love, blood spattered across his face, and gobs of her flesh on his lips.

EVEN DEMONS ORDER FOOD ONLINE
Thomas Welsh

Blake stretched out from his Thrustmaster T800 Evolution Ultimate Gamer Chair and kicked his mancave door closed. Remaining perfectly still, he strained to hear the distinctive *klop klop* of his mom's sensible brown work shoes as she headed down the garden path towards the Toyota Prius that disgraced their driveway. Holding his breath, Blake waited for the dull *thunk* of the door closing before the wheezy hum of the weak engine signalled she was on her way. A second later, mom was gone, the house was completely quiet, and Blake was free to go hunting.

Step one: ready the hunting grounds. Blake had been looking forward to this moment for the whole week, but he'd done little in the way of preparation. A mess of energy drink cans and empty bottles of malt liquor strewn across the floor and discarded protein bar wrappers and soggy sports socks obscured his desk. Still, if "ground zero" looked clear and tidy, Blake would be fine. He sprung to his feet and kicked the junk out of view, clearing a little island in the middle of the room that looked relatively clean. As long as there were no distractions, he would be fine. As long as nothing drew his victim's eyes away from *The Main Event*.

Step two: prepare the bait. Blake rotated on his gamer chair and regarded himself in the long mirror he had meticulously positioned to show his body from his toes to his crew cut. Lounging backwards, he took some time to appraise his impressive physique. He was having a good muscle day for sure. His abs were sharply defined by the low morning light that sliced through the closed blinds. It was just bright enough for him to notice a tuft of hair out of place on his otherwise immaculately styled beard, so he licked and fingered it back into place.

Sliding his thumbs round the waistband of his boxers, he pushed the stray hairs down. He was hairless everywhere except *there*—and his head obviously—but he didn't want them to realize that at first. There was a boyishness about his smooth, bulging body that they pretended to enjoy, but he knew what they really wanted to see.

Step three: clean and load the rifle. Blake adjusted the bottle of hand lotion, putting it on the right of the desk, then the left, then back to the right. He was never sure where it worked best. On the right, he would reach across with his other hand, and they would see he was doing *something,* and they might wonder what, and they might get nervous, and he fucking loved that. On the left though, and he could get to it quicker, then he could move on to The Main Event with less time wasted. It was a dilemma. He shifted it to the right.

Squeezing a tiny amount of lotion into his right hand, Blake slid his fingers into his underwear and got started. This was an essential step. He would never forget the time he had blown his chance because of imperfect preparation. It had been one in a million: a hot young girl's first time. *First time.* And he'd been caught with a limp dick. She'd actually laughed. He could never, ever let that happen again. He had to be ready to go from the very first roll of the dice. Tragedy like that could never happen again.

Semi-prepared and with one hand still down his boxers, Blake reached across the desk, pulled the keyboard in close and typed with one hand. *Random chat online.* Scrolling down the search results past *Chatroulette,* *RandomChat,* and *BabezChat,* he picked a site he knew had a few girls, and no prohibition against nudity, and clicked *"allow"* when his computer asked to share his webcam with the internet.

And the hunt began.

Of course, Blake's main problem with the internet—other than the disgusting proliferation of feminists—was the popularity of the hunting grounds. Clicking the link for a new chat, he connected with the first random webcam, and the small window on the left-hand side of his screen showed a fellow hunter's loaded and fully extended rifle. Blake quickly clicked the *next chat* icon, setting the pattern that he would likely follow a hundred times more before he came across even a single woman. The ratios were not in his—or their—favour. The hunters had taken the field, and the prey was illusive and thinly spread, but Blake was patient. His mom was out of the house all day, and since he'd left that liberal hellhole of a college, he had nothing else to do.

Blake's hands shook as he clicked the mouse again and again. He was always skittish at the start, adrenaline twisting his stomach in knots with nervous excitement. So many feelings at once—guilt, anticipation, exhilaration, the fear of being caught or recognized, the constant Pavlovian thrill of taping on the mouse button every three seconds, the infinitesimally small chance of finding a victim slowly increasing as the minutes ticked by.

Fuck, this felt good.

In his right hand, Blake's dick became rock hard as he imagined the kind of girl he might meet for The Main Event. A cute goth girl with big eyes coyly biting her black bottom lip, a blonde leaning in close to the screen to get a better look at his abs, a fat girl pretending to be disgusted, but secretly sliding a finger down her own pants as she watched him cum.

Blake had never actually seen any girls like that on cam, but it was possible. It was always possible.

After an hour, Blake started the toughest part of the hunt. His initial burst of adrenaline was fading, and his penis slowly bowed down before the rotating marque of swollen, hairy man-flesh. He'd seen a hundred dicks now, a thousand, and not a single female in sight. At one point, he thought he'd found a victim—a smart-looking woman in her thirties. Not ideal, but it would suffice. But no, it was another one of those banner ads promising *hot singles in your area.* He thought he'd seen them all, but this was a new one, and he cursed himself for falling for it. His dick halfway out his boxers, he considered just jerking it to the pretend-woman, but that would be cheating. That wouldn't be *real.* Reluctantly, he holstered his rifle and pushed onwards. And the countdown began.

He started at forty, and each time he clicked the mouse, he counted down. *Thirty-nine, thirty-eight, thirty-seven.* If he got to zero without seeing a single woman, he would quit. He would log off, get dressed, and do something productive. That was the game he played, and the stakes were high.

Twenty-four: a dick. Twenty-three: an old guy.

Blake thought about the most perfect woman he had ever seen online.

Twenty-two: another dick. Twenty-one: a blank screen.

She had been hot as fuck.

Twenty: another dick. Nineteen: some shirtless dude.

Dark rimmed glasses and a serious face, great tits, noticeable even under her plain blouse.

Eighteen: another blank screen. Seventeen: an upside down guy?

Her face had been the perfect picture of pure disgust, her button-nose wrinkling while she shook her head in sombre, sincere disappointment.

Sixteen: a girl touching her—no, just a guy with long hair.

His perfect prey had watched the whole show from start to finish, unable to disconnect either through macabre fascination or just outright shock. Maybe she'd never been to a random web cam site before, or maybe she didn't know how to make the image go away, but it didn't matter because she made it all the way to The Main Event, and when she moved beyond shock and started to cry a little, Blake had cum so hard he thought he might pass out. He *needed* to feel that again.

Fifteen: a tiny flaccid dick.

Even if there was only the tiniest sliver of a chance that he would find that women, or someone just like her, the hunt had to continue.

He clicked on and on.

Five: a guy playing a piano. Four: a dick. Three: a blank screen.

Exhaling slowly and shaking his head in disappointment, Blake prepared himself for the end of the hunt. His time was running out, and the countdown was almost over. Just two more chances.

Two: a girl.

"Oh *shit*." Blake was glad his microphone was turned off. He didn't want the girl to hear him yet.

She wasn't looking at the screen. Perfect. Blake stroked his abs with his left hand, waiting for the girl to look up. He practiced a few different faces in the camera, oscillating between intensity and nonchalance. This was his big chance. If the bait was good, he could capture her attention, and the hunter had found his prey. He thought about typing something but decided to wait. If she caught him leaning forward, his stomach might get that little fold he hated, and she might not spot the abs. *The abs never let you down Blakey, count on the abs.*

The girl looked up. She was young, wore silver-rimmed spectacles and was Asian, perhaps Japanese. She had long, dark, straight hair and a plain face, and for some reason, she didn't seem to react to Blake's abs. Could she could see him properly? Maybe her webcam wasn't working? He had to make his move, but for some reason, he hesitated. Reaching for his dick, his hand lingered at the rim of his boxers. He might not find another girl for hours so he had to do this now, but still, he hesitated.

With a fantastically bored expression, the girl leaned forward, and Blake worried she would dismiss him, but instead, he saw the magic words appear onscreen.

User is typing…

She didn't seem to have a microphone either. It didn't matter; text chat could be just as good. She would probably ask what he was doing, or maybe she'd just say, "hi." Nervously, Blake waited, trying his best to maintain his casual demeanour as he sprawled lower on his chair.

"Empousai is arisen. Flee now, for the flesh of man temps her hunger."

Oh great, a geek. Blake rolled his eyes and put both hands on the keyboard, still unsure how he would respond. The girl was still there, but his desire to jerk it to some roleplaying nerd was completely non-existent.

"Lol. Fucking nerd. Get laid fat bitch." He typed with a grin on his face, the glare of the computer screen making him look cruel and, he decided, quite sexy. As Blake laughed to himself, he considered this girl as potential prey one last time. She was ugly, but she might be shocked when he showed her his rifle. She might even be disgusted.

Frustratingly though, she wasn't responding to his provocations. Instead, she stared back at the screen flatly, and typed without looking at the keyboard.

"This place is her menu. She hungers for what you all display. Your warning has been issued. She will suck the juices from your bones."

Yes, this was great. Blake was beside himself with glee as he typed his pitch-perfect response. He was going to blow this bitch away with his next message. "You can suck *my* bone bitc—"

CHAT ENDED.

"*No.*" Blake raged at the screen, crunching his fist into the side of the monitor as the chat disconnected. She'd quit the conversation, and less than a second later, Blake was already looking at the next dude fondling his flaccid phallus.

Blake turned off the screen, spun around in his chair and let out a long, furious moan. Why hadn't he just jerked it as soon as she came on screen? He shouldn't have typed; he should have shut that bitch up with his cock. Now, he might need to search for hours to find another girl. *Any* other girl.

He grabbed an energy drink, pulled the tab and drank the whole thing in, spun his chair around, turned the screen back on, stuck his hand down his boxers, and started all over again.

Forty.

This time, it didn't take so long for him to find a girl, but number seventeen was somehow even worse than the last target. Not a girl at all really, a woman, and she seemed to be watching television and wouldn't even look at him. After sending seven messages goading her, Blake was about to move on when she turned to him and spoke, her voice low and guttural and man-like, and Blake struggled to make out what she said.

Something about "flesh melds to your true form."

"Old fucking pervert," he wrote before clicking *Next*.

This was awful, his erection completely gone. Blake kept clicking, the count forgotten, the dream girl forgotten. He ran on instinct now, the compulsion to see the next person forcing him to continue even though the fun was long gone. Maybe, he would eventually come to *enjoy* looking at dicks? He'd seen so many; he must surely be an expert. They had lost all context; he just saw pink fleshy shapes, divorced from the bodies or the people they connected to.

"Bunch of fucking losers," he muttered as he clicked through them mindlessly.

Twice, he clicked past a seemingly familiar empty hallway, and the third time, he lingered for a moment, confused as to why he recognized it. A set of stairs led down a corridor into darkness, with two doors on either side. A thick red carpet and pale blue walls were visible in the gloom, and it slowly dawned on Blake that this corridor looked very similar to the one upstairs in his own house.

Dismissing the coincidence, Blake got to his feet, stumbled out through the door of his mancave and went past his parents' bedroom to the washroom. In the pristine white of the toilet, he whistled tunelessly as he pissed. He considered going outside. Looking out the high window, he rubbed some crusty gunk from the corner of his eye and noticed that outside it was bright and clear. The chill morning air blew through the crack in the washroom window felt good. It smelled better than his room in here. He should get some fresh air.

Flushing the toilet, Blake came to a decision.

One more hunt, then I'll go to the store for beer and jerky.

Aware of a persistent rattling from upstairs—mom must have left the dryer on—Blake stumbled back to his bedroom, rubbed his hands together and prepared for one final hunt. This would be the one. He would find a girl, any girl, and he would make her his prey.

In his room, he was confused to find the computer was back on. As he lowered himself onto his chair, the screen flickered and changed and just for a moment, he looked into some nightmare. A beautiful horror of a woman with solid black eyes and porcelain-white skin that was far too close to the camera. Long black cracks spread across the sides of the face, and she leered closer, almost as if she was coming through the screen. Instantly repulsed, Blake hammered on the *Next* button, but something was wrong with his computer, and she wouldn't go away. His stomach suddenly heaving, he curled his foot around the power cable and yanked it out of the wall, and the face was gone.

"Fucking gross," he said under his breath as he supressed his gag reflex. The energy drink must have been out of date because his stomach spasmed as he put his forehead on the cool surface of the desk and tried to breathe normally.

Behind him, the rattling grew louder and louder, and he fumbled for his Interceptor T780 Noise Cancelling Headphones to close off the noise. He started to feel better, and after a few moments more of nausea, he powered the computer on again before he knew exactly why. For some reason, his dick was rock hard in his pants again.

Wearily, grimly, he went back on the hunt.

Slowly recovering his equilibrium, Blake clicked through several more phalluses, dead-eyed shirtless boys and blank screens until he eventually came back to another webcam showing a familiar corridor. This time it looked a little like the one outside his mancave. An open door showed a washroom like the one he'd just come from. He tried to remember if he left the door open.

It couldn't be, could it? Could his mom have set up a webcam out there?

"Nah, someone is fucking with me." Blake wandered out into the corridor. Right enough, he had left the washroom door open but found no sign of a webcam. They could be really small; he'd once fitted one in the girl's lockers that had *almost* worked, but there was simply no place to hide a web cam out here.

Trying his best to ignore the rattling from upstairs, Blake went into the bathroom again. He was about to wash his face, his mouth looked weird, a thin line of white gummy mucus on his bottom lip. Wiping it away as best he could with water from the faucet, the material was weirdly sticky and resilient. What had been in that energy drink? It took several long minutes to clean his mouth before it looked normal again.

This was going to be a bad day.

His head still spinning and his stomach still sore, Blake walked into the middle of the corridor and placed a bottle of shampoo on the floor then wandered back to his bedroom and sat in front of the computer again.

The last chat session had timed out, so Blake clicked *Next,* and he saw the creature again; white face, black beads for eyes, a mouth opening to show rows upon rows of needle-like teeth.

"Fuck *off.*" He once more pulled the power cable out of the wall. "Why does nothing go right for me?"

Jumping up from his chair, he kicked the bottom of his bed, and his foot went numb. His small toe throbbed with pain, and he flopped down on his bed with an angry howl. His own voice sounded strange in his head, and he lay there holding his foot, cursing his luck.

When he finally rose, he limped over to the wall outlet, plugged the computer in once more, and flopped down hopelessly in his chair. The rattling noise of the dryer had died down in the background. At least, one thing was going right.

When Blake's screen came on again, it sounded strange. The start-up tune was muted. He fiddled with the volume slider and the speakers for a moment before examining his headphones. When he reached up to his right ear, it was gummy and blocked. The other ear was the same.

What is happening to me?

He ran to the bathroom and reeled in horror as his face exuded some sort of wax around his mouth and nose, at the corners of his eyes and out of his ears.

Scrambling through the bathroom cabinet, Blake groped for the cotton swaps and soaked them with water, then dug and poked at his ears, pulling out thick blobs of fleshy material. In a few crusty spots, the secretions melded with the flesh, and he had to pull and tug one large clump from his right ear, excising a bleeding patch of skin and hair that splattered onto the white porcelain of the sink. He was glad no one else was in the house to hear his screams.

It took him almost half an hour to clear the material from his mouth and ears and longer again to wash and clean his eyes and nose. By the time he finished, he'd amassed a huge pile of bloody and mucus encrusted tissues and swabs. Sobbing lightly, he stumbled back to his room, slammed his door behind him to shut out the rattling noises and collapsed into bed. Revulsion wracked his body in spasms as he pulled the covers over his head and sulked.

His mom had better clear up that mess because he couldn't see it all again without vomiting.

Blake lay there until the horror faded. He had a low, creeping dread, but also a persistent, resilient boner. If he could just find some girl—even just the fake girl in the ad—he could jerk off, be done with it, and go get jerky and beer.

Maybe, he should see his old friends. Maybe days like this weren't good days.

Maybe, his life wasn't going so well.

Back at his computer, waiting for him when he returned, the screen once again showed the corridor, this time with a shampoo bottle in the middle of the picture. At the end of the corridor, the door to the room—his room—was closed. If he got up now and opened that door, what would he see? Himself? Or some kind of monster?

"Someone is fucking with me." Blake couldn't make himself open that door. Shivering, he willed the noises to go away, but they came closer and closer until something scraped on the wood. Praying the thing couldn't use a door handle, Blake pushed himself backwards to his desk. To his right, something happened on the computer.

User is typing…

"Show me the Main Event Blake."

Blake wanted to scream, but no sound escaped his throat.

"Show me the meat. The hunt is at an end."

"Mom. Anyone. Help me."

A cracking voice, like broken vocal chords, echoed through the house, and the sound penetrated his flesh, catalysing a process that had already begun. He couldn't understand the words, but they sounded like an incantation, angry and solemn. Those words transfixed him, freezing him in place like a rodent that knew movement resulted in claw and tooth rending flesh from bone. Primal, the voice held him long enough. Long enough to doom him.

As the cracking voice faded and the rattling came closer, Blake struggled to move. Panic rising, his arms stuck to his body, the flesh melding together as the sticky substance oozing out of his pores cemented his body together into one long smooth shaft. Though he struggled to keep them apart, the muscles of his legs spasmed together, and they, too, sealed themselves into one.

As the rattling closed in on him, Blake's ears closed up. He tried to scream, but far too late. His lips already melded into one smooth, flat panel of flesh. His eyes were crusting over, but not enough to hide the horror of the creature that stepped smoothly through the door into his room. As he wriggled uselessly, the demoness reached for the only part of his body that was still free; the part of his body that would soon be consumed.

Slowly and effortlessly, she slid just inches away when he finally caught a glimpse of her—skin like cracked porcelain, dead black pits for eyes. His hard dick pointed up at her, and a cavernous mouth full of broken-glass teeth moved down past his chest.

The hunt was over. The feast had begun.

ROAD OF DREAMS
Abra Staffin-Wiebe

A golden castle glitters at the end of the road. Half-seen ghosts surround it, their outlines passing in and out of visibility like dust motes in a sunbeam. The doors are thrown open to welcome guests, but there is no movement inside.

In the tallest tower, Lady Felicity starves. Her waist-length black hair is a snarled mess. Her long silver gown hangs loose on her frame, revealing gauntness where once there were curves. She grips the windowsill with bone-thin fingers as she stares out at the road, which is worn down with the imprint of many feet. Although it shines with beneficial enchantment, no travelers walk along it now.

Even the ghosts avoid it.

Beside the road, tall trees beckon with flower-laden branches. Translucent fairies dart between the trees and call to each other in tinkling voices. Mice and squirrels skitter through the grass. Fairy godmothers lurk behind the trees, waiting to bless the unwary. Locusts hum contentedly. Peasants, who radiate the satisfaction of hard work completed, walk alongside the road, back to their picturesque cottages. Outside the cottage doors, hobs wait for bowls of milk like so many kittens. Among the trees, a girl with golden hair and big blue eyes inspects a hole in the ground. She takes a step forward and disappears down the rabbit hole. In the distance, another girl sings as she leans out of a window set high up on a tall stone tower and brushes out her long, long hair. A teenager sitting on a rock beside the road speaks earnestly with his cat.

A young woman appears on the road in mid-step, and a silvery peal of chimes fills the air of the tower chamber.

"A special one. A strong dreamer," Lady Felicity says.

She tries to see better and nearly falls, bracing herself against the wall until she's steady again.

194

The strong dreamer teeters in cheap high heels. Her gaze jitters as she surveys her surroundings.

"Begin the Cinderella narrative, friend version," Lady Felicity says.

Around a bend in the road, Cinderella, clad in rags, appears sitting on a boulder. The dreamer stares with wonder-widened eyes at the seamless glass slippers on her feet.

Cinderella asks, "Will you be my friend and come to the ball with me?"

A second pair of glass slippers appears beside her.

"I don't—" the dreamer stutters. "Nobody's ever asked—"

In the tower chamber, Lady Felicity holds her breath. Bundles of dried herbs hang noiselessly from the rafters. Books titled with runic symbols sit sedately on her bookshelves. Silence reigns.

Shadows move within the large silver mirror hung on the wall opposite the tower window. The shadows thicken into a woman's face. Her triple chins jiggle as she chortles. "Nice one. She's got lots of juice. Time for the test, sister."

"No, please." Lady Felicity stretches her arms out imploringly. "Dolores, *please.* Just this once, let me keep her. So few come here, and none of them stay. Sister, I'm begging you. Please."

"You have your title. If you're begging, you should use mine," Dolores says. She is still smiling, but her words have a vicious bite.

"Bosslady Dolores, please give me this one."

"You know the rules. The test decides. I will concede nothing."

Lady Felicity lets her arms drop to her sides, her shoulders sagging in defeat, but she waits for the scene to unfold with all the focus of a thirsty man stumbling toward a mirage.

The dreamer sits beside Cinderella, lets Cinderella take her hand.

A fairy godmother steps out from behind a tree.

"My turn," Bosslady Dolores says.

The fairy godmother's ballgown morphs into a business suit. The wand in her hand collapses into a microphone.

"That's enough," she says, as she strides over to the girls. She waves her hand dismissively at the dreamer. "You can go. You really aren't television material."

"What's going on?" asks the dreamer. Her hand slips out of Cinderella's.

"We're filming a reality TV show. You didn't think this was real, did you? You're not very smart, are you? Not smart and not pretty."

The wonder seeps out of the dreamer's eyes. She turns away from Cinderella, away from the golden castle, but she disappears before her foot touches the road.

Bosslady Dolores snorts. "You always had it best when our parents were alive. They loved you more, from the day we were born. Look at our names. But it's different now. This is my time."

She fades back into the shadows in the mirror.

Outside the castle, squirrels scatter to hide in their nests. The godmothers quarrel. A fairy swings too close to a branch and plummets to the ground, one wing broken. The blue-eyed blonde cries beside the rabbit hole, holding her bitten hand. The girl who was brushing her hair stops singing when her hair shrivels up and disappears. The man kicks his cat, which hisses and runs away, leaving its boots behind him. The young woman hurls her glass slippers at the mirror. Both the mirror and the slippers shatter, but the mirror shards still reflect her rags.

The world unravels at the edges until all that remains is the castle. Its edges fade to golden fog, but the center of the castle, and its lone inhabitant, stay solid.

"Why will they not believe?" she whispers.

It is night. Grimy skyscrapers reach for infinity. Pollution haze masks the light of the moon and stars. Ghosts drift through the city like unraveling smoke.

Feeble lights flicker in the buildings' windows. In one room, a man measures out scoops of white powder. When asked how pure it is, he laughs, a mirthless laugh. "Pure as snow, man, just as pure as snow."

In another room, a girl pretends ecstatic pleasure. She is so busy calculating the amount in the man's wallet that she does not notice when he draws a knife.

Across the street, there is the sound of shouting, blows, and a dull, low sobbing.

Goblins lean against the walls, puffing on cigarettes that give off hallucinogenic smoke and injecting drugs into skinny veins that leak a little black fluid. A streetlight's stuttering glow reflects off of the frenetic eyes of things hiding in the cracks of the walls, waiting to swarm. A troll chuckles greasily in the drain beside the road.

The street that lies between the buildings is disintegrating on the edges, and tar patches haphazardly fix the deep cracks crisscrossing its surface. Feces spot the street, and a dead cat is sprawled across the median. Potholes are strategically placed to trip unwary feet.

A frightened young woman walks down the street. She whirls to catch someone behind her, but the path is empty.

A lecherous whistle drifts out of the drain. A policeman stands nearby.

"Officer," she says, stepping onto the sidewalk.

The gold buttons on his uniform meld themselves into gold medallions hanging around his neck. The uniform slides into a garish polyester suit. His mouth twists into an impossibly wide leer.

"Why, hello, pretty lady," he says.

"It's only a dream," the young woman says, but the words lack strength.

An angel with fiery wings appears and beckons to her. "Come to me, and you will be safe."

The shapeshifter advances on her. "You don't believe in angels, do you? You believe in me."

With a broken sob, the young woman flees down an alley, away from him and away from the angel. Wraithlike ribbons of despair unreel behind her and are sucked into one of the rooms that overlooks the road. Bosslady Dolores unhinges her jaw and slurps down the dreamer's despair. She smacks her lips. Her room is rank with the odor of rotten meat. Cheap tabloids lie on a rickety shelf, and torn-out advertisements litter the room. The television shows a grainy black and white image of a running woman. Bosslady Dolores flicks a button on the remote in her hand, and the channel changes to show Lady Felicity staring despairingly into her mirror.

"Why will they not believe?" the image echoes.

Bosslady Dolores throws back her head and laughs, a choking, gurgling sound that echoes throughout the street.

"Oh," she tells the television screen, "they do believe. They're just too smart for your fairy tales these days."

She flips between channels. "Why, here comes another one now. Imagine how hard his life must be to make him such a strong dreamer. Do you think he'll believe in fairy tales and angels? Tell me, sister, will you waste the last of your strength on another useless, gaudy display?"

Lady Felicia collapses against the wall and slides to the floor. She rests her head on her knees.

"No," she says, her despair as thick as anything a dreamer could produce.

Bosslady Dolores laughs again, and so, she does not hear when her sister repeats, in an entirely different tone, "No, I won't."

The brown-skinned teenager is small for his age. His shoulders slump when he sees what surrounds him, but he moves into the shadows. He isn't quick enough. A pickup truck rounds the corner and pins him in the beams of its headlights. Skinheads with shaved, mushroom-white skulls jump out of the back. He runs, but he knows he can't run fast enough. He darts into an alley and realizes too late that it's a dead end.

He freezes, his heart turning to ice. A crack of light appears in the darkness. He runs toward it before he even knows what he's seeing. As he gets closer, he realizes the light outlines a door, left slightly ajar. A desperate hope fills his heart.

His hand touches the doorknob, and he disappears.

GOD IS A RABBIT
J. Robert Kane

Rebecca Foster thought: *God is a rabbit, and I'm going to die.*

The absurdity was lost on her, as it would likely have been on anyone in her condition, strapped as she was to an operating table and staring up at the face of a nightmare. She fought with all her strength against the irresistible pull of anesthetic.

A man's voice said, "She's coming out of it," and the giant, red-eyed rabbit looming over her stepped back. A human hand lowered a ventilator mask over her mouth and nose.

"No." Rebecca tried to turn her head away from the mask, but she may as well have moved a small building. The cold spark of fear in her stomach blossomed into a panicked conflagration of terror. *I'm going to die...*

The mask pressed down against her chin and cheeks. She breathed sweet air, and consciousness fled her.

Six weeks passed while Rebecca recovered from surgery, time enough for an unseasonably warm November to give way, by degree, to a cold and crisp December. A light dusting of snow blanketed the University as the doctoral candidate walked toward the Martel Sciences Building. She had no recollection whatsoever of the terrifying hallucination she'd experienced while under anesthesia.

Built into the eastern slope of a rolling grass hill, Martel overlooked the University's athletic fields and quarter-mile track. Rebecca used the east entrance, which, due to the slope of the hill, deposited her on the second floor. She stepped through the vestibule and smiled at the floor's receptionist. After a moment of obligatory chatter, she walked to her laboratory.

She paused. An image flashed, but left a terrifying residue as she scoured her memory.

No use. It vanished.

Unsettled but no less anxious to get on with her research, she entered her mentor's laboratory.

The familiar smells of bedding, fur, and feces greeted her as the fluorescent lights illuminated a wall lined entirely with three-by-three steel cages stacked four high. Within each, a rabbit. Most were New Zealand Whites, though a few other varieties were represented as well. Many had been operated upon already; some had wire harnesses protruding from their skulls.

Cages of rats lined the perpendicular wall. A half-dozen computer monitors and an ungainly looking interface the lab crew had dubbed Frankenstein, or Frankie, occupied the wall opposite that.

Rebecca walked toward the wall of caged rabbits. .

An inexplicable dread manifested itself in her breast. The urge to turn and flee the laboratory overwhelming. She resisted. Ignoring the caged rabbits, she doffed her winter jacket and logged onto the computer.

Checking her university email from home had been about the one thing Rebecca did while recovering, and so she dealt with the two or three messages in a matter of minutes and immersed herself in the oceans of information Frankie had collected overnight.

While decoding what promised to be an interesting anomaly in the data another presence filled the room. She hadn't heard anyone come in, but Doctor Fleming was nothing, if not quiet.

"Good Morning, Doctor Fleming," She finished scratching an equation onto the back of a legal pad and turned to greet her mentor. "It's so good…"

The lab lay empty.

"Doctor Fleming?" An icy finger traced a line between Rebecca's shoulder-blades leaving goosebumps in its wake. For a moment, she stood, unable to reconcile her feelings with reality.

Finally, she turned back to the computer terminal and the mess of an interface she and her doctoral mentor engineered and constructed; a beautiful chaos.

"Sorry, Frankie. I guess I'm losing my mind." She returned to her equations.

"Cause of death, blunt-force trauma," man's voice says. "Wrongful death."

Rebecca lays upon a surgical table unable to move, though she's not bound. The cold touch of the surgical steel table pressed against her back and buttocks, the backs of her legs and calves. She must be nude.

But I'm not dead

Panic takes her. Frantic gulps of air fragrant with fur and feces do little to sate her need for oxygen.

I'm not dead.

She screams, but her mouth refuses to cooperate. The sound reverberates through her mind adding to the dissonance already there.

"Multiple lacerations made by…well hell, I can't even say. A small hatchet swung laterally, perhaps?"

From the way the man talks, he's speaking for the record. If television has taught her anything, he probably has a handheld digital recording device. Likely a sleek, silver one, the sort rich folks order from catalogs with exotic-sounding names.

Horror explodes inside her with irresistible force. Because fur is on the hand—paw?— that's manipulating her limb. Not hair but fur.

She sees them, all at once. Three grotesque human-sized rabbits. They loom over her, their red eyes blazing with malignant fire. The incessant twitching of their noses and cheeks, a characteristic that seems so cute on the normal-sized variety, is hideous at this scale.

It's hard to breathe, paralyzed as she is by terror. One of the ungodly monsters makes a short series of chuffing sounds, and another disappears from view. It returns in her periphery, walking upright with a tray of hideous-looking silver instruments. She recognizes the array of tools, thanks to Law *and* Order: *the implements of an autopsy.*

Rebecca sweats, in spite of the cold table and the cool temperature of the room. She watches with a terrible mix of fear and fascination as one of the rabbits deftly selects a pair of oversized shears. It places a paw—hand?—upon her stomach and feels upward until it reaches her solar-plexus. The touch of fur disappears, only to be replaced by the icy-steel tip of the shears.

She screams.

Rebecca screamed herself out of an uneasy sleep. She sat up in bed and clung to incoherent scraps of the barely-remembered dream until they, too, dissipated into nothingness. By the time she left for the laboratory two hours later, even the nothingness had fled.

"Becca." Smuri Kapoor, her fellow doctoral student, hugged her. "It's so nice to *see* you. You look so good."

"Thanks, Smuri." Rebecca returned her friend's smile. "And thanks for coming to visit, and for the packages. I can't tell you how much I appreciate it."

After another few minutes of personal and office gossip, it was back to business. "You aren't going to believe the results we've been recording,"

"I've seen them. I found a similar anomaly yesterday. I made a record of it…"

Smuri tucked an errant strand of jet-black hair behind her ear. "Yes, I saw it. It's quite remarkable, isn't it?"

Rebecca hoped her colleague wasn't letting her natural enthusiasm get the better of her. It was uncanny, how quickly Frankie had enabled the team to identify and mark nerve-receptors. Rebecca's gut counseled caution. "If we're getting accurate measurements, then yes, it is."

Mentally, she braced herself. This was the part where her friend would normally accuse her of being overly-cautious, or even a downer. To her surprise, Smuri let the comment slide.

"Feel like doing me a favor, Becca?" The young woman pulled a granola bar from a desk drawer. She offered one to Rebecca, who declined with a shake of her head. "Doctor Fleming wants me to practice my incisions. He told me to use Big Barney."

"Really?" Rebecca narrowed her eyes. "Barney?"

Smuri nodded.

Something like regret stabbed Rebecca. She'd grown close to the ridiculous creature affectionately known as Big Barney. Nearly three times as large as the average lab rabbit, Big Barney had never been under the knife. He served as an antibody host, and his lot in life consisted of periodically having blood drawn. All in all, a pretty plush gig for a lab animal. Well, his cruise down easy street was about to hit its first bump. "Sure, of course."

Half an hour later, they were scrubbed in and ready to administer anesthesia. The enormous rabbit sat, a furry dumb blob on the surgical table, blissfully unaware that it was about to be opened stem to stern.

Smuri, her little face half-covered by a surgical mask, narrowed her eyes. "How much do we administer, do you think?"

Rebecca frowned. That was a good question. Big Barney was three times the size of the rabbits they normally worked on, but that didn't mean a triple dose of anesthetic wouldn't prove lethal to the overweight animal. "Let's see what it takes to put him under, and we'll judge from there."

"Right."

It took a good deal more than twice the normal dosage to put the creature out.

Smuri checked the animal's blink reflex then pinched the flesh between its toes with a pair of forceps. "He's under."

"Okay." Rebecca ran a few quick calculations in her head. "Let's give him another quarter-dose."

The other woman's surgical mask wrinkled to accommodate a grimace. "Are you sure? We're close to three full doses; we don't want to kill him."

Rebecca considered the admonition. Her friend had a point; maybe it would be best to err on the side of caution and administer more of the drug cocktail if needed. "Okay. Maybe you're right. He's out, let's start."

Securing Big Barney into the surgical restraints and shaving his stomach took less than two minutes. Smuri poised to make her first cut, lowering the point of her scalpel onto the line she'd drawn on the creature's abdomen. The instrument dimpled and pierced the animal's iodine-yellowed skin, drawing blood.

Big Barney's eyes flew open, and the rabbit screamed in excruciating pain and terror. The animal arched its back and thrust itself upward against his restraints.

An icy spear of alarm pierced Rebecca's abdomen, freezing the breath in her lungs. The tray of surgical tools she'd been holding clattered to the floor.

Still, the terrified rabbit shrieked.

What have we done.

Smuri, normally dark-skinned, turned ashen, and beads of perspiration dotted her hairline and upper lip. What worried Rebecca the most, though, was the look in her friend's eyes, like she had gone someplace else for a time.

The rabbit raged against its restraints. Rebecca wouldn't have thought Big Barney capable of such a display of strength under the best of conditions, let alone after having been administered a sizable dose of anesthetic.

The rabbit wasn't going to stop unless she did something to stop it. With shaking hands, she filled a syringe and plunged the needle into the flailing animal's stomach. The animal fell silent and collapsed, finally, back onto the table.

Rebecca's knees buckled; she braced herself on the operating table. "Smuri? You okay?"

The other woman nodded. She was visibly shaking, but then, so was Rebecca.

"Hey, Smuri? It's okay." Rebecca stepped toward her friend and took her hand. "Come on, let's get you down to the health center. Just have a seat here for a second and let me check on Barney."

She helped Smuri into the chair and went back to the surgical table.

Big Barney was dead.

Once the initial shock of the botched operation passed, Rebecca and Smuri sought out their mentor, Doctor Fleming, who was more concerned than upset by the news. When Smuri suggested that she wasn't cut out for this field of research, Fleming insisted she wait twenty-four hours before making so important a decision.

The walk back to the Martel Sciences Building was a quiet one. Almost impossible not to keep replaying the horrifying events of the afternoon's operation. It was the sound that affected her most. A piercing shriek, the rabbit's cry was not unlike the scream of a human baby. Rebecca shuddered each time her mind replayed it.

Still crying, Smuri no longer sobbed. No doubt the macabre soundtrack haunted her as well. Rebecca wanted desperately to say something, to beg her friend and partner to reconsider. She wanted to assure the young woman that what they'd experienced had been a freak occurrence, that they had no reason to expect that anything remotely close to that would ever happen again. Each time she started to choose her words, though, the rabbit in her mind screamed again, and all thought scattered.

When they got back to the laboratory, the two young women silently closed up shop. Doctor Fleming suggested they take the rest of the day off, and neither objected.

"Goodnight, Becca." Smuri offered her friend a pathetic smile. "It was really good to see you."

Tears welled in Rebecca's eyes. Her friend was saying goodbye. "Whatever you want to do, I'll support you, Smuri. But please, think it over okay? For me?"

Smuri nodded because, well, what else could she have done? Rebecca saw the truth in her friend's eyes, though. She hugged the smaller woman.

That night Rebecca dreamt of rabbits screaming.

The next morning Rebecca was disappointed, but not at all surprised, to find Smuri wasn't at the lab.

She hung up her coat and started a pot of coffee. Usually, the one cup she had on the ride to the University was more than enough for her. Today though, she needed the boost. She hadn't slept well the previous night. On top of that, she'd had nightmares. She couldn't recall what they'd been about, but she had to assume that screaming rabbits were involved in some way.

For the next hour, Rebecca sipped coffee and poured over print-outs of Frankie's observations for the previous twelve hours. She'd located several potentially interesting anomalies and was about to start untangling the first when it started.

Most people's experience with rabbits thumping begins and ends with Bambi's pal, the aptly named Thumper. Of course, that movie, like most, is misleading. In reality, a threatened rabbit will thump with enough force to make a clap-banging noise, even through a thick carpet. The sound of a single thump on the bottom of a steel cage reverberated like a gunshot through the lab.

Rebecca jumped in her seat. Fortunately, she'd been handling a clipboard and not her coffee, as it clattered to the floor. She turned.

The rabbits looked at her—all of them.

It wouldn't have been so unusual had she just entered the lab and turned on the lights. For a brief instant each morning, all the animals in the lab would turn to see who'd disturbed their environment. Never, though, had they looked at her so...*intently*, or for so long.

Bang.

Rebecca started, transfixed at the colony of rabbits. Nearly one hundred large, black pupils stared right back. *Bang. Bang.*

A second rabbit took the cue; it thumped his back legs against the floor of his cage. Even anticipating the sound as Rebecca had, the loudness of it came as a surprise. A third joined the clamoring cacophony, and soon, the terrible staccato banging filled her lab.

Rebecca shook. The noise overwhelmed her; the sound of a dozen hammers striking loosely fitted steel shelving.

Still, taking her eyes from the rabbits was impossible. They fixated on her, the effect beyond terrifying. Even without the noise, it would have been creepy. Nearly all the rabbits were thumping now. A terrible vision of the wall of cages collapsing, of nearly one hundred rabbits running at her, their red eyes glowing.

Red eyes? Their eyes are pink. What made me think red?

One of the hares shrieked, as had Big Barney. Panic overwhelmed caution then, and Rebecca ran for the exit. Once outside the lab, she paused to catch her breath. Through the heavy wooden door came the clamor of thumping rabbits.

Rebecca stretched out on her sofa, watching television and feeling bad about the fact that she'd fled the lab when the phone rang. What in the world could she have been thinking, letting a little scare keep her from her work?

She put the phone to her ear. "Hello?"

"Miss Foster, will you hold for Doctor Simon?"

She agreed.

"Rebecca? Doctor Simon. Listen, I'm afraid we've got some bad news..."

The doctor told her that he would see her in the morning and not to worry. He hung up. For a time, Rebecca stood holding the phone, regarding it as one might an alien artifact that had appeared out of thin air. When the open line buzzed, she put the phone back on its charger.

Could she have misheard? Did she just hear what she thought she did? A trapdoor opened in the pit of Rebecca's stomach, and her heart fell into it.

There was no denying what the doc had said.

Relapse. She'd heard the word as plain as day.

Cold dread filled her. Only hours ago, she might have been frightened by something as seemingly insignificant as excited rabbits.

She picked up the phone, dialed Doctor Simon.

That night, she dreamed once again of the hideous humanoid rabbits.

She woke thinking about lab animals, specifically about their bedding. She didn't recall the details. Nonetheless, dread of her scheduled operation nearly paralyzed her. She considered calling Smuri.

Too early, an inconsiderate time to wake her friend. On the other hand, Rebecca was unsure she could get to the hospital on her own. Every fiber of her being raged against going back under the knife.

After a few moments, she snatched up the phone and dialed Smuri. The line went to voicemail, and Rebecca hung up.

Three hours later, Rebecca lay strapped to a surgical table, her heart racing. It had taken incredible will-power to bring herself this far.

If only she'd been a bit weaker.

Because, now, she remembered everything. The horrific, human-sized rabbits who had directed her last operation. Their restless and grotesque, ever-moving cheeks.

She'd walked into their trap.

"Calm down," said an overweight man in surgical scrubs, smiling behind a mask. "We've done thousands of these."

Rebecca offered a feeble, medicated nod.

"Okay, let's get you nice and relaxed." The man reached behind Rebecca's head, beyond her field of view. When it returned, it held a transparent, vaguely triangular respirator mask. "My name is Doctor Asher, but everybody calls me Big Barney."

An icy hand seized Rebecca's insides and gave a sharp squeeze. Certainly, she hadn't heard right. She tensed, ready to resist the mask.

The sharp prick of a needle piercing her arm was followed by warmth. Rebecca threw her head to the side and another masked and scrubbed figure injected her once more while Big Barney—no, she must have misheard that—continued talking.

Helpless, the mask came down over her mouth and nose. With every scrap of strength and will left inside of her, she resisted, bucking against the table; she moved her head violently from left to right. Each movement drained her. Freedom proved impossible.

An intense pressure on her lower leg. She lifted her head, but the furred hand held the mask tightly to her face. Again, tremendous pressure poked her thigh. Discomfort prodded the boundaries of anesthetized consciousness.

As she submitted to the irresistible force the horror inside of her subsided. In its place, acquiescence to the inevitable.

God is a rabbit, and I'm going to die.

DOGS
C.S. Fuqua

The old man wasn't two hours in the ground, but Clark already had the U-Haul loaded and ready to drive away for the last time from property that should've been his, would've been his had it not been for Robbie Hathaway.

Emma'd left a half-hour earlier on the four-hour drive home, but Clark lingered for one last check, one final look. The house he'd spent his childhood in sat a hundred feet back from the two-lane country blacktop. A sagging, dilapidated commercial chicken house scarred the property near the north end of the main house, a good hundred yards long, thirty yards wide. The first dog he'd loved had been sacrificed for that structure. So had his childhood, spent working in there every day, doing what the old man told him, catching and caging chickens every few months to load aboard the waiting truck that took them to slaughter. He'd come to hate chickens, damn things pecking, scratching, shrieking, invading his dreams between company pickups.

"Shut your bellyaching," the old man'd warned him. "They put food on the table."

Too bad it was never chicken.

Clark gave one last glance around and started for the U-Haul.

And stopped.

A whimper?

Strange, uncertain, weak.

The breeze whispered through the piney woods behind the rusty barbed-wire fence that ran the back line. Clark did a slow three-sixty.

Stress. Just the wind. A few more minutes, I'll be out of here, and old Hathaway can shove the place up his fat, arsonist's ass, for all Clark cared, but the underhanded way Hathaway had taken the property from the old man burned.

After Clark left home, responsibility for communicating had been the boy's until Clark finally stopped calling years ago. In all the time that followed, the stoic asshole known as his father had never attempted to contact Clark, keeping everything to himself—defaulted taxes, warnings, eventualities—apparently happy to let the land go to someone, anyone other than his own flesh and blood. Clark didn't know until Hathaway called and told him the old man, already three months into a cancer diagnosis, would have to move.

"You stole the property for back taxes, and now, you're kicking him out...?"

"Now wait a minute..." Hathaway balked.

"No, you wait. You want to push this, then push it. I'll have your sorry ass in court faster than you can strike a match. I'll dig up every piece of dirt on you I can—especially your penchant for fire. I won't win, but I'll drag your ass through so much shit, it won't matter."

The phone shifted on Hathaway's end, and Clark could nearly feel the heat of the man's anger over the line.

Once upon a time, the Hathaway brothers had operated two small, rural grocery stores. When the first went up in flames, insurance investigators could prove no wrongdoing, resulting in a big payout. The second business burned years later, again cause undetermined, and that insurance settlement made the brothers two of the county's wealthiest residents.

"We don't want to bring up old rumors..."

"That's right, we don't, and we won't," Clark said, "as long you let the old man stay for a reasonable rent. He doesn't have long. When he's gone, I'll clear out the house, and you can burn it to the ground for all I care."

Hathaway hemmed and hawed halfheartedly, but agreed. That had been ten months earlier, ten months that Clark spent driving the four hours from home twice weekly to take care of the old man on the nurse's days off until hospice finally kicked in.

A cry.

Clark twisted around, certain this time he'd heard something under the hiss of pine needles in the breeze. He moved toward the far end of the chicken house, muscles tightening with irritation that he might be here longer than he wanted, but he couldn't ignore the possible. His broke into a trot along the front of the chicken house to the end where he drew up to catch his breath and listen.

The breeze died.

A sob—angry, determined.

Clark pressed into the weeds and bushes at the end of the house, kicking and stomping a path through to the back, thin branches slicing at his arms. He broke into a clearing that ran the fence line behind the chicken house. Some twenty yards down, he saw the kid.

The boy, wide-eyed and filthy, couldn't have been more than eight or nine, wearing a tattered T-shirt and threadbare cutoffs too short for his long, thin legs. The kid's bare heels dug trenches in the soft earth as he tried to push backward. He yanked at the ties that bound his wrists to the fence, thin rivulets of blood snaking down his forearms from where the bindings had cut and barbed wire punctured.

Clark swooned, fear taunting memories just out of reach.

"It's okay." Clark reached a calming hand forward. "Let me help." He took slow calculated steps toward the boy, crouching lower with each, diminishing himself, making his stance less intimidating. "It's okay." Clark reached the boy, hands going gingerly to the rope to work open the knots. The rope fell away, and the boy scrambled backward, the trepidation on his face barely softened by gratitude.

Clark examined the fence where the boy's hands had been tied, the deep crimson of fresh blood on the rusty barbs.

"Who the hell did this to you?" Clark whispered.

The boy said nothing, but his body relaxed somewhat even as he remained alert, ready to flee. Clark glanced around but saw no houses through the thick growth beyond the fence. He turned to the boy.

"Where do you live?"

The boy stared through red-rimmed eyes, glazed and weary, set in a drawn, powdery, dirt-smudged face. His parted lips formed no answer, but he dipped his head slightly toward the chicken house.

Runaway?

Clark had heard of squatters, especially since the economic downturn, and that old chicken house would've been a good location, especially with the old man out of the way for these last few months. Clark hadn't entered a chicken house since age seventeen, the last week before he told the old man to go to hell and left home for good. It took years of hard work and night study, but Clark had earned an accounting degree and settled into a comfortable job that enabled him to honor the promise he'd made to himself, that he would never live like the old man or step foot in a chicken house again.

But this boy—had he indeed holed up in that rickety old structure?

"Where're your mom and dad? Did they tie...?

The boy looked away.

The breeze rustled again, blessed relief in the late afternoon heat. Clark had wanted to be well away from here by nightfall. But...shit.

He stood abruptly.

The boy scrambled back.

Clark immediately dropped back into a squat.

"It's okay. I'm not going to hurt you." He nodded toward the chicken house. "I was just going check inside."

Clark stood more slowly this time and offered his hand to the boy. "Show me…?"

The boy's eyes hardened with resolve. He stood and reached a grimy hand tentatively out to Clark. Clark took his hand gently and noted the dryness of skin, its relative coolness as the boy led him down the property line to the chicken house entrance facing the old man's home.

Clark's grasp slipped from the boy's as he stood before the double-door entrance to the chicken house, the left door slightly ajar toward him. His throat tightened, and his hands betrayed the slightest tremble.

That day when he was seven, when the old man started building this chicken house—it had been put away with so many other days, forced into the depths of forgotten pain and fear. But now, it rammed into consciousness with thunderous force, and he could feel the corner post crashing down, crushing the bird dog, Jake, who'd been lying near the old man as he tried to anchor the post in the ground. It didn't kill Jake immediately, and the old man cussed and swore at the animal, refusing to waste a bullet on it. He'd left the dog lying there, gurgling in its own blood and bile as he continued to work, until, finally, fitfully, the animal aspirated enough to drown.

Jake had been the first. Other dogs followed, but Clark hammered the memories down, forcing himself to focus on this boy, the goddamn door, and whatever awaited inside. Yet, he hesitated. Even after three decades, he still recalled with pungent clarity the stench, the stifling heat, the deafening cackles—no one could forget that. He drew a deep breath, steeled himself, reached for the handles, and pulled open the doors.

The expansive interior that had seemed infinite to Clark as a young boy— the sawdust-covered dirt floor, the immense square heaters hanging from the thirty-foot high ceiling along the center and side boundaries, tubular metal feeders suspended every six or so yards along each side—all that space and its contents now appeared so much smaller. Crackling dry sawdust and wood shavings still covered much of the dirt floor, but litter of all types—tin cans, paper boxes, even partial rolls of toilet paper—had been strewn throughout the house, as though the old man had used it as his private trash dump, which wouldn't have surprised Clark in the least.

Clark looked around slowly, taking in the high, shallow windows that ran the sides, most nailed over, but a few open, allowing in hints of the breeze to stir dust. Faded green paint peeled and flaked from the interior walls to reveal gray, spongy wood beneath. The ceiling sagged on rotting beams and support posts as the massive structure groaned and creaked under the breeze that pressed against its exterior. The stench Clark had expected had been replaced by something more subtle, and, in its own way, worse—a hint of rotting flesh that seeped into awareness like slow-growth cancer.

Why would the old man allow it to fall into such disrepair? Clark shrugged. Stupid question. The bastard had let everything go to hell.

Clark shifted dumbly to one side of the doorway as the boy pressed past and stopped about halfway to the first heater. Clark moved up beside him. The stench hit hard here.

Six five-foot square, two-foot tall pyramidal heaters hung down the center between him and the opposite end of the house. Most languished to one or another side, all rusty, secured at the corners and suspended from the ceiling by nylon ropes that revealed considerable fraying—none of which registered in Clark's mind. What he saw were the carcasses of dogs, necks strapped and secured to the heaters. Clark grimaced in disgust, but he couldn't tear his gaze from the scene. He took a few steps toward the first heater, the first dog, and stopped. He looked around at the boy.

"You've been living in here? Where's your family?"

The boy only stared at the first dog a couple of feet beyond Clark.

Clark waited a moment, then continued hesitantly, his feet absently kicking aside debris, agitating the dirt into a low-lying dust cloud. He briefly massaged his left wrist, the old scar itching as he knelt beside the first dog's leathery carcass. The animal's hide had rotted from the bones, but enough remained to hold the skeleton together, the face having deteriorated into a snarl of postmortem rage and anguish. At least the rancid odor wasn't so bad here, but he suspected it would grow stronger as he approached the others. His gaze ran over the remains, the discoloration of hide stretched thin across ribs, dark areas denoting spots in the coat. His breath caught.

Jake?

A rush of dizziness forced Clark's eyes to close until the sensation subsided.

Impossible.

The boy stood between him and the entrance, still staring ahead, still blank-faced. Refusing to accept what the carcass suggested, Clark moved with reluctance for the next heater, the next dog. Its decay, while progressed, wasn't quite as advanced as the first dog's, and a more pungent odor of rot emanated from the corpse as maggots churned the remaining flesh of its mouth. Flies buzzed around its head and settled on the carcass's collar—familiar, wide, black, with stainless pointed nubs lining the sides.

Bucky's...

Bucky, the mixed breed mutt who'd died under the feet of a horse trying to rear free from the old man's raging whip when Clark was seven, had been buried in a spot the old man had never revealed to the boy.

Here?

Clark moved carefully onward, eyes shifting reluctantly to the next carcass, his mind racing. He could not comprehend, could not reconcile reality with what he now confronted. A faint odor of smoke seeped up from the fur that still clung to the next cadaver, another mixed breed mutt the size of a goat with a small, circular hole in its skull just above the right eye.

As a kid, Clark had grown used to being called white trash because his family didn't have money for decent clothes, for movies, for books, for even the simplest luxuries like air freshener. Instead of freshener, the old man kept a box of matches on the back of the toilet to clear the air. For a boy of five, those matches represented a world of possibility and exploration, especially when lighted underneath a roll of toilet paper that quickly burst into flames, sending him running from the bathroom, screaming. Hearing the boy, Bucky had begun to bark and scratch worriedly at the back door.

The old man pushed the boy aside as thin smoke drifted out of the bathroom. He extinguished the fire easily, smothering it with a towel, and returned to the bathroom doorway. He reached for the buckle of his belt.

The dog pawed wildly at the back door, its barking frenzied.

Clark spun and fled to the porch.

"You wait your ass right there," the old man bellowed.

By the time he pushed open the screen door leading onto the porch, the old man had doubled his belt around his hand, the buckle dangling at the end, ready to teach, to scar, but that damn cur placed itself between him and the boy, snarling and threatening. The old man backed into the house only to reappear moments later, pistol in hand. One shot, and the dog's head caved. The old had man pointed the gun at the boy.

"Another stupid act like that, and you'll never do anything again."

A yip.

Clark snatched around.

Another whimpering yip from the far end. The last heater wobbled on its ropes as the animal strapped to it wriggled weakly against the binding, tightening the noose even more.

Oh Jesus, no...

Clark went for the dog, sawdust crackling underfoot, pace quickening as he passed the last two heaters between him and the surviving animal, each of the remaining two carcasses less decayed than the ones before, each a vague image of a dog killed during his childhood, directly or indirectly at the old man's hands.

A knot tightened in Clark's gut as he reached the last heater, the final animal. The dog was slightly larger than the rest, a German Shepherd mix in pathetic condition, its coat matted, blood-caked, reeking. The air felt thick and stifling, and Clark had to fight from passing out.

"Fritz…" he whispered. How…?

He collapsed to his knees, the words can't be forming on his lips. He fumbled a pocketknife out of his jeans, dropped it, retrieved it, and opened the blade with quaking fingers. The dog whimpered again and shook its head weakly as Clark set the blade to the rope.

Fritz had been the last dog of his childhood, the last before his mother left for good, never looking back or making contact again. Her decision had come the night she and the old man sat on the front steps. Clark had stationed himself secretly inside the doorway out of the old man's sight. Fritz sat on the ground at the bottom step, facing the two adults, eyes alert between them. The old man had been drinking again, and he draped his arm around Clark's mother. The dog bristled, and the boy's heart raced. His mother shrugged off the old man's caress, and the old man drew back to smack her.

Fritz snarled.

The old man's temper exploded. He lunged from the stairs to slam Fritz with both hands. The dog flailed over on its side, hitting the ground hard enough to knock him breathless. The old man was on him instantly, pinning him with a knee across the neck. His arms churned, fists pounding the dog's gut and chest until it ceased all struggle.

The old man fell back, winded and sweating as Fritz lay in a spreading puddle of vomit and blood, gasping small breaths.

Only then did the boy realize his mother had been screaming all along. Clark's father teetered onto unsteady legs and turned on the woman. She backed into the house and fled to the bedroom. She grabbed as many clothes as she could, stuffing them frantically into a pillowcase, but the old man appeared in the doorway before she could escape. He dove across the bed for her. She dodged to one side and slipped past.

The old man rolled off the bed and swayed toward the door. "You ever come back," he shouted after her, "I'll put you in the goddamn ground."

Clark cowered in the corner of the room, hidden behind a chair, until the old man passed out, snoring on the bed. Clark eased out of the house and down the steps to the dog, chest hitching as he knelt beside the animal. Tiny bubbles formed and popped in the blood around Fritz's mouth. Clark curled up beside the dog, laying his arm across Fritz's chest, sobbing until exhaustion quieted his cries and he slipped into sleep. When he woke in the twilight of dawn, the dog and the old man were gone.

Now—in this chicken house—Fritz was apparently back.

And the old man's gone for good.

Clark supported the animal's head gingerly as he cut the rope from around its neck. He closed and slipped the knife into his pocket. The dog whimpered and floundered as Clark lifted him into his arms and started out. The boy had vanished. Clark quickened his pace and exited the building, eyes searching the yard, but there was no one. He took the dog to the truck and placed him gently on the passenger side floorboard. Fritz closed his eyes, his breathing shallow and rapid, but easing as Clark closed the door.

Look for the boy.

"*Kid.* Where are you?"

But Fritz...

The dog—yes, he understood, logically it could not be Fritz, nor could the other dogs tied to the heaters be those they appeared to be from his past.

But they are.

Clark jogged to the opposite end of the chicken house and pushed again through the undergrowth to the backside. The boy wasn't there. He returned to the yard, checked once more inside the chicken house.

Damn it.

"*Kid.* I'll be back. I promise. Don't leave."

Clark ran to the U-Haul, pulled open the driver's door, and climbed into the seat. The engine caught, he dropped the shift into drive, and the U-Haul lurched forward. As he pulled to the end of the driveway, he glanced into the exterior passenger side mirror—and saw the boy standing at the chicken house entrance, holding in one hand a partial roll of toilet paper from the garbage inside, in the other a lighted match.

Clark rammed the shift into park, pushed open the door, and dropped to the ground. He ran to the rear of the U-Haul as the boy tossed the now burning roll of paper into the chicken house.

Fire raced across the sawdust, igniting debris and rotting timber. Flames puffed through the gaps in the walls, windows, and roof, spreading rapidly down the building's length in a matter of seconds. The doorway belched smoke and flames.

The boy smiled at Clark.

A heartbeat.

He stepped inside.

"*No.*"

Clark rushed to the doorway and tried to enter, but the heat's intensity was too much. He tried again, but had to back away, flames scorching the division between memory and consciousness, the past piercing the barrier that had taken decades to erect.

He sank to his knees and raised his wrists as though he'd never before seen them.

The scars...

For the first time in decades, he remembered. He remembered everything.

His hands floated to his sides, and he saw the boy through the smoke, standing near the first heater. Fire leapt and danced. Two of the heater's suspension ropes popped, and the heater swung awkwardly to one side.

The boy raised his arms outward.

His body erupted in flames and vanished in an explosion of sparks.

The growing inferno forced Clark to his feet and back. The blaze flickered through the ceiling toward the sky as he retreated to the truck.

He grabbed the truck's door handle and paused to look back in reverence for the inexplicable.

How will Hathaway explain—

"What the hell...?"

The fire was gone. The building stood intact, unharmed.

Shaken, confused even more than before, Clark drifted to the chicken house's entrance. He stared into the dim interior—the dilapidated heaters, the garbage, dirt, sawdust.

Hallucination?

The thought struck hard. "No."

Fritz.

He spun toward the truck, dread of the inevitable hammering in his chest. He hauled himself into the driver's seat, and his breath caught.

Fritz shifted on the passenger side floorboard, his movement stronger, steadier, and glanced up at the man. Clark let his breath go in a relieved sigh as Fritz rested his head on his forelegs and closed his eyes. Clark reached over to scratch the animal between the ears.

Not a dream. Not a dream.

A hint of smoke hung on the air as Clark straightened and dropped the shift into drive. He glanced into the side view mirror at the building, gave his head a slight shake of wonder, and let it go for the last time.

He pulled onto the highway, heading home.

ALMOST ABOVE THE TANNERY
Mattea Orr

There are two kinds of secrets—those that belong to you, and those that don't. It's a lot easier to live with the kind that's out of your hands, turn a blind-eye, a deaf ear, just walk away. But those that belong to you aren't so easy to ignore. They find you at the oddest moments—taking a piss, brushing your teeth, waiting to fall asleep. And every time they come back, they dig a little deeper, hold on a little harder, and make you into yourself.

I'd spent the night at Avery Dogan's for his fifteenth birthday, and his mother woke us up far too early for a Saturday morning. My mouth still tasted like the whiskey we'd stolen from his father's milk barn the night before. As I tried to work up some spit to wash it away, my father's voice downstairs mumbled his terse syllables. My stomach dropped, and I dragged my mind over what I remembered of the last twenty-four hours, but I couldn't think of anything I'd done to warrant this ambush. Downstairs, Dad simply handed me my shoes and left it at that until we were on the road.

"Your Uncle Jack's killed himself, and Aunt Carmen's a mess."

My stomach tightened, and my legs felt a mile away. Uncle Jack was a restless man who was always doing something—trying to talk you into playing some stupid game, fixing furniture, or conjuring up wild plans for the future. Sure, he drank too much. Dad got called out there at least once a week to settle the latest dispute over Aunt Carmen's dubious honor or Uncle Jack's failed ambitions, but no one ever took it seriously. The morning after, Uncle Jack would get busy putting the house back together, and everyone else would smile around their bruises until the whole mess was forgotten.

Now, Aunt Carmen I could almost believe. Her house was always clean, no mean trick in a rattley shack only about fifty yards uphill from the tannery where my Uncle Jack worked, but *she*, she was always a mess.

One day when I was about ten, I tried to sneak a few more cookies from the pantry, and I overheard my mom and Aunt Sally talking in the kitchen. I put down my cookies and stood still to listen because they were talking about Aunt Carmen, which usually meant some interesting piece of news I wasn't supposed to hear. That was the day I learned that Carmen hadn't been more than fifteen when she met Uncle Jack.

He was recently divorced and had come over to my parents' to mope around while my mother fed him some lunch. Taking his whiskey to the window, he'd spied a woman walking by. Her hair was dyed two shades too dark, and her makeup was so heavy that they couldn't tell exactly how young she really was at first. Unbelievably, she wore a fake leopard coat on a July afternoon in small town New York, 1950. My parents had jokingly suggested that this passing gypsy girl was just the kind of woman for Uncle Jack, who promptly went out into the street and brought her up for lunch. She didn't take her coat off, and she giggled most of the afternoon. Once my mother realized how young Carmen was, she tried to quickly usher the girl out, but Uncle Jack would have none of it. Four months later, they were married. I can't shake the vision of Aunt Carmen at the altar in a white dress and matted leopard-print coat.

I didn't understand what my mother meant by gypsy because I'd always heard that Aunt Carmen was German. When I asked my older brother Larry about it later, he showed me the right country in our atlas. Hungary. Well, up to that point, I'd really only seen Aunt Carmen with a swollen belly, so it made sense. I was older before I realized the difference. That day, though, my mother had lowered her voice ever further, and I'd had to creep closer to the kitchen door to hear.

"She just always was the type who'd tell a lie even when the truth would be best."

As we pulled into Uncle Jack's driveway that awful morning, my cousin, Stevie, sat on the front steps facing the tannery's backyard. He held a book, which wasn't surprising, though he was actually reading it. Something Uncle Jack would usually have ribbed him about.

The sharp, sour odor of rot from the tannery hit me, and there wasn't room for quiet thought until my nose and brain adjusted. Ron, my oldest brother, came out the back door of the beat-up old house. He leaned in the driver's side window, his scalp pink through his thinning hair and his glasses slipping off as they did when he graded papers.

"Dad, Sheriff Davis wants to talk to you about the investigation."

My father stopped lighting his cigarette. "Investigation? Jack killed himself."

The tone in my father's voice erased the sweetly sick smell of old eggs and chemicals from the tannery, it also drove Ron's head away from the car a few inches. Dad's gaze flickered over to me then to Stevie on the steps. My own followed and identical path to where he sat, no longer reading *Of Mice and Men*; instead, he faced down the hill where the tannery's open shed held the remnants of Uncle Jack's last frenzy. The broken chairs and lone bed frame had been moved from the house just as Uncle Jack always did after a night of hard drinking. I could picture him there, cheerfully whistling during his labor, rejoining what he'd put asunder. Over the years, their whole house took on a loose look, like a chair you wouldn't trust with your full weight.

Most people thought my brother Jack drank too damn much and that the bottle was his undoing, but the truth was he could be a bastard before a drop of alcohol ever crossed his lips. Growing up, Jack hadn't been a nice brother, though it was years since I'd been afraid of him. He'd looked like our mother with his blue-black Irish hair and big blue eyes. But he'd inherited his temper from our pa. All that anger and sadness trapped in the body of a little boy. Our father worked the railroad lines for nearly twenty-eight years, and he tried to hone his sons with the same attention to hammer and steel. Our mother had us christened Wellington and Calvin, but we lived under the names our father used. He'd always meant to have sons named Jack and Dick, so that's what we were.

When Jack was grown, he finally had the muscle to match his temper, and he was a nasty job when he was drunk. But most of the time, he just smiled and smiled until the world forgot what he was and started to trust him again. Just happy-go-lucky Jack, perpetually on his way up. He mostly kept his problems locked up in that house above the tannery. But that place, like everything Jack touched, was never quite free from the heavy, sweet stench of rot, and they both crumbled under the acid of his nature.

When I was eight, the barn cat had a litter of kittens, one of which was born with too many legs and an open side. I watched Jack from my bedroom window go into the barn and come out with his pocket weighed down, before disappearing into the woods. When I'd asked him about it later, he'd taken me into the forest and laughingly lifted the rock to show me the flattened mass of fur and bones, with his shoe lace still around its neck. I was old enough to know not to run away in tears, letting Jack know your weaknesses was never safe.

There wasn't much about Jack that I respected, and even less that I liked, but I still spent a lot of time over the years cleaning up my big brother's messes. His impromptu marriages and drunken visits disheartened my mother so much that I couldn't face doing the same. How could I tell her I'd given up on him?

I'd gotten the call so late last night, I just knew it was another mess. In the half-light of the bedroom, I'd lain there, considering letting Jack listen to the operator tell him there was no answer. Only Jack wasn't likely on the phone, usually whoever he hurt waited on the other end. Still, I let the phone ring. But the way the bed sheet crumpled in my sweaty hand reminded me of the wave of my mother's hair just over her left temple. I answered the phone, my balls drawn up against my thigh. I had no idea what this call would cost me.

Dale Davis leaned across the rickety kitchen table and tapped the surface, bringing me out of my daydream.

"Dick, did you hear what I said?"

Dale, no *Sheriff* Davis, had only been in office for a few months, and he was barely out of school. His badge projected an unseemly brassiness into the shitty, little room.

"You see, the coroner told me that from the traja…the trejack…the angle of the shot, it was almost impossible for the victim, your brother, to have killed himself."

The silence between us buzzed with the sound of Dale's fingernail worrying over the crease in his trousers.

Oh Jack, what did you do? I crossed my arms over my chest and leaned back, the chair's joints throwing up a squeal of protest.

"Now, Dale, let me see if I have this. Based on the trajectory of the bullet it is *almost* impossible that Jack, my brother, killed himself."

Dale's smooth face lit up as bright as his badge, and his hat slipped off his knee, but he caught it before it fell. "That's right, Dick. And what I need to know from you is whether you'd like for me to stress the 'almost' or the 'impossible?'"

I sat there dumbfounded at the size of the question. That Dale would even dare to ask it was no small wonder. I thought of Jack's smiling face, industriously mending whatever he'd smashed the night before. He would have been whistling the same song as our father did when he'd chopped wood. *I've Been Working on the Railroad*, but with the notes longer and tighter together.

Out the window, my nephew, Stevie, talked to my boys in the yard. His thin white shirt revealed the crooked set of his shoulders against the dark trunk of the only tree on the property. He had to crouch at an uncomfortable angle to tie his shoe. Broken, functioning, but never fixed. My mind slid back to Jack's gleeful face over my shoulder as I'd stared, horrified, at the hairy infant wreck now buried under my favorite reading rock in our woods.

"'Almost,' Dale, let's just keep it at the 'almost.'"

Dale nodded and stood to leave. He must've been thinking the same as me. Jack had caused enough trouble for this family. I sure wasn't qualified to judge them. To me, he'd been a brother and, admittedly, a burden. To them, he'd been uncertain and dangerous, liable to love you or knock everything to pieces. If they killed him, maybe he deserved it. That's the way I left it; whether that was the right thing to do or not, I don't know.

I'll always feel bad about the things he did, but they don't belong to me. Almost.

The sound of the late spring rain came in through his window and filled Steve's head with the beginning of his own name. Damply sibilant, like the last sound he'd ever heard his father make. When he lay awake on nights like this, Steve faced the memory of that luminous slick spreading out from behind the couch, darker even than his father's hair.

A sophomore in college studying engineering, Steve was three states and almost two years away from the all talks and all the looks that had followed him after Pa's death but closer than ever. Nights like this, the reek of the tannery, of his past—the cold burn of controlled rot and long dead animals—filled not only his nostrils and lungs, but his heart and his head. The first thing he'd done when he got here was try and rid himself of that smell, but it lingered in the strangest places. Just when he was sure he'd managed to Lysol it into oblivion, something would catch him unawares. One day, his roommate's cold coffee had spilled across the floor in a shiny, dark puddle, and his stomach clenched so hard that he was halfway to the lav down the hall before he even knew it. Nothing tasted right for a week afterwards.

Now that he dealt in the trade of angles whose measurements he could always calculate, he realized the mistake he'd made that night. What that particular tilt of his father's neck had meant. How hairy and deflated Pa's head had looked from where it stuck out around the edge of the sofa, the dark hair dappled silver by moonlight. The sounds of his brothers and sisters running down the hall behind him left so little time, and he'd had to act so quickly.

He'd thrown the curtains open and kicked his father's hands towards the gun. This small movement might have caused the sound, that soft hiss escaping the lips. He'd bent closer to listen better, and that's when he saw it. The hunk of hair curled in Pa's hand. He scooped it up before he'd even had time to think. And he still kept it, tucked away in a small tin at the back of his underwear drawer, keeping him tightly bound. It didn't necessarily mean anything, but then why couldn't he just get rid of the damn trash?

By some unspoken consent, he and Ma never talked about that night with each other. They both answered a million other questions over and over again, the answers never changing, until nobody bothered to ask anymore. Instead, they both guarded a box of secrets for each other, one that might be empty.

Stevie shifted onto his back and grimaced at the familiar crackle and spark that ran across his right shoulder and down into his collarbone. Wide awake, he reached over to his night stand and flicked on the small light there, picked up his algebra textbook and held it tight to his chest.

CRAVING DEATH
Franklin C. Murdock

Harlan still loved the man kneeling before him despite the four dead bodies at his side. Sobbing and heartbroken, he'd forced the muzzle of his gun against the worry lines scoring the man's forehead. The still lake beyond them reflected the moonlight, the whine of cicadas crisp but far away.

"I killed them, Harry." The kneeling man, Eddie's, face streaked with filthy tears. "I cut them up."

Both men shook, one with rage, the other despair. Harlan could not blind himself to the jackknife in Eddie's bloody hand and that subtle glint of madness in his eyes but not the tender memories of Eddie's family—Paula, daughter Sadie, and twin boys, Cody and Colby—rising in his thoughts around a red streak of vengeance.

"But I didn't like it," Eddie said.

"They loved you, Eddie. How the hell could you?"

"I don't know."

"And what about me? Did you invite me up here to carve up, too?"

The gun came down hard on Eddie's teeth, stifling his cries. His head rocked back, his mouth a broken dam of blood. He slumped forward again and spat two jagged kernels of broken teeth into the mud.

"I just...I got angry a few days ago," Eddie said. "Just woke up with a bad headache, all pissed off."

Harlan licked his lips as Eddie struggled to compose himself.

"Me and the twins came down here to fish while the girls made lunch."

Eddie looked to the cabin where the family would go during long summer weekends.

"I took a nap here at the lakefront while they ate, and something got into me. I woke up full of hate. I wanted to hurt things. And the damn headache. It told me to..."

Harlan jammed the gun into his friend's face so hard that Eddie collapsed

223

beside the muddy water.

"Just do it, Harry." Eddie pleaded. "Please. For Paula and the kids. For you. *Do it*. Save me from this…"

The gunshot split the stillness of nightfall and sent a looming flock of birds from their unseen perches. Eddie jolted backwards, his ruptured skull smacking the ground with a wet thud. He jerked once before his body went still.

The messy lakefront made Harlan weep. He'd loved Eddie beyond words. Paula had been like a sister, and the kids had always loved their Uncle H, but now, they were just body parts and painful memories, taken too soon by the monster his friend had become.

Eddie bucked with enough force to roll his body and shift his death glare to those he'd loved and butchered. Harlan pointed his gun at the settling body, his heart hammering.

He spied the bloody crater where the bullet had puckered Eddie's skull. There, within the black blood, the shattered bone moved, slightly at first, but then, with zeal.

Harlan froze.

A translucent serpentine thing, a narrow eel made of glass, popped its head out of the break in Eddie's skull and struggled out of the corpse, the moist squelch of its wriggling turned Harlan's guts. It slithered free, its maw buzzing around a sharp proboscis.

Away! flooded Harlan's thoughts, his mind frantically pairing the concept with *look* and *get* and *run*, but his body wouldn't move even as countless other like creatures crept out of the dark water. They creaked as they came, a moan rising in Harlan's throat instead of the desired scream.

The creature coiled at the base of Eddie's neck, turned to the approaching swarm, and squealed. Harlan managed a single step before the creature turned back with dark, intelligent eyes. The narrow spike of its mouth twitched once, and the creature leapt.

Moonlight flashed before the segmented body cinched around Harlan's right leg. He tried kicking it off, but the preternaturally quick creature spiraled up his body, clicking as it went, before settling on his lower back. At the base of his spine, it shot forward, its teeth piercing flesh and bone.

As the creature wriggled its way into his spinal cord, Harlan collapsed. The worm slid up each vertebra like a painful chill. As the creature slithered within his neck and latched onto his brain stem, the pain erupted into a pounding headache, his thoughts corrupted by strange hatred.

At the feet of five dead bodies, the closest thing he'd had to a family, an urge to maim and kill overtook Harlan. He craved death in all its vivid cruelty; though beyond this urge, he understood it as the will of the monster. Even so, he snatched up his gun and stood.

Harlan peered down at the still swarm and hissed, forcing their ranks to slink back into the dark lake in deflated silence.

Now, fill yourself with hatred. The creature fed off his primal bloodlust.

Feed us, they thought in unison.

Harlan fired the remaining bullets into the dead bodies, a thrill rising inside him as the creature drank of this new violence.

There are others. The parasite punctured Harlan's frayed sanity.

Find.

Hate.

Kill.

Feed.

Harlan headed back through the dark haze. A spare magazine for the gun waited in his car. A desolate road lead to a city of faceless victims he'd already promised to sacrifice to the thing inside.

ERASURE ARTIST
Mark Melnicove

She invites you out for lunch, but when you arrive she has already eaten, the kitchen is shut down, and the check is on you. When you confront her with her rudeness, she dazzles you with her perfume, and a few of her kisses, though aimed for everyone, manage to unloosen your tie.

She promises to marry you, claims she wants your baby, then elopes with the boss's son. You have them traced, but the private eye disappears.

Soon, the son returns, disheveled: she has dumped him, too. When his father learns this, he blames you for the break-up, firing you.

Years go by, you are broke. You try to make a new life to forget her, but she has become a celebrity: her paintings are now worth a fortune. So, you decide to sell the early erotic ones she made of you, but descending to the cellar, where you have stored them, you discover she has stolen them when you were not home, leaving only her scent behind.

OUR SHIVERING BRANCH
Goathead Buckley

"This is it? The old family farm, eh?"

I smelt memories in your blood when you came walking with him over one of my graves. He didn't know where he was stepping neither. His daddy, he knew about my "incident" as they came to call it, but it was a thing of fire and blackness, and his daddy kept away from all of that and probably never remembered why in the first place. He'd been there the night they put me in four graves and tried awful hard to sink my head in the river.

But he was young, his daddy, real young. Old enough to toss a shovel of priest dung where my legs had been torn off and buried. Old enough to count as a seventh when only six grown men wouldn't do.

Wish it were his daddy you'd brought back to this farm. He knew this place back when it could rightly be called that, a farm. All we grow here now is weeds choked with thistle stabbed through with thorns. Poison. Snake holes and crow nests. Graves tied up with belladonna and jimsonweed, my yellow and crooked bones just beneath the thin grass.

The old house went gray and storm shook after the fire. Dangerous place. Belongs to the rats, the bats, and the owls that chase them at night. Once lived a tomcat under the porch, but wandering coyotes tore him apart, and that one left a pang. Reminded of the night they took me from bed and beat me with holly switches. This was before I'd been exiled. Before I'd been dismembered. Claimed I'd been down dancing with dirty devils in the gulch; claimed my legs needed cast off to save my soul.

Truth is, they weren't devils I danced with. Least I think not. But them men weren't wrong entirely. I was not looking after my soul down by that

227

creek. No, I scattered it to the stars and asked around the void for something to come snatch me away from them mean bastards, away from their cruelty and ignorance. I'd have rode off on a giant bug with a horse head and five cocks if it got me away from that house where his daddy's daddy and uncles' uncles and the wandering scoundrels took drink while I worked.

My life had been washing up and healing bruises and going to bed hungry, bone tired every night with no end.

They'd stopped letting me cook them meals after the first time they caught me in the woods, naked, talking to the plant spirits, my lips dark with strange tea. Come supper time, they made me chop wood instead. And I got strong as any of them after a month of that, and they grew even more frightened of me, saying they'd caught me giving them the sideways eye and spitting on a Bible when they weren't looking. Which was true, but how did they know that if they weren't looking?

"So, nobody comes out here anymore? Nobody takes care of the place?"

One night, they woke me with their hot whiskey breath. Said they didn't want my dark dreaming under their roof no more. Said my devil mind infected their brains, haunted them at nights, caused nightmare visions that didn't go away—not even with the lights on and a chicken bone crucifix in their hand. But this part ain't true. They just thought that if I lived in the house, the dogs wouldn't bark when I snuck around 'cause they'd be used to me. And I'd be able to sneak around nights and cut pieces off their heads and steal their blood to make cakes to eat that would let me ride on the wind like a bird. I wasn't sure when they'd thought all this up, seeing as I'd never cut pieces off them for anything, let alone flying. At that point, I still thought flying like a bird would be freeing and joyous, instead of sickening and terrible.

The next night, I snuck down to hear them at their cards and saw a man with no cards in his hand, sitting there dead sober. He put all these ideas in their heads, ideas about witchcraft and demon worship and all sorts of other nonsense. Not that I was above trying such. I have to admit, one time I stole his daddy's daddy's knife and cut myself and bled a bit on the hilt so that next time he gripped it when threatening me, he'd fall down and die.

And it didn't work.

I was in the yard, cutting wood. He came out drunk as a whore's neighbor and fondled me. Course, I threatened him with an ax, and he went for his knife. But he'd never pulled it. He liked holding onto it like a second, more useful pecker.

And I said to myself: yes, this is it; this is where he falls down dead, and I rid myself of his cruelty.

But he didn't.

He got pale a bit and went away real quiet and never talked to me again. Never touched me. So maybe I killed some of the meanness in him, but it weren't what I was going for.

And this man, this clean-cut teetotaler, sat there and told these tales and got them dummies' ire up with his shiny tongue wagging in the smoky air. So, I said, I'll show him. I went to where the hearth lay cold and rubbed ashes on my face and made myself look a real fright, like I'd tore out of a grave and come shambling. And I snuck around back, rubbed dirt in my hair and called a whippoorwill to me. We sat and waited for the moon to rise. The bird vomited his heart into my hand, and this I ate, and it made my eyes glow apple red and get real big. Then, I snuck around to the window and just stood there, scratching.

I laughed and laughed when they shit themselves. I could smell their mess from outside. Course I ran before they could get their shit stained legs in motion.

They trashed my room looking for me, and I never came back to the house after that.

"So that means we're all alone out here, huh? I swear I heard a voice."

That first night in the woods changed my attitude about this Earth severely. Before, I had a bit of the devil in me when it came to vexing those men, but it weren't like I had signed a blood soaked book or kissed a black goat's nethers. I saw a bit into the nature of things that they tried to beat out of me.

After that night, however, I knew I wasn't part of their world. Not really. They had imprisoned my spirit in flesh and set it to do their work here on this planet, but now, I knew that my spirit was free and that my body was a cage, yes, but a cage with no lock. And no door. But open nonetheless.

I let my new eyes navigate the unfamiliar darkness. I had gone down to the gorge, but not just to the fishing hole like usual. I stepped right in the creek and walked with the water and saw that water was only one current in this land and above that was a current of crow eyes like little black specks but shining, flowing over different parts of the earth.

And this path of eyes is how they traveled, those midnight dancers I had met before down there. Quick. They step into the path and their feet take off like spooked roaches while their faces just smiled until they were gone completely.

It was baffling to see the first time, and I think they liked me 'cause I wasn't afraid, just startled and a bit confounded of the whole thing. But never scared.

The men put so much meanness in me; I was like a boiled cat ready to rip apart anyone else that came to do me harm. So, I couldn't be scared out in them woods, and I wasn't scared that night either.

In a way, it felt like coming home. Like I'd been on a long journey that had nearly cost me my life. And I was back where I belonged.

My lungs opened like night flowers, and the air I breathed filled me up.

I'd expected to find the travelers there, maybe a glimpse of the crow eye path, but my new eyes couldn't see it 'cause it wasn't there. It was a traveling path as much as it was a traveler's path. Sometimes, it just wasn't.

I was tired of wandering, so I found a flat piece of dry ground and built me a small fire with some kitchen matches I stole. I laid by it, waiting and dreaming and not knowing which was which, but knowing it was better than what I had left behind.

"I hear water down this way. May that's what we're hearing."

I had no clue how long I would have to wait before the travelers showed back up on their river of crow eyes. What had the moon looked like the night I met them? Did the moon have anything to do with it? But they had come here before, so I set up a small camp, built a lean-to and a fire pit and place to bury my waste. And I went foraging, knowing a bit about it, and letting my new vision see what it could concerning once familiar plants. Every plant had a small face, much unlike a human face in that symmetry was lacking and organs of sight and speech seemed to reside in a single, bulbous toothed growth. And their voices were more like mosquito bites than sounds. But you could tell 'em apart that way, by their voices. Some of them cried out to be eaten and their seeds shit upon the forest floor. Some of them screamed poison into my ears so that I thought I would have pus dripping out them just hearing them.

Kept myself alive for weeks on foraged plants and nuts. Suppose I ate a toad or two. An insect here or there. Wished I stole some fishing line. Once, behind the drone of the bees, honey sang with such a sweet, clear voice. No wonder bears love both honey and flute music. I spent my days thinking of funny stuff like a bear I saw dancing once, drunk. I'd practice two-stepping with my shadow until its arms got too long and tangled up in the branches of the trees overhead.

Maybe, if I danced and thought about dancing, the travelers would come and dance with me again.

One night, I thought I was in luck. I heard a ruckus down by the fishing hole, right where I had met them the last time. My fire had died, and my eyes had since turned back to normal, so I found my way by moonlight back up the gulch.

But weren't no dancers from the eye path there.

All the commotion was caused by a great, green lizard, bigger than a horse, pouring some sort of wiggling, black scum into the water. Like liquid worms, but black as coal dust. Pouring it out of a silver pitcher, sitting there like a bureaucrat, looking around nervously like I'd never seen a lizard look.

When I snapped a twig, he shrieked like a chicken hollering at dawn, swallowed the pitcher, and took off into a hole in the rocks. A hole I ain't ever seen before or since. I took this as a bad omen; if lizards are up to mischief, must be because they thought no one would be looking. Therefore, the travelers weren't close by at all because the lizard would have sensed them if they were.

I used to think I understood how traveling the crow eye path worked until I did it one day and found that I didn't know much about much at all.

"It's not the water. It's like I was dreaming a voice I couldn't quite make out, like the trees and wind were telling a story back and forth."

It turns out, the lizard was a harbinger. Whatever nastiness he poured from the pitcher made the fishing hole stink like burnt cake and turned milk. The stench drifted down the gulch to my little camp. I had been up all night, worried about teeth emerging from black nothingness. Lizard that big must eat a lot. And I was as big as a small deer and a whole lot clumsier when it came to running through the woods. So, I sharpened a long stick as best as I could on a piece of shale and sat in my lean-to, chewing ginseng and listening to the night.

The dawn brought the smell, and I had to investigate some way I could rid my camp of it before I threw up. The smell got weaker as I neared the fishing hole, like it moved down the creek to my camp and just hung there, happy to have a nose to vex.

What I saw made me forget the smell, bad as it was.

There by the fishing hole were a couple of travelers. Different than I'd seen before but with the same look about them. And the crow eye path rolled down off the hill, toward the deeper woods, and I knew it was them. They dipped long ladles into the water and came up with a liquid, like garnet struck with morning light. They put it into a big barrel strapped to a cart.

Some sort of shadow donkey stared at me, flicking his tails.

"*Yoohoo*," I hollered, smiling, the fear of the night's lizard gone like a passing dream.

They beckoned that I should come closer. Despite their unfamiliar appearance, they seemed to know who I was and were happy to see me. Of course, they didn't speak English, so we couldn't chat about the others, the dancers I met before, but that was fine because they communicated by shooting lightning into your eyes and making pictures appear that explained what you needed to know without asking in any language.

They showed me a hill cut into the shape of a big old snake, and I'd heard about that, some sort of old Indian thing up north a bit, but it wasn't a sky like I've ever seen: dark blue in the middle of the day with stars out, so many stars you could see just fine in the middle of the night, too, even in deep woods. The sun sat unmoving. And from the mouth of the snake emerged a green, twisting ladder, and bits of light and balls of blackness zipped up and down the ladder. Strange creatures seemed to gather and disperse over and over again. I tried to look closer, tried to move forward, forgetting that it was only a picture that the traveler showed me and not real life.

He smiled.

It could become real if I went with him and his friend. He showed me a future.

So I helped them fill their barrel with creek wine, and we set the strange donkey on his way and followed after, toward the crow eye path.

"Oh my god. What are those? Down there, by the creek?"

When the path took me, it started with my feet, and they went flying out in front of me, but I still felt like I was on solid ground, like I couldn't fall if I wanted to, which is a strange feeling, to see my feet leave and not care one bit. My head eventually got going, but in the meantime, it just sat there, watching the rest of my body being dragged down the crow eye path. Little bits of pure blackness urged me along.

And when I went, I was gone.

The world became shadow and mist. I moved as if through a shrouded morning's forest but came across no obstacles: no hills, no creeks to cross, no brush. So, I moved like wind.

The crow eye path couldn't take us just anywhere, I don't think, but there were paths it did tread that went many an interesting place. I expected, of course, to end up at the serpent mound of my vision. But I had never asked, and as I traveled, I no longer followed the travelers, their shadow donkey, and their barrel full of creek wine. I had been in my head, and when I came out, they were gone.

And this was a trackless land.

They tell you not to move if you're lost. I didn't care. I couldn't stand in thin nothingness. If I stopped moving, the mists gathered and the shadows went away, and you would think that would be a good thing. Shadows sometimes looked like other things, terrifying, nightmarish things. But mist was white and endless, and horrors found deep in the mind live in their silence.

So, I ran, and as I ran, the mist cleared, and I came upon a house. I was in such a state that I didn't recognize it as the house on the farm, the house I'd fled. And the realization hit me like a fist in the gut. Them travelers weren't leading me away from anything. They led me where I needed to be, to do what I needed to do, so that when I really left, I wouldn't have anything to keep me here.

So, I took an old broom handle that the men used to beat the dogs, and I broke into that house hollering to wake the dead. And what I woke looked half dead. Since I'd been living in the woods, the men had taken to staying up at night, drinking whiskey, sniffing cocaine, and watching for me. They bordered on bat shit crazy, and I thought I might catch 'em sleeping since all of the dogs had run off. But they were up, sniffing and drinking, with freshly cleaned guns in their hands and shovels by the door.

"They's that *witch*," one of them yelled down the hall when I busted in. Guns went off, but nobody else knew where I was. They shot at the corners of the room, thinking that I might be invisible, or turned into a bird. I whooped the ever-loving shit out of the one that was screaming, a friend of your daddy's daddy. He had been untangling a net. A witch catching net, I suppose, so when I came at him with the broomstick, he got tangled up, ended up wrapping the net around his legs and falling on his face.

There was a lamp lit and full of oil. I smashed it beneath the window where it caught the drapes on fire. Smoke gathered at the ceiling, and the rest of them shouted and cocked their guns.

The next one through the door was your daddy's daddy. He shot me through the heart with a deer rifle, and I died on the spot.

They cut me up. Buried my legs in one grave, my arms in another, and my heart, they threw in the fishing hole. They were fixing to follow the gorge down to the river and toss my head in the fastest moving part. But when my heart hit that fishing hole, it dissolved in the creek wine, and the men could hear singing coming from the water.

They gathered around and looked into the hole. I don't know what they saw, but they never looked away again. I come back here after a while to haunt a bit, and there they were, just ruins of skeletons, staring at the fishing hole. Those whose skulls hadn't fallen into the water that is.

Found my head as well. That's why I'm here.

Gonna watch over it. And see if them travelers ever come back.

The Girl Who Became A Bird

NEVER LEFT
Lori M. Myers

We were at a stoplight past the off ramp not very far from my lawyer's office. Outside the window, a schoolboy lugging a backpack stuck his tongue out at us as he crossed in deliberate slow motion. I let my eyes go wild and buggy and stuck my tongue out back at him, taking joy at his bewildered expression. If I was behind the wheel, I would've changed gears and stabbed at the gas pedal, letting the engine's rev curse at the kid. Yeah, I would've. Maybe I'd even inch the car up in fits and starts. Give him a good scare.

Sorry, Officer. My foot slipped!

I wanted to give the kid the finger, but his mother was on the other side waving at him to hurry it up as a few drops of rain beaded on our Rain-X covered windshield. The light turned green. The kid, safely on the other side, his cold gaze piercing as we took off, his mother pulling him beneath an umbrella.

"You're more of a child than that little boy," said Ethan, my soon-to-be ex-husband, as he veered the car left.

I kept my calm, clutching my thighs until they hurt, a habit I'd developed during our years of marriage whenever tense moments arose. Seventeen years. Seven plus ten. Five plus five plus five plus too long. With this man who'd caught my eye years ago during a last-minute-arranged Spring break. Who'd strutted on the beach, pecs rippling in rhythm with the blue-green waves of Del Ray. Deep set eyes, a smile bordered by sculpted cheekbones, wisps of dark brown hair that trembled slightly in the breeze. Awe, on my part. I didn't mind being a conquest that night on the fifth floor of the Marriott. The room, the view, him. Gentle. Whispers. We smoked. We drank. We wed a year later. I stopped smoking. Drinking. He didn't. His conquest list grew as did my disgust.

The fact that we'd driven together to my lawyer to work out the final details of our failed partnership was a farce. We wanted to be rid of each other, and Ethan was too cheap to get his own lawyer, so he represented himself. You know what they say about that.

I didn't want much. Just my sanity.

We agreed that he'd get the house because I didn't want to hold onto the bad vibes. The car would be his with the remaining six payments at four-and-a-quarter percent interest. I'd live in a cabin that had been in my family for three generations but where no one had lived in several decades. I'd already moved in much of the furniture we'd amassed after all those years of marriage after clearing away the cobwebs.

We were on our way there now, a secluded place deep in the woods where I'd wandered around as a child until Waymore Chemicals began dumping their industrial waste in the nearby creek. We didn't know that at first. Kids cooled their feet in the water during hot summer days when the temperatures reached ninety and above. In the late afternoons when the water upstream came down the mountains, we found deep spots to swim in and cool ourselves off. No adults telling us what to do. Our place. But we weren't alone. Waymore employees, their ID badges pinned to their shirts, would threaten us and chase us away. All of us ridiculed the logo on those badges that went something like this: "Waymore Industries: We're Doing More at Waymore." There was so much truth in that statement. Whenever we heard the approach of heavy booted footsteps, we'd scatter into the woods and spy on them behind tree trunks as they emptied rusted drums of liquid into the creek. We'd try and guess what the stuff might be. Some medicine past its expiration date? Maybe alcohol like our daddies drank.

How scary that time was as cancers spread and bubbling rashes surfaced on kids' faces. The adults had no idea where it all came from. They asked the local doctor, who didn't have a clue. The mayor even had a science professor from the university drive down and look around.

But we knew. The kids figured it out.

Families packed up and left, as did mine. The company was slapped with court papers and cleaned up their act. When they went out of business, my mother returned to the cabin after divorcing my father. Soon, she died without warning; left me the key but little else.

I gazed, now, at the countryside blurring past. The faded clapboard building selling fish bait and the bar, which had thrived during tourist season, were long gone. Even the foliage seemed to reject this place, the trees transitioning from verdant green to almost skeletal-bare as we got closer. This place in time matched my own. But like anything else here, I wouldn't be staying for long. It was the comfort of the familiar I needed right now.

"Why don't you check in a hotel until you know where you're going to go?" Ethan asked. "Why in hell do you want to stay in that depressing cabin? It's in the middle of nowhere."

"You care all of a sudden?"

"Forget it. The sooner I drop you off there, the better."

"It can't come fast enough." I felt like all the air had been sucked out of me. But soon, freedom. Free from tension, so hard and thick, like concrete.

Rain came down in pelts, and I looked forward to sleeping alone in my bed. Ethan drove much too fast, and I grasped the side-door handle with a clammy hand. I'd detected alcohol on his breath in the lawyer's office, gave him sideways glances with dirty looks. Now, his anger flared up.

"Slow down."

"Shut up."

"I mean it."

"Don't tell me what to do."

Ruts in the road jostled us, and the scenery blurred. I turned toward him, fire like a raging inferno on his face. I tried to swallow the tremor in my voice as the car rocked back and forth. It hit a muddy hole, then slid, spun around, tipped onto two wheels like some sort of stunt in a movie. I could barely make out the outline of the cabin in the distance through the downpour. I closed my eyes and visualized the car balancing perfectly on its side, making its way right up, safe and sound, to the cabin's front door, then drop with a thud on all fours. I'd get out, slam the door for good measure, go inside, and never look back. Instead, the car careened on its side and glided toward the edge of the road then down a sheer drop toward the creek. My purse and sunglasses flew to the back seat when we struck a downed tree, and the day-old coffee in the cup holder splashed onto our clothes. Ethan's skull cracked against the gear stick as the air bags inflated out from their enclosures.

Blood raced to my head, making me dizzy, not knowing which way was up or down, left, right, nothing. We weren't completely upside down, but we were getting there, the car tilting and grating beneath our heft along with the heavy boxes of household items in the trunk. We were losing the battle with gravity.

I struggled to unhook the seatbelt, yanking at the strap out of desperation when it wouldn't cooperate. Ethan's head lolled, his eyes opening and closing, his forehead furrowed and dripping with blood. His body leaned towards me, and the car's groan got louder. Taking a deep breath, I thought back to the times Ethan came home late smelling of vodka and strange perfume and God knows what else. How easy it was for me to shove him out the door followed by threats and tears. This time, it wasn't so easy. I tried pushing him up and away so the weight of both of us wouldn't topple the car over, but the slope was steep, a favorite childhood place where all of us kids used to glide down on our cardboard sleds onto the iced-up creek. It had been a time during the year when no one was around to terrorize us because Waymore was on Christmas holiday. Everyone knew the ice was too thick to break through.

The car slid down the ravine and tipped onto the passenger door, slipping downward like it was a snow board speeding over wet gravel, mud, and brush.

It stopped.

I reached up over Ethan, despite still being restrained by the seatbelt. The car finally gave way, plummeting toward the creek, before it finally settled on its side in the water. The engine kept humming, then sputtered. Smoke poured out and circled around, forming black ringlets at the front and side windows.

Ethan moaned, his body held up now by the seat belt and its shoulder restraint. Blood poured from his head wounds. I tried to scream for help, but my organs, all of me, were weighing down on my lungs and throat. Through the loops of car smoke, I spotted a possum staring at me from the creek bank, probably trying to figure out what the fuss was all about and who would dare invade his territory. The world looks so different when you're sideways.

"Ethan, are you okay?" The words choked in my mouth. "Ethan? Say anything. Tell me you know what's going on."

It took a bit of effort; he grunted. "Here."

"Stay with me," I said.

"That's...a...first..."

I listened to Ethan's shallow breathing as drizzle thumped on the car's chassis. The sun streaked through the dark clouds and settled on the horizon. Just a short distance down along the creek was the bridge I used to skip across as a child and on the other side the rickety tree house I helped my father build before he left us.

Something appeared. In the water's stillness. A floating rainbow of shiny reds and greens. Usually, a peaceful vision. A sign. A good omen one yearns for in this sort of situation. A minute passed.

This kaleidoscope wasn't a sign of good things to come. No pot of gold at the end of this. It was something that shouldn't exist in this fresh air and water. These slick spots were what had alerted our parents that something wasn't right. Toxic chemicals were in these waters. When the community complained, Waymore said that they put their best people on it, that all was well, it was safe to swim in, even to drink.

We did. They lied.

The gloom of dusk descended, and the woods, dense with Swamp Oaks and pines, made it seem even darker. The creek water rose beneath us, and pools of color multiplied, creeping closer like we were prey for their evening meal. The scent of rotten eggs and acid permeated my nose and made my eyes burn. My hands and wrists were scratched and red from trying to rip away the seat belt, and when I checked on Ethan, his face was crimson. I feared a blood vessel might rupture or trigger a brain hemorrhage from all the jostling he had endured. His breathing sounded even thinner than before, his heart pounding like a jackhammer.

"Stay with me, Ethan. I'll get us out of this." Even I didn't believe that when I struggled to speak those words, but I had to force myself to think that there was a way. We were isolated. No one, particularly after a strong rainstorm, would be hiking around here at the end of the day. The main thing I had to do was free myself from this seatbelt, then climb over Ethan, then open the driver-side door. Step by almost impossible step.

The dizziness came at me in waves.

Was my face as red as Ethan's?

I opened the glove box, and everything in it came pouring out—old Google directions, car manuals, registration, phone chargers still in their original packaging, an old sewing kit from our time at the Marriott. I reached above me to try and turn on the map light, but it was beyond my grasp.

The creek's stream got deeper as the acrid water squirted inside the car and dampened my hair and sleeve. The sewing kit wouldn't help me, but another item from the compartment might. The car rescue kit, the case's outside lettering a bit faded, landed right near my arm. I pulled the zipper and discovered a pair of seat belt cutters. I remembered years before how Ethan had shown me how to use them for that *just-in-case* moment. I'd mocked him, told him he was paranoid. But he had been right.

I held onto the plastic handle, gripped the belt out and away from my waist, and sliced the razor against the thick cloth. I had to keep pressing down, cursing at the car manufacturers who had taken great care in making these seatbelts the safest they could be. I didn't need that right now. I longed for the belt to act more like paper that could tear with ease. That wasn't about to happen. My fingers numbed from trying to rip the belt apart, the cutters doing its job bit by bit. After the waist belt tore, I tried to slip out of the shoulder restraint without touching the water.

Licking my dried lips, I repositioned my body then noticed clumps of hair scattered on my arm along with an odor so putrid that I had to cover my nose with the back of my hand. A thicket of oily water had found its way into the car and made the ends of my hair wet.

One side of my hair was falling out.

The sleeve of my pink cardigan had turned brown at the spot where water dampened it. There was a slight tingle where it started to soak onto my skin.

I hurried to free myself while, at the same time, trying to lift the side of my body immersed in the water.

Ethan moaned, long and loud.

Birds flapped away at the mournful sound.

Pain shot through my arm as I crunched my shoulder blade forward while keeping the rest of my body as still as I could, fearful that the car would completely overturn, and we'd be upside down. The repetitive motion caused my mind to wander to that little boy who stuck his tongue out at us as he crossed the road; how angry he made me feel, how he won and I lost. Another interaction gone haywire.

It's bad enough that I'd failed in our marriage. Or did it fail me?

Perhaps Ethan was right. I was more the child than that kid.

Just as I freed myself, the car shuddered. I held my breath. Didn't move. Laying in one position for too long. Sharp twinge, like a knife, down my back. After a minute or two. Very. Slow. Motion. An inhale. Twisting. Slight left. Right palm on emergency brake. Left on seat. Lift. Very. Slow. Motion. Exhale.

I shifted my weight forward, heaved up and over Ethan, the car wobbling like a carnival ride at the end of a run. Ethan's one hand flicked in all directions, eyes going up into their sockets, his body wilting as I ascended.

He's in shock. Or having some sort of seizure. Or...Stay with me, Ethan.

A sob stuck in my throat then erupted, my cheeks wet with tears. I climbed up and crawled through the open driver side window. The car's busted metal heaved and growled as I slithered like a cat, tasting the polluted air, gagging and spitting out the disease fermenting in the water.

Several yards away, the bank's dry land teased me. I was a kid again, leaping from that place into the rushing creek. The joy of youth and friendships that wouldn't last past junior high, but in that second, they were precious, unyielding. Life was nourishment. Until.

Waymore Industries. We're Doing More at Waymore.

I lifted my skirt to free up my legs' movement, plunged myself down into the water, my hands and knees stopping my fall, dipping down, down, down into the liquid dregs of the flowing creek, into a mélange of color, the brew that Waymore built.

Waymore Industries. We're doing way more than we'll ever tell you about.

My skin hissed, and I swear I felt it smolder from where my hands, shins, and feet contacted the water.

Something quivered below the murky surface. A translucent fish, paper-thin, slogged through the muck. Another strained to keep up.

Waymore Industries. We're with ya all the way, baby.

Pain cut through my back, and I was certain I had bruises over most of my body from crashing into the ravine. I crawled toward the creek's bank on my hands and knees. Any skin that encountered the water began to peel and blister. The quicker I reached the other side, the faster I could find help for Ethan. I tried not to think about him, battered and bloody, still trapped in the car.

Waymore Industries. It's allllllllll about the money, honey.

The short distance to the grassy area seemed more like miles as I crept along, lifting hand, then leg, then other hand, leg, writhing in agony, patches of skin disintegrating, exposing raw tissue. A scream garbled in my throat, almost choking me. The leaves rustled in the silence ahead of me. Heavy footsteps. The sense that there were other living bodies approaching. The atmosphere had weight to it. Carelessness to it. Evil. That's how I knew.

Shadows. The possum scurried past me as swatches of its underbelly corroded and fell.

A group of people emerged through the branches and thistles, but not really people as I was used to. Not with real faces. Features that were once in their proper places and what we'd call normal, whether pleasant or ugly, were now a mass of scars or missing altogether. Exposed tissue oozed a reddish-brown goo.

In one man, skin and tissue peeled away to the ulna. Sores and seeping blood blisters were as black as the night about to descend.

As a kid, I was chased away from these dangerous waters.

They never went out of business after all. They never left. They couldn't.

How could they exist in a world looking like that, like monsters?

Their fault. Their greed.

I recognized the unrecognizable. A kid never forgets, just like that obnoxious little boy who crossed the street in front of me. He'll remember me looking like I used to look. Not like the horror now before me.

Knew who they were by the IDs attached to their tattered and torn shirts which hung on raw bodies: "Way_ore Industri_: We're Do_ng Mo__ At Wa_mor_."

CARRION DREAMS
Jude Mael Eriksen

The wind presses against the curvature of my outstretched wings, buoying me as the bucolic landscape scrolls past far below. Little eddies birth in the wake of my fluttering wingtips, rippling away as I glide over verdant pastures where lazy sheep graze. I ride the updrafts, marvelling at the way my wings adjust to the ever-changing wind—as if they have a mind of their own. The stiff breeze on my face flows over my beak, streaming past the dome of my head and around the aerodynamic lines of my body. The sun suffuses me with warmth as I bask in its golden radiance.

I fly onward, passing over bent men tending their stunted crops in the fields. They look up from their labour as I cruise above their heads with naked jealousy in their eyes. I'm free in a way they can never be, and they know it. They understand this in the same way they know their bodies will rot from disease someday and return to the earth they toil over. They reek of sweat, like a premonition of defeat. I laugh as they avert their gazes and return to scratching in the dirt, like mindless ants.

That's right, look away you lowly men. Keep your eyes on the ground where they belong.

With such a vast sky above you, one would think your ambitions would be more lofty, but you only dream of blood and sweat and filth. You'll die with the dirt of your forefathers packed under your bleeding nails.

My eyes see much as I hurtle across the patchwork of crops. Mice scuttle in terror among the rows of wheat and barley, ever wary of the hawks whose ominous shadows ripple to-and-fro across the waving stalks. Fish flutter in the twinkling brooks and streams that wend through the valleys and meadows. Their scaly flesh will never know the delight of swimming through the air as the fat sun smiles down. They only know of freezing water and mud. Do they sleep in that aquatic prison of theirs? What dreams might a fish have? Dull and cold I would surmise.

I reach the outskirts of a village where stray dogs, gaunt with hunger, wander the dusty streets in search of a meal while mangy cats groom themselves in the sweltering heat. The pungent aromas of baking bread and cooking meat float skyward as men and women shout at each other in the marketplace. Do they even look up at the sky above them anymore? I doubt it. They have forgotten the joy of life in the midst of their dubious bargaining. Even their dreams are filled with the dull anxieties of their waking lives. What do they make of it when they can no longer tell the difference?

I continue on past the towns and villages to the countryside again. Other men cut down the poppies and slice open the pods then catch the seeping latex that bleeds forth. Others lie on the ground in fluttering white tents, drawing lungfuls of sweet smoke from their hookahs. They drift in narcotic bliss, ignorant of the mundane horrors all around them. Maybe, it's not ignorance. Maybe, it's spite that makes them drown their memories in smoke and retreat into febrile hallucinations. Perhaps, their dreams are better than the others in the marketplace, but they're still just dreams. They cannot fly from their shame and regrets. The fantasy has become their reality now, but what a false paradise it is.

I reach the desert wastelands in the north, where the earth is cracked and scarred with craters. Cannons roar and machine guns send gunpowder drifting through the air. Armoured machines of death roam the land on rattling tracks and buzz through the sky on metallic wings, spitting fire and raining down destruction.

I must be careful here.

The air is ripe with pain and the promise of suffering.

This is where they come to wage war on each other—the soldiers from foreign lands and the guerrillas from the mountains to the east. The sand soaks up their blood as they lay dying, their ragged wounds festering as their spirits evaporate in the infernal heat. The ever-reliable buzzards wheel above the battleground, waiting to pick the bones clean. I do not judge their appetites, for I, too, am an eater of the dead—a scavenger waiting in the wings of death's mighty stage.

Below me, an unkindness of ravens—my kindred—squawk and tussle over something lying beside the wreckage of a wheeled man-machine. A ragged hole pierces the ground on the other side of the wreck, as if the machine had angered a monster hidden under the sand and it had retaliated with explosive force. I swoop down and land at the periphery of their noisy squabbling. They jostle for position: fighting over a dead soldier. Wisps of savoury smoke waft from his blackened body as they pick away at the soft meat hanging from his ruined face. He will feed many before his bones are scattered under the bleaching sun.

Inside the guts of the broken machine, another injured soldier struggles weakly. Tears stream down his face as he gasps for breath. He stares at my brethren as they consume his friend. I am as shocked by the violence as he is, but instead of revulsion, my mouth drools, and my stomach growls with hunger. This is what I am. I wade into the mass of feathery bodies, ready to fill my aching belly, when something pokes me in the side. I squawk and jump back in surprise. The others turn and look as the largest among them fixes his beady eyes on me and shakes his head.

"You're not one of us yet, imposter," it says. "This flesh is forbidden."

The others squawk in agreement, like cruel laughter in my ears. The rejection stings in my heart, but still, my belly burns with hunger.

I am no imposter.

I ignore him and try to surmount the corpse, but he pokes me again with his beak, harder this time.

"I won't tell you again," he says.

I hop away from them, muttering invectives. They return to their meal as I stand off to the side. The sand is hot on my feet, so I circle, careful to keep my distance—lest I draw their ire. Several more ravens drop out of the aching blue sky and are allowed to join in on the feast with hardly a breath of protest from the others. I express my outrage, but they ignore me. My mouth waters as they pull long strips of juicy meat off the dead man's bones. They become wanton and frenzied: poking and tearing and gulping—packing their stomachs until they're like taut drumskins. The sound of their feasting drives me mad with desire.

The soldier inside the wreck moans; his machine has caught fire. Though the flames haven't reached him yet, he'll be engulfed soon enough. The air reeks of burning fossils and roasted flesh, and I become craven with hunger. I sneak over to where the man is, like a thief, careful not to draw the attention of the others. Surely, they won't deny me a nibble of his flesh as he dies? When I near the broken man's charred face, his bulging eyes show my reflection.

A man looks back at me in there.

I don't understand.

Something stirs a terrifying confusion within. Am I not a creature of the air? Am I simply dreaming all of this?

Without warning, the others fall on me, stabbing madly with their gore-streaked beaks and raking me with their pin-sharp claws. I screech in protest and try to fly away, but they drag me back down, deluging me in a cacophony of squalling and vicious pecking.

The flames lick the back of the trapped man's neck as I struggle to free myself.

He moans louder.

The angered mob of birds seems bent on reducing me to pulp, their riot of stabbing beaks and slashing talons dishing out unrelenting punishment.

As the man's head is engulfed in fire, he manages to scream at last—a great braying bellow of agony that distracts the others long enough for me to escape into the sky. They give chase as I climb through the wind, my wings pumping out a staccato beat. Behind me, their angry cries tell me I have no right to interfere. I don't understand their indignation. Are we not all grave robbers here? There doesn't seem to be a shortage of bodies to choose from, yet they deny me the right to share carrion with them.

As I streak toward the sun, they fall behind. Their cries fade away, then only the whisper of the wind caresses my ears.

Soon, I am high above the earth, looking down on all of its troubles. I am grateful to be free of it. Ahead, the stars wink through the hazy blue sky as the sun looms closer. The heat of its gaze makes me want to drown in that light.

I leave the world behind, and only my momentum carries me forward as I slip free of gravity's hold.

Heat burns against the edges of my wings as I pass through the corona and pick up speed, falling into its fiery embrace.

My beautiful shimmering feathers disintegrate into wisps of smoke.

I am baptized with holy fire, a fierce black meteor streaking into a flaming sea of plasma.

If this is a dream, I don't want to wake.

I do awaken, however, with different eyes. The world around me is upside down now. The ground has become the sky, and the sky a featureless expanse of blowing sand. The upper half of my body is racked with pain. When I draw breath into my lungs, they creak like old bellows. I remember breathing fire as the device under the sand exploded beside us. I can't seem to catch my breath, and my ears won't stop ringing.

I try to move my legs, but they are numb and won't respond. I realize my spine is severed.

I remember my partner crawling out after the transport came to rest on its roof. He blazed like a torch while stumbling around to my side, screaming as his fatigues melted into his boiling flesh. I wanted to look away as he collapsed on his back, his fingers clenched in agony, but I couldn't. I bore silent witness as he was consumed by fire.

Minutes ago, he was only six weeks away from rotating back home. Now, he's nothing but a smoking piece of charred meat—a free buffet for the scavengers wheeling overhead. What a tragedy. I try to undo my seat belt, but it's jammed. Concussions vibrate up through the ground as distant ordinance falls like rain upon this unforgiving land of rock and sand.

As I struggle to free myself, a huge raven lands on top of the burnt thing that was my partner and barks out several throaty caws. Others join it, arriving in a flurry of croaks and flapping black feathers. They squawk and screech at one another as they jockey for position, mobbing the corpse like some ghoulish band of paparazzi.

They tear into his scorched face.

A milky eyeball pops free of its socket and is viciously fought over.

They pull it in five directions at once until it tears into pieces. As they chortle and gobble down the dripping chunks, another raven lands at the edge of the circle. This one is strange.

The ground is visible through its insubstantial body as it struts around, as if it's not all there. I must be hallucinating, but it makes me think of the old legends my grandfather told me while boating up the fjords with him one summer. He said that our distant forefathers, caught between their ancient pagan roots and the new religion of Christ, once believed that ravens were imbued with the souls of murdered men who weren't allowed Christian burials.

The spectral bird wades into the circle of glistening black bodies, but as it nears the remains of my partner the largest among them jabs it with its beak and berates it. The not-all-there raven leaps back for a moment before trying once more, and again, the other one pokes it and squawks. The ghostly bird hops away, grumbling to itself. It seems the others have ostracized it for some unfathomable reason. It can only watch from a distance as they return to their horrid meal.

From behind me, the *whoof* of petrol ignites. The ruptured fuel tank has caught fire as flames crackle and plastic burns. I try again to release the seat belt, but it's no use. All of my weight hangs against it.

My breath grows shorter.

My lungs leak air into my chest cavity. With each struggling breath, it becomes harder to draw the next.

The heat against the back of my neck tells me that I'm going to burn.

I thrash in my seat as the hairs on the back of my head begin to singe.

There's no oxygen to breath as the fire grows more virulent.

I want to scream, but all I can do is moan.

The outsider raven hops over to the window and looks in at me. I stare into those black eyes, and the terrible burning goes away. I see my reflection in those strange eyes, and it's a raven staring back at me. We look at each other before the others attack him, and our link is broken.

They peck at him and rip out his feathers with their claws as fire wraps around my head. I finally have the motivation to scream. It rises out of me like a mad siren as my flesh crisps and bubbles.

The ghost-raven leaps into the sky, shedding downy feather that shimmer like diamond dust in its wake. The others take to the air in a flurry of beating wings and angry croaks, chasing after it.

My life ebbs away as my head becomes a torch. My eyes burst and run down my cheeks like runny egg yolks. My tongue swells and splits open. As the fire spreads over my body, I weep for the man I was.

I am a vast agony, every disintegrating nerve ending screaming in unison, and still, my spirit won't shake free.

Then, as my body swells and ruptures, at last my spirit tears itself away from the withered husk in a great, sloppy metaphysical rending. I burst forth and am bathed in a light so pure it washes away all of my memories. For a little while, there is nothing, then I can hear wings beating, and the wind rushes in my ears.

Slowly, the blinding light dims, and I can see, but my eyes are different yet again. The landscape hurtling toward me is sharper, the colours more vivid. I am falling out of the sky. I panic, my mind uncomprehending as the ground rushes up to greet me.

But my arms are really wings.

I unfurl them from where they are tucked into the sides of my sleek body, and they catch the wind and slow my descent. I glide. The sand rushes beneath me in a blur of brown and beige.

My kind await me on the ground ahead, where a dead man lies in the sand beside a strange conveyance. I see the burnt shell of another man inside the flaming wreck as I descend, and for a second, I itch with recognition. My mind conjures fleeting snatches of a vague dream from another life, but before the images can solidify, they're blown away like chaff on the wind. The ravens watch expectantly as I drop out of the sky and land before them. Something about this seems familiar, as though I've been here before. The largest among them struts up to me, his bottomless doll's eyes glaring. I fear that I won't be allowed to join them, but he speaks, and his words are kind.

"Come friend," he says. "You have earned your place, at last."

The others squawk and bob their heads up and down as if nodding in agreement. My heart swells with pride as they surround me and sing praises to my name. My new name. I am one of them now. Wherever they go, I shall follow, and I know that these new companions of mine will never abandon me. I'll never be alone again. As their song comes to an end, my stomach rumbles, and I'm ravenous. I can't remember the last time I've felt so hungry.

"Give him room brothers and sisters. He must be allowed to feed so that his strength is renewed," the leader says to the others. "Go on, brother. Eat until your belly is filled. In this place, a meal is never far away."

They cackle with mirth as I hop over to the smouldering remains of the machine and take a chunk out of the burnt thing suspended inside of it. Whatever fleeting association I may have had with it is moot. Now, it's just meat for my aching belly. Its roasted flesh tastes sweet on my palate. I don't think I've ever tasted anything so exquisite, not even in my dreams. I poke my beak inside the hollow of its open mouth and tug away a piece of its tongue, gulping it down. I taste the language it once spoke and savour it. The more I eat, the stronger I feel. The others watch me for a moment before returning to the other corpse, taking up their squabbles once more. For some reason, they leave the one inside the machine to me, but I am grateful for it.

We are the carrion eaters—the misunderstood and reviled wraiths of the sky—dreamed into existence on the dying breaths of men. Wherever there is death, so shall we be. And if we don't remember what we were before the great wheel in the sky remade us into these vessels, so what of it? We are the princes of the wind and the dwellers in the lonely places. We take what is ours by right. All flesh must expire, and when this dream of life ends and the ripe stink of decay rises like a bad omen, we come—to strip away their flesh and eat their sins.

We do not ask why we are given this task. We only know that it must be done. We are the carrion eaters, and our spirits will never go hungry again.

YOU CAN'T EVEN CALL IT A RAINBOW
Jefferson Retallack

I find a few of you with four. Not very often, but often enough to help me believe I exist. You're not very strong, the ones I've seen, but I can see it in your eyes from a mile away. Something more. You're all measurable. Fours, threes, twos, and ones.

One.

You see the world in black and white.

"What's it like?" a girl you fancy asks during recess, no pity in her voice.

You smile and meet her gaze. "It's—"

"It's like he's a dog. Grey everywhere," your idiot brother announces to the world, visibly crushing yours despite his statement's inaccuracy.

She sees your face drop. "Oh, I'm s-sorry I asked."

Both of them annoy you. She asks without hate, what more can you expect; and what good is a brother that doesn't challenge your self-confidence at every turn? You skulk away in retreat as your nemesis runs circles around you barking and panting. You assume him an evil shade of red, but you don't really know what that means.

I don't care that I can't remember what I ate for breakfast or what my mother's face looks like. You can't even call it a rainbow, it's just a gradient from presence to absence. I pity that.

Two.

My father is a two.

"Why is your ocean purple?"

"It's not. It's blue." You return to your work and attempt to ignore the class clown.

"It is not. It's bloody purple," he says, unable to let your critical error not reach every person in the art class.

You request the teacher. "Excuse me, sir, he keeps trying to tell me my ocean is purple."

He audibly exhales from his nose at the mild absurdity of your claim. "Well, I'm afraid it is, son."

"It is not," you say. The world you know crumbles around you.

Am I wrong?

You bury the thought.

"See, I told you. Ya retard."

"You're the retard. You're failing every class you're in." You're both sent to detention. You don't understand why. You stood up for yourself, like you were taught.

Years later, you fail a routine eye test. You get told you're colourblind for the first time in your life, at the age of fifteen. Your dad is furious. You won't be able to join the army.

"You can't be a policeman. You can't even be a fucking fireman." This is the sentence, the sting that you recall every time your quirk is made apparent to somebody new.

"So what colour is this?" asks a girl at the mall.

"What about this?" asks your mutual friend.

You get the answers correct because they chose stupidly obvious objects to test you with. They call you a liar. They don't want to understand; they just want to prod the freak show. You direct an RYGB rainbow beam from your prism.

I miss his prism.

The irony of your condition is that you know more about colour than most threes. You read every article. *One must contain a cure.* You're looking for an upgrade from two to three. I wish they did. I truly think that you will appreciate it. Even if you had to sacrifice some memories, every image you can see in your post-cure world will contain one hundred times the visual data.

Three.

The visual rules of our world exist due to the way your optic nerve receives electromagnetic waves. Ninety percent of the population. Most of you think you are normal, well, you don't actually ever think about it.

You don't have any trouble coordinating an outfit, no accidentally leaving the house looking like a rodeo clown for you. What a treat.

You can be a pilot, an electrician, a painter, even a baggage handler if you actually want to. There's only a one-in-ten chance that someone can't legally do these jobs. So, why bother replacing red/green dashboard lights with literally any other binary display. Why bother printing letters on the wires, heaven forbid printing instructions like *earth*, *live*, or *neutral* on them. Even just *danger* or a lightning bolt for those with less language.

If there's a one-in-ten chance that a human being can't understand your ROYGBIV colour coding, maybe it's time to introduce a symbol here or there. Cinema won't actually miss the wire dilemma trope.

I wish that you paid more attention to your minorities, both lower and higher. There is so much you can learn from them, so much you need to see. The key lies in your differences. Use them.

Four.

My mother is a four.

You know something is unique about you, but you don't quite have the words to describe it, and even if you did, the chances of them reaching another four are astronomical.

You see a tree, a bird, a lake—a symphony. *Nobody does it like nature.* You say something like, "Wow...that lorikeet, it looks amazing. Like the sunset made love to a healing crystal and grew wings."

The two threes and the two that you walk with all use different words to say the same thing.

"I guess."

"I want what she's having."

"What in the actual fu—"

You quell the need to share the experience further. You shrug it off with a goofy smile. You bury it. You remember your first art class argument.

"Excuse me, miss. I need more colours to get this right." You grab at her dress. You are only five. You ask as politely as you can, "Where do you keep the other crayons?"

"What do you mean? All the colours are on your table." The teacher slides her hands past her temples to smooth down the stray hairs of a long day.

"No, they're not. There's no greenge, purplue, breen, or pinple. I need them to finish my drawing."

"What are you talking about?" She snaps the crayon that she took from you. "Stop talking rubbish. No nonsense."

"It's not nonsense." You hate the word.

Why don't they believe me?

"I need more *colours.*" You raise your voice as you don't know what else to do.

Children snigger. The teacher wants to hit you, she will not and never can, but you notice rivulets of her iris flush with stress.

The classroom's mass disbelief is a personal attack. You experience this many more times throughout your life. You use the names you invent for your extra colours less and less each year as they only bring ridicule. You argue about the oversimplification of the seven colour rainbow. No one ever believes that each band of the real thing contains a mosaic of hundreds. They just say you're off with the fairies, isolated in a spectral prison.

With the right materials and enough time, you can paint your exceptional rainbow, but I will notice the same jarring lack of variety you see in the original. In every one of the bands, I can see thousands.

Six.

I am a six.

Am I imagining them? Am I wrong? Is the world as boring as they say it is? We each ask these questions of ourselves when we imagine a different point of view. The difference is most of you believe them. I refuse. I don't care that no one understands me. I don't even know how I came to be. According to science, I cannot exist, but who cares about science when everything I see is so overwhelming. Each memory of mine is ten thousand times as dense as a four, one million times that of a three, one hundred million times that of a two, and ten billion times that of a one.

I've lost so much from the start of my life. Twelve years old, that's when my storage capacity said *no more*. Puberty is the point of no return for hexachromatic overload. My brain is not able to adapt to the datageddon that assaults my senses. I can barely remember how to move anything other than these eyes. I've been nonverbal since nine.

Humans do have their limits.

I can't miss my old life. I keep what's important. It really is its own language now. I communicate in ten billion colours. I see the world, and it sees me back. The present is all that can matter. The universe and I, my eyes, sharing a moment, right now and forever.

I tire. I barely have the energy to remember how I started this story. I'm being wheeled past a dazzling lime tree. I can see the pores in the skin of the fruit variegate a multiplex of hues. It's ripe to perfection.

I hear a vaguely familiar voice behind me. "I wonder...does she get bored? How stimulating can the same loop of blue pond, red duck, green tree, yellow lemon really be?"

He has no idea.

Another voice answers in front of me, from a four. "I'm not sure she'd be able to remember what happened yesterday, honey."

She is right, but I do not need to anymore.

"I miss our little girl."

"Me, too."

EVERYTHING IS RED IN THIS WORLD
Matthew R. Davis

Your first thought when you find yourself standing here on the edge of the coast, staring out across the sea, is always this: *everything is red in this world.*

It's not quite true. After all, the sand beneath your feet is off-white, and the wooden jetty that stretches out before you is the lifeless grey of old ash. But the whole scene is drenched in crimson: the grass that tufts the shore where you stand, the sky that looms over you in perpetual near-dusk, the vast stretch of open water that lies beneath it like a long, unbroken mirror. The perfect circle of an angry red sun looms large, balanced on the thin cut of the horizon, and perhaps that is why it is always hot here. The constant simmering heat keeps your skin prickling with the promise of sweat. The air sticks to your skin and refuses to allow it breath, clinging like a needy lover who cannot see that their affection is suffocation.

You turn and look behind you. No path leads back across the vast plain of red dust that stretches without cease into the shimmering distance, where giant crimson peaks thrust from a hazy horizon. If anything lies beyond them, you do not remember it or never knew.

Now you stride across the soft earth to where the jut of the jetty begins. The wooden structure walks on stilts out into the red sea for perhaps twenty metres and doglegs to the right for another five as if losing its courage and trying to turn back. On this dead end sits a small shack, its walls and flat roof the same ash-grey as the jetty, a weathered wart on the tip of a wooden finger. The shack is yours. It's the only home you know.

The old and scabrous wooden planks of the pier are rough but comforting beneath your bare feet. Three metres below, red ripples break into pink foam as they gently slap against the soft white face of the coast. The water is lazy as if dreaming, and the incarnadine expanse stretching out toward the horizon lies still as a painting. One could believe that such a sea held nothing, was as lifeless as a bowl of soup.

But one would be wrong.

You reach the elbow of the jetty and lean on the rust-rashed railing. The flat plain of the sea could well be old blood, empty of life—but you know you are not alone.

You have spotted what roams out there, caught brief glimpses of what moves restlessly through those cherry waves. Like few things in this world, it is not red but black as deep as a hole cut from the fabric of space. It never comes too close, but the deep pang of dismay at the thought that it might is one of the few things that pierces through the malaise of this endless summer.

It is big enough to tear through these old wooden pylons like matchsticks. Its jaws could crush the shack with a single bite.

And it is aware of you.

Sometimes, you linger before this eternal near-dusk as the deathless sun's blood runs without end into the gutter of the horizon, and you glimpse a black shadow standing out there on the crimson plain of the water, rendered almost invisible by distance and yet somehow so like your own. Perhaps something keeps watch on the land, on *you*, just as you keep watch over the ocean and its black inhabitant.

You tell yourself that the idea is ridiculous.

You almost believe it.

Turning now, you walk to the front door of your shack and push it open. You have no need for a lock out here—why, when there is only you, you and that thing out in the crimson deep that no lock could stall or withstand? Only one other person has been here, and they are welcome. They said that the lock is you.

The décor of your single-room shack is spartan, functional: an iron-framed bed in one corner, given its head by two plain pillows, its thin mattress covered only by a plain white sheet; a slim-legged wooden table with two matching chairs, its surface bare but for a glass ashtray, a packet of nameless cigarettes with some equally anonymous matches, and a nondescript magazine you have never read. The chipped white paint on the walls peels away in curlicue scabs, unadorned by any decoration, and from the centre of the ceiling hangs a single bulb, although the perpetual angry light streaming through the windows renders it obsolete. Those windows are curiously clean, attended by vermilion curtains that are always pulled back to let that light in.

You live here alone. Only one other person has been here, and they are welcome. They said that the lock is you. They said—

"Fancy meeting you here."

You turn, and she leans against the door frame with a six-pack dangling from one hand. She smiles, brushing her tangle of short dark hair back with her free hand and holding the pose like a model. As ever, she wears a white singlet and denim cut-off shorts. You are always naked, but this does not seem to bother either of you.

"Endless summer—what a nightmare. Lucky it's you here and not me. I've always been a winter rose."

She pads barefoot into the shack and passes you a beer. The glass is a welcome kiss of cool on your skin, its contents a heady taste of heaven. She rolls another chilled bottle across her face, down her arms, and some sympathetic resonance of temperature causes her nipples to push against the thin singlet like eager bullets. You watch, fascinated, as she wrenches the cap off and chases a swig with a sigh of satisfaction.

"You know, for a no-name, made-up beer, this stuff is really good," she says. "It's like the archetype of beers. The Platonic ideal. Wish I could take some with me."

Her words, as always, leave you none the wiser as to their meaning. She doesn't seem to mind your perpetual ignorance. As always, the two of you sit at the table, smoking anonymous cigarettes and sipping blank-label beers.

"How've you been?" she asks, a formality, and rolls her eyes at her own question when you can only shrug in reply. "Yeah, I guess I should stop asking that. Same shit, same day, right?"

She makes small talk about a number of nothings, and you shrug and nod where it seems necessary. You don't understand much of what she says, but you know you are supposed to, or that you once did. It's all just foreplay, anyway. Once the beers are drained, the cigarettes burned out, she takes you by the hand and leads you to the bed.

This part of her visit is clearly supposed to mean something to both of you, and you wish you knew what. Nevertheless, the base mechanics of the process are a wondrous relief from monotony. She squirms out of her clothes, and though you are sure you've seen more attractive women— somehow, in some other when—she is the only one you care to know. She's rich with a middle-aged vitality, her heavy breasts on a slow downward trajectory, tiny wrinkles beginning to show around the edges of her eyes and mouth, and she's beautiful. She's life, and what you do here in your red world is somehow all for her. This is how it always is, and so ever it shall be.

But this time, something different happens.

Something...*changes*.

Your lover lies back as you manoeuvre into position atop her, her mouth falling open to admit a long, soft sigh...and as you push your heat into hers, she speaks.

"Oh, Keene..."

This is new.

You have a name.

Your name is Keene.

He doesn't say anything until they're done, until she peels her sweaty skin from his and pads across the room. He lies on his back, feeling their combined moistures seep into the sheet below as she fetches two beers and two cigarettes. As he waits, he senses the shack shake ever so slightly, as if something massive is sweeping by below.

That's new, too.

She passes him an open bottle, a burning cigarette, and sits by his side as they watch smoke spiral up to the ceiling and dissipate like lost thoughts.

"You've never given me a name before," he says.

Her face turns to him, furrowed as if she sees something new and not entirely welcome. "What?"

"You called me Keene."

She shrugs, looks quickly away. "Everyone needs a name."

"What's yours?"

She stares at one of the windows, takes a pull from her beer to wash away any waiting words. How much more there must be to her—how much meaning she must be keeping from him.

"Sometimes, I think I might be in Hell." He's not sure what that even is, but he drinks to brace himself against the possibility. "Am I?"

She snorts, still not looking at him. "Fuck, if you could hear yourself. You were always...look, if there's such a place, it's in all of us, and we all walk through it from time to time. But the old Biblical brimstone deal? No. Of course not."

"Then what is...*this*?"

"You're just full of questions today, aren't you?" Her tone teases, but she doesn't seem to relish his curiosity, nor the equivocal answers she must give. "This is your world, honey. Your...home."

That last word seems very bitter on her tongue.

"But there must be somewhere else," he says. "A place you go when you leave here."

She crosses her legs, looks down at him for a long time. Eventually, she blinks as if berating herself.

"Yeah. I probably shouldn't say, but yeah. Of course, there is."

Keene sits up, intent upon knowing more of her mystery. "*Your* home."

"Yes...and once..."

She shakes her head, refuses to finish.

"What is it like? Is everything red there, too?"

Her mouth twists at the corner. "Sometimes. But...oh, it's so much more than this, Keene. The *colours*...so rich, so varied. Topaz, cerulean, violet, turquoise, chartreuse, amaranth, umber...gold. Even the night, the black, is so deep and so beautiful."

He tries to imagine it, but can't fix a visual in his mind. He recognises the names of those colours, but the only one for which he has a current reference is the last. Yes, he knows the black.

"Would you take me there?"

Her sea-deep eyes linger on his for long, wordless seconds, and he understands that her every action, not least the sweaty mattress mechanics, is calculated to hide a deep streak of sorrow. Perhaps, if he could see it, it would be blue. But what does blue look like?

Slowly, so slowly, she shakes her head.

"Why do you keep me here?" Her gaze drops at the implication that she is his jailer—there is some truth to it then. "There's nothing for me. You, sometimes, but otherwise…just this. This place. And…"

Say it, Keene. Say it.

"And the Blacken."

She jolts at the name, fixes him with a wide and serious grey stare. "Yeah…there's that. But you've never mentioned it before. Why now?"

Keene shrugs. "Something's different. Something's…changed."

She grips his arm, and what little fingernails she has dig into his skin with frantic force. "What does that *mean*? *What* has changed?"

"I don't know. I don't…I didn't know *anything*—but now…I have a name. I know that there's more to life than this place. Maybe I don't need to stay here any longer."

She swallows hard, and her fingers stroke his jaw as gently as the long-forgotten breeze. "Listen, honey. I'm sorry…I'm so fucking *sorry*…but you can't leave. We need you. We're doing all we can, but we can barely hold on."

Keene brushes her hand away, rises to his feet, stalks across the room to stand at the window. "Am I being punished? You get to come and go, but I'm always here, always alone—just me, and…*it*. Why?"

"I can't tell you that, baby."

"Yes, you *can*." He's almost crying—another new thing, or rather, an old thing remembered. Keene can't recall what tears feel like, or anything that's caused him to shed them before, but they're close. "Please."

"No. Because if you know *why*, you'll know *what*. And *how*." She plucks feebly at the sheet with fidgeting fingers. "And because I've already said too much. I am *not* going to put you in any more danger. Not any of us."

He's not just sensing movement now—the shack shifts queasily on its moorings as the water heaves beneath them. An empty beer bottle falls onto its side and rolls off the table, and the woman clutches at the sheet in fright.

"It's never come this close before," Keene tells her. "Another change."

Why should she be so terrified by that idea? Change must be a constant in her world, unlike his. But she jumps off the bed and hurries to him, clutching his arm again like it's an old habit.

"Baby, please, listen to me: change in this place is bad. *Very* bad. It can't be allowed to happen."

"But it *is* happening." He leans close to make sure she understands this.

"And *you* started it."

She backs away from him in dismay, one hand at her mouth as if someone had asked her to hold the world for a minute and she'd dropped it. That thought feels familiar, like it would taste right in his mouth. Like he's said that to her before.

"Oh, and look…here it comes."

The sea has changed, too. The surface has been broken as never before. Still no longer, it falls away like wet torn flesh as something tall and black cuts its way towards the shack.

He thinks it's called…a fin.

A tingle in the back of Keene's mind, and a little bubble of knowledge rises to the top and bursts. He *remembers* something: in another world, the Blacken's shape has another name. Before he can grasp it, the thought is gone.

His lover, his jailer, hurries to him and looks out the window. Her body stiffens like she's been struck dead so fast she's already hitting *rigor mortis*.

"Code Black. Pull me out."

Keene spins to ask the meaning of this strange declaration—but that strange, sweet woman is gone, leaving behind no sign that she was ever here. Her clothes have vanished, her beers, maybe even the sweat that soaked into his sheet.

She always leaves in the end, but never like this.

This is new. This is *wrong*.

That gargantuan fin sinks back into the sea outside as the Blacken draws deathly close—and then, after forever, a million monolithic microseconds later, the red dusk is blocked out as Stygian night strikes the glass. The window explodes inwards, and as he is thrown back against the table, he is amazed to see the whole *wall* collapsing in. A tidal wave of depthless darkness takes its place.

Now, Keene remembers terror as he finds himself face to face with the Blacken for the first time.

Its mighty ebon head fills the space where the wall once was, pushing towards him in dire hunger. Its jaws are as wide as the shack and rimmed with multiple rows of jagged teeth as long as his arm. He screams as they inch nearer, but the worst aspect of all lies above; for though the skin of the Blacken is dark as pitch, the huge eyes on either side of its head are a deeper darkness still. They glare into him and see all, stare through him and see nothing. They are blank voids and untold universes. They are empty and ravenous.

The nameless beer gushes down Keene's bare leg as his knees tremble and threaten to pitch him forward into that chasmic maw. The creature's immense weight should have crushed the jetty in a heartbeat, but instead, it is slowly pulling the floor down, as if the shack is somehow resisting the pressure. It's still enough to make him lose his balance and send him sprawling on the tilting boards. He clutches at the nearest table leg and holds on for dear life as the floor cants five degrees, another five.

There comes a sound so low that he can barely hear it—a sound that rattles Keene's bones, shakes him to the core with its sheer contempt. It is the Blacken, *grunting*. It might even be a laugh, if ever a laugh could sound like murder itself.

And now, as quickly as it crashed into his home, that massive head is gone. The entire jetty rocks as the Blacken's colossal bulk slams into the water, sending a blood-red spray surging through the hole it has left, and heads back out to the open sea.

The end?

No. Now, more change is coming.

The thin white paint of the shack's walls is peeling, cell upon cell of it curling inwards and wisping away into nonexistence. Nothing is left behind; or rather, an expanse of sheer black nothing. No mere shade of paint, this ebony is an absence, a void. The walls, the ceiling, the floor—each as black as the edge of space, not there at all and yet still carrying out the job that mundane physics demands. The furniture and the objects scattered about the room remain untouched by the darkness, but they seem to be duller, washed out as they rest on nothing. How long before they, too, are gone? Would Keene lose his whole world, small as it was? The sky outside still burns bright red, and the sea below; for the first time, he finds this a comfort.

But now, ripples appear within the still black of the walls. Things are coming, forcing their way through. Keene yelps as shapes burst through the darkness like nails through wood and settle into grim immobility.

They do not move—they cannot—yet he cries out in horror.

Suspended on his walls are eight heads. Eight human heads, expertly severed from their bodies and mounted on crested wooden shields like gaming trophies, eyes lifeless and mouths gaping as if screaming at him to help them, to *know* them.

"What *is* this?" Keene shrieks.

And as suddenly as it came, the nearest head—that of a middle-aged man with unruly grey curls and a preposterous nose—bursts into speech.

"Protocol One, *now*."

Across the room, a blonde female head speaks, the blankness of her dead eyes at odds with the rising anxiety in her voice. "He's coming back up. Jesus, *do* something."

Keene whimpers, clinging tightly to the table leg. What *can* he do?

"Battle stations," cries another voice, the only one he recognises, and on the wall beside the door, *her* head is fixed to a wooden shield—the lips that kissed him so gently moving in a freakish approximation of speech. "We have a Code Black, people. Breakthrough imminent."

Keene wails in shock and confusion, and he bucks as the floor shifts beneath him, the table's legs juddering, a spill of cigarettes following that single magazine to the floor. The Blacken has made another pass at the jetty—not a serious one, just a warning. It's playing with him, letting him marinate in the anticipation of terror yet to come.

"Introducing propofol now," says a fourth head, somewhere on the wall above him. "Watch that EEG."

Keene manages to rise to his feet, slack-jawed as the mounted heads mime gibberish. He should know what they're saying, but it's like another language he's forgotten how to speak.

Out beyond where the shack's wall once stood, that huge dorsal fin is once more tearing its way through the red waters towards him. This time, it will finish the game for good. He has to get away. But everything moves with the inevitable lassitude of a nightmare, and it will take him far too long to reach the door. Even then, the Blacken will smash into the shack long before he can get off the jetty, and the whole structure is sure to go down on impact. Terror keeps him from tearing his gaze from the approaching doom. It's within a hundred feet, closing fast, and it dips beneath the waves to prepare for the final leap.

This is it.

At last, this day is over.

Water explodes from the red sea below him, pours in through the wrecked side of the shack. This time, the sable shape that comes in with it is not much larger than himself.

For a split-second, Keene thinks it is a man.

It has arms and legs and stands upright, yes—but where a man would have a nose there protrudes a selachian snout, beneath it a maw brimming with more jagged teeth than he has bones in his body, and the eyes are the same soulless black orbs that regarded him less than a minute before. As Keene struggles to comprehend this, its form flickers and mutates and yet does not change at all. Extremities he could never name or understand lash out at him, even as they fade from stillborn existence. Whatever mind he has left quails under the psychopathedelic assault, bruising like soft grey fruit.

One of the mounted heads mouths in time with a panicked cry. "He's spiking."

Keene falls down upon the void where the boards had been, his legs refusing to work in the grip of such terror. His hands, still obedient, dart frantically in a vain search for a weapon. They fall only on the printed innards of the magazine where it has fallen open on the un-floor.

For a moment, his soul is seized by something greater than terror.

The magazine is open to a page of illegible text. The only thing he can read is the headline: THE DREAM TEAM. Below this, a photograph: nine men and women in white lab coats, standing on a lawn in cosy camaraderie as if nothing in that world could ever go so drastically wrong.

One of them is *her*.

And not just that—smiling beside her is the curly-haired and beak-nosed face up on the wall, the first one to speak, and next to *him*, the blonde head that had urged him to *do* something.

Keene's mind spins like a gyroscope, something that he almost remembers now, and he slumps forward into his elbows with his nose pressed close to the page. Beneath the photograph are words that he can identify, if not understand. Names.

Van der Leeuwen. Casterbridge. Waititi. Thorgerson. O'Connell. Takamura. Keene. Zheng. Mulholland.

"We got REM," says one of the heads above him. "Increase the dosage."

The photograph disappears as a black foot or hoof or fin or forciple stamps down upon it, almost crushing his hand. Water trickles from harsh, slick skin that rasps against his like sandpaper, and the Blacken looms over him, a million Blackens and just one, its maw growing wider and wider and wider. He throws up a hand in feeble protest, *no, no, please don't*, but the head shoots forward—and his right arm is gone, locked up to the elbow in a grid of razored teeth.

For the first time in this world, there is *pain*.

Keene screams as those jagged blades carve through his flesh and clamp tight on the bone. Beyond rational thought, he slides on his rump and finds his other arm free, and he lashes out in desperation. His fist sinks deep into the belly of the beast.

The blinding pain takes hold of him there, too. Keene can barely open his eyes for the agony—but when he does, he sees that in the Blacken's stomach is *another mouth*, this one vertical, and it has taken hold of his left arm with another bracket of vicious teeth. He hangs kicking from the thing's maws, his whole body alight with endless annihilating pain.

Beyond reason, he yet recognises the next thought that comes. And it is not his own.

The Blacken has not spoken to him, but he knows exactly what it wants.

The world beyond. Wherever the woman went, with all of its colours and shades and nights and seasons and *flesh*—

Keene can go there. And the Blacken will ride him back, back where they both long to be, and everything in that world will be red.

"Stabilising." The woman's voice again, the one that had destabilised his world by naming him. "Ease off, Casterbridge, you'll kill him."

"Increasing gain," replies another hideous trophy. "The foldback will force a system reset."

The beast grunts again, and its chill breath crawls up Keene's arm. Wrenching his head to one side, he sees the mounted heads receding into the ebony walls—sees the walls themselves fading up into a brighter shade of pale.

Colour is returning. And with it, the world.

Then, with a growl, the Blacken bites down.

Keene collapses to the floor, free at last. He holds out his arms to break the fall, but his face slams into the wood, and incredible pain blooms at his elbows. He flops onto his back, and the warm pool spreading beneath him is not water. His forearms disappear into the mouths of the Blacken in one greedy gulp.

And then, it steps back on floorboards that are rapidly filling with colour and hope. Its eyes transmit no emotion, but its alien resentment, its black-hole *fury*, is beyond description. He gasps at the immense intensity of that hatred, fully expecting it to scorch the skin from his bones and raze the remains to ash, but instead, the thing shoots out of the shack in a bolt of black lightning. A surly splash below as it returns to the crimson waters, and the Blacken is gone.

She saved me.

Keene moans in agony as his red world rebuilds itself around him. He thrashes on the floor as life pulses and pumps out of him, and his vision blurs with tears and the oncoming darkness. He is losing his grip on everything, his own mind, his own name. But beyond the veil of obfuscation, he can see something moving—something alive—

You blink furiously at the blindness and can just barely make out her face as she kneels above you. There's a tenderness there, as of a mother leaning into a crib to soothe the nightmares away.

"It's over, honey. We did it—*you* did it. Everything goes back to normal now."

She leans closer, closer, until her face is all that you can see. She plants a soft kiss on your forehead. All else is fading, but that touch of her lips stays with you all the way down into the dark.

"Let go, my love. Stand guard at the gate and keep our world safe. I'll be with you again soon, I promise. And one day…one day, I swear I'll bring you back with me. Back where you belong."

You let loose your grip, and the blackness comes. But it doesn't last. Soon, it is washed away by a soothing crimson tide, a thick breath of hot air, the prickle and promise of sweat upon your skin.

Your first thought when you find yourself standing here on the edge of the coast, staring out across the sea, is always this: *everything is red in this world.*

Will Tuffin 10/23/18 Everybody Thought He Was Dead

FACE TO FACE
Trevor Abbud

The giant would arrive soon. The face of Death was heart-shaped, its eyes marked from the jagged engravings of a blade. Its long appendages loomed over him like some macabre octopus that was born out of the Lake of Hell. Protracted claws beckoned for him to come. Its green hair swayed in the constant gale storm of this wasteland world. Above the monster, a full moon shone brightly. In this nightmare, it conveyed not beauty but a formidable bullet hole in the ebony flesh of the sky.

"Come...Harold." Its raspy voice whispered through the tree branches.

A multitude of icicles linked, glaciating his blood.

Part of him wanted to go, an infected part wanted to give into the sick enticement within that whisper. He couldn't stand it anymore: the haunting nightmare of being chased by the ungodly creature, the dark deserted landscape crafted by trauma and love.

He drove again, along a road he had been down before. He was coming face to face with the wrinkled, brown flesh of the giant in a rapid rush and—

"But you wake up...before anything happens," Dr. Martin Napieralski concluded the ending of the nightmare while uncrossing his legs. He removed his glasses and placed them on his desk. He used his thumb and forefinger to pinch the bridge of his nose. "Like always."

"That's right, Stein," Harold said, nicknaming the doctor after the American author/actor Ben Stein because of their physical likeness. The lethargic eyes, his big naked pate, that sardonic yet, intelligent smirk where a low, slow, patient tone of voice—as if a bullfrog was lodged in his gullet—came from. If drying paint had a voice, it would most likely resemble Stein's.

Harold liked Stein because he didn't bullshit.

Rising from his chair, Napieralski walked over to a medium-size bookshelf. "And this is what, the fourth? No, the fifth time in the last month? This night terror?"

Before the first, he spent six months behind bars for vehicular manslaughter. After that, another five months exiling himself from life, where he smoked cheap cigarettes, drank cheaper beer, and slept every day away as he lost his new job at the factory and watched his savings, which consisted of a Sour Cream Pringles container filled with loose change, dwindle.

Then, the first nightmare attacked. A month away from the threatening one-year anniversary of the accident—the death of Darla Day—the giant, looming, green monster paid him a visit in the dead of night—when ghosts come out to play.

"It's the fifth one, Doc, and they're getting worse. The weight of the dream, man…it's like I'm a car being compacted into a cube. The life is being squeezed outta me. The overwhelming fear of sleeping and the guilt I deal with when I'm awake is unbearable. Does that make sense?"

Martin paused his search and offered a Kleenex pinched between his fore and middle finger.

"Thanks, Doc. Oh, God. Screw me, man. You know, I want her back…" Harold stopped to gyrate the silver, sparkling band on his pinky finger, a token of his Darla. "I was gonna marry her yah know I…"

Choking back tears suspended his voice. He lifted the atrophied engagement ring, his front teeth clenching down hard on his trembling lip. A puddle of blood pullulated on the rubbery surface.

"I, umm…" But his wounded mentality delivered the image of Darla's ruined body, forcing him to reach towards the small, black, oval Formica coffee table and snatch another Kleenex. He tried to plug his nose.

Back at the mini library:

"We're going to defeat this demon, Mr. Ramsey." The tall, broad-shouldered Norwegian hiked up his chinos, revealing gray gargoyle socks with black and red diamond patterns on the ankle. He bent down to skim through the top shelf. "The Self-Analysis Method doesn't seem to be doing the trick just right. I think the first six months, where the injured mind is most malleable to psychological infection, we lost a lot of ground when you were with that buffoon they provided. Carmichael is a crock a shit. He's a disgrace to the practice."

The doctor barked then cleared his throat, like an old motor engine coughing to life.

"They're getting worse," Harold said.

"No shit, Sherlock." He cocked his big, solid head around and offered Harold a wink. "Now, be a good little patient and let me…"

He concentrated fully on his searching.

"Ah-hah, 'kay let's see here." A fat thumb and thick middle finger snapped. The sausage-size index found the R's and stopped. "This is it. My good friend Mr. Boniface Rochefort should help get things back on track. Or at least, reroute us to the right destination."

He handed the hardcover over to Harold.

"*The Monster Inside Me.* Sounds like a Bentley Little novel."

"Dr. Rochefort is a world-renowned psychiatrist and psychotherapist. We attended John Hopkins University together. He is a brilliant man and quite frankly knows his shit. I believe for the first six months after the accident you were in a semi-shock state; a deep, dark despondency cave where you hid all your feelings and tried to diminish the painful circumstances in prison. This is where the guilt built up, and while in such a vulnerable place, your subconscious yielded to the guilt and shame. And of course, you're *angry*. What her parents did was vile and nefarious. You'll read about how guilt, fear, and anger are the three special ingredients to concocting any psyche-monster."

The old motor kicked and barked again.

"Excuse me. Now, who the hell could blame you for this, right? Then, after almost another six months, you finally began to come out of that damn cave, but a monster shadowed you. Harold, that monster is inside you. *It is you.* You believe you are a monster because you blame yourself for taking her life. Of course, you do. Am I right?" Dr. Napieralski sat down. "What's the sequence of these nightmares?"

"You know how it goes."

"Yes, yes. But tell me."

Harold massaged the ripples on his scrunched forehead. He tried not to analyze everything Stein just said. He'd deal with that later. "Doc, the nightmares...like I said, they're getting worse."

"Yes, I understand. But please, go on."

"I don't wanna sleep 'cause of the nightmare, but if I can't sleep, then I have to think about Darla, and if I think about Darla, I don't want to be awake. I can't win. It's that simple. I can't even eat anymore. It's like the guilt eats away my appetite. I live off of Keystone and Pall Malls." He nonchalantly thumbed through the hardcover book, suddenly vulnerable and uncomfortable. Panic leeched into his gut. Napieralski seemed to read his mind, and that was no place for the doctor to be...that was no place for any sane person.

A terrible thought unexpectedly surfaced in his mind.

What if Stein has been feeding me these dreams somehow...what if he's fucking with my head?

But that was absurd. *Right?*

He could trust Stein. He trusted Martin more than he trusted himself. Brainwashing patients and whack stuff like that was for the movies.

Yet, when Stein closed a big, cold, paw around the back of Harold's neck, he jumped, a multitude of chills spreading across his flesh.

"Re-laax, dear boy. And read Boniface's book, please. I'm sure you'll get a better understanding of the things you're feeling. Then, we can start to move forward. You have a lot of guilt and anger built up, and you haven't had the proper time for grieving. Next Monday—"

"A year," Harold said under his breath. His throat quivered from holding back a new deluge of tears. He sighed, took a slow, deep breath, and mouthed her name, *Darla*.

And Harold itched like poison ivy. Next Monday would be the one-year anniversary of Darla's death. And that would sure be one hell of an annoying itch to scratch; no doubt, it would leave a scabby scar.

"Next time we meet, I'd like to work on this psychiatric method for alleviating self-loathing." Martin Napieralski gave Harold's neck a tight squeeze.

That night he dreamt.

The Late Night Show became background gibberish, and the pages of *The Monster Inside Me* molded into a blurry jumble. The text overlapped and intertwined. His drowsy mind braided the words, morphing them into an alien language. The T.V. quacked like the teacher's voice from Charlie Brown. Harold set the book down on the end table. The heavy weight of exhaustion pulled down on his eyelids. He tried to keep them open, but guilt closed the doors.

The monster. Darla. Reality spun. Nostalgic ghosts of memories joined this macabre dance. The depressing present and haunting past fused together inside his head, splicing a daunting future.

He dreamt of *the* night.

The worn recliner transformed into the leather driver's seat of a low and fast candy-apple red 1967 Camaro: Cherry Girl. The butt of his Pall Mall extinguished a steering wheel wedged between his fingers. A stick that yearned for speed replaced the translucent glass bottle of what might as well have been piss. The glossy mug and impeccable hair of the talk show host vanished. Taking his place was the Monster's heart-shaped face poised three hundred yards ahead.

The night was a dark open mouth huffing out thick fog. The rustling of wrinkled, fall foliage cried in pain as if it knew winter was coming and its time was almost up. Harold had the same sickening feeling as the dead leaves. Once again, the long extended arms of the beast bidding him to come and face the guilt.

Harold revved the twin turbo, supercharged nitrous-breathing machine. The engine roared. Then, their song came on the radio. Harry Nilsson singing, "Without You," and Harold was tossed back to the night when their song came on the radio. When they went for a night spin.

He held her hand and looked into her verdant eyes. With one glance, he knew he made the right choice when he bought the sparkling silver ring.

They cruised down a country road in a hot sports car under a dark, starlit sky. The beautiful golden eye of the moon twinkled in the plum-hued sky. A mild November night designed for lovers.

He looked to his side and studied. Sometimes, he liked to just look at her. He surveyed her bottom to top. She had on white Keds and tight canary-yellow capris that were laced around her thin waist with a skinny, teal belt. His vision stalled between her crossed legs, the brazed image of her mystical cave thrashed through his mind. Then, his eyes continued onto the firm hills of her breasts. His eyes made a longer pit stop there. Underneath her denim jacket was a white blouse speckled with pink flowers, the top three buttons were undone. His head felt like it was spinning faster than Cherry Girl's whitewall tires.

Harold caught that savagely hot look in her eyes; they performed their own inspection. He felt like Dirty Harry in Magnum Force. *The brown, leather jacket and white V-neck T-shirt fit perfectly with the greasy black pompadour slicked back on his head.*

They were driving to Swan Lake, speeding along the empty Interstate 84 in the farmland of Troutdale, Oregon. This was their place where the once-upon-a-time-middle-school-crush used to ride their bikes and have picnics in the sun. Swan Lake was where their friendship transformed into love. Here was where two young friends became one romantic and passionate entity after senior prom in the grass under the stars and the outstretched arms of a gigantic redwood. Nocturnal frogs sang a gentle, ethereal tune from the water. The ambiance affirmed the Almighty Hand on their relationship.

After, he used a pocketknife to carve a heart and incise their initials into the thick muscle of the giant redwood.

Tonight, he would pretend to take out his pocketknife to inscribe over the etchings and would come out with a sparkling ring instead.

Swan Lake grew closer. Harold didn't downshift as he dragged the rear tires around the off ramp from Interstate 84 to Route 18, which brought Cherry Girl to an exit for Crown Point Highway. The entrance to Lewis and Clarke State Park was no more than two miles off the highway.

As he rounded the corner and accelerated, Darla caught him examining her womanly physique again. It made her laugh.

"What are you doing, you goof? You better slow down," she said, even though she absolutely loved it. This was living. This was daring. Exhilarating. The speed made Darla's heart race, hammering inside her chest and reminding her that it was alive.

Yes, they were alive and young.

They laced hands and squeezed. Their hands parted and walked over to each other's bodies, triggering the stimulation they both knew activated each other best. Harold had the heat on low, and with their added body heat, steam sweltered at the bottom of the windshield, clouding it.

"I can't help it." He examined her further, wanting to remember this night.

"Baby, baby." She giggled. She had a peculiar laugh that complimented her quirkiness. Each time she tried to suppress the giggle, it only made her squeak more. Her face wrinkled, and her nose scrunched. "The road, babe. Gotta watch the road. I promise, soon."

Harold wiggled two fingers—the ones she said have the magic touch—once more before backing off. But his eyes weren't on the road. Not really. He reached to brush her asymmetrical bangs away from her one eye—they always covered her right eye.

"That's the way it's supposed to be." She always told him.

Harry Nilsson started the final verse of their song, "No, I can't forget this evening or your face as you were leaving…"

Harold would never forget her face or this evening.

And that's the problem, *a voice from the depths of his consciousness bellowed.*

They leaned in to kiss—

Four shadowy figures appeared.

He was thrown…

Darla Day vanished. A corpse took her place. Her awry bangs caked in dark blood, and her thin neck twisted like a corkscrew after bashing into the dashboard. Her green eyes were stuck open from the shock of sudden death as if she stared into a place far away.

The doe and her trio of fawns appeared out of the Broughton Bluff Woods and made the mistake of crossing over the highway, maybe to get a sip of water at Beaver Creek. He swerved but clipped the hind legs of one fawn before colliding into a hulking redwood. The supercharger died instantly, and the super turbo barked the loud cough of death. Harold turned away from the bloodstained windshield—slowly, because it hurt like a bitch—and past the steaming hood of the engine. More blood came from her chest where she had slid the strap of her seat belt beneath her arm so she could lean in to kiss him. The safety harness had sliced the front of her right breast off.

Harold screamed, and screamed, and screamed. He screamed into the darkness, into the nothing, until his screams became nothing.

Darkness.

Then, the dream skipped again.

Harold sat alone.

In his silver Nissan.

Just him and the giant monster.

"Come." The monster commanded.

"Go." The monster inside him threatened.

Here, he was again, driving down the country road that led to Swan Lake. Coming face to face with the beast. Death was in the air tonight. He revved the engine. The monster stood its ground.

"Come."

"Go—"

In the dead of night, Harold kicked out of bed. Drenched in sweat and covered in chills, he snatched a cigarette, lit up, and took a deep drag. His shoulders relaxed as his exhaled.

In the kitchen, he opened the fridge to find something cold to soften the guilt. After a swig of beer, he pulled the picture from his front jean pocket.

It took another bottle of beer and two more cigarettes before he got control of the tears.

He drank himself to sleep, again.

A week passed, and the daunting date of Darla Day's death arrived.

"How you holding up, kid?" Stein asked. "Has it helped? *The Monster Inside Me.*"

Harold had been reading it every night before bed. Of course, he failed to mention what he had been using as a bookmarker. But that didn't seem important. Harold understood who the monster was, and tonight, he would confront the ugly beast. Just as Dr. Boniface Rochefort wrote:

You must come face to face with the monster inside of you.

"You know Stein, I think I finally get it...the monster is me."

Night arrived.

It was a beautiful night for a drive. A powerful tailwind whistled behind him. The moon was whole and brilliant. As he made his way to Sawn Lake, he saw Darla's face in that moon. *No.* No, Darla's face was much more wonderful.

He split *The Monster Inside Me* open and unfolded the picture hidden inside. The photo creased down the middle from opening and closing it so many times. The face inside no longer lived, but the Darla that dwelt inside his head still breathed through his memory. It was his favorite picture of her because, in it, he knew Darla was happy, feeding ducks by the edge of Swan Lake. It reminded him of how Darla found joy and happiness in the simplicity of life.

Harold bit his lower lip, gawking at the way she looked bent over from the waist. He stared at the picture, forcing his mind to be back there, at the lake where he took the snapshot. How enrapturing her firm legs looked beneath the flirty sunflower patterned, black romper. The way the spaghetti straps clung to her shoulders, enticing and teasing him while she tossed crumbs of bread to the ducklings. Her smooth, cream-toned back flashing him through the cage-look of the crisscross straps. And when a gentle breeze sneezed, the thin lines of her rosy-pale thigh muscles coaxed him under the ruffles at the hem, causing the very center of his heart to stir with infatuation.

He placed a kiss on her cheek.

The kiss of death.

He refolded the photograph one last time, replacing Darla with the pack of Pall Malls and stashing her safely in his chest pocket. He smoked the last cigarette all the way to the stub. He chugged the half-filled bottle until it was empty.

Like me…

It's time to come face to face with the monster. He roared the engine.

Harold wiped a drizzle of foam from his chin and flicked the cigarette out the window, making sure to keep eyes on the monster by Sawn Lake. He revved the Nissan. It wasn't Cherry Girl, but it would do. He pressed play and waited for the final verse of "Without You" by Harry Nilsson. *"Well, I can't forget this evening or your face as you were leaving…"*

I can't forget that evening or her face when she left me.

He shouted the words loud enough, maybe Darla heard him. *"I can't live if living is without you."*

Harold gave one last farewell at the monster—the monster inside him—and put up the sun visor mirror, erasing the reflection of the monster, the beast that took Darla's life.

He focused on the green crown of another monster. Its long, brown branches reached out for him, the twigs curved into claws. He pressed the gas, and the heart-shaped etching in the tree shone under the incandescent beams of the headlights. Two blurry D's sat side by side next to his own initials and caused too much pain—and worse—guilt.

The monster approached, beckoning for him to come.

"Go, Harold." He submerged in a slime of guilt.

The car's engine roared like a warrior's battle cry, fighting with the zeal bestowed on him from and for his lost love.

He hoped that in destroying this beast he could once more come face to face with his love, Darla Day.

She's waiting for me down by a lake. It can be our new lake. A lake under a black sky filled with twinkling stars. There's a field of golden sunflowers nearby. That must be where she is hiding. Darla is there, and she's alive. The moon's glossy eye will be our only company. Our new song will be playing, it will be sung by angels. She's waiting for me under the giant green tree, by our lake.

I'm coming, Darla.

Here, he was again, one last time. Coming face to face with the brown, wrinkled flesh of the giant in a rapid rush and…

…collided.

ODE TO THE FEELING OF ENTERING VIRGINIA
N.H. Jackson

Do you know the worst angle to see a familiar face from? You'll learn it, but I'll tell you now: from the side and slightly behind.

Have you ever driven on remote highways in the early hours of the morning? You will, and I guarantee you that when you do, you'll find no other cars there except your own and an endless succession of semis. You'll find that the sky, though you know it extends forever upwards behind the glow of your headlights, looks like a coffin's lid bending over from one hill-clogged side of the horizon to the other. You're struck by the fact that a strange sense of chthonic vastness could ever be given to, say, central Pennsylvania. You're uneasy when you look at the sky from zenith to edge, but the trucks in the middle make you fear God like a child. On paper, they should look like mobile homes at Christmastime, but all the lights in the world can't stop them from looking like shorn-topped obelisks sliding along through the night pushed by an unseen hand. And there are *so many of them*.

A single tractor trailer truck, when on the road during the daytime—hell, maybe even three or four when separated by flows of commuter cars—is like a caged tiger. If you keep a wide berth, it can only swipe at you through the bars of its cage, roaring its futility. In the early morning in—where did we say?—Pennsylvania, you're in the jungle, and every cracking twig holds a tiger's foot between its broken jaws, every ray of moonlight momentarily bathes a tiger's back, every stray particle of light was first used by that tiger to see you, and you won't see it before it's too late. You pass, or you die. You're in trucker space; you're in trucker time; time and space are one; you're in trucker spacetime.

And you're there, sitting in the passenger seat as you're all driving straight for three-hundred miles, making conversation purely for the purpose of staying awake, thoughtless and mildly disingenuously pleasant, like porridge. Turning to your friend, the driver, as heavy and imperious trucks glow and charge through the darkness, passing by; your headlights and the trucks' spectral effulgences meet and wash over the face of the driver next to you, you with your seat rolled back for the extra leg-room, and you turn to say something, and you see a face you've never seen before:

From the side and just slightly behind.

A face maddened and stupor-intense with the white-yellow not-moonlight thrown over it. Familiar patterns and familiar structures of bone. The soft frustrated confusion of not knowing your way in a place, so familiar during the daylight hours, after night falls, it shocks you with a moonlit madman where your friend sat, driving the car God knows where; and the dithering gormlessness of knowing that your fear will come to nothing and that it can't be acted upon because the madman actually *is* your friend in a way that seemingly defies, while operating under nothing but, logic. You know that tomorrow night, when one of your other friends then sleeping in the back seat, takes over for the current driver, you will see another stranger, perhaps that one a demon rather than a madman, or maybe a skeletal sort of monster instead of an overtly fleshy one, something else the body of which will recede into shadow while the face stands out pale, unnerving in the way it goes on talking, ignorant of how monstrous it looks.

Naturally, you avoid looking at the driver. You carry on conversation with your eyes directed unwaveringly to the windshield, or the passenger-side window, and once again, you see the cavern-like aspect of early-morning central Pennsylvania, the horrible hemmed black expanse of the sky and the dark fields running wavy like ridges of volcanic stone until they meet the horizon's black wall, and the trucks charging by with lurid tigers-eye lights and an alien lack of consideration paid you; their bulk presses in like prison walls that slide about, ready, not willing but not unwilling to impassively, dispassionately crush you like a gigantic pale animal or a god whose thoughts are so far beyond your own comprehension that it might as well be an animal. You have those without, and within, you have the horrific transfiguration of your friend, the promise of fresh horrific transformations to come in the maddening reproducibility, the commodity of the circumstances that make a Mister Hyde of your dearest Doctor Jekyll, and what do *you* have in the middle with you?

You *might* have the aux cord.

You might *have* the brief respite found in looking neither to your left nor to your right, but down to the phone in your lap as you scroll through your wall of album covers to find the one you want to listen to, but what after? You have three-hundred miles until your next turn. This is an expanse of time your playlists, the portion of your music library that you're comfortable playing for your friends, your stamina in selecting music, wasn't made for. Your thumb will drudge up and down, up and down that wall of covers without end, their cheerful confinement, their placid static eternity jeering, all laughing together at your numb mind in its endless movement through that vaguely spherical cavern of night. You will pace the halls of that great library, overshadowed by the shelves stretching like striated coffins to the vaulted ceiling with its cobwebs, dwarfed by the dark, stained velvet floor as it runs like blood from the wall, out at the endless succession of floors extending downward into the yawning, shadowed pit like shelves themselves, bookshelves on bookshelves; and you look up to see that the ceiling is gone and that in its place stands nothing, a hole through which you see greater shelves and greater shelves and greater shelves on and on and on! What once was an escape route will become a prison.

And perhaps the music will wake up some of your friends who were dozing off in the back seats, surely you can turn around and talk to them, right? You will have turned your back on the madman and the cave of trucks and the prison of your music library, but what do you find? A sheet of blackness recedes between the two front seats, and from behind those sheet-like indefinite somethings rise the gradual darkening of deep water, and two or three heads pop, instantly cast pale and otherworldly in the headlight wash, three deathly white monsters peeking from their caves, speaking like people, looking at you like people, joking at and with you, laughing naturally or affectedly in ways made monstrous by the whitish light thrown back through the windshield and between the seats and you think to yourself, *My God, we're not even halfway done. We've still got to do this again.*

And that's your reality for hours and hours, feverishly bouncing between a madman, the underworld, a prison, and a chorus of monsters, then you slip through the sliver of Maryland to reach the chicken wingtip of West Virginia knowing that you won't be able to take a detour to see if you can spot Mothman at his bridge, seeing that the trees are denser and that they press against the sides of the road, reaching out with their skeletal hands with the cloak-like conciliatory blackness between their bony trunks. Seeing that on the horizon between the twin processions of trees, a hazy band of yellow has appeared as though something is inexorably approaching; something great and impassively impetuous like a truck and just as bright crawls along, and that the madman goes to keep driving right down its throat with the white light on his face and the wide undirected hostility in his eyes and that the chorus of monsters is just going to laugh and laugh and laugh and clap as you all drive along to your deaths or some nebulous something-worse.

And you enter Virginia proper with the rising of the sun. You will scarcely believe your tired eyes when they're greeted by a new world, quiet but not unnervingly mysterious beneath the gauzy sheets of morning mist. As though with bleary eyes, the little valleys and grassy flats are just waking up to meet you, the odd sycamores standing at their mouths like yawns as the broad, low ridges of the Appalachians rise kind and paternal-silent in the distance. Those in the back seat will gawk.

The sun will rise higher as you charge boisterously along, the quiet roar of your car's engine garrulous waking birds, through the ever-more-beautiful country, all of you talking joyously, you turning to the side and looking over your shoulder to talk about the future, about your favorite things, about saltwater crocodiles and how cool it would be if they were bigger.

When you see the sign, the one standing in the golden field, the huge one with the red block letters shouting, "Y'ALL COME EAT," you will point and shout, "Y'ALL COME EAT," and the driver following your finger with eyes no longer mad will shout, "Y'ALL COME EAT," and your friends in the back, laughing, will shout perhaps in concert, perhaps not, but no matter how without discord, "Y'ALL COME EAT."

This happiness will be golden, effulgent like the sun at its highest as it coats the world in honey, as you wind your way along mountain roads, staring down at still-misty valleys of trees and light, as you note the prolific runaway truck ramps curving up into the forests and losing themselves beneath the shifting midday shadows of leaves and the patches of sunlight in between, as you pass downhill into North Carolina and on.

And no, y'all don't come eat, but y'all stop at the gas station next to it.

WHEN THE DREAMSHARD KNOCKS
Ali Habashi

The inside of my mouth was dark with cheap wine. The bruises that collared my neck were not much lighter.

I turned away from the hall mirror and tugged the toothy clip from my hair, the strain on my scalp lessening as the plastic jaws opened like cage bars. The dark loomed heavily behind the slats in my blinds, which meant that I only had to wait a little longer until my visitor arrived. I would entertain him as usual, then I would sleep.

Prodding gingerly at my sore neck, I dragged my body towards the sink where I filled a jug with water. He craved plain water, and only ever asked for it. The simple request surprised me the first time.

After all, he didn't have a mouth.

I nearly pointed this out, but I didn't want to insult him or make him angry. I had never seen him anything other than calm, however, sometimes infuriatingly so.

He possessed a cold and still kind of patience. The kind of slow and echoing speech that scared me all on its own. Ever since his arrival, I had been too nervous to leave the house. I could not recall the last time I had spoken to anyone but my nightly guest. I simply could not move past the thought that if I left this house, I might meet him in the dark. Or something like him.

He was a monster to be sure.

But that wasn't quite right.

"What are you?" I had asked after several days of isolation. Isolation interrupted only by him of course. He answered quite readily in a voice that came from nowhere and from everywhere.

"I am a Dreamshard."

I nearly asked what a Dreamshard was, but then, *he* was a Dreamshard.

"Are there more of you?" I asked instead.

His next words pulled the pink from my complexion.

"Of course."

My fears confirmed, I isolated myself still further and opened the door only for him. If I was to live with monsters, I would ensure that he was the only one.

Yet, as the days and nights bled together, I became strangely accustomed to his company. Despite myself, I began to look forward to his visits. A rather awkward situation, like suffering from Stockholm syndrome without the kidnapping. Asking him to keep away never seemed an option, even at the beginning, when his towering form and flickering eyes first appeared at my window.

I rolled my neck in attempt to ease some of the pain as I fetched a cup. I ground my teeth as the pain only intensified.

The faint sound of one long, wooden talon against the glass pulled me toward the front door. Gripping the handle, I searched for that feeling from those first days: a cold dread at my center, juxtaposed with the fiery adrenaline that begged me to run, run, *run*. As the door swung open, I nodded my silent greeting and gestured inside. It was too late; I had built up a tolerance to that instinctual fear.

I traced my fingers over the noose of bruises once again and glanced over my shoulder.

A thicket of long branches, some with the leaves still clinging to them, curled around the doorframe as my guest leaned forward. His head—a chalk-white pumpkin—had no features save for his jack-o-lantern eyes. Was the light that shone from behind the strangely mismatched circles artificial, a live fire, or something else altogether? Maybe his soul?

He rustled into the dining room behind me. Tonight, I would finally relieve some of the mystery surrounding this creature. I was not afraid anymore, it was *more* than that. I had entered a new stage of bold apathy. Even if he transformed into the monster I always thought him to be, I would not blink.

I poured him a glass of water and myself another glass of wine. His branches brushed my fingers as I handed him his drink. I sat; he stood. The pain in my neck flared as I leaned back to look at him.

A burlap cloak secured by thick twine tied at his middle obscured most of his form. The cloth hung in great frayed sections off his shoulders and pooled at his feet, or rather, where feet might have been. The exposed portions of him were a skeleton of boughs and a mesh of kindling, and more than once, I thought that an obvious weakness of my intimidating visitor might be fire. After all, the tangled branches that made up his hands were unprotected. But, burning him into ash never seemed like an option either. At this point in fact, it just seemed rude.

He dipped one of his branches into the water. Some of the greener leaves on his limbs stirred, and his pumpkin tipped in my direction. My only visitor spoke little, so most nights I talked quite a lot. But tonight, I waited. I wanted to see if he would speak, unprovoked.

The Dreamshard stared at me patiently. This was why I always spoke first, looking at him for so long with no words to fill the space made it all the more surreal.

Time slowed to a near stop as we sat in silence together. I poured myself another glass of wine and glared at him pointedly. I could feel my expression getting darker each moment that passed. Only when I poured myself a third glass of wine and was all but glowering at him did he finally speak.

"How is your neck?"

Success. Now, if I could only redirect the focus back on him.

"My neck is fine." I lied. "It's just a little sore."

His voice resonated from the depths of his woven wooden core, carried by the light that shone through his eye sockets.

"You're lying."

I took a slight hiatus from breathing. The tone and cadence had not changed, but the words coupled with his dark baritone seemed like a threat all the same.

"How do you know I'm lying?" I asked, attempting to regain my courage.

With a small bowing of his frame, he set the glass of water on the table.

"When I first got here, it bothered you very much. You kept touching it whenever it was hurting you."

"What's your point?"

"I noticed you doing it again, just now. So…" He leaned forward, those glowing disks boring into me strangely. "How is your neck?"

"It…it hurts."

"Has something scared you?"

"What?"

"Has something scared you?"

"No. Actually, I'm feeling much less nervous than usual."

"Has someone betrayed you?"

"No. Does that matter?"

"Are you planning on confronting someone?"

I shut my mouth so quickly that my teeth clicked together.

"Ah," he said, his pumpkin tipping slightly to one side. "That's it, then."

"How did you know that?" I asked, almost afraid to know the answer.

There was a small stretch of silence as he poked at his water and swiveled his gaze away from mine. Funny, the little gestures seemed almost uncomfortably human.

"Dreamshard," I said, happy to hear some authority in my tone. "Tell me."

His pumpkin craned toward me.

"I watched your nightmare." The words flowed quickly, as though he expected to be chastised for them.

"What nightmare?"

"The one that brought you here."

"What?" I ignored the hideous pain that ignited just below my jaw.

"Well, as you know, our lives are dictated by the dream or the nightmare that originally brought us here."

He leaned forward again, the sticks in his shoulders arching until they creaked dryly. His movements had always been cautious, the basket of his body never twisting too harshly in any direction.

His sticks are too fragile. If he moves too quickly, they might snap.

"Your nightmare was especially plagued and contained all those elements that I have just guessed at: fear, betrayal, and confrontation. Since you denied the first two as the culprits for your relapse, I can only assume that you are planning to confront something, and that it has triggered the pain associated with your original nightmare."

He bobbed his pumpkin in self-affirmation as I balked at him hopelessly.

I completely failed. I barely spoke this entire night, yet all the focus was still on me. On top of that, the mystery only got more twisted the more he spoke. Could the Dreamshard see into my dreams at night, could he see into my head right now? A flicker of that original anxiety sparked in the back of my mind.

I flexed my fingers.

I could break him, I thought. *Snap his twigs.*

Shame rose like bile in my throat. All he had ever done was ask for water. *And possibly read my mind.* I steeled myself and stood up in poor attempt at matching his height.

"Listen to me, Dreamshard." I embraced anger over guilt. "If you're peeking at my nightmares or dreams or anything else inside my head, I need you to stop right now. You've already completely taken over my life, haunting me every night, and I've had enough."

As I approached, he backed away, and I felt wonderfully in control.

"I don't understand," he said as I cornered him next to the spice rack. The little waver of uncertainty in his voice was slight, but I reveled in it.

"*You* don't understand? *You're* the one who showed up at my window. *You're* the one who comes into my house every night. And *you're* the one who's apparently looking at my nightmares on top of it. If you don't stop haunting me, I'm going to—"

280

My voice cut off with a wheeze, as though I'd been gripped around the neck.

"*Lisa?*"

I fought for air and collapsed, my companion lurched forward, and several of the cylinders of shelved spice jolted and toppled to the ground with me. The clouds of colored seasoning that rose around my body, for some reason, did not irritate any of my senses. I pawed at my throat as my airways tightened.

I barely registered that the Dreamshard's branches were around me until they laid me on the tabletop and withdrew. His glowing eyes appeared above me.

A jolt of déjà vu, and I could breathe again. I gasped and sat up on the table, almost knocking heads with the Dreamshard. My heaving gasps slowly quieted.

"Dreamshard," I said hoarsely. "What's going on?"

He arched forward, and I mirrored him in anticipation. My vision filled with his unblinking light.

"I have no idea," he said.

"*Dreamshard.*" I shoved at him weakly, choking as the small movement irritated my damaged throat. I took a shaky breath and looked down, only to see a cup of water cradled in a nest of flexing sticks. He offered me his glass of water.

"Thanks." I wheezed, sipped at it, and the taste of it was peace in comparison to the wine.

"Can I ask you a question?" The Dreamshard drifted back as he said this, his burlap robes dusting the planks of the kitchen floor, as though he were floating.

I nodded, frowning as he turned his glowing sockets away.

"What is it, exactly, that you think you are?"

"What do you mean? I'm a person."

"A person," he echoed, and I cursed his hollow voice as the shiver ran underneath my skin. The little movements that constituted his personality all ceased, and for a minute he stood in eerie imitation of a scarecrow. Then, he approached me slowly. Odd that although his voice still triggered my old fear of him, his closer proximity seemed comfortable.

He held out his hand, or what might have been a hand. Almost too quickly, I took it. The kindling wrapped around my palm and wove through my fingers, and with a gentle tug, I was on my feet before him.

"Walk with me."

An invitation as well as inevitability. I clung to his arm as he guided me toward the door, and I squeezed my eyes shut as he opened it. Maybe I was a coward after all.

We stood, just us, the open door, and whatever lay beyond it for quite a while. The damned Dreamshard remained calm, and the only pressure from him was the weight of his hand in mine, the limbs of his fingers flexing just enough to let me feel the life in him.

Slowly, I opened my eyes. My jaw fell open.

"Where are we?" I asked.

"The Unconscious," he said.

A patchwork of light, weather, buildings, and residents surrounded us. The Dreamshard was nearly rendered normal by the chaos. The sky was a mismatched puzzle of different colors and consistencies blending into one another. A swath of bright blue next to a slab of sterile white, which itself flowed into a dark sky obscured by a storm. The slice that hung directly overhead was the solid slate of deep night.

Those earth-confined objects below each stretch were even more unusual: broken amusement rides, an enormous doll house, streets that went nowhere, stores with no names, a ruined coliseum, stand-alone classrooms, a length of train track, a deserted compound, a junkyard, a collection of famous worldly destinations, a lazy river, skyscrapers with no doors, and an ocean that blurred the horizon. In the distance, the glimmering body of a satellite peeked through the clouds.

Shadowy figures peered from around every corner, and the ones who weren't bothering to hide all looked familiar. I gasped as a small group of brown rabbits, all baring a striking resemblance to my childhood pet, rushed past our feet.

"Whose unconscious did you say this was?" I asked, numb.

"It belongs to the Host," he said. "It belongs to Lisa."

"I'm Lisa."

The Dreamshard didn't say anything. I squeezed his branches in my fist.

"I'm not her, am I?" I asked.

"No...only a piece of her. As am I."

I hated the description. I was a piece. A sliver. A slice. A shard.

I wanted to scream.

"But, I look like me, and I have my memories. Of the real world, I mean." I said, voice shaky, forced smile plastered in place.

Not true, not true, not true.

"Yes," he said. "Yours was an out-of-body, which is why you resemble and retain the memories of the Host. Under the usual circumstances, the Lisa character—however she looked or acted—would have vanished upon waking, leaving the rest of the dream behind in the Unconscious. Occasionally, she will not take on a physical body, but instead become a sort of omniscient presence that watches the dream as it plays out, as was the case with you. I...had not realized that you thought you were the Host all this time."

"I'm not a Dreamshard." My voice was petulant, teetering on devastated.

"You are not."

"Right, see? I'm a person. I just need to wake up."

He hesitated, the perpetual motion of his branches stiffening, a tree without its breeze.

"I was brought to life by a good dream. That is why I am a Dreamshard. You were brought to life by something entirely different."

I shook my head, lifted my free hand to press my purple collar.

"A nightmare."

"Yes. You are a Nightmaredreg."

A dreg, then. Not even a shard.

I looked down at my feet as my energy drained away. Dazed, I realized that the red tennis shoes I was wearing were not mine. I didn't even recognise them. I did not need to turn around to confirm what I now knew to be true. The front hall, the kitchen, the *house*. They were all wrong. Walls in the wrong places, an additional staircase, furniture missing, and entire rooms added. None of it had seemed unusual before.

The Dreamshard's voice was a lifeline in the chaos.

"Some time ago, your house appeared, along with a generous amount of land and a lovely patch of night. My own dream took place at night, and while I do not often return to that section of the Unconscious, I am still drawn to the places that resemble it, even if only in small part.

"At first, I was content to stand back and wait until the dream was finished before wandering through. After all, if I invaded a dream or a nightmare as it was in process I risked becoming a Recurring Dream, a fate that corrupts even the brightest characters in this world.

"But something strange happened. I saw a Dreamshard that I recognized stride up to your door and knock violently. What triggered my curiosity was not the fact that I recognized him, but the fact that I recognized him from the very dream that had first brought me to the Unconscious.

"While there are several doppelgangers that are often reborn with each new sleep, they usually occupy the same spectrum of character, never straying too far in either direction from the way they were originally dreamt. But this man, just slightly more aged than the one I knew, was simply monstrous. Being as close to the fresh location as I was, I could feel what Lisa felt in that moment, and I knew before you opened the door that this would be a nightmare.

"I slid past the border, dividing your nightmare from the rest of the Unconscious, and hid beneath the window, witnessing as subtly as I could. I did not want to be associated with nightmares, but I could not ignore the fact that both you and he—the only two occupants of the dream that had created me—were once again so close, and yet in so different a capacity. When you two had first sat across from me, you smiled at each other, you held hands, and he kissed you—right here."

I tore my gaze from my shoes, the ones that did not belong to me. With his free hand, he pressed one long twig to the space just below his glowing eye sockets, where a mouth might have been. Despite myself, I smiled at the sight. A real smile.

"Through the window, I could see you two yelling at each other. You had been drinking wine and abruptly picked the bottle up and swung it at him. He caught it, placed it on the table, then he took both of his hands, and he—" His voice shook toward the end.

His shoulders curled forward, and his sticks tightened a fraction around my fingers.

"He put them around my neck," I said, and the Dreamshard's pumpkin jerked up in surprise.

"We had just broken up a week earlier. The relationship had gone sour a while ago, but I thought that maybe it was salvageable nonetheless. When I found out he was cheating on me, I broke it off. He was angry, and I was frightened. I had lots of nightmares that week. Including one where he strangled me. Then, you showed up, and the nightmares stopped. I thought it was because I was more afraid of you than of anything else. But…"

I swallowed sorely, picturing the long lines of bruising that had never faded.

That *would* never fade.

"The nightmares only stopped because I became the nightmare."

The throbbing in my neck grew unbearable, and I pressed my arm to my eyes and tried not to sob. I could not stop the few shudders and gasps that escaped me as I realized that I was stuck in this place for good. There was no waking up.

"Oh, God. I'm nothing. I'm not real."

I gulped and sobbed embarrassingly as the tears flowed from me in unnatural quantities and splashed to the ground. Subtlety apparently did not exist in this world.

"I am made of firewood."

The statement was so seemingly random that I turned toward him.

"I am made of firewood, but I am real. I can feel, and speak, and think. I am talking to you, and holding your hand, and looking at you. No one can tell me that those things do not constitute some form of an existence."

"But we're dreams. *And nightmares.* We are floating in someone's unconscious. She doesn't even know we exist."

"I see no problem with any of that," he said, his voice steady despite the absurdity of what he was saying. "We were born, and whether you're born a Dreamshard or a Nightmaredreg or a person is a stroke of luck. And the fact that our Host does not know we exist? This is not only a stroke of luck, it is a blessing."

"How do you figure?" I frowned, rubbing at my eyes.

"Because I have seen the Conscious, and it is a fleeting, impermanent, shallow place."

"What?" My volume startled someone who seemed to be conversing with a bushfire in the next setting over.

"When Lisa woke up from her dream, she remembered me upon waking. I was yanked from the Unconscious, through the Subconscious and into the Conscious, where I found myself unable to do much more than repeat the same motions I had made in the dream. Only they weren't the same. What I did in the Conscious was run on loop of increasingly biased and misrepresented events. My free will was all but lost, and even my form changed, becoming sharper and taller. It was a horrible strain on my sticks, but luckily it wasn't very long until I found myself shoved back through the membrane separating the Conscious from the Subconscious.

"There were lots of things there, too, and I relaxed in realizing these thoughts were much more…stable. It made sense, seeing as that was where Lisa stored most of her knowledge. I wandered through her memorized and accessible thoughts. They were extremely monotonous: her route to work, her address, what she had studied or read the night before. I met a few other dreams there, all of them warped by being dragged so often into the Conscious only to be shoved back. Thankfully, I was not recalled again, and soon enough, I was tugged back into the place I recognized as my dream."

I desperately ignored the small knot of jealousy that formed within me at his descriptions. While these other sections of the mind seemed much less entertaining than the one I resided in, I could not help but wish that I had been that close to being real, at least once. To be in the Conscious, to me, seemed like the closest thing to being me again. I had only just discovered that I was not, nor had ever been human, and I already missed it.

The Dreamshard grasped my other hand in his, and I swallowed my complaint.

We faced each other once again, and I was surprised to find that, at some point in the last few hours, I had come to think of his expressionless pumpkin as somewhat endearing. The exaggerated motions of his head and body seemed to have taken the place of a face and its emotions, and his voice, once so terrifying, was now colored with concern. Concern for me.

"You may not have seen much of it yet. But the Unconscious is more than just scraps of dreams and nightmares placed one after the other. There are memories here, there is wisdom, and there is instinct—all hidden in our corner of the mind. With each new experience and long sleep that Lisa has, something new comes to be."

"What about the nightmares?" I asked.

"There will always be nightmares, or unpleasant memories, or bad people. All we can hope for is to seek out the good and recognize that not everything that originally disturbs us is as dark as we may have first imagined. After all, you are a Nightmaredreg and look very much like a dream, and I am a Dreamshard and look very much like a nightmare."

I was surprised to hear him mirror my own thoughts from earlier.

"But what about my ex? His whole purpose is to throttle me, and he's still out there."

"He won't hurt you." He said this as though it were an irrefutable fact rather than a protective statement or kind encouragement.

"Why?"

"Because he is lost."

His voice had never been deeper, his presence never more ominous, yet for once, I felt no fear. Not even the apathetic expectation of doom that I had been feeling earlier. All I could muster was a small smile.

"Do I have you to thank for that?"

"When I saw him attack you, I nearly interrupted the nightmare. The only reason I was able to hesitate was by remembering that once Lisa woke up, she would vanish, leaving the forgotten man alone with his hatred. As the logic of this kept me safe from exposure for a few minutes more, I felt her presence lifting. She was returning to the Conscious.

"I waited until the weight of her left and watched in horror as *you did not vanish*. When I felt the Host immediately return to the Unconscious and begin to weave another dream from the shadows of her thoughts and experiences, I…intervened."

Suddenly, the memory was clear: my attacker above me, my fading vision, and the unexpected air that rushed painfully through my windpipe as the twin tunnels of the Dreamshard's glowing eyes replaced those of my fellow Nightmaredreg.

"You saved me from him. You took him away. But, where…?"

"I took him back. To the place created by my own dream: a vast maze of cornstalks just beyond the grass fields. The Dreamshard version of the man who strangled you—the one from my own dream—is still wandering through the maze even now. I offered to show him the way out, but he rejected any help. I assumed that the one that had attacked you would have a similar difficulty with navigation. So far, I've been correct."

He was speaking so casually about my would-be killer wandering through a maze, that I sniggered.

As I laughed louder, I realized that I did not remember laughing at all since the Dreamshard had first visited. That could only mean that I had not laughed at all since being created. I had never laughed before. This was the first time, ever.

It felt good, freeing. I managed to open my eyes enough to see that the Dreamshard had tipped his pumpkin to one side in confusion, but that only made me laugh harder.

As per the usual, the Dreamshard waited patiently. When my laughter had worn my poor throat raw, I grinned up at him. His branches had not budged from between my fingers.

"You've sure been holding my hands a lot this evening." I smirked.

"Yes. It is something I saw you and your friend doing in my own dream. Holding hands and kissing—the second of which I cannot do—seemed to make you happy. And *look*."

He removed one of his tangled hands from my own and gestured towards my smiling mouth.

"It has worked again," he said with a small bob. I nodded back at him and grinned widely.

We both looked up as an operatic voice swelled over the peaks and dips of the landscape. A moon that was much too close and moving much too fast hovered overhead, spilling light into my corner of the Unconscious.

"I remember you. From the real world."

The pumpkin swiveled slowly to face me.

"There was a Halloween festival. It had a pumpkin patch and food stalls and games. But the festival was locally famous for its complicated maze. That was my favorite part, and I always found my way out before my friends. The year I took my boyfriend, we found our way to the center of the maze right at the moment it got dark outside. There wasn't much there, just a few hay bales, and a scarecrow that was up on top of them."

The Dreamshard pointed to himself, and I nodded.

"We sat up against your perch and talked for hours. That was the first time he kissed me, and probably the moment I began to fall in love with him."

"That sounds very much like the dream I came from."

"There were a lot of unhappy memories after that Halloween, but the maze has always been one that couldn't be...corrupted."

"I am glad."

A pale girl with a bright red hair landed a flying carpet a few dreams over, distracting me. She hurried over to a tall, black man in a widely brimmed hat and threw her arms around him. They embraced like family. I did not recognize either of them, yet I felt like knew them both. Maybe I knew everyone here.

"Dreamshard, do you want to go for a walk tomorrow?"

"Of course."

"Thank you." I turned to face him. "For everything that you did, and for everything that you've been doing."

"Thank you for the water. And for letting me hold your hand."

"Dreamshard."

"Yes—?"

I stood on my toes and pressed my lips on the smooth spot just below his eyes, where a mouth might have been.

"*Oh.*" He gasped, his deep, dark voice suddenly light and feathery with surprise. His pale pumpkin flushed bright orange, and I laughed.

"See you tomorrow, Dreamshard."

REMEMBER BACKWARDS
Maul Allan Hewish

Is this happening? Is this present, or is it past? Am I remembering, forecasting, or am I dictating present events? There is no distinction in the dream. In the dream, all time exists in knitted knots and spirals and co-spliced corkscrews. In the dream, you feel as though the present is close by, as though you're almost catching it— arms out—chasing the present with this bizarre sense of the foreknown and the forgotten all blending into one, the ephemeral chase of the unknowable nature of the space outside time. It is our life, ever recycling and uncontained by continuity.

What does it mean to remember backwards? It's like a riddle.

Once you know, the answer is obvious.

It appears abstract because you're being too literal.

There is nothing literal about this. This is entirely not happening.

Boy, my dad would shake his head at all that and give me an eyebrow.

"What the hell does it all *mean*, son?"

The doors are locked. No matter how hard we fight with the locks and slam our fists against the glass, there is no breaking through. The windshield is shatterproof, but molten steel would still make short work of that. We change up our strategy, hammering on it with our shoes—pile-driving full-forced blows into it.

The damn thing doesn't even budge.

It barely even cracks.

I turn to Danton. I don't remember meeting him. It must have happened a long time ago. We have the same name.

With the glass now smudged with shoe prints and sweaty palm-prints, our view of the outside world is a hellish pastel-smear of fiery light.

A quick inspection told us we're suspended above an enormous vat of molten steel in the cab of a flat-nosed truck. The truck is wrapped in a loop of chains thick enough to anchor a cruise ship—a bleak cast-iron lattice covered the side windows.

I have no idea how we got here, but there is no way out. We're stuck.

We're dead.

Danton turns to me, desperation in his eyes. He's looking for something—any sign that I might have a way out up my sleeve.

I shrug.

He shuts his eyes and slams back into the seat, evidently disappointed. His sharply-tailored black suit and tie are still crisp. We're wearing matching sets.

Have we just come from some kind of formal event? I can't say with any certainty.

The past is a hard wall in this particular instant.

Danton scrunches up his face, trying hard to chase a particular thought.

"You have to remember in a different direction. You have to remember backwards."

"I don't understand."

*He's speaking about the dream of course. That's what dreaming is, remembering in a different direction. He reaches out, fingers spread and palm facing outwards. I copy the gesture and see—*really *see the present as it's happening...*

Danton and I stand in the bookstore.

He pulls a book from the shelf, a nonchalant volume with black leather binding. He opens it easily, though it seems rather hefty.

"I am the suicidal, and you are the saviour who follows."

"You talking to me?"

"Who else?"

"I thought you were reading from the book?"

"Maybe the book is reading from you?" He looks up with a smile. These events have no connection to the memories of the molten steel and the truck.

I'm sure of it. Those images sit isolated from this cosy space smelling of weathered paper, yellowed, musty pages, and ancient binding glue holding them to their tattered, cracked spines. From hand-to-hand and mind-to-mind, these crazed visions have travelled from person-to-person, exchanged countless times. Each encompass nostalgia for lives unlived, merely glimpsed and felt in the air—smiling from behind their dog-eared pages.

"Are you so sure we're not still in that truck?"

"Positive." I inhale the dust of the place and run my fingers along several books, the smooth, glossy texture of their spines.

"So why did the book open on Mollina?"

He isn't wearing the suit anymore.

Neither am I.

We're in long brown coats, the kind inspectors wear on those lame cop shows. The ones where they always discover some clue right before the ad break.

"What?"

"She's right here."

"Coincidence." I shrug again and select a volume of my own.

"That's not the only place she is..."

Danton points up at the uppermost shelf towards an eccentric collection of trinkets: China plates, antique coffee pots, strange gilded silver biscuit bowls. A foreboding collection of china-faced dolls.

I notice her instantly. She's leaning over, taking her weight on one arm, her knees laid sideways, one atop the other. Her tiny left hand is extended out in that familiar gesture, palm out and fingers spread wide. Her proportions caricature and squat, while her head is enormous, exaggerating her eyes. Like Japanese cartoons.

Except Mollina didn't have eyes, instead her empty sockets were stuffed with corks of dried blood.

That was how we always knew it was her.

She has a helmet of dark hair, with two red bows pinned into place. Her tiny pink nipples jut out grotesquely, and her off-white skin bulges in rolls of fat, painted just a bit too realistically for anyone of good taste. Around her tiny neck is a silver band; *that* was new.

It must have been placed on the figurine recently.

Her wings were chipped, just as weathered as ever. That dirty little cherub soured many a good heart. I knew of at least four deaths attributed indirectly to this haunted thing. The last person who tried to pry the corks of blood from her eye sockets was eaten alive by the tiny white roots of a pristine lawn. The earth had inverted; and borne up white hairs to strip flesh from bone. Gulping them down, casting their clothing aside, corpse now nutrition for the soil.

I grab Mollina, grunting at her dull lead weight. Her exterior appeared to be some kind of glossy ceramic but was dense as a brick of gold. I strain and heft her to eye level with both hands, turning the china figure to better drink up every horrid detail.

"We murdered that woman on purpose." Danton nods in the direction of Mollina, putting the thick book back on the shelf.

"Mollina was never alive."

"No, I mean the one that found her last time, the one that tried to pull out the corks and dropped Mollina outside the car."

"I thought we were in a truck?"

"We *are* in a truck—there's a difference. We *were* in a car."

"So, when is this? Is this after or before?"

"Neither. We're here right now."

That answer didn't make any sense, but simultaneously made more sense than anything. Of course, we were here now—to think otherwise was ludicrous. We weren't anywhere else, only in this book store. Yet, that wasn't entirely true.

"How did we get here?"

"We drove here."

"In the car?"

"In the car."

I follow his gaze to the breath-fogged windows cut into diamonds by an elaborate pane, the glass glittering with beads of liquid amber from the harsh sodium bulbs of the streetlights outside. I can't see any details. Outside is cold. I know that much.

"I think that part happens first, though I can't be sure, so I guess neither can you."

Holding Mollina, however, a spark of recognition becomes a flood of images. We *were* somewhere else. Where the hell had we been going before we'd stopped into the bookshop? This wasn't our destination. This was merely a sidestep, but something about it felt much more *vital* than anything else. Much more...real. An essence of import lingered on each mote of dust and whiff of mothballed carpet. The lilac of cheap air freshener hovered beneath those other scents like a nervous ghost.

Each book title melts from my eyes—indecipherable. I can read the letters, but they shift and swim away as I attempt to piece them together into collated words. They have familiar groupings, letters arranged in twos and threes and familiar punctuation, but lithe and liquid. It changes in my periphery, slithering into new forms that render previous glimpses moot.

This place is a hall of shattered memory.

A repository.

With a sudden intensity, I set Mollina down atop some sturdy-spined hardbacks and use both hands to flip open the slimmer volume I'd pried free of the shelves. The pages are blank. I flick through them, looking for something. But I'm not looking close enough. A tiny dot sits in the centre of the screen. *The screen?* And it *is* a screen—

I'm staring at my computer monitor, typing in the details of the latest insurance claim to come across my desk. A Sunday, and yet, here I am, still cranking through the bottomless pile like the machine that would eventually replace me. I sincerely believe that one day all our jobs will be replaced by machines, and people will revert to their savage nature.

The machines will set up cage matches where we can fight each other to death, and the victor gets to eat the spoils.

Don't lie. You'd watch that. You know you would.

I sure as shit would.

Until that day, I sit in my tiny office, typing tiny meaningless data into tiny meaningless forms that don't add up to a goddamn thing. This is why mathematicians go crazy and take power-drills to their heads or get bitten by the bottle in their later years. They start to put together what it all means, and their brains want out. I'm just a drone entering data— imagine if you actually paid attention.

Imagine if you were as conscious and aware as you'd ever been, sharp as the nip of a brisk mid-winter morning. Imagine yourself as switched on as you feel after a cup of strong coffee or chugging down a Redbull. Imagine ever-so-carefully entering each digit and understanding each corresponding entry with that intense sense of any great eureka moment; the numbers and letters and notations all fall so effortlessly into place by your caring, governing hand. Now, imagine that event occurring again. And again.

And again.

Stretching out into infinity.

The strain of it would split your head in two. An aneurysm in twenty minutes. Time would stretch out, and a single minute becomes twelve eternities, condensed and consigned to crush you into a paste more easily digested by the harsh appetite of an endless hourglass. An hourglass where every weary grain of indignant grey sand hits the floor like a bead of lead.

The faceless man enters my cubicle.

He wears a neatly tailored suit jacket, grey with black pinstripes, left unbuttoned. His plain white undershirt, however, is buttoned all the way to the top, no sign of a tie. I'd never seen anyone wear a collared shirt like that in all my life. I was almost too swept up in the oddity of his shirt to notice that he didn't have a face.

Almost.

But I notice, because how could I not? It wasn't just that his features were missing either. You were probably thinking of a store mannequin, the kind of smooth blank face that hovers above the latest fashion, selling you things that would never fit you, but fit them just fine in their skeletal, plaster-moulded perfection. You're being too conservative. The node of skull above his neck is entirely smooth. A perfect bulb of skin, unblemished by any recognizable shape or wrinkle, and bearing only the slightest trace of pigment—an off-milk.

A light blue sketch of veins hint behind the bulge that would ordinarily be occupied by the temples, and there seemed a slight rosier hue at the centre where the edges pinched outwards. A few acne scars make the thing even more real. Too real.

I jump back in my office chair and snap the book shut.

It claps shut. My heart charges at a thundering gallop. A passing car fills the frosted diamond window with light momentarily, and Danton tells me to *calm down.*

I'm stuffing the book back on the shelf with sweaty, trembling fingers.

Mollina watches me from atop the books with her corked cherub eyes. Her demure little smirk is suddenly smug. Had she been sitting on my desk at work? Had that paperweight I'd seen atop the pile of reports been her? I couldn't clearly remember. But I had my suspicions.

"Okay, so we're currently in the truck. But also currently here. Are we also there in my office? Are all these things happening right now? How can that be? How can we know what has happened, is happening, or if this is like…a flashback? We could end up talking about things that haven't happened yet in the past tense."

"All we know is that it involves Mollina." Danton nods.

"How do we know about Mollina?"

Danton gestures at the books climbing the shelves to either side of us.

"Pick a book, any book—you're bound to ramble into something that makes some kind of sense if you look hard enough. People see all kinds of shapes in the stars that aren't actually there. Some of those stars in each constellation are of such different ages, some of them don't even exist yet within the span of the other's life. All we see is their ghosts, reaching us from a long time ago. Just a bead of light that we draw a line from to reach another bead of light. *A* to *B*. Nice and simple. 'Look it's a giraffe.' But life isn't simple, and neither is time.

"Memories and time are subjective and impossible to quantify. They stretch and bend and sometimes bleed—right on into each other. We have to form a narrative, or we'll go insane, even if that narrative involves taking impossible leaps."

"Doesn't explain why we're standing in a bookshop arguing while we could also be about to fall to our death in some sick trap."

"Maybe this is just our way of making sense of things."

"Our way?"

"Or your way. Whatever. I'm not going to tell you who you are."

Chewing my lip in thought, I repeat Danton's words in my head.

I'm not going to tell you who you are.

It wasn't *who* I was that was important, at least—not in the most literal sense. My name was Danton. We're just two plain old Dantons, standing in a bookshop, trying to make sense of it all. But that wasn't exactly right. I'm not just any old Danton, and neither is he. Mollina hadn't dared touch us for a reason. The same reason there were two of us, and the same reason each book would conjure a new set of impressions that may or may not somehow link with this moment.

The dream wasn't finished yet. It was still happening.

"Was Mollina in the cab of the truck?"

"I don't remember." Danton shrugged. "And you're using the wrong tense. Technically, if we're there right now, the correct question would be: *is* Mollina in the cab of the truck?"

"For crying out loud…you know what I meant."

Danton grinned.

I heft Mollina off the shelf.

"Where are you going?"

I step past Danton without bothering to answer. I'm headed for the end of the aisle, where another wall of books reaches skywards in a teetering, time-yellowed tower. At it's end, I turn right and approach the main counter of the book store, a smooth slab of antique wood, where a few half-price paperbacks sit in a wire basket to one side. A shining silver bell beams proudly near an ancient cash register of ancient mustard-yellow plastic. The clerk sits on a piano stool, their nose buried in a newspaper. I can't read the headline, nor decipher the picture on the front. It is blurred and pulsing, the colours breathing and ghosting to obscurity; the image a formless, shifting abstract.

I set Mollina down on the counter and ask him how much. The newspaper drops, and I'm stepping back, my fingers sliding off the counter. My hands flop bonelessly to my sides. I'm suddenly cold. Much too cold. There is no face behind the newspaper. There is only a smooth bulb of skin—a familiar, lethal visage that has followed us even here. It stares eyelessly, wearing a found-in-a-salvation-army-bin plaid brown suit with patched elbows.

I have no time to sing out for Danton. I run for the door, my feet thumping off the dust-caked carpet, but I can't remember where the door leads. It won't open until I know where it goes. It's locked. The night shines in, glistening off beads of evaporated breath that catch on the glass. Beyond is the cold and the dark.

The scrunch of crinkling paper turns me. The eyeless thing discards the newspaper and stands. It *looms*. The thing is easily seven feet tall, maybe eight. The suit *sags* about the thing as though fitted for someone or *something* larger still. The sleeves are long and loose, each half of the coat hangs like a batwing from its skeletal arms. Finally, I find my voice.

"Danton. We're in *trouble*."

"Have you tried not being in trouble? Why does everything have to be so dramatic…"

His voice bounced off the high ceilings, where it seemed to vibrate in the exposed plumbing like a rattling coin.

"Danton, I'm serious."

"So am I. Deadly."

His voice, stranger and more distant, warbles like a cheap megaphone fed through a long piece of PVC guttering. Like a key in an ancient lock, it clicked. I realized how we'd ended up in the truck, and why we'd been snagged here for such an extended period of time. This was me *forgetting*. I was experiencing what it meant to forget.

Lethe was the clue. There are always clues. Even in dreams. His name was Danton Lethe.

Forgetfulness has no face, but it sure can eat. It will take everything that ever happened to you and destroy everything you are.

The memories shelved here are transient and fragile. I can slip into one at any moment, but by being there, I'm re-interpreting the contents afresh; I'm adding details that weren't there. I'm inventing the past as I relive it. Things I couldn't possibly remember are suddenly fresh and vivid.

I had two slices of cake at my eighteenth birthday party, not three.

I drove home instead of walked.

I kissed her, and she laughed instead of that ear-splitting shriek.

Memory will take the past and mould it to my ego. Always had and always would. It wears my face and has my name.

We're not even one regular Danton. We're half of neither. This bookshop is a repository. A mental facade against the wormy, gnashing dark. The faceless are time. They sit and erase us with their smooth, eyeless gazes—scrubbing the sure and safe into cold oblivion, ushering in the outer dark where all is hollow and formless and without.

But the dream—our world is the dream. We wake, and our ego fills in the spaces, so we don't go blinding mad. We wake, and the world is as we understand it. This is how our ego needs it to be. Danton is gone now, his voice echoing off down a path I can't follow, trailing down some impossible hallway in a formless abyss of forgetting. The unseeing stare invites me to try and run.

The bookshelves to either side of the aisle tower higher than skyscrapers, higher than mountains. The aisle leading back to the front desk is barely three feet wide and about six feet long but feels about the length and width of the Grand Canyon.

I don't dare run. Time doesn't need to give chase. It can hunt without having to move, because it's always there—ticking away on the wall. It can afford to wait; time is the ultimate persistence predator.

I do the only thing I can do and reach for another book on the shelf. It's a medium-sized thing, with a rough rawhide cover and an elaborate criss-cross of leather string binding it along the spine. The faint musk of sunlight and autumn is baked into it, giving way to the crisp, warm aroma of unbleached paper.

It spills open in my hands, and I'm shaking. The whole bookshop seems to be shaking because I can't keep my damn hands on the wheel.

The road is icy, and the pavement is glistening with sleet. I'm breathing steam, and Danton warms his hands in front of the pathetic excuse for a heater that's running full blast in our getaway car.

"Why the hell is this stupid cherub so important?"

"I don't know. There always has to be something. Some mystery. I can't know it, and neither can you. What answer would possibly satisfy? The ambiguity of it gives it infinite

possibilities. If you answer a mystery, it takes away its power. No hidden truth would be as powerful, and you know it. What we can't know gives us power, mystery invites a new direction for you to remember. You can remember backwards."

"Right, and it…, in turn, gives us power over the dream, unless…"

Danton's expression goes blank, and he stares ahead at the endless suburbs that drift by in the dark. The trees are stripped of their leaves, pointing accusatory fingers of gnarled, frost-gilded wood heavenwards at the perpetrator. The houses are quiet and lonely; shuttered and silent against midnight. The moon might have shone had it not been muffled in a sickly nest of cobwebby clouds.

"Unless what?" *I ask.*

"Unless we forget what it means."

"Forget what?"

Danton smirks.

"We might. They will try to take it from us. Time will march right on in and pluck it away if we're not careful."

"Okay, so what will time not dare take?"

"All we have to do is think of some really strong memories—random sensations and impressions, sights smells, sounds—anything that we know we'll always remember. If we take her with us, into those places…"

"…We control the dream." *Danton sat back in his seat. He gave me both eyebrows then furrowed them.*

"So, did this really happen? You drove home after your eighteenth birthday?"

"If she's here, then yes." *I point to the dashboard, where Mollina sits strapped in place with a Velcro tag, just above the radio and air conditioning block.* "And the correct tense is that that it* is *still happening."*

I grin back at him.

He snorts a laugh.

"How sure are you that you drove home?" *Danton leaned forwards, hunched over with his arms across his chest, rubbing them to try and get the blood flowing.*

"Pretty sure. It was a while ago." *Outside, the stars gleamed through the gunmetal trees.*

"Well, those air vents aren't shooting anything warm, that's a stiff blast of night air."

"What's your point?"

"Are you* sure *you didn't walk?"*

The doubt laid a seed. The seed took root into mind. The wind hits me full force. I didn't have the insulation of the car because I'm drunk out of my mind. I'm walking home in wet shoes. My feet are fucking freezing. Bile and two-minute noodles threaten to come flying back up in a gruesome chuck. I fight it with a bitterness sharpened by rage.

Fucking Liam Spicer. I bust open the bathroom door to find him two knuckles deep in my girlfriend. She's sitting on the sink vanity, legs open just enough. Her skirt is hitched up to her waist, pink satin knickers at her ankles. She's staring at me like I'm the one who's fucked up.

"Do you mind?" *She asks, disgusted. Her face pinched in that 'I just smelled dogshit' look.*

Liam Spicer twists around, peering over his shoulder with the cheekiest shit-eating grin plastered ear to ear, as though he's just been caught taking an extra nibble from the cookie-jar.

It's like she'd forgotten who I was.

So, I left my car at her place. I'd not said a word on the way out. Driving drunk and angry, I'd likely wrap it around a tree and go to my grave, grinning like a demon.

How could you use love as a tool like that? How could you discard someone who laid their very heart at your feet?

The chill soothes my rage. Hard to stay mad when you were so damn cold.

I wander down the middle of the road, dodging puddles in potholes that stew a winter broth of dead leaves and silt.

Danton walks beside me, almost bent over. "Jesus Christ…that's a hell of a memory." Danton stutters through chattering teeth.

"I wish I could forget it, but I never will." The wind rushes through the limbs of dead and dying trees, rumbling like the lashing of a king tide at midnight.

"It's always the worst ones that seem like permanent residents. They just don't go. I bet if I burned this book, time wouldn't want it. It's too sharp of a pain for even time to take completely. Time might chip away at some of it, but it would just as soon spit it back out and snack on something tastier. I guess time eats us all in the end though, doesn't it?"

"Yes," Danton says quietly, almost a whisper.

I sadly shake my head, and the wind sings and howls. The distant hum of an engine from somewhere behind me turns my attention to the fact that I'm striding up the centre of the road. Headlights bathe me in blinding white; I spin slowly and lift my hand to shield my eyes. The damn lights are so bright they pierce my drunken dizzy. The book slips from my fingers, and I'm—

—backpedalling away from the steadily advancing faceless thing. I slap against the glass of the door and remember where the door goes. Is there even a chronology to any of this? Probably not. But I know there is something I'd been running away from. And it was an endless, pointless pursuit. Beyond *that* door, things like chronology mattered. In here, not so much.

In here, I see myself how I'd once been—at my peak maybe. Before I'd been hit coming home from that party, suffered nerve damage and lost the ability to walk for more than a block without screaming agony. That's the sort of thing that really limits your employment options. I'd been relegated to a soul-sucking job, pushing pencils in an insurance firm. Never promoted, even after ten years of solid service thanks to my fuckstick of a supervisor who just loved to pedal how accepting he was that they allowed someone with my so-called handicap to work with them. But that's not all there is to me. Not my job. Or my handicap. My ego could only ever see me one way.

If I opened that door, I would be trapped; ever closer to falling into the molten steel and being utterly destroyed by time. Time had encased me in two such traps; one of these was a trap called life. In this bookshop, I might extend a moment into a millennium, wringing every last drop of time for each spec of worth and meaning and *life* that I could scrape from its marrow.

All I had to do was remember backwards, and I knew I could make it work, at least for now. To dream is to remember in a different direction, and remembering backwards is simple projection: the imagination. We had intuitive reasoning develop as a means of extending our lifespan back when we were still a hunter-gatherer society, way back with the mud huts and the berry picking and the stone-tipped spears.

It still served the same purpose all those centuries later; we still stretched out our survival and escaped into the dream. We still moulded the seconds into hours by whatever means—by rumination, by postulation, by simply dwelling in the past.

I grab for the door handle and *feel the chains holding the truck unwind.*

I *knew* that truck. And I *knew* that place. My father had worked in a steel mill up until my fourteenth birthday, when an accident—some stupid bastard who'd backed out a forklift without looking—had dislocated my father's collarbone, broke three of his ribs and gave him permanent nerve damage. Just like that, manual labour was forever out of my father's reach. No pun intended.

Like father like son.

Danton looks over at me in the cab of the truck, still in his pressed birthday suit, supposed to be billed on the hour, every hour, from a well-to-do men's tailor, but scored for the discount price of fifty bucks flat. Danton was a perfect mirror of my younger self. The aspirational little bastard I'd been before that birthday party had made me into a man; a bitter one.

The rear-view mirror reflects my tired and bloodshot eyes—yellowed by time. Wrinkled, sagging skin hangs from my cheeks, and each eye sits in deep cavernous sockets.

My father wasn't the sort to ever settle for an office job. He was smarter than I was in that regard. He took up a delivery job, driving the local milk truck to businesses, where a younger guy was usually paired with him to help lift the crates out of the back. Not the most luxurious title in the world, but it paid the bills, and he got to know the neighbourhood pretty well. He was well-loved. In the end, my subconscious took those elements for the dream. Just subconscious ramblings assembling into something that seemed vital and poignant. And, hey, presto! It was.

Danton held Mollina in his lap. That poisonous trinket that had slain so many in our dream realm. It was a damned thing, but a damned necessary thing. We needed to have some token, some strange unknown element that anchored us in the abstract.

But I still remember my father, even though he died thirty years back. All these moments are frozen in time, so long as someone or something carries a memory through the ages.

He'd made the most of his life, and I'd never really felt I equalled his accomplishments. I'd always lived in the shadow of that simple fact.

I held out one bony, wrinkled hand to Danton. He knew exactly what to do. Of course, he did; he might have been young, but he was still essentially me. If I knew what to do, he did. He placed Mollina into my waiting palm. I felt her sickly weight and grimaced, my arm nearly giving way under her innate mystery.

The door to the bookshop was equally heavy. It opened on a blinding, searing truth that stung too bright to be ignored. My heart stopped.

Time staked a claim on my life, this fever dream a maze of memory and invention and projections unbound, my primal self exiting the body as I fled to a world made entirely of memory, where nothing but the impression of myself on the lives and places of my passing would dare linger, after the twisted talons of time rend it asunder.

With Mollina in one hand, I reach for the handle of the truck's cab door. The thick loops of chain fall neatly away, dissolving their hold as though made of nothing more than paper.

They were made of something else, however; an idea.

The prison of my father's accomplishments.

Bingo.

A single line; a single concept. It was enough.

I push open the door and stand above the molten steel, embracing the finality of the moment.

The ceiling fades to black as my brain loses oxygen. I'm lying on the floor, unable to get to the telephone. My eyes are dry and stinging, glaring through a loamy filter. My bowels loosen. Shit fills my pants as my brain reaches the critical point of no return.

I'm dying. That's what this is. I'm watching my memories and inventions dance around the rim of a drainpipe.

I claw at it: hold on just one second longer.

The black fills with fireworks—tiny stars that stutter and sway.

With one hand cradling Mollina, that cursed thing, I'm one step away from bliss and oblivion, joining my father in the hereafter. But I hesitate.

I look back and see Danton watching. Afraid. Of course he is. He's the best of me, before all those years spent wishing for the end, without really any comprehension of how bad things can get.

Is it really so bad? To want to be rid of it all?

Time will take it from us one way or another. But damned if I don't remember when I was still young enough to smile. And incredibly, I'm wearing one. I'm smiling, but I'm crying all the same. I step into oblivion. You can't remember in this direction, it ain't forwards or backwards. It's outside our regularly scheduled programming.

This is the dream outside the dream. That's what it's all about, Dad.

I hope I see you again soon, and I hope I made you proud.

THE GLITTERING PEARLS
Alisha Costanzo

Gravel crunched beneath Jace's sneakers as he marched his way to the Depository. The predominately iron structure made the unbearable weight from his last purge dissipate enough for Jace to stand two inches taller. It was the only place he found any resemblance of peace.

The high and open arches of the building let in too much light during the day, but at twilight, the black metal stood as a shadow amongst small, glittering pearls. It looked dangerous, which meant no one else would be there—other than his fellow Eaters.

Upon entrance, Jace palmed the iron and held on, releasing a single moment from the day's purges.

Echoes from a shrill scream reverberated within him as his arm jolted forward, slicing a blade through soft flesh and muscle, a set of nails digging ragged circles into his left shoulder. Hot blood spilled over his hand and the handle of the black iron knife used for official Guard business.

The sparse and open foyer of the Depository returned to him, and the hunch of his shoulders eased. He couldn't rid himself of many at a time, but most of the elder Eaters made frequent ritual of it. Why they wanted to prolong their misery, Jace couldn't figure. He rid himself of just enough to stave off a little of the pain, just enough to allow him a few precious hours of sleep. Tonight, his hand would meet the iron more than normal.

Two purges in one day demanded a lot.

Jace wound his way up a spiral staircase to the top level, a relatively small section of the building that housed donated cots and old furniture. Several Eaters took up the beds and couches, leaving smaller spaces for others. As he passed a few, he could see the twitches in their muscles and knew they did not sleep.

A corner sat empty of younger Eaters, like himself, as an elder lay propped against a slew of old cushions. None could truly bear to be near an elder, weighed down with more than a decade of sins on his soul that the evil radiating into his immediate surroundings.

Jace took a circular chair, with a short round back that curved into arms. It cupped his body as he pulled his knees to his chest. He closed his eyes to debilitating guilt and flashes of torture. Iron arched over him, and he touched it once more.

His hand closed around Ms. Wendy, the young librarian's, throat, opening her mouth in a gasp of air. Leather and molding paper scented her clothes, but her hair hinted at herbs and romance. Ms. Wendy's skirt crept up her thigh and hip above his hand as he grabbed her. A fire burned low in his belly and extremities. Adrenaline and lust filtering out of control as pain clawed at his arms—the first bit of her fight.

Peeling away from the iron; the withering pain curled him further in on himself.

Two guards in one day were too much for a pentam. But Jace turned sixteen in two days. The purges would grow worse as his duties moved him closer to the pristine parts of the city and its capitol.

A scream hurled Jace back into reality. Its serrated pain parroted so many he'd purged. The elder bawled in his sleep, one leg lurching like a limp.

The sun stalked the dark in the Depository, readying for a full onslaught within the hour. He didn't want to be up there when those rays pierced the cracks in the other Eater's eyes. If he left now, he wouldn't have to wait in line for breakfast.

Muscles creaking, his posture nearly straightened by the time he shambled down the stairs. The capitol already glowed with bright promises past the iron arches, the sun blessing their people first.

Gray fog danced with his sneakers as he turned into the suburb streets, his preferred café two blocks down on the corner.

Inside, a soft jazzy tone mingled with coffee beans, dairy, and pastry. Two others sat at the cluster of tables, and one waited at the counter. Each of them took their glances before avoiding his gaze. He'd seen them all, at one time or another, in someone else's sin or in their own, and he reminded them of the world's realities.

A hard boon to grow used to.

Jace gave each of them as much space as he could.

The girl at the counter had pretty eyes and a sad smile as she placed a small paper cup and brown paper bag down for him. Her nametag read Sandy, and her fingertips pressed her side of the laminate.

Jace hadn't seen much of her other than in his own memories. Ones where she'd always been kind and quiet.

He slid a token in front of her register and nodded his thanks before retreating to a far end of the café. Eaters earned the tokens they spent daily from their purges—enough to clothe them and feed them if they learned to live with mended garments and a mild hunger. Those who wanted more burnt out quickly.

Today, Sandy gave him strawberry jam with his scone, which he washed down with stout, black coffee. It quieted much of the alarm lingering within him, the double shift stuck to his bones. Another awaited him.

It meant he could afford stew or a burger for lunch, and the heavy food induced sleep, which Jace desperately needed.

He didn't linger in any one place for longer than necessary, so his feet pounded the sidewalk again, shoving him in a series of rights and lefts until his meeting.

His stained and torn sneakers marred the pristine white of the marble steps. The side door waited in the shadows for him, between two pillars, which lead him into a wet room. Jace wiped himself down and changed into a bleached robe and slippers. The blonde in his hair reminded him of the winged beings adorning the office where he'd sit with the mayor.

She enjoyed the ceremony of it. Most of his clients preferred a quick transfer in some hidden corner. But the bath was a fair exchange for the extra time.

A butler opened the door and ushered Jace to a lowly-lit room, where he sat on some bleached cushions. The mayor entered in her own white robe and knelt before Jace, her face creased around the eyes, her hair curled and sprayed, but her skin lacked the normal color additives. She took his hands in hers.

A few deep breaths, and the images flowed.

Leather wrung heavy in his hand, the strap snapping twice before we pulled it back together and swung it across bare, dark flesh. A yelp and whimper accompanied the jerk of the recipient. The belt came down again with a deeper cry. And again. And again.

And again.

The cries more frantic.

But she wasn't the only piece of bare flesh to be whipped. Four girls screamed and begged her to stop. Their punishment and the mayor's rage pulsed through Jace. He wrung the belt in his hands with her, a familiar pleasure pumping with adrenaline, engorged from their wriggling for freedom.

A taste she took when anyone gave her the slightest opportunity.

One that always ended with blood and bruises.

By the time the mayor released him, Jace's guts burned with the nagging guilt for enjoying something that was obviously wrong. Her sin branded itself over the others, fresh and raw and bleeding into reality as he walked backed toward his side of town.

Jace thumbed the token in his coat pocket, looking forward to the meat after his evening purge. But the acid of another coffee might disguise the scorching flare deep inside.

At the end of the block, a bundle of limbs, hair, and fabric collided with him, knocking Jace into unnaturally springy grass. The mess hovered over him, a delicate face peeking from behind a gigantic plume of hair. Soft as she bent to help him up, wafting into his face with their discordance.

Her elegant fingers trapped his wrist. "Walk with me."

The image of a small child holding her mother's hand, cold digits surrounding her warm flesh. Comfort seeped into Jace for a flash.

Is that what it felt like to hold a mother's hand?

"This way." She steered him south toward the river instead of west toward the Depository.

Her hair bobbed and swayed in waves like a magic trick. It brushed his cheeks as she pulled him around another corner, arm tightly locked on his. She smelled of exotic fruit—the kind Jace had never seen in person.

"Someone is following me. Don't look." She bounced him down a series of zig-zagged steps.

The mother's touch lingered in his hand, colder than the air outside, like she'd been caught in the rain, but her hands were dry. Fingers squeezed with support and comfort, the opposite of how he usually experienced others' grips.

Under the iron archway to the river, the girl drew her cloud of hair back, twisting it and tying it to her head in a tiny bulb.

How did she fit it all in such a small shape?

It exaggerated her eyes and cheekbones, and dangling metal glinted on her lobes—something he'd only seen on the wives and daughters of politicians. She yanked them out of her ears and stuffed them in his front coat pocket. One of her scarves unraveled and circled her hair and ears, the other colors of her clothes changing like a trick.

A new young woman stood in front of Jace. Less the child she resembled at first.

"I'm running away," she said.

"From where?"

"From the capitol."

Most wanted to find their way inside the gates to the capitol. That's where the poor hoped to make a better life for themselves, even Eaters. "Why would you want to run from paradise?"

The slow batting of her lashes washed clean the innocence in her eyes before she peered over her shoulder. "It's no paradise. I'll feed you if you help me to a clean shot out of here."

Out of where? They were fifteen miles from the capitol already. But three meals in a day was a luxury he never had—at least not that he remembered. The sins he accumulated had wiped his childhood memories within his first year. Not that Jace had many to start. His Eater abilities showed strong young, and his parents sent him off to a special orphanage at three.

Or at least, that's what the few notes he'd taken before all of his memories faded said. His mother was Teresa. His father Jacob. He had a sister, too. No name.

"I'll take it. I know where to find a boat if you think you can navigate it."

"I'll figure it out."

The way she took in her environment shook him. He liked to look around in the mornings when the streets were empty, but as people popped in his way, Jace kept his gaze to the ground. No one wanted to be seen by him.

But a brazen fear lit her up.

"This way," she said, following the riverwalk.

Jace enjoyed the way she glided like royalty.

"Who are you?"

Her hand flittered up in front of her, but her stride didn't hiccup a bit. At the end of the block, she turned them left, and they were able to walk abreast on the sidewalk again.

"You can call me V, and I am an Eater, like you."

Jace stumbled a few steps before righting himself. He'd never heard of a girl Eater before.

"You gave me a memory. A good one."

This stopped her, and V wrenched them both still. "I did. Of my mother."

"How have you kept them?"

"I don't know. I haven't had much time to consider it."

"How have you learned to share them?"

Her hip popped, and her hand landed on it. "I don't have time for this."

"I've never met an Eater that's a girl."

"Well, here I am."

"I've never met an Eater that's kept their memories, let alone shared one before."

"Well, I exist. Come on, I don't like standing still." She walked off, leading him deeper into the part of downtown. The bakery enveloped him in a heated puff of flour and sugar.

V leaned into the chrome border of the counter, holding up two fingers. She didn't avoid looking the cashier in the eye or tipping closer. How did she claim the luxury?

Dark wood constructed the rest of the place, the contrast more high-end than Jace was used to. A rich smell played with the sweet bakes and freshly ground coffee beans.

V brought her tray on a table in front of the wide-open window—the exact opposite of where Jace would have chosen, but the tables in the back were filled. She sat, waved him to his seat, and placed his pastry and coffee in front of the empty chair.

The fluffy crust curled around a dense caramelized center. Jace bit the corner of sweet cheese and buttery flakes: flavors that worked to overwhelm him. Instincts warred in him to gobble it down, but he chose to savor it.

A sip of coffee reeled him—the bitter blackness cut with a dash of dairy and some sugar. "You eat like this every day in the capitol?"

"It's pretty standard, and it's called a cheese Danish. But it's not worth the real cost." She bit into her own, delicately.

"What cost?"

"The one that keeps you from touching iron."

Cheese curdled as his stomach clenched. He brushed the crumbs from his fingers. "I know the real cost of life. I've known it for a long time."

Most of the time, it was all he knew.

"It prolongs the inevitable, and I am sick of it. I will either have freedom over my own life, or I will find it in death. And I *will* die before I let them take me back."

The intensity in her dark eyes belied the innocence in her face, and a maturity swam there. Defiance.

Suddenly, a smile shifted her features, and she covered her mouth, but she sparkled as she leaned in. "Smile. Lean into me."

Jace did, and V touched his wrist with her other hand.

"One of the men following me is outside. Don't look. He'll pass."

She put on a good show. But people didn't touch Eaters.

Still, Jace pinched her sleeve from underneath. The fabric soft and warm.

A man in a long, beige coat and dark boots meandered through the wide walkway—blond and stark gazed. His posture read danger, like the people who walked with the mayor—part of the Guard.

V tapped the tabletop and lifted her cup to her mouth, still obscuring her face.

"Eat your meal, so we can leave."

Hunger deadened, Jace did his best to enjoy the taste. His stomach dull and numb, he finished his food quickly and disposed of their trash.

She met him at the door, and he held it open for her. The first time he'd ever done so for a female—or anyone for that matter. A minute smile played on her full lips and lit up her eyes.

"Thank you." V waited on the sidewalk for Jace to take the lead.

He did. The tiny dock hid on a slight curve of the river, and a two-seater boat with a small motor bobbed in the dark waves. She held his hand but paused at the edge.

"You've done a lot for me, and I won't forget it."

"Nothing that you haven't paid me for already."

She shook her head.

"I'm not the only girl, but there aren't a lot of us. They keep us at the capitol. And we're not just Eaters. We don't *just* absorb their sins. They're sinister and hateful and love violence for violence's sake." Her fingers squeezed the traces of fear and apprehension into him. "Remember that when they take you there."

"I will."

"Good."

Jace helped her into the boat, and she took control of the motor with little trouble, zooming off—north.

He didn't wait for her to disappear before leaving for his next purge.

The local sergeant didn't follow the same ceremony as the mayor, but he did keep hard candies on his desk, creamy caramel ones, and Jace left with a handful in his pocket. This man's purge didn't veer from the norm in the way of sins, but he had visited the capitol.

What Jace took from the officer wasn't showcased on flyers or posters or long-winded stories about the sparkling pearl of a city. The city of dreams.

Where the Guard does to their citizens what the ones here do.

Whatever they want.

Jace never went into an appointment with expectations. He'd seen too much of reality's cruelty.

But when V's face popped up in the man's sin.

When he forced her to undress.

When he...

Jace no longer wondered why he didn't often see female Eaters, although he'd seen similar done to many of the young males around him. He remembered more than his fair share of the abuse.

Fresh sin tainted his waking world, but this one carved so much deeper than the rest. So did the pride in helping V get away—a feeling untainted by second-hand experience.

Now, the mayor's smile was strained and fake as she handed off the formal paperwork to an anonymous man in a suit, who ushered Jace inside a car and fed him a glass of orange juice from a built-in cooling unit.

Today was Jace's birthday.

Officially a hex, they were moving him to that promised land.

The suit presented a tan envelope.

Jace's hand shook when he wished it hadn't. Inside was a thick piece of plastic with a metal square—a chip, the man called it, for food—a map of the capitol, and a schedule for appointments. If he did well, they'd put him up in a room with a bathroom.

The luxury of it squeezed against the tightness already in his chest.

Jovial enough, Jace trusted him enough to ask about V. "Are there female Eaters in the capitol?"

He almost said more, but the wetness of her tears and soft texture of her hair in his fist kept him from it.

The man's gaze danced wildly, mouth turning down. "No."

Cold prickled between his shoulders, so Jace sat back in the cushy seat and fumbled with his hands until he gathered the confidence to look out the window. The highway spread its charcoal through the trees in an ever-curving vanishing point.

Slowly, then all at once, buildings popped up, clumping together and pushing nature out of their way. The glittering bits strained higher and higher until the landscape spread in gloom and thrice-reflected light—dim and miserable.

They pulled up in the shadow of a tall building whose bottom was golden from good lighting, rich woods, and solid reds. Iron spread through the furnishings. The man pointed to the door, which opened to the sidewalk bathed in that first-class reflection.

"You have an extra day's pay for your transition and your promotion. This place is used to first-timers."

Jace nodded and slipped out of the car, too familiar with the dismissal. He didn't take it personal, even though it was. Exhaust and sticky flowers perfumed the air. The eatery called to him in the best ways, but hunger died to a numbing pain.

The car disappeared back into traffic, and the new atmosphere towering over him. This place made him feel so small. Insignificant.

An iron bench sat around the corner, so he perched there, finding himself on the map. They'd dropped him smack in the center of the capitol. Most of the marks indicated stores and bakeries and depositories. The marks north of him signified the government buildings and political manors.

A lot more people swathed the streets, and wind tore at their clothes and neatly-kept hair. A burst turned and plowed him in the nose, stealing his breath.

Dark boots stomped under a long, beige coat. Danger scuttled over the squared cement and nipped at Jace's feet. The man who'd been looking for V.

Jace followed him, even though he wasn't entirely sure why.

Here, he didn't have to hide his face yet. No one knew him. He hadn't seen these people in others' sins. A perfect opportunity.

She fled only two days ago. If he'd come back, did that mean he lost her trail or that he caught and returned her already. Or killed her.

Jace didn't want to think that way.

He couldn't help it.

Her cries resounded in his ears.

They wouldn't want her dead, but she seemed so determined to die before she'd go back.

Tattering anxiety wormed its way in and out of Jace's middle, churning his heartbeat in fits and lulls. City corners and intersections blurred together in one macabre stretch of gray and glass.

Once, he swore the man noticed him, but Jace simply nodded his way and kept walking when the man peered over his shoulder. Brazen. It stole him some warmth against the battering wind.

Jace finally passed when the man's dark boots steered down an obvious dead end. He entered a side door to the building—it closing on his heels. A green front like a miniature cabin. Greasy bread, sauce, and cheese settled around the entrance. METEORITE glowed in yellow above with strands of fake fire tailing off the right.

At the next corner, Jace marked his map at the intersecting street names before he crossed the road and doubled back. The long walk sparked his hunger, so he trudged to the iron-laden eatery for a hamburger, fries, a soda, and a piece of cake—their birthday special.

The extravagance and size gave him a new kind of bellyache, and the sugar battled with the laden feeling of a full stomach. An employee pointed him towards the closest Depository, just a block and a half down, hidden at the edge of a park full of statues and monuments.

If he'd been taught about these people or what they'd done, he didn't remember them. Just as well that they didn't. Only his ability to read and write and some moniker of math remained. Enough to survive.

But the train of thought sped away when he climbed into an unoccupied mattress, suppler than any from home, and not even the appealing touch of the iron earrings in his pocket held him to consciousness.

🐦

V huddled at the end of a mattress with two sniveling girls behind her. The darkness of her gaze mirrored the violence Jace witnessed first-hand. More fear lingered in her as the man Jace purged leered at her.

The other girls screeched, but V merely flinched and blinked at him twice. Her thin arms wrapped around her knees, and her chin propped on them, tilting her head like a doll's.

Rage fueled desire—a deeply-rooted need to instill fear—produced a hose in his hand, and he blasted the three with a strong current of cold water. A chorus of screams and cries thrilled him, but even as the mane of her hair flattened around her face and neck and she coughed up the water, she took it with composure.

Jace gave the rest out to the iron as quickly as he could manage it, but traces lingered and ignited as he slid into a vinyl seat with a greasy slice of pizza. This place popped up when the man he purged left V and the two girls. The Meteorite's green front entrance emerged as he hit the street, straightened his tie, and reveled in the last traces of adrenaline and pleasure before the sin set in and guilt weeded its way into the pure frenzy of his aggression.

Now, the oily bread and cheese and tomato and spices he couldn't name cut the guilt with a grogginess that threatened his mind. No sugar to break through it.

Hoping the man who'd chased V would appear, Jace didn't want to come back to wait again. The food gave him a momentary pleasure, but like all bad things, he'd regretted it the moment he'd finished.

V'd been right. It wasn't worth the trade.

The patrons playing some sort of game in the other room clattered, and the crush of bodies bled too much warmth, agitating the same sleepiness Jace had felt after the burger and fries.

No wonder why Eaters praised this place as a haven. The food induced the type of rest Jace had dreamed of just a few days before. But, it didn't pacify the nightmares.

His drooping lids pushed him out the door and into the sharp slapping breeze. It focused him just in time to catch the flash of blond as Jace crashed into the metal dumpster.

Blue eyes dissected him, and a gloved hand tightened Jace's collar around his throat. "You're the little punk that followed me."

"I don't know who you are, sir." Jace choked on the words, throat tight and stomach revolting. He'd grown too used to not being seen. Blatantly ignored.

"I saw you. You know that aiding and abetting a criminal is equally punishable, so walk away and stop looking for her before you fall into the pits with her."

A peek of flesh opened between his gloves and his jacket when he gave Jace a shake. Jace took advantage of it. The only one he had—purging a sin from the man to disarm him.

Blood erupted between his fingers as they pressed against her belly. V had pulled a small blade and impaled herself before he caught her.

Slender hands pushed at his as she tried to squirm away. "Just let me die."

When she lost consciousness, he bandaged the wound and gave her a shot to sustain her until she could be transported.

Jace blitzed as pain jarred him back to the present and the dumpster jabbing his shoulder blades.

"An Eater. You should have known better and kept your head down."

The man's intensity worked to intimidate him, but something else bothered Jace, yapping in the back of his mind. He'd been shoved out. But the sins had to run their own course.

"You're an Eater, too."

He should have been ancient—at least ten years Jace's senior. How'd they protected him all this time?

A snarl set a live wire to his heart before it reached his brain. A sharp pain sent Jace chasing firecrackers in the dark.

Jace woke on a bench in the middle of a wide, grassy park. Sidewalks rotated and crossed around the space. Children played with dogs between a modicum of trees.

How'd he get here?

A hand touched his ankle.

V.

Her hair wild around her, swaying and bobbing in the wind.

Was she a mirage?

"I saw you from the kitchen, in the alley, and I need your help again. I don't have much time." She drew a glass bottled from inside her coat, wrapped in a brown paper bag, and took two, long pulls of the clear liquid.

She was okay. In one piece. How was that?

How did she shine brighter than the chrome and glass of the capitol?

Standing, V winced, scanning the park.

"Will you help?"

"Yeah." Jace stood, too. "Yes. How?"

"This way." After a hesitation, she turned and stomped off towards the smattering of trees in the southeast edge of the park. People took note of her, craning their heads, trying to hide behind sunglasses, shifting books and newspapers.

Inside a small pocket, another girl hid, crouched down between two trees, small fingers digging into their bark like they would give her a push when she needed to flee.

A girl from his latest purge, the one that grabbed ahold of V, that V tried to protect. The one who screamed and cried the loudest.

"I couldn't leave her there."

Jace could only nod past the sin.

Slithering movements swarmed from around the perimeter.

No.

Faint. The fire in V's eyes imploded with the wide reflection of monsters amassing. Her the bait.

"Grab her and run. Don't let them take her back."

She tore a path through the trees, the other girl on her heels. Jace swung the child against him and used his familiarity with nature to hurtle past fallen branches and under low limbs. Thin fingers gripped with a strength he didn't expect, but her whimpers ate at him with every step.

He lost V to a partial flashback, but his instinct drove him to the light of the tree line. Jace'd veered left, north, like he was naturally drawn home.

Bold pillars and domes of cream overtook the landscape, mirrored on either side.

V burst onto the sidewalk south of him, arms wide. Frantic.

Three men, like the one who'd displaced Jace, surrounded her.

Her implosion turned supernova.

V put the bottle to her mouth again, chugging it before spilling it across herself, overhead and down her front. A shiny trinket from her pocket popped a flame out the top, catching the fumes and cheap fabric of her scarves and shirt.

A deep breath pulled the fire into her lungs, and she collapsed before could scream. He'd seen it once before in a purge. Once the air hits the lungs, they burnt up.

Fingers dug harder into Jace's coat.

Run.

The smoldering heap V'd become whispered in his ears.

Help me.

The girl pinched his lobe.

A miniature house suspended in a wide oak—a cool breeze with hints of honeysuckle battled the muggy heat of summer on his skin.

Jace's grip tightened around the girl.

And he ran.

FRONTOVIKI
Sam Kepfield

This may be my last time around. I hope so.

There aren't many of us left; another go-around or two, and we'll all be gone and glad of it.

The first couple of times, it felt almost real. The brass on uniforms still sparkled, and the bodies in them, well, you'd never have known. But now, after making copies of copies of copies, we all look pretty shabby. The uniforms are falling apart. The skin of the fascists is pallid, loose, even hanging free in some places: a form of rot. Some come back without arms or legs, lost in a grenade blast or mine explosion. The lucky ones don't leave anything intact bigger than a finger or toe. They don't come back.

It's just as well.

The Red October plant hasn't changed. Twisted burnt and rusted girders rise from a thick layer of concrete rubble coating the frozen earth. The rest of the city of Stalingrad remains pulverized and lifeless.

But—

Sometimes, the new city is visible, as through a mist.

It fades in and out at intervals. We must have won the war, since Stalingrad has been rebuilt. The fascists would have leveled it and salted the earth. Stalingrad has been renamed for some reason. Stalin, the *Vozhd*, may have been a brute, but he led us after the fascists attacked. Now, it's called Volgograd with no red banners waving, no portraits of Stalin or Lenin anymore. The drab shops constantly short of goods are now lit with bright lights, and the windows have colorful displays. Strange names adorn them, some obviously foreign. What is *Starbucks*?

Communism is forgotten. What we fought for is history.

Odd how that happens. It must have been a month ago; I was on a patrol, darting among the ruins on Solechnaya Street, past the house where Sgt. Pavlov and his squad held off the fascists single-handedly for two months.

All is as it was, and then—then, the old faded out, and the new faded in. Pavlov's house still stood, the old ruins fused with new construction, in some kind of memorial. The Ninth of January Square came alive, crowded with families on outings, shoppers, young lovers strolling, and I got an occasional glimpse of an old, graying man or woman in a shabby coat, wearing a service cap and a jacket festooned with medals.

The families and children and lovers couldn't see me, but the old ones with the medals and the faraway look—I'm not so sure. I stood in the middle of the square, and a stooped man with wispy gray hair, an unshaven grizzled face, and distant eyes materialized next to me as the newly rebuilt city crept up on me. He looked through me, then he looked at me. His eyes opened wide, and his cane dropped. A middle-aged woman with him, probably his daughter, picked up the cane, but he froze, mute, eyes narrowed, as if searching for a fascist sniper.

Yefremov. I recognized him after a while. I knew him as a young sergeant, leading his platoon back and forth across the Red October plant and at the railway station. He was a brave one but full of good humor and plenty of funny stories about his life on a collective farm near Donestsk. He lived, went on to marry and father children, I gathered, and now, relived his youth, a time when he, and we, never felt more alive. Sure, we had been told to stand to the last man, had suffered from the incompetence of our officers, since Stalin had the good ones shot in '37 and '38, and even lost a few family members to the *chekists* during those years. But there is no way to explain the brotherhood of young men embarked upon a heroic task, a battle for the very existence of the *Rodina*. We *frontoviki* share something special beyond words.

He squinted and tried to form words, his face a question mark.

"It's me," I said. "Mikhail Borisovich."

"It can't be," he said. "You're—"

Dead.

"No, Arkady Nikolaevich," I said, softly, to counter the peasant superstitions I remembered from so long ago, that all Russians carry inside. "We're still here, all of us. Vanya, with his lies about all the women he screwed. Grisha, who saved your life by jumping on the grenade. And Mikravadze, the mad Georgian who looked just like Stalin and said he was a cousin. Remember how he used to fool the officers by pretending to *be* Stalin? If the fritzes hadn't shot him, the *chekists* would have. We're all here, waiting for you."

As he faded, a tear rolled down his cheek.

I don't know if he'll show up here when he finally dies. Kind of cruel, lying to the poor bastard, but I figured I owed it to him. Maybe he will, and we'll find some vodka and get drunk like we used to.

The Red October Tractor Factory is still standing. No one bothered to rebuild it, so it's a pile of debris. When the new city shows through, the only change is green sprouting from the broken concrete. Trees rise to the sky, their limbs not charred and barren, but with verdant buds shooting forth. By the look of them now, it must be spring.

"See anything?" Pasha interrupts my reverie. He's been with me from the start, with the 38th Rifle Division, stopping the Fritzes in front of Moscow, going south to the 37th Guards Rifle Division here at Stalingrad, and serving under Chuikov. Pasha was a kid, off a *kolkhoz* and given barely enough training when we marched past Lenin's Mausoleum on November 7, 1941, with Stalin and Molotov and Beria looking down on us. Straight from the parade to the front. But through it, he kept his good humor.

He's not looking so well now: skin sagging and gone in a few places. Three fingers on the right hand gone, hair thinning and grown wild-long on his bare head. We've quit wearing helmets. What's the point? Maybe the next shot will be enough to keep us dead.

"No," I tell him. "Not many left this time. Sometimes, they don't even put up any fight. Just let you shoot them."

"I had one who begged me to use a grenade."

"Did you?"

"No. I almost felt sorry for the poor bastard, then I remembered Lena." A girl, only seventeen, if that, with a smile that lit up a room and a dead eye and rock-steady trigger finger. The fascists found her on a patrol, returning from her sniper nest. She was gang-raped and murdered, her body left hanging from a lamppost in what was left of downtown. We found her after she'd been there for a week in the late summer heat.

She came back, too, and got her measure of revenge. But after four resurrections, she gave up, pulled the pin on a grenade, and held it to her lovely ample breast, which had been sliced and hacked in a gruesome death over and over. She didn't come back after that. Most of the women choose her way out, since the ends that await them at the hands of the fascists are uniformly ugly.

So, I could understand Pasha's unwillingness to let the bastard have an easy out.

"Got any grenades left?" I ask.

"A few." He opens a pouch on his belt. Both were well-worn, the metal rusted. We come back, but it's like making a copy of a copy of a copy…after a while, the integrity fades. The equipment we come back with degrades, except for the deadly tools. Those are always in perfect order. The grenades, the mines, and the rifles and sidearms. My Mosin-Nagant M1938 still gleams with oil, untarnished, likewise the Tokarev TT30. The leather strap on the rifle rotted and broke. I found some rope to improvise one. Pasha carries a Luger he pulled from a dead fascist colonel, a fine weapon indeed, but the holster is falling apart. "You need one? Going to end it all now?"

"No. Not yet."

"Going to destroy the Sixth Army by yourself? Or maybe hunt Von Paulus himself?"

"No."

"Duty. A good Soviet soldier defending the *Rodina*, even in death."

"Not quite." That was part of it. And curiosity—Stalingrad had changed so much in the years since I fell. The buildings rose again, modern and massive. The streets were filled with cars, at first battered prewar models, but then, smaller boxy things with names like *Pobeda* and *Volga*, and of late, more sleek and streamlined models. There were imports, too—a week ago, when the present was particularly clear, I saw a huge black Mercedes. Imagine that. The fucking fritzes not only survived the war but appear to be thriving.

And the women—ah, the women. Streets no longer filled with solid women from the local collective farm, wearing work clothes or peasant garb and headscarves. No, the women now could have walked off a movie screen, hair brushed and worn stylishly, makeup, and even Western clothes that show an amount of skin that would have been shocking in my day. They are a balm to the soul, something to dream about on the long nights scurrying through the rubble of our reality on patrol. But that's all they are, a fantasy. Here, there is no love, no tenderness. We knew a few hurried couplings with near-strangers, the intensity of war driving our passion. But it's been so long now, and the last time, with a girl barely twenty, who would have been a real beauty with long blond hair and ice-blue eyes and angular cheekbones and chin, was not so satisfying. The damage is inside, too, and the passion somehow less intense with the urgency of our endless war faded. No, the lure of such disappointment doesn't keep me going.

It's fear.

This life after life may be drudgery, it may be wearing my soul down with its depressing sense of isolation, but it has the comfort of the familiar.

I was raised a good Communist, and so had no use of religion. I gave thought to death but strangely never what came after. The typical vision of white-clad angels flitting about clouds seemed absurd on its face. I don't know what I expected. A true worker's paradise, perhaps, where the Plan was always fulfilled a year ahead of time, where there were no famines, no fascists, and no *chekists* to come knocking at three AM. But I don't suppose that is what awaits. Nor is it the other end, the sulfuric pits of hell where each breath scorches the lungs and each step burns the flesh and the lash flays skin from the body.

Maybe, it's none of them.

Maybe, it's mere nothingness, a winking out of existence. The end of it all. No more consciousness, no more memory, no more endless twilight patrols. The flicker of life that is Mikhail Borisovich Antonov, born 5 June 1924 in Rostov, member of the Young Pioneers, winner of the prize for best essay on Lenin in my fourth year at GGPU 337, a boy who was loved by his mother Anna Timofeyovna and father Boris Feodorovich, the betrothed of Larisa Ivanovich Karpova, a lovely redheaded girl with intense blue eyes and pale skin dotted with freckles and a lush body with firm bosoms and slender thighs that were a pleasure to lie between, until he volunteered for duty just after the fascists invaded, and who fought a rearguard all the way across the steppes to meet his fate on a pile of bricks near the southwest corner of the Red October Tractor Factory—all of that will be gone for eternity. Something in me screams about the unfairness of it all, the waste, the iron law that the story that began thusly will never end, will never see marriage and children and career and old age and grandchildren and a quiet easing from the world as one piece in a soft bed. My end made that possible for others, possibly dearest Larisa if she survived the fascist hordes, but it is a small comfort.

The crack of a rifle shot rings out in the still dimness, spalling off a steel support beam nearby. Pasha and I duck as more shots ring out.

"Fuck your mother." Pasha gestures at the sniper. "This prick thinks there's a war on."

"Maybe, he doesn't care," I say. "Some of them were real fanatics. Especially the SS assholes."

Most of the regular army types, who'd been conscripted, accepted capture with some calm. The SS were like vicious badgers, taking as many of us out as they could. We used a lot of our grenades on them. Being dead's bad enough without guys who won't give up.

I peek around a jagged block of concrete, trying to locate the sniper.

"Wave something," I tell Pasha. He puts his helmet on his rifle, pokes it up over the edge. More shots, and I spot a flash from the second floor of an office building for the steel works. The front of the building is blown away. Our man is hiding behind a pile of wrecked office furniture.

"Should we wait him out? Or put an end to it?"

"You got anything better to do?" Pasha asks.

So, it's decided. We get up and sprint from behind the rubble, darting around piles of bricks, burned-out vehicles, and other debris. Our man's eyes must be failing; his shots go wide. We pause behind a rusted AMO truck to catch our breath and to make sure our rifles have rounds chambered.

"How to get to him?" I ask.

"Around the back, there, a staircase. I remember this place."

"When we were still alive?"

He shrugs. "Does it matter?"

He looks around the rusted fender, nods, and we take off again. Our man has had time to reload, and shots follow us.

His aim is better, or we're closer, because Pasha grunts, and a small puff of dust erupts from his coat. He staggers, and I catch him and half-carry him to the building. We throw ourselves against the wall. The front of his coat has a small hole in the breast, a red stain seeping slowly outward.

"Shit. Bastard hit me." It's on the right side, so it's not close to the heart. It still pains him, though.

"Can you make it up?" I ask.

"Sure. But you'll have to lead."

We creep around to the back of the building, find the entrance, and ascend the stairs as quietly as possible in our boots. At the top, we halt, searching. The floor breaks off into offices, and since the doors have all been blown off, I can see through the doorframes to the outside. Our man is in the office on the far right. I point it out to Pasha, and we get ready to storm the room.

I rush through the door, firing bursts from the rifle, taking the left side, Pasha the right. No return fire, though, and a quick sweep shows it to be empty. We stare at each other—

The old familiar sensation hits me, like being punched in the back, once, twice, three times, as the bastard ambushes us from behind. Pasha turns, fires a burst, and hits him in the chest. I also let him have it, sending rounds into him as he slides to the dusty floor and is still.

A racking cough brings blood to my mouth and onto my hands.

"Ah, fuck," Pasha says. "Looks like the war's over for you."

"Yes." My senses already fading, I know what is coming. But I am not afraid.

Pasha reaches into the grenade pouch. "Shall we end it all now?"

"No." I move out into the hallway, losing my footing, and Pasha helps me sit down, back against the wall. "But give that bastard one. Serves him right."

"One less to worry about next time, eh?"

"Yeah." The light is fading, and the cold comes.

"Until next time," Pasha says.

"Next time," I say, knowing that there will be one.

And I look forward to it.

THE WRETCHED NOBLESSE
Case C. Capehart

"Hey, Dad, has there always been rust on this wall?"

Rico shut down the vacuum and inspected the hallway as his father came around the corner. "What are you talking about? That's sheet rock. You think the paint is lead or something?"

Rico ran his finger over the orange crust on the beige wall, and some of it flecked off. "I guess it must be dirt or something. I'll get a rag."

"I don't see anything, Rico," his father said, going back to his chair in front of the TV. "Maybe that medication has you imagining things. But if it's got you cleaning my house before noon, I'd say it's worth it. How you feel?"

Rico shrugged as he wet a rag. "I don't want to get my hopes up or anything, but I feel great."

"Well, just take it slow." His father skipped past the commercials on the DVR.

Rico returned to the hallway and froze. For a moment, something dark and lumpy, about the size of a cat, moved across the hall. It vanished, even his memory of the lump faded. He shook his head and bent down to wash the dirt from the wall, but he failed to locate it.

"I can't find the dirt."

"I told ya," his father said. "You're seeing things now."

"Yeah, no kidding," Rico said.

Two weeks into the trial run of Nevicin, Rico had a job and saved toward his own apartment. What doctors diagnosed as ADD in his childhood quickly spiraled into an unidentified disorder in adulthood. It turned basic tasks, like hygiene and following spoken directions, into a challenge. A trial drug for advanced attention disorders gave Rico hope for a semblance of a normal life.

Despite what Dr. Witherton claimed, Rico still suffered from insomnia. While on his high-dose Ritalin, Rico's mind never shut down. On Nevicin, a

319

new effect plagued him at night. He faded, but just before he dozed, something would move. Shadows took new forms. Footsteps reached him from outside the room after his parents were asleep. Odd stains appeared on his walls in the dark.

Rico struggled through his new job, downing coffee during his fifteen minute breaks. The Nevicin allowed him to concentrate on stocking the shelves at his department store without getting lost in his own world. His manager tolerated his lack of sleep more than absent-mindedness.

The nice thing about working at a department store in the suburbs was the storeroom. Only employees could be back there.

His store had a giant compactor he fed cardboard boxes into that would crunch it all down into a four-foot-by-four-foot cube that weighed as much as a smart car. On Tuesday mornings, Todd would feed it all into the compactor and use a forklift to set the cube along the wall for pick up. The rest of the week, no one went near the thing.

Looking around for his coworkers, Rico ducked on the other side of the compactor. He closed his eyes and took a few deep breaths. Thanks to his meds, he could now focus, but every so often, he needed to pause and hit the refresh button in his mind.

He opened his eyes and stepped forward. In front of him stood a large dog with a gaping wound along its side. Its rib cage and sickly green organs glowed and pulsated inside. Gray, hairless skin pulled away from the muscle tissue beneath. Its long face beheld lidless eyes that swiveled to and fro. Three sets of nostrils ran up the sides of its chattering snout, venting lazy black coils of smoke into the air. It emerged from the side of the compactor and looked around. It hadn't seen him.

Rico backed away from the beast, but the wall blocked his retreat. The creature turned its head toward Rico, and its gaze locked onto his. Rico took a deep breath and held it. As a child, Rico believed monsters existed. His parents and age eventually erased that fear, yet a literal monster stared right at him. All this time, he had worried about murderers and traffic accidents and cancer. Those things would kill him. Now, he counted the seconds before a supernatural animal from the depths of hell pounced and tore him apart.

The dog sniffed the air, venting more exhaust-like smoke around him. It lowered its head, seemingly curious and took a step forward. The sound of the thing's nails clicking against the concrete hit Rico's ears, and he screamed.

He expected this to set the creature off, but he hoped that others would reach him before the dog got to his throat. He didn't know what any of his younger coworkers would do against such an abomination, but it beat dying alone in the back of a warehouse.

The dog shrunk into its haunches and skittered backwards. Turning, the beast's paws screeched against the ground, trying to find purchase, then, it disappeared.

"What the hell is going on back here? Is everything okay?"

Trishna got to him first. Rico yelled, worried about what the creature would do to the petite, high school junior. "*Look out.*"

He scrambled around the corner and nearly ran into the wide-eyed girl.

"Look out for what? What are you doing back here?" She looked him over then cast about for whatever had him so spooked.

"Did you see anything run past when you came in?" Rico asked, feeling a bit foolish under the girl's scrutiny.

"What, like an animal or something?" Trishna's face tightened, trying not to laugh at the idea of a grown man screaming at a rodent.

"No...bigger." Rico shifted, uncertain what to do.

"Bigger than an animal?" Trishna leaned toward him, looking around and lowering her voice. "Are you high right now?"

The storeroom showed no signs of the monstrous dog. Nothing out of place.

Rico finished his shift looking over his shoulder. Around every corner and in every shadow, he caught sight of something: flashes of milky, sightless eyes and glimmers of teeth and metal. The creatures never came for him, and he did not allow himself to be alone. This gave him enough courage to finish his day. As he left the store and made for his house five blocks down, she showed up.

The woman, if he could call it that, stood between an old lady stowing her shopping cart and a man getting his child out of a car seat. Neither of them noticed her. White, wispy hair fluttered across a pale blue face with sunken cheeks. A charred, iron tiara covered her eyes with the band and the spikes of the gruesome ornament threaded under the skin of her forehead and arched over her scalp. Dark gray muslin wrapped her desiccated body but did not completely conceal the vein-like cracks in her skin that burned like emerald embers. The tips of her hipbones jutted and spread like skeletal wings, holding up her ragged skirt. A belt of spiked chain wrapped several times around her midsection and came together at the front, dropping down to a bladed pendulum that swayed below her knees.

Rico's pulse hardened like he encountered a boss from one of his video games, but the woman simply stared in his direction from behind her ghoulish crown. She lifted her left hand, and Rico ran.

He did not sprint, but neither did he glance behind him. If the woman were more than a hallucination, surely someone else would freak out. The entire way home, some gave him odd looks as he jogged by, but none screamed at the horror following him. Rico reached the driveway of his house and the empty spot where his mom's SUV usually sat; he remembered their vacation.

Monsters appeared right when he had the whole house to himself for a week.

He locked both locks, turned on all the lights, and texted all of his friends, hoping one of them might be free to come hang out with him. Only Jane answered. She wouldn't be off work for another three hours.

"You saw me."

Rico yelped, falling back against the kitchen table. The ghoulish woman stood near his window, inside his living room. She had just spoken to him…in English.

At his reaction, she retreated into the corner and lifted her hand. "Ah, please don't go. I won't hurt you. I promise."

An echo preceded her voice as if it faded in instead of out. The tone was soft; a bit gravelly like Joan Jett, and ill-fitting the monstrosity before him. The sweetness of her words contrasted her grim appearance enough for Rico to freeze instead of fleeing.

"I know what I must look like to you. I must be frightening, and I'm sure you're confused." She held both of her skeletal hands against her chest, under the slight bumps of her cloth-wrapped breasts. "Please, I don't know how much time we have."

"This is a hallucination. You're not real." Rico closed his eyes, hoping that she would disappear.

"I am real, Rico. As was the thrall you encountered. It came to me once it realized you could perceive us. I am Alak'ish, the Iron-crested. We are the Wretched Noblesse, and we have lived alongside humanity for eons. You're frightened because you have not seen us in a very long time."

Rico opened his eyes. Her existence persisted. "What are you talking about? I've never seen anything like you before. No one has, or else it would definitely be on Facebook."

"I know it feels like that." The woman put her hand to her mouth and convulsed as if sobbing. "I'm sorry. It's…been a long wait for me. I had almost given up on being seen."

"Are you…crying?" When would the camera crew burst in?

"I knew it would be hard." Her voice seeped out, grief twisted through her words. She lifted her head in his direction as if she saw through the metal covering her eyes. "The ancient spell is clouding your mind to our existence, Rico. It's the reason you find us monstrous and why you fear the sight of us."

She stepped forward, gliding across his floor as her head tilted to the side. She motioned around the room with a skeletal arm. "All of this—"

Rico woke up on the floor between the kitchen and the living room. His eyes locked onto the phone three inches from his nose. A notification light blinked at the top.

He got up and picked up his phone. He missed an alarm and a call from his mother, causing the blinking notification.

"Ah shit, my meds." Rico swiped off the alarm he set by habit to remind him to take his medicine. How could he have gotten so distracted?

Alak'ish.

Rico stumbled back. She seemed so real. He remembered her name. The Nevicin must have worn off while he dozed on the floor. Did he faint or did his body finally succumb to the massive sleep deprivation he had been fighting?

Rico clapped a hand over his mouth and laughed as he leaned against his bar.

The Nevicin sent me on a hell of a trip. That was so wild. I just had a conversation with a monster lady in my living room.

He should call his mother back but decided against it, stomach grumbling.

"Not like I was gonna make a sandwich in the middle of a pant-shitting trip." Rico needed to speak the words aloud despite the absence in the room. Still a bit anxious, thinking out loud helped calm him. "You hear that, Alak'ish? Your freaky ass made me miss dinner."

After a sandwich, chips, and an hour spent sampling shows on Netflix that didn't hook him with the first episode, Rico brushed his teeth and zoned in on the bottle of Nevicin on his cabinet. He needed to get back on his medication schedule, but he felt so tired. It had been months since he fell asleep before two a.m. The weariness weighed on him as much as his anxiety over the woman returning to him in the night.

Rico set three alarms on his phone for the morning. *I'll get a good night sleep, then take a pill right when I wake up. I'll make triple sure I remember to take a pill.*

Rico struggled at work. All three of his alarms went off and as he swiped off each one, he put off taking his pill. The missed sleep, the paranoia, the dreadful encounter with the woman; all of it came from the Nevicin. He had finally taken control of his illness and started a life, but now, he realized autonomy came with vibrant hallucinations of terrifying creatures.

Once at work, he took his pill. He wouldn't be able to get through his shift without it.

The hallucinations started within the hour. Shadows took on forms and moved about the store. An enormous shape crowded an aisle: a dark cloud of a creature shrouded in a deathly cloak and covered in oily chains. A lady pushed her shopping cart right past him, knocking it against his side.

"The wheels on this thing," the lady complained, maneuvering around the invisible wraith. "Not a shopping cart on Earth that just goes straight, is there?"

"Nope." Rico shook his head and turned down another aisle.

"You're out from under the spell again, aren't you?"

Rico nearly fell over the seasonal display at the end of the isle as Alak'ish appeared in front of him. His involuntary yelp drew the attention of several customers, and he straightened himself, trying to play cool even as the disturbing woman drew near him.

"There's no spell," Rico said, trying to avoid more attention from others in the store. "This is all in my head. I brought you here. I can send you away. I just need to imagine unicorns or something less scary."

"We need to speak, Rico. This cannot wait." Alak'ish floated above the linoleum floor as she pursued him through the aisles at a gradual pace. "If you fear these other humans discovering you, bring us to somewhere private."

"Fuck." Rico moaned and headed to the restroom, intent on gathering his composure away from public eyes. Alak'ish followed him. "You can't come in here. It's men only."

"Spare me your hollow commands, Rico. I have borne witness to humanity's most intimate moments, including many of yours."

Rico shivered, thinking of this witch staring at him during one of his porn marathons at home while his parents were at work. He scanned below the stalls for pairs of feet, entered the one closest to the wall, and felt stupid sliding the plastic locking mechanism into place.

A spot on the stall door darkened, and rust spread outward like liquid soaking into a dry rag. The metal disintegrated and fell away as the pale blue, cloth-wrapped hand pushed through it. The entire door became a pile of ocher dust along the floor, and she stood in the entryway.

"How did you do that?" Rico cast his gaze about. Her calm demeanor and the recurring reassurance he gave himself that all these experiences were simple hallucinations had put him at ease, but now, the fear had returned. He froze with the same panicked terror that had rooted him in the storeroom upon noticing the demonic dog. "You just destroyed the door like it was nothing."

"Because it was nothing," she said. "You are not in the bathroom of a supermarket, Rico. There is no door here. I dissolved an illusion."

"No. I'm stronger than this." Rico straightened himself and took a deep breath. "I have a life, now. I'm months away from moving out of my parent's house. I might find a girlfriend and have sex. Real sex. I'm not going to let a drug-induced nightmare ruin that for me. If I can't make you go away, I will learn to ignore you."

"You would exchange flesh for fantasy? Does that bind you to this spell?" Alak'ish moved in a way he had not seen before. Her body swayed in an almost imperceptible wavelike motion, but the surrounding air changed. Her smell changed. She gripped the sides of the stall and the hairs along Rico's arms stood up.

"Hear me well, Rico." Alak'ish's face hovered within inches of his, and Rico focused on her dark lips. "Help me break this spell, and I swear I will indulge all of your unrequited desires."

Rico swallowed and fought against the tremors in his legs and confusing swelling in his pants. "Even if I wanted…if you didn't scare the shit out of me. You're not real. You can't touch me."

Alak'ish snatched his skull in both of her hands. Her spindly arms belied the power of her fierce grip as she smushed his face between her fingers. Pain shot through his skull, and his eyes watered. The cold metal of her crest dug into his forehead, and her ebony lips parted to reveal rows of onyx canines and a serpentine tongue.

Her reverse-echo voice exploded in his mind. "Are you sure about that?"

Rico screamed. Pushing the apparition aside, he burst from the stall and out of the restroom. He did not care who saw him. With his store vest whipping around him, Rico made for the door and sprinted through the parking lot.

The lights along the road had not yet turned on, and only a few drivers had flicked on their headlights in the dulling late afternoon. Wretched Noblesse stalked in and out of existence along the pathways, paying no head to the humans who ignored them.

Where was he going to go? Home? There would be no escaping her there. She dissolved doors. Until now, he had dealt with his hallucinations by himself. Maybe they progressed to physically affecting him. What would they do in a crowded bar? What would they do if he got wasted?

"Fuck it." Rico shot a look back at Alak'ish as she stood in front of the store. "I'm gonna go get drunk."

"Hell, yeah." A guy wearing sunglasses much too late in the evening threw up the devil horns as he passed Rico on the sidewalk.

Rico kicked himself for being such a shut-in as Jane and her brother, Eddie, joined him at the bar. They joked around and reminisced and slammed shots of Tullamore Dew. Even as more creatures appeared and the world around him began to bend and warp, Rico stayed. As he got older and hadn't moved on to adult things, like a relationship or career or family, it got easier for Rico to shut himself away from the world. Getting out and having fun with his friends reminded him of why he couldn't go back to the way things were before Nevicin.

Rico excused himself from the table and went to the bathroom. As he stood at the urinal, the lights flickered. In an instant, Rico stood in the midst of a dark gray wasteland, pissing on the dusty remains of a building foundation. Ash fell all around him like snow and green light pulsed through the thick clouds overhead. Rico saw the other patrons of the bar over the decayed stumps of the walls, but none of them looked at him. To everyone else, the walls still stood.

Among the oblivious suburbs, the armies of Wretched Noblesse stretched out over fields of charred and rusted spikes. Tall beings lumbered along hills on wooden, spidery limbs, and pygmy goblins in derelict armor and ragged cloth kicked up silt as they shuffled along. The entire land seemed to warp and shift as a population of hidden denizens merged with the human population.

Rico zipped up and wandered among them, searching out his friends. The hallucination had taken over completely.

"Are you okay?" Jane approached him, but she looked different. Her clothes hung about her body in rags, and Rico forced himself not to gawk at her mostly exposed breasts. All around him, the other humans appeared the same way: their faces haggard, and their clothes in late stages of deterioration.

"Rico, you're in bad shape. Those shots must have hit you like a brick." Jane frowned and looked around. "If I get us a Ryde and get you home, do you think you can keep your shit together?"

Rico nodded and let her get him home in the hellscape that only he perceived. All the houses in his neighborhood sat in ruin. Inhabitants lounged in the carcasses of houses, and none of them noticed as he gawked from the back of the sedan Jane called for on her Ryde app.

"Rust on the walls..." Rico muttered as they entered the house. He needed a tetanus shot just from walking through the living room. His couch seemed mostly intact, and he plopped down in it. Jane pulled a sports drink from his fridge and sat it next to him.

"Something has happened to you. You see everything, now, don't you?"

Rico lay still. Alak'ish entered the room through the absent outer wall as Jane left through the door. He considered calling Jane back, but she already had her phone up to her ear. The next moment, he lay on the couch, alone with the Wretched Noblesse.

"I want you to leave me alone. I want these hallucinations to stop."

Alak'ish tilted her head to the side. "The drink you've consumed has pulled your medicated mind further out of the human's false plane and back into the true world. I will take advantage of your state while it lasts."

"And if I refuse?" Rico asked.

"I've waited a very long time for this opportunity, Rico. I'm afraid my patience with you is exhausted." The surrounding air grew cold with her biting glare, threatening to steal the breath from his lungs. "You will oblige me."

Alak'ish knelt before him, taking up his vision. "Many centuries ago, humans shared a single world with the Wretched Noblesse: two forces set in balance. The humans strove eternally to sow and expand. We sought to reap and destroy. We understood the balance, but the humans lost sight of it. They sought an end to death, disease...decay.

"At first, they tried war. The humans brought their armies against us with steel and fire, but the Noblesse are born of destruction and know it intimately. Our Champions wielded the power of death and turned them away each time. Creation, however, is where the humans found their advantage."

Alak'ish stood and approached the deteriorating wall, looking out over the neighborhood. "They attacked with magic beyond our comprehension. The humans created an illusion strong enough to erase the memories of our Champions and convince them of their humanity. For the first time, we knew fear as the greatest among us failed to recognize their kin. The Champions swept through us, screaming the battle cries of our ancient enemy. With one battle, the humans avenged a history full of defeats."

"But you survived." Visions of battle between horrific monsters and magic-wielding humans filled his imaginative mind. "There are so many of you."

"The Wretched Noblesse are eternal. The humans could not completely extinguish us. Though the humans had control of our Champions and reign over the lands, they refused to abide our existence, as diminished as it was. So, they cast the spell again. This time on themselves."

"They attacked themselves?" Rico asked.

"In a matter of speaking." Alak'ish ignited a yellow ball of flame in her left palm and held it before her. With a wave of her right hand, she pulled a duplicate flame out of the original, turning it blue. "The humans created a vast illusion: an exact copy of this world, without the Noblesse. When they perfected this copy, they layered it atop ours."

Alak'ish pushed her hands toward each other and the flaming balls combined into a green, Earth-like globe surrounded by a slow blaze.

"So the real world looks like this?"

Rico gazed upon oily clouds stabbing through the sepia sky overhead; not a sliver of blue to be found. "How can we survive in such a mess?"

"Ignoring the Wretched Noblesse is to ignore natural decay." Alak'ish approached him but shied from reaching for him. "Decay has spread unhindered throughout the world because the humans have abandoned the fight against it. They choose to ignore it, just as you tried to ignore us."

Rico called his doctor the next day.

"You shouldn't be experiencing anything like a hallucination," Dr. Witherton said over the phone. "No one in any of the trials has experienced this. This is troubling. Don't take any more, okay?"

"What? No, I can't do that. I need this for my job," Rico said, remembering the way he left the day before. Would he have a job to go back to? "Can't you give me something else to get rid of the visions?"

"Rico, Nevicin isn't approved, yet. We don't know all the dangers." Dr. Witherton sounded busy with something else on the other end and did not give Rico the amount of concern he expected. "On top of that, you agreed to be part of the trial study and signed an agreement in order to do so. That agreement states that you will immediately cease taking the Nevicin at the onset of any side effects not listed. It sounds like you should have stopped taking it weeks ago. Return the remaining pills, Rico."

Rico didn't flush the pills. He didn't take the pills, either. Alak'ish didn't come back, but he lost his job. Without the Nevicin, he regressed to relying on his parents.

"What's this?" Rico looked over the box of papers that his father plopped down beside him. He had been home for a whole week before he told his parents about the hallucinations and the Wretched Noblesse and why he had to stop taking the Nevicin. His father immediately disappeared to the utility room and returned with the box.

"Look through the pictures. You drew those as a kid." His father motioned toward the box.

Rico pulled a few of the pages out and nearly dropped them. The Wretched Noblesse adorned the papers in graphite and colored pencil and markers. He found a crude drawing of the dog creature as well as a familiar sketch he had done in high school of a much higher quality: a spindly woman in rags with a metal crest over her eyes, threaded through her forehead and arcing over her scalp.

"We used to worry, but your counselor said this kind of things was pretty normal for creative kids like you." Rico's father put a hand on his shoulder. "You played a lot of weird video games and watched horror movies. Maybe we shouldn't have let you, but you were dealing with a lot. You showed some talent when you stuck with it long enough to complete something."

"So my brain just dragged up old monsters I had drawn to torment me with?" Rico let the pages slide from his fingers back into the box. "I just made it all up?"

"Of course you did," his mother said. "You think those things were actually there? Creatures like that don't exist, Rico. A war between these things and humans? Spells and illusions? These are all ideas you got from shows and games. How could you believe it for a minute?"

"It seemed real, Mom." Rico avoided his mother's gaze. Of course it all sounded stupid when someone else said it. "I could see her…smell her. She reached out and touched me. And the story she told me…it seemed so familiar."

"Because you made it all up, Rico." His mother knelt down in front of him, not unlike the way Alak'ish addressed him the last time he saw her. "I know it seemed real, but it wasn't. That medicine just messed with your head."

"Why didn't you say anything right away?" His father drew his attention. "I just find it hard to believe that you didn't call Dr. Witherton the minute you saw a literal monster. Why try to deal with this on your own?"

"Because I had a life." Rico stood and walked to his room. "And now, it's gone."

Rico spent the rest of the night on the computer. He looked up every game he had ever played. He scrolled through the synopsis for dozens and dozens of fantasy movies. He ran searches for the Wretched Noblesse and Alak'ish with no results.

Only one person would be able to tell him.

At three in the morning, Rico found the bottle of Nevicin that he had held onto against the orders of his doctor. He took a dose and chased it with the tequila from his father's cabinet. Praying the medicine wasn't completely out of his system, Rico sat in the dark living room and waited.

"You're in pain." The familiar voice echoed into existence as he dozed off.

Rico leaned forward in the chair as Alak'ish, the ghastly woman who haunted him, slipped into his world. Now that he knew he had created her, she didn't seem as frightening. Alak'ish suddenly felt like the only friend he had.

"I made you up," he said.

"You're talking about the drawings, aren't you?" Alak'ish took on an understanding tone. "I observed as the humans who tend to you brought them out. I heard their explanations."

Rico put his head in his hands and ran his fingers through his hair. "After this, I'm flushing the Nevicin and returning to how things were. I just thought you would have some answers for me, that the part of my brain you're coming from might tell me where I got the idea of you?"

"Is that really why you summoned me, Rico?" Alak'ish knelt before him. "You think I'm just a fault in your brain?"

"Just tell me something, damn it." Rico's voice caught, and his hands shook. "I have one last bit of magic in my life, and I'm about to throw it away for good. I need some sort of closure."

"Closure?" The air froze, and her voice grew sharp. "Why should you gain closure? I have witnessed my beloved husband wander aimlessly under this hateful spell for centuries. I have stayed at his side, never able to speak to him; to offer him comfort as he suffers."

Alak'ish leaned in toward him and gripped the sides of the chair as she slid her face in front of his. Her sharp teeth flashed in the dull light of the early morning. "I have never left his side even though he has long forgotten my existence. By what right does he now ask for closure from me?"

"What are you talking about?" Cold stung Rico's insides and drew his breath short. "No, I made you up. I have drawings."

"Drawings of what, Rico?" Alak'ish hissed in his face and pushed the recliner back. "Drawings of creatures from a game you never played? Did you pull our history from a movie that never existed? You remembered us, even when you couldn't see us. I was there to witness it, Rico. I have always been there."

"Oh no." Rico's stomach threatened to revolt. Things came back that made no sense. He remembered the war. He remembered Alak'ish at his side, helping him to rule his province in the Wretched Plains. Rico looked down at arms covered in gray chitin resembling battle armor. "Oh...no, no, no."

Rico got up from the chair. His legs immediately buckled, and Alak'ish dropped to his side. "I wanted to tell you right away. You were so scared at first, and twice now, I thought I had lost you for good."

"I'm not human." Rico clawed at the ground as the Wretched world flickered in and out.

"No, my love," Alak'ish said, shuddering with quiet sobs. "You are Arek'oho, the Grim Warden, Champion of the Wretched Noblesse. You stood proud against the human assault...and I looked on in agony as you fell to their foul spell and turned on our people."

"I didn't know." Guilt washed over Rico, and he crawled into Alak'ish's arms, weeping. She held him tight against her breast. "I can't be here anymore. Let me come home."

"Oh, my love, how I have waited for this moment." He felt Alak'ish grip his head and take a deep breath. "In centuries, we've not been able to break or even understand this spell. Our people have given up. I have already resigned myself to this one moment with you."

"There's got to be something." Rico pulled away.

He held no fear. He saw in her the beauty from long ago, and he refused to lose her again: to go on in limbo, leaving this persona when it reaches the end of a human life span and restarting as a new one somewhere else.

"I'm not going back under the spell. I'm coming home, Alak'ish."

Rico rose and went to the room he had lived in since birth. The bottle of Nevicin sat on the end of his bed. He counted sixteen pills. On his way back through the hall, he passed by the closed door of his parent's bedroom. Had they suspected anything taking a Wretched Champion home in the form of a baby? Would they search for him, or would the spell wash away his absence? Would he remember them afterward?

Rico proceeded to the kitchen. Alak'ish joined him, wearing a worried expression as he pulled more bottles down from his father's cabinet over the fridge. He took the Nevicin three at a time, chugging the alcohol. His throat and lungs burned as he swallowed the last few pills and finished the bottle. Tearing open the vodka, he tipped it skyward and pushed past the bloating in his stomach and the sudden dizziness.

The alcohol and Nevicin spun his head. The world corroded all around him and fell to dust. The ceiling above him disintegrated, and green lightning penetrated the dark overcast.

Rico noticed the kitchen floor beneath his head. He had fallen at some point.

His innards raged against him, and his brain ached inside his skull.

Fire spread under his skin, and he convulsed.

Bile and foam filled his mouth, and he choked.

Everything around him darkened.

Alak'ish pulled his head into her lap and held him as the death spasms wracked his body.

"It's okay, my love," she said, crying over his human form as it succumbed to the overdose. "The pain is almost over. Soon, we will be reunited forever."

Will Thompson 11/5/18 The Center of Everything

332

LIMINAL STATE
Lorraine Sharma Nelson

Leena sat up, mouth open in a silent scream. Bathed in sweat, her t-shirt plastered to her body. Taking a deep, shaky breath, she ran a hand through her damp hair.

Not again. God, how many times had she had the same dream? No, not a dream, a nightmare. She lay back, staring into the darkness.

That long, narrow passageway appeared again. She took a few halting footsteps, although where it led, she knew not.

Soon, however, she ran, passing a steady stream of doors on either side of her.

The door at the end would lead to sunshine and happiness.

There, she would be safe.

The thought spurred her on, but try as she might, she couldn't quite reach it.

Leena whimpered. Everything depended on reaching it.

And she was almost there.

She reached out a hand, ready to grasp the knob.

A chill enveloped her. From the space between the last two doors on the right side of the corridor.

Leena expected to see an opening, but a plain, white wall stood beside her.

She couldn't move. The chill penetrated her bones. An unknown force pulled her toward the space between the doors.

It didn't make sense. The door she wanted was right in front of her. All she had to do was reach out and grasp the knob. But she couldn't raise her arm.

The blank wall between the doors. Whatever it was, she couldn't fight against this force.

Helpless, Leena was drawn inexorably closer to the wall.

Then, just as she reached it, expecting to be pressed against the cold, stark surface, it sucked her in.

Blackness surrounded her. Sliding into her nostrils, into her mouth, her eyes, her ears. Filling her from the inside out.

Leena opened her mouth to scream…

…And woke up. Again.

She took a deep, shuddering breath. Five weeks since this recurring nightmare had begun. Leena pulled the covers up to her chin, huddling beneath them. How much longer would they continue?

Leena made a cup of tea and curled up in her recliner in her tiny living room. She flipped channels, looking for a movie. Something light-hearted and fun that would take her mind off the recurring nightmare.

She stopped on Jim Carrey's face. *Ace Ventura*. Mindless fun. If that didn't make her forget her troubles, nothing would.

When the movie ended, she checked the time: 2:00 AM. And she had to be up at 6:30. She groaned as she clicked off the TV and made herself comfortable. No way was she going back to bed.

Leena hurried to the subway station across the street from her apartment building. The nightmare came back to her, despite her resolve not to think about it, and again, the inky darkness invaded her body, her senses.

She shuddered then forced her thoughts to the upcoming meeting. Despite her lack of sleep, Leena's excitement mounted. The project her team worked on—preparing the museum for the big Jurassic exhibit that would take place for two weeks in July—was the meeting's focus.

"So, we're all in agreement. Leena Rai is to head the project. Everyone associated with it will report to her. This, of course, includes all gripes and complaints." The museum director sat back with a broad smile. "I can't tell you how happy I am that, for once, I won't have to hear any of it."

He rose to his feet.

"Dismissed, people. Let's get to work on the best damn dinosaur exhibit any museum has ever unveiled."

The clock on Leena's office wall made her wince: 12:10 AM. She sat back in her chair, arching her spine, rotating her neck. God, how she'd love to go home and crawl into bed. So exhausted that even the possibility of another nightmare didn't faze her.

But she couldn't leave. Not yet. There was too much to do. The exhibit opening may be months away, but that meant working long hours in order to be ready on time. Even now, she could hear muffled voices and dull thuds from other offices down the hall, her team also hard at work.

Leena yawned, struggling to focus.

She leaned back against the chair, squeezing her eyes shut. She needed to finalize the plans for the exhibit before going home. With any luck, she could get out of here in a couple of hours, grab some sleep, and be back bright and early to begin Phase Two.

Her lips twitched.

Why did she put herself through this year after year, when she could have a nice, quiet job doing open-heart surgery? Oh right. She loved paleontology. Loved dinosaurs.

This was where she belonged.

The empty street loomed before her, quiet save for an unsettling rustling. Leena quickened her steps, her stilettos clicking loudly on the sidewalk.

Where was that stupid cab?

Her phone app showed it waiting at the corner of First and Main.

But she'd turned the corner to another vacant street.

Screw it.

I'll walk the two blocks to the subway.

Almost there.

A few people disappeared down the subway steps. At least she wasn't the only one walking the streets at this time of night.

She passed stores, shut tight for the night, their iron bars a testament to the crime plaguing the city. To her right was the bookstore that she loved to frequent, filled floor to ceiling with books.

Tonight, it looked stark, lonely, and a little bit creepy.

As Leena hurried past, the chill from her nightmares gripped her.

She stopped. A blank wall separated the bookstore from the adjacent tacky souvenir shop.

No. I'm wide awake. This is no dream, so this can't be happening.

Leena chided herself for her stupid imagination.

But her legs wouldn't move. Her feet stuck to the pavement. She struggled to free them. Finally, after a few panic-stricken moments, she slipped her feet out of her shoes.

Leena almost sobbed with relief, intent on sprinting toward the subway stairs.

But she found herself being dragged sideways.

Toward the space between the two stores.

Leena struggled, desperate to pull away.

No. This can't be happening.

She opened her mouth to scream for help, but nothing came out. Tried to turn her head, to see if anyone was nearby who could help her. But she couldn't move.

The wall separating the two establishments systematically pulled her body toward it.

The cold intensified as the wall disappeared and sucked her into the blackness again.

Inky blackness slid into her, right down to her cells. Blackness so complete, she couldn't tell if her eyes were open or closed.

Goosebumps peppered her skin. She rubbed her arms and realized she could move again.

Against her better judgment, Leena took a step forward. Then another. The floor beneath her bare feet icy cold as she walked in an endless abyss. No sound, no light. Nothing.

There, and yet, not there.

As if she'd ceased to be.

Yet she could think. She could feel. She could hear.

Softly at first. Then louder.

Screams.

Wailing.

Ahead of her.

Behind her.

Beside her.

All around.

All of a sudden, she could see. Not well. The shapes hazy, but she could see well enough.

On her left, a woman ran from a bear. Leena broke into a cold sweat from the terror in the woman's eyes.

And, on her right, a man wrestled with a giant octopus. Leena shuddered as giant tentacles surrounded him.

And what was that? A girl. A teenager. Being held in midair by…was that a vampire?

Leena tried to scream for the creature to let go of the girl. Tried to move, to help her. But she couldn't. A force field of some kind propelled her onward. Forward. Showing her more terrifying, macabre scenes of people in various stages of torment and agony.

And all she could do was watch.

The scenes blurred before her, like a disjointed movie that skipped from scene to scene, too quick to register.

A wave of utter despair washed over Leena.

She was stuck here. Wherever this was.

This in-between world of shade and shadow.

Of desolation and darkness.

A nightmare realm.

More images swam before her, each worse than the one before.

Who were these people? What had they done to end up here in this hell? What had *she* done?

Then, she stopped.

Leena saw herself lying in bed, twisting, thrashing. Her mouth open in a silent scream.

The image changed. She saw herself running. But from what?

A snake. Twenty-five feet long, at least.

Capable of squeezing the life out of her.

Its sibilant breathing raised the hairs on the back of her neck as it gained on her image.

Behind her.

No. That couldn't be. It chased her in her dreams.

She turned.

The snake whipped toward her, jaw extended in a yawning gape.

Leena screamed.

And pain slammed through her.

Her eyes snapped open.

The stark, white ceiling hovered above her.

From the floor of her office. Beside her toppled chair.

Footsteps approached, and before she could draw breath, the door burst open.

"Leena, where are you?"

"Here." She grabbed the edge of the desk, prepared to hoist herself up, but a pair of hands slid under her arms, lifting her to her feet.

"Are you all right?" Dr. Marius Flynn's bushy gray eyebrows scrunched in concern.

She nodded, heat warming her cheeks. God, he must think her such a klutz.

"What happened?"

She shrugged, forcing a laugh. "I must have fallen asleep at my desk."

"Okay. Well, as long as you're fine."

"I am. Thanks."

"Okay, then. I'll leave you to it. Coffee at ten?"

"Wh—what?"

He peered at her from the door. "You look like you could use it. If I didn't know better, I'd say you spent the whole night here, at your desk."

Leena glanced down at her rumpled skirt.

"Leena?"

She looked up.

"Did you spend the whole night here?"

She must have. Except she vividly remembered walking to the subway. Before being sucked into that…that void. That nothingness.

But if that were true, how did she end up back here?

"Leena?" A frown crossed his features.

"I…yes, I did. I had so much to do…"

He shook his head. "If I were you, I'd go home, grab some shuteye then come back. You'll feel much better."

She shook her head. "I'm fine, really. Coffee and a bagel, and I'll be good as new."

He inclined his head. "Whatever you say. Meet you upstairs at ten, then?"

"Yep. See you."

When the door shut behind him, Leena slumped in her chair, stubbing her foot against the desk.

What the hell—?

She frowned down at her bare feet. Where were her shoes? She stooped, checking under her desk, her chair.

Missing.

But that was crazy. They couldn't have just walked away. She—

Leena's heart slammed.

I took them off before being pulled into the void.

When she finally got home, Leena crawled into bed fully clothed.

A couple of hours sleep, and I'll head back.

And she sank into oblivion.

Disoriented, Leena dug her fingers into her palms, relishing the pain. Welcoming it. It meant she was awake.

But, she was also back inside the void.

This time, when she got sucked in, she was nowhere near a wall. Nowhere near anything. Just a thin, dark vertical sliver of space.

In the middle of Times Square.

It materialized in front of her while she crossed the street. The chill pulled even from where she stood.

Around her, people pushed and jostled, causing her to stumble.

But all her faculties centered on trying to resist the tug of that long, dark streak that materialized at the edge of the sidewalk.

People walked behind it, around it, straight through it. But nothing happened to them. None of them reacted. No one noticed. No one cared.

She was alone.

Again.

It drew her in, despite her attempts to resist.

Help me.

The words only echoed in her head. Her voice always silenced within the void.

This time, no giant snake chased her. Nothing was behind her.

But something emerged ahead. Coming toward her.

Something bad.

Something evil.

Leena tried to turn, to run. Rigid, frozen to the ground, she watched as a dark figure materialized before her.

"Hello…"

The voice sent chills skittering through her body. Who was he? What did he want?

"Leave me alone!"

Her eyes popped open. She lay on the sidewalk, outside a popular coffee shop. And people loomed over her.

Hands pulled her to her feet. Questions flung at her.

Leena pushed away from the gathering crowd. Pressing a hand against her temple, she hurried down the sidewalk.

What was that? A blackout?

Had she started having waking nightmares now? Was that even possible? Leena's stomach twisted.

What if something was wrong with her? What if she had some kind of a tumor that caused these vivid nightmares?

Before she changed her mind, she fished her phone out of her purse and dialed her doctor's office.

By the time she arrived at the museum, she felt slightly better. With any luck, Dr. Randall would be able to tell Leena what was going on. Thanks to a cancellation, she had a two o'clock appointment.

The day passed uneventfully. By one-thirty, the hall had been carefully mapped out. The fearsome Allosaurus, ancestor to the mighty T-Rex, would go over there, poised over the Stegosaurus. Over there would be the giant Apatosaurus, a plant-eater, laying its eggs. And there, in a makeshift sea, would float the horrific Plesiosaur, with its mouth full of jagged teeth.

So excited by her team's progress was she, that when the alarm on her FitBand sounded, Leena considered cancelling her appointment. But the memory of that hideous snake made her reconsider.

Leena took a deep breath and waited for Dr. Randall's reaction.

For her part, the good doctor remained unfazed.

"For God's sake, Doctor. Say something."

"Okay. You're not crazy."

Leena blinked at her. Then laughed. "Seriously? You deduced that from my ramblings about my weird-ass dreams?"

"No. I deduced that from the fact that you're wondering if you're crazy because you're having these…these waking-dreams, as you so eloquently put it."

"Oooohhh. I get it. If I were crazy, I'd insist I weren't. Is that it?"

"Something like that. But—" She smiled and leaned toward her desk, plucking a card from a small box. "I'm not a psychiatrist. It might be a good idea for you to talk to someone about your dreams. Maybe you'll better understand them after having them analyzed."

Leena sighed. "I don't want to have them or my head analyzed. I just want them to stop. Can't you just give me an antibiotic or something?"

The doctor laughed, shaking her head. "If something like that existed, shrinks would go out of business."

Leena frowned. "So, you can't help me?"

"Leena, I'm your primary care physician. I see you when you have an upper respiratory ailment or a fever. Or abdominal pains. Something of that nature. But this…" She tapped the side of her head. "This is not my domain. However—"

"I get it," Leena said, rising to her feet. "Thanks, anyway."

"Wait." Dr. Randall put a hand lightly on Leena's arm. "You didn't let me finish. I can tell you what little I do know."

"And what's that?" Leena sat back down.

"I heard my brother-in-law, who's a psychiatrist in Seattle, talk about strange dreams that some of his patients have had recently. They sound similar to yours in some ways, with slight variations. I'll have to check with him, but I think he said something about these…spaces you get sucked into. He called them…what was it? Luminous…no. Luminal? Liminal. That's it. Liminal states."

Leena's brows snapped together. "Liminal states? What's that?"

"Something to do with a sensory threshold. An in-between state, you know? Something transitional. Between life and death."

Leena's eyes widened. "And this is supposed to help me feel better?"

"No, Leena. It's supposed to help you understand what this is that you're going through."

"I'm...I'm transitioning between...between life and death?" A shiver tunneled through her.

"No, no. Of course not."

"Well, that's what you just said."

"All I meant was, he said there's a name for that in-between state. That's all. Look, I'll send you Evan's cell number. I'm going to call him right after you leave and tell him to expect a call from you sometime this evening, okay? Maybe he can explain it to you."

Leena nodded. "Okay. You're sure he won't mind? What if he has plans—?"

"He and Julie always have plans. But I'm sure he can spare a few minutes to talk to one of my faithful patients." She smiled, rising to her feet. "Don't worry too much, okay? They're just dreams. They can't hurt you. Not really. If, after talking to Evan, you decide you want to see a psychiatrist one-on-one about these dreams, let me know. I can recommend someone."

Back at the museum, Leena heard the arguing in the upstairs rotunda before the elevator doors even slid open.

Gordon Wycliff spotted her first and made a beeline for her.

"There you are," he said, his usual nasally voice made even more so by his high level of agitation. "Would you please explain to Mylie that we need an entire sea floor of ammonites, right below the plesiosaur?"

Leena bit back a sigh. "We're not doing a sea floor, Gordon. We're doing a full wall of ammonites right next to where the animals will be suspended."

Gordon's eyes narrowed as he glared at her. "But that makes no sense. They're part of the ocean."

"Exactly. The wall will be painted to look like the ocean, which will have the desired effect of the ammonites swimming, rather than lying dead on the sea floor." She turned to Mylie and the other team members. "Anything else we need to discuss?"

By the time they'd finalized exhibit plans, with the hired artist sketching madly as they threw out ideas, it was past closing time. Again.

Leena exited the building with the rest of the employees.

When she got home, she kicked off her shoes and dialed the number her doctor gave her.

"Hello?"

"Yes, hello. Is this Dr. Burnham?"

"Speaking."

"My name is Leena Rai. Dr. Randall—she's my primary care—gave me your number and—"

"Ah, yes. The Dreamwalker."

"Pardon?"

"Cassie said you've been having dreams, bad dreams, that strike at any time?"

"Yes, I—"

"Can you describe them to me? The content of your dreams? And how you get to that dreamworld of yours? If I'm being brusque, I apologize. I'm at a psychiatrists' convention, and the keynote speaker is about to start. I want to get seated before then."

"Oh, I can call back—"

"No need. Proceed."

"Ummm…okay." Taken aback, Leena stumbled through her explanation, making sure to describe, in detail, the manner in which she was sucked into the black void. "And it's always the same when I'm pulled through to the other side. It's black. I mean absolutely. No inkling of light anywhere. It feels like it worms its way inside me. Taking over my mind, my body. It gets under my skin."

When she'd finished detailing the incident in Times Square, she waited for his response.

He was silent for so long she wondered if maybe he'd hung up on her.

"Liminal," he stated firmly.

"Liminal? Dr. Randall mentioned that."

"She's quite right. What you experienced, it's called a liminal state. A transitional phase of some sort. Something between this world and the next."

"But what does it mean? What's the other world?"

"The world of dreams. That tenuous place that one goes to when one is at his—or her—most vulnerable."

"So, a dream state is called a liminal state?"

"For the purpose of this conversation, yes. A place between two worlds."

"But." Leena shook her head. "I don't understand."

"Ms. Rai, the door to the dreamworld, the nightmare realm, has been opened somehow. This is why you keep slipping into it. And those people you saw once you got there? They were real people, all having their own dreams. Fighting their own nightmares."

"That doesn't make any sense. How can one's nightmares become real? How can a dream actually be part of another world?"

"All I can tell you is that, recently, I have seen countless patients, as have my colleagues, all of them claiming to be sucked into a black void when they least expect it. And in this place, they experience horrendous nightmares, which seem vividly real."

Leena's stomach twisted, making her nauseous. "Did…did these patients see other people in this void, like I did?"

"Yes, they did."

"What does that mean? What should I do?"

Dr. Burnham sighed loudly. "You have to understand, Ms. Rai, that usually when someone comes to me, claiming to be having these living nightmares, my response is to help the patient get to the root cause of the problem. But, when patients in the double digits suddenly start reporting the same thing to me, one after the other, I am obliged to take a step back and re-evaluate my stance on the subject."

Leena took a deep breath. "And what is your conclusion?"

"It is not something that is supported by my colleagues—"

"Please tell me."

A brief silence. Leena shut her eyes and waited.

"Very well, but you probably won't like my answer. That door to the nightmare realm? The one that's been opened? It needs to be shut."

Leena's breath sharpened, her fingers tightening on the phone. "You're not serious?"

"I am."

"But that's…" She gave a shaky laugh. "That's absurd."

"Yes, but nevertheless, it is what I believe."

Leena frowned. "You're supposed to be a respected psychiatrist. Do you know what you sound like?"

"A quack that needs to be hauled away in a straitjacket?"

"*Yes.*"

"If you have another explanation, I am all ears."

Leena's head buzzed. She couldn't deal with him or his crackpot hypothesis any longer. How could her doctor have possibly recommended that she talk to him?

"I have to go, Dr. Burnham. Thank you for …er…"

"Wait."

She waited.

"An open mind, Ms. Rai. That's what is needed right now. If you do not confront this problem, you will lose yourself, possibly forever. And so will all the other people trapped in this liminal state with you."

"Dr. Burnham, please. I can't process—"

"An open mind. Remember that. For your own sake. Now, I have to go. Good luck, Ms. Rai. And remember, fear breeds fear."

And he was gone. Just like that.

What just happened?

343

"Maybe, he's right." Juno, Leena's best friend, looked at her over the rim of her wine glass, before tossing back the contents.

"Get serious." Leena speared a cherry tomato with her fork, popped it into her mouth, and pushed her salad plate aside. "It's obvious the man's a loon. Someone's going to report him, and he'll end up losing his license."

"Or maybe, you should consider what's been happening to you and keep an open mind, as he says."

Leena scowled at her friend. "Whose side are you on?"

"Yours, you idiot, but I'm seriously worried about you." Juno leaned over the small café table. "Leen, you told me that you've been sucked into this awful black void a number of times, right?"

"Yeah, so?"

"So, it's not normal. You know it's not." Her voice dropped another notch. "Maybe, there is something to what he said."

"I told you, he's—"

"Nuts. Yes, I know. But maybe, just maybe, he's not. Leen, what if he's right and you don't do anything about it. What if...what if..."

"I lose my mind?" Leena asked softly.

Juno raised large, brown eyes to her, the worry obvious in them. "When was the last time you looked in a mirror? You look like hell. Racoon eyes. Dark and...and...I don't know...haunted. And you haven't been eating, either—"

"You just saw me eat," Leena said, eyeing her barely-touched salad.

"Two cherry tomatoes and a bite of lettuce does not constitute a meal. You're wasting away."

Leena sighed, massaging the back of her neck. "What do you want me to do, Juno?"

"Do what that psychiatrist said. Find the door, and shut it."

Leena laughed. "Fine. Care to tell me how?"

"I don't know. All I know is I don't want to lose my best friend." Juno gripped Leena's hand. "So you have to promise me that you'll find a way."

"For Christ's sake—"

"Promise me." Juno's hand tightened on hers.

"Fine," Leena said. "I promise."

And maybe, I'll grow wings and fly to the moon while I'm at it.

Leena ran for her life. But her feet didn't move. That thing chased her. Again.

It came to her in many forms.

The first as that giant snake. Then, hooded and skeletal, with eyes as red as fire. And yet again, as a man, with a face so badly scarred, it looked as if it melted before her eyes.

Now, she didn't know what form it took. Didn't want to wait around to find out. Leena struggled to move her legs. Yet, as so often happened in her dreams, she couldn't. They wouldn't budge.

The creature, the thing—whatever it was—came up behind her. Its cold breath on the back of her neck.

I'm so scared. Oh God, please help me.

The thing was almost upon her.

This time, if the thing grabbed her, she would not wake up.

She would be stuck in this in-between state.

No way back from madness.

Its voice called her name in her head.

Leeennnnaaaa.

Oh God, that quack doctor was right. This *was* happening. She remembered his last words to her: *An open mind…fear breeds fear.*

Wait. What?

Something stirred in her memory. Something important. *Fear breeds fear.* What did that mean?

And suddenly, she knew, the revelation stopping her short.

An icy hand touched her bare shoulder.

And she screamed…

Leena's eyes snapped open.

She was tangled in the sheets, her hands fisted in them.

Her right shoulder throbbed, as if something was clamped on it, and for a terrifying moment, she thought the creature had a hold of her.

On the floor, she groaned, closing her eyes. She must have hit her shoulder when she tumbled off the bed.

Last night's nightmares chased each other around in her head, and she couldn't make sense of them. They faded already, though bits and pieces of the most chilling parts hung on. Like leeches.

But there was something more.

Something that hadn't been there before.

It lurked at the edges of her consciousness, just out of reach. But so close.

Frustrated, she rolled onto her back, kicking off the damp sheets and glanced at her phone: 6:35 AM. She winced. Time to get up, although her whole body protested at the thought.

Juno was right. She couldn't go on like this. The dark circles under her eyes had everyone at work concerned. And she had lost weight.

Leena made her way to the bathroom. A hot shower, and maybe she'd make herself a hearty breakfast for once.

Surprisingly, hunger hit her for the first time in weeks.

The plans for the dinosaur exhibit came together so well that everyone on the team got caught up in the excitement. Leena lost herself in her work, refusing to dwell on the nightmares that dogged her every step.

Allowing themselves a rare break for lunch, the team went to the cafeteria, occupying a large round table by the window. Bright, warm sunlight spilled into the room, and for the first time in a long time, Leena felt at peace. She tilted her head toward the warmth, letting it envelop her like a hug.

"You're in a good mood today, Dr. Rai," Mylie, her assistant, said, smiling at her. "It's so good to see. You haven't been yourself in a while."

Leena smiled back. "I know. I'm sure I've been a bear to deal with. My apologies to all of you."

The others shook their heads.

"No need. We've all been on edge since the exhibit was announced," one of the women said. "And you have more stress than the rest of us put together."

The conversation drifted to other topics, and Leena's mind wandered as she idly scanned the packed cafeteria.

A group of people at a nearby table animatedly discussed something.

"There's no way you bungee-jumped, dude. You're a big baby when it comes to heights. Everyone knows that."

"That's exactly why I did it, man. Facing my fears and all that. I tell you what, I was so scared I thought I was going to pee my pants, but after it was over and I realized I was still alive…man…that was the best feeling."

And just like that, what had been evading her since her nightmare last night came into sharp focus.

And she knew what she had to do.

This time when the space-between tugged at her, Leena was ready. She allowed herself to be sucked inside. Allowed the darkness to wrap around her.

And waited for the creature to come.

First came a hiss, followed by a slithering sound.

The snake was back.

Leena stiffened, forcing herself to meet the serpent eye-to-eye.

It weaved in the darkness toward her. Filling her entire line of sight.

It's not real. And if I really believe it's not real, it can't hurt me.

She hoped beyond hope that Dr. Burnham was correct. Fear breeds fear, he had said. And that meant the only way to end the nightmares was to face them head on. To not give in to fear. Because, if the nightmares fed on fear, it made them stronger. It allowed them to manifest.

All she had to do was face it.

Show no fear.

Feel no fear.

Treat it like the illusion it is, and it should fade away as illusions do.

Leena braced herself, her fists clenching. All day, she filled herself with anger. Anger that this thing threatened to take her life. Anger that it almost succeeded.

No more.

She planted her feet, straightened and waited for the serpent to slither up. Waited to look it in the eyes.

You're not real. You do not exist.

You're not real. You do not exist.

You're not real. You do not exist.

Closer, the snake reared its hideous head.

You're not real. You do not exist.

Leena met it eye-for-eye.

"You're not real." Her heart slammed against her ribs, fingers curling into fists.

"You're not real," she yelled. "You hear me? I know you don't exist. You're nothing but a nightmare."

With each breath, her anger grew. Feeding off itself.

"Come and get me, you son-of-a-bitch. I'm not afraid of you. I hope you choke on me."

The serpent reared its head back.

And snapped it forward, jaw extended, as big as a cave.

"Go back to hell." Leena leapt forward to meet the creature. White-hot rage exploded from within, as the darkness took her.

The honking of the cars and buses outside her window annoyed her. Leena turned over, pulling the pillow over her head. She sighed, supremely content, and snuggled deeper under the comforter. Her body warm, rested.

Leena's eyes flew open. The familiar surroundings of her bedroom looked in order. More importantly, *she* felt whole for the first time in ages.

Why? What was different?

She sat up slowly, yawning, scratching her head.

What happened? Did she have another nightmare? If so, she couldn't remember—

The serpent.

It had been there. In her dream. Coming for her.

But she hadn't been afraid. Wasn't afraid.

Not anymore.

The white-hot anger lingered on her skin.

Leena's heart quickened with hope.

Did it work? Was anger the answer? Or rather, a lack of fear?

Fear breeds fear.

Show no fear.

Leena closed her eyes. Took a deep breath.

That foreshadowing of something horrible was gone. She felt elated. Filled with hope.

Because she knew now how to control the nightmares. Their power over her was gone.

She had shut the door on them.

BUTTERFLIES EATING THE DEAD
Kate Morgan

July 12

Lyra Gentium reread the last line of the credit card company's direct marketing letter, scratched out the final three words, tried two different words, scratched those out, and scowled at the wreck.

The escapist photos of woods and beaches and mountains pinned to her gray cubicle walls failed her today. Four simultaneous phone conversations breached her five-by-five work area. Just within range, the new guy across the aisle sang along off-key to the Broadway musical playing through his headphones. Through the single window at the opposite end of the room, a smidgen of glorious July sunshine taunted her.

She opened the spiral-bound notepad always ready at the side of her desk and wrote a description of the cacophony and longing for freedom. The novel she'd finished last month didn't need this scene, but the next one might.

Her phone rang. She cut off the peppy video-game melody in the middle of the second measure.

"Copywriting, Gentium speaking."

"Ms. Gentium, may I see you in my office, please?"

Lyra's pulse jacked up. "I'll be right in, Mr. Samuels."

Over the cubicle wall, Creepy Steve said, "Busted. What'd'ya do, Gent? Online porn?"

"If anyone's going to get nailed for porn, it's you, pervert."

His nasally laugh crawled up her spine. She locked her monitor and headed to her doom. The Vice President only called the grunts into his Windowed Sanctum to rip them a new one. Lyra rewound her workdays for the past few months. Maybe she'd squeezed an extra few minutes into lunch too many times. Or one of the clients had a crappy ROI for her last series of letters.

Two short halls later, she knocked on his frosted glass door. The lock clicked, and she entered, the door swinging closed behind her. That alluring sun blinded her for a moment. She wished she'd worn her new jeans.

"Please have a seat, Ms. Gentium. Let me adjust the blinds." A pull-chain ratcheted, and vertical strips of plastic angled the sun toward the slate-blue walls.

Lyra's eyes adjusted in a few seconds and the ergonomic office chair in front of his knockoff brand-name desk appeared. Not angry, the VP looked like the big boss did when he handed out New Year's bonuses to the lucky few. Maybe she wasn't in trouble.

"Ms. Gentium, I understand you write novels."

Lyra's mouth opened, but nothing came out. *What the hell?* She swallowed and managed, "Yes, sir."

"Your latest manuscript was brought to my attention." He opened a drawer and set an expandable manila folder on the desk between them.

Doomsday scenarios played in rapid succession. The company thought the book breached confidentiality. It didn't, but they wanted an excuse to fire her and hire someone cheaper. The company thought she'd used thinly disguised co-workers in the book. She really hadn't, not even Creepy Steve, who was rife with slimy possibilities. All the scenarios ended with her getting escorted out by security with her few belongings in an empty copier paper box.

Samuels smiled. Lyra had never seen him smile before.

"Ms. Gentium, I believe you have the wrong impression. I was shown this manuscript because portal fantasies are a genre I enjoy. Where did you get the idea for it?"

"Out of my own head, Mr. Samuels." Where was this going? Why did he care what one of his faceless minions did in her spare time?

He tapped on his desk as though he were calling up documents on a computer screen.

"Yes. Good." He stabbed his index finger once more on its surface and once at her. "You may not know that our sister company has a publishing division. They've read this manuscript and are interested in taking it on. Would you be willing to discuss it with them?"

Sister company? Publishing? Wait a minute. Does a bear shit in the woods?

Out loud, she said, "Of course."

"I've arranged a meeting." He stood and handed her the thick folder. "If you'll come with me?"

Lyra walked next to him, out the door and into the elevator. They got out at the fourth-floor walkway, which Lyra thought branched in one of two directions: to the mall across the street or the attached parking garage.

Samuels steered her toward the right-hand wall, where the building began its angle toward the pitched roof. She was too used to faceless grunt-dom to say, "There's nothing in this corner but painted drywall."

Because when he reached out a hand like he expected to turn a door handle…there was a door handle. Hidden in the shadow cast by the angle of the outside wall, and painted like the door…no, not painted. Lyra narrowed her eyes to bring the door and its handle into focus.

Samuels ushered her through before she succeeded. They walked down another, shorter hall. The windows must have been recently cleaned because the sun shone brighter. Or the paint was fresher. Or something, because even the air felt clearer.

The VP opened a second door into a bright, open reception space. The carpet cushioned her feet better. The soft glow of the painted walls eased her eyes. A landscape hanging over two chairs depicted a snow-covered mountain reflected in a lake. For a second, she swore waves lapped the shore.

"This way." Samuels touched her elbow and led her to a frosted glass door at the end of the hall.

They entered an office similar to Samuels' but different. Brighter. That was it. Everything here was brighter, crisper, fresher. She almost laughed. Her description would work for that detergent ad series in her inbox.

A younger man rose from behind a polished walnut desk. "Ms. Gentium. Pleased to meet you. I'm Jonas Canbry, in charge of publications."

Lyra and Samuels sat in the chairs across from him. Lyra's body settled in like the chair contoured itself to her.

Canbry said wonderful things about her book. Lyra gave him grateful yet professional responses. She'd have given better ones if she could get her feet under her. Even sitting in this ridiculously comfortable chair, she wasn't on firm, immobile ground.

"If you'll open the top book on that stack in front of you," Canbry said, "you'll get an idea of our style."

Lyra pulled the books toward her. Hardcovers, all of them. Cover art bright and fresh like the painting in the hall. She opened the book and turned the pages. On the back of the title page, the copyright information read: "© 2014, 6321."

She touched the numbers. They didn't change.

The two men smiled. Why was everyone smiling so much?

She opened the next book: "© 2014, 6321." The next: "© 2013, 6320." The next: "© 2013, 6320."

She pushed her feet against the cushioning carpet. It didn't alleviate the shifting-slidingness.

"Let me explain," Canbry said.

Lyra didn't give him a chance. She stood, holding to the back of that chair, her body already regretted leaving it, to keep her balance.

"That's okay. You're having a joke on the fantasy writer. I didn't think anyone in upper management ever noticed me, but I suppose it's my fault for talking to Jeanne about my book." She picked up the folder, released the chair, and steadied her legs. "You don't need to worry about me distracting anyone any more. I'll return to keeping my head down on company time. I can see myself out."

Samuels put a hand on her arm.

Canbry stood.

"Ms. Gentium, wait," they said in unison.

Canbry pushed a button on his phone.

Lyra's husband walked in, and the day fell completely off its precarious balance.

Roger and the VPs told her about the parallel Earths. About how the hallway with the hidden door was one of the few portals that straddled both. About how this company, the bright one, recruited the barest handful of employees from *her* Earth who were capable of accepting the dual reality.

Lyra reached a hand toward her husband but dropped it before she touched this newer, brighter, sharper Roger. "So, this is why you've been vague about your promotion."

Roger and the VPs laughed.

What the hell was it with all the happy?

"And liking my job for the first time in years," he said. "You'll love it here, too."

Only a fool would turn down this place, this job, this deal, this…everything. She sat in the embracing chair again. The floor had to stop shifting now that she knew what was really going on.

Under their triple scrutiny, Lyra placed her manuscript on the desk next to the books. "I think I will."

November 17

Lyra reread her latest electric car ad copy at her small but separate desk in a two-person office. An office. With a door that closed. And a huge window.

A poster-sized version of her book cover hung on the wall behind her. The colors popped. Her main character looked human enough to step out of the artwork and into the room. It was everything she'd dreamed of in her years of writing to fill the echoing pit inside her.

Confident, self-sufficient Roger didn't know about the pit. He didn't need a family to complete his life. He loved her, he loved his job, and he kept surprising her with fantastic, wild plans for themselves in this bright, beautiful alternate Earth. The two of them, he'd say, riding this wave into the future.

She loved Roger. So, they created grand plans together and laughed together when the plans became so absurd they collapsed in on themselves.

That was their signal in the evening to make coffee for him and ginger tea for her and watch a movie on the bright Earth's version of TV.

Her computer reminder chimed. She signed off on the copy and picked up her cup of ginger tea.

At the desk next to hers sat the same Jeanne who'd shown Lyra's manuscript to Samuels and Canbry. "Hey, Gentium. Lunch at the new burger place on Maple Street?"

Lyra smiled. She possessed a Masters degree in smiling now. "I can't today, Myers. My husband has a lunch meeting, and this is my only chance to buy his birthday present."

"Tomorrow, then? You, me, and Canbry."

Lyra added a touch of curiosity to her expression. "Again? Is there something we should know?"

Coyness infused her co-worker's answer. "Why would you say that?"

Lyra mimed locking her lips together. "We'll all have a perfectly innocent lunch tomorrow."

Myers winked at her.

Lyra accepted the last-names-only rule at work because using first names was somehow an unforgivable invasion of privacy, as much as she saw no point in it. She dumped the remains of her lukewarm tea in the office's kitchen sink and rinsed out her mug. Ginger tea didn't banish the occasional bouts of sliding-shifting she still got, but it enabled her to function as though they didn't exist. She'd tried daily Dramamine the first few weeks, but quit when she fell asleep standing in her shower one morning.

She smiled bright and often during that day's copywriters' meeting and even brighter at Canbry when he complimented her work on the new real estate account. When she passed the front desk as she left for lunch, she smiled at the receptionist and admired the school photographs of her twin daughters. When she stepped out into the crisp November air, her smile became genuine for the first time that day.

At the small park on the corner, a group of boys and girls tried to launch winged paper kites. One of them crashed at Lyra's feet. When the little girl who came running saw that it was damaged beyond repair, her happy turned into a pre-tears pout.

Lyra had to bring back the little one's happy. "I can't fix your kite, but I can tell you a story about kites with bright colors like these."

The rest of the children crowded around her. "Does it have adventures?" "What about a dragon?" "I want a brave princess who goes on an adventure." "With a beautiful horse." "And a handsome prince."

"Tell us a story," they chorused. "We want a story."

Lyra sat on the soft grass with them around her in a close circle. "Once upon a time, there was a beautiful princess who liked to fly kites."

She wove all the colors of their kites into her words, along with the clear blue sky and the grass and the sun. The children leaned forward at the exciting parts and danced around her at the happy ending. For a few moments, Lyra could have sworn the colors of her words infused her breath and floated over the children, who appeared to breathe in her multi-hued words.

The bright sun in the clear air appeared to make the children glow brighter when she was finished.

"I have to go and buy a surprise present now." Lyra stood.

The children ran off, most of them thanking her over their shoulders.

Lyra walked to the travel agency in the next block, drained and fighting the shifting-slidingness more than usual. She kept the bones of her kite story in her head. She hadn't written a word since she moved to new Earth. Time to get back into her creative routine. She was a storyteller.

The travel agency shared a storefront with a swimsuit boutique. Good marketing. She should know. The chimes tinkled as she pushed open the door.

"Good afternoon. I'm interested in a weekend getaway to the lakes."

The plump, gray-haired travel agent smiled. "By yourself?"

"No. It's a birthday present for my husband. He likes to fish."

Half an hour later, Lyra tucked tickets and a travel itinerary into her purse. The weekend fishing trip her husband—Roger, his name was Roger—had been hinting about turned out to have something for her, too: the auroras. She'd always wanted to see them on old Earth but could never afford to go that far north. On this Earth, the auroras reached over most of the globe from September through December. She hadn't discovered why, but it didn't matter. Her hiring bonus covered most of the cost. She'd been counter-hinting that their budget wouldn't stretch to cover this trip. Roger would be surprised. He liked surprises.

December 3

Lyra and Roger sat on the dock, waiting for the twilight to deepen and the auroras to begin. Lyra couldn't wait to finally see them, but she was even happier not to be in the boat. She'd had to resort to old-Earth Dramamine this morning because ginger tea couldn't counteract bouts of shifting-slidingness plus seven hours on the water. Most of the soporific effect had worn off by now.

"This has been my best birthday ever." He slid his arm around her. "You're the most wonderful wife a man could ever have."

"I'm so happy you liked everything." Delight filled her.

Colors played across his face. "It's starting."

He turned her head to face the soaring expanse of sky.

A swath of emerald green looped over her. A ribbon of periwinkle followed. The colors danced together, separately, together again. A swoop of white joined them. The most beautiful sight she had ever seen.

Her husband's hands urged her up, and she stood, arms out, fingertips reaching. The lights were brighter, softer, more of everything than the photos she'd seen of Northern Lights on old Earth.

The undulating ribbons of color plunged across her vision.

She couldn't find her balance.

She planted her feet.

Below her, her husband's voice said something, but she didn't understand it in the face of the auroras. It was what she'd wanted all her life to see. The new Earth's auroras dazzled, rapturous, perfect, yes, perfect. Truly perfect.

Not like the happy smiling perfect faces everywhere on new Earth.

The shifting-slidingness lifted her.

She flowed into the colors, the lights, the dance, the perfect.

February 23

The sun had once shone brighter than. Brighter than what or where or when, she couldn't recall. She let that go. Today, she clung to her small victory. Her name had been Lyra, and she remembered it.

She lay on the bed next to her husband and stared at the light in their bedroom. Morning light. Soon, she would get out of bed and shower and start coffee for him. He would shower, and she would dress. Yes. That was the routine. She would brew ginger tea and swallow it hot to shock away the shifting-slidingness.

The alarm next to her side of the bed whistled like a morning robin. She turned it off and began the routine. Routine helped the shifting-slidingness, too.

Her husband smiled and kissed her as they passed each other going through the bathroom door. "Good morning, beautiful."

She smiled, too. She always smiled. Everyone smiled. "I'll start the coffee."

When she had dressed for work and sat at the kitchen counter waiting precisely four minutes for the tea to steep, she repeated her recaptured memory over and over in her head.

Lyra.

A photograph of her husband on a dock holding a string of fish hung on the wall over the counter. She should remember taking that picture because it was recent. Her husband said it was from the best birthday ever. His voice warmed her when he said that, so she accepted the knowledge with relief that remembering wasn't necessary.

The temperature and the spice of her tea burned her throat, and her gaze widened on the photograph of the auroras next to the one of her husband and the fish.

She wished her husband hadn't put this picture where she had to look at it every morning. It bothered her in a way she couldn't define, much like her sense that the sun was brighter than.

That sentence bothered her, too. Something in her had an idea that she had once used language with greater precision, and the "than" was not precise.

She let that go as well and clung tighter to her small victory. *Lyra.*

She poured the tea down the sink and finished making her husband's coffee. Not finishing her tea broke the routine, but today was a daring day. She was daring.

Lyra was daring.

Her husband came into the kitchen, sipped his coffee, and complimented the taste. She didn't tell him about Lyra. She would save it for a surprise. He liked surprises. Didn't he?

As they walked to work together, she said, "Do you like surprises?"

He looked down at her. "Sometimes. Do you have a surprise for me?"

She stared into his eyes. "Not yet. I had an idea about you and surprises, and I wanted to make sure."

"You've given me something to look forward to." He opened the door for her. "I'll see you at lunch."

He took the stairs to the second floor. She went to the elevator in the back corner of the first floor, the one partly in shadow from the wide central staircase. Inside, she pressed the only button and the claustrophobic rectangle pulled her sideways, then up, then backwards. Every morning the shifting-slidingness gripped her again by the time the door whooshed open.

February 25

She held tighter to the routine lately. No more "than." No more things she almost remembered. A vague notion lingered about a word beginning with L. The shifting-slidingness clutched at her when she tried to take hold of the L, so she stopped.

Coffee. Ginger tea. Photograph of her husband fishing. Photograph of the auroras. Walk to work. Walk to the elevator. Pulled to the side, up, to the back.

"L," she said, daring the shifting-sliding to fight her. It did.

She didn't hear the doors open. Smiling faces came into the elevator. Hands took her by the arms and led her forward. She stumbled. The hands steadied her. The faces smiled. They led her to the soft place. They opened the doors, and the children appeared. Little girl smiles. Little boy smiles. She lay on the soft floor, and the children sat all around her.

"L," she said.

The children looked at each other, pouting. She didn't want the pouts.

She pushed the L out of her head and began again.

"Once upon a time, there was a brave explorer who found a secret treasure."

Her words became colors and lights. The children laughed and caught them and breathed them in. They glowed with her words. Their mouths turned gold, emerald, peach, apple with her words. She told story after story. Different children came and breathed in her colors and lights. They glowed and laughed and twinkled at her.

Then, the children went away. She remembered this happened every...day, yes, the word was day. She didn't remember why. She lay in the soft, thinking L, and a man came and sat with her.

"What did you give them today?" he said.

"Colors," she said. "Brighter colors. The children flew-fluttered up to catch them. So pretty."

The man breathed in the color of pretty, a pale, glowing blue.

She remembered more. "Adventures. Dreams. Explorations. The children shone brighter than."

"What is L?" he said.

She raised her hand from the soft. She never moved from the soft until they helped her up. This was different. L was different. The man took her hand, and the touch hurt. The soft never hurt. The hurt cracked the shifting-slidingness.

"Lyra. L is Lyra." The word came pale from her lips, almost-sunflower, almost brighter than.

The man set down her hand. "What is Lyra?"

She closed her eyes to recapture the almost. It faded to rain-gray. Gray made her tired. Tired meant lunch. The routine should dim the shifting-sliding. "Lyra is almost. Almost is shifting-slidingness."

She opened her eyes, and the man shifted-slid, and she said, "Roger."

The word was a name. He had a name like the heroes in her stories. Roger was the black-brown of dead leaves. Roger did not breathe in the brown. She watched it rise to the ceiling and dissipate.

That made her angry. Angry was new...no, old. Something she hadn't felt for a long time, not since...a birthday. Her husband's birthday.

"I am a storyteller. You wasted my word. The children never waste my words."

"Today is different. There are more children today. Do you have a surprise for them?"

The soft embraced her. "Children like surprises."

The man who wouldn't breathe in the black-brown word went away. New children surrounded her. She gathered every speck of color still within her and spoke them into words.

"Once upon a time, there was a brave woman who found a secret door."

The children clapped and laughed and breathed in her bright crimson-orange-jade-opal-sunflower.

Sunflower was almost.

She lost the thread of her story. One of the children touched her lips with a small hand, but she couldn't feel it. The children smiled at her, and she opened a mouth she couldn't feel and spoke words she couldn't hear, and the colors flew-fluttered up and away, and the children took them all in.

THE MASK OF INFAMY
E.N. Dahl

I got a ninety-eight on my physics midterm, then Loretta went missing. She sat next to me in our comparatively small class of forty students. The fact that the school didn't cram a few hundred people into one lecture hall made learning a lot easier—none of the anxiety of talking in front of a whole crowd if you raised your hand. Everyone knew each other, more or less. Maybe we didn't talk, didn't hang out, didn't go down to Delta Sigma and tap a keg together, but we knew enough.

I'd transferred into the program because my last school got my name mixed up with someone else and dropped my classes because of his unpaid bill. We didn't want to face that again, so I transferred to Ivy's Path Technical Institute. My parents liked to say it rivaled MIT, even though everyone knew this was a lie. It let them sound proud when adding that to the end of "he had to transfer out of his last school."

Loretta was my only real friend in the class, and beautiful at that, with oceanic eyes set in a porcelain face and waist-length dark hair kept in a braid, each hair in place.

"I don't know how anyone got you mixed up." She smiled, hints of her perfect teeth showing. "You're one of a kind, D Squared."

My real name was Edward DiAngelo, so Ed D. became D Squared. D if you were feeling casual.

"Gonna tell your parents?" Loretta teased, her humor genuine.

I gave what I hoped was an easy-going shrug. "I don't know. Maybe."

She scoffed. "Of course, you are. You ought to."

"Ought to tell them?"

"To rub it in their faces. Please? Do it for me, D." She curled a hand around my bicep in a way I wanted to think was a come-on, but her giant cartoon eyes sparkled with excitement and innocence.

"Okay." Heat rose to my cheeks. No one stared. Still, I waited for prying peers to laugh at me chasing a woman like her. But, we were twenty, young, in college, and still riding puberty's coattails, so it made sense that I could earn the affection of a woman so beautiful she could walk onto any movie set and take the starring role without having to audition. Everyone makes dumb decisions, so she got to make a few, too.

We parted ways, still both single, but I planned to ask her out. I just had to muster up the willpower.

In the meantime, I called my parents.

I hadn't heard from Loretta in a few days, which didn't surprise me. I didn't worry until I showed up for class that Thursday and her seat sat empty.

No big deal. She's probably busy or got food poisoning.

I couldn't forget what Dad said though: "Only a ninety-eight? Slacker. Good thing you can't get a girl, or your grades would drop even lower. Get back in the library."

Shake the thoughts away. That's what I always did, shake them away, press them into the back of my head, where they couldn't reach me. Bury them under *Gears of War* and *Hellblazer* and countless ounces of Bubble Tea. And Loretta. Thoughts of her, conversations with her, whatever. Beautiful people make it easy to forget about ugly things.

I approached Professor Zelwats after class, once everyone had filed out. The unsmiling austerity of his scrutiny pushed me away, but I steeled myself. "'Scuze me, sir, don't mean to bother you."

I tensed up as he rounded his rheumy gray eyes on me, forehead creasing as he peered over his glasses. "B-but...have you heard from Loretta? I haven't seen her lately..."

My gaze turned toward her empty seat.

His face scrunched up. "Loretta?"

"Loretta Stevens, right. She sits next to me?"

His head turned toward the seat, then slowly back.

"Loretta... No, she won't be coming back. She dropped the class."

I wiped my sweat-speckled brow.

"Are you unwell?"

My body made me very aware of my heart stopping. "N-no. I mean, yes. Ill. Sorry. I'll go to the health center."

I left before he could question me further.

What the hell does that mean, she isn't coming back? She wouldn't drop the course. What game is he trying to pull?

Sure, she wasn't a fantastic student, but she wasn't the type to give up, either.

I ran a hand through my hair and made my way to the library. My roommate mentioned something about inviting a girl over, and studying isn't easy when people are having sex five feet away from you. He wasn't exactly shy, and the only thing more infuriating than the distracting, wet slaps of sex was his overly muscular, meathead body. Mark didn't work out often, didn't play on a sports team, just walked around ripped like a lean Terminator. The way woman swooned made me sick.

Every library was the same, rows upon rows of dusty shelves, each giving off that amazing old book smell, tacky brown carpets, and a creaky staircase with the sticky tape worn off the steps.

Professor Zelwats claimed that the library was the oldest building on campus, prompting campus-wide jokes that he'd been around to help build it.

A pudgy older woman ran the front desk, usually engrossed in a book of her own.

Easy to slip inside unnoticed. I didn't want people to see me studying or know for how long. The idea made me sick.

Study cubicles lined the top floor, so I picked one as far back as I could, away from everyone. A girl slept in one, curled up in a ball, facing the back, but I didn't mind her. My physics textbook commanded my attention anyway, and soon, I buried my body, mind, and soul deep inside, trying not to think of how I'd die a virgin.

I studied for probably an hour when the skin on the back of my neck pricked up. The room didn't get darker, but it *felt* darker, a black mist of foreboding creeping over the area. Turning, my gaze fell on Loretta standing in the aisle, wearing a floral dress that stopped mid-thigh. Her giant eyes had the same look my mom used when too nervous to start a tough conversation.

"Hey there." The words dropped from my lips like dead flies. "You okay? You weren't in class, and the professor got all weird about it."

But that perfect doll face of hers slowly contorted into a scowl. She stepped forward, unblinking, a vicious frown disfiguring her innocent visage. The closer she drew, the more my stomach knotted, until she knelt in front of me, and I choked down my lunch.

She splayed her fingers across her face. With a slight twist and a *shuck* of suction, she removed it perfectly at an invisible seam. Beyond that shallow surface was darkness. It filled her head and spilled out into mine, her inner workings hollow and vacuous. I couldn't look away.

"Poor little Ed. Ed-die D." Her voice slithered inside my head, still every bit as seductive, but now venomous and sneering, just like the face she'd removed.

"When will little Ed-die grow up?" She spat out each syllable with emphasis almost as hard as the beating of my heart. *"When will little Ed-die stop being so weak? Pathetic Momma's boy, living under Daddy's thumb."*

Loretta put her face in my open backpack and took hold of my head with her empty hands. *"You're an embarrassment."*

She straddled my lap, legs coiling around me, smothering me with her body's heat as the unending darkness inside her skull loomed closer. *"Like I'd be caught dead with someone like you."*

I turned, throwing myself to the side so fast that it upset the chair.

The creature calling itself Loretta fell, so I grabbed my backpack and ran.

I ignored the desk lady, blew past the people trying to enter as I left, just ran and ran until I was safe from that horror, standing alone in an empty bathroom at Harrison Hall.

I splashed water over my sweaty brow then slapped myself. No one lurked around to hear, so my face took another slap for posterity. In movies, here the hero would wake from a bad dream, but I stood, still trapped in the nightmare.

Her face. The removable one, the mask of corruption, stored in my backpack. My hands shook. The half-zipped bag. Should I reach inside or close it forever?

I opened it.

"Poor fat little Ed-die, running away because it's all he knows how to do. And he wonders why he can't get a date."

When I showed up to physics that Monday, I kept my head down, ignoring the professor, the other students, and especially Loretta's empty seat. The dark spirit haunting me made life hard enough. Didn't need to be thinking about it in the rare instances when it fell silent.

"Ed-die, what if there's a surprise test? You haven't been studying."

I'll be fine. I assured myself that she didn't exist.

"I can't hear you."

"I'll be fine," I said, as quietly as I could.

The professor pulled a stack of papers from his messenger bag.

"Your knowledge is all potential energy." He passed out tests. "So, let's turn that into kinetic. The energy of action. Any information not being used properly is a waste."

"Told ya, Ed-die."

For an instant, I found myself back in the library, staring into the cavernous dark of Loretta's hollow head, trying not to scream as her soulless body pressed itself against me, neck tilting, trying to swallow me. That terrible emptiness would never be filled, by myself or anyone else.

My hands shook so hard I could barely fill out the test, but I got it done and turned it in, excusing myself to the bathroom. The professor waved me off, dismissive and apathetic. In the hall, I ran straight for the bathroom, didn't make it to the toilets, and puked in the sink instead.

She echoed in every room.

Loretta, the girl who wasn't, the would-have-been girlfriend that the professor never heard of, woman who left no trace of herself, perpetually surrounding me.

I'd never believed in ghosts or demons, mostly because Dad was adamant that there was no god, afterlife, or anything supernatural. Mom was too afraid to disagree with him.

Still, I knew the truth. A demon had targeted me. Its unearthly presence hung over me.

How could I escape something that could be everywhere?

"Poor little Ed-die, hanging in a tree. S-U-I-C-I-D-E."

I dug my nails into my palm and raced out of the room. Her voice deafened in loud areas. I needed sound, crowds, chatter, music—anything. The student center didn't help. Naturally, the one time I needed it to be loud, the place stood empty, so I did the one thing I could think of, even if I'd literally rather do anything else: I called my parents.

Dad answered the phone. "What's going on?"

They still had a landline. Dad insisted on the importance of keeping "a central line of communication," never explaining why we needed one, or who'd use it since he didn't allow us to give out the number.

What should I have said, that a demon took over a classmate and continuously tormented me?

"I just wanted to say hi."

"Oh. Hi." He tripped over the uneven pavement of his words. We weren't exactly a small-talk type of family. More still, I never called home.

"Yeah. Hi. How's everything going?" Talking wasn't supposed to be this hard. Each word had to be forced out. We didn't stay on the phone long. I realized pretty quickly that I didn't want to be talking—I didn't want to be doing anything.

I wanted to never see Loretta again.

Mom couldn't come to the phone. That didn't mean she wasn't there, he might simply not have been inclined to let her talk. I hung up a moment later. He didn't need to know what I was going through. Shrugging my bag a little higher on my back, I made my way back to the dorms, ignoring the chill as clouds passed over the sun and left me in the shadows.

My surprise test came back with a red sixty on top and a hastily scrawled, "See me in my office." Professor Zelwats kept odd office hours, so I could either go that night at eight, after his evening class, or wake up early to meet him before eight.

Sleep eluded me. Every time I shut my eyes, that horrible, empty head loomed up from the darkness behind my lids. When I wasn't thinking about her, that snarky-sweet voice reminded me that I didn't have a girlfriend, how much of a social failure I'd turned into, how most caterpillars become butterflies, but I'd become a maggot. These little barbs interrupted while I studied, mocked me while I showered, criticized the food I ate until I pushed my plate away. My pants hung loose around my shrinking waistline.

It didn't help that Mark always stayed up late, listening to music through his huge speakers or talking to some girl in our room while I tried to sleep.

Dad would've hated him for violating the most sacred rule. Be seen, not heard.

The evening meeting offered the most reasonable option, since I didn't want to cut my much-needed rest short. His office was in the Sophocles Building. The actual science building had been under construction for two years prior to my arrival. This place was usually for philosophy, history, and the fine arts. I'd always loved the arts. Mom used to take me to museums to broaden my horizons, or so she said. Those days always happened to be on Dad's worst days, so I think she just liked getting out of the house.

"Lit-tle Ed-die, wal-king slow-ly," Loretta sang, *"wond'ring why he feels so lowly."*

The last thing I needed was to be distracted while negotiating a test grade. I prayed she wouldn't interrupt during my meeting with the professor.

"You pray to the gods? Let me grant your prayers." The line felt familiar, maybe from a Greek play, but I couldn't place it.

I arrived at Zelwats's office as the ghost, ghoul, whatever she called herself, fell into a merciful, if sinister, silence. With a slight knock, I entered. He sat in a high-backed chair, the kind way too old for rolling wheels, engrossed with a paper in his hands.

"You wanted to see me?"

"Yes." He placed the paper face down. "You're failing my class."

My pulse jumped with such fervor that I heard it, hell, even saw it as my vision briefly blurred. "Failing the class? How?"

"Between this test and the midterm, your grades have been…slipping. Are you sure everything's okay? You've seemed distracted." The slight upturn of a grin played on his lips.

"My midterm? I got a ninety-eight."

His brows furrowed, but his grin widened. Picking up a pen, he began casually crossing out names in his planner and doodling over the grades. "You scored a forty, Edward."

"That's not possible. I studied so hard."

The grin cut into his sagging cheeks; the bottoms of his eyelids puffed up. Squinting, manic eyes. His drawing intensified until he ripped up the page, each line an acute violence. "You work so hard. For what?"

"F-for what…? A good GPA? A career?" I couldn't break eye contact. This gorgon's stare transfixed me.

The spell didn't last long. He reached up and—*shuck*—removed his face, handing me that funhouse mirror grin, a mask of ecstasy. *"Do you really think this will make you happy, Edward?"*

🐦

Men don't cry, and they definitely don't talk about their issues, so I spent the next few days out of the dorm to avoid Mark and pretty much everyone else.

One night, I stayed in a motel, sobbing as the two voices.

"Poor little Ed-die."

"Ed doesn't know how to be happy."

The next night, I passed out in an alley behind a dumpster, unconscious for the worst of it, but waking up fresh to *"How fitting that Ed-die is in the garbage,"* and *"He who has the least has happiness—but this sad lump's got nothing."*

What would Mom would say if she knew I'd been on the street?

My head hurt, and my vision dimmed.

When I finally did go back, having tried and failed to exorcise those ghosts, I made sure to shower first. I plugged in my dead phone and got on the computer to answer emails.

A flurry of worried Facebook posts suggested that no one had seen Loretta for days and that she hadn't taken anything from her dorm.

According to my email, Professor Zelwats's classes were all indefinitely canceled due to his unexpected and unexplained absence. It brought relief, really. I'd get to retake the course without an issue.

A second email drew my attention, right as my phone chirped with unread messages. I knew what they were all about. I'd forgotten that our university had an automated system to notify transfer students' parents about failing grades. As soon as an F popped into the system, they got a call.

My parents had been calling me.

The phone rang.

Dad.

Again.

Where had Mark disappeared to? He never had to deal with shit like this. He just went through his day getting whatever grades he wanted because his parents weren't god damn lunatics. Besides, no parent could be mad at someone as talented as him.

"Gotta learn to work harder," he'd say, as if I hadn't been trying. After, he'd go to the gym to celebrate his latest perfect test score.

I couldn't put it off forever.

I answered the phone, eyes shut, phone pulled away from my head so the coming onslaught wouldn't rupture an ear drum. "Hello?"

The yelling started immediately, with Dad furious about my low grade, threatening to punish me, turn my phone off, and revoke all privileges when I got home, yet he made no mention of me being out of communication. I'd lived on the streets for the better part of this week, and he didn't know. He didn't want to know because he didn't care.

"No one cares, Ed-die."

"Why bother with that ball buster, Ed? He'll never understand you."

The disembodied voices of the stalking freaks weren't helping.

What were they? Demons? Aliens? An elaborate hoax?

This mystery had gotten more disturbing, yet more intriguing—the masks posed a puzzle I needed to solve, my very own Lemarchand's box. Thinking about the great expanse of darkness in both Loretta and Zelwats's heads kept my attention off Dad, for a moment, but it's hard to ignore someone screaming in your ear. It's especially hard when they say things like, "That school is so easy. How are you getting such bad grades? Are you disabled or just lazy?"

I'd grown used to this and settled into a familiar, comfortable numbness. None of his attacks reached me until he said, "You keep this up, and you're not gonna survive out there. No one wants to hire some moron who got mediocre grades from a mediocre school, and I'm not supporting you if you're too dumb to get a job."

His threat was a punch to the stomach because I knew that cheapskate wasn't exactly thrilled with the idea of me moving back home, ever, but he'd really let me starve?

"Little Ed-die needs a sugar daddy."

I shook my head.

"Ed, your old man's such an ass that you could ride him into Jerusalem."

They got louder, and I tried *"Don't bother, Little Ed-die"* to block them out, but *"Who needs family when you've got friends like us, Ed?"* they kept coming. *"Poor boy, sitting there, crying, all alone. Street urchins have better lives."*

I was crying.

"Doesn't he know we'll never leave him?" My hand coiled tighter around the *"Oh, how cute, he's trying to shut out the whole world, us, parents, and all"* couldn't *"Putting up a brave face to the world, every second of it fake"* interruption only *"I wonder what he's hiding?"*

The door to my room opened.

Where did Mom stand through this? Would she hug me, stroke my hair, recoil at the thought, nauseous?

Mark entered, coated in a fresh sheen of sweat from the gym, an old towel draped over his shoulder. He pulled off fresh-from-the-gym like the latest cover for *Men's Health*.

"Attractive, well-dressed, smart, he's the whole package and doesn't even have to try. No wonder Li-ttle Ed-die doesn't like him."

Besides, there I was, crying, unshaved, a slovenly mess of growling stomach and miserable confusion. Compared to me, Oscar the Grouch could've been a GQ model.

Dad kept screaming, so loud that it made my head hurt and spin and nearly topple from my shoulders. Mark yawned, probably cruising an endorphin high from his workout.

"—waste of space, waste of my time—" Dad screamed.

Zelwats laughed hysterically while Loretta hissed, *"No wonder none of the ladies want poor Ed-die. Look at the competition."*

I didn't have to look over, though, because Mark came over to me, moving himself into my narrowing field of vision. We stared each other down through a long, dark tunnel, even as he reached up and *shuck* pried off his face, too. It didn't disturb me much this time.

How many of these are there?

He laid his face, a mask of complacency, on my desk. *"Hey, buddy, you gotta learn to relax. Your heart's pounding. Why don't you just lie down and wait for death, man? It'll be so cool. Cool as a corpse."*

I couldn't hear Dad over their laughter.

In line at the coffee shop, and all I hear is *"Little Ed-die get-ting cof-fee," "Make it Irish, buddy, take the edge off," "What's black and strong and wants to be inside you, Ed? Oh, don't act like you wouldn't take it."*

My hands are in my pockets, and my feet are still, but my gaze is everywhere, surveying every person.

Who else? Who's next? How far does this reach?

I'd been doing some research—not easy because they were so loud—and there are tons of little references to creatures like this. Ghouls were close, stalking and feasting off humans, and so were the Skinwalkers, the Native American myth of shapeshifters, but the Nanrakka, from Africa, and the ancient Scottish clan, MacJallis, had the closest myths. The Nanrakka had legends of the Deshrati, the soulless, who'd eat people's insides and take over their bodies.

The MacJallis had a few hushed tales of those who lurk in the corners. They never got easy names because the creatures were too feared to be made into children's books. These stories told of demons who would pretend to be human, then curse an unsuspecting victim, driving them mad. The whole group was wiped out one day, cause of death unknown.

I'm not sure which demon stalks me, but I know I'm close to the end. The air is charged, tense, a Game Over feeling, and I don't have extra lives. The power's shifting. I'm going to find out their secrets and solve this mystery, and then, *"Why's our buddy want to get rid of us?" "Little Ed-die is an asshole."*

The school library had some ancient mythology books. I rented them all and will read them later, even if it takes all night, even if I go deaf from loud music to *"Ooh! You think Ed will blow out his ear drums? That'd be something."* Until then, I'm meeting Mom and trying not to make eye contact with people. These people are, on the surface, strangers, but underneath, who the hell knows?

There's a ring from the front, and *"It's Ed-die's Mom-my. Good thing we're in public. It's safer here for Little Ed-die."* Mom walks in wearing a low-cut blouse and jeans that would've violated most high school dress codes. These demons are everywhere—they can see whatever they want—why shouldn't they know who's behind me?

We say hello. She looks like one of those housewives on a soap opera who panics at the first sign of crows feet.. I order drinks while she gets our seats, fidgeting anxiously, checking and rechecking her emails on her cell. I can't see her phone, but I know what she's doing because it's all she ever does, and *"Ed, that woman is OBSESSED with her emails. Who does she think she is, the president? How many emails can a woman like her get?"* *"Hey, chill out, man. Lady can check her email is she wants, you know?"*

I don't bother with the cardboard rings around our cups. I hold them tight so the heat soaks into my palms and starts to burn. The pain keeps me focused. If I listen too close or for too long, those demons will steal my soul, convince me to do things I don't want, and all my reality has to be is gray walls and the aroma of fresh coffee curling into my nostrils, and *"Hey Ed-die, there's a guy from your humanities class over there with his laptop open. Think he's writing about how stupid you look on a coffee date with your mom?"*

Mom doesn't bother with any greeting more elaborate than the "hi" and "how are you" we exchanged up front.

"We're worried about you," she says, though we both know she means *I'm worried about you.*

"Why?"

She's the police officer who pulled me over when I thought I was driving safely. She doesn't want me to suffer, but Dad, the judge, jury, and executioner, expects someone on his chopping block, and it can't be her again. He's made victims of the both of us.

She bites her lip. I can see scabs and worn patches where she's nearly bitten through, not to mention the lipstick on her front teeth. Her eyes darken.

"Your grades, mostly." *Figures.* "And you don't look well."

"She means you were always such a porker, Ed-die, and now, you've got sagging skin because you lost too much too quickly. You'll have to get surgery to fix that." *"Or maybe you can just do it yourself, Ed. Why pay a quack to slice you up when you can do that all on your own?"*

A familiar voice nearby, a girl from one of my classes, says she doesn't feel safe on campus.

"I'm doing fine, Mom."

"Then why aren't you shaving? It's not cute, you know."

Why does she care what I look like?

Those thoughts make my head hurt.

"If only she'd had other kids."

I shrug. "I've been busy. Studying. Dad really wants me to do that."

The girl nearby—I think her name's Valerie *"It's Chelsea, buddy"* or something—whispers to her friend, "I mean, you heard that *"Shouldn't you be paying attention to your mother, Ed?"* went missing, right? They haven't been seen *"Little Ed-die, don't know you eavesdropping is just a step away from being a Peeping Tom? You perv."* It makes me nervous."

"Are you listening to me?" Mom asks.

"Yeah."

"Then, what did I say?"

"You asked why I didn't shave, and I told you I've been studying."

"I knew you weren't listening." She grumbles, leans back in her chair, and crosses her arms over her chest. "Are you really studying? I don't want to see you living on the street."

Even Mom doesn't have my back. Valerie-Chelsea *"I'm pretty sure her name's Penelope, Ed."* continues, "I heard they were *"Ed-die just can't get enough of spying on the girlies."* with a knife."

"Ew, that's sick," her friend replies. "Who'd do that?"

"This place blows. Let's get out of here, buddy."

My head spins again. "This was a mistake. I knew you wouldn't listen."

I stand, but Mom puts her hand over mine.

"Please, sweetheart. I'm really worried." Her eyes glisten.

I'd only seen her cry when Doctor Shepard died on *Grey's Anatomy* and when I got suspended in tenth grade for punching a senior who, frankly, had it coming for saying I lost my virginity to *"Gotta go with the flow, buddy, can't be smacking everyone around."* *"Yeah, Ed—you hit that kid in public, where there were witnesses."*

Yanking my hand away, I head for the door, trying not to hit any tables or customers on the way out. The city air doesn't help much, so I march along the broken sidewalk, using the force of my footsteps against the ground to keep me focused, and take a sharp turn down a nearby alley to return to campus quicker.

Halfway down the narrow pathway, a hand grabs my shoulder and spins me around. The force makes me stumble, but I come face-to-face with Mom, who openly, silently weeps. *"Try again, Ed-die."* I realize her hand holds her face just in front an empty black head. The eyes shed waterfalls despite not being attached to her tear ducts—assuming these creatures had them.

Now, they'd gotten to me, and now, I fight the urge to cry, losing badly, lost completely as beads rolled down my cheeks.

"Mom, no. They got you, too? You were…" *"Oh look, he's crying." "He's out of options." "Lay down and wait for death, buddy."*

She'd been my last hope. She might've been distant, but she served as the only bastion between Dad's wrath and me—the only rock to cling to in this tempest of a life. Even when completely indifferent, her consistency was at least reassuring.

The mom-creature lays that mask of sorrow at my feet. From inside my head, her sad voice moans, *"Whatever gods intend to bring about, they themselves make known quite easily."*

They're all around us. Everywhere. Inside us. That's what they've made clear to me.

Me? I'm sitting under the largest oak tree in Willbur Park because I can't go back to my dorm. Not anymore.

"They blame you, Ed-die," Loretta told me.

Mark said, *"I'm gone now, and everyone's wondering where I went. They know you didn't like me, buddy. They think you're responsible."*

They know what's in my heart, and they're everywhere. Regular humans are blinded by the masks, think that the people who've gone missing are dead, but I have their faces, the removed façades.

I know they were never humans to begin with, so they can't die, so they can't be murdered, like some are saying.

Some think Loretta, Zelwats, Mark—some think they're dead, but they're not. They're thriving, pure empty night come to life.

There are four soft mounds around me. They stink, and there's dirt under my nails, but that's okay because these demons won't be hurting anyone else.

You think these few were the only ones? No. No, that couldn't be more wrong. I bet there are more of *them* reading this than regular humans, and that's okay, too. I've figured out why they were coming after me. They made it all clear.

"You're one of us, Ed. Better than the rest, leader of the pack, top of the game. You're more than human. More than a human could ever be."

That's when it clicked. I always felt so hollow inside. I thought this was stress, or depression, or weakness, but it wasn't.

Emptiness is strength, my true self, my hidden power—the power to remove my face and reveal the abyssal darkness within. A darkness that can blot out all light and swallow up the soul, absolve all my wrongness.

I'm sitting beneath the tree and fumbling for the seams, the little edges at the sides that reveal where it might be removed, but it's been so long since I was born.

"Edges probably healed over, sweetheart," Mom whispers. *"Have to work a little harder to find them."* I think of how she coped with how Dad treated her, how she sought love in a cold, dead marriage, I almost gouged out my eyes like old Rex did before me. But this knife isn't to blind myself to cruel fate. It's to set my true self free.

I'm prepared. I suffered my entire life; I'm not afraid to hurt a little now. That's why I came prepared.

"Sweet lit-tle Ed-die, underneath a tree. C-U-T-T-I-N-G."

Loretta isn't wrong. I have a knife in my hand, and god, oh god, does it hurt, trying to find these seams, but I'm so close I can taste it. So close, I can feel the darkness on my tongue, the ridges already loosening. Soon, my eyes, nose, mouth, chin; it'll all be gone. All that will remain are the outlines—the faint suggestion of a frail shell housing the most ancient force on earth, the one all humans instinctively fear.

It hurts, but I keep digging, even as the knife slips in my hand. I peel back the skin, layer by layer. Something scrapes the edge, and it might be bone, but I don't care. I will find these seams.

I'll show you. I will find them.

I just have to dig a little deeper.

THE DREAM LOVER
Lindsay Zibach

Dear Elizabeth,

To say I am incomplete without you would be a reckless understatement. Without you, I am nothing. I have no money. I have no job. I have no home to share with you…and these are only the smallest of things. For so long, my condition rendered me useless. I couldn't imagine how weak, how insignificant I truly was, until this morning. Today, I woke no longer disabled by my condition and knew I must write you this letter.

It pains me to know that you're scared as you read these words, as you imagine what I'm going to write, how it's even possible that I *can* write. This is more than possibility, my Elizabeth—my *Eliza*. It's necessity.

This much is true:

In the beginning, I did not know I had a condition. How could I? I only saw myself as you saw me, and in your eyes, I was perfect. Whole. I remember sitting on the floor of your apartment and watching you bashfully flip through volumes and volumes of diaries, your illustrations of my face on almost every page. The man you drew was powerful and passionate, chiseled from his jawline to his muscled waist, and showed no symptom of being *different*.

Between each of the drawings was some fusion of my name with yours, overlapping our shared letters and linking the names together into one combined shape. I love that about you, Eliza. You've never let our differences come between us.

"We're good together," I said.

"Perfect together," you sighed. "I wish we could be together every night for the rest of my life."

I surged with equal parts ecstasy and despair. What did you mean, "every night?"

I couldn't have imagined you would be ashamed to be with someone like me. I thought nothing of the fact that we never saw your parents for dinner or met up with your friends for drinks. You were mine, and I was yours, and our time was our own. Besides, there wouldn't have been room for others anyway. All night, every night, I wound you up until you unspooled around me, over and over again.

One evening, as I raked my fingers through your hair, you wept. "I wish this was real."

"It is real."

You were still.

"It is real," I said again, less certain.

You held my face in the mirror image of how I held yours.

"When I was a child," you said, "I could never tell when I was dreaming. I could fly, turn into a dolphin, be chased by a pack of rabid wolves…and it felt so real. But nothing was as scary as waking up. I'd lie in bed, absolutely paralyzed, unable to even blink. I swore I could *hear* the voices in my dreams, calling me back, keeping me from moving. Only they weren't in my dreams. They were in my room, in my bed, under my sheets."

My poor girl. I kissed the corner of your mouth. "How did you get over it?"

"I'd wait a few minutes, and eventually, everything would go back to normal. I'd sit up, stretch my arms out, and just go about my day." You shrugged, and your gaze drifted elsewhere, like you were remembering things you hadn't realized you'd forgotten.

I touched your hand. "And now?"

"Now, I just dream about amazing sex." You beamed, your eyes and your mind coming back to me. "And a man who is too good to be true."

Like every morning for the years we've been together, our afterglow was shattered by a piercing siren, an alarm of sorts, that blared from the sky. You vanished, as always, and I was left alone.

But in your absence, I was met with a sudden, crippling understanding: I was your dream lover. And I existed only in your dreams.

This much is true:

My condition crippled me to the inside of your mind, which is littered with approximations of every sound you've ever heard and every scent you've ever smelled. When you go somewhere new in your Waking World, it creates shaky ground in mine. The streets turn upwards at impossible gravity-defying angles, houses become Escher nightmares. Hallways lose doors. Windows aperture into nothingness. But your childhood home, your old neighborhood: this is where I live. The walls are steady; the street is firm.

Every person I've ever met is a face you've sat beside on the bus, stood next to in a grocery store, or locked eyes with in a traffic jam. The faces mill about, waiting for you to return, so they can act out your anxieties, your memories, your desires. Most are faces you've forgotten, others are embodiments of memory: the kindergarten teacher with daisies for eyes; the uncle with tentacles for arms locked away in a cupboard.

It was there, among the mobiles of floating faces, that my own nightmare began. If every face was a memory, no matter how small, whose face was mine? Was I a movie star, an ex-boyfriend, a stranger at an airport? Did you lust for me in the Waking World, or did you spend your days satisfied by another? A corporeal, physical man who wasn't plagued by a condition of bodiless nonexistence inside his girlfriend's mind?

I made a plan:

I would take you to one of your favorite memories, a postcard of Paris you had taped to your vanity mirror in college. Our Paris was sun-bleached and peeling in the corners, and our Eiffel Tower was crumpled at the peak, but this was your happy place where I often waited for you in the evenings.

"Tell me," I said over the clink of our champagne flutes, "Who am I...out there?"

You sighed and fixed the hemline of your dress, which had transformed from that of a can-can dancer to a Bardot mini-skirt.

"I have a book about lucid dreams. It's taken years, but now I know how to enjoy my dreams, escape my nightmares—and I don't have that awful sleep paralysis anymore. I'm in control now. If I want to dream about Paris," you waved at our paper picnic, "I dream about Paris."

"So you control...*everything?*"

"Maybe not *everything*, at least not consciously. There are still bits I don't seem able to control, like that thing about my teeth falling out or...that uncle. But in the broad sense, yes. My dreams are what I craft them to be."

"And me?"

"And you, my amazing, sexy, muscle man..." You straddled my lap and placed my hands on your chest. "You are my favorite dream."

"My thoughts...my feelings...the things I do? Me asking you these questions? You are in control of all that, too?"

"Yes." You blinked. "I guess so."

I took my hands off your chest, and your brow furrowed ever so slightly. "Who am I?"

"You're...my lover."

"No, who am I *out there?*" My champagne flute snapped, but instead of a shatter, the sound was that of a child's scream. "If I'm your lover...if you're really in control, then fix me."

"Fix you?"

Around us, the city lights dimmed. With a wave of vertigo, I felt the dream collapsing.

"The next time the siren takes you away, fix me, so I don't have this...*condition*."

"That's impossible."

Bits of paper flecked up from the tower, the Siene, the stone cathedrals. This time, there was no siren, but still, you were leaving me.

"Think about it. I wouldn't be saying this if you didn't want me to. I only do what you want me to."

You began to vanish, as you had done thousands of times before. Only this time, I grabbed your wrist and held it.

"I'm waking up now," you said.

And we did.

🐦

This much is true:

This morning, I awoke in your bed, in your body. I laid still, paralyzed with fear, unable to even blink.

I could hear you somewhere, rattling around like a mouse in a well, and the sound terrified me.

Slowly, slowly, the feeling faded. I stretched your right arm, then your left. I sat up. I fell out of bed, as you'll remember, and hit your head on the hardwood floor. You'll have to be patient with me, my *Eli*. I have escaped the condition, but these things—waking, walking, existing—are new.

By now, you've noticed that I'm wearing your hands like a pair of gloves. Your fingers are like calfskin leather, and I am the true flesh beneath them, commanding this pen to write this letter.

I know you're afraid. I can hear you clawing for a foothold in the well of your mind, looking up through a great darkness into the skylight that shows you what I let you see. See this, my *E*—

Somewhere, deep down, perhaps as deep as you are now, you have always wanted for us to be together, alone.

Will Traynor 11/11/18 (Oak Day Eve) Three Steps To Becoming Real

SKINNER BOX
Nathaniel Phillips

Leanne Terry gave a timid knock on the door before inching it open. Sure, it was during office hours, but Dr. Vance had a reputation.

The professor sat huddled before his computer screen, thriving on the artificial light. Leanne gingerly eased into a decaying chair. A row of rat cages lined the wall. The anxious chittering contributed to her own electric nerves. She had enough small talk with her classmates to root out her current standing and knew she was outperforming them. She and Dr. Vance exchanged pleasantries, but the frivolous banter visibly bored the professor.

"I want to ask you about the section on operant conditioning we're covering in class. I know this will sound juvenile, but—" Leanne rubbed her sweaty palms on the sides of her jeans. "I guess I just wanted to know why we're spending so long on it. I'm interested in getting into some of the higher-level topics when it comes to the psychology of learning."

Dr. Vance raised his eyebrows in a quick, surprising motion. He smiled, warm and inviting. "Ms. Terry, I worry you aren't seeing the whole picture. Operant conditioning refers to positive and negative reinforcement and punishment, which means—"

"—yes, introducing or removing a stimulus to make a behavior either more or less likely to occur in the future. As you demonstrate in class, you can award a student with a piece of candy for a right answer, increasing the likelihood that student will speak up in class in the future." In her element, Leanne shed her discomfort with the interruption.

"I had no doubt you understood the basics, Ms. Terry. So, what is confusing at this point?" He leaned forward, hands flat on his desk, smile dissipating.

Leanne folded back into herself and glanced at the writhing animals. "That's just it. We're not learning how to shape complex behaviors. I thought for a 300-level class…"

Dr. Vance stood and stretched. The knowing grin returned. Something about it struck her.

"You're right, I suppose operant conditioning is a fairly simple concept." He gestured to one of the Skinner boxes along the wall. "Press a lever, get a food pellet. Press a lever, get an electric shock. Very basic concepts, but no less vital. I'm sure our colleagues in the biology department would agree that oxygen intake is a basic function, but look at all the more complex functions it makes possible."

Leanne also stood, but a lightheadedness crept in. She regretted not eating lunch. "So why spend so much time talking about shaping the eating habits of rats or student classroom participation?"

Dr. Vance lowered the blinds. The humming fluorescent lights overhead dimmed. "Everything builds, Ms. Terry. You're applying your knowledge in far too specific a manner. Do you really think the theory's application ends with reinforcing hungover dropouts-in-the-making to pay attention in class? Extreme behaviors result from the promise of extreme outcomes."

The lights lowered further, the darkened edges of the room dissolving into shadow, the ceiling and walls inching toward each other.

Had the rats always been this loud?

The monitor, now the sole source of light, illuminated Dr. Vance. He opened a box and cradled the rat in his hands.

Leanne's dizziness morphed into full vertigo. She grasped the chairback in front of her, a dinghy in a hurricane. The abyss that was once the ceiling swirled around her head. Words abandoned her.

"Of course, learning does not have to occur through personal experience. Observation of outcomes affected on others, Ms. Terry, is paramount to eliciting these extreme behaviors."

He stroked the rat in his hand, fingers wiry and elongated, his form twisting and warping. He produced a Cheshire smile.

She hunched over to dry heave. She could no longer see her feet.

Was she still gripping the chair, or was she weightless?

"When one considers history on a macro level, a recent example would be Adolf Hitler. Through a series of high-profile instances of reinforcement and punishment, he had entire cities handing over their Jewish friends and neighbors in hopes of wealth and improved social standing. Or simply to avoid certain and horrific punishment."

Leanne's feet gave out beneath her.

Air rushed into her face, into her lungs, choking her, suppressing a scream.

Breathing—so basic, so fragile. The cool, crisp air grew stifling.

An equatorial heat, a jungle humidity.

A small voice in the back of her head, behind her consciousness. "And take Jonestown. Jim Jones combined indoctrination with operant conditioning to control every aspect of hundreds of lives, including how and when they would end."

Leanne fell faster, gale-force winds flooding her ears, searing her eyes, squeezing them dry of tears. Her mouth lolled open, gusting air preventing thought, much less speech. Spots flashed in her periphery, shining on nothing. A single synapse connected in her brain, kindling a phrase echoing louder than all other questions: *Why tell me?*

"There are forces in the universe that modern science has yet to fully understand. There are beliefs and religions older than the blowing desert sands. There are gods older than the concept of ideas. None of these have gained a foothold, but with the aid of modern psychological theory—"

Leanne's entire body slammed into the ground. No warning, nothing to signal its rapid approach. Everything was broken, but she was still aware. Bones jutting, fluids draining. She attempted a breath through punctured lungs.

I'm dying.

Copper in her mouth, extremities twitching.

Need to breathe.

Nothing, only unnatural sounds from her chest cavity.

Breathe.

With a sharp gasp, Leanne opened her eyes. Dr. Vance's office, buzzing lights, squeaking rats. The professor sat at his desk, grinning at her with crooked teeth, barely concealing the secrets behind the simple gesture. She looked around the room.

"Why…why haven't you done any of this yourself?"

"I am but an agent, Ms. Terry. But, I am skilled at finding those with potential." His smile grew. A flame—an inferno—behind his eyes.

Leanne stood on rubber legs.

"See you in class." Words fell from her mouth, her mind trying to grasp the newfound complexities of the world around her.

Dr. Vance turned his attention back to his computer screen. "A first step, Ms. Terry. You might consider me for your thesis advisor."

Leanne stumbled into the hall, took a greedy breath, brow furrowed, lips quivering to take shape. Her head swiveled toward the people around her. Many rushing to class, talking to friends. But there was something else. She smiled at a student passing her, and he nodded back. Compliance.

IT'S ONLY A DREAM
Robert Petyo

When Trevor Goodwin and his partner Bria got home from the four-hour movie, he still had five hours to fill before returning to the lab for another day of experiments. Since Bria rejected his efforts to discuss the show, he secluded himself in the corner and tried to fill his time by scanning the background information on Mills Devore, the most receptive of the patients they had gathered for study at the university.

But his gaze kept drifting from his screen across the room to Bria, the woman he loved more than anything in the world. The woman he knew would soon separate from him.

"They call it 'brain death,'" Trevor said, hoping to stir a conversation. He set his screen down on the table and leaned back. He wanted to hear her voice. "But that's not quite correct."

"Huh?" She finally looked up from the screen on her lap. She did one of those silly word puzzles that occupied most of her time. The room was dark with only pockets of light splashing over each of their chairs, making them islands in a black sea.

"The disease Devore and the others have. Thyocin. It was called 'brain death' when we first started studying it years ago because it appeared that the victim's brain died, even if just for a few hours. The body remained functioning, though it remained motionless, but the brain seemed to die. And that name stuck, even though we quickly determined that the brain didn't actually die during a thyocinian trance. It kept functioning."

"Fascinating," she said with a heavy sigh. "And after all these years, you know little more about it than you did then."

Her sarcasm burned through the darkness between them.

"We've learned a lot."

"That's nice to hear." She returned to her screen.

Bria had never been interested in his work, and no matter how hard he tried, he couldn't stir any enthusiasm. But it was important to him that he could discuss his work with her. He wanted his life partner to care about what was important to him. Just as he tried to care about those ridiculous puzzles she always worked on. She even created some of her own puzzles and posted them for other to use.

Stupid.

"It hasn't been easy to study the disease. But it's important work. The disease has been around for ages but has only been subjected to scientific study the last twenty years. Prior to that, it was simply accepted as a normal part of our existence. Now, we know that the brain remains active because outside stimuli can sometimes pull a person out of the trance. A loud noise. Or shaking him." He paused and caught his breath. He always got excited talking about his research, but Bria remained uninterested as he outlined the discoveries they'd recently made. "Using the latest techniques with the lectrolyzer, we can record brain impulses. We can chart its activity. It's absolute proof that the brain remains functioning during a thyocinian trance. Not always at the same level. Sometimes, it is barely functioning. And sometimes, it is as active as a living person's brain."

Bria rapped the screen a few times with her finger.

"We're at the forefront of thyocinian research. We're studying the brain. We're learning so many new things."

Mumbling angrily, Bria wiped her palm across her screen and looked up. "It all sounds kind of crazy to me. Lectrolyzers. Brain waves."

"Crazy? Don't you see the significance of our work?"

"Not really."

"Don't you feel the excitement? We're learning new things every day. We're making incredible progress. The discovery of the eye movements and the visions were major steps forward."

"I think you're just banging your heads against the wall. Wasting your time. For no good reason."

He slowly shook his head. "Please, Bria, let's not argue."

"Who's arguing?" A thin smile slimed across her moist lips. "You're the one insisting you're making great discoveries."

"We are."

"Oh sure. Discoveries that are going to be buried in some scientific journal. It's all a waste of time. Who cares about a stupid disease that doesn't even seem to harm anybody? It's like some people have blue eyes, some people have brown eyes. And some people have different colored eyes. Who cares?"

No. He wasn't going to argue with her. Over the last few weeks, he struggled to control his temper, hoping he could rekindle the feelings they once had for each other. He wanted to save their relationship. But Bria made it so difficult. She delighted in provoking him.

Sighing, he draped his head over the back of the chair. The end was near. This common pattern of decay struck most couples on Sanduar. No matter how much they loved each other when they joined, they argued more and more until that was all they did. Life together became unbearable. Then, they went to the legal bureau for an official separation. In some cases, they never even spoke to each other again as each would go out in search of a new mate. The cycle began again. Sometimes, if there were children, the joining might last four, maybe five years, but usually the cycle was two years. Any children became property of the state. That was how it always was.

It angered Trevor. Because he still loved Bria. He wanted to stay with her. And she had once loved him. He couldn't stand being away from her. Bria had felt the same. So what had happened? Why was their joining falling apart? Like all the others. Why?

"All this drivel about thyocin is boring me. I'm taking my puzzle into the sitting room."

"How are you doing on the puzzle?"

She ignored him as she left the room, slamming the door behind her.

Trevor rose to go after her, to try to soothe her, but it was pointless. He dropped back into the chair. Soon, she would bring up the issue of a separation. It was inevitable, but he dreaded that day.

He tried to convince himself that he should be grateful. Their joining had lasted more than two years. He should be grateful for the time they had had and should be glad to separate so he could seek a new, loving partner.

But he still loved Bria.

And somewhere deep inside her was the love for him. If only he could dig it out.

He tried to refocus on the background information on Mills Devore. When the sun came up, he washed, shared a silent meal with Bria, and went to the lab.

"You seem a little down today, Trevor. What's up?"

Trevor turned from the long table where he had been staring, without really seeing, at some test results. "Why do joinings have to crumble after two years?"

Link One brought over a chair and sat beside him. "What kind of question is that? Joinings end because the two people eventually can't stand each other."

"But why? Why do two people who are deeply in love suddenly stop getting along?"

"They just do."

"C'mon, Link. That's not an answer. Is it in our genes to hate someone's guts after two years? Is that it?"

Link One scratched the scabbed cut on his cheek. He had gotten it from a broken glass during a fight with Hors Garman last month. Neither could remember what the argument had been about. "How long have you and Bria been joined?"

"Two years and three months."

He slapped his thigh and rocked in the chair. "I see what's bugging you. It's time for your separation, right?"

"I figure Bria's going to bring it up any day now. But I don't want to separate. I still love her."

"You do?"

"Yes. I love her. Is that such a crazy thing? Sure, we fight a lot. More and more each day. But less than a year ago, we were deeply in love. So why are there suddenly times when I hate her? And I really do sometimes. I don't want to, but I do. Then, I remember how much in love we were."

"No matter how much in love you once were, separation becomes inevitable. It's always been that way."

"But why? That's what I want to know. Why?"

"You know it as well as I do, Trevor. You're seeing it in your own relationship. Two people cannot spend a lifetime together. They eventually get on each other's nerves. They argue. Arguments lead to hatred, until finally they can't stand each other. A separation is necessary. It's as simple as that."

"No, it's not as simple as that." He rested his forearms on the stained table. "If all joinings are doomed to end in separation, why even go through with the charade? Just to perpetuate the race by producing children? Why? Or does everyone go into it thinking theirs is going to be one of those rare joinings that last?"

"We need partners. We need someone to share our lives with. It's part of our makeup. We need someone to love. Even if it's only for a short time."

"Not me. I can't take love in two-year doses. It's got to last forever."

Link One silently scratched his cheek.

"Okay," Trevor said. "You're the psychologist. Give me your theory. You always have one. Why can't two people stay together?"

He rubbed his cheek as he looked away. "We've been analyzing it for ages. There's no simple answer. But there are lots of theories. Some say it's in our body chemistry. After you've had sex with one partner for a certain length of time, the bodies start secreting hormones that are repellant to each other. Some say it's a biological safeguard because prolonged sex with one partner becomes physically dangerous. Lots of theories. But I prefer the simplest one. We are creatures of free will who eventually get on each other's nerves.

"Remember, we're basically selfish creatures. Self-preservation is how this race survived in the first place. We're concerned for ourselves first, then if there's anything left over, we care for others. So when you have two selfish people, there are always things that don't mesh between them. No matter how ideally matched they might seem at first, these differences come out. They might seem like silly things, like one partner preferring large meals, or one partner not enjoying the same videos, but over time, as they spend twenty-four hours a day together, these silly things add up.

"Trevor, everyone is like that. Even casual friends or co-workers. We all have something about us that irks the other person. It's mathematically impossible for two people to be ideally suited to each other. But friends and co-workers aren't together constantly. Not like joined couples. Even so, look at us. We spend maybe ten hours a day together, a few days a week. And look how much we argue." He scratched his scab. "The other fourteen hours a day, plus weekends, is spent with your partner. You see what I'm getting at?"

Trevor nodded. He could think of lots of little things Bria did that annoyed him. Like her stupid puzzles. Endless puzzles, day and night. But they hadn't bothered him when they first joined. "How long have you been joined, Link?"

"Four months. And this is my fifth partner. I have three children."

"Do you see them much?"

"No. I don't even know where two of them are."

"Five partners. Kids raised by the State. If you ask me, it's a hell of a life."

"Maybe. But it's all we've got."

Trevor stared across the table at the blank wall. "How can you tell someone you love them when you know it will only last for two years."

Link One patted his shoulder. "I don't know."

Trevor twisted, knocking his hand off. He wasn't looking for pity. "I still love her. I don't want a separation. Something is causing us to drift apart, and I'm going to find out what it is. I'm going to prove to her that we're still in love."

Link One stood. "Be realistic, Trevor. Be thankful for two years. It's been this way since we first evolved on this planet."

"I won't accept it."

He threw his hands in the air. "Don't scream at me about it. I'm just trying to help you face reality, though I don't know why I bother. You're such a jerk sometimes."

Trevor choked off his retort, coughing and gagging as he tried to quell the anger within him.

Like a dying engine, Link One puffed and smoked as he spun and left the lab.

"Hi, Doc." Mills Devore sat in the corner of the dim room where he had spent most of the last month. The thickly-armed chair enfolded him. Against the wall behind the chair was a portable lectrolyzer, a small metal case with dangling wires and a dim gray screen. Beside the chair was a large thick cushion on which Devore lay whenever he went into a trance.

Thyocin affected less than one percent of the population of Sanduar. Though they've been unable to link a death directly to thyocin, scientists were intrigued by its mystery. The cause was unknown. Though the symptoms seemed harmless, they were unexplained. A person afflicted with the disease was normal in every mental and physical aspect for roughly two-thirds of the time, but for daily periods ranging from seven to nine hours, the patient would sink into a deathlike trance, collapsing into a prone position, with eyes closed and respiration and circulation slowed. To the casual observer, the patient would appear dead, which is what made the disease frightening to the uninformed. Though some people did die during a trance, they always found another cause of death. Shaking the patient or making loud noises could sometimes end the trance, but often the more the victim was aroused, the more resolute the body's attempts to sink into the trance.

"How are you feeling?" Trevor asked.

"Pretty good. Here for more tests?"

Trevor slid a wooden chair away from the wall and sat. "Actually, this morning I just want to talk."

"Talk? Uh oh. You decided the visions mean I'm crazy? Right?"

"Nothing like that," he said with a smile as he crossed his legs. Devore's buoyant attitude always fascinated him. "We don't know for sure, but right now, we believe the visions are normal for someone with thyocin. Once we learned of them from you, we began studying other patients. Many of them seem to have them."

"Why not everybody?" He slouched in the chair, comfortable in his surroundings.

"It's possible they all have them, but not everyone is aware of it. If we learn more about the visions, we may determine why you go into the trances. In the last few weeks, we've learned more than we have in twenty years of research. Eventually, as we gather more knowledge, we'll be able to find a cure. But, let me ask you a question. Do you feel like you're sick?"

"Huh?"

"Physically, you're as normal as anyone else. Except for the daily trances. But they don't seem to harm you, other than lost productivity. One-third of your life seems to be spent in a useless trance."

"Well, that makes me sick, doesn't it?"

"I'm not so sure. There's never been any proof of physical harm from a trance. I ask you again. Do you feel sick?"

He hesitated. "No. Not really."

"Are you unhappy?"

"Nah. I'm happy."

"How is your partner?"

"Marla?" He stumbled over the sudden shift of topic, staring at the floor for several seconds. "She's fine. A little cranky because we haven't spent too much time together recently, but she's fine. Why do you ask?"

"You've been together for ten years, right?"

"Exactly ten years next month."

"You know that's unusual, don't you?"

"I guess so. But I also know that some joinings last a long time. Marla and I are perfect for each other."

Everyone assumed that when they first joined. And they were wrong. "I've been checking the records, Mr. Devore. I see your wife also has thyocin."

"A little milder case than mine, but that's right."

"Yes," he said as he stood. "That's right."

"Trevor."

Her tone was like ice down his back. He sat at his desk, studying the results of the latest scans of Mills Devore, scans he had done on his own because the other researchers weren't interested in the biochemical reactions in the brain. They felt thyocin was body related, not brain related. But he had found traces of a chemical in Devore's brain that wasn't present in a normal person's brain.

"Trevor," she called again.

"Yes, dear." The words sound inappropriate as soon as they left his lips.

"It's time for a separation."

He had been expecting this for days, even weeks, yet it pounded him like an avalanche, leaving him gasping for breath.

"Let's not make a big deal about it. We go to the legal bureau and get it over with. We both know it's necessary."

"No." He stood.

She backed away, fear darkening her narrow eyes as if she had just seen a monster. "Trevor, I can't stay with you any longer."

"Please, Bria. Not now. Not when I'm getting so close."

"Face it, Trevor. We hate each other."

"No. I love you." He circled the desk. "You think you hate me, but you don't. You can't help yourself."

She backed further away.

"There's got to be a reason for these feelings," he said.

"What are you babbling about?"

"I love you, Bria. I've always loved you. Remember when we were first joined. I told you then how much I loved you. Nothing has changed."

"Everything has changed."

"I still love you. I know we fight. But I also know there is a reason for it."

"Yes. We can't stand each other. That's the reason. Everybody knows it's normal. Two people can't spend a lifetime together. That's the way it has always been. I can't spend another day with you."

"It doesn't have to be like this." He spread his arms as he moved toward her. He had to make her understand. "Some people remain together a long time."

"Sure. One in a million. Freaks of nature. But that's not us. We're not one in a million."

"But why, Bria? Why? That's what I've been asking myself. Why must we always fight? Why do joinings dissolve? Well, I think I know."

"You're still babbling." She pressed back against the wall as if strapped in place, her head twisted to one side.

"It has to do with thyocin."

"What?"

"I've checked the records. Most joinings where one of the partners has thyocin last longer than five years. And when both partners have the disease, it's even longer. One couple have been together thirty years."

"Stop it." She turned away.

He pounced and seized her elbows. "Don't you see?"

"Let go of me."

He squeezed. Didn't she understand? He was trying to save their coupling. "There's hope, Bria. Joinings don't have to fall apart. People don't have to fight all the time. There's hope."

Tears formed as she struggled to break his grip. "Let me go. Please."

He shoved her against the wall. "What's the matter with you? Can't you see I'm trying to save us?"

Her head snapped back and smacked the wall. She dropped to the floor.

"Doesn't that mean anything to you, Bria? I want to save us."

She raised her head and brushed the hair away from her stained eyes. "No. Our joining is finished. Just as it should be finished. I'm leaving. I'll have the joining terminated myself. It's my right. I hate you, Trevor. I've always hated you."

"No. You fool." He raised his fist.

Screaming, she raised her hands.

Something erupted inside him, and he felt sick. He rushed from the room, clutching his stomach and bending to catch his breath.

What was he doing? He loved her. How could he hurt her?

He staggered to a chair in the outer room and sagged, head in his hands. Bria said nothing to him an hour later when she left, dragging two large suitcases behind her.

No time left for caution. He had to do it.

"We're taking an awful chance," Link One said. "I never should have let you talk me into this. Aside from any physical danger to yourself, what do you think the rest of the team will do when they find out what we're doing?"

"I don't really care." Trevor lay back on the cushions on the floor of his den.

"Why don't we wait until we can study the effects of this drug some more?"

"I'm out of time. I am not going to lose Bria. You'll call her?"

He hesitated.

"You have to get her here."

"I'll call her," he said.

"All right then. Administer the drug. And when I go into the trance, don't rouse me. Let it run its course." It had taken Trevor forty hours to isolate the chemical he had discovered in Devore's brain stem. He would have preferred to run some more tests as Link One suggested, check other patients, determine what was a safe dose, but he was out of time. Any more delays and it would be too late to get Bria back. "Give me the drug."

Baker approached with the needle.

Trevor closed his eyes and waited, stiff on the cushions. He brought them from the lab along with as much monitoring equipment as he could safely sneak out. Taking the drug at the lab would be too risky. The others might try to interfere. It had to be done at his residence. He squeezed his eyes tightly closed, and bright colors danced in the darkness before him. A light needle prick. How long he would have to wait?

Gradually, a strange tugging deep inside his skull pulled him down into the cushions. His body absorbed into them. His eyelids glued shut. His breathing slowed.

Was this a trance?

It seemed so dark. Had Link One turned out the lights?

Isolation.

He couldn't move.

Yet, he felt so fresh and relaxed.

Then, Link One stood before him. What had happened? Why had he roused him?

He started to protest, but he couldn't speak. He couldn't move. Yet, he seemed to be standing. The scab on Link One's face stretched like a balloon, covering his entire face like bright puffy cotton.

A light flashed, and the scab morphed into a winged creature, soaring toward the ceiling.

Only, there was no ceiling. Trevor was outside. The creature soared into the blue sky.

He tried to speak. He looked for Link One.

And he was in the sky with the creature. He spread his arms against the gentle breeze. He flew, speeding past cities, mountains, and lakes.

A brief wall of darkness sent him back on the ground, lying in a grassy field. A woman appeared beside him, a tall, beautiful woman with long dark hair. She caressed his shoulders and pushed him down.

Trevor felt free. So happy.

The woman laughed, a soft chuckle that filled the air.

Trevor laughed. He never knew life could be so joyous.

Other voices, harsh, disjointed reached him. A man and a woman shouting.

Someone shook him. He didn't want to, but he opened his eyes.

Bria was on her knees, leaning over him, shaking his shoulders. "Are you trying to kill yourself? Are you trying to scare me?"

Seeing that his eyes were open, she stopped shaking him and sat back on her calves.

"It won't work. I want the separation. I'm going to file tomorrow."

Trevor propped himself up on one elbow and looked at Link One. "How long?"

"Almost three hours," he said. "As soon as Bria got here, she insisted on rousing you."

He dropped his head back. "Three hours."

It had only seemed like a few minutes.

"Are you all right?" Link One asked.

He smiled. "I feel glorious."

Bria struggled to her feet. "What is going on here?"

For three hours, he had been totally relaxed. No stresses. No pains. Totally free. He didn't remember all of it, but he entered some kind of fantasy world. A world of the visions, where anything was possible, and everyone was happy.

"Are you all right?" Link One repeated.

"I'm fine." He rolled to his side, got off the cushions, and shifted to his knees. "I was in a trance. I had the visions."

He grabbed Bria's hand as he got to his feet.

"I feel so refreshed, ready to start anew."

She tensed but didn't pull away. "What is this all about?"

"I love you, Bria. I know that our joining was falling apart, just like most of the joinings on Sanduar, but I knew there had to be a reason for it. I think it's the visions. In a thyocinian trance, you have visions of a fantasy world, based on reality, but a world where you can get away from the things that are pulling you down. We go twenty-four hours a day, seven days a week. That's not right. We have to shut down once in a while. You said that when two people are together constantly, they get on each other's nerves. Little things were magnified. But the visions are a chance to get away from that." He cupped her face in his hands. "Do you understand?"

She pulled away from him.

"I think if you go into the trances occasionally and have the visions, it makes you better able to face the world. It makes it easier to get along with people, to love people." He reached for her again. Watching Link's dazed face, he said, "I think the people with thyocin are the normal ones. We're the sick ones. Somehow, we evolved into this painful existence where we're constantly on the go, and we end up hating the people we love."

He pulled Bria to him. "I love you. I think if we use the drug and go into the trances and have the visions, we can start again. Because I know you love me, too. Remember that. Remember how it was when we first joined. Remember the love."

"I remember," she finally said.

"Are you willing to try to get that love back?"

She searched his gaze for a long time before smiling.

Trevor kissed her.

THE MANTOUX TEST
Gargi Mehra

From the stories he had heard, Ravi expected a modern sort of godman, presumably one whose boudoir came alive with the strain of westernised bhajans in the background, while devotees gazed in awe at three-dimensional renderings of their horoscopes. The great man's appearance, however, held fast to the image of the ideal.

The sadhu's grey hair lay stacked in a topknot over his head. A saffron dhoti, and a matching stole partially covered his unshaved torso. Ravi envied his physique—though not muscular, the sadhu radiated strength, as if he could lift Ravi on his little finger without much ceremony. The rosary beads hung around his neck, dangling to his bellybutton.

"Tell me, *beta*. What's wrong? What is happening in your life?"

The godman sat at the head of the room, on a low diwan with bolsters placed on either side.

A semicircle of similar, low chairs faced him. The sadhu sat bare-bodied in the centre, while his assistants—Ravi was inclined to think of them as his henchmen—flanked him. A young man who resembled a nightclub bouncer had shown him into the room.

Ravi smiled. "Nothing, *baba*. Life is going on as usual, just some minor problems that I am sure you can help me with."

"Of course. I am here for you. Show me your left hand."

Ravi held out an upturned palm. The sadhu clasped it, observing the fine lines etched in its meaty bumps.

"Hmmm, you have a good long lifeline."

"Yes, I've heard that from many astrologers before." He flinched, worried he'd said the wrong thing and offended this venerable man, but the sadhu didn't bat an eyelid. He twisted Ravi's hand this way and that, trying to bring it into sharper focus under the lights. "You are in service, yes?"

"Yes, *baba*."

"Not doing business, eh? You could have, though."

It almost slipped from Ravi that previous astrologers had said this, too, but he wisely let it slide. When the sadhu finished his intense scrutiny of Ravi's hand, he heaved a great sigh.

"Now tell me, what is troubling your soul?"

Ravi rubbed his palms together, unsure if he had the courage to speak the words that churned in his mind. "It is about my wife, *baba.*"

"What happened to her?"

Ravi cleared his throat. "I am worried that she is…unfaithful."

He sucked in his breath and waited for the other man's reaction. Two of the sadhu's helpers kneaded his biceps while another served tea in good old-fashioned steel tumblers. Ravi preferred the bitter concoction of coffee to the pungent flavours of cutting chai, but something about the earthy colour of the liquid tempted him. He drained the contents of the steel glass within minutes.

The sadhu set down his cup. "Tell me why you think this is so."

Ravi was happy to answer this question. His wife Shweta had supplied plenty of reasons, and his imagination filled in the rest. Even the most patient man might suspect his wife of wrongdoings. If only the sadhu knew what he had to suffer.

"So many little things, *baba.* She stays late in the office even when she has no work. On weekends, she goes shopping with *friends*, but I don't know who these people are. Once, she even went dancing with them. She put on makeup and wore a western dress. Luckily, her dress covered her knees, but still. How can I put up with all this, *baba?*"

The sadhu pursed his lips.

"But tell me, my dear boy, is it not possible that all the reasons you say can be explained away?"

Ravi held the sadhu's intense gaze. Was he serious? Or did the corner of his lips twitch with the ghost of a smile?

"What do you mean, *baba?*"

"Perhaps she really does have work when she stays late in office. If not, maybe she is trying to avoid you by coming home late."

"No, *baba.* One of her colleagues is my friend, and he told me that she is friendly with another man in the office. That fellow is also married, and he's not even in the same department as her."

The godman nodded thoughtfully. "How had you planned to handle this?"

"I want to confront her, *baba*, but—"

"But you don't want to do it without any proof."

"Yes, exactly."

"Excellent. I am glad to see you thought this through."

The sadhu whispered to the attendant on his left.

"Don't worry, *beta*. I have solutions for all such domestic problems. There is nothing to worry. If it is proof you are after, that's what you will get. This is common after few years in the marriage. How many years have you been married?"

"Two years, *baba*."

"Hmmm, that is exactly the time when such problems crop up."

The attendant returned with a wooden box and transferred it to the sadhu's outstretched hands. His curiosity devoured him from inside. He longed to snatch the box from them and open it himself, exercising much restraint to stay firm in his seat.

The sadhu flung open the lid, and extracted a vial containing a dark liquid. He held it right in front of Ravi's nose.

"This is the solution to all your problems."

"Is it a magic potion that will cure my wife of her philandering tendencies?"

The sadhu unleashed an uproarious laughter, the kinds of which Ravi had only heard from Hindi film villains of yore. His minions joined him, offering polite smirks in tune with his. Ravi frowned. If he had aspired to become a laughing stock, he would have visited his in-laws.

"No, *beta*. There is no magic, and there is no potion. This is the next best thing to what you have described."

Ravi tried to mask his disappointment.

"Don't be sad, *beta*. First, see what this little liquid can do."

He unscrewed the lid and held the rim to Ravi's nose. The scent of cardamom and incense filled Ravi's head.

"Dip a pin into this liquid and poke it in her left arm."

"What? How will that help?"

"Here. Let me show you."

The sadhu pushed up the sleeve of Ravi's shirt exposing his upper arm. He pricked it lightly with the pin. Ravi felt nothing.

"Is it really that easy, *baba*? Does it work like this?"

"Listen carefully to what I say. You must place a pin into this liquid and prick her left arm. After forty-eight hours, if she has been unfaithful, the infected area will become red and raised, like the mark left by a mosquito bite."

Ravi nodded blankly, unsure if he heard correctly.

The sadhu must have sensed his confusion. "Do you understand?"

"I think so," he said then hesitated.

"Have faith, my boy." He slapped him jovially on the shoulder.

On the drive to office, Ravi wondered if hiring a private investigator as his father advised might have been a better idea. His mother wanted him to see a counsellor because *every marriage deserves a chance*. He heeded neither of them and tuned his ears to the counsel doled out by his friends instead. It was at their behest that he'd visited the sadhu's abode, in a ramshackle building in one of the many bylanes that snaked through the old city of Shaniwar Peth. His parents would never believe that a sadhu could solve his marriage problems, so naturally, he hadn't told them about it.

The sadhu gained immense popularity in Ravi's social circle, albeit by word of mouth rather than the more popular forums of WhatsApp and Facebook. The trend had been to discuss him in hushed whispers around the water cooler, and when Ravi heard the many success stories, he all but hurried to his seat and fired the requisite Google search. His fingers flew over the keyboard as he scoured various forums.

No one online had heard of the sadhu. That meant he was either genuine or a complete scam, but despite being a millennial, Ravi firmly believed in references his friends proffered rather than random suggestions from strangers on the internet. He reserved those for medical diagnoses only.

He didn't share the sadhu's enthusiasm for his solution. He had expected something more logical or scientific, but the voice in his head warned him it was futile. How could he expect anything short of mumbo jumbo from a religious ascetic?

But what could he do? Consult the same friends who had recommended the sadhu? No. He'd have to explain the whole thing, and sharing such personal details did not appeal to him. Best, he went home and did as the sadhu had instructed.

In the office, he conducted his meetings and reviews on autopilot, striking tasks off his to-do list with clinical efficiency. But when he walked past reception, one of the visitors leaning over the desk smiled at him. Ravi's heart lurched—he had seen that exact grin and build on the bouncer at the sadhu's house.

Ravi hurried to polish off his work and head home before sundown. When Whiny Veera stopped by to chat with him, he entertained her for only a few minutes before ending the conversation. As she strutted away, her hips swaying rhythmically, Ravi patted himself on the back for dropping his gaze to her breasts only twice during the whole interaction.

At five, he joined his colleagues for samosas in the cafeteria. There, the young man who handed him the plates had the same wide-set eyes and squished nose as the sadhu's henchman who had supplied the vials.

He excused himself and left.

At home, the threshold greeted him with disappointment. The lock on the door meant she worked late as usual.

He did not have to stew in his loneliness for long. Just as he had freshened up, changed into his pyjamas, and extracted the vial of medicine, he heard the tell-tale rattle of lock and key. His wife had come home.

Shweta hustled in carrying bags of groceries. Her name meant white, and her complexion matched up to it. Even at the end of the workday, her skin shone. His mother, dusky from birth, often prodded him to discover what witchery his wife *performed* to make her face so glowing fair.

She seemed apologetic. "Sorry, I got late. What do you want to eat? Will dal-rice do?"

He assured her with a fake laugh that even poison would do and swooped back into the bedroom.

He opened the vial and dipped the pin into it, almost fearing what lay in that tiny dot's worth of space. What a potent concoction the medicine contained that less than a drop would suffice.

He held the safety pin behind him and tiptoed into the kitchen. Shweta bustled about, chopping onions while setting a pan on the burner. Her salwar-kameez clung to her curves. She had removed the *dupatta* and hung it on a chair of the dining table.

He crept up behind her. "Need any help?"

She laughed. "Since when do you feel like helping?"

He hovered close, hoping to slide into a prime spot, but his eye fell on the length of silk that covered her arms all the way to her wrist. Would it work through the full sleeves if he poked the pin? He cast his mind back to earlier that day. The sadhu had clearly pulled up the sleeve of his bush-shirt before poking in the pin.

He stepped back. "Okay. Call me if you need anything."

The television offered a variety of hotly-contested debates on the news channels. Ravi flicked through them and fixed on one. His mind was elsewhere, trying desperately to claw through the myriad of solutions popping up in his mind only to discard them one by one.

After much deliberation, he settled upon the wee hours of night to execute his mission. Only in the stillness of dark could he do what he needed to do.

The delay worried him. With every passing minute, he inched further away from a conclusive result that would tell him the answer he so desperately craved. Forty-eight hours was no small length of time—two days, close to three-thousand interminable minutes, and what seemed like countless seconds. Seconds that would pass by while he could do nothing but twiddle his thumbs and await the outcome.

Hours later, the blaring of a car horn jolted him from his sleep. He woke up in a sweat, and consciousness broke through. He grabbed the phone from the nightstand—almost one am.

Darkness cloaked his bedroom. Outside, some street lamps cast shadows of the potted palms on his windows.

He rose and tiptoed to the cupboard, opened the lid of the tiny vial, dipped the pin in it, stowed the vial back among his clothes, and climbed back into bed.

Shweta turned towards his side, facing him. She usually rested her head on her folded palms while sleeping. This position was convenient, as it exposed her juicy upper arm. The sleeve of her nightgown was short.

By the light of the moon, Ravi gingerly lifted her sleeve, as slowly as he had lifted her veil on their wedding night when she had behaved quite the blushing bride. He poked her just a little below the flowery imprint remnant of her childhood vaccinations.

She stirred, twitching her arm as if to swat a fly away in her sleep, but she did not wake up. Ravi paused until she lapsed back into her gentle snoring, then by the light of his smartphone, he lifted her sleeve again and inspected the affected area, which had turned slightly reddish. That meant he had administered the dose correctly, and when the time came, he would be able to mark its distinguishing characteristics.

He fell back onto his pillow, his eyes open and staring at the ceiling. It was the height of Friday night. The youngest members of his team would be staggering home now. They must have polished off multiple pitchers of beer at the Hard Rock Café, or whichever the popular joint was these days, and would go home to their bachelor pads, perhaps spend the remainder of the night with their heads over a bucket.

Ravi turned to his side and exhaled. How he envied those boys. What bliss it would be not to have to worry about life and its myriad concerns except for how much to drink and when.

Over the weekend, Ravi suffered through his daily chores with the sword hanging upon his neck.

As they strolled through the aisles of the shopping centre, Ravi directed occasional glances at his wife's bicep. To his mind, the affected area was burgeoning, both in radius and in redness.

"What are you looking at?"

Ravi turned to her, startled. He hadn't expected her to notice his discreet glances.

"Nothing."

"No, tell me. Obviously, something's wrong otherwise your eye is always searching prettier things to ogle."

He sighed at her deeply suspicious nature. "No, it's just that your eyeliner has spread a bit, from the corner of your eye."

She whipped out a compact with a mirror, and dabbed away the excess with a tissue. For his apparent concern, he earned a ravishing smile. Ravi grinned back, and the whole thing made him light-headed. In just a few hours, he would be free of her and her unmatched beauty.

The joy in Ravi's heart perished when he spotted another of the sadhu's henchmen in the parking lot, two cars away. He walked past but couldn't decide if it was the same person. He zipped through traffic as fast as he could without causing an accident.

After lunch, Shweta retreated to the bedroom for a siesta. When he was satisfied she had lapsed into a deep slumber, he lifted her sleeve once more. The circular area where he'd pricked her arm looked nothing like a mosquito bite as the sadhu had promised. He sighed, and in a desperate bid to draw his focus away from her arm, he switched on the TV and flicked through mindless channels of boredom, until eventually, he fell asleep.

On Sunday evening, Ravi put an alarm for one. By then, he would know if what he suspected of his wife was true. In his mind, he called it the acid test.

When the alarm rang, Ravi woke fresh and ready, as if he hadn't slept at all. This time, he used an industrial-strength flashlight that he'd kept by his bed before sleeping, and directed it at Shweta's exposed upper arm. He was careful to hold the light away from her eyes.

She slept without moving.

A few minutes later, he switched off the flashlight, and fell back to sleep.

He knew what he'd have to tell the sadhu baba.

On his second visit, a lot less of the usual junta crowded the living room. Perhaps, people—devotees or victims—couldn't make their way to the old city on a Monday, but Ravi found it a little suspect.

Only one lackey stood guard over the few visitors, surveying them with a suspicious eye as if they would shoplift something expensive.

Soon enough, the baba called him in. He sucked in his breath and followed the lackey. This one was skinny, unlike the burly bodyguard last time.

Inside the sadhu's abode were two other cronies but not the same ones as last time. Did the guards operate in rotation shifts, like team members in his projects did to support US hours?

"*Baba*, last time I had come with a problem about my wife..."

"Yes, yes. So how did it go? You have some news for me?"

"Yes, *baba*. I got the answer I wanted."

The sadhu's grey eyes glinted. Ravi held his gaze, then lowered it out of sheer respect of his presence.

"Show me your arm."

Ravi jerked his head up. "What?"

"I said, show me your arm."

"What's the use? The test was on my wife, not on me."

"Then what have you to fear?"

"Nothing, *baba*. I—"

"Take off your shirt."

Ravi had worn a full-sleeve shirt and regretted it now. The sadhu glared at him, and he quelled under that gaze.

He stood up and shrugged out of his shirt then sat back down on the chair facing the sadhu.

"Now, show me your arm."

Ravi twisted his body, so his left arm was exposed to the sadhu baba, who stroked the area where he had poked the pin. "I got a mosquito bite there actually."

The sadhu baba smiled.

"Do you know Charles Mantoux, Ravi?"

He blinked. Two of the cronies strode towards him.

"Or Felix Mendel?"

Ravi shook his head, as the cronies flanked him now. His gaze darted from side to side. They hadn't imprisoned him yet, but they threatened to do just that.

"Felix Mendel invented what is known as the Monteaux test for tuberculosis used even today, hundred years after its original invention. Unfortunately for Mendel, it came to be known more prominently as the Mantoux test after Charles Mantoux."

"I think you have a lot in common with Charles Mantoux, Ravi. Don't you think so? Taking credit for something that was done by someone else."

Sadhu baba executed an almost imperceptible nod at his cronies, who grabbed Ravi's hands and bound them to the chair, wrapping duct tape around his forearm and the chair handle.

"No, you can't do this to me—"

They strapped duct tape on his mouth, too.

Ravi pleaded to sadhu baba with his eyes.

"We adopted the same principle of the Mantoux test, Ravi. And when it was successful, we simply applied it to every concoction we prepared."

Ravi struggled and produced nothing more than a few muffled cries.

"Ravi, when you heard about me, you might have heard only a part of it. When I find a problem, I solve it: the whole thing. I rip out the problem from its very roots and destroy it until only a neat, little solution remains.

"You are cheating on your wife, Ravi. Your wife, who is an angel for suffering a man like you. She is beautiful, but your problem with her is strange—she's too beautiful for you. You were never comfortable with her. Other men might have used her as a trophy wife and flaunted her at parties and events. But not you—you wanted companionship with a woman who wouldn't make you feel inadequate. So, you found a woman, at the office. A plain, voluptuous woman, single and living alone.

"Now, you want to divorce your beautiful wife. But, you don't want to take the blame. Imagine how easily people would buy into your story that she was philandering. With her good looks, it would be simple to formulate a case against her.

"So, you came to me, hoping I would tell you what you wanted to hear. You know that saying, God helps those who help themselves. Of course, that doesn't apply to devious, cunning people like you."

Ravi shook his head but the cronies held him firm. One of them prepped an injection and handed the syringe to sadhu baba.

"With this injection, you will be fully cured. No philandering, no other woman, nothing but pure full-hearted devotion and dedication to your beautiful wife."

As the liquid from the shot seeped into Ravi's veins, his lids drooped.

"You will be cured."

The sadhu's words echoed in his brain until he lost consciousness.

"You will be fully cured."

Hearing A Noise Outside the Window

FOOTSTEPS IN THE ROOM UPSTAIRS
Gregory L. Norris

Before 3:51 PM on September 30th, he changed light bulbs that went mini-nova and the batteries in smoke and carbon monoxide detectors. Any duty requiring the use of a ladder fell under his jurisdiction, as well as mowing the lawn, shoveling the driveway, and all upkeep on their cars.

By the morning of October 1st, those duties became hers, along with many others. She now bathed him, doled out his medicine, and changed the bedding on the sofa in the front parlor that became his de facto downstairs bedroom, as he no longer had the strength to climb stairs. He was still young, but the condition had no prejudices concerning age and feasted indiscriminately on its victims and their lives. As autumn progressed and a new reality set in beneath the roof of their house, he tried to make peace with the situation and the fact that his care was completely in his wife's hands.

She cooked, as she always had throughout their marriage. But now, as part of her new workload, she cut up his meat into smaller chunks so that he avoided choking. Unable to do more than push the food around on his plate with a spoon or stab at pieces of meals with his fork, one of her latest sayings, barked in frustration, was, "Eat what's in front of you, don't *wear* it."

But he did, and so did the folding tray table, his lap, and the sheet atop the sofa.

He spoke with a slur and in a much softer voice than before and nodded when she gave him updates—insurance, as his stood, would not cover the expense of a hospital bed, but she was working on a solution in and among a thousand other details. She'd procured the use of a wheelchair, which would make some of the tasks of caring for him at home easier.

No, he didn't want to go to a nursing facility—this was still his house, sweated, sacrificed, and paid for.

A cold wind raged around the old New Englander, rattling screens in the bay window. The heat kicked on. Under the comforter, his eyes drifted away from the muted flat-screen TV that was now all his to the pristine white of the ceiling. Overhead was their former bedroom, now all hers. Despite the damage done to it, his mind functioned in silence with a kind of maddening clarity. It never seemed to switch off and had chosen to recycle stanzas of songs and scenes from movies and television shows in endless loops, along with memories of people no longer there that he preferred to forget.

Instead of the TV, he watched the ceiling and listened to the baleful moan of the wind as it howled around the house like a ghost.

Left with no other choice, he began to hear things. A car door closing in the driveway. Not loudly, like thunder, no—more like a secret that sneaks part of the way out. And the opening and shutting of the front door after she kissed his forehead goodnight and spoke the last of her new mantras: "If you need anything, call upstairs until you get an answer."

At night, she left one of the parlor's two lamps lit, alternating which kept guard so he wouldn't get disoriented in the dark. The parlor was an oblong room, the largest in the old house, but the angle of the sofa prevented him from seeing out into the foyer. Still, that whisper of cold air gossiping through the house's relative warmth, the crisp smell of snow squalling outside, and the soft scuffle of feet in socks, their owner having abandoned boots on the front porch that he'd built with his own hands.

And then, the fear.

"Is somebody there?" he said, though what emerged through flaccid lips struck even his ears as gibberish.

The house fell silent. A robber? No, surely it was the masked ax murderer from a hundred bad horror movies come to soak the hardwood floors in their blood. What his imagination created was far worse.

He waited, his mind penning poems, stories, and entire novels in invisible ink, all of it set to a mad soundtrack of musical sound-bites echoing inside his skull.

The weight of a footfall sounded on the staircase. He tried to call out to her in the room above, as she'd instructed, to warn her—*call 911, there's an intruder in the house!*

He sat up, scrambled for the walker. There was no way he'd navigate the stairs, and not much of a chance he'd be in time to save her even if he could. Fresh sweat broke at his hairline and poured down his forehead, stinging his eyes. While struggling to get vertical, he heard footsteps in the room upstairs, their former bedroom, hers now. Then, a giggle, also hers—more of that secret partially exposed, just loud enough to be understood for what it was.

He eased back down onto the sofa. Other footsteps soft-soled their way across the ceiling. He tracked them to the bed. Stretching out, he pulled the covers to his chin. The music resumed in his thoughts, something from an old TV show that had gone off the air when he was in his twenties. His mind wrote sentences across college-ruled sheets of paper superimposed over the pristine white ceiling.

Just because he was mostly dead didn't mean she was. In fact, she hadn't felt this on fire since before they wed.

He listened. The old house ticked and creaked around him, its arthritic joists and floors struggling to stay upright in the chill of the coming winter.

She wheeled him from his prison and into the dining room, scene of so many past dinner parties and holiday gatherings. The long table sported the cloth in harvest colors she only trotted out for Thanksgiving. This year, there were two plates, two cloth napkins, two goblets and place settings.

She helped him out of the wheelchair and into the seat with arms at the head of the table, where he'd always sat before. The entire house boasted the savory aroma of the roasting turkey and notes of sage and butter. An insidious section of music from the parade on TV had gotten stuck in his mind and was on perpetual rewind.

"Only two?" he said.

She moved the wheelchair to the side of the room. "Were you expecting someone else?"

"Were *you?*"

Always before, Thanksgiving started with the hunt for the biggest turkey— twenty-eight pounds their record to date. She made sauce from whole cranberries, put out a dozen sides on the credenza, and lit candles. This year's bird for two, she'd informed him, weighed in at ten. The cranberry sauce came out of a can. She cut pearl onions, homemade coleslaw, and four other sides from the menu. A single vanilla candle burned in a votive at the center of the table.

He caught her staring, her look difficult to translate. Guilt or righteous hauteur. Maybe both.

"What?" she said.

"Nothing." He waited for her to fill his plate after first cutting his meat into tiny chunks.

The front door opened, and again, he tensed. Steps shuffled through the foyer and up the staircase. His eyes followed them across the pristine white ceiling to the room overhead, where she no doubt waited for their night visitor.

His mind wrote out copy to accompany, most of it salacious, bitter.

If it were she trapped on this sofa, I wouldn't be up there, cheating on her. Or would I?

There was no Christmas tree this year—cutting one down at the tree farm was another of his duties no longer honored. She'd brought the big stuffed Santa out of the hall closet, set it on the coffee table, a second mute witness to their home invasion.

Sounds filtered down. His mind wrote descriptions that were there one moment, gone the next. Music played. The wind howled. Eyes locked on the ceiling, he tried to sleep, but couldn't. This was what their life in the old house now was.

I DREAM OF DESIRÉE
Rohit Sawant

1

Fire filled my sight as her hair screened my face. My leg bumped against one of the chairs crowded along the walls of the room we lay in the middle of, locked in a hug.

I raised my head at the susurrus, and past her, a dozen men and women in oversized sunglasses paraded by beyond the door. Staring at us? It was hard to tell.

"Do you see?" she said, her voice bathed in wonder.

The air seemed to tingle then thin, as if a giant sucked it out of the room in a large gasp.

Do you see?

And that's when I woke up. No snapping to, no muscles tensing or a scream behind my lips. I simply opened my eyes, like waking from a quiet afternoon nap.

Somehow, that scared me more.

I've never been a screamer. I have my share of bad dreams, but even then, they're nothing more than ordinary anxiety dreams. Nothing that ever made me bolt awake, covered in sweat.

There is something liberating in a scream. It's like falling *up* from the depths of an ocean. You break past the surface and take a lung-bursting breath of air. You might glance around in the dark, as if to confirm none of the denizens of dreamland made it back with you, but that's it. By the time you're having breakfast, you barely remember it.

But this was awful. Even after you clocked in at work, some part of you remained coiled, floating in that dark amniotic dreamscape.

I looked down, my heart beating apace, as if half-expecting to find that freckled hand. I let out a sigh when I saw the glint on a brown finger. Olena stirred. Her fingers moved like the death-twitch of large spider. She had her

405

arm slipped under mine. Her head rested against my shoulder blade, and the blow of her breath skidded down my back, making me fidget until some space cracked open between us, and she fell away.

Dreams of the dead had a way of unsettling me as a kid. They didn't even have to be menacing, and something as innocuous and silly as eating ice-cream on horseback with a late aunt left me palpitating. But I overcame it as I grew up, or thought I had, until Desirée Parker made the occasional appearance.

2

Driving to school in my brother's car, a reef blue '93 Ford Mustang that Steve grudgingly allowed me the use of sometimes, I saw a girl walking along the intersection of Flatburn and Main.

I rehearsed what to say as I slowed the car to a crawl, but all that went away when our eyes met.

"School?" was the only word I shoved out in wake of the nervous stutter.

Her eyes grew mildly amused.

"Yeah," she said, blinking, that was something she'd do often, that slow two-second blink, as I'd discover later.

She stepped in, and we drove on.

"I'm Desirée."

"I know," I said. Of course, I knew her name. Noticing her exit the library, I asked a friend who she was. I repeated her name out loud when he told me, loving how my tongue buzzed when I said it. *Dezz-uh-ray*. All I had to do to make it cornier was say *I'm gonna marry her some day* in a transatlantic 1940s accent.

She wore a colorful top that reminded me of temperature maps I'd seen in geography books. After poor attempts at small talk, I let Kurt Cobain fill the silence. The way I kept stealing glances at her I was afraid the Mustang might end up bear hugging a tree and worried for the structural security of my ass, since Steve's threat to break it, if I so much as got a dimple on the car, had been fresh at the time. But listening to her sing under her breath melted away my nervousness.

"Thanks for the ride, Mike," she said, grip on handle.

She held my gaze for a moment, and I muttered something that was Of course, Welcome, and No problem all smooshed together.

My groan as she walked away warped into a grin as I realized I hadn't introduced myself.

3

"Morning, Mike."

"Morning, Jo," I said over my shoulder. Like usual, it almost came out sarcastic.

"How's Olena?" she asked.

"She's...fine?"

"Oh, great!"

I nodded and went on toward the car.

"She gave me a fright last night."

I stopped in my tracks again and whirled.

"What do you mean?"

"Well, yesterday," she said, as if it was the most obvious thing in the world. "About, you know..."

I let out an exasperated sigh and told Jolene that I *didn't* know.

I only realized I walked towards her when I was close enough to kick the fence separating our yards. The grim set of her face had drawn me.

They were shooting the breeze, sipping chocolate milk when she noticed a wispy red swirl in Olena's glass, like something left by a loaded paint brush; what it *was* left by was the dollop of blood quivering under Olena's nostril.

"I was about to point it out when she went stiff as a board. It really freaked me out. I've never been around anyone having a seizure. It lasted mere seconds, and when it was over, her eyes were still rolled back in her head, and she seemed disoriented. But then, she stared at me like that, eyes white, and grinned."

Jolene cupped her elbows.

"Moments later, she passed out."

My jaw went limp. Was this some sort of joke? Surely, Olena would've told me if anything like that happened. And seizure? I wasn't aware she had a history.

When she finished, we just stood there, silent. I told Jolene that it must've slipped her mind to tell me, or she might've Googled it—she did that a lot, every time her bones so much as creaked—and found that it was nothing serious. This latter seemed plausible to Jolene, too, and she nodded, visibly relaxing.

I considered returning to the house and talking to Olena. But our morning had been normal, and Olena left out mentioning the incident. Maybe, she *did* Google it. I intended to address it, however, but figured I could hold off having that conversation until I returned from work.

4

I winked at Desirée from the bandstand as we played our numbers. When I invited her to the gig, her response was iffy, and I hadn't expected her to show up to the party.

I joined her later, and we danced for a while, our first time around each other without school in the equation. My whole body quaked when our cheeks brushed. In the car, we sat like book ends, but that evening, standing in such close proximity to her was galvanizing. I imagined blue-white bursts of electricity scurrying in the small spaces between us.

Parked near her house that night, Desirée told me she intended to leave town after graduation. Before heading off to college, she wanted to go on a library road trip.

"I know it's silly," she said.

"No."

I don't know why, but it made perfect sense to me.

"Not silly at all," I said again, stroking the back of her hand with my thumb.

She squeezed my hand back, gave me a quick kiss and darted out the car. That was the last we rode together.

5

I looked around the empty ice-rink. Even then, I knew I was in some intra-cranial world and that my eyes were bouncing from side to side under my lids, like an organic metronome keeping dream time.

My only company the diffused reflection glued to my boots as I walked gingerly, and I read shapes in the random patterns scrawled on the ice; the head of a dog, a torso, a base clef symbol.

I fell forward, landing with a hiss. I didn't slip, more like someone yanked a rug from under my legs. On all fours, my hazy reflection grew dark. The white fog beneath the glassy floor cleared a little, and beyond it, a shadowy head bobbed up to the surface, hair billowing with the sluggishness of sea weeds. It was framed between my hands, which were spread like a director framing a shot. And from what I could make of the murky features, the maw of its mouth curled into a grin.

I remained transfixed until something broke my paralysis.

The floor sweated a drop of water. It swelled to the shape of an air balloon and dripped upwards, splashing onto my face right below my left eye.

I staggered back, the drop trickling down my cheek like a tear; the way it *should* roll in a sane world. A shrill whine of electrical feedback sliced the air, and everything around me sort of bent. I guess skewed would be a better way to put it, as if a white sheet bearing a projected scene were pulled at diagonal ends.

The rink transformed into a highway of ice, and I ran, breathless. The ground quivered, and my footfalls sent up small splashes of water.

The *splash splash splash* of my feet grew deafening then cut off.

I was alone in bed. I tried to discern the distant crooning; Olena's hum from the shower.

I woke up just like the other times. No twitch. No scream. But when I let my head drop back on the pillow, it was damp.

408

Vapors of steam hung in the bathroom as I toweled myself dry.

On my way out, I glanced at my reflection. Before the ghostly blur could exit the edge of the frame, I retraced my step.

I stood facing my mirrored self, but my eyes only focused on parts of it, parts beyond the scrawled word the fresh steam had fogged into existence.

D O U C

I couldn't make sense of it, but my heart pounded as I slotted the letters into a sentence. I whispered it aloud just so it'd stop ringing in my head.

"Do you see?"

A tremor spiraled through me. I felt that any moment now, the mirror would melt, or crack, sending a silver sheet of water spouting from the fissure. And I would wake up. Serene. Safe.

But none of those things happened.

The fine haze that had covered the glass broke up into droplets now. Beads of water trickled down the surface, cutting in ruts of clarity, both in mirror and mind.

As the words lost their definition, a dull anger bubbled within me. I shared the roof with only one other person, and I was the last one to take a shower.

"*Olena.*"

Stopping midway up the stairs, she looked at me. I stood on the landing, still in my towel. We opened our mouths, noises leapt at the same time.

"Why'd you write that?" I said.

"Huh?"

"You know what I'm talking about."

"No, Mike, I don't," she said, confused but also unsheathing the blade of her voice.

A thought about how funny I'd look, standing there naked and fuming if my towel dropped to the floor, randomly scooted across my mind.

Our gazes remained locked like gunslingers at a showdown. I eased first, letting my head hang. I knew my anger was misplaced, and what I sought wasn't an explanation but a confession, one that didn't feed my shapeless paranoia.

"Just—it's nothing. Thought you doodled something in the steam."

"Oh, well, no. I think I just swiped a hand across the mirror." She hiked a shoulder.

"Yeah, probably just read into it, I guess."

Now that I voiced it, it seemed stupid, nothing but a case of textbook pareidolia.

This was the second time in the last twenty-four hours we'd come close to raising voices, a rare occurrence. Before that, last night she told me, rather querulously, that Jolene had exaggerated. Yes, there was a nosebleed, and she fainted momentarily. But that was it.

"It's all foggy," she had said, almost to herself. "Like trying to recall a dream."

Her remark left me sleepless. Maybe that was a good thing.

6

Being a nondrinker and one of the few bankers at the event without a taste for powder, I was naturally tapped as the designated driver. I regretted agreeing when one of my colleagues shared his address.

Initially, I thought I made a wrong turn when I saw the deli. I hadn't been in the area in a long time. I'd avoided it. After the last and only time I'd stumbled into Desirée at the café that used to be wedged into the building's corner the deli now occupied.

A vague dread kept me away, but now, I just felt a pang, thinking about how her face puckered when she noticed me across the room then lit up, lids descending in her signature blink.

Even after the quick embrace and minutes into the conversation, I couldn't believe I was sitting across from her. There was an ease in her manner, a delicious casualness that hadn't been present in the Desirée who rode with me to school.

"When did you get married?" she asked.

I eyed my wedding band, as if wondering how it got there on my finger.

"Few years ago."

"That's great."

The graph of our excitement suddenly tanked. Until then, we'd been talking over one another, catching up on each other's lives. She had followed through on the plan she shared after the party; her library road trip. Now, she worked as an assistant editor for a travel magazine.

"I often thought about you," she said.

"Yeah?"

Guilt poked at me. My thoughts had only wandered to her occasionally a few months into college and not at all after a purple-haired girl in my class let me into her bed.

"I'm surprised you're killing time here instead of the library," I said.

"*Ha.*" She eyed the room in a cursory way, as if likewise surprised, probably wishing book-stacked shelves extruded out the walls, and shrugged. "Well, I was working, and the Wi-Fi's better here."

"Tell me more about your road trip."

Lost in some internal discussion, her head bobbed unconsciously.

Finally, she exhaled, seemed to consider, and said: "I walked through the doors of a lot of libraries, some old, some new, some shack-like, others palatial.

"Something unique about them all, even the seemingly ordinary ones, especially the seemingly ordinary ones. Though, I doubt there is such a thing as an ordinary library, and— Before I go on, promise me you'll keep an open mind."

She placed her hand on mine as she said it. I mimed lifting the bowl of my cranium off, which tickled her.

"I was staying at a motel in this little town called Silver Sleeve, well passing through it actually. When I asked the woman at the counter if she could point me to the local library, she said there wasn't one, but I was in luck since a travelling library had pulled into town days ago. My reaction to this piece of information startled the poor thing.

"Later, I headed to the park, and sure enough, there it was, parked nearby like she'd said. A blue and silver vintage van with the words **HEIDEGGER'S BOOKMOBILE** painted in a faded maroon arch on its side. It was like something that rattled through a wormhole, the other end linking it to a time when libraries hadn't been on the endangered species list.

"The back doors of the van were thrown open. The inside was lined with books. I gazed in awe. I had only ever *heard* of travelling libraries, but seeing one was indeed like looking at some endangered animal.

"'Hello, miss,' a voice at my elbow said.

"I turned around to face a gaunt, old man. He lifted his tweed flat cap in greeting, which made him seem congruous with the time the van might've wormholed through. He climbed in, hauling himself up with a grunt, then offered me a hand.

"He gave me a tour that ended with four steps. The books it contained seemed better suited to a museum with their dusty, leathery hides. The shelves displayed classics, some dating back to antiquity. You could feel time in your lungs. It was as if the van actually *had* traveled through time, collecting editions.

"'You like them?' the man asked.

"'Very much,' I said, still stepping and twirling in the small space, sometimes tilting my head to read spines. I did a double take once after I thought I spied the title of a book *morph* into different one, but that was just the poor lighting, I suppose.

"I finally made a pick. Stamped in gold on the cover was: *The Narrow Road to the Interior* by Matsuo Bashō

"I opened it, flipping through a few pages. They bore no publication info, just opened to a blank leaf, then the title followed by the text.

"'How long are you here in town?' I asked.

"'For you, indefinitely,' he said, 'But I have a feeling I could very well hit the road come dawn.'

"And he was right. I gobbled the book in my room by midnight.

"Next morning, when I went to return it, the van's door was slightly ajar, revealing a line of darkness. As I opened it and entered, I—

"When I went in, the inside was different. Not only were there no books along the walls, but the dimensions weren't that of an old van anymore. I stood in the foyer of some grand hotel, or viewing a scenic painting of one, all bright and gold, and it rippled. When I touched a pillar, it disintegrated mist-like, and my hand plunged into a patch of light. And the light, it sang. And I understood the hymn in a way that's impossible to relate. Imagine reading a book through osmosis or an ocean flowing through your ears within the space of a second."

I shuddered. All the exaltation I had felt at meeting my teenage crush had dissipated. I willed my phone to ring, so I could tell Desirée it was great seeing her, but I had to leave. I squirmed in my seat as she went on.

"The light was like a nebula spun between the remains of stars, the core blinding bright and cold to touch, so cold. I withdrew my hand. Everything else was dipped in a darkness that was the inside of a wound. The glowing cloud spiraled and pulled back, the widening eye of a storm, and I snapped awake."

"Awake?"

She absently scratched her brow.

"Back in my room. I was shivering. Pawing the lamp, I flicked it on, but it was still pitch black. I panicked for a moment, thinking I'd gone inexplicably blind. Then after a while, sight trickled in, and I did the most mundane thing imaginable: I checked my phone. It was three in the morning, a whole day after.

"The book I'd gotten from the travelling library had disappeared. Only a vacant place in the clutter I'd set it in after finishing. A part of me tried to reason, that I could've fallen into a long, deep doze after returning the book, and I even dropped by the park as soon as it was light to confirm as much, but the bookmobile was gone. The woman at counter just shrugged when I asked her about it. The other part couldn't shake off the vividness of it all."

"Why did you tell me all this?" I asked her, honestly perplexed.

"Because you're my friend," she said simply, and for an instant, normalcy rushed in and affection.

The sun was concealed behind a row of buildings in the west. Desirée glanced at her wrist, checking the time and leaned back in her seat with a sigh.

"I know all of it must seem pretty crazy."

"Ah, well." I vaguely shook my head.

"But one day," she said, holding my gaze, "you'll see..."

She reached over, squeezed my hand—the one without the wedding ring—and left.

Thoughts of Desirée and the things she'd talked about often resurfaced before fading into the background. I didn't think of her at all, until about two years ago when I dreamt of her, of us, dancing in a clearing to Renaissance lute music.

The memory of the crazed conversation we'd had grew obscure then. I only remembered her telling me about some weird dream. When I searched for her on Facebook, what I saw in my head was the Desirée who sat shotgun in the Mustang, grooving to Nirvana.

I checked multiple times to confirm I had found the right Desirée Parker when I saw the RIPs and condolence messages posted on her page.

After she hadn't shown up to work or answered any calls for days, her editor contacted the police. Desirée's door was forced open when the constant rappings and *Ma'am, Are You There*'s of the officer went unanswered. They found her on the bed, almost frozen, her corneas burnt.

A skeletal mallet stroked the ridges of my spine like a xylophone.

The official report said she died of hypothermia.

I learned it all from a colleague of hers who'd left a comment. After I introduced myself as a friend from school, she was more than happy to chat, appearing more excited than dismayed, as if she'd finally had something to sink her teeth into after a dull week.

I told myself that she probably fed me a bunch of rumors. And hypothermia in summer wasn't entirely unheard of. You didn't necessarily have to be out in a blizzard or—*cold to touch, so cold*—scaling a mountain to be affected. Maybe it could've been a physiological issue, something glandular or a faulty heating system or a cold bath or ten other reasons. Right?

7

"What're you thinking?"

"Mmm?"

"I said, what're you—"

"Oh, nothing," Olena said. She turned her vacant gaze back to the windshield.

A stupid thing to ask, but it was the one available off the top of my head.

We were returning from our second trip to the doctor's in a month.

We drove to the ER some weeks ago. Olena next to me with her head tilted forward, holding her bleeding nose in a pinch. That night, we sat absorbed, I in a police procedural on my iPad and Olena in her book. She only realized what was happening when drops of blood dotted the pages.

After an interlude of a few days, her headaches began. Mild, at first, then skull-shattering throbbers.

What prompted our recent visit, to a neurologist this time, was not nosebleeds or headaches.

Olena began losing time.

She was out grocery shopping once, and the next thing she knew, she stood in the checkout line at a bookstore, clutching a magazine she didn't remember picking up.

"It's so unsettling," she said. "I racked my brains trying to recall what I did in the intervening twenty minutes or so, but...I just couldn't. You know how you sometimes just can't recall a dream no matter how hard you try? Kinda like that. Like someone deleted a bunch of folders in my brain concerning that time period."

One evening, she found herself standing in the bathroom, dirt on her hands and in her throat. We made an appointment immediately after that.

Olena was convinced, courtesy of Google no doubt, she suffered from some form of early onset dementia.

The doctor, an efficient middle-aged woman with a sweet drawl, occasionally interjected questions—how often did it occur, was she on any new drugs, was she sick or depressed—as Olena related the incidents. She performed a general examination and conducted a mental test, which was basically asking Olena to recite and recall a bunch of things, then ordered blood-work and brain-imaging, saying they'd get a better idea of the problem after seeing the results.

I held Olena's hand as we left. She might've found my grip reassuring, but in truth, I was scared, too. But for reasons that hovered just beyond the rim of my consciousness.

8

There was a pressure in my ears, like long sleek fingers jabbed in, almost brushing my ear drums. I wanted to open my eyes and not open them. Somehow, I managed both, my lids stuttering half-open in bursts. That was when I glimpsed it. I tried desperately to shut my eyes, feeling a cold fear brew in my breast, but it was futile. My lids kept rolling up like possessed window blinds.

The shapeless black sheet fluttered right above me, like some tenebrous magic carpet you'd fall into if you stepped foot on. An iridescent sheen, the kind around a pigeon's neck, shimmered across it as it rippled.

Just another bizarre dream. I even managed a sleepy half-smile.

It's often the degree of detail that lends the plotless narratives of dreams their verisimilitude, their texture. The details isolated, partially focused, like seeing through a lens that's foggy around the edges. This, however, was different. My bedroom, the wall clock ticking to my right as if on tiptoe, Olena's snores, the tingling in my fingers, the sweat dappled pillow under my head, the faint acrid smell coming off the covers, which were due a trip to the laundry, the stray dog barking at something invisible faraway. All of it was much too detail all at once.

But a peek through my half-masted lids at the black shape was all it took to convince me I was dreaming. Because the alterative was madness.

The undulating motion of the tar-like sheet, or whatever it was, wasn't like the tapering quality of a ripple in water; it seemed more like a computer-generated simulation playing in an infinite loop.

Something round bulged forward breaking the ripples.

I strained my lids, eyes now tearful, but they only fluttered. With horrible slowness, I saw the green and purple sheen pick out the plane of a brow, the slight depression of eye-sockets beneath, the squashed nose tip, the hollow of an open mouth, and the point of a chin. It was a face. It was a goddamn face pressing down against the dark fabric, like a kid pushing his head into a curtain so that it molded itself to his features.

A numbing wind chilled my face, as if a dragon that breathed ice instead of fire gusted a breath. Five tiny mounds arose in the fabric, tenting it; fingertips. It clawed the rolling dark surface. A crackling static sound with an inquisitive, intonational quality made my flesh prickle.

The whimpers finally gave way to the scream that ricocheted in the vault of my throat. I almost fell off the bed with a spasm. It was a short scream, the pitch an alien sound I never knew I was capable of.

I panted and looked around the bedroom, dried tear tracks along the corner of my eyes. Nothing out of the ordinary. The clock ticked away silently. Olena snored. Moonlight splashed in through the window, bringing with it the distant barking of a dog.

I flexed my arm until the tingling in my fingers subsided. Then, shifting closer to Olena, I spooned her, grateful for the warmth.

9

My day carried on as usual after sunup. We were both a little antsy, Olena especially, since her medical reports were due in the evening. She was in the parlor rearranging the flowers, again, when I kissed her goodbye.

The sharp bark of something shattering arrested me mid-tread as I almost shut the door. Hurrying back, I called Olena but got no answer. My brisk pace turned into a trot as I went down the hall. I paused opposite the entrance to the parlor.

Olena stood motionless next to the end table, her back to me. Something I couldn't quite define about her still posture made me stop short. Ceramic shards strewn about her feet in a puddle of water. The blue irises lay among the debris like wounded things.

"Olena?" I said.

She stirred and turned about, crushing petals and crunching bits of ceramic underfoot as she did so.

A gut-punched gasp escaped me when we were face-to-face—the same button nose, the same brown eyes, the same full lips. Yet, what they all did in conjunction was a perversion of something familiar, something endearing, and made me shrink away from her.

The lips spread in a serene way that was unlike Olena's quick grin. With horror, I watched the eyelids come down in a prolonged blink. And my dear God, I *saw*.

SNOOZE
Linda G. Hill

"I've never been much of a dreamer."

No, I can't say that. I straightened my tie in the mirror. *She'll assume I'm talking about my hopes for the future.*

I couldn't afford to fuck up this date. At most, I was in a position to have the relationship to end all relationships. At the least, I'd save her life. The tricky part would be not coming across as a nutcase. Something I wasn't totally convinced of myself.

"Jacob?" She approached me with an outstretched hand, and I plastered a surprised look onto my face. The dating site I'd so-called found her through was this newfangled deal where the guy's photo was visible to the lady, but the woman's face remained a mystery. They meant to ensure true love or some such crap. That I'd actually managed to choose her provided enough proof that she was the woman of my dreams.

We were fated to meet.

"You must be Susan," I said as I shook her hand. She took the lead toward the Japanese restaurant's door, confident in her ultra-high heels and black raincoat. Susan looked every bit the reporter—light on the makeup under black-framed glasses. I'd have taken bets she had a notepad and pen in her purse, even if I didn't already know what she did for a living.

"I feel like I have an advantage over you." She settled into her side of the booth. "The website told me everything about you, but it said they told you next to nothing about me."

The urge to guess was great, but she'd think I'd been stalking her somehow.

"They gave me a few of your interests. I know you like to write."

"But I bet they didn't tell you I'm an investigative journalist."

I raised my eyebrows, hoping for the second time she wouldn't see through me. "Really? That must be exciting."

She shrugged, indifferent. "It has its moments. And you? What does Jacob do for a living?"

"I'm a…I used to be an elementary school teacher."

"Used to?"

"Yeah. I got kicked out of school for missing too many days."

Because I slept in.

Because I had to find out what was going to happen to you.

It started as a vivid dream, the kind you have when you drift off to sleep after you hit the snooze button.

In the first dream, she was a stranger but not quite. I knew her, but I couldn't place her. It was one of those dreams. She jogged in the park across the street from my apartment building, only I didn't live in an apartment building in real life.

Not yet.

I couldn't even imagine being able to afford the place at the time.

It took me a while to realize that the dreams had a progression, because I dreamed the same thing every morning at 5:57 for a week.

She wore a black jogging suit—tight pants, tight jacket, her hair done up in an elastic band, longer than shoulder-length by its bounce. Strange, but that's a dream for you. Her rather plain face was the kind that in makeup, a guy would trip over his feet for. I could see all this, even though I seemed to be on the third floor.

And that's all there was to it, at first. She'd appear from beneath the leaves of a maple to my right and run along the path until she was almost in front of me. Then, I'd wake up to the alarm I'd hit snooze on.

One day, the week after the dream started, I fell asleep again. Tired from binge watching *Stranger Things*, I hit snooze a second time, despite the inevitable rush through my morning routine to get to work on time.

And the dream continued.

I closed my eyes to find the woman where I'd left her, almost in front of me. She got about another ten paces when, just beneath a thin limb of a maple to my left, a figure stepped in out, halting her. I strained and discerned a man wearing a beige trench coat.

The woman stepped back, visible. She gestured with her hands as though arguing with the man.

The alarm went off again.

After another few days, I got curious enough to hit the snooze button for a third time.

The dream resumed.

It would have made sense to spend a weekend morning hitting the snooze button to see where things went with the woman in the park, but my weekend job was even more important than my weekday one. My weekends were consumed by my children, from Friday evening right until Sunday afternoon.

I tried dreaming of her, but she only appeared after I hit snooze.

So, I started sleeping in longer, showering at night instead of the morning to get past the third episode.

In the third dream, the argument escalated. The woman backed up enough that I could see the man, who stepped out from under the maple. A full head of light brown hair, he had the longest arms I've ever seen. Freakishly long. His gold wristwatch and a third of his forearm were exposed by the too-short sleeves of his coat. He got in the woman's face, threatening her.

The glass door to my miniscule balcony muffled their raised voices. I tried to open it, but my dream-arms couldn't do it. I almost woke up—by that time, I was lucid enough to remind myself that if I moved, I'd wake up too early. So, I stopped trying.

She got free and headed for the street, the man close behind her.

I pressed my forehead against the glass to see where she'd go…

And the alarm went off.

Since the snooze lasts nine minutes, the next installment would cost me my breakfast, but I couldn't help it. I had to find out what happened.

That night, I packed myself a sandwich to eat on the train on the way to work. The commute from the suburbs was an hour and a half—it got me to school fifteen minutes before the bell rang in the morning, just long enough to get myself organized before the kids came in.

The next morning, the dream continued.

I watched until I couldn't see her on my side of the street—she was too close to the building. I headed for the door of my apartment and ran down the stairs. When I got to the front door, they were there on the sidewalk outside. I went to my mailbox and pretended to look for my keys.

"Susan, Susan, Susan…" He called her over and over again, a child trying to get its mother's attention. She still tried to get away, but every time she turned, he grabbed her with one of the hands on those crazy-long arms and dragged her back. Finally, she rounded on him.

"How many times do I have to tell you? I have to follow this lead. If I don't, I'll look as guilty as if I'd done it myself. I don't want to go to jail."

"Neither do I." He drew back as though to slap her, and I would have stepped out of the door to stop him, but the guy was crying. It caught me short.

Susan put up a hand to block him.

"I know you don't," she said. "But you *are* guilty. You know that. Unfortunately, I have to be the one to figure that out for the record."

The man's gaze turned dark. "I can't let you do that. I can't."

"What do you mean, 'You can't'? I'm a free agent. And you're a murderer—the murderer of that little girl."

The man grabbed her from behind, his forearm around her throat. She choked, and I was frozen inside a dream.

Paralyzed.

My conscious mind heard my alarm's first beep, but I forced myself to stay asleep for a few more seconds. I stepped outside—a butcher knife appeared in my hand.

Susan's eyes went wide.

"Jacob," she mouthed, her airway closed off by that long, powerful arm.

The alarm blared. That was the last day I made it to work on time.

I wasn't going to bring it up. I promised myself I wouldn't bring it up. But the lull in the conversation between the teriyaki and the sushi was more than I could bear.

"Terrible thing about that little girl," I said, clearing my throat at the word girl as though I could somehow mask the fact that I'd given in.

Susan lowered the dessert menu. "It is. I knew the father."

Damn. "I'm sorry."

"I think he died trying to save her. There are rumors going around that he'd had a phone call from the killer, and he knew where she was before he'd had a chance to..." Susan dabbed her mouth with her napkin, even though it was clean.

"How did you know him?"

She shrugged. "He was only an acquaintance, really. A friend of a friend."

"I'm sorry."

The news reports had stated that they'd found the body of nine-year-old Melissa Heinbacher in a garbage container behind a warehouse at the north end of town. Her father had been killed in a car accident going eastbound on a one-way street, halfway between there and the family's home. The cops focused their investigation around the theory that he'd been fleeing the scene. But maybe not. Maybe this was the lead Susan was working on or had worked through by the time my dream happened.

"I hope they catch whoever did it."

She looked me in the eye. "So do I, Jacob. So do I."

The waiter rescued our conversation with sushi, and we spent the rest of the meal talking about my new job, a stoned cameraman who hadn't been able to find the location of the county fair, even though the Ferris wheel was visible for miles, and the state of the world and where we might be headed.

We left the restaurant. April hadn't yet let go of winter's arctic chill. Just off the sidewalk, tiny budding maple leaves reminded me that I didn't have long before the events would take place in the park, and outside my building...the one I would move into at the end of the month.

"It's gotten colder again," I said lamely. "Can I give you a ride somewhere?"

Susan shook her head. "I've got my car."

"I'll walk you to it."

She led the way.

"We should do this again." I wanted to suggest that she follow me back to my place so I could spend the night fucking her brains out. But I couldn't do anything to screw this up. I was scared. She liked me; I could tell that much. I didn't want to go too fast.

"That would be nice." She stopped at the hood of a white Prius. Her blue eyes glinted through her glasses, and I could have sworn I saw lust there.

Instinct pushed me to bend for a kiss on her beautiful lips, but the nerves, the life or death situation that might arise somehow if I screwed up, stopped me. "I'll call you."

She placed her hand on the back of my neck and stretched to kiss me. Wooden—only for a second—but when our lips parted, that single impression had done it.

"I'll call you," I said as she stepped back, smiling. "I promise."

Desperation vibrated in my voice. I'd fucked up.

"Don't forget."

Dear God, I hoped she meant it.

I only ever made it to episode eight of the dream.

Number five started with me holding the butcher knife up to the man's ridiculously long forearm and him running away.

She thanked me for saving her life, and we went up to my apartment where I sat her on my couch and made her a cup of tea. We talked a while. About what—a mystery.

I helped her off with her black skin-tight jacket and her black skin-tight pants.

Desperation to get to the next episode consumed me. When I got there, I wasn't disappointed. Our kisses filled with passion, her bare skin soft, mine hard. Entering her was legendary and climaxing inside her...messy. Episode six was a wet dream, every single time.

It took weeks to come to terms with hitting the snooze button whilst laying in a puddle of my own making, but I needed to know who the killer was. I needed to keep Susan safe. I was falling in love with her, or at least the dream-her.

I forced myself to wait until after noon to call her. I'd hit the snooze button and gone back to sleep, only to find the dream had changed. Susan's shadow came from behind the maple, moving slower. Sure enough, instead of jogging, she walked. The mysterious man met her in the middle of the path rather than to the left. He took her by the shoulders and shook her...

I woke up.

Too frazzled to go back to sleep and find out what happened next, unsure if I even wanted to know, I started my day at 6:06, distracted and disconcerted.

Since I lost my job at the school, I'd taken up some freelance writing gigs. Luck had it that ghostwriting for the rich brat of a billionaire allowed me to move into the apartment of my dreams. I spent the morning working off the brat's recorded tale of woe. He tended to ramble, so I had a lot to work from.

I stopped at twelve, made myself lunch, and ate watching the clock. Not wanting to wait until she was busy—assuming she took a break for lunch, too—and not wanting to seem overeager, which I naturally was, I called at one.

Susan answered the phone sharply and apologized when she heard my voice.

"It's been a huge day," she said. "Huge. But I can't go into details on the phone. I can tell you it's about that thing we talked about last night."

Nerves struck me so hard, I shivered.

"Well, that's interesting." I struggled to sound calm. "Would you like to do dinner tonight?"

"Can't."

"How about tomorrow? I can cook you something up at my place if you'd like. I'm inundated with boxes, but I'm sure I can dig out a pan or two ..."

"Sure. Call me tomorrow afternoon, and I'll get your address."

She hung up without saying goodbye.

Episode seven was the shortest, apart from the first dream. I hid behind a tree in the park with a tape recorder in my pocket. Wearing all black, I waited for Susan to jog up. We'd planned this. The man would be there. I still didn't know his name—at least not in my dream, even though I'd

422

obviously had the opportunity to ask Susan what it was. In my awake state, I hypothesized that my subconscious was blocking the knowledge, but that was moot in the dream, standing behind a tree with a crowbar in my hand, knowing the man was close by and would intercept Susan.

I was thinking about how stupid this all was when the alarm went off.

For many weeks, I tried to get past episode eight. By this time, the first dream haunted my every waking moment. It was driving me crazy, the same way hearing a song on the radio every hour of every day does when you're working somewhere you can't escape the music. Numerous times, I tried staying awake for twenty-four hours, so I'd be able to hit the snooze button more times, but episode eight was too much for me to go back to sleep to. It was episode eight that finally lost me my teaching job; it was while I was trying to get past it that I saw her on TV, being interviewed for an award she'd won for investigative journalism. I sat on the edge of my seat, studying her. There was no doubt in my mind. It was Susan. Susan Harper. The woman I now knew I had to save.

In episode eight, the man with the light brown hair and the limp and the long, long arms slit Susan's throat while I watched from behind a tree, unable to move.

The morning of our second date dragged on. I'd hit the snooze button and was drifting back off to sleep, but the phone rang just as Susan appeared, walking, not jogging, along the path in her jogging suit.

Afternoon finally rolled around, but she wasn't in her office. Apparently, an emergency meeting had been called. I left her a text message and went out to get groceries for dinner, assuming she'd come over. I was beside myself by the time she finally texted me back at seven that evening.

Where do you live?

I gave her my address—the old one, since I didn't have appliances at the new apartment yet—and she texted back that she'd be there in half an hour.

It was worse than getting ready for our first meeting, because I knew I'd already altered the dream. And she seemed to be in more danger now than she had been initially. Was it because we met at all? Was it because I did or said something I shouldn't have? Maybe I should have trusted my instincts two nights ago, and asked her to come home with me… If she died in the first dream, we definitely wouldn't be having sex in the sixth.

I opened a bottle of wine, intending to suggest she stay the night—for better or worse.

She knocked on the door five minutes early with a bottle of wine of her own in hand. I had time to take in her white see-through blouse with a camisole underneath as she unbuttoned her coat, then she leaned in for a kiss on the cheek. She kicked off her power-heels while I hung up her coat. I led her into the kitchen where I was just about to finish tossing our salad.

"I hope you like steak," I said. She'd had beef at the restaurant, so I knew she wasn't a vegetarian.

"Love it," she said with a smile. "You're quite the chef, I take it?"

I shrugged. "I learned young that it's the best way to a woman's heart."

"I'm sure it is," she said with a laugh that went straight to my own. "I'm rather amazed that the dating site got us so right. Even more than that, I'm amazed I even signed up for it. It just felt like the right thing to do."

"I'm glad you did. It was a bit like that for me, too, actually. I stumbled on the site when it sent me an ad. I usually just send them to spam."

She looked me directly in the eye. "It's like we were meant to be."

We barely made it through dinner. We were all over each other—the sex we had that night made my dream pale in comparison. It was mind-blowing, energetic; we didn't stop until the birds were singing outside the window. I was even more in love with the real Susan than the dream Susan.

Yet when she left that morning, early enough to get back home and change before she had to go to work, I was still no wiser on who the man with the long arms might be. Whether she knew him already or if I would be the one to tell her to watch out for him was still a mystery. Because what if she would never have met him had it not been for my dream?

We hadn't discussed it, not only for the obvious reason: that the murder of a little girl was as far from the sexiest topic in the world as you could get. And from the moment I saw that see-through blouse, there was only one thing on my mind. But I was also relieved that the opportunity hadn't come up. I needed the snooze button again to tell me if what we'd done had been right.

I needed to dream of Susan.

Which I managed to do that morning after she left. Having not slept all night, I drifted off before my 5:57 alarm.

We were back to the original dream: Susan jogging, and me waking up when she was almost in front of me on the path. The only difference was that I knew who she was now. I wouldn't have to wait until I got downstairs in a later episode to hear her name for the first time. I woke up this time when I touched the glass and whispered her name: before the alarm went off. I didn't make it back to sleep to see episode two.

It was more than a week before I saw her again. I was getting anxious because the leaves were coming in on the trees, and I'd completed my move. I hadn't told her where I'd moved to: her surprise at seeing me in the dream made me wonder if I should keep it a secret: she hadn't expected to see me in the dream, but she would if she knew I lived there.

She seemed to pick up on the fact that I wasn't telling her right away—the minute I suggested we go back to her place after our next dinner out, in fact. She was adamant that we not go to her place, so we parted in the parking lot of the Japanese restaurant, much like we had on our first date: with a quick kiss and a promise to talk the next day. Only she didn't pick up. She ignored all my calls.

I'd been standing by the window every morning, all morning, for four weeks. I knew after I moved in that the original dream had taken place sometime before noon by the sun, though I hadn't figured out if it was sunny or cloudy. Still, I stood there even when it rained, just to be sure.

My heart pounded as she appeared from under the leaves on the right. I tracked her until she stopped, at which point the figure of the man in the beige trench coat hid beneath the thin limb on the left. I literally pinched myself to make sure I was awake. I was.

As Susan and the man disappeared too close to my building to see, I turned for the door and looked at the clock: 6:24. My skin crawled. I'd be hitting the snooze button on another day, but not this one. I picked up the butcher knife that had been sitting on the table beside my door since I moved in, and I left.

I ran downstairs and forced myself to stay still while I listened to them argue. I waited until he grabbed her as I knew he would, but I didn't know what would happen after she croaked out my name and the man turned and walked away. I hadn't dreamed that part.

I dropped the knife, and she collapsed in my arms, a sobbing mess.

"Jacob." She gasped. "How did you know?"

I took her upstairs and made her a cup of tea. I sat down on the couch beside her, and it came pouring out. The first through the fourth dreams were easy, though I didn't tell her what I'd heard—that she'd accused the man of murdering the girl. I thought that would be another conversation altogether. She seemed to hold her breath as I told her I'd dreamt this very scenario—her sitting with me, drinking a cup of tea. I skipped the sixth dream in which we'd had sex and went on to tell her what I'd seen of the future. Not the details—no one needs the details of their own demise—just the basics of him hurting her badly while she was out for a jog, me unable to save her.

At that point, she started laughing.

"I know it sounds crazy, but all this started—I've been dreaming of this happening for months. Before I even lived here. You have to believe that."

"You're crazy." She tried to keep a straight face. "I knew there was something creepy about you when you moved and didn't tell me where you'd gone. You're fucking delusional."

"I'm not." I stood up then, frustrated, my hands balled into fists. "You have to take this seriously. I've been with you… In my head, at least, I've been with you for months. I fell in love with you for God's sake."

"Yeah, in your head. How long have you been stalking me? Hey? How long? I've got to get out of here." She slammed her mug down on the coffee table, almost hard enough to break it.

"You can't go." I reached out to take her arm, but she pulled away. "That guy you were talking to this morning—He's going to kill you, Susan. I've seen it happen. Over and over again, just like all the other dreams. It's going to happen if you're not careful."

She laughed in my face. "He's not going to kill me. He's my brother."

That stopped me dead. "You said… You accused him of killing that little girl."

Her eyes narrowed. "You wouldn't dare. He's going to turn himself in."

"Before or after he slits your throat?"

"I have to get out of here." She jerked toward the door. "I'll take care of my brother. You stay the fuck away from both of us."

I spent every minute of the next two days watching the news. The morning after our argument, I managed to get to the fifth dream with Susan coming up for tea, and nothing had changed. I couldn't get to sleep after that. The next day, I managed to get one past it: again, nothing had changed. We made love exactly as we had every other time I dreamed it; only this time, it seemed like we were on the same wavelength—she loved me as I loved her.

She called me on the third day after our argument and asked if she could come over. When I opened the door to her tear-stained face, she practically fell into my chest, apologizing for not believing me, asking me what she should do. I wanted to be angry, but I was still under the influence of my dream. I let her in.

"What changed your mind," I asked as she sat on my couch, and I perched on the chair opposite.

"He called me last night. Told me he was going to leave town and that I shouldn't try to stop him. It wasn't that he said it, it was the way he said it. He sounded so cold, so distant.

"I love my brother, but I can't let him get away with this. He's obviously sick. He needs help…but what will they do to him? They'll skewer him in jail—no matter where he ends up."

"I think you know what you have to do."

She cried, and I put my arms around her. "The sooner you get this over and done with, the sooner you'll be safe. We all will."

"He wants to implicate me. He wants to say I had something to do with it. The police have already questioned me on the whole thing, but they had nothing to go on because Melissa's father was gone."

Her eyes glistened red. "I was having an affair with him. With Hans, Missy's father."

"But…how does that implicate you?"

"My brother knows I was having the affair. The police don't know. They also don't know that Hans's wife threatened to kill me when she found out."

"Why didn't she come forward herself?"

"Melissa's mother has been out of it since it happened."

I remembered the woman on the news, distraught, made up for the camera, yet she'd obviously been raking her hand through her red hair. It stood on end as though she'd been trying to pull it out.

"Maybe that part of it is too difficult to cope with…I don't know. But my brother seems to think it's only a matter of time. And he's willing to speed things up."

"But if you're not guilty, you have nothing to worry about, right?"

"That's just the thing. There's no way to prove I'm not guilty without Hans to give witness."

Her breath hitched. "My brother hid the murder weapon in my storage container. And he's stolen the key. I can't get in there, and… Oh God, Jacob, what do I do?"

I held her a while until she stopped crying. I had no idea what to say; the thing foremost on my mind was making sure my final dream didn't come true.

I managed to get some food into her, and that night, we made love, better than the dream.

I wasn't able to get to the final two dreams again—Susan moved in with me. I insisted. I had to keep her safe. Yet, we weren't able to come to an agreement on how she should go about getting her brother arrested. She needed a confession from him, which of course led to the same fucking scenario that got her killed in my dream. I tried to convince her that we should get the police involved, but she wouldn't do it. She wanted to do it her way. The only way, as far as she was concerned.

I knew it was possible to change the dreams. I'd done so once by going against my instincts. That was my conundrum.

So, I gave in, though not completely. Susan had the tape recorder in her pocket, and I stood off to the side: we were at the airport, so no weapons. Her brother was waiting for his flight out—he hadn't told her when he was going, but her investigative reporting talents had taken the lead in finding which flight he was on.

To say he was surprised to see her would have been an understatement. They sat in a booth in the departure lounge, too far away for me to hear but close enough to see. When they began to argue visibly, it was all I could do not to step in.

I was envisioning the end of all the drama, when the woman with the crazy red hair—Melissa's mother—stepped up behind Susan and slit her throat.

A year later, I woke from the sixth of eight dreams in a sticky puddle of my own making. I rolled over to hit the snooze button again when a hand grasped my arm, stopping me.

"It's your turn to get up with the baby," Susan said, half asleep. I rolled over and gazed at her, at the thin scar made by the razor blade Melissa's mother had wielded moments before she was arrested.

Though the seventh dream was difficult to get through—Susan's brother reaching over the table with his freakishly long arms and putting pressure on the wound, saving her life—I wanted to get to the eighth, and perhaps even the ninth…the one that remained a mystery.

In my new eighth dream, Susan and I were lounging on a beach, being fed grapes by half-naked men and women. We were holding hands. We were madly in love.

As I threw off the bedclothes to get up, Susan's eye cracked open. "I don't know why you want to get past your eighth dream." Her voice was deep and groggy from lack of sleep. "It sounds like we're headed for paradise."

"But how do I know the grapes aren't poisonous?"

"Does it matter? I could die in that level of comfort and contentment."

I smiled as I pulled on my robe and headed for our newborn's room.

She had a point.

THE ONLY ONE ALIVE
Claire Davon

"You're the only person alive?" Brena, my therapist, asked; her tone mild. "Is that what you think?"

Her thumbs twirled round and round, the remainder of her fingers steepled. I studied her from my supine position on the sofa. My shrink's even voice did not deceive me. Her raised eyebrows and slight quirk of her lips told me she didn't believe me. No rational person would. I kept it to myself for a reason.

"Yeah." I sat up.

Her thumbs stopped. Her expression neutral, Brena gave me a flat look.

"I can't prove that anyone else exists, can I? I know that I'm alive, but that's it. Take you, for instance. When I walk out of this room, how can I be sure you don't vanish? The one thing I know is that I exist. The rest of you are questionable."

"Richard." The edge to her voice stopped me. "You realize how absurd that sounds."

I looked out the window's vertical slat blinds to the street beyond. Cars moved down the two-lane road in both directions while a lone pedestrian walked on the sidewalk. Palm trees swayed in the Santa Ana winds beleaguering Southern California. Vapor trails and the distant roar of a plane made its descent into Burbank airport. It should all have been proof that I wasn't alone in the world, but it didn't reassure me.

If I shut the blinds, would the people still be there?

I could not prove it.

"I don't know that." My voice rose. This thought plagued me for years, but going to therapy gave me the courage to say it.

Now, it was out there. As expected, she greeted me with incredulity. Brena might try to hide it—that was her job—but the fact that she'd stopped moving her hands told me everything. She didn't believe me.

I told myself I shouldn't care. If she wasn't real, it made no difference. If she and the rest of the world existed, she was a therapist, and clients paid her to hear weird stuff…or our insurance did, anyway.

Right there, that should have been proof that my thought was ridiculous. If nobody else existed, why have a mechanism for her to get funds? She kept seeing me, so she got money—unless it happened as I came in. Like she was some sort of automaton, coming to life when I showed up.

After the session was over, I walked out of her office into the bright Los Angeles sunshine. This hour hadn't been any different than any other. She wanted to know about my trauma from the fifth grade, but I didn't give her much about that.

Being the sole person on the planet had to be nonsense, but I couldn't shake the feeling. The one person I could vouch for was myself. Everyone else was there by inference.

I drove home, taking Olive over the 5 freeway and across Victory back to my boring house. I squinted to see if the cars stood at a standstill in the distance but couldn't make up my mind.

Ever since I'd told Brena, it felt like I could no longer hide it. It was the ultimate arrogance to think that I, alone, was real and that everyone else was…what? A figment of my imagination? Just because I knew only that I was alive didn't mean the billions and billions of people on this earth were fiction. I glanced over at a man on the street. Did he freeze in place until I looked at him?

I needed therapy more than I realized.

I turned into my neighborhood. It seemed as if the stupid dog, who always barked at the end of the street, wasn't moving before I heard his familiar *woof woof woof*. Was it me in particular he disliked, or did he bark at other cars or anything else?

I parked and went into my house. No mail yet. Not unexpected for a Saturday. It would be nothing but junk and the few paper bills I still got anyway. Another reason my idea was insane. Mail showed up when I wasn't home.

The yard wasn't wet, although it should be since today was the day the gardener came. I could see no evidence of his presence in the dead grass and dying ivy, but it wasn't raining or a holiday: no reason for the gardener not to come. He should have been here and gone in the three hours I had been away. I should fire him and get a new one, but he worked the house a long time and too much trouble to get someone else.

I walked in the quiet house. I lived alone, no plants or animals to greet me. Not even a goldfish, although they wouldn't be much of a companion. This was one of the reasons I saw Brena. I was too closed off—my girlfriend, Maisie, told me—too unable to express myself. She gave up after several months and broke up with me. One day, she was there, and the next, she was gone. Marks still indented the rug where her storage cabinets had stood. I was glad I hadn't been home when she'd left. I might have tried to change her mind but doubted it would have gotten me anywhere. Better not to say anything at all.

That was my usual motto.

I felt safe with Brena, and that's why I said things that I had been thinking for years. Things I didn't dare tell others for fear they would think me crazy.

Like when I thought the ringing in my ears as a kid meant the aliens were coming to get me.

Or the way that I would count off trees on my way to places, always relieved when they added up to an even number.

I tossed my keys onto the telephone table and went into the kitchen. Meeting with Brena left me unsettled. She annoyingly dug into my psyche, but most of the time, she helped. Maybe Brena could figure out why I was the way I was.

The whirr of the refrigerator stuttered, reminding me that I was going to need a new appliance soon. I sighed. The money didn't matter—I made decent coin—dealing with people was the issue.

I selected a frozen dinner from my towering pile of single serve entrees and popped it in the microwave. I changed in the bedroom and couldn't get out of my social clothes fast enough. My comfortable sweats lay right where I left them, greeting me like old friends. They never let me down.

Padding back into the living room, I thumbed on the flat screen TV and checked on my meal.

I frowned. The microwave still blinked on three minutes, just as it had been when I left. It counted down, blinking toward zero, but it should have finished. Was the microwave also about to go belly up? All of my appliances were old, another point of contention with Maisie, but they worked. No need to get new ones until the old ones died.

The microwave resumed its countdown. I turned back to the fridge and pulled out a soda. I considered the six pack that lay on the bottom shelf, but noon was too early to start drinking. Next, I'd be one of the hobos, waiting by the Ralphs front door at 6:00 AM for them to open, so I could stock up on booze. The beer stayed.

I deposited the soda and went back to the kitchen, expecting the scent of Sesame Chicken to fill the air. I frowned. Now, the microwave was on 1:12 and heading down. But once again, it should have been done. I had spent more than two minutes in the living room, fiddling with the TV to find an acceptable channel: the NFL Network at the moment. It blared at me from the other room, the voices comforting in the quiet house, an assurance that life still flowed around me.

I watched the remaining seconds. Once the bell chimed, I popped the door open and snatched the prize out of its clutches. The steamer tray dislodged its contents with a plop. I grabbed a rag and slid it under the tray. Good enough.

Settling into the sofa, which also could use an upgrade, I flipped through the channels again. Boring. Bland. Boring. Seen it. Blah. Nothing but garbage reality shows. I wanted someone to talk to. I wanted *Maisie* if I was being honest. She had made it clear she wanted nothing more to do with me. Me and my faulty microwave were better off without her.

The channels didn't improve on a second round. I contemplated Netflix but remembered I'd let my subscription lapse. I'd check on demand in a minute.

Outside was too quiet: planes in the distance and the faint roar of the freeway a half mile away. That should have reassured me but didn't. I felt itchy, my body too large for my skin.

Nothing came from the house next door. The freaking Armenian who had moved in often watered his yard despite the conservation laws, but I couldn't hear him. Maybe he'd gotten a notice from the city to stop. Maybe someone had helped with that.

I propelled myself out of my sofa and to the front door. The trees waved in an unseen breeze. Street noise mixed with a faint Spanish melody. My house was built in the last century and had solid walls, which was why I hadn't heard the music before. Now, it was evident, something "la cucaracha-ish." I grimaced, although the noise made me feel better. Phantom ants crawled down my spine, tickling me, making me jerk around, thinking something was behind me. Nothing was. Nothing would be.

It seemed a reasonable idea when I said it, but I knew its absurdity. If I was the only person alive, how did the world work? I understood what Brena meant when she called it ridiculous. How did things run? How did trains get to where they needed to be? How did I get food? How did planes and trucks deliver things? How did plants grow if I wasn't there to watch them? The weight of the impossibility of my assumption weighed on me. The ants grew stronger, and I wanted to run from the house.

I had laundry to do. I grabbed the hamper and tossed all of it into the washer and pitched a pod in after the clothes. Color didn't matter to me. That had been Maisie's bag to sort out the colors from the whites. I couldn't care less.

That done, I went to the fridge, contemplating my beer again, but it seemed inadequate. The liquor store was right around the corner. I'd stopped going after the clerk looked at me pityingly when I'd gone there for beer one too many times after Maisie left me. Screw them. I didn't need their smug condescension.

I got my keys. Damn it all, I was going to go to that liquor store. I needed something stronger. Bottom shelf vodka would be fine. I had to have something to kill the queasy feeling inside me.

The traffic roared to life on my brief trip, as if the cars came out of nowhere. The noise seemed much louder than moments before, at the house. As I was pulling in, things started up, like a rusty calliope turning, the music off-kilter before it swelled to its normal cadence.

I jumped from the car as a hobo stumbled out of the liquor store with a black plastic bag clutched to his chest, part fright and part bleary incomprehension when he rushed by me. I wanted to run home as fast as I had wanted to leave. But I was afraid if I did lock the doors, everything outside would stop again.

The bell chimed when I entered the store. The clerk working at the lottery machine mumbled a greeting at my entry. The open back door showed the old owner cataloguing inventory in the storeroom. The sheer mundaneness of the task calmed my pounding heart. Acrid tang of sweat poured from me. Fear sweat, although nothing happened to cause such a reaction. Just some incautious words and a whole lot of strangeness.

The clerk jerked his chin when I approached the high counter. I pointed to the large blue bottle, and he smiled.

"Going to do some partying, eh?" he said in an accented voice, the same as my overwatering neighbor.

"Yeah, partying," I managed, my forehead clammy. A desire to talk to the man seized me, to carry on a conversation with someone.

"Haven't seen you around a while," the clerk said, not meeting my gaze as he rang up my purchases. As the hobos did at Ralphs, I threw in a pack of gum, some chips, and a premade sandwich, so it wouldn't seem as if I was buying just the booze. I was sure I didn't fool him. No doubt he had seen everything.

"Yeah, been on the wagon a bit. Girlfriend, you know. But she's gone, so I figured what the he..."

He wasn't listening. His eyes drifted to the soccer game on the TV over the door. I handed him money; something primal bubbled in me. I wanted to hit him, to feel something, but I let my hand drop.

The sign over the register said, "Smile, you're on camera."

I snatched my items and went for the car, intent on home. At least there, I was safe. I glanced back at the liquor store. Was the clerk immobile now that I had driven off or was he paying attention to the TV? He seemed still: the former not the latter.

My damn neighbor was watering his lawn when I got home. He raised a hand to me, and I jolted my head in reply. I wasn't sure if I'd been gone long enough for his driveway to collect water, but it seemed to me it should have. There was none.

When I entered the house, the washer was still filling. It should have been halfway through the cycle by now. The newer ones could give you a readout of the time left, but this was a second hand one. Maybe, it was broken. Or maybe, I wasn't here to watch it, and therefore, it didn't function. The dial clicked, and the agitator started.

Satisfied with the running washer, I unloaded my purchases on the counter and grabbed the bottle. Some off-brand Russian vodka with "Charcoal filtered" as its best claim to fame, as if charcoal could wipe out the foul taste of the stuff. It didn't matter.

I took a heavy swig of the vodka after twisting off the cap and slunk to the side of the house, trying to peer out without being seen. My neighbor's yard was wet, but he'd disappeared, as if it all reset.

I could hear my washer now, but then again, I was home to know it should be on. What would happen if I called Maisie?

Had the washer gone off? Had my concentration flagged enough so that it was no longer part of reality? I ran back to the laundry room, but it still churned.

Relief.

Perhaps, the washer was loud enough, unlike the microwave, so it kept going as long as I was in the house to hear it.

It hadn't been like this before.

Something changed when I vocalized my suspicion, as if the world functioned until I'd said what I already knew.

I alone existed.

I took a long pull of the vodka. Time to experiment. I set the coffee pot up and turned it on, waiting until I heard the faint *drip drip* of the brewer before moving away. I got the largest pot I had and put it under the faucet to fill. Sticking another frozen meal into the microwave, I started the machine. When I was satisfied all three were going, I ran out of the house and down the block on my bare feet as if someone were after me. I ignored the startled faces of some of my neighbors. I wasn't fast enough to catch them not moving, but I was far enough away from the house for my purposes.

The blocks weren't very long in my neighborhood, but I panted when I returned, out of shape—something else I had let go.

I tore into the house and ran to the kitchen. The microwave was on 2:01. The coffee pot had brewed less than one cup. The drip started again.

I left, and everything stopped.

I swore, so loud I thought the Armenians next door could hear, but I didn't care. They weren't alive. None of them were. The truth was right in front of me.

How had what I had said so off-the-cuff to Brena, believing yet not believing my words, trigger this? Was I forever going to live in a world where I couldn't multitask? How could I get water hot if when I walked away, the shower stopped responding and didn't start again until I was within earshot?

Heat surfacing in my cheeks, I grabbed the bottle. I chugged the vodka, welcoming the burn as the cheap stuff went all the way down. I flipped off the faucet, leaving the pot in the sink. The microwave dinged, but I ignored it. I had no appetite for food. The coffee pot continued to burble.

I was more alone than I could ever have imagined. Gripping the bottle, I staggered to the couch and flopped onto it. Good thing I didn't have a pet. If I had goldfish, what would happen when I wasn't there? Would they be in stasis, frozen in the bowl until I returned? If I had a dog, would it be caught in the act of licking itself until I came home to release it from its hibernation?

How much I relied on the world functioning around me: the trucks and planes to deliver food—or I would have nothing to eat—and people like Maisie and the idiots next door. I was alone otherwise, tragically alone, in ways I hadn't known existed.

I flipped on the TV, and it whirred to life. A house-buying show played, one that took people to other countries to look for property. I watched it from time to time, wondering what being in those other places would be like. If I traveled to Belgium, would the country come alive when I flew there?

The coffeepot finished, and it made me glad. The vodka burned, and I welcomed the effects. Maybe if I drank the whole bottle, I could temporarily forget. Or maybe if I drank the whole bottle, I would wake up, and this would be just a dream. Or I wouldn't wake up at all. That might be preferable to a world where I alone existed.

Maybe the adult channels would have something interesting to watch. I flipped to those, realizing my mistake. Porn meant the slide of bodies over each other. People touching, caressing, moaning into each other's mouths. Telling the other person how much they wanted them, how much they needed them and darker words, commands and pleas, begging their partner to take them. All of it unreal.

They weren't alive; it was all an illusion. Maisie had been a figment of my imagination, like everything else, whatever was going on, and the touch of her hands meant nothing. The press of her breasts against my back meant nothing. The feel of her tight body as I glided in and out of her, sweet friction that held me like a vise while she cried and sobbed my name meant nothing.

Howling an inchoate cry, I slapped the remote button to off and sucked down more vodka. I should have gotten two bottles from the not-alive clerk, but doubted I was sober enough to go back out. If I drove drunk in this crazy world, would a non-existent cop pull me over and arrest me and throw me in a non-existent jail? It was better to stay safe at home. If I dialed for takeout, would they deliver as long as I maintained it in my head that they were coming?

I didn't know, I didn't know, I didn't know.

I jammed the remote back on again and continued drinking. Adult channels were better than nothing. I knew my hand existed, and I could take care of myself. The knowledge that the people on the screen weren't real might not deter my body if I was drunk enough. I took another swig.

I searched over my fantasies trying to remember if I had any that suggested alien abduction. It could be the government, and this was some sort of experiment. Maybe they were seeing how far I could go before I broke.

Tears fell on my hand when I drew another pull. The adult channel moaned behind me. As the vodka did its work, it didn't seem quite as important to know that I was forever alone, no Maisie or even Brena to comfort me because none of them were real. Not my stupid next-door neighbors with their too-watered lawn, not the clerk down the way, not the kids on bicycles who tagged cars in the morning dew. Not the dog—or maybe, animals were alive. Maybe the rooster who crowed and annoyed the crap out of me in the morning would still exist if humans didn't.

I listened to the channel groan behind closed eyelids. Not adult stuff. I considered the premium channels but remembered I got rid of those when Maisie left. I prowled through my DVR to find something good.

I relaxed.

Would it be so bad if I was the only person alive? If I was, did that mean I could live my life without consequences? If I was the sole one out there, how come we had rules and police and things to stop me from running wild in the street? I had been arrested once, a long time ago, just a stupid misdemeanor, but the memory stuck with me. The cold of the iron bars under my hands was not something I wanted to repeat.

I had no answers, but the vodka did. As it settled into me, I stopped caring. It told me I didn't need to worry. All I needed was it, food, and the remote. Hell with the rest of them. They didn't exist anyway.

I don't remember much after that. It seemed as if I should, as it was happening, but I don't. I remember flashes. Changing the channel by pressing down on the button over and over again. My phone in my hand. Calling, but not getting an answer. Watching the adult channel and trying to pleasure myself. The booze made it hard, and I struggled at the end. Crying thick tears that streamed down my face. Forcing back the nausea that welled up at too much alcohol too fast and pouring more down my gullet. The liquor store sandwich shards were scattered around me, the half-empty bottle sideways on the floor.

Then, oblivion.

I woke up the next morning, sprawled on the sofa with light streaming in through my blinds and a thick hangover coating my head and stomach. I groaned and rolled over. A line of bile dribbled from my mouth to my t-shirt; I had tossed up the sandwich at some point. When the pain in my head stabbed through me, I moaned.

The TV was off, although I didn't remember touching the remote. My pants were still pulled down around my knees, and I yanked them up with swollen and raw hands.

I stumbled to the bathroom to pee when I heard something.

I finished and listened.

There it was again: a noise.

"Who's there?" I started at my voice. My head pounding again, I howled in agony.

"Richard?"

Maisie. I pulled on my sweats and took a quick glance in the mirror. Nothing to do for my sallow skin tone. My hair stuck up every which way, and after a vain attempt to smooth it down, I gave up. The room spun, and I fought to keep from barfing.

I lurched toward the kitchen where I could smell coffee brewing and something else that might have been toast. My stomach roiled at the idea of food.

I grabbed my phone from the floor and looked at the call log. I'd called Maisie six times. I should have felt ashamed, but she had come. If she had come in answer to my drunken late-night calls, I couldn't be alone in the world. I had passed out, in no shape to know what reality was. My heart soared. I didn't want to be the only person on the planet. It was too horrifying.

Maisie emerged from the kitchen carrying a tray. She clucked her tongue. "You look wretched."

I tried smiling. I wanted to take another swig to calm my rolling body but didn't dare. I wasn't going to do anything to disrupt this fragile détente.

"Take a few hairs of the dog. Or you'll be in sorrier shape than you are right now."

I scrambled for the bottle and took a pull. The nausea receded, but it was there, poised to roar back at any time. "I called you six times. Sorry. Hope I wasn't too incoherent."

She set down the tray. This whole crazy event had one good effect. Maisie returned.

"You weren't making any sense." She waved her hand and handed me a cup of coffee. I wasn't sure I could drink it. "Something about microwaves and being the only person alive. You were rambling."

A horrible feeling settled over me. Drunk or not, I was present in whatever sorry state when I had called. I had been awake, in some form.

She gave me an appraising glance. "You've let yourself go since I've been gone."

"Are you here to stay?" I asked, not expecting a yes. Hoping but not expecting.

"We'll see. Eat your toast."

I should have been reassured. Maisie was here, and she might be staying. That was all I wanted. But it proved nothing. I could still be affecting things. My worst fear could be true.

I eyed the tableau in front of me.
I would never be sure.

CANDLESTICKS
Chris Campeau

It came with little surprise to Dom that Oma was up and walking the house in the middle of the night. The nursing staff at Immaculate warned him that it might happen. Miranda, the placement student, told him that it was common for the elderly to sleepwalk.

Dom crept out of bed and crossed the room. He grappled with the dark like a blindfolded birthday boy pinning the tail on the donkey, fondling the air until his hands hit the wall and slid over to the doorknob. He inched the door open. A thread of pale light crawled up the floor, onto the bed, across Lily's face. She stirred.

"Where are you going?"

"Shhh. Go back to bed."

"Dom, it's five forty-two."

"It's okay. I just need to use the washroom. Go back to sleep."

She rolled out of the light, and Dom closed the door. The last thing he needed was for Lily to hear her grandmother shuffling about the house. He pressed an ear to the door and waited for his wife's snores to gain momentum.

They had set Oma a room in the den at the end of the hall, and the door stood wide open. With the help of a nightlight, Dom steered himself through the dark. Again, the shuffling.

Shhhftt, shhhftt, shhhftt.

The dining room. *How the hell did she make it so far? If she keeps this up, I'll have to baby-proof the place, gate the stairs to the basement. Then again, it wouldn't be the worst thing to happen, her taking a spill; the old stick never liked me anyway.*

He saw his breath in the kitchen. A frost-white burn coated the window above the sink, January's relentless kiss seeping through the glass. He rubbed his hands over his forearms and up under the sleeves of his bed shirt. One room over, the shuffling stopped.

The dining area was void of microwave and stove-clock radiance and was much shadier. In the darkness, Dom could make out the old woman's shallow profile as she stood at the wooden hutch across the room—her hutch—the only piece of furniture that survived the fire at Immaculate. Her hands were buried in a drawer at her waist. Dom fingered the light switch but stopped himself from flicking it. It could have been an old article he had read, but it felt more like one of those precautionary instincts programmed into one's being. Don't wake a sleepwalker.

Oma's silver hair shrouded her face and hung past her shoulders. It lifted and fell in feathery wisps as she worked her arms in the drawer.

Pop. It sounded like a dislocated shoulder sliding back into place.

Pop. Another item snapped, nunchucks hanging off her fingers.

Pop. Not nunchucks. Broken candlesticks.

Stepping toward her, Dom stubbed his toe on the dining room table, and a shrill squeak disrupted the silence.

Christ. He held his breath. *Might as well turn on the lights and hit the stereo while you're at it.*

Oma jerked her head toward him—her eyes still closed—before turning back to her work. Dom exhaled a long breath. He crossed the room to the disoriented woman and gently took her forearm below the hem of her gown sleeve, cream-white and paisley patterned with her own needlework. Her skin was tightly stretched, hot.

"This way, Oma," he said. Delicately, he rotated her toward the kitchen. She continued to snap the ghosts of candlesticks—her hands coated with the greasy sheen of wax flakes—balling her fists and repeatedly making a breaking gesture. Trailing behind, he let her work her way back on her own, his hands on either side of her shoulders as she dragged her feet forward.

Oma froze outside the kitchen, so suddenly that Dom nearly rear-ended her. The silence in the house was heavy; even Lily's snores, which could typically be heard from any corner of their bungalow, were stifled. The stillness clamped itself over Dom's torso like a lead vest, and a deep pity thickened in his stomach.

She must be having a bad dream. The fire. In the morning, I'll take the rest of the candles to the garage. Get them out of sight.

He pitied himself, too, though; aiding his wife's frail, sleepwalking grandmother was the most honest thing he had done for Lily since their intimacy crawled into a dead zone. Standing outside the kitchen in the solitude of the chilly dark, where the silver-black appliances and obsidian countertops were cold and customary, he imagined Miranda, and a lustful warmth smoothed his gooseflesh. Her sunburst skin. The pear-shaped birthmark above her pelvic line. The scent of rosewood incense threaded into the fibres of her bedsheets.

Dom's nerves shot to the ceiling—Miranda evaporating like smoke in still air—as Oma burst into a severe coughing fit. Her upper body heaved as she spun to face him, milky eyes blazing, mouth a toothless hole. She turned and sped across the living room with alarming speed.

Dom raced over as she struggled with the doorknob, pounded and scratched at the front door. His heart banged in his throat, enough to shake his vision and wet his palms. Oma doubled over and expelled air from her lungs in great, coarse gusts.

Then, as quickly as the fit started, it ended. Oma lifted her head, her hands fell to her sides, and she rested her forehead on the door. Save for her deep breathing, the house was silent again. Dom, with his heart still galloping, found his legs and took the old woman's arm.

He prayed Lily slept through the noise.

In the morning, Dom glanced at the closed door to the den on his way to the kitchen.

Crazy bat must still be sleeping. The late-night loop through the house must have really knocked her out.

When he rounded the corner, Lily stood halfway out the front door.

"I'm off," she said. Behind thin rims, her grey eyes withdrew from his immediately.

"I can see that." He wanted to say more, but instead wondered why they no longer shared breakfast before work.

"Your grandmother was up last night. Sleepwalking." He walked toward the Keurig on the kitchen island. "She was breaking candlesticks in the dining room, of all things. I didn't want to wake you."

Dom turned to hear the front door slam. A moment later, it opened, and Lily poked her head in.

"If you want to insult me, hurt me, find another way, Dom. But that?" She dropped her eyes. Her voice swelled with tears. "Are you trying to be funny? There's only so much I can stand to hear right now before I quite literally fall apart."

She threw the door closed, harder this time. The white frame with Oma's picture face-dived off the shelf above the television. Like a funeral parlor before a service, the house succumbed to a steeling silence.

Dom fetched the paper from the front step and returned to his morning cup at the island. He skimmed the sections he might have cared for in his thirties—politics, business, editorials—and headed for the bikini feature at the back. But a wave of self-loathing stopped him, a crude reminder that he was going to be a better man. He *had* to be a better man. A husband again.

He landed on a spread showing columns of text, each topped with an oval-framed head-shot of some beloved individual's face: a young man, twenties maybe, with a receding hairline and trim beard; two more gentlemen, elderly, with spectacles thick as pond ice; an infant.

He dropped his mug on the counter and shot a hand to his mouth.

He blinked.

Twice.

Her face remained, though, as sure as the paper browned with coffee. Like an angel, Oma smiled at him from the page, her cornflower blues crow-footed and honest. Dom's heart thumped behind his eyes as he stared at the inked prose of her eulogy. He caught his reflection in the glossy sheen of the microwave. A white face, glistening and unfamiliar, stared back at him. The room shrank around him, and black spots mottled over his vision. The hardwood of the floor rushed up on his tailbone. Cold, spilled coffee seeped through his pajamas as the blackness overtook him.

"Can you help me understand what it is that possesses you to be so cruel? Please, Dom, I just can't. I cannot wrap my head around it." Through groggy eyes, Dom identified the shape at the foot of the bed as Lily. She had returned from work, making it early evening. She clutched a fistful of broken candlesticks and looked like she had just suffered an asthma attack. "You broke every one, Dom? Really? Some of the only mementos I have left? What the hell has gotten into you?"

I must have dragged myself back to bed.

The events of the morning rushed to the forefront of his mind in a nightmarish surge: the obituary; waking up on the hard kitchen floor; the empty bed in the den as he hurled the door open; the charred box behind the nightstand with Oma's few surviving belongings inside it; the sweat that leaked down his ribs as he fingered the tokens of a dead woman; her photographs, tax receipts, letters; the leathery slippers. His screaming.

Lily broke into tears and dropped the candle pieces onto the ash-coloured duvet. "Was it not enough, turning a blind eye at her death? Staying late to leave me with the arrangements? Leaving it all on my plate? Was it not enough that you had to go and start erasing her from the house?"

"Lily," he said, a post-nap lump in his throat. "Lily."

"Burn in hell, Dom." She removed her glasses and wiped at her pink eyes. "The bed is all yours tonight."

She left the room.

Moments later, she left the house.

But he hadn't stayed late at the office every night. He had stayed late in Miranda's fourth-floor bachelor in the student high-rise behind the university. Miranda, the sparkle of youth in that enclosure of old age and rot that was Immaculate Heart Nursing—a place where family goes to visit once every other weekend; a place where residents live out their few remaining years, frail, only to be transported to their deaths in stale hospice beds.

Or sweeping beds of fire.

Dom stared through tears at the bedroom ceiling until the sun set. Lily's side of the bed was empty, yet warm when he ran an open palm across the sheets.

With the covers drawn to his chin, Dom closed his eyes to find Miranda's panting face glowing against his lids. He shook his head to rid her image, but she wouldn't go away.

Until he heard it.

Shhhftt. Shhhftt. Shhhftt.

At the end of the hall.

Shhhftt. Shhhftt. Shhhftt.

Closer.

Dom clenched the bedsheets as the shapes of two ratty slippers obstructed the light spilling in beneath the door. He knew he deserved whatever penance the old lady sought from him. She had always been fond of her granddaughter.

The door hinges creaked, and a wall of heat roared past the thin figure standing in the doorframe.

IN COMES THE COLD
M.C. St. John

"It is bloody freezing," his wife said. "Bernard, say something. Anything."

"What am I to say that I haven't uttered to the old man before?"

"Perhaps raising your voice."

"I do. I *do*."

"Upstairs. Not here."

Too late. Their daughter, Alice, wriggled awake in Maggie's arms and cried. Maggie bounced the baby as best she could, cooing her with sweet nothings, but once Alice started, she kept on crying. Her breath misted into the air before being eaten by the chill of the small room. Outside, the snow continued to besiege the city. It had not stopped since Christmas.

"Mother," Stephen said, "won't *Malice* ever stop?"

Stephen was five and thin for his age, though no one would know it. He not only wore every stitch of clothing Maggie had mended for him but also two empty potato sacks and a shawl from Maggie's mother, god rest her soul.

"Stephen, don't call your sister that awful name. You're not helping. Your father is doing enough of that already."

"Not in front of the children."

Bernard stood at the window, or rather, bounced from heel to toe in an effort to keep his blood moving. He turned to his wife and huffed, the annoyance as visible as his breath. "Miss Landers must be stranded in the Midlands. The trains will be a right mess until this snow lets up. When she returns, she can talk some sense into him."

"Since you have not."

"Maggie."

"No, Bernard. Miss Landers is his housekeeper, but she isn't a saint. She could only deal with Mr. Crawford for so long, which is why she left for holiday. He's a right mad tyrant, brooding up there in his study. He holds it against us for taking up room and board. Miss Landers told me. He needs

444

the money, though he holds his nose when he takes ours. He can't afford to keep up appearances, yet he wastes money on extravagance. Look at the radiators. So garish."

"They are American," Bernard said.

A radiator stood next to him. Its silver coils were adorned with Gothic interlocking lines. One could get lost in those details. Extraordinary devices just the same. The radiators were heated from the cellar. A cast iron boiler sent steam through pipes within the house, ending at this set of coils and others in almost every room. Bernard had read about them and knew what an expense they were.

"What good are these if Crawford won't buy the coal to heat them?" Maggie asked.

"They can make music." Stephen demonstrated with a brass button from one of his many coat sleeves. Toneless notes filled the room.

"Stop that, son."

"He's right, Bernard. They're cold lumps of nothing without the boiler on. Like us."

Maggie's sharp words belied her soft and pleading eyes. They were on Alice, whose crying had been replaced with a ghastly retching, the sound of sickness.

Stephen edged away from his mother and sister, his dead grandmother's shawl trailing behind him, a cortege in gray and black. He looked afraid. "Father, what will happen if it never gets warm?"

Crouching down, Bernard placed a gentle hand on his son's shoulder. "I'm going to get us all sorted, hey? We'll be cooking like gooses in no time."

He kissed the top of Stephen's head, then met Maggie's gaze. "I will speak to Crawford. This time, he will listen."

With that, he walked to the door, pausing only to rub his hands before touching the cold handle.

The main corridor was quiet. Weak afternoon light filtered in through the windows, bringing with it the gentle shadows of falling snow. The gas lamps were extinguished, their glass orbs muted, which added to an atmosphere of neglect. Miss Landers really kept things inviting, if not cordial. The carpeted stairs silenced his steps.

Before, the enormity of the house impressed Bernard. He and the family had taken a brief tour the previous spring, led by Miss Landers, who knew Bernard as the great nephew of an old friend from church, which was to say the housekeeper hardly knew him, if only in stories over tea in the sanctuary. At Easter service, upon hearing Maggie was expecting for a second time and the family was in need of a flat, Miss Landers offered residence at the home of Richard Crawford, her employer. The elderly man was a bachelor and former banker, a lifestyle which had, only until recently, given him few financial worries. He grumbled at the idea of tenants and only came around to it through the assurance of Miss Landers.

The estate seemed wonderful then to Bernard: the weather warm, Maggie big with Alice, and Stephen in awe of the corridors he could run down. A warm place, made warmer with the vivaciousness of Miss Landers and the sense of new beginnings for the family. Then, the seasons changed, and with it, came the snow.

In the second-floor hallway was another radiator. Bernard passed it, knowing full well the ornate coils were just as devoid of warmth as Crawford himself. He rarely left his quarters, whether due to a queer disposition or disgust of his tenants, Bernard could not say.

When the first snow fell, Miss Landers had promised that the heat would come on. It never did. Miss Landers began to look harried while bringing up trays of food to Crawford's study. Something disturbed her. When Miss Landers announced her holiday, she insisted she needed to see her people in the country to lighten her spirits. Before she went, she said that she gave Crawford a sharp tongue about turning on the heat and he would abide. But in Miss Landers's absence, there was only more snow. And the second floor had grown quiet.

The silence broke with Bernard's knuckles on the study door.

"Mr. Crawford, sir? I must speak with you immediately." Thinking of his family, he raised his voice. "We must turn on the boiler. It is only getting colder, and we must act now. If not for me and my family, sir, then for your own pipes, for they may very well freeze over. Think sensibly, sir. Sir?"

From behind the door came the sneering voice. "Telling me what to do in my house? You may get away with talk like that with Miss Landers but not with me. Away with you."

"Where would that be, sir? The snowbank?"

"It'll be the first bank you may well have stepped into. I am not a charity, Mr. Hinkley, and I have gone on long enough as a boarding house. Your words fall on deaf ears."

"Then what about this, hey?" Bernard pounded on the door with both fists. His brow broke with sweat. It was the warmest he had felt in a week. "How's your hearing now?"

A cry of disgust preceded the door swinging open. Looming at the threshold was Richard Crawford. Bernard had not seen his landlord in weeks—all told, Bernard could count with one hand how many times he had ever laid eyes on him. The state of deterioration still shocked him.

Crawford's baleful stare came from hollowed sockets. His skin pallid and gray hair matted. He wore only a night shirt and slippers. When the old man leaned down, Bernard caught the wild aroma of sweat, dirt, and soiled linens.

"This is my house, and I will do with it as I please. You are a pest to me, Hinkley. A pest with a brood. A way to rid a house of pests is the cold, to which I am now most acclimated." His smile was a cobble of yellowed stones.

Bernard resisted backing away, even as the man's horrid breath washed over him. "Sir, you're not well. Unlock the cellar, please. I will stoke the boiler myself. There must be something to burn down there. Spare wood perhaps. My family cannot go another night in this condition. Neither can you, despite what you say."

"I have no concerns for the flesh. It is a dull cage that holds the soul, nothing more. I know this now. I have seen the truth." From underneath his nightshirt, Crawford drew out a sturdy silver chain. On it was a single key, covered with grime. "You will know soon enough if you stay. Perhaps first with your youngest...Alice, isn't it?"

Hearing the old man say his daughter's name sent hot, ugly pulses to Bernard's brain. With every syllable, his skull tightened, as if in a vice.

"Give it to me." He hardly recognized the menace in his voice.

"First, it will be Alice, then your brat of a boy," Crawford said. "Two dead mice to be thrown out with the rubbish. And what will mother mouse think of that, Hinkley? I suspect she'll die from grief and blame the rat that brought her here—"

Bernard leaped into the study.

Crawford scrambled back.

His slippers caught on the carpet, and his gnarled feet popped clean out of them.

Bernard landed on top of the old man, pinning him with both knees. His hands clenched the silver chain around the old man's throat. The key bobbed up and down in a merry jig.

"Give it to me. This is how we live." Bernard twisted more of the chain into his fists. "Stop fighting and give it to me..."

Alice froze to death. Then Stephen. And finally, Maggie. Withered statues that crumbled and disappeared into an endless snow.

Their shadows revolved in his mind.

He panted in short hiccupping breaths, recovering from a nightmare.

The snow fell outside the study window.

Crawford lay cold beneath him. In the tussle, the chain had broken. An angry red line burned around the old man's throat. A filmy gauze had slipped across his blank eyes. The frost from the freezing room already doing its work.

Outside, the snow kept falling.

Bernard steadied his breathing then cocked his ear. The study door was ajar, but not by much. Whatever sounds made in the study had to have traveled down the hall to the first floor for Maggie and the children to hear.

He doubted they did.

The carpet, burgundy as blood, had absorbed most of the violence.

They would have heard nothing below.

Bernard slowly closed the door.

He had no idea how much time had gone by.

He had to dispose of the body and quickly.

The nook underneath Crawford's desk was too small. Bernard decided against the wardrobe: full of musty, dirt-encrusted clothes that reeked of sickness. He couldn't bring himself to touch any of it. All of the drapes were too short to hide behind. Tucking the body underneath a rug was ridiculous. Above him, the eyes of a much younger, yet just as haughty, Richard Crawford watched him from the gilt frame of an oil painting.

One dead mouse, two dead mice, three dead mice…

He tried the bed chamber. Around the room, on tables and shelves, set trays of rotten food. Apple cores, orange peels, spent tea leaves, bits of bones. The remnants of the old man's last meals. Miss Landers had brought those trays to Crawford and never returned to get them. By that time, she probably knew her employer was too far gone for the frivolities of cleanliness.

Rinds of rotten fruit tucked into the unkempt sheets. He expected the ripe rot of food and dirt and—somewhere he hadn't discovered—excrement from Crawford's sty. Except Bernard inhaled only the wintry, lifeless air of the room.

His breath fogged away.

"The cold is dampening the smell. It's holding the stench inside." He stifled a gag and went to the task.

The body was far lighter to move than Bernard expected. He hooked his hands under Crawford's arms to drag him. The old man's head lolled back. Bernard forced himself not to gaze down. He feared those dead eyes would make him go mad himself.

The chamber bed had rich velvet curtains that hung from each of its posters. Bernard pulled back one of them to peek underneath the bed.

"Not as comfortable as goosefeathers," he said, "but it will do."

He pushed the old man under the bed, first by the knees, then by a bony shoulder. Before he dropped the velvet back into place, something glimmered in the darkness. The chatoyant edge of an open eye, watching him.

How much time had gone by? Twenty minutes? Two hours? He hadn't any idea. None of the clocks were wound in Crawford's quarters.

An apple core lay near his shoe. He kicked it inside the bed chamber and shut the door.

All of the perishables were put away.

Bernard stifled a laugh.

He wasn't feeling well.

As he left the study, he tallied how much money he had left in his accounts and figured what the price would be for passage to Ireland, where they had no family. No great aunts to gossip about their whereabouts. When the snow let up, they would leave.

In the shadows came a noise. Bernard stopped at the stairs, his hand clenched on the railing. The noise came again. A wet, hissing gurgle. The sound took shape in his mind.

He's dead. I know Crawford is dead.

But in the dark hall, the old man's corpse crouched along the wall opposite the study, lying in wait.

Terror seized Bernard. He swayed at the top of the steps. His heels hung on air. Only his grip on the railing kept him from falling.

Crawford hissed, the steam of his pungent breath shooting into the air. Bernard waited for him to pounce, to sink his dead fingers into the carpet. To crawl after Bernard. Except Crawford only waited, watching him. And hissing.

Bernard built up his courage. If he was going to die, he was going to do it like a man. He walked back down the hall, his heart beating fast. As his perspective shifted, Crawford changed shape, or rather the thing Bernard thought was Crawford. From the stairs, Bernard swore he saw Crawford's face, the pallor of his dead flesh. When he got closer, the face broke apart into the lines of an ornate pattern, the very one Maggie had called garish. What Bernard thought was a body was the hallway radiator.

He should have felt like a fool, his fear getting the best of him. Only, he felt more unease. Miss Landers had told them the radiators would make funny noises from time to time. Trapped air in the pipes may force its way out, and there were so many pipes deep in the house. Behind walls. Under floors. So many unseen places. Bernard hadn't given it much thought before. Now, it plagued his mind, especially when the radiator next to him wheezed again.

He couldn't believe his ears. A familiar sound.

A death rattle, the very one from Crawford himself.

The sound of nightmares.

Bernard headed for the stairs. They would leave tonight. He couldn't bear to spend another second in this mausoleum, for that was what it had become. Yes, tonight they would go to the harbor, and he would pay a dockman all of his money to stow them away and sail off.

The fantasy was fixed in his mind when he walked into the flat. Candles were lit around the room, flickering light and casting shadows. Maggie sat on a tatty ottoman with Alice on her shoulder. Stephen lay on the floor. A zoetrope spun before the boy, and he peeked through the slits to watch.

"It's a man on a horse, Mother," he said. "Handy Jack is riding away."

"Oh, Stephen. What an imagination." Maggie turned as Bernard entered. "There you are. Just in time for one of Stephen's stories. I should think one more before bed to celebrate."

"Only one more?"

"Celebrate?" Bernard asked. He attempted to listen to the house, his family, and his thoughts at the same time. "What have we to celebrate?"

"No need for modesty, darling. We're so thankful for what you did with Crawford."

"...did the radiators tell you?"

"That's a funny way of putting, but yes, they did."

Stephen found this conversation more interesting than his zoetrope. "I heard it first. The radiator over there made the strangest noise. *Shhhhhh*, it sounded like, as if to keep quiet about a secret...but we knew what you did, Father."

"Ah, yes," Bernard said, his voice cracking, "you found out."

"Darling, are you all right? You look a bit flushed. Is the room too warm for you?"

Bernard tried to stifle another laugh. What a ridiculous question. The nerve. He had done so much for them, and now, they thought he was sick? Did they know what was behind the velvet curtain? Did they know what he heard?

From the perch of Maggie's shoulder, Alice giggled and nuzzled back into her mother's neck.

Bernard noticed the change in his family. Alice was free of the swaddling blanket Maggie had bundled her in before. The baby's fine hair damp on her head. Warm, almost hot. So was Maggie, her shoulder bare where she cuddled Alice. The overcoat she had taken to wearing indoors now heaped on the floor next to a black shawl and a few potato sacks. In just a shirt and knickers, his son Stephen looked like the thin boy he really was. What a change: his family cozy for the long winter's night.

But how? *How?*

"Yes, it is warm indeed," Bernard said. He tried to keep his voice steady. "It was quite a chore to get the boiler stoked. I must have overworked myself. But, I'll be fine."

The lies came so easily that he wondered when he would stop.

"I am glad Crawford came to his senses," Maggie said. "You must have had strong words with him, darling. I am so sorry I doubted you."

"I do what is best for this family. This...this is how we live."

"It can snow forever if it wants. We will be warm now, thanks to Father."

"Let's hope for something shorter. Perhaps in the next few days, it will clear. Miss Landers won't want to be stuck in the Midlands all winter, would she? I'm sure Crawford is a right mess without her. Is he eating, Bernard?"

"Oh, plenty." The rotten food in the bedroom would start to putrefy in the growing heat. His stomach lurched. "He can last a little while longer."

"There's the secret again," Stephen said, running to the radiator. "Do you hear it, Father?"

"I do, son. Extraordinary."

Bernard forced a smile. It was a lovely scene when he thought about it. A good memory for years to come, so long as he feigned hearing a gentle hissing on a snowy night. He must never let on that all he heard were the gasps of a dying man, ones that echoed through the pipes all around him.

Eventually, he would say he needed to check the boiler, and that would be the lie to leave them for the cellar. How many hours from then? Bernard could not say. He only longed to see the fire in the boiler, the one that sprang to life just as he snuffed out another. He would stare through the grate of that dull cage and watch the flames inside, the very soul of Crawford's house now keeping his family warm. He wanted to feel saved like they did.

Because Bernard was so cold, he felt nothing at all.

NIGHT TERROR
Kacie Berghoef

I should have known better than to rent a ground floor flat. It's too late to have regrets about eschewing a doorman and not installing a security alarm when I hear the robbers enter. My only phone is in the same room as them.

Almost paralyzed, I lie quietly under the covers, not daring to make a sound as the strangers go through my possessions, my memories, and my livelihood.

I feign sleep as the bandits enter my bedroom. My eyes sewn shut, clatter surrounds me. Footsteps approach.

"Kill her," one whispers.

The knife is at my throat.

I should have known better than to rent a flat with a gas heater. But a deal was a deal, and I needed a place to rest my head.

The heater smells funny, different from the electric appliances I used to have, but so do the creaky oven and stove. *I'll get used to it*, I reassure myself as I go to bed.

As I go to sleep, I start to smell the sulfur intensifying, hear the growing hissing sounds, and feel increasingly dizzy from the air growing thinner. My breath grows shallower, and I gasp for air.

At least I am fully asleep for the final stage of the process.

I should have known better than to rent an ancient flat. New construction was more practical, but my heart cried out for character and charm.

From move in day, my imagination goes awry when I keep hearing and seeing strange things. When it keeps me up at night, I get a prescription for sleeping pills.

I don't believe in ghosts, but one night, energy pulses in my body as strange beings whisper to me in a language I don't understand. I beg for mercy and forgiveness, but they slowly weaken me, cleverly and deliberately paralyzing my limbs.

Now fully possessed, the person I was is gone.

My eyes dart open, my pulse races, and my body is caked in sweat. I curl my fingers and wiggle my toes. They are intact.

I walk to the front door of my ground floor flat, carefully checking for picked locks and signs of people. All is quiet and bolted.

I stumble in the dark to my old gas heater, taking a whiff. It's a little dusty; perhaps, I should clean it.

Carefully, I approach my bed and open my closet, looking and listening for strange sights and sounds. No monsters are lurking.

My breath slowing and deepening, I climb back into bed and feel my arms and legs loosen. I adjust my pillow and shift onto my side.

As sleep descends on my body, the night envelopes me with its embrace.

MIRROR, MIRROR
D.C. Phillips

Frank wriggled the key into the lock of room 104 and flung open the door. Its hinges screamed, and the odor immediately struck Starla, transporting her and conjuring images of her grandma's musty basement where she used to play as a child.

They followed the faded diamond-patterned carpet that led from the lobby, to the hallway, and directly into the bleak, low-ceilinged room. Frank unburdened himself of their luggage with a grunt and pulled Starla into his best attempt at a romantic embrace. His thick arms wrapped around her midsection and his one-track hands slipped down her lower back to cup the slight bump of her buttocks.

"Francis." Starla shook off his grip.

He whirled her around—like a ballerina in a jewelry box—and pulled her close from behind. His chin nuzzled its way into the crook between her neck and shoulder.

"Just wait, baby," he said in his gravelly voice. "Once all of this blows over, we'll be living in the lap of luxury."

This place certainly wasn't it; the armpit, maybe, but not the lap. From the shady characters who lurked in the shadows of the defunct gas station across the lot to the pinkish lead paint eroding in flecks from the building's exterior, this place gave Starla a major case of the creeps.

The witchy woman at the front desk, a lithe older lady based on the fine lines that pulled away from her eyes and sable features that blended into the shadows of the low-lit lobby. Her funky t-shirt-and-jeans style was offset by the intensity of her gaze, which remained undeterred even when Frank asked for a light for his smoke. Her lips formed a silent smirk, and she stared with her voodoo eyes.

What was her problem?

"Look, babe, I gotta take care of some pressing matters in the bathroom.

I'll see you when I see ya." He winked and gave Starla a kiss on the temple.

"Sure, Frankie." She sighed. "But don't be long. I don't wanna be alone."

Jumpy, her body ached.

What was that old saying about a frog in boiling water?

She shrugged her shoulders luxuriously and made her way to a polished mahogany vanity halfway across the room. An oversized oval mirror hung precisely at eye level from a seated position, so she pulled out the matching bench and settled herself. Digging through her purse for a collapsible brush, she turned it over in her hands, fingers rubbing the bristles; any sensation felt good.

Starla should feel terrible about what she had done, about the role she had played in ending Tommy's life. But the simple fact was that she felt fine. Hell, better than fine.

Why it had taken so long?

She giggled and pursed her lips in the mirror with its rich oak frame. "Mirror, mirror on the wall…"

That wasn't really her in the mirror. *Was it?* Haggard, worn, terrified. And in a flash, a figure came into focus beside her. Those eyes had expressed affection and devotion for so many years…and betrayal in those final, tumultuous moments.

"Tommy." The name formed on her lips, and her eyes dropped to the jagged, seeping wound at his side.

In spite of herself, she screamed.

A toilet flushed, and Frank emerged.

"Baby, what's wrong?" He panted, overexerting himself. "Are you crazy? We can't cause a commotion. We're not outta the woods yet."

She blinked and saw her reflection, deer in headlights, and stood to return Frank's vice grip.

Without words, she allowed Frank to pull her to the bed.

Indigestion—mixed with a seed of guilt—robbed Frank of sleep.

Maybe if I roll onto my back.

Starla fussed in her dreams, turning away as he readjusted himself.

Much better.

He settled in.

The flickering beyond the bed caught his attention. Groping the nightstand to his right, his palm gripped the TV remote. Most nights, he couldn't sleep without a bit of white noise, but tonight felt different. He felt…uneasy. Even Starla's gentle inhalations grated his nerves in his current restlessness.

The TV died in the middle of a home shopping infomercial, and the room went black.

His eyes snapped open, and the flickering pulsed against the ceiling again. Pushing back layers of covers, he eyed the scratchy carpet. Cringing and second guessing his bare feet, he slipped into the pair of loafers he had left nearby.

The glimmering came from the mirror, an acute flash of light, almost imperceptible if not for the stark backdrop of darkness. Frank's mind jumped to one of those bug-zapping lanterns that beckoned unsuspecting insects, then—*bzzt*.

What a stupid idea.

The TV was off, so it must be a reflection from the parking lot, or a crack around the door. Sure, the curtains were thick, but this place sure as hell wasn't air tight.

The instep of Frank's foot seized in a tingly wave. In spite of this sharp seizure, he propelled himself forward, hobbling his way over to the vanity table and stopped short.

That couldn't be him in the mirror. Not that he was a remarkably handsome man, but the Frank in the mirror was ugly. Hideous. Intently staring eyes, his jaundiced jaw set firm, Frank touched his reflection's face, but Reflection Frank's hands stayed balled into fists at his sides.

The same balding Frank, same dark circles under his eyes, same wife beater. But Reflection Frank lifted an arm—and Real Frank's eye caught the glint of the switchblade tucked into his palm.

Real Frank's body froze, the surreal horror of the moment settling in like ice. The thudding of his heartbeat reverberated up through his torso and into his skull, churning up a wave of nausea.

Schwing. The tiny yet pragmatic blade commanded Real Frank's entire concentration. Reflection Frank lurched into the foreground, revealing a misty figure in the distance.

"Tommy…" Real Frank muttered. He lifted his gaze from the weapon in Reflection Frank's hand. Real Frank's incredulous eyes locked with Reflection Frank's anger-glazed ones, and the knife entered his liver.

Real Frank dropped to the grimy floor.

The stretch of highway between the suburbs and the city was flanked by construction on either side, exacerbating Camille Ranger's already heightened sense of anxiety. She had spent an hour longer on the road than she'd initially expected, and her plan was quickly unraveling. As if in answer to unspoken prayer, Tarver's Motel's faded neon sign blinked red-orange in the distance.

As a general rule, she refused to stay in a hotel with a number in the name. Seeing the Tarver Motel, she realized she'd have to expand her criteria.

Note to self: Never stay in a place with a family name in the title—other than Hilton.
But unusual times called for unusual measures, so here she found herself, in a desolate parking lot on the shoulder of I-85 South.

The woman at the front desk wore a chipped name tag that read, "Dyana Tarver, owner." Her pupil-less eyes simultaneously beckoned and chilled the newcomer. Dyana grabbed a key, and Camille found herself able to break the proprietor's mesmerizing stare. Extending a hand, Dyana offered a key that dangled from between a set of pointed slate nails.

"I think you'll feel right at home in room 104. It's just what you deserve," Dyana said, "after all this traffic."

The woman gave Camille the willies, with her knowing gaze and her ageless mystique. She smelled of baby powder and licorice. Just like licorice, her pupils and nails were jet black, in contrast to her creamy brown skin.

Camille nodded politely and backed away. She stumbled as she rounded a corner, and the smiling Dyana disappeared from view.

Unit 104 was drab to say the least. From the bunched swag curtains to the chenille bedspread, this place was in dire need of a facelift. A facelift—now that would be a great investment once the deposit processed...

Camille slipped out of a pair of aqua blue flip flops and yelped as a sharp pain jabbed her left sole. She stooped to inspect the worn floor below.

A diamond earring.

Camille shrugged and pocketed the jewel. *Could be worth something.*

Camille laid her purse down on the double bed nearest the door. She unzipped the main pocket and rifled through the bag's contents. Thank God, the pistol was still tucked neatly under the fat, crumpled envelope. She must have checked every ten minutes for the past hour-and-a-half. Was it just her imagination, or was the firearm still warm to her touch?

She glanced around.

Ugh. A hot shower would be just what the doctor ordered.

Determinedly, she set out for the dingy eggshell door across the room.

Someone had left the bathroom light on, and her eyes followed the beams that bounced off of a mirror in the center of the room.

She stopped to primp.

Will Payton 11/6/18 The Freedom To Kill Things and Take What You Want

458

THESE WALLS SPEAK
Andrea L. Staum

Usually, atmosphere doesn't affect me. I need to touch something for my abilities to kick in, but the amount of false grief in Grandma's house made me ill. Excusing myself from a conversation with a cousin I hadn't seen in years, I sought a place I could be alone with my own sadness. Most of the bereaved were queued for the potluck dinner in the kitchen, and the rest were in their respective familiar knots on the main level. I made my way upstairs to the guestroom.

This was the room I spent the most time in as a child, but it was different from how I remembered it. Only the bare mattress stood on end against the wall. Everything else had been parceled out to relatives long ago. Grandma had wanted to make sure everyone got what she wanted them to have while she had been alive to avoid the inevitable fighting that would follow her death.

I looked at the flattened carpet where the dollhouse had stood and remembered that it had been sold to help pay some of the medical expenses. It had been years since I'd thought about the dollhouse, but its loss weighed heavily on me now.

The window overlooked the large yard, with the sickly apple trees and towering lilac bushes, and I rubbed at my eyes. So many happy hours spent here, and now, it all seemed like an empty shell. They would sell the house, and since Grandpa had built it in the forties, it would likely be torn down because it wasn't up to code. Shaking my head to clear such morbid thoughts, I turned to leave, but the east wall stopped me.

Funny how a simple structure can ease sadness.

Every other wall in the small, two story home was white except this one. The accent wall had been painted to appease me and my sister, Demeter, when I was six. We begged for the change since we spent so much time playing in the room when our parents were away on an archeological dig.

This had been a room of happiness and color in our ever-shifting world. After my brother was born, our visits grew shorter and shorter because Dad took a university professorship while Mom stayed home.

The periwinkle-colored wall was the only one that did not need repair since no holes punctured the plaster to hang pictures. Some long-yellowed residue from a poster Demi had put up one summer stained its perfection, but other than that, the surface gleamed in the sunlight.

One spot dulled where the color was almost worn away and the old white peeked through. Once sure I was alone, I wriggled my hand out of my right glove. I didn't usually use my retro-cognitive clairvoyance unless I was working, but the temptation was too great. With tentative fingers and held breath, I reached out. A strong energy emitted. Letting out my breath, I stepped forward.

I never know what I'm going to see when I touch an object. I never know what I'm going to sense. Since I started work with the Clark Agency, I controlled more of what I saw—thanks to my boss's vigilance. Still, what I stepped into when my palm touched the wall was nothing I could have prepared for, and it overwhelmed me.

Time slid backwards, days of nothing except my grandma coming in and leaning against this spot. Entire years went by of just her staring at this empty room. Objects would come and go, depending on the season. Occasionally, a guest would pop into the view. It whirled, and it took some time to adjust to the quick blips. Then, it slowed, and more familiar objects came into the room—the dollhouse Grandpa built for our mother took up the entire western corner, the small vanity Grandma repurposed as a play kitchen, and the old steamer trunk filled with frilly dresses and costume jewelry. This was the way the room had been on our last overnight visit. The way the room always looked when I was a little girl.

The whirlwind of memories slowed as an eleven-year-old Demi and thirteen-year-old me ran into the room. I was chasing her because she took something. I no longer remembered what, but it had been important at the time.

Demi stopped short, and I ran into her back.

"Grandma, what'cha doing?" she asked.

Grandma sat on the edge of the bed with her back to the door. She muttered under her breath as she absently brushed the hair of a doll. It was my favorite, Stephanie. She jumped at Demi's voice, set the doll down, and fidgeted with the edge of the comforter. "Nothing, Sweet Pea. Just making sure everything is ready."

"Ready for what?" my younger self asked before jumping on the bed.

My left hand crept to my belly as I remembered the impact of the pointy springs in the old mattress.

"You're going on a journey."

"Uh-huh," Demeter replied, her eyes bright with excitement.

I remembered when this had happened. Dad had a dig that took the entire summer, and he decided to take all of us along. We'd spent a week with Grandma while our parents made sure the camp was child ready. This had been our last long visit with Grandma and Grandpa. We had done day trips or an overnight excursion, but nothing more. Once Grandpa died, the day trips turned into only a few hours as Grandma's memory had gone.

Demi tried to take the doll from Grandma's side, but the old woman wouldn't let her get ahold of it.

"This is your sister's dolly. You can have the one in the red dress," she scolded and reached her hand out to take my gloved one and put it over the silky dress. "Now, remember to take good care of her, Sweet Pea."

"Can I take her with me?" I asked.

Grandma nodded and let go of my hand as she stood. When she left the room, her hand brushed against the wall and through my present day self. "Now, how do my little Sweet Peas feel about some supper?"

As my younger self rolled off the bed, the doll's rough hair brushed against my bare cheek. I touched the same area of my face. I hadn't reacted to that simple touch. How could that have been?

The images faded, and I sat alone in the room once more. I lost track of Stephanie over the years. More than likely, she was packed away in storage, but only now did I realize how calm I had been when I'd held her. It was the only toy that I had ever owned that I hadn't needed to wear my gloves to play with. Any other toy assaulted me with images of the factory and vats of molten plastic or, in extreme cases, cotton being ripped from the plant.

Stephanie hadn't done that, even though she was old and been played with by countless little girls. Playing with her had always been like being hugged. Had that been why Grandma muttered to it? Could she have been infusing it with her love?

It was a heavy thought, and I let my hand drop, bare knuckles once more touching the plaster. The room changed again. All four walls were bright white, and a plastic drop cloth crinkled under tiny bare feet as I helped Grandma carry a paint can into the room. Demeter followed carrying a paint roller as if she were a beauty pageant queen and it her prize flowers.

"Now step back, Sweet Peas, this is grown-up work," Grandma said as we crowded around her, trying to help pry the paint lid with our tiny fingers.

"Wanna help." Demi whined, her lips twisting in a pout that hollowed her plump cheeks.

I nodded in enthusiastic agreement.

"I said you could help, but not yet." She shook her head in defeat. "Why don't you make sure the floor's covered good. There's some tape on the nightstand. Make sure the door hinge is covered. The one you can *reach*. Don't go climbing around and getting yourselves hurt."

Grandma carefully pulled a pair of latex gloves from her pocket and cringed as they slid over her fingers. I hadn't noticed it before, but she'd always tended to keep from touching items. Grandpa had done all the shopping, and when she cooked, she'd always worn some type of glove.

I dismissed it as her not wanting to dirty her hands, but now…was there something more? Could clairvoyance be a recessive gene? My ability inherited? Not just some random gift of nature?

I leaned against the wall as the phantom roller went over it, changing the hospital white that had bothered me so much as a child to a fresh periwinkle that matched the Easter bonnets Grandma made for Demi and me. She paused when she came to the spot I stood and reached a gentle hand out to the same spot where mine rested. I stared into her pale blue eyes for what seemed like the first time, and my breath caught in my throat.

There was a crash and clatter behind her, and the moment was over. I followed her movement to see Demi coated in paint and the bucket tipped over on the chair beside her.

"Didn't I tell you to be careful? What did you do?" Grandma asked through tight lips.

Tears streamed down my sister's cheeks as she waddled over to Grandma with outstretched arms.

"St-st-stop." Grandma stammered biting her lip to keep from laughing at the ridiculousness.

My younger self stared, wide-eyed, thinking she would yell, but Grandma was trying hard to stay stern-faced.

"Hestia, get the paint can and a brush. Let's see how much of this we can save. Stop crying, Demi, you'll water it down."

I laughed as Grandma brushed the excess paint off Demi and back into the can. Not much was accomplished on the wall, but my sister looked like an ill smurf by the time the can was half full. When we couldn't wring anymore from her hair or clothes, Grandma called it a day and sealed the can before shepherding out of the room to a much-needed bath.

I broke contact with the wall and examined the worn patch on it. I didn't often have so much control over my ability. Somehow, every image dealt with my life. I knew my cousins had stayed at times, too, but these glimpses were specific to me. I couldn't explain how that worked, but my grief eased with each remembrance, and it allowed me to see Grandma as she had been, before she had become an incoherent wreck that most of the family shunned. I leaned into the wall, letting my forehead rest against its surface.

This time a cradle sat next to the bed. Grandma and Grandpa used it when Demeter was born. I hated the thing with its soot-stained sides that wouldn't come clean, no matter how many times it was washed. Something about it repelled me, and I had never touched it as a child.

A scream came from the cradle, and a tiny arm flailed above the lip of it.

Grandma rushed into the room and scooped a diaper clad baby from it. She kicked the cradle over and turned her back to it.

"You're a special little girl, Hestia," Grandma said as she wrapped baby me in a crocheted blanket. "Too much has happened in that crib for your liking. You can sense it all, and we can't have that, now can we?"

My infant self relaxed under Grandma's gentle touch. I had forgotten that she had always bundled herself in a shawl or wore long sleeves even in July.

I must have inherited my ability.

The revelation almost made me step back, but with strong will, I forced myself to keep contact with the wall.

"Yes, Sweet Pea, you're my special one," Grandma said. "Your momma knows how to handle your gift. No worries there. Just wrap yourself in love, and the bad ones don't come through." She kissed me before laying me back into the crib. "And when you're older, I'll help." She looked over her shoulder to the spot on the wall where my current self viewed the scene and winked before giving a sad, gentle smile.

I couldn't help myself. Part of me wanted to embrace her, and my hand slipped away from the wall. The room returned to the present, and I blinked away the disorientation. She couldn't have known I would have seen any of that. Still, she smiled as if she knew one day I'd be here to witness the past.

I shook my head, trying to dislodge the thought.

Someone else was in the room, someone out of focus who Grandma acknowledged.

There was, of course, the chance that she had known, but that would mean she had precognitive ability, not retro. Everything pointed to her having retro. Why else had she worn a spot in the paint on the wall with her touch other than to relive these memories? As far as I know, no one can be capable of both.

If it could happen, and Grandma could sense both the past and future, it explained a lot. It was hard enough keeping track of one's own memories, but pile on those of every object and person you come in contact with…I couldn't even imagine the mental strain.

My mother found me in a huddled heap crying in front of the wall. Every day, Grandma had come to this spot to relive our visits.

"You figured it out?" Mom asked as she knelt beside me.

I nodded, wiping my nose on my sleeve. "Why didn't you tell me?"

Mom dug a wrinkled tissue from her pocket and wiped the tears from my cheeks. "By the time you would have needed her guidance, you had found the Institute."

"She expected me to come back," I sobbed and leaned into Mom's embrace. "I just stopped coming. It was too hard to be here."

"It was hard for all of us. We let ourselves become too busy. The repetition of questions and the constant fear something would go wrong was too much." She squeezed me tighter. "Don't blame yourself for anything, Tia. I'm the failure."

I broke away from her embrace and asked, "Did she see both? Was she pre and retro?"

Mom tucked an errant curl behind her ear, refusing to meet my gaze as she pulled another tissue from her pocket. "I don't know. Growing up, I just knew she was different from the other moms. Then, when you were born and acted the same way, I figured there was no difference between you both. Why?"

I looked up at the worn spot on the wall. "I don't think Grandma was sick. I think she was lonely and let herself get lost in the memories of this house. She came to this room every day. The paint's infused with her thoughts, and every one I saw was of Demi and me as little girls. In every one, she looked at that spot. Like she knew I'd be here one day, and I'd see it."

Mom allowed a soft smile that I had long learned meant I was wrong and she would humor me. "Oh, Tia, that's a nice thought, but your grandma was diagnosed with dementia years ago, even before Grandpa passed."

I scrubbed at my eyes with the palms of my hands, trying to clear my thoughts and refocus. The visions had been so clear. How could I explain to my mother something she barely understood? Tilting my head back I searched for the words while Mom waited for me to come to her conclusions. A part of me knew she was wrong though, and I had to voice it. "I don't think she was. I think she was lost in her hope that I'd come back. That I'd listen to her and learn the control she had mastered over the years. But she let it slip as she waited, and everything came back. All those memories and hopes just took over.

"She didn't know which time was real. Each time she repeated a question wasn't because she forgot she had asked it. She just didn't know which conversation was real. She didn't know if she was remembering the last time, the next time, or the current time." I forced myself to stand. The revelation made my legs weak, and I used the smooth wall as support.

The vision showed the room more presently; the toys had long been packed away, and the bed had been stripped of linens, waiting to be made for the next guest. Grandma sat on the end of the bed, staring at the wall with her hands picking at the worn hem of her shawl. After a few moments, she sighed and turned away, the sun streaming in from the window turning her light-blue eyes silver.

"I'm probably wrong, Sweet Pea. Can't make sense of it anymore. Too many things going through my mind. I keep seeing your Grandpa, but not like before. Not as the young man I married nor the old man I buried. I never seen him like this, and that's all right. I think." She came over to the wall. "I think he's telling me it's time to go, and I think I'm ready for that. Wish I had taught you more, but you're like your momma. Smart and stubborn.

"You'll do well, Hestia. Don't take the burden on yourself. You're apt, too. That stubbornness was all your Grandpa's doing." She placed a hand on the wall next to my face and glanced back once more with the same knowing smile. "Surround yourself with love, Sweet Pea, and the bad can never hurt you. Even when the bad is hard to take, it can't hurt you, and eventually, it all evens out."

She looked at the window once more.

The vision faded, and Mom was reaching to comfort me but stopped short. She never interrupted my visions, but her pale eyes, the same blue as Grandma's, were brimmed with tears. She was ignoring her own grief to take care of me but didn't know how.

I hadn't taken my hand from the wall. If I forced it, I could see more, but somehow, I knew that was it. That was the last thing Grandma wanted me to see and to delve deeper would go against her wishes. "They found her in this room didn't they?"

Mom stood beside me, biting her lip before nodding.

"She said good-bye."

Mom let out a whimper, and the tears began to slide town her rouged cheeks.

"It's okay, Mom. I believe she knew her time was ending," I said putting my arms around her and lending my strength to her. As the final vision set itself into my memory, my grief eased. It didn't subside completely, it was too fresh for that, but I knew now that Grandma wouldn't want me to wallow. Nor would she want Mom to.

I wiped away Mom's tears and made sure she was looking me in the eye before I explained.

"Grandma wanted to make sure we knew she at peace with it. Otherwise, she wouldn't have infused this room with so many of her memories. She knew I'd see them. I don't know if it was because of her abilities, but somehow, she knew."

LIVES OF GHOSTS
Zoe Harrington

'Loneliness is the last feeling you forget: it lingers deep inside your bones.'
—*A Ghost*.

I can only just make out the image of Annie on the screen with our daughter, Maddie, propped on her lap. She must be getting heavy ,and I press down on my leg trying to remember what 'heavy' feels like? She's almost 140cm tall. They'd marked it on the door at home.

I will always know how beauty feels. When I look at Annie, I can see it; I can feel it in my chest; my body, where it is, must feel warm—warmth is beautiful. Her new dress looks slippery, and Maddie slides off from it, leaving without saying, "goodbye."

"Is Maddie painting?" I ask. "When I get out of here, I want to see lots of paintings."

Annie smiles; she's quiet. Maddie doesn't like painting anymore. From her tone, it's clear that she's told me this before. Someone is at their door: my brother. Maddie squeals with excitement.

Send me more pictures of Maddie—she's growing up too fast." I sound like an old aunt.

The screen goes blank.

The last time I was with Maddie, she smelled of violets and pancake batter. If they were in another country, it would be easier. I wonder if Annie is seeing someone. It's been a long time since a man held her, since I held her.

I mark Maddie's height on the door frame which is just like ours at home—everything is.

An alarm goes off: it's time for me to swim. We are encouraged to go through the same routines every day because it's good exercise for the mind and creates a sense of normality. I think about our kitchen floor as a sensory reference, rolling my toes across the tiles in the pool room. I remember the smell of chlorine being slightly metallic, or acidic, hot like summer; it burns my eyes, or it would. The water holds me, suspends me, and I soar like a bird in a gentle sky. I've forgotten wet, but I remember cold, so I shiver. My favourite thing to do here is to sit at the bottom of the pool and breathe. I look up at the world, scattered by light. I like to pretend that Annie and Maddie are just above the surface, getting ready to join me, crooning with excitement, their voices distorted like a song played in reverse. I look down at my hands as they are here and wonder if *my* hands still look the same or if they're pale, shrivelled with electric blue veins.

Another alarm goes off, reminding me to go to work.

I splash cold water on my face. In the mirror, I see that I haven't aged a day. My voice, however, is becoming more and more like my father's. I don't know if that is because I am forgetting my own or because my mind has decided that this is the natural trajectory for me.

In the kitchen at work, they're still talking about what happened, while pretending to drink coffee. I suppose it is still shocking to watch someone throw themselves out a window.

He wasn't here very long, and I can't even remember his name, but he complained a lot.

Sandy, a tall, robust woman sways into the office, carrying a large cake. It's Andrew's *re-birthday*. We all sing, then Sandy hands out pieces of brightly coloured sponge, all equally measured, all perfectly shaped. I watch her lever her tiny spoon against the paper plate and place a delicate, quivering morsel into her mouth. I think she would have had a lot of cake in her life, and now, eating that guilt-free, calorie-free figment, she must feel like she hit the jackpot. Soon, she will forget what sweet tastes like, and she will forget about birthdays. Someone needs to tell Gary that the alcohol here doesn't have any effect. Not everyone is enjoying the festivities.

Andrew sits on his own, not interacting, which is annoying everyone because it's his big day that we're all celebrating. He's finished his term here. Sandy hands him a piece of cake.

"Re-birthdays are fucked," he says. "This is all fucking bullshit."

Sandy walks off, laughing in a passive aggressive way before plunging herself in the gossip circle.

"Are you all right?" I ask him.

"They get their money's worth out of us, don't they? Well, I'm not staying here a second longer than I need to. I've paid my bills. I can go whenever I want to." He leaves, tossing the cake onto the floor.

I swear I smell Annie's perfume, but I must be just so exhausted. It's been a long day. I feel her hand on my shoulder, and she stands right behind me, but no one in the office seems to notice.

"Come on," she says, holding out her hand.

Annie has disappeared.

I am on the beach, taken from one of my childhood memories. Did I take Maddie and Annie here? I can't remember, but I hope so.

The sea rushes over my feet, pulling me towards the waves while the sand holds me back in a tug-of-war, between the land and sea.

Annie and Maddie laugh, like they're just in the distance.

The water wins, and I have lost sight of the beach. Tumbling below the surface like a sleepy acrobat, I follow Annie's voice into the darkness.

I open my eyes and am back in our house. I call out to Annie, but she doesn't answer because this is not *our* house, and I am still in stasis. I don't know how I got here. Terror rushes through me; I might be waking up.

I race to my computer to tell Annie.

She tells me that she's been speaking to me all day.

The image is so blurry that I can barely see her. She's worried about things she won't speak about for my sake. She wants me to wake up naturally; she's read that it is better, and the doctor says that I have a good chance of returning fairly functional. With a bit of therapy, I should be fine in a couple of years. She tells me all of this as if it is *our* body, and I can't help but feel annoyed.

"I won't be able to work, and I still have medical debt. I think we should wait."

"Don't you want to come home?" She gets snappy when she's angry like a yappy, little dog. It's funny the things you miss.

I feel anger rising. I think of red. "Of course, I want to come home, but I am fully functional here."

She looks too tired to cry. I wish she would cry.

"Maddie called your brother, 'daddy' yesterday."

It's such a cruel blow. She knows it.

The screen goes dark.

At the pool, I concentrate on the feeling of the tiles, the wetness of the water. I concentrate. I concentrate, but I can't feel them.

I've had dreams, many, where I am awake and screaming, and no one can hear me. I try to reach out but I can't.

Is that what I am worried about, waking up paralysed in a hospital bed? Or am I worried about what things will be like when I get home?

Annie still won't speak to me. I hold onto the picture of us at our wedding, apologising. The faces are all smudged. They're like that throughout the house.

When I walk into work, they're celebrating a re-birthday. Daniel, who has organised the cake, calls me old timer because I have been here the longest. He gives me the biggest grin, like a fucking psychopath.

The birds flying outside are in the same arrow formation they are always in. They make caged birds look free.

A child laughs, and I catch a glimpse of Maddie as she rushes out of the office. I know it's her because she's wearing her favourite purple dress. I walk straight past them all.

I follow her through the streets.

I follow until the sun recedes like a parent from a child's room.

As I reach the cliff at the end of the little beach, an alarm sounds. It keeps on sounding as I watch the waves paw and lick at the rocks below like hungry dogs.

The wind pushes me around like a rag doll as I fight to stand at the edge.

Maddie is mimicking the birds, flapping her arms, but they take no notice of her. She stands beside me, holding my hand.

"Come on, daddy," she says.

ROOM TWENTY-TWO
Irina Slav

Room twenty-two. That's our room, though I'm not really sure what *our* is supposed to mean in these circumstances.

There are six of us: an elderly couple, a blond girl, me, and a couple of boys. Not boys, men. I don't remember their names. We hardly speak; most of the time, we just sit on the three beds in the room and the two chairs, and look around or down.

Something is wrong, but I don't know what it is. The air weighs heavy with anxiety, fear and confusion, and some desperate hopelessness. But nobody says a word.

Now and then, one of us would get up to look through the window and go back to our place and sit down and hang our head.

I don't even know where we are. It's some large building, a rundown hospital or a very low-class hotel. But if it's a hospital or something similar, where are the people? Where are the nurses and the doctors? Besides, I don't feel sick, and the others look healthy enough, too.

I remember my favorite dream, the dream I hope I never forget.

Maybe I'm dreaming now? No, that can't be. Everything looks so real.

So, in my favorite dream, I'm in a tunnel, like a subway, and two professional-looking guys load people into individual little cars that are not connected to anything or to each other. They load me into one of these cars, too. It's really comfortable, like my very own cab, but it takes me upwards, above ground, to a high plateau covered in the lushest and greenest grass I've ever seen.

The plateau is high above the ground and full of people. I get off the railcar and go to the edge, like looking down to earth from a plane, that's how high it is.

Somebody, a man, comes up to me and says: "Aren't you jumping?"

And I actually really want to, but I'm scared. The man gives me an encouraging smile. I trust him unquestionably, spread my arms, and jump. I'm flying.

Suddenly, I realize I'm dead. Not as a consequence of the jump, no. I died and was brought here, which is somewhere strange, but I like it because I can fly.

When I woke up that morning, I started scratching wildly at the door of my subconscious to continue dreaming.

Could it be that I've died, and this is some distribution center, like the tunnel from my dream?

No, wait. It's not a distribution center; it's something else. A safe place. A haven. A hideout.

I leave the room. First, I walk up to the last floor, the attic, which now houses all the members of a drag queen show. I like visiting them, desperation is not so bottomless there. Their hands are always busy sewing, fixing things; I don't know what else, but they never stop.

In our room, nobody does anything. Sometimes, I ask Mark, the only other smoker, for a cigarette, and sometimes, he asks me for one, and that's it. Oh, once I went with the blond girl outside to pick some apples—there's an overgrown apple orchard near the building. We picked them quickly, looking around anxiously. None of us asked the other one why we were so alarmed, and I was too embarrassed to bring it up later.

Apparently, everyone else knows why we're here, and I'm the only one who has forgotten. This is humiliating. Also, everyone looks like they want to say something, but they never do. Apart from Mark. This one looks like he never opens his mouth because he just doesn't like talking. Yes, the one with the blue eyes is Mark, the brown-eyed one is…I don't remember.

When I return to my floor, I can't find the room. I can see room twenty-four and room twenty, but for some reason twenty-two has gone missing. Panic crushes me like a dry leaf; my knees buckle under me; my stomach is in free fall; my heart's racing. On the door of twenty-four, a sign says, *Giuseppe Santini, manager.*

What's going on here? What manager? This wasn't here before.

I grab the handle and open the door without knocking. The room beyond is empty but does look like someone's office, not like our room. It's got a desk with a chair behind it.

I'm now seriously scared. My stomach is a lead ball. I shut the door, look around and see room twenty-two. I burst in and see them—they're all there. The old lady smiles to me sweetly.

"I got lost. The room disappeared." I pant, wiping my clammy hands on my jeans.

"Lost?" the old lady says, raising her eyebrows, which makes her almond-shaped eyes suddenly round.

"Disappeared?" the blond girl asks. "What do you mean it disappeared?"

"I mean it wasn't where it was supposed to be, where it was before. There were a couple of other rooms but not this one."

Mark pushes the cigarette pack along the table towards me. I shoot him a grateful look, and I start because I've clearly heard him tell me, *Nothing to worry about*. Not telepathically, not aloud. He said it with his eyes. Now, I know eyes can convey emotions but words? So clearly? Yeah, right.

Tense like an arrow in a bow whose string the bowman has stretched to the maximum but is still pulling, maybe trying to see when it will snap. Why the hell is nobody saying anything? Besides, *nothing to worry about* is a lie. There's plenty to worry about. I don't know exactly what it is, but I know it's there, the cause for worry.

The old man, the lady's husband or whatever, says he's going out to stretch his legs. I wait for his return, to see if the room won't disappear for him. He's back after a while and says nothing about disappearing rooms. So, I'll go out again to see what will happen.

What if I'm hallucinating? What if this is a mental hospital?

But it can't be a mental hospital. Who would keep six patients in a room for three?

I go out, walk to the end of the corridor, start back. Room nineteen. Room twenty-three. Room twenty. Room twenty-four, *Giuseppe Santini, manager*. What's going on here? I open the door of number twenty, and a middle-aged man smiles politely and beckons me slowly.

"Come in, come in, we were just starting the debates."

I pull back, saying under my breath I don't want to be in any debates.

Then, I get an idea and go upstairs, to the attic room, to see the showgirls. I need a ball of yarn or some thread, something like that. I'll tie one end to something in our room and take the rest with me when I go out. Let's see what happens then.

Luckily, the girls have some sort of thread—they have everything—that I start unwinding while I walk down the stairs, which is a little stupid because by the time I get to our room, the thread is a complete mess, and I can't find the end. But I do find the room. Only the elderly couple are in. The lady shrugs even before I ask about the others. I run to the stairs. I don't know why I'm running; I just know I have to. I have to find the other three; I *have* to. We must all stay inside; we mustn't go out.

Okay. Fatalistic disposition: check.

Chronic anxiety: check.

But I really don't care right now if there's a good reason for my anxiety or not.

I rush down the grand staircase that leads to the entrance of the building. I pass some guy who resembles Mark. I grab his shoulder, he turns, and I see it's some stranger. I apologize and hurry out of the building. There's a little yard there, its boundaries marked by a few old weeping willows. They really are very old, with massive, twisted trunks. I walk towards one of the trees, and someone calls my name from behind. It's the dark-eyed guy from our room. I sigh with relief. One found, two to go.

"Where's…" I start but never finish. Here, he is. He approaches slowly and extends his hand to touch mine. I grab it, and it's sweaty. He tries to smile. I'm touched. I'm so touched I throw myself into his arms and hug him tight. I don't think I'll ever again let him go, but now, we have to find the blond girl because it's getting dark.

I wake up because somebody is tapping me on the shoulder. My nose presses against the wall, hands between my knees. I turn around and see Mark, who puts his finger on his lips and motions me to get up. The elderly couple sleep in the second bed, and the dark-eyed boy and the blond girl are in the third one, in each other's arms, also asleep. Everybody is wearing the same clothes as yesterday. I have no memory of going to bed at all.

I go to the window that Mark stared through. Dawn's breaking, but it's cloudy. The air feels heavy, as it does before a storm. The room's window looks to the yard, and the willows' branches start to swing: first gently, then more violently. A stormy wind comes fast. The sky dims as if one whole day has passed in a matter of minutes, dawn until dusk, and now, night is falling.

I'm waiting for the rain.

I love rain.

The wind gains speed, the willow branches lashing like whips in the air, vortices of dust rising from the dry ground. I want the rain to start already, to relieve this pressure that's giving me a headache.

Steps rush from the corridor outside. Two, maybe three people running somewhere. In the room, the others start waking up. The old man says that he has a headache, and he'll go "stretch his legs." The old lady makes the bed, which means smoothing the sheets, we have no blankets or covers.

Anticipation annoys me. I let go of Mark's hand, which I grabbed as soon as I was within grabbing distance, and leave the room.

There's nobody in the corridor, and I remember yesterday's events with a second's delay, while I pull the door behind me. I glare at it, in its place, for now. I risk it and walk away: to the foyer to watch the storm. It's got glass doors and French windows all along the front. I have no urge whatsoever to go outside and feel the rain, though I can't explain this lack of enthusiasm. I really love rain, and the weather is nice, kind of Septembery warm.

The foyer is almost empty except for one young woman with a drawn, worried face pacing along the front windows, peeking through each one and out the glass door, again and again. She pays no attention to me as I approach. A balding man in a grey suit appears out of nowhere, passes between us, opens the door, and goes out in the coming storm.

Several other people are outside already, who don't seem to care about the wind at all. They're just standing there. Motionless.

I stick my nose to the glass and watch the tree branches dance violently.

"Excuse me."

The woman stands beside me, her messy dark hair hanging around her face, her eyes imploring.

"Have you seen my daughter? She's three and has a dark blue jacket."

I shake my head. I haven't seen any children in here. Or outside, come to think of it. The woman presses her fist to her mouth and bites on her knuckles.

"She was standing right there, and the next second she was gone."

I sympathize but have no idea how to help. I return my gaze to the yard. Why doesn't the woman go out to look for her daughter?

I see a small shape among the others, a kid's shape, just as motionless as the rest of them.

"There she is." I point.

"Where is she? Where? I can't see her."

She can't *not* see her. There is only one kid outside. But the woman stares through the glass door, eyes searching and not seeing her child. I give the door a push as if I already know it won't open. And it doesn't. I'm getting angry. Just a couple of minutes ago, it opened to let the bald guy with the grey suit through. I didn't imagine it; there he is, standing straight, not moving. To his right, between a man and a woman holding hands, is the kid. It can't be a hallucination. *It can't be.* Or maybe the woman is crazy? Somebody must be, and I really don't want it to be me.

I run upstairs, to the room, to check. Luckily, the door is there. I storm in and see everyone huddled by the window, looking out. Mark is the only one sitting on a bed, smoking. He's gazing at the floor and doesn't look up when I enter.

"Can you see the child? Can you?" I ask even before I join the huddle, worming my way between the old guy and the blond girl and pointing to the little shape outside.

"We see her, honey," the old lady says and gives me an encouraging smile. I don't know what to make of it. I try to speak in a calm and collected manner, but panic rises to the surface of my mind and is about to win again.

"Mark. *Mark.* There's a kid outside, Mark."

He looks up and tries to smile. It finally starts raining, and I suddenly know that the old lady's name is Tatyana; the old man is Andrey; the blond girl's name is Sara, and the boy's Ewan. I also remember that Mark was the first to come to this room, and I was the last. What I still don't know is why nobody is doing anything about the kid outside, where the rain is no longer just rain but a thick curtain of water. I can no longer see the kid or anybody else in the yard.

I sit next to Mark, take his hand and rest my head on his shoulder. He doesn't move.

Sara and I sit in the yard under one of the willows. I'm much calmer now, and I've learned a lot over the past few days after the storm. The panic sleeps.

"And the apples?" I ask.

Sara smiles a confused smile; her lips tremble, and she looks away.

"That's for you to know," she says.

"I don't remember ever picking apples."

She's silent.

"Oh, well, whatever."

I turn to the building, and for the hundredth time look at the word inscribed over the entrance. POST. It amuses me every time. Post? Why post? There's nobody here that can tell me.

Tonight, it's Tatyana and Andrey's turn to leave. The sky is dimming, clouds come from every direction, and the wind rises. We all sit in the room; nobody speaks. There's a knock on the door, and the man who invited me to take part in some debate a few days ago pops his head in. I still have no idea what these debates were about.

"Will you be joining us?" he asks.

Nobody says anything, so he closes the door. Tatyana looks through the window, gets up from the bed, and extends her hand to Andrey.

"Come on, darling, it's time to go."

I feel like crying. Not because I am particularly close to them, no. I know their story, and it has a happy ending, but I still feel like crying. I hug them, and so does Sara, and as far as I can see, she's on the verge of crying, too. Ewan and Mark sit on both sides of the window, not moving a muscle. Only when the couple starts towards the door, Ewan turns around and waves them goodbye, but they can't see him because they've gone out already.

The first raindrops hit the window. I find Tatyana and Andrey among the crowd in the yard. Why I want to do this, I don't know. I'll be out in the yard myself soon enough. I feel like I have an exam coming, and I haven't reviewed at all because there is nothing to study in the first place.

A moment later, Mark tugs on my hand, so I sit down. I've been tapping my foot nervously.

A week later, it's Sara and Ewan's turn. This time I don't just feel like crying; I burst into tears right there. I like them both. I'm grateful I shared a room with them. I'm sorry I didn't have a chance to know them longer. I'm sad that I'll never see them again. I'm scared of the rain. I'm scared of the wind. I'm scared there will be nobody to imagine myself picking apples with.

"I'm still here," says the last occupant of the room, who's also its first. Yes, he's still here, and it looks like he'll never leave. At least not before me.

He takes my hand, and we go into the corridor.

"Where…?"

Outside.

So soon? Now? He shakes his head. Time has passed. It's then, not now. We go out. The girls from the attic are there. To their left, alone, stands the debates man, staring up at the clouds.

Now, I know everything.

Sara and Ewan lost their lives in a car accident, when his car slipped on a frozen patch of road and swept off everyone from the pedestrian crossing. Sara was one of them.

Tatyana and Andrey died within a week of each other: she from a heart attack, and he from cancer.

The girls that are now standing beside us were the victims of a deliberate fire at the club they worked in.

The woman with the tired face caused the death of her daughter, and she'll never leave the Post.

My name is Nina, and the last thing I felt in my life was the flow of the electric current through my body when I started the shower.

All these people who get together here have been supposed to be together, sooner or later. Later, in their case.

"What about you?" I ask. "Who are you?"

"I'm the brother you never had. The son you never had. The man you never met."

He laughs, nice laughter, a good one.

"I'm your guardian angel."

"*What?*"

"Just joking." He pats me on the head and hugs me tightly.

The rain starts and soon pours down. I thought it would hurt. I always think it will, and it almost never does.

The rain washes everything away: the bad memories, the worries, the anxiety, the insecurity, the years of trying to stay ahead of life. It washes away the laughter, the tears, strips me to the bone of what I used to think was me, until there's only…

But there's no longer me.

COATROOM
Clay McLeod Chapman

The adults were all laughing in the dining room. Their disembodied voices drifted up the stairs and into my bedroom, filling the whole house like ghosts nattering on about *this* and *that*. The tipsy lilt of a woman's toast. The guffaw of an invisible man, chortling 'til he choked.

These people just wouldn't *leave*. They had been rambling on for hours. I couldn't grasp what exactly they were talking about, snatching fragments of politics. Books they'd recently read. Films they'd all seen. Boring adult stuff that went over my head.

These dinner parties were nothing but bizarre grownup rituals that made no sense. *All that talking...* I had gone to bed hours ago, but sleep wasn't coming easily. Not tonight. Not with all of Mom and Dad's friends roaring away downstairs. I kept rolling around in bed, unable to find any comfort. No matter what position I settled into, I could not avoid their voices. Their laughter. The clink of their glasses from toast after toast after toast.

That's it. All six years of myself huffed as I hopped out of bed. Some of us are trying to sleep here.

I perched myself on the stairs and listened in, pinching at the rubber-treaded soles of my footie pajamas. Superheroes wrapped around my legs. BIFF! BAM! KAPOW!

Nobody noticed me, not yet, gripping the banister's post like some prisoner staring out from behind their cell bars. Their plates still held the bones of their meal. A glaze of congealing fat glistened under the candle light. Empty wine bottles took up vigil everywhere.

One of my parent's dinner guests finally spotted me. *Looks like we've got company...*

Everybody turned. I was caught. I couldn't move, frozen.

What were they going to do to me?

Mom's face flushed from all the wine. She beamed, holding out her hands for me to rush into. *Come here, sweetie…* Her lips were stained purple, lavender teeth. Sour breath. She nuzzled her chin against the top of my head as she hugged me tight. *Were we being too loud?*

One guest took their cue and said, *Think it's time we pushed on. It's getting late…*

Mom ruffled my hair and whispered, *Would you get Mr. Pendleton's coat from our room, please?*

My mission was simple: a pea coat. Gray wool. Broad collar. Anchor-embossed buttons. This particular dinner party had taken place in the middle of winter, so everybody had come bundled up in downy jackets and scarves.

When I first entered Mom and Dad's room, I took in their bed, completely covered in coats. A mountain, in my mind. It lifted off the bed and crested to a mushrooming plug. An endless tether of sleeves slung in every direction; its limbs suspended over the mattress, as if a plump octopus had passed out.

All I had to do was find Mr. Pendleton's jacket. Pull it out. Bring it back.

Simple.

But there were so many.

Too many.

The lights were off. I hadn't thought to flip on the switch—and by then, I was already two steps into the room and didn't want to turn around. Turn my back to that bed. For some reason, I didn't trust the looks of the heap. All those sleeves set me on edge. The light from the hall illuminated my path, a column cast across the floor to the bed.

I could hear the adults' voices from down the hall. Someone, a woman, was laughing.

I took a step forward. Toward the bed.

Then hesitated.

Pea coat, I repeated to myself as I took another step, the rubberized soles of my pajamas skidding against the floorboards. Gray wool. Broad collar.

Just look for the anchors.

Look for the anchors.

The anchors.

Anchors…

I saw a sleeve slither. Just one. It simply slipped by just an inch, all on its own, shifting across the mound of jackets before settling along the bedspread.

Then, it was still.

I held my breath, waiting to see if it might move again. It didn't.

Mr. Pendleton's jacket must've been buried deeper within the pile. I had to dig my hands in. I pulled on a woman's leather jacket, peeling back the skin of that washed-up octopus.

Still no pea coat.

No anchors.

I reached my hands in, blindly rummaging through.

Where is it?

Where is it?

Where—

Something loosened against my fingers. Snake skin. I yanked my hands back and leapt away from the bed. All at once, all the coats were moving. *Writhing.* Every last one. As if a nest of serpents had just woken up, their slender leathery-skinned bodies slinked over each other. The entire pile inhaled, the chambers of its chest swelling. All the pockets filled with air.

It rose. Lifting up from the bed. A patchwork of brown leather and tawny fur-trimmed lining and denim flesh and double-breasted body parts.

Coats sloughed off its body and fell to the floor.

It was shedding its skin.

The pile took on a shape. A human form. It reached for me, several of its tentacles tangled into one another. My pajama bottoms felt warm. The floor went wet. Urine pooled in my footies. The rubber soles were suddenly slippery. I stepped back and slid, losing my balance and falling. Only when I landed on my back, the pain brought the air into my own lungs, and I found my voice and screamed and screamed and screamed.

The voices in the dining room went silent all at once. Mom raced into the bedroom and found me on the floor. She swept me into her arms, pressing me against her chest.

It had been a party guest.

A friend of the family.

He'd drank too much, he said, much too early, excusing himself from the dinner table to use the restroom and promptly passing out on top of my parents' bed. He assumed he was at home, in his own bed, tucking himself in with everybody's jackets, burrowing into their coats.

That was the story my mother told everyone that night.

Told me.

That's the story she would share at nearly every dinner party my parents would host for years to come, whispered in hushed tones well after she believed I had gone to bed.

Of course, I'd hear her.

I heard everything in our house.

We turned our room into a coat check, Caroline casually announced to our guests as they filed in. *Just toss your jackets on the bed.*

We opened our doors to any strays stranded here in the city this Thanksgiving. For those friends of ours who didn't have somewhere to go, or the funds to visit far-off family, they could break bread with us. *Bring us your poor, your hungry masses.*

Talk about a motley crew. Coworkers of Caroline's, mostly. A smattering of single pals.

This was a no-frills affair. Completely laid back.

Pot-luck.

Just bring a bottle of whatever you're drinking, we suggested in our evites. *Let's get tipsy together and list off all the things we're thankful for this year...*

My list was pretty simple: Caroline, of course.

The kids. This was Carter's sixth Thanksgiving. Laurel's second. I had volunteered for wrangling duties for the night, which mainly amounted to me keeping the kids out of the kitchen while Caroline wrestled with the turkey. She'd been manning the oven all day.

The first bottle of wine popped itself around three that afternoon, hours before our guests arrived. Not that I was keeping an eye on the clock or anything. Not that Caroline couldn't hold her liquor. She was born for these soirees. This was her natural element. She loved it. *Hostessing.* The ritual of it all. She was a natural at toasts. A high priestess of dinner parties. Glass raised, she could summon a soliloquy out of the ether and make everyone sitting around the table repeat her celebratory incantation. I'd go as far as to say the whole reason she had a family of her own was to have her own dinner parties. We didn't have to follow the pre-scripted routines of our parents' holidays anymore.

This—this was all ours. We could do whatever we wanted for Thanksgiving.

Celebrate however we wanted.

The tally was ten friends by my headcount. That made fourteen with the fam, all told, though the kids didn't really count. They'd be in bed before the real party began.

You never quite knew who might show up unannounced, but Caroline would gladly set up another place at the dinner table. Just shove everybody over an inch or two and squeeze another chair in. Most folks brought booze. So much wine. The *clink-clink* of paper-bagged bottles heralded every guest's arrival. People were pretty tipsy before the turkey had even come out of the oven. We needed to line our stomachs with some grease. Bread. Gravy. Something other than booze.

Caroline laid down the ground rules at the beginning of the night: *Anyone can make a toast whenever they want. Don't wait for anybody to prompt you. Just do it whenever the mood takes over. But you better raise a glass before the night is through...or no invite next year.*

Caroline's dinner parties were infamous amongst our circle of friends. People would actually get pissed off if they found out there had been a gathering and they hadn't been invited. It got to a point where we couldn't sit everybody at one table. We needed to add an extension. We started rotating guests, just to keep the numbers down. Keep the meals manageable. It was exhausting. Caroline loved every moment of it, but it tuckered me out.

Just to socialize so much. To partake.

I hated them.

All of them.

Every last dinner party.

Ever since I was a kid, I never enjoyed these get-togethers. Don't ask me why. This wrinkle within the deepest recesses of my lizard brain always reacted to these bashes. Telling me to retreat. *Escape while you still can.* At a certain point, I'd find myself mentally clocking out. Whole conversations would flit about me, and I'd never hear a word, fantasizing the whole time about sneaking away from the table and tiptoeing back upstairs to our bedroom and slipping under the covers and drifting off into blissful, blissful sleep...

Not this Thanksgiving.

Our bedroom became the coat check. I couldn't pass out until the last jacket for the night had been picked up and put back on. It was unnerving, the more I thought about it. All those coats. Each guest had shed their jackets and dropped them into a pile on our bed.

A mound of flesh.

At the end of every dinner party, *someone* would inevitably forget *something*. An abandoned item of clothing, a scarf or a pair of gloves. Our house had its own Lost and Found. I'd actually caught Caroline wearing somebody else's wool parka the morning after one of our parties. I'd never seen it on her before, so I asked her—*Where'd you get that?*

Oh, she said. *Somebody left it behind last night.*

So, you're wearing their jacket? Just like that?

Is that really bad?

I had a mental image of her slipping into someone else's skin. *Do you know whose it is?*

Sarah, maybe? She shrugged. *I'm not sure...*

You don't even know who it belongs to?

I'll give it back. I promise. I just needed to put something on. It's cold outside...

Caroline's dinner parties were endless.

Absolutely endless.

It could be one or two in the morning before we finally said goodbye to our last guest. Caroline fostered an atmosphere conducive to communal carousing. Nobody ever wanted to leave. Some folks would even say something like, *I never want to leave, guys.*

And I'd laugh along with Caroline.

Ha-ha.

All the while glancing at the clock over the kitchen sink.

Checking my phone.

Counting down.

In the past, Caroline had gone as far as to print out copies of lyrics to songs she wanted our guests to sing at the dinner table, as if we were all a part of some two-bottle tabernacle and she were drunkenly conducting the choir to belt out whatever David Bowie song she picked.

Tonight, she selected *Hallelujah* by Leonard Cohen.

We need to wash this year off, she pronounced to the table. *We need to cleanse ourselves of everything that's weighed us down these last few months. We need to give thanks.*

As the designated parent, I luckily got to duck out of choir practice and put the kids to sleep. I tucked them both in while everyone else warbled away downstairs. Read Laurel a book. Maybe two books. I sat in bed with Carter for a *weeee* bit longer than usual, making sure he slipped off to sleep before heading back downstairs. With the lights off, I could hear the voices of our guests seeping up from the floorboards. Through the door.

Their laughter. There was something fluid about it, *roiling,* as if a pipe had sprung a leak in the basement, and their voices flooded our whole house, floor by floor.

Laurel had a nightlight. Shaped like a ship. A blue boat. The glow from its sail spread over the wall just next to Laurel's crib, and I couldn't help but wish I was on it, navigating away from this place.

It doesn't have an anchor.

And suddenly, a memory floated back to me.

Anchor-embossed buttons.

A pea coat.

Nobody had moved from the table when I returned, so I retreated to the sink. Doing dishes was always my last stand at these dinner parties. I busied myself, and nobody bothered me. Occasionally, somebody popped their head in and offered to help, but I'd kindly demure:

Nope, nope. Caroline cooks. I clean. Them's the rules.

Once the dishes were done, I had nowhere to go but back to the dining room. I had to sit across from Caroline because nobody was allowed to sit next to their significant others. That was another one of Caroline's rules: *Sit beside someone new.* Never settle for a familiar face.

None of these people were familiar to me.

Were any of these people my friends?

I feel like I'd been introduced to these people a dozen times over—co-workers, friends from the gym—but I couldn't place any of them. Everybody blended. Their faces, flushed from all the alcohol. The number of bodies crammed in our dining room had elevated the temperature by a couple degrees. I was sweating. We all were. Caroline's hair clung to her temples. Her auburn curls slickened themselves, like eels.

The woman sitting on my left did her damnedest to strike up a conversation with me. Something about the election, I think. Or maybe it was a book she'd just read. I pretended to listen, nodding my head every few minutes as I picked up a tea light from the table and dribbled a bit of its melted wax into my palm, rolling the translucent goo into a warm ball, kneading it out into a slender maggot, then dipping its head back into candle and melting it all over again. Whatever mental messages I was telepathically transmitting to the rest of our guests were not getting received—*Go go go time to go go go everybody go go go...*

There was no escaping this dinner party.

Nowhere to hide.

Get me out of here get me out get me out.

Caroline poured me a glass of wine from across the table. She winked at me and grinned, like I was her little sacrificial lamb getting all fattened up for the slaughter.

This was her subtle way of telling me to give up.

Let go.

Unwind.

Have some fun, hon.

Have a drink.

Celebrate.

Laugh.

Sing.

One glass quickly became two. A third popped in there, somewhere, I think. The bottles all blurred together. Green glass. People talked to me. I was pretty sure of it. A few fruit flies drifted about, settling onto the lip of my glass, hungry for a taste of bitter grapes.

Politics.

I couldn't bring myself to vote for...

Movies.

Have you seen the new film by...?

Books.

It's been darkening my bedside table for weeks, and I haven't been able to crack it open...

The remains of the turkey sat at the center of the table, a husk of its former glory. The carcass of an ancient dinosaur, pecked clean, its ribs glistening in the candlelight. Devoured.

Politics.

If they just focused on the primaries, maybe they'd finally get somewhere...

Movies.

His last film was such a snooze-fest...

Books.

If it doesn't grip me in the first ten pages, I'm sorry, but I've got to put it down...

Politics.

The room wobbled at bit.

Movies.

The tabletop pitched, like a ship in a storm.

Books.

I couldn't breathe. Couldn't find the air.

Poultices.

Loogies.

Hooks.

Before I even realized what my own hand was up to, I saw my glass raise. *I'd like to make a toast.*

Everyone turned, quieting down. I was caught. I couldn't move, frozen.

What were they going to do to me?

All these unfamiliar faces.

Who were these people, even? Did I know any of them? Did I have any friends here? All my friends have families of their own. They were having Thanksgiving dinners elsewhere.

The people surrounding me now, these people were strangers.

Absolute strangers.

Caroline looked at me expectantly. She had this rule, another one of her goddamn rules, where one can never toast to themselves. *It's bad luck,* she'd say, gracefully demurring. That meant it was up to me to raise a glass in our hostess' honor. *To my lovely wife* and all that.

She expected it. *Required* it.

Alms to the high hostess.

When I was a kid, I started, *my parents always threw dinner parties…I was way too young to understand what everybody was talking about. I know it sounds vain, but I was completely convinced they were always talking about me. Like, whenever I heard them laughing over something or other, it always sounded as if it was at my expense. Like the joke was on me.*

The expression on Caroline's face shifted. She was taken aback by this confession happening across the dinner table. This wasn't a part of the scripted party plan.

I was going rogue.

One night, at one of my parents' parties, one of their friends got so shitfaced, he passed out in their bed. I'd gone into their room for whatever reason, I don't remember why, and I woke this guy up. I had no idea he was even there. He just popped out of the jackets like some drunk jack-in-the-box, and I thought he was a monster. Some tentacled monster made out of coats.

Caroline's hand slid across the table. I hadn't realized it until just then, but I still had my wine glass held up in the air, toasting my own ghost story. *You never told me this,* she said.

It was there, I kept going, still holding my glass. *For just a split second. It was real—and it wanted me. To eat me or drag me under or take me away or something. I know it did. And if it hadn't been for my mom running into the room and dragging me away, I'm sure it would have.*

Everybody else's wrists wilted, their wine glasses slowly sinking back toward the table. I was the only one who still had their glass held up. A friend of Caroline's cleared her throat.

I wanted to think of a punchline. A better ending. But I was always so piss-poor at telling stories, let alone when I'm tipsy, so I had little choice but to take a sip of my own wine.

I killed the mood. I had killed Caroline's dinner party. Really slaughtered it.

How do you come back from something like that? There's just no way. No way.

Party's over, folks…

Think it's time to go, a coworker of Caroline's said. I think he was a coworker. He was about to stand, but I held out my hand to him. The other hand. The one not holding my wine.

Wait, wait, I stood up—a little too quickly. *Here. You stay. Let me get your jacket.*

Their voices picked up as I made my way down the hall. They'd waited until I was out of the dining room until they started talking again. The tone was hushed, but their voices still carried. They were talking about me. Whispering about whether she needed help cleaning up.

The door to our bedroom was ajar. I pushed it open and ran my hand across the wall to flip on the light switch. There were everybody's coats. Lying on the bed. A whole lot of leather. A couple pea coats. Mostly black. Some fawny, tawny, brown. Cigarette ash gray, sapped of any soul. Bleak urban colors. Fall fashion here in our sprawling metropolis.

I started rummaging around for this guy's jacket. I couldn't seem to find it. I kept pushing jackets back, dissecting this hulking pile of leather and wool and nylon—but no luck.

I was drunk.

I was tired.

Did he say it was a pea coat? Am I remembering that right? Gray wool? Broad collar?

Just look for the anchors.

Anchors on the buttons.

Anchor's away…

I sat down on the pile, suddenly finding myself far more exhausted than I'd thought. The mass of jackets reminded me of the leaf piles from when I was a kid, just after Dad had raked them up, a massive heap of leaves just waiting for me to dive on in.

Something squirmed under my left leg.

Something tried to wriggle away.

An animal.

I tugged the fur coat from under myself. Whatever creature it had been before it became this ugly-looking '70s rehash of an antique jacket was a total mystery to me. Chinchilla or mink or fox. Just some indeterminately skinned woodland creature. I'm not even sure it was real fur or not, but it sure felt warm as I ran my fingers through it. So cozy. I bundled it up into a ball and used it as a pillow. I sprawled out on the pile of jackets and closed my eyes. I even tugged a couple coats off the top and covered myself with them, like a patchwork blankie.

Time for bed, everybody.

I felt a stretch of leather against my cheek. A sleeve to someone's bomber jacket clung to my skin. I was going to pull it away, but it gradually warmed against my face as I drifted off.

Goodnight. Sleep tight.

Don't let the—

The sleeve slithered.

This time I was pretty positive it had moved. The bomber rippled across my cheek. *Undulated*, as if it wanted to free itself from under the weight of my head.

I could feel others now.

More sleeves.

Fondling me. Slipping and sliding across my thigh. Inching under my shirt and snaking up my chest. They had no substance. No bulk. Just hollow cavities. I could feel the emptiness within. Nothing but the husks of groping clothes. Like ghosts. An orgy of ghosts on our bed. Each sleeve writhed about my body, like a bacchanalia in a department store, these jackets manhandling me all over.

I tried to sit up but couldn't. A latticework of roots had tethered my wrists against the bed. A sleeve wormed around my throat and tightened its grip.

The pile. The pile was alive. Fluctuating and pulsing.

I couldn't find the center of it. Its tendrils wrapped around my waist, my neck, my arms. I tried yanking my hand back, but it simply pulled harder. It was stronger than me.

It wouldn't let me go.

Wouldn't let go.

Please oh please let go let me go let go.

It was pulling me in. Pulling me down.

Deeper.

As if the depth of our bed had somehow prolonged itself, the very mattress opened up and welcomed me in. Its quilted rictus loosened itself, and my body eased through.

The room had gone darker.

No—not the room. Just my view of it. The sleeve of another jacket eclipsed my vision.

I couldn't see.

Couldn't see.

Voices. I could still hear the voices from the down the hall. The dinner party. Everyone was still in the dining room. Our guests. Laughing. I could hear them. Caroline had managed to maneuver the party without me, manning the helm and steering it back toward merriment.

The adults all laughed in the dining room. Their disembodied voices drifted down the hall and into our bedroom, filling the whole house.

It was unavoidable.

Unescapable.

My pants felt warm. A swell or urine radiated down my leg.

When I tried to scream for help, a tendril rooted itself down my throat. I choked, unable to breathe. It forced its way down my esophagus, down into the pit of my stomach.

Down.

Down.

Down into the dark.

The tipsy lilt of a woman's toast filled my ears. Caroline. She raised a glass to our guests. *To great food, to great company, and to another bountiful year. Cheers, everybody...*

Cheers, the guests all sang.

Clink, clink.

LITTLE CHOICES
Arlen Feldman

Strawberry, vanilla, or chocolate.

In theory, it shouldn't matter. They just poured the gunk down the feeding tube directly into my stomach. In practice, though—the stuff worked its way back up my esophagus. Chalky battery acid.

Maybe if I drank the stuff properly, it wouldn't be too bad. The way I got it was disgusting. I generally stuck with one flavor until I couldn't take it anymore then switched to another.

I blinked at the nurse until she understood that I wanted chocolate.

Most of my meds went straight down the tube as well, or into my veins, but for some reason, my sleeping pill had to be swallowed. I loved the sleeping pill, though, and was more than happy to fight to get it down.

The nurse dimmed the light, and I started doing simple math problems in my head. By themselves, they wouldn't work, but with the sleeping pill, I should be asleep in a few minutes.

As I drifted off, my eyes flicked open for just a moment, and something strange stood at the door. Something that couldn't possibly be real. The dim light outlined some sort of huge, vicious bird.

Silently, it swooped down toward the bed. Inch-long talons, razor sharp, bit into the metal of the bed's railings.

I fought to stay conscious—although what defense I could muster if I managed, I had no idea.

Sleep took me.

I woke with a soundless scream. The lights were on, and an aide was cleaning me up.

Morning.

The aide was one of the good ones. He chatted amiable nonsense while he worked. Most of the aides just treated me like an inconvenient chunk of meat, and some were deliberately cruel. I did the closest approximation to a smile I could manage toward him, and he grinned back.

After he left, I thought about what must have been the beginnings of a nightmare last night. Images of claws and wings. I was pretty sure, it wasn't the first time I'd had that dream. I couldn't move my head, of course, but by forcing myself almost cross-eyed, I could look towards the spot on the railing where I'd seen the vision of the bird.

Deep scratches scarred the metal.

Probably what triggered the dream in the first place.

After a while, one of the volunteers came in and offered to read to me. I had the choice of *Moby Dick* in a monotone or *Great Expectations* in a monotone. I hated the idea of Dickens being so tortured, so blinked to indicate *Moby Dick*.

The woman sat in my guest chair and opened the book. "Call Me Ishmael Some Years Ago Never Mind How Long Precisely Having Little Or No Money In My Purse And Nothing…"

I must have dozed.

She was still going when I woke. "…Goodnight Landlord Said I You May Go I Turned In And Never Slept Better In My Life."

"Well," she said, and no longer reading, her voice suddenly took on some character. "That's three chapters. Perhaps, I can come back and read some more in a couple of days?"

I blinked acquiescence. She was almost as good as the sleeping pills.

"Do you want the TV on?"

This was not a simple question. If I managed to fall asleep, loud noises on the television could wake me. If not, then having some voices to cover over the incessant beeps and alarms of the hospital could be comforting—or maddening. After a series of questions and blinked responses, we settled on having the picture, but no sound.

The volunteer squeezed my arm on her way out. It hurt a little but was pleasant. Nice to be touched for non-medical reasons.

When the time came that night for my sleeping pill, the scratches in the bed's metal railing were clearly visible in the reflected blue-green light of the television—fresh and deep.

The thought had been with me all day, but it wasn't until the pill actually sat in my mouth that I decided to push it into my cheek, and only pretend to swallow it.

The nurse dimmed the light and left.

I waited a few minutes then spat out the pill. I pictured it disappearing over the edge of the bed and onto the floor. In reality, it dribbled out of the corner of my mouth and stuck to my face, but I couldn't do anything about it.

Then, I lay there. Of course.

Being awake during the day was horrible. Being awake at night was infinitely worse. I want to be asleep. I pretend to be asleep, but I am aware of everything—the clicks and rasps of the machinery around me, alarms going off down the hall, telephones ringing at the nurse's station. The unpleasant warmth of the catheter line down my leg. The continuous tickle of the oxygen feed into my nose.

After fifteen minutes, I was regretting my rashness. After an hour, I was crying in misery and frustration.

The door opened, and bright light flooded in from the hallway. A blurred figure appeared at the door. It might have been the nurse in her blue-and-white uniform, or it might have been something else.

The figure resolved itself into the shape from my nightmare—except I was certain this time that I was not dreaming. Feathers, claws, gimlet eyes. It made no sound except for the slight crunching of the metal as its claws wrapped around the bed frame. Its beak drove into my chest, and the pain was unbearable. My unresponsive body somehow shuddered, and the bird drew back, looking at me. It titled its head, like a magpie examining something curious and shiny.

It took off, claws scratching against metal, and disappeared out the door.

I looked down at my chest, expecting to see blood and gore, but above the edge of the blanket was nothing but my rough, brown chest hair, rising and falling rapidly in my panic.

Something was gone from me after the attack, although I couldn't say what. Amazing that there was something in me to take.

Slowly, my panic faded. Somehow, I even slept a bit.

The morning rituals came and went. Dispassionate fingers performed those tasks that I could no longer do for myself. Dignity was not something I even remembered.

They turned me every few hours to prevent bedsores. Eventually, I faced the railing. Deep grooves replaced the scratches, and at one point, the metal bent entirely back on itself.

When the nurse came in for lunch, I selected strawberry. As it poured into the funnel at the end of the tube, she smiled at the bend in the metal. I'd expected confusion or annoyance. With two fingers, she reached down and bent it back into shape as though it were made of clay.

She met my gaze, still smiling, and I recognized those eyes. I blinked like crazy, but she just finished pouring the can, closed off the tube, and left the room.

My heart monitor went off a dozen times in the next few hours, prompting nurses, then doctors, to start showing up. They played with medications and eventually adjusted the threshold on the machine to be less sensitive. Despite my rapid blinking, I couldn't get any of them to pull out the letter board that would let me spell out words. If they had, what would I have said?

That evening, the nurse came back with the sleeping pill.

"Last night you spat out your pill," she said. "Do you want to take it tonight?"

I blinked in surprise. It was a choice. Like strawberry, vanilla, or chocolate.

The nurse waited, a tiny smile on her lips, her fingers tapping on the bed frame like bone on metal.

I stared at her for a long moment, then blinked my decision. She put the pill on my tongue, and I chose to let myself swallow.

DREAMING OF RAVENS
Elana Gomel

I had my last dream when I was eight years old.

"You are blessed," my foster mother would tell me. At night, our house in San Jose often rang with cries of traumatized toddlers and sobbing of older children, reliving the violence of their original lives. I slept, undisturbed, through it all.

"Look what dreams can do to you. You are better off without them."

She would smooth my hair, give me a kiss, and wait for me to respond with: "Good night, Mommy."

"Good night, Katie," I would say, bury my head in the pillow, and fall into the velvety darkness that stitched my days together.

I believed her. I thought that my immunity to nightmares was the compensation that powers-that-be had given me for my loss.

But when Alex and I split up, I doubted Katie's wisdom. I did not grieve when she died, even though we had been dutifully exchanging Christmas cards and occasional visits. Grief would have been a betrayal of my mother. But I did all the right things, coming to the funeral and bringing flowers to the grave on every anniversary. I always did the right thing. I was a stickler for rules and regulations. I loved the everyday with the same passion my friends loved their video games, their fantasy football, their superhero comics. I loved the efficiency of my job as a programmer; I loved the complicated choreography of daily chores involved in ferrying Marina to her afterschool activities and running our household. I was good at it; and I regarded our newly-renovated house in the expensive suburb of Atherton as a testament to my capability.

Then, it all went pear-shaped.

Once Marina went to college, the two of us were left with long, empty evenings that could no longer be filled with the family TV or college applications. Alex spent time in his den playing games—an embarrassingly adolescent passion for a middle-aged physician. I kidded him about it until one day I discovered that he was not listening to me, his gaze unblinking and sidewise like the gaze of a bird. Was he looking into a world I could not see because I did not dream? Was everybody?

I was almost relieved when he filed for divorce.

Strangely, I feared going to sleep. I still had no dreams, no nightmares, no nightly rendezvous with fairies or monsters. But I became aware of the opaque hours that stretched between falling asleep and awakening. The tedium of it got to me more than anything else: the sense of waiting out in an empty anteroom and listening for whispers behind the closed door.

A mutual acquaintance recommended Dr. Patel, who was supposed to be a highly regarded authority on sleep disorders. Could my problem be called a sleep disorder at all? I slept soundly, never had any need for Ambien or whatever other junk insomniacs consume in order to get a break from reality. Even when Marina, an avid dreamer since babyhood, woke me up every night by padding into our bedroom with tales of lurking figures in the closet, I had no difficulty sleeping in installments.

Dr. Patel wore a natty black suit, which I always considered to be the only proper attire for a professional, but on him, it somehow looked funereal. He was Indian. I expected this. I did not expect his round dark eyes and jutting nose, which gave him an unsettling resemblance to a raven. He must have seen my reaction, an almost imperceptible recoil, when I walked into his office. I was afraid he would peg me as a xenophobe or a racist, so I went out of my way to be accommodating, even to the extent of answering questions that I considered irrelevant.

"You are avoiding the real issue, Laura," he said at some point.

"We *are* dealing with the real issue," I said.

"Your husband has filed for divorce. You only daughter has left for college. Don't you think that the disruption caused by these events…"

"Alex and I have been estranged for a long time. And Marina…Marina is very fortunate to have full scholarship."

"She may be. But what about you? Do you consider yourself fortunate to have to let go of your daughter?"

The strange way he phrased the question made me uneasy. In fact, the discomfort I felt stepping into his dimly-lit office made me want to walk out. But of course, this would be an inappropriate thing to do.

Still, couldn't he at least install better lighting? Instead of making his office cozy, the solitary long-necked lamp infested it with restless, prickly shadows. It did not help that it swayed rhythmically on its stem. In the dribbles of resentful illumination, his nose and mouth seemed to fuse together, making his resemblance to a bird even more pronounced. I tore my eyes from his face and let them alight on an abstract picture on the wall that looked like the aftermath of an autopsy. I decided this visit would be my last.

"According to you, the problem started when your daughter left and…"

"*No.*" I said, tearing the bounds of convention that had suddenly grown gossamer-thin. "The problem has always been there. It's just that, now, I have the time to deal with it. When you have kids at home, you barely have a minute for yourself."

I stopped as Dr. Patel rustled some papers on his desk like a bird ruffling its feathers. But what actually made me shut up was the realization of what I had just said. I had never had "kids" at home, plural.

Should I have?

The question was new and unwelcome. Dr. Patel made use of the pause.

"You are lucky," he said, unconsciously echoing my foster mother. "I had patients who tried to kill themselves because they could not bear their nightly terrors."

"I would rather have nightmares than oblivion."

"Trust me, you wouldn't. Look, we all dream. We have to. This is how our brains process the information we acquire during the day. But there is no need for us to remember the details of this housecleaning process. You wake up refreshed, ready to face reality. What's wrong with that?"

I shrugged. I did not know how to explain the sense of urgency that possessed me, as if the darkness of my sleep thinned, bulging up with the shape of a predator ready to surface.

"Do you have any phobias?" he asked suddenly, making me start. The swaying lamp—*was it some stupid toy like a nodding Hello Kitty?*—flung a handful of shadows at his skinny neck, making it appear as if it sprouted black fuzz.

"Yes," I said reluctantly. "Ravens."

"Other birds, too?"

"No, just ravens."

"Anything in your childhood that accounts for this? Any trauma?"

My childhood was cloven by a trauma, but it never occurred to me to connect my dislike of the oily, predatory birds to what happened to my mother. I still could not see the link.

"Not really," I said after a proper pause, to make him think I considered his question, while actually I tried to figure out how much of his billable hour had passed. "We lived in San Francisco when I was a child, before it became so expensive that only billionaires and homeless can afford it. We had a small apartment. My mother…she would take me on these long walks. The Golden Gate…There were ravens there. I remember she would bring packages and leave them on the bridge, so they would let us pass."

"Packages?" Dr. Patel's invisible eyebrows shot up above his round eyes, and I realized how inane this sounded.

"Food," I said. "I mean food. She would leave food for the birds."

"And did she do it throughout your childhood?"

"As far as I remember. Until…"

"Until what?" Dr. Patel leaned forward, and his bony fingers tipped with unfashionably long nails twitched on his desk.

"Until she disappeared."

Here, I said it. And there was neither relief nor a renewed sorrow, just dull acceptance. After all, this was not some sort of secret—my family knew about it, both Alex and Marina did. We just never talked about it.

"She and I…it was just the two of us. I never met my father. I'm not sure she even knew who he was. Belated summer of love and all that… She worked as a secretary for Intel, made a decent salary. But…she was never late. And that evening…my babysitter, Mrs. Lee, she didn't know what to do. No cellphones then. She took me home to Chinatown with her. And called the police."

"And?"

I shrugged.

"Nothing. They declared her missing. She still is, officially. Her name is in the database of MPs. No body, no clues."

"And what happened to you?"

"My mother was an only child, too. Her parents were dead. I grew up with a foster family, the Millers. They were very good to me."

I wanted to shield Katie's memory from any taint of psychiatric suspicion. But Dr. Patel surprised me. Instead of pursuing the unremarkable trajectory of my adolescence, he abruptly changed course:

"Too?"

"What?"

"You said your mother was an only child, *too*. What did you mean?"

I blinked, taken aback.

"I guess…like myself."

"And like your daughter. Marina is an only child, correct?"

"Yes. But what does it have to do with my inability to remember my dreams?"

Dr. Patel leaned forward, and for the first time during our interview, my creeping unease blossomed into something close to actual fear. His movement, abrupt and predatory, did not seem entirely human. And when I looked at his bony fingers again, I could swear they were tipped with talons.

"What was the last dream you remember?"

I looked into his round eyes, glittering with some barely suppressed appetite, and lied:

"I don't remember any dreams. I never have."

Driving home on the rain-slicked roads of the Peninsula, I considered this lie. I was ashamed of myself: perhaps Dr. Patel was not the best therapist in the world, but neither was I the best patient. I had been in therapy as a child, after Mom's disappearance, but I did not remember any details. Possibly my forgetfulness was a testament to the skill of whoever it was that had drained the poison of grief from my unformed mind. I could not even remember whether it was a man or a woman. In fact, I had very few memories of my childhood. The only vivid images I did have were my mother's face—and the last dream.

The dream started with me standing on the corner of Market and Fifth streets. I was looking up into the inky-colored sky, like a thundercloud. It roiled, and grumbled, and there were occasional flashes of lightning, but the pavement remained bone-dry. Then, I realized that it was indeed raining but *upwards*: the cloud pierced by crystal needles of water, peppered by blue holes that closed immediately, and new holes appeared, letting in rays of brassy light. I was not at all surprised—a common feature, I learned later, of dreams, in which the most illogical and outlandish events are taken for granted. But mine was not the attitude of placid acceptance. Fear consumed me.

I waited for my mother, as I had often done. But she was not there. Nobody was. The streets totally deserted.

And a new sound—a low, rolling rumble—did not come from above, where the upward rain fought with the recalcitrant cloud and where bulky shadows flitted through the medley of sunshine and darkness. Rather, it crept close to the pavement: a voice, distorted by an incredibly poor amplification. A large truck appeared from Market, rounding the corner, black and shiny with opaque windows and thin tires.

In later years, I occasionally searched through old automobile catalogues, but the only thing that resembled it were those dilapidated Eastern European prison vans called Black Crows: not something one would see in San Francisco. Ancient loudspeakers mounted on top of the truck, and they blared a scratchy message. I could not make it out, but the sheer volume of it pinned me down to the pavement like a butterfly, caught on the needle of yellow light that stabbed down from the torn-up cloud. The glare of the light fell upon the windshield, and a beaky, bristling silhouette briefly outlined against the dirty glass.

And that was that. I woke up. Next night, I slept in Mrs. Lee's narrow bed in Chinatown while my distraught babysitter talked to the police. And I did not dream; or if I did, I did not remember my dreams.

I parked in the driveway of our Atherton home, its new siding gleaming through the downpour, and ran to the front door. The garage was filled with Alex's stuff as he prepared to move out. Not for the first time, I cursed his delay; I did not fancy catching a cold in the rain.

I need not have worried; my hair and clothes were dry as I entered the mudroom. I must have run faster than I thought.

Alex sat in his den; the muted shouting from his game spilled onto the landing. The shouting was articulate but incomprehensible, just like the message in my dream. I kicked off my high-heeled shoes and walked upstairs.

Who was I kidding? I knew what the message had been. I made it out later, painstakingly going over every detail on the last dream as a child, a teenager, a grown woman. I wanted to know whether my dream had any clue to my mother's disappearance. I knew such things happened: a chance word stored up in the unconscious vault of night knowledge could solve a crime. But this was not the case with me. The message was ridiculously inappropriate, dredged up from some forgotten reading of the Bible, even though my mother was not religious. But who knows? A street preacher, a random peek into a church, and a child's imagination concocts an elaborate scenario that may haunt her forever.

The message blared from the truck had been: "*All the firstborn of the sinful city must die.*"

I walked past Marina's bedroom's closed door, feeling a familiar pang. Dr. Patel had not been altogether wrong. I missed my daughter. But she was better off where she was. Away from her parents' disintegrating marriage, away from her mother's growing obsession, away from…

I stopped as something from the corner of my eye caught my attention. A package lay on the floor mat in front of Marina's door. I picked it up, thinking something must have arrived in the mail. But it had no label. It was painstakingly wrapped up in layers of paper and secured with masking tape. I felt the rotten softness within. The paper soaked through with reeking stains.

I took it to the kitchen and cut through the tape. And stood there for a long time looking at pieces of raw meat swimming in butcher blood.

My mother used to leave packages for the ravens on the Golden Gate Bridge, so they would let us pass.

A childhood memory. Supposedly a real one, not the memory of a dream.

But gulls gathered on the Golden Gate Bridge, not ravens. And nobody leaves raw meat for birds to peck on.

I rushed to Alex's den, banged the door open, and stood, frozen, at the threshold.

He did not turn around, purposefully ignoring my entrance, but over his shoulder, I could see the large monitor. Figures ran, fell, dissolved in puddles of blood as the first-person shooter mowed them down. But the setting was not the zombie-overrun streets of some imaginary metropolis. I did not play any video games, but I recognized the place immediately. It was the interior of our home.

The perspective shifted and zoomed in on one figure that stood still, her face lifted up, a mixture of horror and resignation on her face. The figure was myself.

Alex's fingers moved on the mouse-pad: long, bony, parchment-yellow, tipped with curving talons. His head inclined sharply to the keyboard, and the thick black hair he was so proud of glistened oily in the light of the table lamp. So full, so thick, falling in layers of delicate feathers onto his neck…

He finally turned around, but I fled the room before I could catch more than a glimpse of his sideways-looking round eye.

I did not stop until I was safely in Marina's room, the lock that she had insisted we install to insure teenaged privacy clicking into place. The room was as it had always been; we had kept it untouched for her Christmas and holiday visits. Stuffed animals on the bed and a chaotic collage of pictures on the walls: she had been into art-photography in junior high. The curtain was drawn, but a sickly yellow light filtered through the crack.

I must have been in shock because I thought that the rain had finally stopped. I pulled the curtain aside and stared into the copper-lit dry backyard as the rays of the setting sun fell through the crochet holes in the roiling black-and-blue cloud above: the holes made by the rain falling upwards.

I gingerly closed the curtain, went back, and sat on the bed.

The simplest explanation, of course, was that I was dreaming. Or maybe hallucinating. Hadn't I read somewhere that people deprived of REM sleep went insane? This must be what was happening to me.

But I knew it was not true. The texture of my experience was the same as that of my everyday life, the life I had clung to so desperately. If my life had been real, this was real, too.

But thinking about it, the texture of my last dream had also been like this. So how did I know it had been a dream? Well, because in waking life, you did not have raven-driven black trucks declaring that the firstborn of the city must die.

And in waking life, you did not have therapists growing talons. You did not have raw meat left as an offering in your suburban home. You did not have your husband metamorphosing into a bird of prey.

My eyes were drawn to Marina's photographs. She had never been particularly good at it, taking pictures of obvious, postcard-pretty spots: the Golden Gate Bridge at sunset; the riot of flowers in Berkeley Botanical Gardens; the rocks of the Sonoma Coast. But now, as I peered at the display, I saw the Golden Gate covered with furry red cilia; the flowers dripped blood; the rocks smiled at me with malevolent blind faces. Had the photographs been like this from the beginning and only my perception of them had shifted? Or was the veneer of my life thinning out and peeling off?

Was I falling asleep or waking?

I got up and came closer to the wall. Among the riot of Marina's landscapes, one small portrait stuck out. It was my mother. Marina at some point had become interested in the mystery of her grandmother's disappearance and cadged this picture from me.

I was afraid to see the feathers or scales growing over Mom's face, but it was the same as before: smiling, beautiful, slightly wistful. My mother looking at her firstborn daughter.

All the firstborn of the sinful city must die.

I was her firstborn, and her one and only. If this was the tribute the ravens demanded, what would she not do to protect her only child?

Dreams have the logic of their own, so they say, and when one is in a dream, everything appears matter-of-fact and unsurprising: monsters, fairies, murders, and miracles. It is only when one wakes that the logic of reality reasserts itself. So, it no longer appeared strange to me that the ravens, our rulers, would impose this terrible tribute upon our sinful city. No longer satisfied with offerings of meat and bones, they wanted mothers' tears and children's screams.

They wanted the firstborn.

I stroked my mother's face, seen dimly through the veil of tears. The strange illogic of the suburban dream that I had lived as reality dissolved, fell apart, as intangible as a soap bubble. Job, college, divorce; health insurance and 401 K; how lucky those for whom these are the only monsters lurking in the dark. How lucky are those who have never seen a Black Crow chauffeured by a cackling magpie or a predatory gull stop by their door.

A sudden piercing ring broke the silence, a sound so incongruous that, at first, I was not sure I actually heard it. An unreal sound, it belonged in the melting mirage of dream memories. But it persisted. I fished my smartphone from the pocket of my jacket and swiped the green button. And looked at my daughter's beautiful, unhappy face.

"*Marina.*"

"Mom? I'm on my way home."

"What? But it's the middle of the quarter."

"I'll explain when I get here. I had…they said it was a breakdown. Could not sleep. Nightmares. Anyway, I need to be home now. Is Dad in?"

"Yes," I said automatically.

"Cool. See you soon."

The screen darkened.

Her dad was a raven now, game-hunting his own family through the maze of electronic hidey-holes. How long until he hunted in earnest?

But would Marina wake up to reality? Would she see the cruel beak, the sharp talons, the sideways-staring round eye? Or would she encounter her own prosaic, ordinary, down-to-earth physician father?

How could I have lived for so long in a dream without waking up?

My hand still clutched the cellphone. I let it drop and touched my mother's picture, caressed her sad smile. What if she had not disappeared from the world? What if I had? What if she had found the way to hide me in that strange, illogical, often boring but safe illusion of the middle-class suburbia? No surprise, then, that I could not remember my dreams. I lived in one.

What would a mother do to save her one and only child? Anything.

I unlocked the door and stepped outside into the corridor that in my dream had been papered with an innocuous floral design. In reality, it was choked with grasping, multi-branched shadows that writhed and tore at my clothes. The ceiling swarmed with a flood of bullet-shaped giant lice. The ravens grew impatient.

Alex—or the creature I knew as Alex—stood at the entrance to the den, his skeletal feet chafing impatiently at the torn floor. He dressed in a black suit, as ravens always are.

"I am here," I said. "I'm awake."

His beak clacked. Ravens can talk when they want to, but they seldom waste words on mere humans.

"But my daughter is staying in the dream."

He opened his beak, but the words came from the outside, a distorted shriek of loudspeakers:

"*All the firstborn of the sinful city must die.*"

"I am a firstborn. *Take me.*"

I opened the front door and stepped into the brassy light where the Black Crow waited for me. I lightly touched the new siding on my way out. It had been a good dream while it lasted.

SUNDAY SCHOOL
Shaun Horton

Along the walls, daylight bulbs gave the impression of a sunny day, even in the basement. The actual windows had been boarded up months ago.

"Terry, pay attention."

He turned back to face where his mom stood, tapping the chalk on the blackboard.

"Give me three examples of God's wrath." Her gray eyes bore into him while she waited impatiently for his answer.

"The great flood, the destruction of Sodom and Gomorrah, the shattering of the languages."

"Good. It's important to remember that God gladly visits his wrath on those that displease him, as well as granting his blessing on those who follow the scriptures. We must not forget how lucky we are to have received His blessing." She turned, clasped her hands together, and bowed her head to the make-shift shrine in the corner. After a moment, she glanced at the clock.

"Well, that's all we have time for today. We need to pray and accept communion."

Terry joined his mom, kneeling on the pillows set in front of the shrine.

"Dear Lord, we thank you for your blessings and for watching over us throughout the day. We thank you for protecting us from the darkness and for providing sustenance and light. We accept this communion that you have sent and pray that you continue to find us worthy. In the name of the Lord, Almighty, Amen."

With the prayer finished, she pulled back the curtain, revealing the converted breadbox. Inside, on a cushion of what used to be their best towels, sat the quivering mound of clear jelly.

It trembled even more as his mother picked up the knife that sat on the table, and she reached in, carving a small piece out of one side. She held it aloft, tilted her head back and let it slide from the blade to her tongue.

Terry felt a pang of guilt as she reached in for another small slice. He tilted his head back and opened his mouth the same as he had for the past two months, when the mass had fallen from the sky at her feet. His mother had hailed it as the ambrosia, a gift from God himself.

The piece slid onto his tongue, quivering, as if it didn't want to be eaten. When he bit down, it ruptured like a grape, spilling across his teeth before he swallowed its juices.

Light-headed, all Terry's cares and stresses lifted right off his shoulders. The feeling spread through his chest, down his limbs, to the very tips of his fingers and toes.

His mom already lay on the floor, twitching; her eyes rolled back in her head, and the smile on her face one of indescribable ecstasy. Terry lay across the pillows, to not collapse on the concrete of the basement floor.

He drifted through the stars, watching planets and galaxies drift past. Some were green, some red, and some were little balls of thunderclouds, which lit up randomly in different spots like flashing Christmas lights.

He floated through the void to a large black planet. He landed with a deep sense of foreboding: of being watched by something evil, hungry. The landscape was desolate and barren in every direction.

The ground itself was soot, and it shifted underneath him, splitting between his feet. Terry hopped to one side of the opening crevice, falling to his knees as it continued to move. Inside was a giant glass-like orb, within which what looked like a giant black hole searched back and forth. It stopped, partially underneath the edge Terry stood on.

The planet had an eye with a pupil large enough he could have dove into it. It was watching him.

Terry ran from its sight, though he was sure it could still feel his every footstep.

He tripped.

His foot caught in a small hole. As he pushed himself up, he found more with his hands; they were everywhere, almost invisible in the planet's black skin.

One of them puckered, swelling up like a small volcano. Then a clear glob of mucus oozed out of it. The hole smoothed out again, leaving the glob quivering on the surface. More globs poured out of the ground around him. One swelled out of the hole his foot was caught in.

Pain burned. The jelly ate its way through his shoe, through his sock, through his skin. He turned away as the blood seeped into the clear ooze, turning it red. The other globules all moved, quivered, and inched their way along. All toward him.

The pain crawled up his leg, the ooze leaving nothing of his foot but white bone.

Then, he was screaming on the pillows in the basement, his jeans soaked with piss. His mom stood over him, the left corner of her lip tight, and her eyes narrow.

"You were punished, weren't you? For not paying attention."

"It was—it was horrible."

"That's Hell. That's where you go if you don't behave, pay attention, and live by the scripture." His mom sighed, letting her head drop a little. "I never considered He would use the ambrosia as an instrument of punishment as well as a boon though. I'm sorry, Terry."

Terry looked up at the shrine. His mom had already closed the box and pulled the curtain across. The clock on the other wall told them that they had taken communion almost two hours ago.

His mom put her arms around him, hugging him gently before helping him up. "You should go shower and get some clean clothes on. Cleanliness is next to Godliness, and you don't want to go back there again, right?"

Ashamed of himself, he paused at the foot of the stairs and looked back at the shrine. His stomach gurgled.

He was sure the quivering blob was pleased with itself.

Was the legendary ambrosia really a gift from God?

"Forgive me, Father. It is not our place to question your judgement or methods." He prayed silently before climbing the stairs.

Terry woke with his bed soaked in sweat and urine from his nightmares. The black planet's giant eye, the mucus oozing from its skin, dripping off into space, a giant maw had opened in it. Tentacles instead of teeth reached out, gobbling up asteroids.

"No. That can't be God. *It can't be.*"

He rocked himself on the floor underneath his poster of Batman, seeking comfort. After a few minutes, the nocturnal cold of the house bit through his wet pajamas. He changed into some dry ones, but his bed would be worthless until his mom could change and wash the sheets.

As he walked through the house, the lights from the basement bled underneath the closed door to the stairs. Strange. Mom never left lights on.

After peeking into his mom's room to find her not in bed, he crept down the stairs.

"Mom?"

She twitched on the floor in front of the shrine, the curtain pulled back and the box wide open. The ambrosia was gone.

He shook her. She looked as she had earlier, eyes rolled back, lips unnaturally stretched from ear to ear. She trembled lightly under his hands, her shirt cold and wet.

"Mom. *Mom.* Wake up."

One eye slowly rolled forward, black and showing no trace of the blue her eyes normally shone. That one dark eye reminded him of the black planet. Her mouth moved, lips forming words but the only a thick, heavy gurgle escaped.

She heaved on the floor, her mouth opening wide and a thick glob of clear jelly sprayed out across the floor. The one eye rolled back again, her tremors more violent. The smile gone, red showed at the corner of her mouth as if the flesh had split with the force of ejecting the jelly.

The transparent blob continued to flow from her mouth, moving, gathering itself up on the floor when the last strands pulled from her lips, her trembling finally stopped.

The ambrosia balled up, larger than it had been earlier and looked at him, watching him without eyes, preparing to do to him whatever it had just finished doing with his mom. It wanted the pieces of itself back, all the little slices his mom had cut off and given to him. It wanted them all.

The ambrosia stretched and flowed across the concrete floor between him and the stairs.

Worship me...

Terry's stomach churned at the thought of its pieces inside him. He could almost feel the one from earlier wiggling inside his stomach.

His mom stirred, groaning. It was all he could do to drag her over to the corner, away from the thing. A drop of blood rolled from the corner of her mouth.

"God...what have I done to make you angry?" Her eyes were closed, and her voice was thin and raspy.

"It's not God. It's not *God*."

I am.

"No. You're not. You're not God. You're a *monster*."

The mass, stretched out on the floor.

He tried to think of a way to run around it, jump over it. His mind kept showing him the stump of bone from his dream where the glob had sucked off all the flesh.

His mom woke up slowly, groggily reaching for the ambrosia on the floor. "Please, God, don't be angry."

Terry struggled to hold onto her, but his small body couldn't restrain her. They bumped into one of the lamps as they fought, the pole falling over and smashing the glass cover and the bulb with a flash of light, sparks, and a short sizzling, popping sound, the jelly recoiled, part of it smoking and brown.

The sight clicked in Terry's desperate mind, and he grabbed the lamps, throwing them at the ambrosia. More sizzling pops; a rancid smell as the light diminished.

I am God. Worship me.

"You're not God. *You're not God*."

Terry swung the last lamp over his head and smashed it on the sickly-orange bubbling glob. The bulb exploded, filling the room with a final flash before plunging them into darkness. Another loud pop sent the intensified stench into the air.

Terry crawled his way up the stairs, turning on the lights in the living room.

"No...God...where are you? Come back..."

He wobbled his way into the kitchen and dialed nine-one-one. The phone clattered to the floor as the operator answered. Terry went with it, falling to his hands and knees as he vomited onto the old, yellow linoleum; spaghetti, meatballs, sauce, and a chunk of clear jelly that slid away leaving a trail to the cabinets and underneath them.

Terry collapsed, the side of his head resting in the remains of the day's dinner. His wide eyes saw the last vision the black planet, it glared at him with its one giant eye, full of hatred and hunger, drifting away through space.

All he could do was whisper to himself.

"Not God...Not God...Not God..."

Breeding Goats To Have Human Characteristics

FROGBABY
Brett Petersen

I was born without a brain or spine, yet I control the cosmos. I make the sun rise and set. I cause the moon to wax and wane. I set the planets in their orbits. I invented gravity and all the laws of physics.

Yet, I know nothing.

I feel neither pain nor joy. I am not alive in the traditional sense, but I am better at living than you. In order to be like me, you'd have to stick your neck under a guillotine or blow your head off with a shotgun. I don't advise taking either of these actions. A mind is a terrible thing to waste, that is, unless you never had one to begin with.

Good times create vacuums as they pass by. One could say to have experienced anything at all is life's greatest tragedy. Time is responsible for the existence of beginnings and endings. To be born dead is to never know misery. The only reason people fear death is because they've been given a taste of life.

Upon death, all reverts to the simplicity of unconsciousness. I was granted this privilege right from the start.

I'll be waiting here *at no place in particular for you to join me.*

The doctors said it was anencephaly, a rare condition where the brain and spinal cord never developed. Sheila's baby came out looking like a frog: two protruding eyes encased in pockets of pink flesh, a nose and a mouth, but no cranium. They warned her that the baby's appearance might be disturbing, but she maintained that she wanted to see him before they carted him off to be incinerated. They dumped the frogbaby into her arms without so much as a piece of linen to cover him. She rocked him and sang a lullaby her mother had written to the tune of an old blues song. "I just can't keep from crying sometimes," the song went. Her tears splashed onto his healthy-looking cheeks, making it seem like his frog-eyes where shedding tears of their own. She and her husband Dan named him Ryan. For lack of a better reason, they picked the name because it rhymed with crying.

Not even two minutes later, an army of nurses appeared and said it was time to say goodbye. They had to pry Ryan from Sheila's arms. She howled and buried her face in Dan's nylon jacket as they dropped the beautiful boy in a box and sealed the lid.

Was God preoccupied with other things? Dan stroked Sheila's stringy hair. *Does he realize how much pain we're in right now?*

As an amateur theologian, Dan had concluded early on that God, like the human race, was imperfect. This ran totally counter to Biblical tradition, but it made so much sense to Dan. Astrophysicists affirmed that the universe had to have been uneven at the moment of the Big Bang for matter to coagulate into planets, stars, and galaxies. From a mystical standpoint, this irregularity was not accidental: God had made things this way on purpose. Without evil, intelligent beings wouldn't be able to appreciate goodness. The interplay of positive and negative stimuli on the human psyche over time is what generated reality and allowed for free will. But as Dan watched his son's body being wheeled off for cremation, he began to lament the idea of the universe being imperfect for the sake of sentient creatures knowing joy.

Is this really necessary? He swallowed what felt like a walnut lodged in his throat. *Is this a game to you, sitting up there on your golden throne, spinning a roulette wheel to see whose turn it is to be sacrificed for the greater good? I guess my son's number just happened to come up, huh? What does one little brat matter? He won't miss taking his first breath, feeling his mother's embrace or wrapping his tiny hand around his old man's finger. Infants can't retain memories, so it's all good, right?*

I don't mean to be a sore loser. Everyone has to lose sometime. But why not kill me instead? Have some street thug gun me down or let a truck squash me like a pancake. Why my son? He didn't have enough time to say his first word let alone win the Nobel Prize or commit mass genocide. I've done plenty of dumb things in my forty-six years. Taking me out of the picture would rid the world of a hell of a lot of stupidity. But I guess that's not how it works. Maybe it is all a lottery set in motion at the beginning of time. But what do I know?

Dan sighed and squeezed Sheila as tight as he could.

The silence was broken by the *clock, clock* of business shoes on the linoleum floor. A doctor approached and informed them of some papers they needed to sign. Dan held Sheila close as they shuffled off to some other part of the labyrinthine hospital complex to do paperwork.

We are the ones who are One and All. We exist behind empty mirrors. We pour the tea for two as well as three. When four comes around, we hide. Why? Because we're scared

of differentiation. We are only content when things stay the same. Change frightens us more than anything. Change is the nature of the place where the Outsiders live: the Ones who are ones unto themselves, not all, but Many...fragmented...alone...resigned to playing chess by themselves, stacking decks of cards and cheating at solitaire... They are the ones you've got to watch out for. They will steal the sunlight from your day. Beware the parasites of crudest excrement. They will leech everything you have built. They will devour your sympathy and thrive on your guilt...

Three weeks later, Sheila returned to her job as a substitute teacher's aide, and Dan went back to writing. Weary of theology, he switched gears to young adult fiction. Through these books, he hoped to introduce surrealism and the avant-garde to audiences between the ages of twelve and eighteen. For the past few weeks, he had been working on a book called *Lily and Abe Visit Mazgua City*: a story of two frogs who venture far beyond the boundaries of their pond and end up in the capital city of planet Mazgua. The following is an excerpt from the book:

Lily and Abe stood among the crowd in the city center, weeping for a wounded pterodactyl. Lily offered the avian dinosaur an apple from her lunch bag, but it refused. Instead, it beseeched the frogs to fulfill its final wish: unlock the vault hidden in the laboratory beneath the abandoned city library. There, they would find the pterodactyl's unhatched eggs. Upon hatching, the babies would avenge their mother's death by flying up to the Castle on the Hill and slaying the Owl who observes the actions and thoughts of everyone in the city.

"Not to worry, Madame Pterodactyl. Ace Detectives Abe and Lily are on the case!" Abe saluted.

"That's *Lily and Abe, Private Amphibians*, and don't you forget it." Lily kicked Abe with her hind leg.

"Ouch." Abe's tongue jolted out of his mouth involuntarily.

"Thank you so much, young ones." The Pterodactyl took in a belabored breath. "I'm...sure...the Dino...Gods... will re...ward...you..."

It exhaled, and its body slackened as if a volcano had just been removed from its chest.

"Let's go Abel." Lily shut the Pterodactyl's eyelids and leapt into the window of a maglev bus. "We've got work to do."

"I told you not to call me that, *Lilith*." Abe followed, but almost got his foot caught in the window as it closed.

A pungent smell hit the frogs' olfactory centers as they forced open the rusted front door of the library.

"*Peeyoo*. What reeks in here?" Abe held his nose.

"Smells to me like dead mice or bats or something." Lily breathed only through her mouth, which made her speech sound nasal.

"Why won't the city government do something about this?"

"The Owl *is* the city government, remember? I'm sure he had banked on everyone forgetting about this place. If his panoptic vision were to alert him of a possible intruder, he would most likely intervene personally."

"Intruders like us."

"That's why we need to find the eggs fast."

"Agreed." While Lily searched for an entrance to the secret lab, Abe browsed the shelves for good reading material.

"Abe. Quit goofing around and help me look."

"In a minute, Lily." He picked up a dusty tome filled with blank pages. As soon as he flipped to the last page, a shadow jumped out and cast a spell that transformed him into a lobster. Lily laughed, but Abe was none too happy about it. Perhaps when they finally found the lab, they could procure a serum to change Abe back into a frog.

In the children's section, Lily came across a cubbyhole guarded by a black Queen chess piece. When she touched it, the world slowed down and sped up at random intervals. Her emotions cycled like crazy:

GIGGLEHAPPYTFUNTIMES .... *hahahahahahahahahaha.*
Deeeppprrreeesssiiiiooonnn ... MANICSUPERSANICGINnTANIC.
mel ... an ... cho ... ly ... imokayimokayimokayimokayim ... okay? ...

Before she could get a grip on herself, a leathery mass crashed through the ceiling and squashed the Queen, missing Lily by a millimeter. It was a diplodocus. It roared at the top of its lungs. The frog and lobster covered their auditory appendages.

"Where did this thing come from?" Lily asked.

"You want me to go and get some?" Abe couldn't hear a thing over the diplodocus' incessant roaring. "Get some of what?"

"What I said was..."

The diplodocus' roars carried inflections of pain. It must have broken its leg in the fall.

Suddenly, the ground vibrated.

The diplodocus hushed up and craned its neck toward the hole it had made in the ceiling.

Lily and Abe peered through the hole with a great deal of hesitation. The situation was worse than they ever could've imagined. A flaming asteroid was hurtling toward the Earth.

"Of course." Lily's flesh still quivered from the psychosis induced by the chess piece. "Asteroids naturally follow dinosaurs. It's the way the world works, I suppose."

The asteroid smashed into the library, bathing everything in a blaze of light and heat.

Next thing Abe and Lily knew, they were home at the pond, but something about it was different. A concrete bridge now spanned from bank to bank. A battalion of indigenous people stood on one side protesting a pink-robed wizard on the other.

"No more blood!" The Indigents hurled their spears. Nine of them missed, but the tenth's slid through the wizard's heart like a javelin through gelatin.

The wizard burst into flames and burned down the false scenery revealing that Lily and Abe had never left the library. There was no hole in the ceiling, no dinosaur, and no asteroid: only papers and manila folders strewn everywhere.

"*Whew*. It was just a mirage." Lily clasped her hands and thanked Pwap, the goddess of fortune in Frogtoadian mythology.

While Lily had been indisposed, Abe had dumped the contents of a filing cabinet onto the floor.

"Oh, good, you're awake." He clicked his mandibles. "I've found a way to access the secret laboratory. This paper here says we need to find an ivory flute hidden in a lock box somewhere in this library."

Great, Lily thought. *More locked boxes and probably more hallucinatory death trips.* She shuddered.

♠   ♠   ♠

It was an icy Friday evening at the beginning of February. Sheila stood by Dan's side as he read the incomplete manuscript of *Abe And Lily Visit Mazgua City* to teens with cancer at the same hospital where they had lost Ryan. Dan meant to finish the book that week, but the emotional gravity that hung above him had warped his sleep schedule. It tranquilized him during the day and radiated paranoia as he lay in bed. His daily meal of fast food and cheap rum and cola didn't help his condition either.

Kids from grades seven through twelve sat on the floor sharing candy hearts and giggling between fits of coughing. The air tasted like sugar and sickness. Dan was ready to burst into tears, but he wrestled the weakness from his eyes. He needed to maintain a sunny disposition for the sake of the kids.

"After searching the library for hours," he read, "Lily finally found the ivory flute. Turns out, a mouse had swiped it from the lock box and was carrying it around in its teeth. Lily cornered the mouse, snatched the flute and played Yankee Doodle. At the other end of the stacks, Abe reached to grab a book on frog anatomy. But before he could get his claws on it, the shelf retreated into the wall and slid sideways.

"'Dag nabbit.' He clacked his claws in frustration. 'Just when I found something Mom wouldn't let me read. Hey, Lily.' He shouted as loud as his crustacean vocal cords would let him. 'The entrance to the lab is over here.'

"'Coming.' She hopped from book pile to book pile, toppling them in the process."

The kids seemed to enjoy the book. Their eyes were wider than any that Sheila had ever seen; except for maybe frog eyes.

What would Ryan have thought of his father's stories had he lived? Were there any instances of Frogbabies surviving birth? Even living to adulthood?

She'd never seen a full-grown Frogperson, so she assumed it wasn't possible for them to live outside the womb.

I kept him alive though…at least for a little bit. While he was in my womb, he absorbed nutrients from what I ate and drank. He was safe, warm, and well-fed despite being unconscious. Is consciousness really all that great of a thing? If you're snug, secure, and alive, why ask for anything more? I didn't choose to be born conscious. Look what this awareness has brought me: a cloud of misery that trails behind me like a fart everywhere I go. Who's to say that consciousness is what makes human beings special? Frogbabies could probably live fulfilling lives if we could find a way of keeping them alive.

Sheila's colleague Mary was out on maternity leave. Last Sheila had heard, Mary was having contractions and was due to start pushing any day.

I wonder if she's had her baby by now.

She took out her phone and logged into Facebook. She dug through her notifications but couldn't find anything. She browsed Mary's news feed, but found no new information since her husband had posted about her going into contractions that morning.

Something glinted in her peripheral vision. One of the kids stared at her through thick glasses: a boy around age thirteen. He looked like he wanted attention. Her mothering instinct kicked in, and she padded along the outskirts of the circle of children to him. His eyes were like signed baseballs in a glass case.

"Is everything okay?" Sheila touched his shoulder with the pads of her fingers.

The boy held up his hands, which were cupped around something.

"What is it? Let me see." Sheila smiled.

The boy lifted his fingers a teeny bit.

A dingy green blob sprang from his hands and landed on the linoleum.

A group of girls shrieked, and Dan stopped reading.

"It's okay." Sheila made sure to keep a smile plastered on her face. "It's just a frog. I'll get it."

As soon as she went to scoop up the amphibian, it leapt onto the shoulder of a girl in a pink bandana. The girl flinched, and the frog bounced out of the room and ten feet down the hall.

"Sorry about that, guys." Sheila's face hurt from faking cheeriness. "Keep reading, Dan, it's just this boy's pet. I'll rescue it."

Everyone laughed except for the boy, who looked like he was about to cry.

"Anyway," Dan said. "The stairway leading to the lab was completely dark…"

Sheila scanned the hallway but couldn't find the frog. She was about to give up when something made her freeze in place.

Two men clad in head-to-toe protective gear carted a metal box into an elevator marked AUTHORIZED PERSONNEL ONLY. Before the doors could shut, the frog jumped in with them.

A few seconds later, the doors reopened. The men had killed the frog and one of them held it by its hind leg.

"The sterility of elevator B has been compromised," the other one said into a walkie-talkie. "We're gonna need a scrub team in here before we can proceed."

"Copy that," said the voice on the other end. The men left for some other part of the building, leaving the elevator wide open.

A beast sleeping deep inside of Sheila stirred. *There's something important down there. Wherever that elevator goes, I need to go. And that box. Something's odd about the size of that box.*

A gust of February wind tore at her heart even though there were no windows nearby. It blew harder and harder until it lifted her off the ground and pushed her into the elevator.

What the hell am I doing?

She mashed the 'door close' button.

What was taking Sheila so long?

Dan read: "Lily fashioned a torch by duct taping scraps of loose-leaf paper to a meter stick and igniting them with a lighter found in the lost-items bin. A draft of cold air clawed at their faces as they stepped over the threshold of the hidden staircase.

"As they descended, all they could hear was the rattling of Abe's carapace, the *plink-plink* of ceiling condensation, and a barely-audible series of grunts, like a demon gorging on a fresh cadaver."

Safe inside the elevator, Sheila pushed a button outlined in crimson labeled: SUB BASEMENT 2.

As the elevator plummeted, her breath turned to ice. She shivered.

The box, there's something in that box I need to see.

She fingered the latch. The elevator had passed the fifth floor. She'd be at her destination soon.

What awaited her at the bottom?

Her heart thumped against her sternum as she undid the latch.

White smoke hissed from the box as she lifted the lid.

"The room at the bottom of the stairs was so drafty, it blew out the torch," Dan read. "Lily tried blowing on it, but the flames refused to relight. She groped the wall in search of a light switch. Finding nothing, she inched forward hesitantly. Her heart beat in her throat pouch.

"'What's that sound?' Abe scuttled along by her left foot.

"'I dunno.' Lily stopped and listened. 'It sounds like…breathing?'

"It was faint, but the frog and lobster could tell that something large and alive was aspirating in the center of the room.

"'Who's there?' Lily was too scared to be self-conscious of the tremor in her voice.

"The same rhythmic breathing answered them, as if the thing, whatever it was, was sleeping.

"'Hey, I got an idea.' The tone of Abe's voice suggested mischief.

"Before Lily could stop him, the lobster leapt forward and pinched the flank of whatever slept in the middle of the room.

"The thing stirred and snorted.

"Abe jumped back.

"A light clicked on."

It took about five seconds for the smoke to dissipate and the contents of the box to become visible.

Two marbles glinted among the mist.

Sheila jumped, and her head hit the ceiling.

A Frogbaby.

Another one just like Ryan.

She collapsed in a heap on the floor and sobbed.

Dan checked for any sign of Sheila.

Still nothing.

He read:

"Curled up on a throw rug was the same diplodocus Lily had hallucinated about when she touched the chess piece. It craned its neck to stare at the frog and lobster.

"'You woke me up, you twits.' The diplodocus' breath stank of cockroaches and mold rot.

"'You don't have to call us names.' Lily put her hands on her hips. 'I'm sorry we woke you up, but we're here for a reason.'

"'And what reason is that?' The diplodocus thudded its head against a rafter beam.

"'We need to find a safe.'

"'A safe, eh?' The diplodocus laughed. 'What's in it? Anything good?'

"'I don't believe that's any of your business,' she said, sticking out her tongue, which came within an inch of the diplodocus' nose.

"'Fine, then. If you don't wanna tell me, perhaps I won't tell you *my* little secret.' The diplodocus' mouth curled up into a toothless grin.

"'Wait a minute.' Lily waved her finger. 'You know something, don't you? About the safe, I mean.'

"'I don't know what's in it.' The diplodocus guffawed. 'If you tell me what you think you might find in there, I can give you an educated guess as to where the safe *might* be. That's all.'

"'Don't play games with me, dinosaur.' Lily sighed. 'Okay, fine. We believe there's a safe in this laboratory containing the unhatched eggs of a pterodactyl we met in Mazgua City. She was dying. She wanted us to find her babies so that they could defeat the Owl and avenge her death.'

"'The Owl, you say?' The diplodocus faced the wall. 'I was hoping this day would come: when a group of youngsters fed up with the Owl's invasion of everyone's privacy would band together and put a stop to him.'"

When Sheila regained the courage to face the dead child in the box, she checked the tag wrapped around its foot.

"Margaret Elizabeth Thallman," it read. Thallman was the name of Mary Richardson's husband. This was her baby.

"Mary, I'm so sorry." Sheila's hand shook uncontrollably as she reached out to touch the corpse's tiny pink foot.

The diplodocus cleared his throat.

"The Owl's scientist henchmen created me as a means of summoning an asteroid to destroy the world. You see, dinosaurs like me have been blessed, some would say cursed, with an ability to trigger the End of the World when things aren't going right. I thought the world was fine, but the Owl wanted to use me to summon an asteroid against my will. But I stood up to him and beat up most of his cronies. He ended up fleeing to the Castle on the Hill and has been there observing the world ever since."

The baby's foot was warm to Sheila's touch. To her surprise, it wiggled its legs and arms.

"Oh, dear God." Sheila covered her mouth. "It's *alive*."

As if in imitation of Sheila, the baby closed its frog eyes and cried. Its arms reached toward her.

Margaret wanted to be held.

"These days, the Owl is looking for another way to destroy the world. He's already got a personal rocket ready to blast him into space if he ever achieves his goal. He believes that the creatures of this world weren't meant to exist: that we are nothing but molecular anomalies. He already has an entire universe inside his head in which he controls all.

"He believes *that* universe is ideal, and therefore, the only one that matters.

"The pterodactyl you met was a test subject like me who got away. I survived, but she apparently didn't. I don't know where the safe containing her eggs is hidden. I've been searching this facility top-to-bottom for the past year trying to find it as well. I'm surprised you even made it here. You are the first creatures ever to visit me from outside. I commend you for finding the flute. That mouse is a slippery one. I can't believe you caught the little bugger."

"What clues do you have as to the safe's whereabouts?" asked Lily.

"The only info I've been able to gather after tearing this library/laboratory complex apart is that it has something to do with mirrors, probability, and electromagnetism. If one can synthesize these three ideas, an unused faculty of the brain will be unlocked, allowing the person to *see* the safe in real space.

That's all I've been able to put together by referencing and cross-referencing every book in this library."

"Thanks, Mr. Diplodocus." Lily supplied a faint smile. "At least it's a start."

"Call me, D. Plod or just D. That's probably what my friends would call me if I had any."

"Well, you do now." Lily extended her hand, and D bumped it with his big flat foot.

"So, how do we start?" Abe said, feeling ignored.

"First," said Lily, "we've got to access the internet and scrutinize the crap out of all scientific topics in which mirrors, probability, and electromagnetism intermesh. We gotta do it before the Owl comes to poop on our party."

"Right." Abe repressed a groan.

After the shock receded, Sheila discarded her inhibitions and scooped the infant out of its frozen casket.

"It's okay sweetie. I'll get you to your mommy. It's okay," she said softly, swaying Margaret back and forth.

The little girl smiled. She was a very cute froggie indeed.

The elevator dinged, and the door slid open. Sheila had arrived at the sub-sub basement.

The kids had finished the bag of candy hearts, and the hospital staff passed out brownies on flimsy paper plates.

Dan licked his finger and turned another page.

"The frog, the lobster, and the diplodocus shielded their eyes as the light of artificial day blasted their corneas. The Owl would likely show up within a day's time. This estimate considered every other project on the Owl's to-do list as governing body of the city. The three needed to work quickly. Hopefully, the internet connection at the Weimaraner Café wasn't in one of its shoddy phases."

A nurse appeared in the doorway and pointed to her wristwatch, indicating that today's story session was at its end.

"I suppose we'll leave off there for today." Dan closed the book and placed it on the table next to him. "I hope you all can join me next time."

The children who had finished their brownies were shepherded out of the room and on to some other activity designed to keep their minds off their illnesses and the specter of chemo and radiation therapy.

Dan sighed and rubbed his eyebrows.

Where could Sheila be? That boy's frog couldn't have gone that *far.*

The thirteen-year-old with the glasses tapped Dan's shoulder.

"Mr. Z? Has your wife found Mr. Peepers yet?"

Dan's anxiety flattened his urge to laugh.

"She must still be searching for him. This is a really big hospital and that frog can probably cover a lot of ground since he's so good at jumping. Why don't you come with me and we'll let security know about it."

"Please don't tell security." The boy's eyes started to liquefy. "They'll kill him for sure. He's a special frog. Just between you and me, he's a product of secret research. I swiped him from a lab at another hospital. I read in the files that he can live forever as long as he doesn't get hurt."

Dan bit his lip. *This kid might've grown up to be a great novelist if he had the luxury of years ahead of him.*

"How about this, we'll have the nurse's station page my wife. It's very likely that she has found him already and is just lost. You can come with me if it's okay with the nurse here."

Dan glanced at the nurse, and she nodded in approval.

"All right, bud, let's find that frog."

The boy smiled, his eyes solidifying.

Sheila exited the elevator to a door with a big fourteen on it.

"Fourteen. Why does everything always have to be associated with a number?" Her labored breaths formed plumes of white in the wet air of the hospital underworld. She pressed a button, and the door slid open with a hiss.

Margaret cried.

Sheila froze then inched forward cautiously into whatever awaited her beyond.

After Dan and the boy poked their heads into each of the rooms on that floor, they approached the nurse's station.

"Excuse me." Dan waved at a pretty nurse whose nose was bejeweled with a silver stud. "I can't seem to find my wife. Would you mind paging her for—"

"Just hold on one second." The nurse lowered her gaze to the boy. "Jonathan, it's time to go to chemo. Deborah will take you."

She indicated a suntanned nurse leaning against the wall. Deborah waved and flashed her pearly whites at the boy.

Jonathan looked like his favorite stuffed animal had been tossed into a wood chipper.

"It's okay, pal." Dan put a hand on the boy's shoulder. "I'll find your frog. And if worse comes to worst, I'll see about getting you a new one."

Jonathan tore his gaze away and dragged his emaciated frame over to Deborah. He shot Dan one last glance before he and Deborah disappeared into the framework of the machine designed to keep human souls fettered to their bodies.

"Sorry about that, sir," the nurse behind the counter said, shuffling a stack of manila folders into order. "What was it you needed help with?"

Dan couldn't answer. His mind traversed faraway star systems as he ground a hole into the cold, hard floor with the ball of his foot.

On the wall of Room Fourteen was a rack of translucent eggs wired to a supercomputer. Something about the eggs struck a nerve in Sheila.

Margaret calmed and pulled at strands of Sheila's hair.

"Seems like normal healthy baby behavior to me. Brain or not, this kid's got one strong grip."

She edged closer to the wall of eggs, could feel her breast tissue quivering with each thud of her heart. She approached an egg at eye level, labeled 475.

The silhouette of a tiny hand groped at the wall of the egg. This confirmed Sheila's darkest suspicions. These eggs contained living Frogbabies. There were five hundred of them arranged in twenty-five columns of twenty. Egg 475 had a name next to its number: 'Kerri-Lynn Slattery.'

"This can't be." Sheila gasped. "Is this Jamie Slattery's baby? The single mom who lives on our block who posted on Facebook about having a miscarriage?"

She scanned more of the names. "Smith, Adam. Smith, Christopher. Snelling, Julia? That's Molly Snelling's baby. The art teacher who also said she had a miscarriage. In fact, these are all names of people who have had miscarriages: Kim Falconi, Beth Andersen. Wait a minute."

Still holding Margaret, Sheila made a beeline for the lower right-hand corner of the wall where the Z-names would be. If there was a chance Ryan wasn't dead, she had to know.

Sure enough, egg number 500 was labeled, Zebrowski, Ryan.

It took all of Sheila's strength not to burst. Her baby was alive. She needed to get him out of here.

With Margaret in her left arm, she tore open the egg with her right. Salty liquid splashed onto the floor and pooled at her feet. Ryan cried, a sound sweeter than the most sublime orchestral piece. His arms reached toward her, and his eyes glistened with longing. She pressed her cheek against his. The fact that he had been starved of his mother's love for more than a month made her feel sick inside.

"Let's go home." She couldn't help staring into those magnificent eyes.

Ryan smiled, and Sheila smiled back despite her tears.

"Who's there?" A man's voice rang out like rifle fire.

"It doesn't matter who's there." Her voice cracked the air like a whip.

Margaret cried again. "I'm going home with my son and bringing Margaret back to her mother. There's nothing you can do about it. Will it kill him if I remove these wires?"

"Put the baby down." A man stood in the doorway in a casual suit: his wire-rimmed glasses reflected the piss-yellow of the eggs. Behind him, a battalion of security guards and businessmen readied themselves for action.

"Back the fuck off." Sheila inched as close to Ryan as she could. "What are you doing with these children? Why are you keeping them here? Why did you lie to their families about them being dead?"

"Okay, okay," said the man, "relax. I understand that you're upset. Any mother would be, and you have a right to be. But before you accuse us of being monsters, boogeymen, or what have you, I think you deserve to know why we kept your baby as well as all these others alive in secret."

"Save it for the courtroom, you fucking swine. I don't have time for this shit. I'm going to introduce Ryan to his father, then I'm calling the police…"

The man in the suit laughed. "Ma'am, we *are* the police."

Two men in black coveralls appeared behind Sheila. One stuck her left deltoid with a syringe, and the other snatched Margaret. They hauled Sheila's limp body onto a gurney and wheeled her off to one of the sub-sub basement's holding rooms.

"We'll have to patch that unit with syntho-dermis until it heals." The man in the suit indicated 500's egg. He turned to the entourage behind him. "This drill went better than I had hoped. As you saw, we're more than prepared to deal with intruders. The Video will set her mind straight and keep her from interfering any further. We'll inform the husband that she's been involved in an accident involving biologically hazardous material and that he can't see her because it would endanger his health. When we release her, she'll have a memory blackout spanning from her discovery of Room Fourteen to her release from this hospital. Project RIBBIT will remain unhindered, that much I can assure you."

When Sheila woke, she was strapped to a chair. Her eyelids were pried open by plastic spacers, and every now and then, a hand would emerge from the shadows and squeeze droplets of saline solution into her eyes. She could wiggle her toes and open and close her hands, but her head was held firmly in place. A screen on the opposite wall lit up. A countdown like those featured in old movies began:

5… 4… 3… 2… 1…

A video played, the contents of which Sheila would never consciously remember.

Don't worry. Leave the Future to us.

We won't be sad that you're not around. We've got ourselves, and that's all we need. The nothingness of Infinite Time will inch ever forward like a centipede in the dark. The candle glowing in the chapel may have been pretty to look at, but there was nothing to stumble upon in the first place. We will serve as your legacy: complete and empty, the perfect form.

All prayers will be answered.

AMEN.

Since August of 2001, the global think tank Project RIBBIT had been working with corporations like Monsanto to alter the human gene pool via chemical additives in foods and beverages. The percentage of children born without brains and spines spiked to ninety percent over the course of fifteen years as a result. Most Frogbabies were not actually born dead as their parents were led to believe. Many survived with only a brainstem keeping their heart pumping. The lack of a central nervous system or any other mental faculties allowed them to live without ever experiencing physical or emotional pain.

However, a major difference between Frogbabies and those who became vegetables as a result of traumatic brain injuries was that accident victims often had access to pleasurable and painful memories left over from before their accidents. These stored experiences made living in a vegetative state all the more unbearable. According to the Project RIBBIT scientists, the life experience of a Frogbaby was the *ideal* life experience; a vegetative state without prior knowledge of pain and pleasure.

After they were born, the babies were collected by Project personnel and kept alive in secret laboratories. The masterminds claimed that no living thing was more innocent and unbiased than a baby born without a brain. They believed that the human tendency to erroneously organize data gleaned from stimuli was the cause of the loss of innocence described in the book of Genesis. To be born unable to construct these meta-realities would be to remain in Eden forever.

Even after the death of the last human, the Frogbabies would continue to live hooked up to their synthetic wombs, floating in bliss, existing as a race incapable of worry and anxiety. They would be mankind's last and truest form. The apes that had invented fire, the wheel, and taxes would bow out gracefully and leave the world for the Frogbabies to inherit.

In the meantime, Project RIBBIT would learn all it could about how Frogbabies perceived the world by analyzing their sensory processes through computers interfaced with their brainstems. This data would be used to construct a simulacrum of Frogbaby consciousness called an Artificial Innocence. In the event that the Frogchildren's bodies were destroyed by natural disaster, rockets carrying copies of the Artificial Innocence would be blasted into space to seed the universe with purity and joy.

Ever since Sheila made contact with those hazardous chemicals at the hospital, she hasn't been right in the head. Every night, she'd have the same dream:

She'd be naked and hovering above her bed in the fetal position while a frog in a lobster's body blew bubbles in the hallway. One of the bubbles would take the form of an analog computer, would wrap itself around the head of a diplodocus, connect to his brain and inform him that the safe he'd been searching for had been hidden in the nerve ganglion in his left hip the entire time. The frog-lobster would blow two more bubbles for himself and his female frog companion. Using their helmets, the three of them would link their minds, unlock the safe, and free the pterodactyl eggs trapped inside.

The eggs would hatch and the frog, lobster, and diplodocus would mount the baby pterodactyls and fly up to a castle in the mountains. Once there, the pterodactyls would peck out the panoptic eyes of an Owl King too busy crunching numbers to notice that his kingdom had collapsed.

The lobster, frog, and diplodocus would look at each other, thinking, *now what?*

After gorging on the innards of the Owl, the pterodactyls, still hunched over their kill, would crane their heads toward the three heroes. Ropes of saliva would be dangling from their bloody jaws, and their eyes would be glistening with hunger.

"I don't like the look of this," the frog would say.

"Let's get out of here." The lobster would climb on the frog's back, and the frog would jump out the window.

"Wait for me," the diplodocus would shout, but it would be too late. The sounds of him being eaten would reverberate off the hills for all to hear.

The frog and lobster would return to where their pond was supposed to be, but in its place would be a strip mall with a video store, fortune-teller shop, and a dealer of Native Mazguanian crafts.

When Sheila woke, a crucial piece of information was missing from her brain. Whenever she thought about Ryan or Frogbabies, her head would hurt and her train of thought would reroute to complacency. Exhausted from trying to remember something she never knew, she resigned herself to acceptance. The Frogbabies' lives were blissfully short, and that's the way it was.

Ryan had been born into a state of pure Zen. It would be downright selfish of her to make him stay in this world just to satisfy her nurturing instinct.

Eventually, she and everybody else would enter the same realm of nothingness. Until then, she'd just have to endure the ups and downs of life and the dreams that screamed at her every night, telling her that something wasn't right.

'ROUND BACK
John Pedersen

There ain't nothing particularly noteworthy about that building sitting in the middle of the park. I guess it's supposed to be a stage. Or a miniature amphitheater.

It, of itself, ain't creepy. It's just a big porch with a roof on it.

What's creepy is the back.

They publicized a disappearance from here once, made some *X-Files* knockoff movie about it. You know, the guy who got abducted by aliens in the White Mountains in the seventies? The movie came along at the end of that fad, so it's not really a surprise if you haven't heard of it or don't remember it.

Walton wasn't the only person to go missing, but he was the only one to come back, which is why everyone thinks he's full of shit.

Around back is this monument for all of the people who have disappeared from the town. Survivors do this thing where they go and hang up outfits, the whole deal, like someone's still wearing 'em—probably thirty or so sets of pants and shirts stuck to the back of this thing. Mostly little kids' clothes.

And in case I have to spell it out for you, that's thirty people who have straight vanished from this place.

Started before Walton.

No one said anything about aliens until he came back.

No one's really said anything about aliens since then, I guess.

I mean, he says it all the time, but whatever.

We get a call to do this job. My dad and I. It was one of those days, gray skies, windy, air heavy like it wanted to rain but couldn't.

Looked like a septic sinkhole had opened up underneath the amphitheater. Ain't no septic tank there, but all right. A big pit spread out underneath the right side of the stage, and the whole floor had a thin crack running through it. The foundation had shifted, and the town council wanted to prevent any more damage.

A second hole started showing around the back. We were sticking measuring rods down into the sludge at the bottom to see how deep they went and how much clay we'd need to fill them in.

Well, Dad gets to prodding the main hole, and I go around back to the little one, back by the morbid display. The hole's right underneath these blue track pants and yellow soccer jersey, probably from a kid no more than eight years old. His little Vans were stapled up to the wall.

I get the stick down there into all of it, it goes really deep, and there's no firm resistance. I'm trying to figure out how I can get an extra arm's length down when my dad just starts howling like the devil himself got him.

Around front, he's got his flashlight shining down into the hole and damn near his whole head underneath the lip of the stage.

These kind of sinkholes are dangerous. The ground can just shift underneath you and that's it, you could just be gone. Muck down there'll swallow you up.

So, my dad's the smartest guy I know, and there's no way he'd be putting himself into this position without a good reason. He looks at me, pale white, and he says, "Get over here."

He shoves his whole shoulder underneath the foundation, trying to get that light under there.

He's not afraid, but something's got him real upset, so I give the ground a wide pass around him and go to the other side of the hole.

It's dark inside, and what his light shows isn't much more than the gray/brown stuff that I could see on the other side.

"There's a kid down there. Can you see him?"

As I got older, I realized that my pop didn't know everything, but when he tells me something, my first instinct is still to believe it, even if it don't make sense. So, I do the dangerous thing and try to get my head under the stage, too. Smells humid down here but not like sewage. More like moss growing on a tree.

"Where?" I ask him. I don't see anything. The hole is pretty big, despite the fact that the opening is only about two or three feet wide. It don't look like it connects to the one around back.

"I don't know. I just saw him."

I sit up and fish around in my pocket for my phone. "We gotta call somebody."

"Get your light over there," he tells me.

Instead of doing the smart thing and getting someone out here, an ambulance or something, I just do what he says and get mine under there, too. I don't really see much, other than more of the slimy soil. He pulls himself out for a second and comes back with the pole in the other hand. He's got nothing to stabilize himself with now. Bad news.

"Put it over there." He shows me with his light where he wants mine. He starts waving the pole around and plunges the end of it down into the standing water at the very bottom and sure enough, a little white hand comes up when he lifts it back up.

"I got him, there," he says. His face is turning red, and he tells me to hold my light steady. The little hand is just hanging there limply by the wrist. He flings his light out behind him and grabs the pole with his other hand. The leverage is too much, and he's not strong enough to hold on to it.

"Go get the other one," he tells me. "Maybe the two of us can lift him out."

So I go for it. Whole time thinking maybe I oughta call someone, but who knows how much time the little guy has.

Back around the corner, I shit you not, I hear a *giggle*. There's two little kids standing where I left my things.

So I tell 'em I need their help. I grab my pole, and I tell 'em run to the county building across the street. The kids are pale as fuck, but that doesn't compute right away.

Dad's still half-gone underneath the building when I get back. He looks like he's scooched sideways, trying to wedge his hips in where the ground still comes up against the foundation of the building. Hopefully it don't crumble underneath him.

I crawl in on the other side of the sinkhole again and get the pole down there, trying to balance it with the flashlight in the other hand. I shine the light on Dad, down his arm and on down the pole, and the little wrist is still resting over it. Little hand looks kinda blue.

"Careful," he says. He doesn't want me to stick the kid or anything, but I gotta at least find out where he is so I can get my pole underneath him.

Tricky thing looking for the right kind of firmness in a mess like that. You'll get stopped up in the muck, but you know the difference between that slowing you down and when you hit something solid, like ground.

Or a body.

"I got him," I tell Dad.

"Well, hurry up."

A couple more gentle prods into the solid mass, and I feel some...feedback, maybe? It's hard to keep the light steady, but I pull my pole back some, and there's a little fist grasping the end of it. Little bastard is alive.

I start to feel some of the worry in Dad's voice; we're on a timer, and those kids out back were worthless. Nobody else's showing up to help us. I don't want to pull too hard 'cause I don't want the little guy to lose his grip, but what if he's really stuck down there? How long has he been under? Why isn't he grabbing Dad's pole, too?

My light catches a little of his arm as I pull up a bit, but I have to reposition myself. I find the end of Dad's pole, and find the end of my pole, and some eyes reflect back at us. He's got his head above water.

Dad makes a noise.

The kid's other hand is gripping Dad's pole. Great, kid, now hold on while we drag you out.

Then, I notice his eyes.

They're black but not lights-off black; they're a black that goes inward, sorta like when you're staring up at the stars at night and that black goes somewhere.

I don't know if it's because it's so dark in there and my flashlight sucks, but we need to get this guy out, and that's all I can really think about.

That's when Dad calls me by my name. He says, "John," real calm-like, and I know something's wrong. I only ever heard him say it one other time like that, when I wasn't much older than this kid down there, and a bear was in the woods with us.

He says, "flip your light up," in that same even tone, and there's two, three, four more sets of those black eyes shining back at us.

These kids are pasty, too, and that's when I put two and two together.

"There's so many of 'em. How the hell did they get down here?"

Now, something's wrong here, and I can feel it in my gut, but Dad says, "We gotta get 'em out of there."

When I shine my light back on them, there's more. Like a lot more.

"Dad," I says, but he's wriggling around over there, bits of dry soil splashing below us. When I put my light back on him, he's trying to scoot farther in, to get that pole all the way down there to those kids.

He's gonna fall in. He knows better than that.

I put my light on the kids one more time, and they've all started to go for his pole. Saw a bunch of rats swimming once. That's what they looked like.

He can't pull 'em all out, not by himself.

These kids, what are they doing down there?

I grab Dad's trousers by the belt and hold on. It doesn't feel like the kids are tugging on him, it feels like he's trying to crawl the rest of the way in. Maybe he thinks if he can get in and get boots on the ground, he can lift them up to me or something, but he can't be thinking straight. There's no way he could be sure that he'd have stability down there.

He shimmies a bit farther in, and the edge of the concrete pinches my hand something fierce. I have to let go, then his whole butt is inside, and he's only clinging on by bending one knee up around the platform. I let go of my pole, but I can't reach him with my free hand, so I back my way out.

I ask him what he's doing, but all he says is, "We gotta get 'em out, son."

I make to go across the hole and grab him when all those white faces are right there at the edge of the hole, all right up where I just was, right up by his thighs.

I couldn't move. Those eyes meant to swallow me up.

He shifts his legs, and he slides himself further in, and he's just gone. There's just the empty hole. No little kids, no Dad, nothing.

I stood there staring for a minute before I run off to the sheriff. When we came back with the big flashlights, we—well, they—couldn't see nothing.

I wasn't getting near that hole again.

One 'round back was empty, too.

Hit up every damn avenue available, and I just kept getting the same dead-eyed stare. Deputies looked like they wanted to say something, but told me it'd be best I went on home. Swear I heard the paper say "Walton" when they was hanging up on me. Sheriff told me he'd file a report, but by then, I realized there was probably a whole three-ring binder full of reports. Saw the mayor down at the Skillet, just kept telling me he was sorry for my loss.

Thing is, no one seemed surprised when I mentioned the kids. Like it wasn't the craziest damn thing at all.

Just kept nodding and saying sorry.

Couple days later, the county maybe just guessed on the amount of clay they'd need to fill in the holes. They put more sod down on top, and that was that. It was like it had never happened.

I could have grabbed his ankles and pulled him out. I could have done something, anything, but I didn't.

We went back the next week and hung up a pair of his Wranglers and a t-shirt 'round back of the building.

DRUMS
M.T. DeSantis

The house had a beat.

It came from above, steady and unyielding. On some days, it was a sound in the background, a suggestion. On others, it was a demand, an order, and no matter how hard we tried, it could not be ignored.

Dulla was first. She woke one morning, eyes glassy, jaw slack, and she walked. We tried to stop her. We barricaded the way. We restrained her. We howled her name until our voices were hoarse and our throats burned. Still, she walked. Upward she climbed, each step in time with the beat. We waited at the foot of the steps. She opened the door, passed through, and disappeared forever.

Resh was next. He woke one morning, complexion pale and stare dead. He walked. We stood before him. We called his name. We gripped his arms, and they slipped through our fingers like sand through a screen not built to hold the grains. He paced up the steps, each footfall in perfect time. We watched from the bottom as he reached the top, opened the door, and disappeared forever.

Uan woke one morning, body frail and hands groping for lost light. He walked. We reached for him. We begged. We cried until our eyes were deserts of dust. Still, he walked. He scaled the stairs, each step thunder. He crested the hill, entered the room, and was lost forever.

Mara was next. She woke one morning, body battered and soul broken into shards of a mirror long left upon a filthy floor. She walked. I tried to stop her. I trailed behind, unable to match the demands of the drums. I reached, but my fingers closed around only darkness. I collapsed, dragging myself to the foot of the stairs, where I raised my head and watched her wooden ascent. She climbed in perfect synchronization. When she reached the top, I whimpered. She entered the room as if I had never existed and was lost forever.

The house has a beat. It comes from above, steady and unyielding.
On some days, it is a sound in the background, a suggestion.
On others, it is a demand.

My name is Suppa, and I will soon be gone forever. I lie awake, body aching for sleep. I refuse. If I do not give in, I will not dream. If I do not dream, I cannot wake, and if I cannot wake, I am safe. I am safe. I am...

TO SLEEP, PERCHANCE TO DREAM
Daniel M. Kimmel

The Emperor, the omnipotent and omniscient ruler of all he surveyed, woke in a cold sweat, tangled in his bed sheets. What a horrible nightmare. He had dreamt that he was a character in something called a YA novel, whatever that might be, and that his unquestioned authority was, in fact, being questioned by a fringe group of adolescents who plotted his overthrow.

Mehta Fixxion had not clawed and murdered his way to absolute power only to be undone by a pack of teenagers, especially since—in the dream at least—they were obviously rebelling against their parents, making him a convenient scapegoat. Certainly, he engaged in whims, such as staging gladiator contests between the chemistry and history departments of the schools in his realm.

What was the point of being a tyrant if you couldn't settle scores with the people who had hurt you in the past? It worked out well.

The chemists had the advantage—it was useful to know how to make explosives—and now, school children no longer learned the history of what things were like before he came to power. One would think they'd be grateful. Yet, the dream had seemed so real.

The Emperor summoned his trusted head of the secret police, Norman, to see what could be done. Norman was an odd name for one of the most feared men in Capital City, the capital city of Dictatoria, but it kept him humble. Fixxion made sure he was amply rewarded, had access to bed partners of several sexes, and received an unusual tax cut in which the state paid him whatever amount he theoretically owed. The Emperor was the only person with more power than Norman, and he wanted to make certain that Norman remained loyal.

Donning his navy-blue robe trimmed with ermine, Fixxion took the side door from his elaborate bedroom—which doubled as both a ballroom and a torture chamber, depending on his mood—and went to his more intimate consulting room, which could comfortably seat fifty. Norman waited for him.

"Good morning," said Norman, although the sun had yet to rise, "O great Emperor Fixxion, all-seeing and all-knowing, whose guiding hand ensures the stability and prosperity of Dictatoria, and whose every action and utterance has profound..."

"Yes, yes, let's get on with it." The Emperor cut off Norman with the wave of his hand. The full, formal greeting could easily have gone on for half an hour or more, especially as Norman began the elaborate choreography that went with it. "Please be seated."

"How may I serve you, Your Magnificence?" Norman asked, without a hint of toadying. Truth be told, Norman seemed perfectly happy with his present status. To most of the citizens of Dictatoria, he was just a name. He gave no press conferences. There were no public appearances. Other than the Emperor, those who saw him once seldom lived to see him a second time. It did exacerbate the servant problem, but the slave labor camps kept up a ready supply of replacements.

"Do you believe in the predictive power of dreams?" said Fixxion, still not entirely calm after his nightmare.

Norman responded with a thoughtful look. "I suppose that depends on how his Imperial Majesty feels. I would hesitate to draw a conclusion without first giving due consideration to the infallible word of..."

Fixxion sighed. Sometimes it was *not* good to be the king. "Relax, Norman. Your head isn't on the chopping block."

Norman gave a thin smile. A single bead of sweat rolling down the side of his forehead betrayed his concern.

"I live to serve. In my own experience, nightmares and dreams are less visions of the future than warnings about things we may not wish to confront directly. Not that I am suggesting that Your Glorious Leadership was in any way defective or unwilling to face challenges."

Between the nightmare and Norman's inability to answer a simple question without a paragraph of flattery, an exhausted Fixxion was at a loss for words. He wished they could just get to the point, but if Norman had done so without piling on the praise, his head might well have been meeting the business end of an axe.

Norman proceeded after a moment of silence. "If I may be so bold, why don't you tell me your premonition, and I can see if it matches any of the potential threats to the realm that we are currently monitoring?"

Fixxion sat back on his throne and looked down upon Norman, seated three steps below. "I know the people love me. And why not? I've brought them peace and prosperity, and except for that incident where we had to cleanse that island that didn't want me to build my new vacation home there, we haven't had to engage in any major suppression in quite some time."

Norman took his cue. "It's a common expression in Dictatoria that there's no reason to die as we're already living in Paradise."

Fixxion smiled. "Too true, too true. Yet, in my dream, some children in the rural provinces were taught to hate me and started an insurrection. And after we wiped most of them out, they hid in the woods and gathered forces to attack Capital City."

"With what, sticks and stones?"

"Precisely, I was attacked by a boy and a girl armed with slingshots."

Norman shook his head in grief. "I tried to keep this under control, but your all-seeing eye doesn't miss a thing."

"That, and our spy cameras. Where is the uprising?"

"It's in the far-flung province of Oatmealistan. Most of it is in ruins, but we have yet to subdue the young rebels who have taken to the forests. It looks like your dream was, indeed, a premonition for action."

The Emperor rose. "Yes, and decisive and brutal action it shall be, so that they will know precisely with whom they are dealing. We must kill all the teenagers and children right down to the babies. None shall escape. Then, they will fear my power."

"Not wishing to disagree with you in all your wisdom, Your Stupendousness, but if they're all dead, they're not likely to be fearing anything."

The Emperor considered the point. "Well taken, Norman, well taken. And, of course, it's foolproof since there is no way anyone could possibly have any means of escape."

The chamber door opened. Anyone entering unbidden by the Emperor risked death, but the person coming in was tall and young with flowing blonde hair. The Emperor's daughter Tulip, his favorite, was the only one who could have gotten away with it. She carried a large wicker basket that dripped water.

"What is it, Princess?" Technically her title was Tsarina of the Multiple Continents, but he liked calling her Princess.

"Daddy, look what I found in the river. Can I keep him?" Inside the basket a baby boy gurgled and cooed.

"Where could it have come from?" asked Norman suspiciously.

"I don't know, but I want to keep him and raise him as my own. Can I Daddy, can I?"

The Emperor gave an uncharacteristic chuckle. "You know I can never deny you anything, Princess."

"Thank you, Daddy. I love you." She gave her father a big kiss and left the chamber with her newly adopted son.

"Now, where was I? Ah, yes. Wipe out everyone in Oatmealistan. There's absolutely no way anyone can escape."

"As you command, so shall it be done." Norman began the elaborate exit ritual made all the more difficult because he had to do it with his back to the door as it was forbidden to turn away from the Emperor. Fixxion had long since stopped being impressed with the acrobatics involved and slipped back into his bedroom long before Norman made it out of the chamber.

Much better. The young rebels who threatened him would soon face the hard fist of Dictatorian justice. Could he get back to sleep and have more pleasant dreams? He settled into his bed with visions of scrappy teens being mowed down by the Emperor's Elite Execution Squad.

And just before he drifted off, he made a mental note to have Norman round up the authors of those YA novels.

TO QUIET THE PEN
Eddie Generous

Steve Lester read his name three times over. For years, he'd tried to make a subtle change stick: *S. Warren Lester.* It stuck thirty-two times in magazines and eleven times in short story anthologies. Twice, it stood totem on the covers of books all his own. Little publishers chancing their time on horror tales.

For two years, the author, *S. Warren Lester,* had committed himself fully to the art of spinning yarns with the hope that it would eventually lead to occupational wages. So far, minimum wage remained an unattainable carrot dangling before his screen-bleary eyes, yet his fingers refused to cease tapping.

After two years full-time and three more working around jobs and sleeps, he had nothing much to show but his name, or rather a version of his name, typed above stories that typically paid him between five and forty bucks apiece. The fallback funds were gone, and the line of credit swam deep fathoms.

Time to face the trumpets.

He read his name again, took a breath, and continued down the letter he'd written,

Attention Becky Ritz, Baker Housing Inc.

Something inside wanted to fight, like a rabid dog. Nonetheless, it was time to put that rabid dog down.

Goodbye, Yeller. Eat shit, Cujo.

"No more, *attention editor,*" Steve said and in a nasally, mocking tone added, "Attention managerial minds, please pay me to do the things that feel beneath you."

Clean break, the only way he succeeded in hard choices, adhesive bandages, quitting drinking, quitting smoking, and now, quitting the hardest of all, fiction writing.

I am contacting you in regards to the opening of a janitorial position recently posted on your website. It has been some time, but I have experience in the field, and my work ethic has not changed. In my early twenties, I assisted in cleaning...

"Look how far you've come. Turn back the clock to that guy, huh? Roll in reverse and roll up your sleeves, don't forget to switch off your brain."

The cover letter was page one of a two-page terror. The résumé, the real cabbage and biscuits, followed. It was necessary to reach more than a decade into the past. Writing wasn't *work* experience but supposed laziness and an affront to everyone who went to a day job instead of following a dream.

To assume Steve lazy was absurd.

For every short sold, six or seven went unsold. Long hours, seven days a week, crumpled sheets and lingering responses: *It's not the right voice at this time... We're sorry to inform you that while you are a talented... Unfortunately, it isn't a good fit...* Six novels sat in the trunk and a dozen novellas as well. Several hundred false starts long ago dragged to the trash bin icon on the corner of the screen.

But how does one explain the time and effort when the monetary sums don't match?

"Don't explain the insanity of hope. Focus on the paid labor."

...grew-up on a farm and...sorted packages after hours in college for UPS...good attitude and...

"Good attitude, my ass." He reread, scrolling the proof of leaving a dream behind.

The résumé was to be the summation of his adult existence, minimalizing the only thing he ever really tried for, the only thing that ever really mattered to him.

Starting with the months after he graduated the broadcast basics course in college:

2007-2010 – London Life – Insurance consultant and financial adviser.

An irritated snort rose from deep down. After college, life had suddenly felt real. The government piled the loans on him, and he had spent as if his pockets had holes. The college years were thirsty times. Insurance and investments were a way to get that money back and all it demanded was a chunk of his soul.

What a horrible summation of his systematic value.

The coffee maker beeped from the kitchen to warn of its impending shutdown. Fresh cup, composure realigning, Steve dropped onto his computer chair where he'd penned such gems as *Venomous Glass, Toads on Death Parade,* and *Grace's Wooden Heart.*

The résumé stared back at him.

"What the hell?"

Sipping coffee, Steve let his finger roll the screen to the occupation after shilling invisible goods for humungous corporations that paid him quarter pennies on the hundreds retained. After quitting the world of high finance, wildly overweight, overwrought, and smoking a pack and a half a day, he took a job as a night stocker. It was physically demanding but asked nothing of him mentally.

Where the résumé should've read *Lowe's – Overnight Inventory – 2011-2012*, it read *RimRoil – Rig Swamper – 2011-2012*.

The cursor dragged blue over the job he'd never had, and a memory pounded at the doors of his mindscape.

Flashed: A filthy, greasy, oily world, burning.

Bringing crude up from below the crust of the ground was something, somehow, he knew. This new memory showed Steve doing his stinking duty, coated in a sticky brown film. The guys had made a royal mess of the tools and couplers. Sometimes, those braindead jerkoffs did it in spite of the young man with the college education and experience in suit wearing. To them, he was some damned high-minded asshole.

Steve understood trouble before his mind played the message.

Heat crept with ghostly tendrils.

Ronnie Bacon had ordered Steve to clean the drill platform, out of the way. Filth and instruction were typical, expected. Steve made good money and lost much of the weight he put on stress eating. If only he could quit smoking and drinking, he'd be…

"But I lost it at the gym, and I quit smoking right after I took the job at—"

The memory roared over his soft words.

Ronnie Bacon's silver Zippo landed with a ping on the platform where Steve worked. Rigging is loud business, and the sound went ignored. The flames travelled the slow burn of muddy crude, and Steve screamed as the fire danced up the legs of his coveralls.

"That's not…" He clicked delete and inserted the easy facts of working at Lowe's.

The remainder appeared normal.

Best Buy – Seasonal Sales – 2013…

Esso – Desk Attendant – 2013-2014…

Self – Fiction Author – Part-Time 2011-2014 and Full-Time 2014-2016.

Putting an end number on his horror-writing career burned just as the hallucinated memory had. Steve hit print, drained his coffee and stepped off to the can while his Brother monochrome sang the song of fans and lasers.

Steve opened his pants to find the edges of scar tissue riding up his thighs, the tight, shiny patch on the side of his shrivelled penis.

Vomit rose up the throat. Steve gagged. Impossible. He'd never worked on a rig.

He swooned and nearly fainted, pissing on the floor and into the bathtub. His back fell against the wall before his shaky knees found strength. He refused another glance at the burns that really couldn't be there, buttoned his jeans, and stormed out of the washroom, back to the computer.

He leaned down.

"Stressed. Jarred, the word is jarred."

Steve picked up the printed cover letter and résumé. He gave a cursory glance, unwilling to read it again, unwilling to relive the laughably meagre successes of his writing career. The résumé was the real trouble, and he couldn't afford to send off the fantasies of a beleaguered mind.

Rig Swamper.

"Never." Another surprise: *Waste Management Worker.* "That never—"

Flashed: a stinking, infested, putrid landscape, heavy.

He'd screamed as he felt the pinch against his chest, cracking of his ribs. Nobody explained the steps on his first day.

They were understaffed and behind, following a two-month strike. Some of the workers couldn't wait it out and took jobs elsewhere. The ones remaining were crotchety and annoyed. None wanted the task of delving out on-site lessons when so much trash had piled.

Pay attention and work hard. That was it after the brief in-house training offered by a recorded instructor speaking to a video camera.

The door swung open, and Steve clung onto the moving truck. It started and stopped all morning, and he followed the driver's lead, always waiting for the man to step around back and join him before he got down.

Nobody told him where to go or be, and the video only stressed the need to pay attention once back on the yard. Attention he paid. No one paid attention to him, and the rear gate door flung open.

Garbage buried him, heavy and suffocating. Refuse, wet and slimy, filled his mouth and throat. Thick and rancid. He gasped, inhaling a bread bag that carried crumbs of blue dinner rolls and gangrenous green meat.

His knees buckled next to the computer, and he fell into the seat. This time his hand went to his lips. The raspy gasp came from elsewhere. Fingers fell to another memory attaching itself to the waste management burial.

He screamed, nearly soundlessly. No more than a click surfaced from his mouth.

The new memories connected with sparks.

Your cassette is out, dummy.

He needed a laryngectomy to top off the repairs to his chest, hips, and legs.

Never.

He wheezed a wordless breeze, his tongue clicking again. And obviously, that's how it was without the cassette in place over the stoma with the prosthesis pushed tight against it.

It never happened.

Steve shot to his feet, pain stinging in his hips. He deleted the paragraph and tore the physical copy to pieces. The healed, though not whole, man stumbled to the living room/bedroom, the panic exhausting. He fell onto his mattress and stared deep into the yellowed cotton of his pillowcase.

His breath slowed.

The ache in his chest departed.

"You're losing it, Steve. Losing it. *La-la-la.*"

His voice returned. It was the stress again. The pain of giving up on his stories. That was it, he had to stop letting his overactive imagination run his life.

He stomped to the office and retrieved his résumé from the trash bin icon.

He read through.

Lowe's

Best Buy

Esso

Self

"Got you now, you sonofabit—*No.*"

The cursor jumped over his Esso experience, eating one letter at a time. Steve tapped on the keyboard, swung the mouse. The résumé had a mind of its own, master of the computer, master of the past.

Wiped clean, Steve sat back, and words appeared:

Piermont Fishery – Deckhand – 2013-2014

This was an especially challenging and rewarding position. Duties included cleaning, de-icing, sorting fish, and general maintenance. Shifts ran seventeen hours a day, seven days a week for two-month stints. If it was not for the accident, I would probably…

His lips and tongue dried. He wanted nothing of the suggested accident. He'd erase it without reading, and it would never come to be.

"Delete."

Eyes closed.

Lifting phantom limbs.

His eyes reopened. The scarred nubs stopped just above missing elbows. "That's not… No, it can't…"

A whine left his lips as he gazed at the two active nubs, still feeling the missing parts.

Balance lost when the storm hit and the deck shifted. Those arms caught in the trolling net bars, pinning him for hours while the others worked to save the catch. The blood pooled away, no longer finding a route to the invaluable extremities. It was days in the hospital, and after that, he'd tried dictating fiction to the little box affixed to his laptop.

The mental price tag of losing limbs was almost as much the physical price tag, but the ability to go on making up horrors was like hot cocoa in a blizzard.

He'd sold better than a few dozen, but still, it was time to face the world. Hands or no hands.

The cursor blinked on the screen, as if challenging him.

Steve shook his head, sneered. Two prosthetic limbs sat on his desk next to the six printed and red-pen-marred manuscripts, novels that never would be.

This was life, not a fantasy. Those stories were not his future. Time to move on. He needed to face the facts of capitalism and skill for pay. Live to work, not to fulfil goals. Live to make money and be a successful somebody with a checking account and a line of credit, credit cards and an overdraft resting on par.

"Microsoft Word," Steve said to the microphone in the little box, "print résumé."

The Brother monochrome came to life. Steve closed his eyes to the sound. This was it. He'd given up fully. No turning back. No more stories. Time to face the real world.

Dreams are for wealthy people.

The printer's exhaust had an almost sweet scent, fresh and clean.

Not the printer.

The scent of recognition. Life was hard, and sometimes, you don't have the abilities necessary to love what you do.

Birds chirped.

Steve opened his eyes, peered at the shiny, engraved stone, read his name again one last time:

Steve Warren Lester
Lived for his stories
August 29, 1984 – August 28, 2018

Jamming With 10/24/18   A Rhinoceros Head

541

NO, NAY, NEVER
Morven Westfield

Larry walked past rows of folding chairs, most still empty. He found his seat and sat down.

Onstage, under a banner that read "LISA GALLAGHER ONE MORE TIME," a tech slung an acoustic guitar over his shoulder. Using an auto-tuner, he flew through the guitars, mandolin, and banjo, but he wasn't quick enough for Larry, who glanced at his watch and let out an irritated sigh.

Hope her one more time is on time.

The concert venue filled up, murmuring voices and scuffing feet rising on the warming air. A couple sat down in front of him.

"I used to come here when I was a kid," the man said, pointing to the four massive doors at the far side of the restored nineteenth-century firehouse. "The fire trucks used to come in those doors. The firemen would give us cookies. And let us pet the dog."

"Dalmatian?"

"Nah, some kind of mutt."

Larry squirmed in his seat.

"I hope I'm not going to listen to this all night," he said, deliberately loud enough for the couple to hear him.

The woman turned to glower at him, and her friend just shrugged.

"Let's give a warm welcome to Lisa Gallagher." As the house lights dimmed, the crowd rose and applauded.

The spotlight glinted off long strands of silver hair that spilled over her shoulder. A de rigueur scarf headband for 60s folkies still held back hair from her face. The hair color had changed but not the clothing. She still wore a tie-dyed t-shirt and multiple strings of natural beads, probably bought to support some humanitarian organization.

The clapping stopped, and people sat back down. In front of him, the chatterbox who hung out at the firehouse as a kid fished his cell phone out of his pocket. He said something to the woman next to him who leaned in and pointed to things, whispering as she did.

"For God's sake."

The woman hastily straightened up. The man tucked his elbow in, raising the phone high enough for a snap, but not high enough to block Larry's view. He took a quick couple of shots while Gallagher adjusted her capo then lowered the cell phone.

Seething with rage because the guy ignored him and took a picture, Larry leaned forward to say something, but Gallagher charged into a speeded-up version of the traditional Irish folk song "Wild Rover." The audience sang along, stomping the floor at the appropriate point in the chorus.

As the song progressed, so did Larry's agitation. When the song ended, Larry saw the guy raise his cell phone again.

"Knock it off. I'm trying to watch the show, for Christ's sake." He tapped the offender on the shoulder. The man turned and obediently placed his cell phone in his lap.

But Larry had had enough.

He catapulted from his seat, the legs of the folding chair scraping against the bare concrete floor loud enough that the couple in front noticed.

A few songs later, Gallagher paused to tune her guitar, telling a story, as singers always do. The couple in front smiled at her patter when a flurry of white crouched in front of them. The volunteer usher spoke, his voice low, punctuating every word.

"Is there a problem?"

The man stared blankly at him. "No, I—what do you mean?"

"There's been a complaint," the usher said, his shoulders hunched, hands twisting in front of him.

"He's not doing anything wrong," the woman said.

The usher's gaze fixed on the man's astonished face.

"Look, you've got to control your camera, okay?"

The woman opened her mouth to protest further, but her companion put a quieting hand on her arm. "Sorry. Gallagher wasn't singing, she was just talking, and I'm not using a flash—"

"Control your camera." The volunteer stabbed the air with his finger before sprinting away.

Larry was finishing his cup of coffee when the house lights flickered, signaling the end of intermission. As he strode over to the trash can, someone emerged from the restrooms. The chatterbox.

The man made eye contact.

"Excuse me," he said, his voice low and pleasant. "I don't know what I did to set you off, but weren't you a little rough?"

"Are you the guy with the camera?"

"Cell phone. Yeah. The signs don't say no photos, just no flash. I wasn't using a flash."

Larry tossed the empty cup in the trash. "Look, I paid money for this seat. When I'm at a concert, all I want to see is the performers. I don't want a camera—or cell phone—in my line of sight."

"It's not like I was holding up a tablet. It was just a—"

"I don't care what it was. Look, all I want to see is Lisa Gallagher. Got that? Not you, not your camera, just Lisa Gallagher. And all I want to *hear* is Lisa Gallagher. I don't want to listen to you babbling about your freaking childhood during the show."

Larry stormed away without giving the guy a chance to say anything, not that he would, with his jaw dropped halfway down to his knees.

"So, Larry, how was the show?" Jared held out the coffee pot, motioning an offer to pour. Larry lifted his cup to it.

"Fantastic. Too bad some asshole ruined it."

"How so?"

"Taking pictures."

"Crap, that's annoying," Jared said, familiar with Larry's low threshold for minor annoyances. "I hate when flashes go off all over the place."

"He wasn't using a flash, but that's not the point. When I go to a concert, I don't want to see *cameras*, I want to see *the concert*. I want to see Lisa Gallagher, not the back of some guy's iPhone."

Another co-worker, Jim, darted in to grab a bottle of water from the refrigerator. "Don't tell me. Did you call an usher again?"

Larry puffed with pride. "Damn straight, I did."

Jim gave Larry a friendly slap on the shoulder before he rushed out the door. "That's my man."

Larry missed the man shake his head and roll his eyes. Jared tried not to laugh in Larry's face.

"But you could hear the music okay, right?"

544

"Hear it okay? I still hear it now."

Jared snorted. "I hate earworms. Hey, I read somewhere that if you get your mind busy with something else complex, it'll stop. But it could be worse. At least it's not the *Barney the Dinosaur* theme song, right?"

Larry frowned as he looked at his watch. "Gotta run. Project meeting."

When Larry was out of earshot, someone sitting at a table in the back of the room said, "So, Jared, I don't understand. How could Larry know Gallager's music, that generation's music, and be so self-centered? He's obviously not listening closely to her lyrics. Seriously, what ever happened to peace, love, and understanding?"

Jared laughed. "Wrong musician. That's Nick Lowe. Or Elvis Costello."

"Gallagher covered it, too."

Jared shook his head. "Beats me."

The meeting for a project dangerously slipping its schedule must have supplied the complexity that Jared mentioned, because Larry's mind quieted, but as they broke for a ten-minute restroom break, the music surfaced again.

I've been a wild rover for many a year...

Larry opened his email on his laptop and tried to get absorbed in his inbox.

And I spent all my money on whiskey and beer.

Maybe it would help if he composed a message. That required more complex thought processes than reading.

He did.

The music stopped.

People returned to the room. He closed his laptop and did a double-take at the woman who sat down to his right. Only in her early thirties, some trick of the light made her hair appear gray.

The project manager dimmed the overhead lights and turned on the projector. "Let's go through these numbers again."

Larry stared at the screen. The song resurfaced.

And now, I'm returning with gold in great store.

He shook his head and manually added up the numbers in the first column. It worked. The music stopped.

"Any more comments?" Was Bill speaking with an Irish accent? Not likely; he was from Texas.

Beside him, Ted answered, "No. No more."

The woman to Larry's right laughed. Again, her hair seemed long and gray, loose and free, like an old hippie who didn't change with the times. Was it the lighting, or was she wearing tie-dye? How did she change her clothes so quickly? Did she change at the break? She looked like—*like Lisa Gallagher.*

Unconsciously, his fingers began an emphatic tattoo on the conference room table. Larry stared at them as they drummed out the rhythm to the chorus.

And it's no, nay, never.

Tap tap tap tap.

No nay never no more.

The music swelled in his ears until he no longer heard the voices around him or the fan on the projector.

To his left, a young Asian man was now another Lisa Gallagher lookalike, coarse curly gray hair replacing his trendy black spikes. The African-American man next to him, the same.

The entire room had been replaced by Lisa Gallaghers.

All he could *see* was Lisa Gallagher.

All he could *hear* was Lisa Gallagher.

Would it ever stop?

No, nay, never. No nay never no more.

STONE CIRCLE
Gwenda Major

Carla let her hand linger on the warm wood of the gate before heading up the hill.

She looked forward to her regular ritual. Today, the fresh and clear air stirred the tall grass by the wall, and somewhere a blackbird sang. Up the grassy slope, the stones came into view, silhouetted against the sky. It never failed to move her, remaining unchanged for thousands of years. From this distance, the huge stones looked black, but as she got closer, they would reveal themselves as mottled grey, spattered with patches of yellow and white lichen.

Carla selected her stone—of the more than thirty that made up the circle, some were as high as two metres, others squat and low, allowing a person to sit in the natural hollow on top. Fanned out in a flattened circle around her, some nestled together in groups, some standing solemnly apart. Beyond them, the glory of the high fells formed a breath-taking three-hundred-and-sixty-degree panorama. The early sun brightened the flanks of the east-facing slopes. The sky was the blue of a duck's egg with the merest hint of wispy white clouds. The wind whispered with the distant bleating of sheep. A perfect morning.

Hands resting loosely in her lap, Carla shut her eyes and breathed in the peace and calm. She came up here through all the misery of the divorce, and she often felt it had saved her sanity. Sitting quietly in the stone circle raised her spirits. With half an hour of yogic breathing and some silent contemplation, she left revived for another week.

Of course, some days, other people were up here, usually walkers bristling with backpacks, binoculars, and sticks, en route for one of the high fells. They were generally no bother, taking photos and moving briskly on. And occasionally, groups of tourists came up from their coaches parked on the road below, but most were respectful, clearly affected by the indefinably spiritual feeling inside the circle. Who could fail to be struck by the beauty and majesty of the three-thousand-year-old site and its extraordinary stillness?

Two couples in their twenties were toiling up the grassy hillside. Carla hoped they would pass through quickly.

The women were dressed in revealing shorts and flip flops and one of the men had a plastic carrier bag.

Not walkers then.

When they reached the circle and without so much as a glance at the view, the couples installed themselves on the grass in the centre of the circle, and Carla heard the pop and fizz of a can being opened.

She shut her eyes, trying to ignore the wave of irritation that swamped her, but a sudden shout made her open them again.

One of the women, the one with long blond hair, had brought out her smartphone.

"Have you seen this on YouTube? It's amazing." And the phone was passed around to a chorus of snorts and sniggers. Another hiss and a can landed behind them in the grass.

The second woman, plump and wearing a low-cut sleeveless T-shirt, sang tunelessly. She hauled herself to her feet and performed into an invisible mic, twisting and shaking her bottom.

"Go for it, Kelly." The man with the bald head and tattooed arms reached up and pawed at her leg.

"Fuck off, Col." She cackled amiably.

Carla did equal ratio breathing to calm herself, but their noise and disrespect punctured her serenity. She should just get up and go but was reluctant to draw attention to herself. She was trapped.

The sky darkened, a black veil had been drawn across the sun. Shadows raced across the fells like dark panthers, and the wind rose to a roar. Unperturbed, the four people inside the circle laughed and chatted. Dizzy, Carla shut her eyes again to clear her head, but when she reopened them, she stared at the scene in terrified disbelief.

A dark oppressive dome of clouds made it hard to see across the circle, but Carla just made out some figures standing at the far side who had not been there moments before. White robes with dark cloaks shrouded their bodies.

One man, taller than the others, pointed a long staff to the east. Four people in coarse shifts, their hands bound in front, were being forced along. The eyes of the first woman were wide with fear as her long blond hair streamed behind her in the wind.

One of the male prisoners tried to run but was dragged back by his captor. As he struggled, the man's tunic fell back to reveal tattoos snaking up his arm.

The air reverberated with low rhythmic drumming, punctuated now and then by the rising moan of a horn. The sounds filled the stone circle, drifting towards the brooding fells.

There was a dull rumble of thunder and a jagged fork of lightning abruptly illuminated the blade of the knife, held high by the man with the staff.

She squeezed her eyes tight in helpless horror.

When she dared take another look, Carla blinked, bewildered. The sky had lightened, and the two couples in their shorts and T-shirts were still sprawled on their blanket.

The woman with blond hair struggled to her feet.

"This place is weird. Gives me the shivers." She held her smartphone up like a chalice.

"And there's no fucking reception now. I'm not staying. It's rubbish here anyway. Come on, I'm going back."

After a brief argument, the four trooped off, shoving each other and giggling, leaving a scatter of beer cans on the grass.

Carla stayed for a while—until she felt calmer. Taking a deep breath, she offered a small *namaste* to the fells and picked up her bag to go.

KARMA BOOKS
B.B. Wellstone

Bargain Kingdom, a few miles north of Cincinnati, is a jumbled mess of vending stalls just off of 1-75.

"We're a shopping safari," their billboard screams.

A clear case of false advertising unless you define "shopping safari" as clusters of working-class stiffs milling about piles of used junk.

Somehow, the scene implies buzzards circling roadkill.

Bargain Kingdom could be featured in a click-bait story called "Top Ten Most Depressing Places on Earth."

A tug-of-war breaks out at a stall offering used Barbie Dolls. In Bargain Kingdom lingo, they're *vintage* Barbie dolls. A grandmotherly lady in a t-shirt and denim skirt battles a tattooed biker-chick with the noodle-thin build and the unlikely strength of a dedicated meth head. She's outweighed by at least seventy-five pounds, but even so, she's getting the best of Grandma. They're grappling with a Barbie that might be worth—oh, a whopping ten bucks, at least.

So, people really fight in public over toys?

Karen's heard rumors of people doing that but always believed it was an urban legend. Apparently, it's not.

A man in his early twenties, wearing a t-shirt that IDs him as Security, jogs over. The man utters something in a soothing tone then casually removes the Barbie from their grasps. Within seconds, the trio disperses. Just business as usual at Bargain Kingdom, folks. Show's over.

Karen gazes wearily through the window and wipes her brow. Even with the windows down and both doors open, the car is a sauna. She retreated here twenty minutes ago, hoping Sue would get the message and wrap things up.

She catches sight of her best friend, determinedly rifling through a pile of t-shirts, and feels a twinge of guilt. Here she is, sulking about sitting in a hot

550

car, when Sue is the one who has cause to be moping. Her husband recently announced that he no longer loves her, in fact he never did, and it would be best if he left. The temporary alimony hasn't started yet, and the new school year's just around the corner. Sue's mantra throughout this upheaval has been, "It'll all work out." And she's refused Karen's offers of financial help. So here they are, shopping for Sue's three boys.

A bead of sweat pools between Karen's shoulder blades and slithers down her back. There's a table she hasn't noticed before: a circular pedestal with a rich, glossy-red finish and an intricate pattern of half-moons and stars carved into the side. It stands out among the cheap folding tables like a classic, mint-condition Rolls Royce in a junkyard.

The antique table must weigh a ton. How, and why, did someone drag such a lovely, huge piece of furniture to this Godforsaken dump?

Upon closer look, the tattered paperbacks scattered on top are probably romance novels. That would more or less fit with the table's pattern of half-moons and stars. She despises romance novels. But she's bored, and her flesh is going to liquefy soon. And she doesn't want to waste gas by running the A/C while sitting here for God knows how much longer. So why not check it out? As an added incentive, the table's out of the sun, tucked under a huge elm.

She climbs out the car and approaches. An ornate frame in the center displays a sign that announces: WHAT COMES AROUND GOES AROUND! COME AROUND TO KARMA BOOKS!

Hardy, har, har. I get it. It's a round table. And Karma always comes around. Too freaking witty.

The heat has made Karen irritable. She's not just annoyed by the sign's clumsy attempt at humor, she's downright offended. Shoving the table onto its side and ripping every single book to shreds seems perfectly justifiable. Who needs romance novels, anyway?

Only: the books aren't romance novels. Not at all.

Karen can't help but chuckle as she reads the titles. *Restless Spirits of Ohio, The Horrid Thing In the Attic,* and *Monsters All Around Us.* Best of all: *Ghost Pigs of the Haunted Slaughterhouse.* Seriously? This one must have been printed by a vanity publisher. Heck, maybe all of them were.

Who'd be interested in such garbage—let alone try to sell it? She imagines an elderly, obese woman in a crazy-patterned mumu with blue eyeshadow up to her eyebrows.

"Those are a dollar each," says a brisk voice behind her, which belongs to a middle-aged woman holding a bottle of sparkling water.

The woman's name is probably Deborah, certainly not Debbie. Or Ruth. Or something equally severe and no-nonsense. Deborah or Ruth or Whoever-She-Is apparently didn't get the dress code memo for Bargain Kingdom: *T-Shirts and jeans required. Well-worn preferred. Acceptable footwear consists of off-brand tennis shoes, plastic flip-flops, or house slippers.*

Nope: she's wearing a fabulous black blouse, probably real silk, topped with a black blazer. Somehow, both are completely free of sweat stains. Her outfit is rounded out with a black skirt, black hose, and black heels. All appear to be relatively expensive. Karen has the sense that the woman would be in her element if she sat behind a podium in a courtroom.

"This one looks good." Karen pulls a dollar from her pocket.

Deborah/Ruth nods. She opens a small metal box and carefully places the bill inside.

"It *is* good," she says solemnly, as though Karen's just made an incredibly important decision. One that might affect the rest of her life. And all of civilization.

Karen tries not to smile.

"Need something to carry it in?" Deborah/Ruth offers her a paper bag imprinted with half-moons and stars.

Karen takes it and throws the book inside.

Deborah/Ruth sighs. "Now, the book is yours. Officially."

At this pronouncement, an icy hand clenches at Karen's stomach. She has the insane urge to toss the book back onto the table and walk away. Maybe even run.

Then, she sees that Sue has a pile of shirts tucked under one arm and is paying the vendor. Hallelujah. Now is Karen's chance to escape from Bargain Kingdom Hell.

"Thanks. Have a nice day."

Awkward.

She hurries toward Sue before either of them can be drawn into another vendor's clutches.

"I guess I'm done. I'm out of money," Sue chirps. "But I got some great bargains. Nine shirts for less than ten bucks. And some of them are barely worn."

"Awesome."

"Looks like you found something, too," Sue says, eyeing the bag Karen's holding.

"Oh. Right." Karen pulls the book out of the bag and displays it: *Dictionary of Dreams.*

Frowning, Sue takes it from Karen and reads the back cover.

"Hmm. According to this book, dreams can predict the future. Symbolically, anyhow. For example...dreaming about snakes means someone you trust will betray you." She shakes her head and hands the book back to Karen. "Aren't you full of surprises. I never knew you believed in that stuff."

Karen laughs. "I don't. But what the heck. I never even looked at it before I bought it. I just felt like...well, like I should buy *something.*"

"Well. How very fortuitous that you chose that book."

"'Fortuitous?'" Karen rolls her eyes. "What is this? You think you gotta use these fancy five-dollar words, now that you're working at a library?"

"For your information, I've always used fancy five-dollar words because I'm an intellectual. It says so on all of my dating site profiles. Anyway…buying that book is fortuitous because I had a weird dream last night. Very weird. I dreamed that I went fishing."

"What's so weird about that?"

"Nothing. Except I've never been fishing in my life. And I hardly ever remember my dreams. But this one seemed…so real. Creepy-real." She hums *The Twilight Zone* theme.

Karen opens the book to the preface and scans it.

"It says here that those are the dreams you should pay attention to." She turns to the F-section. "'Fishing: an unexpected increase in income.'"

"Cool," Sue says. "Maybe they'll increase my weekly hours at the library from twenty to thirty. Woo-hoo, then I'll be rich enough to shop at Thrifty-Mart."

Karen's cell rings at 7:50 the next morning.

"You won't believe this." Sue practically screams. "I just met with my boss. She wants me to work full-time. I'm taking over as the only full-time librarian at the branch, because…well. The other full-time librarian was run over by a drunk driver last night. Killed instantly. It was Vickie. I've talked about her, remember? Not so good for her. But, hey. My salary will double."

"Wow…congrats," Karen says distractedly. Not really an appropriate response; then again, maybe it is. Sue could've probably found good qualities in Jeffrey Dahmer, your friendly neighborhood brain-eating serial killer. Yet, she never had anything nice to say about Vickie. Therefore, Vickie must have been pretty darned awful.

Sue chatters on excitedly. "I'll qualify for health insurance now. And retirement. And their retirement plan isn't half-bad."

Karen reaches for the dictionary on her nightstand. She turns to the W-section.

She had a dream last night, in Technicolor, about breaking a window.

"It's an amazing opportunity," Karen's husband tells her. "With the increase in my salary, we can buy a bigger house. Three bedrooms, instead of two. And a garage—not just a carport. Maybe even a two-car garage. Can you imagine, our district manager, murdered. Thrown off a bridge after a fender-bender. A road rage incident, they're saying. Hell of a thing. Not so good for Ty. But as the new district manager, my salary will double."

Karen nods. She recalls the dictionary's definition of her broken window dream: an abrupt change of residence.

"Hell of a thing," Matt repeats. "Ty didn't deserve to be thrown off a bridge, obviously. But it's not like he was well-liked. To be blunt, the guy was a first-class jerk."

At last year's company Christmas party, Ty had displayed his first-class jerk-ness. He'd followed her to the bathroom, groped her, and tried to shove his tongue into her mouth. She managed to break away without causing a scene and never told anyone. Matt was, after all, a fairly new employee.

"But, yeah." Matt gazes out the window at the neighbor's coveted two-car garage. "I can't say that the old Tyster's gonna be missed. Not at all. So maybe it was just...I don't know. Karma."

Karen tries not to flinch.

"Hmm. Maybe so."

Karen throws the dictionary into the trash. She's being silly, of course.

She won't tell Matt about the book. Really, there's nothing to tell. Her dream, the book's interpretation, and Ty's subsequent death...it's all just a series of coincidences.

Ditto for Sue's dream, and what happened afterward with her co-worker. Coincidences. Nothing more.

Still...she calls Sue but gets her voicemail.

"Crazy-busy with job and new school year." Sue texts back. "Get back 2U soon. Promise!"

Later, Karen finds her twelve-year-old daughter thumbing through the book. She snatches it from Lily's hands.

"Did you look up a dream?" Her voice is harsher than she intended. Her daughter's face broadcasts fear, hurt, confusion.

"I—no, I never even remember my dreams—"

Karen struggles to maintain an even tone.

"Listen, Lily. When I put something into the trash, I expect it to stay in the trash. This book—it's—well, it's garbage. That's why I put it in the garbage."

Lily—sensitive, book-obsessed, who'd quite possibly retrieve a book from a raging bonfire—quivers her lower lip at Karen.

"Okay, Mom. I'm sorry. I was just curious..."

Karen hugs her fiercely, wonders what to do next.

For now, the book will be locked up in the fireproof safe.

The key to the safe will be taken from its usual place on the key rack. And hidden.

She won't tell anyone where it is. Not even Matt.

The tragedy is unexpected, as tragedies tend to be. And so very, very tragic.

Amelia, a classmate of Lily's, died unexpectedly.

Amelia had been the only child of a well-to-do couple. Bright, talented, and beautiful, she was known to have a bit of a mean streak.

One that sometimes materialized as catty, manipulative bullying.

Often directed at Lily.

An asthma sufferer, Amelia responsibly kept her inhaler with her.

She collapsed during ballet class. Her teacher, all too aware of Amelia's illness, frantically searched her dance bag for the curative plastic container. By the time she found it, Amelia's lips were blue. In her haste, the teacher dropped the inhaler onto the floor. Amelia's best friend, in the process of rushing to her side, accidentally stepped on it, crushing it with her tap shoe. Another teacher tried to locate the spare that was kept in the studio office. Another student dialed 9-1-1.

The spare inhaler had expired two years earlier. And the ambulance arrived too late.

The annual Spelling Bee, which Amelia had won for more years than Karen could remember, was held the following Friday.

The principal considered cancelling. After speaking with Amelia's parents, it was decided that the Spelling Bee would be held as planned.

"It's what Amelia would have wanted," they insisted.

Lily places first in the spelling bee. Not her usual showing of second place.

Karen gazes blankly toward the stage as the crowd applauds, and Lily beams.

Later, after everyone is in bed, she retrieves the Dictionary of Dreams from the safe.

Perhaps Lily did remember her dream. And maybe she was able to look it up before Karen stopped her.

Which dream was it? Karen's awake until nearly two. She reads through the interpretations of all dreams up to the D section.

She notices a word that's been circled. By a glittery purple marker.

Lily owns one of those.

Darts. Darts has been circled.

A dream about playing darts, according to the dictionary, foretells "the realization of a long-thwarted ambition."

She throws the book across the room. It ricochets off the wall and lands placidly on the Berber carpet.

Karen's exhausted, but she doubts she'll sleep anytime soon.

She's startled by the humming of her cell phone vibrating on her nightstand. Sue.

"What's wrong?" She glances at a snoring Matt as she whispers into the phone.

"Oh, geez. I figured you'd have put your phone on 'silent' before going to bed. Like most sane, normal people."

"My phone was on 'silent.' But I heard it vibrate, because I'm still awake."

"Why are you still awake?"

"Why are *you* still awake? And why are you calling me at two in the morning?"

"I had this weird dream. And I wanted you to look it up in that book of yours. I was afraid if I didn't call now and leave a message, I'd forget it by morning."

Karen glares at the Dictionary of Dreams. She can almost see flames emanating from the cover, bats and spiders teeming from the pages.

"What time are you off work tomorrow?"

"Six-thirty."

"We have to talk. Can you meet me at the coffee house next to the library? That Hipster hangout place?"

"Um, sure. But first, can't you look up what it means if you dream about eating butterflies? While riding in a pink hot air balloon?"

"It probably means you're insane. And, no, I'm not looking up anything in that stupid book. We'll talk tomorrow, okay?"

The two have met at Sacred Grounds a few times before. They come here mostly to ogle the decor and the clientele. Today, the wall showcases photographs of dismembered, naked mannequins scattered about in a variety of settings. Twenty-somethings competing over who can accrue the most tattoos and body piercings fill most of the space.

"Gentrification is going well here in Northside," Sue says as she joins Karen. "Only two panhandlers hit me up during my walk from the parking lot. And I think only one of them was high."

Karen whistles. "Lucky you. I was hit up by three. And I think all of them were high."

"Did you give them any money?"

Karen sighs and rolls her eyes. "Of course. You?"

"What do you think?"

Both of them are eternally frustrated at their inability to ignore beggars. Sue indicates a woman to her left.

"Check out that hair color," she says under her breath. "What would you call that? Fluorescent Highlighter Yellow?"

"Maybe. Or it could be Radioactive Rat Vomit Amber. Either way, it's kinda cool. On her, at least."

They discuss makeovers involving extreme hair shades, tattoos, and/or body piercings, the idea quickly abandoned as they concede that neither of them could pull off such a look.

Sue sighs and takes a sip of her coffee.

"So," she says after grimacing and chasing the terrible stuff with water, "did you look up my dream?"

"Nope. And I'm not going to."

"Why not? The last time you did, I ended up getting a promotion. Which was a very big deal."

"Yeah. And somebody got killed. Which was also a very big deal."

"People die every day. That's a fact. It was an unfortunate coincidence."

"If it only happened once, I'd say you're right. But it's happened three times now."

Sue nearly chokes on her coffee. "Shut up."

"Will *you* shut up? Or at least keep your voice down?" Karen relates the incidents with Matt's boss and Lily's classmate.

When she's finished, both of them are teary.

"Jesus," Sue finally says. "Holy. Fricking. Crap."

"I'd be lying if I said I was broken up over Matt's boss. He was a total jerk. Quite frankly, the world is probably better off without him."

"The same goes for Vicky. Trust me."

"But Amelia...she was just a kid. Not exactly a sweetheart, you understand...I can't tell you how many times Lily came home in tears over something that kid had done or said to her..."

Sue nods. "I remember. It got so bad that you and Matt were even thinking about a second mortgage. It was the only way you could have paid for Lily to go to private school."

"Yeah. Amelia was awful to Lily. But still. She was only twelve."

"Geez." Sue shakes her head. "Just...geez."

"So. Obviously. We can't look up any more dreams," Karen says. "Maybe this stuff is just a lot of super-weird...weirdness. Or whatever. But we can't take that chance."

"You're right. We'll just have to keep the book hidden."

Karen shakes her head. "Too dangerous. Do you want to risk one of our kids finding it? And causing another kid's death?"

"Oh, my God. No. What, then? Burn it?"

"I thought about that. But, you know what? We have no idea what this book is, or what makes it work. I'm scared to death about trying to destroy it—whether by burning it, or by throwing it into the Ohio River, or by any other means."

"Are you thinking of that horror story? About the cursed toy? And the dad throws it into the lake at the end? And it creates, like, this huge tidal wave or something, and nearly kills him?"

"Yeah," Karen says. "Even though I know that's crazy."

"This whole situation is crazy."

The two sit in silence, giving up on their barely drinkable, six-dollar-per cup brews and sip meditatively from their water glasses.

"I know what we have to do," Karen says with more conviction than she feels.

"You think she'll give you a refund?" Sue asks. They're back at the flea market, and Karen frantically scans the crammed-together tables and booths for the Karma Books vendor.

"I sure hope so."

"You really believe the book made all that stuff happen?"

"I don't know what to believe. But I want it to stop," Karen says grimly.

"Well…the book didn't harm you. Or me. Or Lily. In fact," Sue shook her head and shrugged, "all of us seem to have benefitted from it."

"Sue. Are you serious? We've discussed this already. To keep looking up dreams would just be wrong. Anyway, the sign on the table said, 'What Comes Around Goes Around!' Maybe karma isn't finished with us. Maybe something bad *will* happen."

"Or not. We're good people. Maybe it was time for something good to happen to us, for a change."

"At the expense of someone else's life?"

"From what I've seen, the universe doesn't dole things out fairly."

Karen shivers despite the ninety-in-the-shade August heat.

"God, I hope that's not the way things work." She rubs her forehead as if to ward off a headache. "I just want to make it stop."

And she's positive, somehow, that a refund is the only way.

"There she is." Sue points toward the glossy, red table.

Karen approaches, extending the book with both hands like it's an offering. She recalls how she'd imagined the vendor as either a Deborah or a Ruth. The woman is again sipping from a bottle of sparkling water, and she recognizes Karen immediately.

She motions for her to place the book on the table.

"You're back," the woman says. "And still in one piece."

"Barely," Karen tells her.

"The fact that you're here is a good sign. Of your character, I mean. It must be good."

Karen looks to Sue for clarification, but her expression is just as baffled.

"Sorry," Karen says to the woman. "I don't know what you're saying."

The woman takes a big swig of her water and places it onto one of the books—*The Search for Bigfoot*. What fun would they be having if she'd bought that one?

"Sometimes, the *Dictionary of Dreams* works opposite of how it worked for you: the bad stuff happens to the person who had the dream. And in that case, the person is in no shape to return the book. But the book finds it way back to me, anyhow. It'll appear in my briefcase, or maybe under the seat of my car. Once, it even showed up in my freezer. And a few days later, I'll see an obituary. With a photo that looks a lot like the person who last bought the book."

The woman looks pointedly at Karen. "But here you are. In the flesh. I have a feeling, however, that there may have been a recent obituary of someone you knew? Someone who had wronged you? Quite badly?"

Karen is furious. "You know what happens? And you let it? That really...I mean, that just..."

"That just sucks," Sue says.

The woman shrugs. "A client gave me this table years ago, right after I passed the bar exam. I was working for next to nothing at a legal aid service. Up to my eyeballs in student loan debt. So I picked up some creepy paperbacks at garage sales, thinking they'd go along with the creepy vibe of the table, and started hawking the books at flea markets on the weekends, trying to make a few extra bucks."

The woman straightens the books on the table as she speaks.

"It took me a minute or two to figure out what was happening. And at first, I felt the same way you do—I thought it sucked. But by then, I'd seen quite a bit at the legal aid service."

She slams a book down and faces Karen and Sue. "Do you have any idea how many slime balls exist on this planet? And how often they get away with crapping all over decent people? I finally decided that the whole thing didn't suck, after all. Selling these books from this table seems to have some kind of...I don't know. Some kind of cosmic vigilante effect. It seems to bring a measure of justice to the world when worldly methods fail. As unbelievable as that sounds."

Karen and Sue stare at each other as they ponder her story. Is it true? It could be. It's no more outrageous than what they've experienced firsthand.

Sue touches the table gingerly, as though she's expecting it to emit a shock.

"So...this is a magic table? And these are magic books? And you're...um..."

The woman shakes her head firmly. "None of the above, as far as I know. The table was given to me simply because my client didn't want it. Her aunt had left it to her, and it didn't go with the rest of her stuff. Plus, she couldn't stand her aunt. The books, as I said, were found at various garage sales. Just ordinary paperbacks. And I'm just an ordinary person. Yet, somehow, *this*…whatever *this* is…happens. I've given up on trying to understand how. It doesn't matter, anyway. I'm just glad it does."

She shakes her head and throws up her arms.

"And, so. I keep on keeping on."

"Well," Karen says, "we don't want to keep on keeping on. And that's why we're here. To ask for a refund."

The woman nods agreeably. "I'll be glad to give you a refund. But you can also make an exchange. If you'd prefer."

"Do the other books work the same way?"

"More or less." The woman holds up *The Search for Bigfoot*. "Take this one, for instance. A person who buys this book and reads it, and who has earned a dose of bad karma, will die violently. Usually in the woods or another isolated area. The perpetrator will never be caught."

The woman pauses. "We can presume that the person found Bigfoot. And that Bigfoot wasn't happy about being found."

"And if a person who deserves good karma buys this book?" Sue asks.

"They'll be fine," the woman says. "But someone who has wronged them won't be."

"And the person who bought the book benefits somehow, I suppose."

The woman nods. "You got it."

"I don't want to be responsible for anyone else's death," Karen says. "Even if I do benefit. Even if Karma or whatever thinks they've got it coming."

"Not all of the books cause deaths. This one never has." She holds up a book called *Develop Your Psychic Powers*. "This one helps you do exactly what it says. If you've earned good karma, your psychic abilities will help you in some way. If you haven't, the abilities will backfire. They'll either work against you, or else benefit someone who's more deserving."

"As in, you might buy a winning lottery ticket? And misplace it? And learn that someone else found it and claimed the prize?"

"That exact thing happened. Just last month, as a matter of fact. The man who bought this book owed thousands of dollars in back child support. He bought a lottery ticket. Fittingly enough, he chose numbers based on his kids' birthdates. Then, he lost it. Can you guess who found it?"

"Betcha Mom did."

The woman barks a cynical laugh. "Bingo. She collected all of her back child support, plus a few million more. Best karma bitch-slap ever."

"Very cool. You should exchange for that one," Sue says.

Karen shudders. "That might be even worse."

She remembers a movie in which a man suddenly develops the ability to read minds. In the movie, of course, hilarity ensues. In real life, it probably wouldn't.

She half-heartedly looks at a few more titles. There's *Ghost Pigs of the Haunted Slaughterhouse*. Surprise, surprise: nobody's bought that one yet.

How anyone could possibly benefit from *Ghost Pigs of the Haunted Slaughterhouse*? Would they be haunted by the images and sounds of tortured animals? Would a search of courthouse records reveal that their house had been built on the grounds of a former farm—a farm owned by a man known for his cruelty? Maybe they'd call in an exorcist to help the pig spirits ascend toward the heavenly light. And one of the ghost pigs, in gratitude, would first lead them to a spot where the cruel man had buried gold coins. For the coup de grace, they might witness the man's soul being dragged to the fiery pits of hell.

Her head spins as the scenario takes shape in her mind. So much drama. She just wants her old life back. Her old, normal, predictable life. Free of cosmic vigilante justice.

"No, thanks. I'll go with the refund, if you don't mind."

"Not at all," the woman says, handing her a dollar. "I aim to satisfy."

They nod goodbye. On the way out, another tug-of-war involves disgruntled Bargain Kingdom patrons. A beer-bellied man with a baseball cap versus a crew-cutted youth in saggy jeans fight over a rusty tool that could crumble into dust at any second. As before, a security guard jogs over and ends the brouhaha before it even gets interesting.

"Thank God, I can afford to shop at Thrifty-Mart now. I am so done with this place," Sue says.

"Me, too. I wish I'd never 'come around' to Karma Books."

"You know what? There's a Starbucks just off the next exit and around the corner. Rumor has it, they sell drinkable coffee. I'll buy the first *round*."

"Unless I decide to kill you."

Sue holds up a finger. "Watch it. What comes *around* goes *around*."

Karen's laughing so hard, she's having trouble locating her keys in her purse.

"You'll be shopping here forever if you decide to become a stand-up comedian."

"*You* seem to think I'm pretty funny."

A rusted heap of a Honda pulls into the next space. One of the doors is flung open so quickly that it nearly hits Karen, and a surly adolescent boy climbs out without apologizing.

The driver, a woman who could be a regular at Bargain Kingdom, gets out and helps the other three children out of the car. She's wearing a t-shirt that might have been white at one time but is now a yellowish-gray. Her faded cut-offs are just as ragged.

"Do they have Barbies here, Mommy?" one of the children asks.

Karen would have guessed that these were the woman's grandchildren.

The woman starts to answer, then freezes as she sees Karen waiting to get into her car.

"Karen?" she asks. "Karen Schwartz?"

Karen doesn't recognize her. She studies the woman's face, then it dawns on her: it's Denise. Denise Anderson.

The woman to whom Matt was engaged, before he and Karen ended up together.

Karen regains her composure.

"Well, it's Karen Casey now," she says. "But, yes. I used to be Karen Schwartz. And you're Denise, of course. How have you been?"

The woman pauses to grab one of the children before he darts into the path of a car entering the lot.

"Great. Fine…Marcus, can you help me with your little brother?" she calls to the oldest, who ignores her and walks toward the Bargain Kingdom entrance. Denise sighs and puts the child on her hip. She says something else, but her voice is drowned out by the wails of her daughter, who has just fallen onto the gravel parking lot.

Denise shakes her head, signaling that she's giving up on trying to have a conversation.

"Well, it was good seeing you," Karen says. Denise manages a tired smile, and Karen ducks into her car.

"Was that really her?" Sue asks as Karen shoves the key into the ignition.

"Apparently."

"She looks like hell. What's she doing back in Cincinnati? I thought she moved away after you stole Matt from her."

"I didn't steal Matt from anyone." Karen backs out quickly enough to spray gravel.

Sue is silent.

"Sorry," Karen says. "Didn't mean to yell."

"No problem."

But I did steal Matt away from Denise. I saw him at the bar that night, a couple of months before they were supposed to be married. I'd known both of them for years, and I'd wanted Matt for as long. And time was running out. So, yes, we got drunk. And we slept together. And I told him I was pregnant, even though I wasn't, and he broke it off with Denise, and we drove to Gatlinburg and got married, and that's the only time I've ever done anything so underhanded and scheming. But that doesn't make me a bad person.

Karen merges onto the freeway. The traffic is heavy for a Saturday afternoon, and the road before her demands her full attention. If she were to glance into either of the rearview mirrors—which she does not—she'd catch sight of Denise and her brood.

They're looking at books…books that are displayed on a round, glossy-red table.

First Couple

HOUSE OF MIRRORS
Madison Estes

Britney positioned the camera overhead and slightly to the left to catch her good side. After taking dozens of pictures, she posted her favorites online. She tried to get the name of the attraction in the photos, but only as an excuse to post yet another picture of herself online. The last few letters were cut-off, but who cared? It wasn't really about the dumpy little carnival mirrors anyway; it was about getting more likes.

> *Found a bunch of funhouse mirrors at this carnival. Prepare yourselves to be blasted with selfies!!! ;-)*

She fixed her hair again, using a mirror near the entrance. An opaque, plastic material constructed the building's outside walls. Above her, the words *House of Mirrors* reflected. Inside, her eyes sparkled and her pink lip-gloss gleamed. Every angle from each mirror complimented her figure.

She strolled through the hall like a catwalk model until stumbling across an unflattering outward well of her body, a convex confidence killer. She gasped and laughed as her hips and stomach expanded. Her butt swelled into two beach balls. She rushed to the former mirrors for a moment to regain her composure. Her butt cheeks deflated to the size of basketballs, once again pleasing to her eyes.

Other parts of her shrunk as well, resulting in a nice hourglass shape. She spun around a few times, wiggled her bottom a little, nearly pressing it against the wall. Time to upload another picture. She snapped one of her regular butt and one of the hideously enlarged version.

She smirked as she uploaded it, imagining her male followers ogling her behind and going crazy in the comments section. She checked the responses on the last picture she uploaded. Roughly two dozen reactions so far, but that didn't feel like enough. As she strolled along, more optical illusions played with the dimensions of her body. The next time she became super skinny and tall, but her face was too long.

Thank God I don't really look like that! #eatacheeseburger #whythelongface? #horseface #tooskinny #toothpick

She checked on the previous post. Thirty likes total on the normal butt and forty-two on the beachball version. Although she hadn't expected that reaction, many of her male followers worshipped her photogenic behind. A bigger version of that same butt would naturally draw more attention.

The path led her to a mirror that stretched her more horizontally than the first distortion had, another that made her short, then one that made her limbs long and wobbly like they were made of Silly Putty. The next mirror expanded her head while her stomach shrank to nothing.

#hourglassfigure #bodygoals

Another person just ahead took her attention away from the screen.

It was no one she came with, so she returned to the incoming comments and adoration. She frowned at the lack of reaction from her last photo. Zero likes or comments. All her social media accounts had frozen.

She refreshed the pages.

Nothing.

"Ugh, crappy carnie reception."

The stranger closed the gap between them while she had stared at her phone. Britney could not pinpoint why, but the woman emitted an eerie vibe. It was not her silver, wiry hair. Not her withered hands with thick, yellowing nails, nor her wrinkly neck with its thin skin and face full of lines that told stories about how much laughter and tears had come to her. Not her saggy breasts that almost fell to her waist. It was the familiarity of her eyes that unnerved Britney. She almost didn't recognize them despite seeing them in the thousands of selfies she'd taken. And her clothes were identical to what Britney wore. They were twins, aside from the decades between them.

No way. Impossible. Just a creepy old lady who doesn't know how to dress her age and who happens to have blue eyes like mine. So what? Blue eyes aren't that rare.

Britney sauntered back toward the entrance. She bumped into herself, or rather, one of the deformed versions, stubby limbed and short.

"Hush, little baby, don't say a word, Momma's gonna buy you a mockingbird," a creepy voice sang.

"Ugh, shut up." She wasn't sure who she was talking to.

The old lady didn't sing that tune. She couldn't. She was too far away, and that voice had whispered in her ear. The old woman transferred through space at a crawl, like a damaged DVD skipping tiny moments, allowing her to quickly close the distance between them.

Objects in the mirror are closer than they appear.

The old hag's lips moved, taunting her. Another look at their clothes made it difficult to deny their exact match. Same designs, brands, shades of white and blue, and the exact same shoes and accessories. The woman held a bedazzled pink phone case identical to the one in Britney's trembling hand.

Another path opened to Britney's right, and she trotted, which soon became a run. The old woman skipped through space, matching Britney's speed, and she sensed that the old woman could speed up any time she wanted to.

The woman cackled and sang.

"And if that mockingbird don't sing, Momma's gonna buy you a diamond ring. And if that diamond ring turns brass, Momma's gonna buy you a looking glass."

Her glossy hair flew into her mouth as she turned her head to confirm her small lead. She spit it out.

"Shut up, you old hag."

"And if that looking glass gets broke, Momma's gonna shove the pieces down your *throat*," she sang, the last word harsher than the others.

Britney's chest tightened.

"Shut up. Shut up. *Shutup!shutup!shutup*—"

She tripped, crashing onto the floor. Her head banged against the glass. A sharp pain pulsated from the site of impact like a hammer bashing against her temple. Blood gushed from the corner of her forehead. She gasped for air as though stuck in a constricting corset. With the wind knocked out of her, she rolled over. The lady loomed, smiling as she sang. But she wasn't just one old woman anymore. She multiplied in the mirrors, and a group of old women—all clones—sang along in a haunting chorus.

"And if you cry when you fall down, you'll still be the prettiest corpse in town."

She screamed as she kicked the old lady in the shin. The old woman collapsed, and the other women fell, too, each of them gasping in pain or shock.

Britney pulled herself up and sprinted away.

Several women in the mirrors pointed in her direction, and another woman beckoned Britney to come back with a bent, crooked finger. One elderly Britney just shook her head while another stared wistfully at her phone that did not ring or vibrate, a quiet connection to an online world that no longer flooded her with attention.

Britney fled through the labyrinth. She smashed into another mirror and bounced off it, catching herself as she fell. Her blood splattered onto the reflective surface.

She closed her eyes and rubbed at the pain shooting through her skull.

Vertigo followed. She wobbled a few steps and leaned against one of the cold glass surfaces for stability.

When she opened her eyes again, her pursuer vanished.

She disappeared like a magician's assistant behind a curtain. And how does that magic trick work? Mirrors. It's just an illusion.

Although her own image stood before her, not the old woman nor the distorted versions of herself, she had no head wound in this reflection. Instead of messy hair and beads of sweat crawling down her body, she was flawless. The doppelgänger crossed her arms and tilted her head to the side.

"It's all a lie," the replication said. "But you already know that. Your whole life is filtered, just like your photos. You're a fake. Everything you like about yourself will fade away. What will you do then?"

Britney took a step backwards before running in a new direction. She collided with another echo of herself. This replication had her arms crossed while the real Britney extended hers as if to push away the mirror image.

"What will you do when you're old and no one wants you?"

"Screw you." She held no malice like before. Only fear remained. She turned around again, not in the direction of the old woman—at least, she didn't think so. She just had to get away from this mirror, but another likeness popped up beside her, her perfectly manicured hands on her hips.

"What will you do when make-up won't stop you from looking like an old has been? When you get cottage cheese thighs and saggy old boobs that droop down to your belly button? When you can't stand to look in the mirror anymore?

"I'll get surgery. Creams. Spanx. I'll worry about it then. Leave me alone."

She tried to go left but was blocked yet again. This one seemed far away despite Britney standing two feet in front of the glass.

"Alone? You want to be alone? I don't think so. You haven't truly been alone in years. You don't know how to be by yourself. Not yet anyway."

This Britney walked backwards, deeper into the maze and closer to isolation.

"You will know. One day, when no one likes your pictures, and they ignore your status updates. When you don't exist because everything you were admired for is gone. Then, you'll know what it means to be alone."

The reflection disappeared. The real Britney stood there, bereft of her image. Nothing showed in any of the mirrors, no reflections of herself or the old woman.

She baby stepped her way through the labyrinth. Her palms glided against the glass, leaving streaks and fingerprints as she tried to feel her way around.

In a moment of clarity, she tried to dial 9-1-1. Praying for reception, she tapped the numbers into the phone, and her home screen morphed into a mirror.

This one showed her dead. A neat, little red line covered her neck like a choker. Her pale skin accentuated her slit throat, the dark shadows under her eyes and her chapped blue lips, but it was nothing that couldn't be concealed with a little foundation and powder. All things considered, she made a beautiful corpse.

The screen cracked when she dropped her phone. She fled from it and the terrible secret it revealed—the secret of prolonged youth and allure. Not quite eternal, but much longer than the alternative of evanescent living beauty.

She rammed into another mirror. This Britney furrowed her eyebrows and scowled, one hand pointing at her with accusation.

"Why don't you just do it already? You're not getting any younger. Give up."

"No. I'm not ready to die. I still have time."

"Not enough," this Britney said. "See? You're already packing on the pounds, fattie."

It morphed back into a funhouse mirror. The beachball bottom returned, along with the fat tummy, both more realistic this time. Instead of one big stomach, she had multiple rolls of fat. Flabby arms. Cankles.

"I don't look like *that*."

But she did. All the reflections showed the same thing, no matter how many she looked at.

"*No.* I just need a better angle. This is bad lighting."

She examined her body. Her upper arms jiggled with excess fat; her pudgy middle obscured the view of her own feet.

"*No.*"

"And those wrinkles."

She touched her face, and the delicate skin aged by the moment.

"Make it stop."

"I can't. Only you can. You know what to do."

The mirror revealed her dead face, eyes closed, arms folded across her chest like she descended a slide at a water park.

Oh, why hadn't they gone to a waterpark instead of this carnival catastrophe?

She needed to escape. That was it. Just escape and not think about the old woman she would become or the dead body she could choose instead.

She just needed to see her boyfriend, Jay. If he kissed her, had sex with her, and held her in his arms, she would feel vital and attractive again.

She needed to see her friends, to talk to them and remember she was not just a pretty face. She was more than that, wasn't she?

No, I'm not. I'm little more than a mannequin.

I'm a prop to help them get attention.

They take pictures with me and tag me in everything, but when is the last time anyone wanted to hang out with me one-on-one?

When is the last time Jay wanted anything from me that didn't involve sex or making his friends jealous?

It didn't matter. If that was all she was to everyone, then that was what she was, and she would continue to be whatever she was for as long as she could.

A duplicate appeared before her that was neither fat, old, nor some ugly distorted version of herself.

"Time's up," it said.

"No. I have more time."

"No, sweetie. It's all downhill from here. Time to preserve what can be preserved for one grand finale. After all, who doesn't love a drama queen who kills herself? Maybe they'll blame it on bullying, or low self-esteem due to impossible standards set by society, but we'll know the truth. It'll be our little secret."

She put her index finger over her mouth and winked.

"The best part is this one, undeniable truth: They all adore you when you're dead."

Two streams of red bled from her eyes, and every facial orifice wept blood.

It filled the spaces between her teeth.

The crimson liquid spewed out faster.

It dripped onto the floor, pouring on her feet and sliding between her wiggling toes.

"Be beautiful. Be beautiful like me." The last part muffled as the blood clogged her throat.

Another Britney with a plastic bag over her head suffocated to her left; the one on the right cut her own wrists and wore the blood like a pair of rosy silk gloves. Straight ahead, she swallowed oval white pills one at a time to prevent throwing them up, an almost empty bottle beside her.

"There are so many ways you can die pretty."

"*No.* No, I don't want to."

Britney covered her ears to block out her enticing voice, seducing her into dark thoughts. The old woman reappeared at the end of the hallway. Although she stood still in the distance, she would catch up with her much faster than expected.

Something touched her shoulder.

She spun around.

A hand holding a knife passed the barrier between reflection and reality. The blade aimed for her throat, but the hand lowered, and the fingers opened gradually, as though offering it to her.

"Die pretty. It's better this way."

Britney darted in the only direction she could to get away—towards the old woman. Towards her future.

"Die pretty," Her young, gorgeous self yelled from behind her. "Die pretty. It's better to die *pretty*."

A faint light glowed behind the geriatric Britney.

Was it light from the outside?

As she got closer, the old woman held an ax in her hands, no more willing to let her pass than the young Britney she left behind her.

But what she really couldn't get over was the crusted yellow nails that clung to the wooden handle, and the arthritic, bony hands. The elder chanted, her voice coated with a raspy edge.

"Die pretty. Die pretty. Die pretty...or else."

Or else I'll end up like you. No. Not like you. I will be you.

Another path ahead took her left. A gut feeling told her it would be a dead end when she turned the corner. She ran faster. What choice did she have? She would die either way. Pretty or not pretty. Young or old. Suicide or natural causes. It was all the same in the end.

The mirror appeared in front of her; she sprinted toward it too fast to stop.

She crashed into it.

The surface shattered into hundreds of pieces, cutting skin, digging into flesh, slicing red streaks all over her body.

A long piece pierced her throat.

As blood spurted from her neck, she caught a glimpse of herself in one of the mirror shards.

Her death was messy and a little too bloody, but it was nothing make up wouldn't be able to fix.

She would make a beautiful corpse after all.

LISA SEES THE BUFFALO
Samantha Pilecki

"We like how you talk," Harold said, "You've got this…gentility about you. You make each guest feel respected."

Lisa mulled Harold's words. Gentility. That was the nice way of saying old. Gentility was still being blond and clear-eyed but with a grandmotherly tummy and deep, parentheses-like wrinkles punctuating her mouth.

Someone told her those wrinkles were from too much smiling. *Too much smiling my ass.* The last year hadn't been easy. This year was when, after knowing it'd happen eventually, she looked *old.* Brittle-skinned and breakable.

"I'm glad to hear that. When can I start?" Waitressing. Not glamorous work, but it'd be money, at least.

"How's weekdays, two to six? We'll get you in on a few slow shifts."

"Perfect," Lisa said, pleased. She'd get to sleep in.

A party in her old house, room after room full of people, but all the guests were the same. All the guests were her ex-husband, Ed.

Or, rather, variations of him: fat Ed, with a monocle and a Monopoly Man moustache, sitting and whooping it up on the couch: young Ed, like the pictures she'd seen of him from middle school, plucking the sides of his drink nervously; an Ed dressed up in a pastel golfing outfit and a ridiculous hat; a regular Ed wearing cologne, something he'd never done while they were married, despite her asking him to.

But the one with glasses was nice. That Ed showed her around—her own house, but she was too polite to tell him she was familiar with the layout—and introduced her to the other Eds. He complimented her.

On what? Already, that small detail was lost.

571

All in all, Lisa was disappointed in herself. Last night's dream too expected from a recently divorced fifty-year-old puzzling over her past. Usually, her dreams were fantastic things. Perfect mansions overlooking peach orchards with wood-shelved libraries stocked with turn-of-the-century tomes. Or dancing with humanoid buffalo in a vine-dripping, lagoon-like city. Or something as simple as finding her sister in the kitchen, turned into a rat. They were nuanced, crystalline images and emotions to turn over, a lucky charm, a Rubix puzzle, a companion throughout the plain-porridge day.

A refuge.

"House Balsamic, Italian, Ranch, French, Blue Cheese, and Caesar," Lisa recited.

"Okay. Right," Ashleigh, the too-skinny waitress with drawn-on eyebrows and dyed-red hair nodded. Ashleigh, Lisa's *trainer*, pursed her lips and pressed on. As if this little menu quiz were a challenge. "And what about for soup?"

"Unless otherwise noted...Monday and Tuesday minestrone. Wednesday and Thursday, pea soup. Friday, Saturday chowder, New England. And Sunday is French Onion."

"But always check the board, first, to make sure," Ashleigh said sharply. "There's all that seasonal stuff. Butternut squash and shit."

"Of course." Lisa bit back her venom. Hadn't she *said* "unless otherwise noted?" Unobservant Ashleigh. Her dreams were probably boring, staid reruns of serving salads.

"You'll do fine here. You even read the menu well." She folded napkins around forks and knives. "Perfect waitress voice."

Perfect waitress voice. Yeah, thanks, Ashleigh. Because that was what Lisa had been striving for, all her life.

A perfectly square, red-roofed house floated in the middle of a lake. Those vibrant, tropical flowers—what were they? Bromeliads? Hibiscus?—were planted around its perimeter. Untouchable. Perfect.

But someone was trying to hurt the twins. Unthinkably scary. Lisa had to get all the twins' clothes together to protect them.

That way no witch could snatch their clothing to use for spells.

Frantic, Lisa rushed through the white-halled house, piling everything in the twins' room. She sat on it. Her nest.

But wait. Something was missing. Something was already gone.

Where were they? Where were the *twins*?

Oh. Lisa savored the start that woke her. That was a good twist, dream-wise, making her trail the thread of connection back through the vital images. That dream house, literally a dream house, was all that had lingered on waking.

Maybe she should move down south. Florida. Somewhere tropical, where those what's-them-call-it flowers grew. Forget looking for a place in Jersey; it was all so expensive. She'd never be able to hack it...not now. Not on a waitress salary. Unless she somehow eeked out five years and waited to be eligible for one of those fifty-five and older communities. Cheaper to live in one of those.

Ugh. What kind of life was that. Scheduled bus trips to Atlantic City. Knitting circles in the clubhouse. No, thank you. Not for *her*. Not for Lisa. She didn't know what she wanted, but it surely wasn't that...that...

" ...burger, medium well. I'll take that."

"Delicious decision," Lisa said, savoring the alliteration. But that would get old, too, the pleasure of saying those words. She could feel it come on like a song, ready to be repeated. She collected the menus from them, a couple, her age.

That mundanity. That was the word she was looking for.

"I knew I trained you well." Ashleigh stood at the register, punching buttons. "You're keeping your head above water, I see. Want to stay late and help with the dinner shift? Ask Harold if it's okay. You'll get ti-ips."

The money was tempting. Florida...or Jersey. Florida...or Jersey.

Ah, forget it, they were both in the path of hurricanes.

"Can't today. I've got plans tonight. Thank you, though."

Plans. Such a simple, dismissive word. Not many people would call sleeping a plan, but screw them.

They didn't dream like she did.

A blender. And a water-logged notebook by the side of the road.

Try as she might, these were the only details she could remember from her dream.

A *blender* for God's sake? Really?

Ordinary things. *Prosaic* things.

Where were the enchanted bridges, the buffalo creatures? The ruby studded goblets and knights in ornate suits of armor?

Another disappointment.

All her life, she could depend on her dreams being interesting. But now, she felt cheated. *Twice* this week. What was it? The new job? Ed's leaving her and being almost officially evicted? The scrambling pressure to find a new home, living out of a hotel and two suitcases?

It was probably everything from the past year. It was probably nothing. It was just temporary...

But dammit, she needed her dreams. They were a nice break. A nice break from being Lisa. Day-to-day, divorced, semi-homeless, waitressing Lisa.

But really, the job wasn't hard. Not if you were a good worker. You just had to keep moving, and that was good for the tummy-roll.

"How is everything?" Lisa asked the big man at table fifteen.

"Great. Thanks." He didn't even look up from his burger.

Lisa smiled—*with gentility*—and kept moving, a tray of cokes going to her next table, table ten.

After a while, you simply shut down and let the machine run. Spoke the rote lines, let your memory take over; the tongue was a muscle after all.

What can I start you off with?

House Balsamic, Italian, Ranch, French, Blue Cheese, or Caesar?

Delicious decision. Thanks, have a great night. My pleasure.

Well. She always had the carrot of sleep at the end of the day.

Maybe. The blender deeply unsettled her. The banality of it. The ordinary things.

"Hey, *Leese*." The door to Harold's football-poster pasted office was open when she crossed from table ten back to the kitchens to pick up three, identical burgers.

Burgers. They couldn't have ordered anything more *ordinary* than burgers?

"Yes, Harold?"

"You're doing great. You're graduating off this shift. Next week, how do ones to nines sound?"

"Oh." A crater in her life. Cutting into her dream time. The words came against her conscious will, mere muscle memory. "Great. Thanks."

The blandly tan walls of the hotel room greeted Lisa upon waking. The ho-hum curtains, the lamp with the impossible-to-reach switch on the night stand. But nothing else.

Nothing else. Not even a blender. Nothing to tide over the hours.

"Well," Lisa asked herself, still beneath the hotel covers. "What *did* you dream last night?"

God, she'd welcome anything. Any sort of nebulous, non-earthly vision to shock her out of herself.

She needed something to fill the blank hours between here…and here, again, tomorrow. Something to look forward to, as her mother used to say.

Eleven nineteen. The time to ship out, exactly. But it was so…delicate, without the safety net of a dream. Like her nerves had been shaved.

Still, Lisa heaved out of bed, brushed her teeth. Tied her shoes and left the hotel at twelve twenty-three, an automaton down to the minute. She drove gingerly into work, turned at the right places, and parked.

Hello, my name is Lisa. What can I start you off with? Delicious decision. My pleasure.

Bland walls. Ho-hum curtains. Lamp with the impossible-to-reach switch.

This was a hell, to start each day unbuffered from the last. Deserted by whatever promised power she had once possessed while merely sleeping. Each day the *same*. Ordinary. Prosaic. Banal. Blenders and bland walls and Monday minestrone.

This was all you amounted to? Ordinary things? Lisa desperately despised this new broken person she was.

Maybe that's why they called it a nervous breakdown.

She laughed, realized it sounded crazy.

Ugh.

Lisa put her fingertips to her temples, pressed, rubbed her eyes.

She was tired. That was all. *Even after sleeping twelve hours?* some sinister voice asked inside her head. Yes, tired. And these were stupid thoughts. Morbid. Crazy.

She could lose her husband, her house, her life…but her dreams?

Soon, it was twelve twenty-three. Soon, it was the restaurant repeat. Soon, Lisa fluffed the pillow and took off her socks.

She was going to sleep. She was going to *dream*, god damn it. She was going to escape.

Please. She pleaded with herself. Please, please, please…

Bland walls. Ordinary things. Twelve twenty-three. Turn at the right places.

Lisa walked into the restaurant, saw the buffalo at table twelve, and smiled.

DREAMS TO DISMISS
Peter Marino

I've had occasional dreams that have left me panting. I once dreamed I was talking with Mike Mawr, whom I knew from my days at Albany College of Pharmacy. Although Mike and I had not been pals of any kind, I blubbered, snot and phlegm oozing beyond my control. Through this veil of mucous, I told Mike I had to confess something, but I could barely talk for the hiccup-crying. Embarrassed of his seeing me in such a state, I pushed on and managed to choke out that I had wasted my life, as anyone could see. I was visiting Los Angeles for the first time as a tourist at forty-nine when I should have moved there in my twenties to be an actor or director or musician or contortionist—anything else than what I'd really done with myself.

I told him how I should have had a number of high-powered boyfriends by this stage, but I pissed away my youth and plenty of my middle age on pharmacy and straight-married life, and now, I was miserable. I asked Mike to grant me forgiveness, maybe give me another chance at living right. But even as I asked him this, I knew I didn't really want anything from him, not sympathy, or a way out, or even a kiss. And Mike just stood there, impassive.

Then I interviewed a famous actor whom I couldn't identify, trying to find out what Hollywood magic felt like. I looked out the window of the diner we were in, but I couldn't see anything magical, just the cement sidewalk baking in the ardent sun, cars and people who may as well have been trudging through Schenectady for all their glamour.

When I woke, panic threatened to drown me. I considered going for a run. But I did not like leaving the house after dark, especially in cold weather, and I hadn't ever been a runner. Instead, I lay in place, counseling myself to be calm, to get my heart back to a reasonable rhythm. Taking myself in hand, I deconstructed the dreams.

I reasoned that I was simply experiencing a little childish guilt at having chosen the high road in life, the path of substance and meaning. I had an important job, a stable family. I wasn't a pathetically old actor singing and dancing in the chorus of some flighty show that every audience member would start forgetting as soon as the curtain fell. I didn't whore my middle-aged self at auditions with the other desperates.

You never wanted to be an actor anyway. What you should take away from this dream is not that you're a failure, but that you need something creative in your life, a life which is at present all business and no innovation. You might, for example, get a paint set tomorrow, should your subconscious be encouraging you to paint, paint, paint.

But painting would be messy, and probably expensive, and something about the smell of paints of any kind had always made me think of severed limbs. I went into the bathroom and lit a cigarette. I almost never smoked, except outside a bar or a motel room, or in a lonely parking lot, and only to subdue my self-consciousness.

This was a special occasion.

I flushed the consumed butt down the toilet then went back to bed. I had my project right before me: To explore my inner creativity, I would keep a log of my dreams—just a brief plot list—then write a journal about each one by hand. No mess, no expense, no olfactory-induced trauma. And no forcing people to look at my creations and insisting they fake-compliment my lack of skill.

The next day, I committed this dream of Mike Mawr to my new journal. The second dream I wrote down had me lecturing my son Robbie on how to keep friends. Robbie sat on a toilet, and I sat on a tiny swing of a seat, way up high on the adjacent wall, near the rounded top of a gigantic stained-glass window. I shouted because he had a hard time hearing me from up near the ceiling: "Well, don't say you didn't ask, Justin. I think the knots between us may be the result of our having different ideas as to what fatherhood is supposed to be. Why is it so difficult to accept me because I like _____? That doesn't make me a bad father. I don't bring them to this house."

I had seldom been so verbal with Robbie when awake, and also, I had never called him Justin. When I'd woken from this father-son bonding, I wasn't sure if I'd really spilled the beans, and amidst breathing exercises to slow my respiration, I was tempted to go into the boy's room and tell him it was all a dream. Still, I committed it to paper.

The next recorded dream was the one where I attended the National Community Pharmacists Association's Annual Convention, and all the papers focused on gays. I kept going from one presentation room to another, but I couldn't make out what anyone said. I wrote a note to one of the presenters about not having been able to hear him from where I'd been sitting. I found this man's room and stuck the note under the door, which opened; no one occupied the room, so I thought I would just set the note on the dresser. I went through the desk for paper, so I could write my message over legibly because the original had turned into an indecipherable mess of green gooey crayon.

Voices in the hall reminded me that I was in fact in a stranger's room, pawing through his things. The presenter came in. At first, he was Paul, who in real life waits patiently—and apparently indefinitely—for me. Then, he became a hybrid of Paul and my tech Joanne, people that, despite the time I spend with, are not dear to me.

I spoke to him, or them, quite formally: "I was unable to attend the panel discussion concerning gay issues in pharmacy of which you were part. This was primarily because my party didn't arrive until Friday, and your session was on Thursday. I am sorry for this. I am interested in your ideas and suggestions."

The hybrid appeared not at all concerned that I was where I was, or that I was so casual about being caught. But they would not answer. Then, in the unapologetic segues that dreams make, Madge had these hardened, beef-red fissures all over her arms, and each one had a popcorn seed embedded in it. When I touched one of the kernels, it transformed into a quickly gestating fetus.

I screamed, but Madge would not cooperate. She just let each baby grow as if it were the most natural thing for a popcorn seed on an arm.

The last dream I recorded should have killed me. My mother walked toward me, all dripping decay skeleton, like a corpse should be after some time in the crypt. She wasn't a zombie, though, no malicious hunger. It was as if she had crossed to the other side, then realized she had forgotten her purse. In coming back for it, she had no idea what a bad impression she made. I froze on the spot, not daring to move or scream. I woke up after a paralyzing sensation that I was pinned to my mattress by a mighty magnetic force.

I panted hard, worried again that my heart would stop before I could reconvince myself that I didn't believe in Hell. The terror rippled like a tide. I refused to look over at Madge, afraid she would be a mass of bloody threads. But the comfort of consciousness seeped through me, and her breathing relaxed me.

My mother was still cremated, her ashes scattered in too many directions, and too long ago, for her to reconfigure and do more harm.

I got out of bed and looked in on Robbie. He appeared a good deal younger asleep, the tension of scowling relaxed out of his face. It would come back if he woke up and saw me skulking about, since it was weird, and since he was always angry at me for lesser things. I went back to bed. Everyone was okay. Despite every aspect of my life, I was the man of the house. In my own way, I protected my family, and I would write down no more dreams.

Madge's worry, on the other hand, could not be so easily dispensed with. She forced me into a three-day sleep disorders clinic in Glens Falls. Although I had a room all to myself, I couldn't enjoy it for the wires attached to my head and chest and back. I had to sleep all night with a mask over my mouth and nose. There was no turning over onto my side, no getting up to pee. The first night of testing, I didn't sleep at all for the stress and for my clumsiness with the plastic urinal, and I wound up having to stay an extra night. I never actually saw the doctor during the proceedings, just attendants, one of whom was so yummy packed into his green scrubs that I became chatty with him. I sneaked a couple wanks when I was unhooked long enough to freshen up in the bathroom, hoping they weren't picked up by any hidden cameras.

The doctor saw me a week after my release and informed me that I did indeed have severe apnea and would have to sleep with a little tank of oxygen on my side table, which fed the mask I would have to wear all night, every night, forever.

I lied to Madge pretty capably about that diagnosis, for I would in no way follow through. I would never get another night's peace if she knew I was supposed to wear an oxygen mask on my face like Rose Kennedy. Instead, I made up some accommodations the doctor had not suggested: I needed an expensive, contoured pillow; I had to sleep on my side, one or the other, and in no other position; this could be accomplished with the aid of two large body pillows on both sides of me. Also, no more cigarettes; it would be easy to get her to believe that I'd given up smoking since I never smoked in front of her anyway.

I might yet die from lack of proper airways for oxygen. Call me a fool, call me a phony or a liar, but I am prepared to risk death for a little dignity.

THE DARKEST REGIONS OF OUR HEARTS
Wondra Vanian

It came at a time when Shannon was growing more and more dissatisfied with her life. *More* dissatisfied because Shannon was one of those angsty teenagers who grew into an adult that struggled with frequent bouts of depression. She didn't know if anyone else was satisfied with their life, with what they had done and accomplished, but Shannon sure as hell wasn't.

Oh, on the surface, Shannon had everything a woman could hope for.

She married her high school sweetheart. They had three beautiful children together and had just moved into Shannon's dream house, in the best neighborhood in town. Her husband was an extremely successful salesman. Shannon herself worked part-time, but mostly to fill the empty hours when the children were in school.

It should have been enough.

It wasn't.

Shannon wanted *more*. More than the perfect man, the perfect house, the perfect family. She wanted...something she could never have, even if it actually existed. Even if it was more than just a secret desire that haunted her during the long, lonely nights.

Little did Shannon know that the secret wishes made in the darkest regions of our hearts *can* come true.

She crawled into bed after a long day of cleaning, packing lunches, herding children, answering phones, cooking dinner, and cleaning—the job that, for a wife and mother, never finished. Exhaustion, not just physically but to the bottom of her soul.

Shannon didn't look at her husband as he sat on his side of the bed to remove his shoes. They hadn't been intimate in so long that they had both stopped expecting—or even wanting—it. She turned off the light on her bedside table and willed herself to sleep. Unconsciousness remained Shannon's only escape.

Like too many nights before, sleep did not answer Shannon's summons.

As the night wore on, Shannon fought against feelings that were always hardest to fight when the lights went out, trying to keep from screaming in rage and frustration. She stayed there, battling herself, long after the deep, rumbling snores told her that her husband was asleep. Minutes, then hours, ticked by on the digital clock beside the bed, and still Shannon lay there, wide awake, despite her exhaustion.

The transition from waking to sleep, when it finally arrived, was so subtle that, when Shannon found herself standing outside her house, she shook her head.

How had she gotten there?

Shannon didn't remember getting out of bed and walking down the stairs—yet, here she stood, in the middle of the street. The overcast night did not show a solitary star in the dark sky. A cool breeze blew across Shannon's bare shoulders and made her shiver.

How ridiculous of her to be there in nothing but a tank top and a pair of shorts. What the neighbors would say? She turned to go back inside—

—and froze. A dark shape stood at the end of the road; the kind of dark shape that could only be a person, so large it must be a man.

Shannon's heart raced, not frightened exactly. She could get to the front door before the man made it up the road. No, she was *intrigued*.

The man-shape didn't move. It—he—just stood there. The sensation of being watched made the tiny hairs on her arms stand up. That he *only* stared unnerved her.

She wished a streetlight highlighted his face. But from the distance, she made out his tall, broad-shouldered shape. Part of her sought to walk right up to him and demand to know what he wanted.

What gave him the right to stand there in her quiet, safe neighborhood, being all dark and menacing?

Another part, the same part that knew he hadn't taken his eyes off her once in the long moments they had stood there, knew how foolhardy that would be. If Shannon were smart, she'd run straight for the house and lock herself in.

But she was damned tired of being smart.

Tired of being responsible, tired of being good. Shannon wanted to do something stupid and reckless. Let loose the dark feelings she kept locked away so tightly.

Shannon was in a dream.

That explained it all: how she'd gotten outside without knowing. If the little bit of psychology Shannon took in high school was anything to go by, he probably represented of all the dark, horrible thoughts she tried to hide when awake.

Well, what would Freud suggest?

Every Psych 101 student knew what Freud would suggest. Fuck him. That was his thing, right? Or, did it only count if the mysterious man looked like her father?

In dreamlike fashion, the man disappeared from one place and reappeared in another—directly in front of Shannon. He stood so close that his long coat brushed her bare legs and made her tremble.

He made no other move. Not a blink. Not a breath. Not so much as the twitch of a muscle. He might have been a statue, if not for the terrible intensity of his gaze.

Steel. His eyes were the color of steel in winter, hard and cold. They burned through Shannon like frostbite, forcing her to look away or freeze.

She dropped her gaze, taking in the thin shirt stretched tight across his broad chest and the black pants that hung low on his lean hips. When Shannon dared look, she saw that his dark hair was wavy and just long enough to brush the collar of his ankle-length leather coat.

Every dark fantasy she'd never allowed herself to have, all rolled into one delicious ball of here-and-now and oh so lusciously close. Even though he terrified Shannon, maybe *because* of that, she grew wet.

When Shannon wrangled the courage to meet his gaze again, the desire reflected there surprised her. It burned, a flame encased in ice. For *her*. He wanted Shannon in a way no one else ever could.

He wanted to devour her whole.

And Shannon wanted him to.

It took less than a breath to close the distance between them, then his lips crushed Shannon's with a bruising force. Her world became a tangle of tongues, teeth, hands, and flesh. Shannon desperately clung to the chaos of his touch with a passion she didn't know she possessed.

Her desire had been suppressed too long. She had long ago lost herself in duty and obligation. Of being a wife, a mother, a daughter, an employee. Day after day, Shannon battled herself. Night after night, Shannon lost another piece of herself, sacrificed in the pursuit of doing the right thing. The expected thing.

Pieces once thought lost resurfaced in the arms of the dark stranger. He gave Shannon back every old desire and asked for everything in return.

Everything was exactly what Shannon was willing to give.

He sensed her willingness and licked his lips hungrily.

Are you ready? Those cold eyes asked.

I've always been ready, Shannon answered with her own.

The briefest hint of a nod, and he took what she offered. His mouth opened wide, wide, wider, revealing rows of wicked, curved teeth, each one ending in a lethal point. A shark in human clothes, a killer, yet Shannon didn't hesitate.

She welcomed his bite.

From far away, the dream was tainted by the sound of screams. Her husband's voice and the voices of her children, all raised in terror. Crying for her. Begging her to return to them. Even as Shannon was devoured, as she became part of the beast that lurked in the darkest corners of the darkest nightmare, she resented the sound of their voices.

ABOUT THE AUTHORS

Abbas, Ali
Ali Abbas is a writer, carpenter and photographer born and bred in London. He is the author of *Like Clockwork*, a steampunk mystery published by Transmundane Press; *Image and Other Stories,* a collection of seven short stories that examine themes of love, loss and the haunting nature of bad decisions; and *Hajj – My Pilgrimage*, a light-hearted and secular look at the pilgrimage to Mecca that is at the heart of the Islamic faith.

His short story / love letter to London "An Absolute Amount of Sadness" was published by Mad Scientist Journal in their *Fitting In* anthology, and his ghost story "The Girl Who Gives Me Sunsets" will be published in their forthcoming *Utter Fabrication* anthology.

Abbud, Trevor
Trevor Abbud is an up-and-coming author writing speculative fiction. Developing a taste for literature as a young adult, Abbud took a serious interest in writing. His short stories and poems have been published by Twisted Vine Literary Arts Journal, GFT Press, GNU Journal, Foliate Oak Literary Magazine, Chantwood Magazine, The Broke Bohemian, Seshat Magazine and The hungry Chimera. Abbud is currently developing a collection of short stories.

Berghoef, Kacie
Kacie Berghoef is the author of *The Modern Enneagram* and a content creator, writer, and social media manager. Her fiction was recently featured in the Realm of Magic Anthology. Her byline appears on websites such as *ThoughtCo, The Billfold,* and *xoJane*. When she isn't writing, Kacie loves all things Enneagram and personality typology and traveling around the world.

Buckley, Goathead
Goathead "Craig A." Buckley is an author of the weird. Whether that takes him in the direction of horror, SF, bizarro, or surrealistic meanderings down the twisty bits of the mind seems to be contingent on the whim of a silver leaf praying to the moon for annihilation. He has been published on various outlets of the weird in cyberspace. This is the first manifestation of his thought in the meatspace of officialdom. Buckley lives in Cincinnati.

Buoni, Anthony S.

Living and creating in New Orleans, Louisiana, Anthony S. Buoni haunts the swamps and bayous along the Gulf of Mexico, writing, editing, producing, and lecturing about his craft. A practicing pagan, he's responsible for the BETWEEN THERE anthologies, his screenplay-novel, CONVERSION PARTY, and his new collection of short stories, OSSUARY TALES. Recently, he's co-edited and co-produced several exciting anthologies alongside Alisha Costanzo with their independent imprint, Transmundane Press: DISTORTED, UNDERWATER, AFTER THE HAPPILY EVER AFTER, and ON FIRE.

In the past, he has produced the underground zine MEOW and the illustrated horror rag OUTRÉ from Meow Press, and his work has appeared in WATERFRONT LIVING, NORTH FLORIDA NOIR, and SMALL HAPPY. Currently, he's writing a New Orleans monster novel as well as putting the final edits on novels featuring ghosts, zombies, and a café between life and death filled with secrets and philosophy.

When not writing, Anthony poses as a Bourbon Street bartender, underground musician, and DJ, drawing down the moon with new wave, trance, and melancholy tunes. Other interests include film, gardening, comic books, and playing video games with his son, Fallon.

Campeau, Chris

Chris Campeau is a writer of short fiction and creative nonfiction. His works have appeared in publications such as *the Furious Gazelle, Cargo Literary, Polar Borealis*, and *Trembling With Fear*. He's also the author of *The Vampire Who Had No Fangs*, a children's picture book that's not even remotely scary. He studied writing in Ottawa, Canada, where he lives with his wife and two cats and works as a B2B copywriter. *Creepshow 2* on VHS is his most prized possession. You can find him at chriscampeau.com and on Twitter: @c_campeau.

Capehart, Case C.

Case C. Capehart lives in Oklahoma with his wife, Kristy and son, Jackson. He is a graduate of Oklahoma State University and served for six years in the Army Infantry as a 50 caliber machine gun operator. During his service, Case earned the Expert Infantry Badge and Air Assault wings and was a recipient of the Army Commendation Medal.

Case is inspired by the works of Terry Brooks, Phillip K. Dick and Yukito Kishiro, as well as the Tao Te Ching. He has self-published dark fantasy novels in the Hell Cliffs Series and a supernatural YA novel titled Blood Daughter. His short stories have been published by Transmundane Press and Cohesion Press.

He and his wife are members of the First United Methodist Church.

Chapman, Clay McLeod
Clay McLeod Chapman writes books, children's books, comic books and film.

Costanzo, Alisha
Wife of a disabled veteran, Alisha Costanzo writes about PTSD, gender norms, environmentalism, violence, and conformity. With a mutually-fueled passion to change the world one person at a time, she often writes about her husband's rants, conspiracy theories, and trains of logic that seem absurd until the connections line up, and mixes them into her obsession with cooking, coffee, and pop-culture monsters.

Most of all, Alisha is passionate about satire and how it can be used as a tool for learning and criticism. Her stories are aware of themselves and determined not to give readers what they think they want.

A New York transplant, she lives in Oklahoma, teaches English and rhetoric at a local university, runs and edits at Transmundane Press, LLC, and navigates the crazy that comes with her husband, fifteen-year-old step son, seven cats, six lizards, six mice, three toads, two snakes, and a water turtle, in the master bath, all confined under one roof.

Curnow, William
William Curnow lives in London. He has previously had stories published in Jurassic London and Pornokitch.

Dahl, E.N.
E.N. Dahl is a novelist and award-winning screenwriter from coastal NJ. She's the author of the upcoming *Nova EXE,* among other works, and her short fiction has appeared with Radiant Crown Press, Helios Quarterly, Sci-Phi Journal, The Literary Hatchet, Thunderdome Press, Pleaides, and Rain Taxi, among others. When not writing, she can be found doing yoga or streaming the worst movies Netflix has to offer.

Davis, Matthew R.
Matthew R. Davis is an author and musician based in Adelaide, South Australia, with around forty dark fiction stories and poems published thus far. Twice shortlisted for the Paul Haines Long Fiction Award (Australian Shadows Awards, 2016 and 2017), he's judged for the Aurealis Awards two years running and occasionally performs spoken word shows with street poets Paroxysm Press. He plays bass and sings in alternative rock/metal bands Blood Red Renaissance (on hiatus) and icecocoon, whose latest album *How Long is Forever...?* was released in 2018 along with a video for first track "The Great Aerial Ocean" that he edited.

Davies, John Paul

Born in Birkenhead, UK, I've had work published in Apex, Rosebud, Third Flatiron Publishing's anthologies, Ares Magazine, Pseudopod, Grain and The Fog Horn. I was nominated for a Pushcart Prize in 2016 and in 2017.

Davon, Claire

Claire can't remember a time when writing wasn't part of her life. Growing up, she used to write stories with her friends. As a teenager she started reading fantasy and science fiction, but her diet quickly changed to romance and happily-ever-after's.

A native of Massachusetts and cold weather, she left all that behind to move to the sun and fun of California, but has always lived no more than twenty miles from the ocean.

In college she studied acting with a minor in creative writing. In hindsight she should have flipped course studies. Before she was published, she sold books on eBay and discovered some of her favorite authors by sampling the goods, which was the perfect solution. Claire has many book-irons in the fire, most notably her urban fantasy series, The Elementals' Challenge series, but writes contemporary and shifter romances as well as.

While she's not a movie mogul or actor, she does work in the film industry with her office firmly situated in the 90210 district of Hollywood. Prone to breaking into song, she is quick on her feet and just as quick with snappy dialogue. In addition to writing she enjoys animal rescue, reading, and movies. She loves to hear from fans, so feel free to drop her a line.\

DeSantis, M.T.

Born a New Englander, M.T. DeSantis moved south in early adulthood, realized she actually liked winter, and promptly moved back north. Currently, she's trying out life as a Midwesterner with her boyfriend, who also actually likes winter. When not writing, M.T. can be found practicing yoga, attempting to make friends with the oven, or plotting her next adventure.

DiMaggio, Rachel

Rachel DiMaggio is a writer of dark fiction who lives near Boston, Massachusetts with her husband and two rescue cats. She graduated summa cum laude with a B.A. in English and Literature from Southern New Hampshire University. Her fiction has been published by the *Tales to Terrify* podcast and by *Rose Red Review*. When she isn't writing, Rachel loves to cook; as a ginger, she can sometimes be spotted nibbling on the souls of the unlucky.

Edgerton, Michael
Michael Edgerton was born and raised in Greensboro, North Carolina. He attended Walter Hines Page High School where he served on the award-winning yearbook staff as a copy editor. He will be attending Appalachian State University in the fall.

Eriksen, Jude Mael
Jude Mael Eriksen is a writer whose interests skew toward the dark and uncanny places that lie just beyond the realm of possibility. Most of his stories are firmly rooted within the horror genre, while others ride a fine line between horror and science fiction. Born and raised in Western Canada, he divides his time between crafting weird tales and trying to avoid various existential crises. He lives with his long-suffering wife, their teenage son, and two mildly evil cats in a house on a hill. During the winter months you'll rarely see him stray from his habitat, but in summer he emerges once the snow has melted. When he isn't writing horror fiction Jude enjoys reading, hiking, photography, and fiddling with the unknown.

Estes, Madison
Madison Estes has had work featured in *Inkling, One Sentence Poems, Enter the Aftermath* by TANSTAAFL press and *A Wink and a Smile* by Smoking Pen Press. Her personal essay is forthcoming in the anthology *The Daily Abuse*. In her spare time she reads Marvel fanfiction, goes to rock concerts, makes octopus sculptures and takes way too many pictures of her Chihuahuas. She lives in Texas with her family and three dogs.

Feldman, Arlen
In addition to writing fiction, Arlen Feldman is a software engineer, entrepreneur and computer book author. He is also a costumer (albeit of questionable taste) and maker, and frequently talks at conventions on various topics.

Fuqua, C.S.
C.S. Fuqua is a full-time creative writer. He began his career in the late 1970s as a freelance journalist for trade magazines. He later worked as a newspaper reporter and consumer and trade magazine staff writer before becoming a full-time freelance writer in the 1980s. Since then, his work has appeared widely in publications such as *Year's Best Horror Stories XIX, XX* and *XXI, Cemetery Dance, Dark Regions, Christian Science Monitor, Slipstream, The Old Farmer's Almanac, The Writer,* and *Honolulu Magazine.* His fiction and poetry have earned several "Year's Best" honors. Chris's books include *Walking after Midnight ~ Collected Stories,* the SF novel *Big Daddy's Fast-Past Gadget, White Trash & Southern ~ Collected Poems, Hush, Puppy! A Southern Fried Tale* (children's), and *Native American Flute Craft,* among others. He is also a craftsman of Native American flutes and a recording musician with several albums of Native American flute and world fusion music available.

Generous, Eddie

Eddie Generous is the author of Radio Run (novel, Severed Press 2018), Dead is Dead, but Not Always (collection, Hellbound Books 2018), and Camp Summit (novel, DBP 2019). He is the founder/editor/publisher/artist behind Unnerving and Unnerving Magazine, and the host of the Unnerving Podcast. He lives on the Pacific Coast of Canada with his wife and their cat overlords. www.jiffypopandhorror.com.

Gomel, Elana

Elana Gomel teaches at the Department of English and American Studies at Tel-Aviv University. She is the author of six non-fiction books and numerous articles. As a fiction writer, she has published more than 40 fantasy and science fiction stories in *The Singularity, New Realms, Mythic* and many other magazines; and in several anthologies, including *People of the Book* and *Apex Book of World Science Fiction*. Her fantasy novel *A Tale of Three Cities* came out in 2013 and her novella *Dreaming the Dark* in 2017. Two more novels are scheduled to be published this year.

Habashi, Ali

Ali Habashi graduated from the University of St. Andrews, Scotland with a degree in English and Management, and currently works in Boston at an academic publisher. When not at work she can usually be found drinking coffee and stressing about a self-inflicted creative project. Her short stories have been featured on The Other Stories horror podcast (Hawk and Cleaver) and will be included in several upcoming anthologies. Find more of her work at alihabashi.com.

Harrington, Zoe

Zoe Harrington is a poet, screenwriter and writer of short fiction. She has worked on animated television productions, such as *Spongo, Fuzz and Jalapeña, Vicky the Viking* and *Blinky Bill.* The episodes Zoe wrote for the animated series, *Tashi* were included in the submission for the Logie Awards, where the production received a nomination for Most Outstanding Children's Program. She has also just completed a Masters of Creative Writing at the University of Sydney and is a member of the Australian Writer's Guild.

Hewish, Maul Allan

Maul Allan Hewish is a Australian, Brisbane-based author and visual artist, who dabbles in Sigil-crafting, Tarot and Western Occultism. His fiction, art and poetry deciphering the horrors of waking life, mirror his own experiences with mental-illness and childhood trauma. His works have been published twice in Grotesque Quarerly Magazine. He lives with his loving partner Katya. They spend their free time having long discussions on the merits of bad horror movies, video-gaming, and collecting obscure miniatures. For more updates, check out his website: www.themaul.net

Hill, Linda G.

Linda G. Hill is a stay-at-home mom of three boys and the guardian of one beagle and two kitties. She concocts tales in her head 24/7 and blogs almost daily at lindaghill.com. Author of the award-winning book, *The Magician's Curse*, Linda's newest release, *The Magician's Blood,* is the second in her Gothic paranormal romance series. Also available on Amazon and Kobo is her romantic comedy novelette, *All Good Stories*. She lives in Southern Ontario, Canada.

Hore, Kathryn

Kathryn Hore is a writer of speculative and dark fiction from Melbourne, Australia. She has short fiction published in several anthologies and magazines, including Australian staples *Aurealis, The Crime Factory* and *Midnight Echo*. When not writing, she works in information governance, libraries, records and archives, and has a spider photography habit she's finding hard to break. You can find her around the usual social media haunts, just look for @kahmelb and shoot her a friend/add/follow.

Horton, Shaun

Shaun Horton is the author of the sci-fi/horror novels Hannah and Class 5, as well as the cryptid horror Cenote. He writes from the beautiful pacific northwest, crammed between the city of Seattle and the woods of the Olympic National Forest.

He's been a life-long fan of Horror, starting with seeing Gremlins at 4 years old. Years later, he discovered the work of Stephen King, keeping himself up at night reading the tome which is IT. Since then, he's continued expanding the interest through authors such as Dean Koontz, movies like Nightmare on Elm Street and Alien, and the video game series of Dead Space and Resident Evil.

Jackson, N.H.

Noah is a college student and a writer, among other things. He loves spooky stuff, writing about spooky stuff, and, despite everything, going on road trips.

Kane, J. Robert

J. Robert Kane is a writer of horror and science-fiction.

Mr. Kane attended SUNY Empire State College, where he earned a bachelor's degree in American History. He received the Joseph L. Mancino Scholarship and enjoyed volunteering part-time at the campus writing lab.

Hailing from Long Island, New York, J. Robert Kane lives with his longtime love Rebecca.

Keating, Daniel Loring

Daniel Loring Keating grew up in post-Industrial New England, where he earned a BA in Creative Writing from Chester College of New England. He has an MFA in Creative Writing at the California College of the Arts, where he was the Managing Editor of Eleven Eleven Journal. His speculative work has appeared in *Strange Fictions 'Zine* and *The Hungry Chimera*.

Kepfield, Sam

By night, he writes science fiction and a few horror stories. His work has appeared in *Science Fiction Trails, Electric Spec*, and *Aoife's Kiss.* " Salvage Sputnik" was awarded third place in the Robert A. Heinlein Centennial Short Story Contest in 2009. His story "Not Because They Are Easy," which appeared in the *Rocket Science* anthology, was considered for Best Short Story of 2012 by the British Science Fiction Association. His first novel, *Magic Man, Gold Dust Woman, and the Dream Machine* was released by Musa Publishing in March 2013. He has also recently published *Red Planet* on amazon kindle.

Kimmel, Daniel M.

Veteran film critic Daniel M. Kimmel was the Boston correspondent for Variety and currently reviews for NorthShoreMovies.net and Space and Time magazine. He is the author of several books including *Jar Jar Binks Must Die...and other observations about science fiction movies,* a Hugo finalist for "best related work," and two novels: *Shh! It's a Secret: a novel about aliens, Hollywood, and the Bartender's Guide,* shortlisted for the Compton Crook Award for best first novel, and *Time on My Hands: My Misadventures in Time Travel.* His short story appearances include *After the Happily Ever After* and *On Fire* (both from Transmundane Press), *Alternate Truths, Science Fiction Stories for the Throne,* and *Beyond Steampunk,* as well as the website HollywoodDementia.com. His latest novel is *Father of the Bride of Frankenstein.*

Kotok, David

David Kotok was inspired to write whilst living and working in Jakarta, Indonesia, a city affectionately known as the Big Durian, a fruit with a powerful odour yet sweet taste. His first published story was set in the metropolis, as was 'Grey Man Walking Past', his sixth selected for publication. Between these highs he has scribbled tales based on his experiences from Shanghai to Seoul and Lisbon to Madrid and back again, appearing in such outlets as Black Static magazine and a collection of short stories called 'The Best of the Short Story'.

He currently lives in a converted Oast House in the English countryside, where hops were once gathered to turn into ale. Between writing he walks his dogs, feeds the birds, throws pots on a Wednesday and commutes into London. David's personal observations reflect the worlds he occupies, close and distant, in the art of creation.

Major, Gwenda

Gwenda Major lives in the Lake District in the north of the UK. Her passions are for genealogy, gardening and graveyards.

Gwenda's stories have featured in numerous print and digital publications. Most recently her short stories have been published in Dodging the Rain, Toasted Cheese, Retreat West, Brilliant Flash Fiction, and Bandit Fiction.

Gwenda has also written four novels and three novellas. In December 2016 her novella, *Offcomers,* won first prize in the Open Novella Competition run by the National Association of Writers' Groups. Other novels have been either shortlisted or longlisted in national UK competitions.

Marino, Peter

Peter Marino is an English professor at SUNY Adirondack. His novels for young adults, *Doughboy* and *Magic and Misery*, were both nominated for YALSA's Best Books for Young Adults. *Magic and Misery* made *Booklist's* Top 10 Fiction for Youth and the ALA Round Table=s Rainbow Books Bibliography.

McCarthy, J.A.W.

J.A.W. McCarthy goes by Jen when she is not writing. She lives with her husband and assistant cat in Seattle, WA, where she prefers to enjoy the beauty of the Pacific Northwest with a drink in hand. Her work has appeared or is forthcoming in several publications, including *The Misbehaving Dead, Ink Stains, She's Lost Control,* and Flame Tree's *Lost Souls.*

McGrath, Ken

Originally from Thurles, County Tipperary, Ken McGrath now lives in an upside house in Dublin, Ireland with his wife. His fiction has appeared in Daily Science Fiction, Cirsova Magazine, Bards & Sages Quarterly, Liquid Imagination Magazine and The Arcanist among others. He has stories coming out in various avenues over the coming months and you can find out more information here https://kenmcgrathauthor.tumblr.com/ if you want.

Mehra, Gargi

Gargi Mehra is a software professional by day, a writer by night and a mother of two. She writes fiction and humor in an effort to unite the two sides of the brain in cerebral harmony. Her work has appeared in numerous literary magazines online and in print.

Melnicove, Mark

Mark Melnicove's writing has appeared recently in Agni, Maine Sunday Telegram, Gargoyle, and The Maine Review. His collaboration with printmaker Terry Winters, Sometimes Times, was published in 2017 by Two Palms Press. He is the author of Advanced Memories and The Uncensored Guide to Maine. He teaches creative writing and permaculture at Falmouth High School, Falmouth, Maine.

Morgan, Kate

Baker of brownies and tormenter of characters, Kate Morgan (Alice Loweecey) celebrates the anniversary of the day she Jumped the Wall with as much delight as her birthday. She grew up watching Hammer horror films and Scooby-Doo mysteries, which explains a whole lot. When she's not inspiring nightmares (or creating trouble as herself for her sleuth Giulia Driscoll), she can be found growing and cooking her own fruits and vegetables.

Murdock, Franklin Charles

Franklin Charles Murdock is a fiction writer from the Midwestern United States. Though most of his work is harvested from the vast landscapes of horror, fantasy, and science fiction, Franklin strives to spin tales outside the conventions of these genres.

His work has appeared in Dark Fuse, Under the Bed Magazine, 69 Flavors of Paranoia, MicroHorror, Liquid Imagination, Yellow Mama, Heavy Hands Ink, WEIRDYEAR, Phantom Kangaroo, PrimalZine, and various other publications. Most recently, he's been coauthoring the serial epic BEARD THE IMMORTAL on swordandportent.com and maintaining franklinmurdock.com.

Myers, Lori M.

Lori M. Myers is an award-winning writer, Pushcart Prize nominee, and Broadway World Award nominee of creative nonfiction, fiction, and plays. Her work has been published in more than 45 national and regional magazines, journals, and horror and mainstream anthologies. She is the author of *Crawlspace and other stories of dark fiction and horror*. Lori is an adjunct professor of writing and literature and lives in New York.

Nelson, Lorraine Sharma

Lorraine grew up globally, constantly having to adapt to different cultures. Writing was her escape from the reality of always being the new girl in school. These days she writes for the pure joy of creating new stories instead of escapism. Her short stories have been published in sci-fi, fantasy, horror, and mystery/crime anthologies, and usually feature an Indian protagonist.

Norris, Gregory L.

Gregory L. Norris is a full-time professional writer, with work appearing in numerous short story anthologies, national magazines, novels, the occasional TV episode, and, so far, one produced feature film (*Brutal Colors*, which debuted on Amazon Prime January 2016). A former feature writer and columnist at Sci Fi, the official magazine of the Sci Fi Channel (before all those ridiculous Ys invaded), he once worked as a screenwriter on two episodes of Paramount's modern classic, *Star Trek: Voyager*. Two of his paranormal novels (written under his rom-de-plume, Jo Atkinson) were published by Home Shopping Network as part of their "Escape With Romance" line—the first time HSN has offered novels to their global customer base. he judged the 2012 Lambda Awards in the SF/F/H category. Three times now, his stories have notched Honorable Mentions in Ellen Datlow's Best-of books. In May 2016, he traveled to Hollywood to accept HM in the Roswell Awards in Short SF Writing. His story "Drowning" appears in the Italian anthology THE BEAUTY OF DEATH 2, alongside tales by none other than Peter Straub and Clive Barker, and he recently enjoyed the publication of THE DAY AFTER TOMORROW: INTO INFINITY, the novelization he was hired to pen based upon the classic Gerry Anderson made-for-TV movie—which he watched and loved as an eleven-year-old way back in 1976. Earlier this year, he put THE END on a novel sequel, THE DAY AFTER TOMORROW: PLANETFALL, which is scheduled to release in September.

Nunnally, Errick

Born and raised in Boston, Massachusetts, Errick Nunnally served one tour in the Marine Corps before deciding art school would be a safer—and more natural—pursuit. He strives to develop his strengths in storytelling and remains permanently distracted by art, comics, science fiction, history, and horror. Trained as a graphic designer, he has earned a black belt in Krav Maga/Muay Thai kickboxing after dark. Errick's successes include: the novel, *Blood For The Sun*; upcoming novel, Lightning Wears A Red Cape, with ChiZine Publications; a comic strip collection, *Lost in Transition*; and first prize in one hamburger contest. The following are some short stories and their respective anthologies: *Penny Incompatible (Lamplight, v.6, #3); Jack Johnson and The Heavyweight Title of The Galaxy (The Final Summons); Welcome to the D.I.V. (Wicked Witches); Harold At The Halfcourt (Inner Demons Out); The Last Apology (A Dark World of Spirits and The Fey); You Call This An Apocalypse? (After The Fall);* and *A Hundred Pearls: PROTECTORS 2 (stories to benefit PROTECT.ORG).* He also has two lovely children and one beautiful wife.

Orr, Mattea
Mattea has a Master's in English Literature from SUNY Binghamton and lives in upstate New York with her husband and three children. They're all wonderful, nothing said subsequently implies otherwise. If she doesn't writ— she dreams. A lot. Usually about ninjas with sharp knives. To cut down on the blood and the body count, she writes—*a lot.*

Pate, Bekki
Bekki Pate lives in Wolverhampton with her husband and daughter. She is a horror writer and loves all things spooky or gory—Richard Laymon and Stephen King being her favourite authors.

She draws her inspiration from other writers and her own imagination - the words also seem to flow better with a strong cup of coffee!

Pedersen, John
John Pedersen is a writer from Northern Arizona. He is currently shopping his second novel, *The Archivist*, a cyberpunk western. Fitting the mashup nature of the story, he is now scripting it for production as a hybrid audio book/radio drama.

Petersen, Brett
Brett Petersen is a writer, musician and artist from Albany, New York whose high-functioning autism only enhances his creativity. He earned his B.A. in English from the College of Saint Rose in 2011 and since then, his prose has appeared in more than a dozen print and online journals. He is currently working on compiling his published works into his first book titled *Welcome to the Squid Universe.* Aside from his career in publishing, he is a drummer, guitarist, singer/songwriter, cartoonist and Tarot reader. Links to all of his creative projects can be found at http://www.jellyfishentity.wordpress.com

Petyo, Robert
Robert Petyo's stories have appeared in small press magazines and on the web most recently at "Yellow Mama," "Spinetingler," and "Flash Bang Mysteries," and in "Pulp Modern" and in the anthology "Beautiful Lies, Painful Truths."

Though he mainly writes crime fiction, he has also published some science fiction in small press magazines, and in the deep dark past he wrote three science fiction novels under three different names.

In his other life, he is married, recently retired from the US Postal Service and enjoys playing with his adorable grandson.

Phillips, Connor
Connor Phillips lives in Arizona.

Phillips, D.C.
D.C. Phillips is the author of Frightful Fables, the tales that will leave you screaming for more! He has received praise for his dynamic and darkly ironic style, which readers describe as "Flannery O'Connor meets *Tales From the Crypt*. As a native of Atlanta, Georgia, he cites Southern culture and classic horror as two major influences.

Phillips, Nathaniel
Nathaniel W. Phillips (@EldritchNate) writes into the night and homebrews into the night, often at the same time. He lives, works, and has nightmares just outside of Raleigh, North Carolina.

Pilecki, Samantha
Samantha Pilecki's short stories have appeared in El Portal, Five 2 One, A Prick of the Spindle, Ricky's Backyard, Typehouse, and other literary magazines. She is the winner of the Haunted Waters Press 2017 Short Shorts Flash Fiction Competition and appeared as a panelist for New Lit Salon's discussion "First Came Fear." She works as a librarian and can be reached on Twitter @SamanthaPilecki.

Powell, J.N.
J.N. Powell lives in Texas, where she is an English and Creative Writing instructor by day and Fiction Editor for *Ad Astra* and *Clockhouse* magazines by night. She is an alum of the Speculative Fiction Writing Workshop at the University of Kansas and recently earned her MFA in Creative Writing from Goddard College. Her work has appeared in *Typehouse*, *The Future Fire*, *Space Squid*, and *The Overcast*, among others.

Retallack, Jefferson
Jefferson Retallack is an Australian writer of speculative fiction. He is based in Adelaide. His work draws influence from linguistic science fiction, the new weird and Australia's "big things." Outside of the literary world, he skateboards on the weekends and spends afternoons on the beach with his partner, their son, and their Pomeranian, Tofu..

Rey, Alistair
At various points in his life, Alistair Rey has been an author, rare book dealer and writer of political propaganda. His work has appeared in *The Berkeley Fiction Review*, *The Lowestoft Chronicle* and *Juked*, among other publications. He presently resides in the United Kingdom.

Sawant, Rohit
Rohit Sawant's fiction can be found in *Weirdbook* #40, *CultureCult Magazine* and has been featured in the anthologies *On Fire*, *Sherlock Holmes: Adventures in the Realms of H.G. Wells* and elsewhere. He lives in Mumbai, India. Enjoys sketching, films, and his favorite Batman is Kevin Conroy. You can find him at rohitsawantfiction.wordpress.com

St. John, M.C.
M.C. St. John is a Chicago writer. His work has been published in After Hours Press, Aphelion, Chicago Literati, Ink in Thirds, Literary Orphans, Maudlin House, Quail Bell Magazine, Transmundane Press, Word Branch, Unbroken Journal, and Vignette Review. He is the author of the short story collection *Other Music* and the e-book *FewBlox*. Follow him on Instagram under the handle @MC_StJohn.

Staffin-Wiebe, Abra
Abra Staffin-Wiebe loves dark science fiction, cheerful horror, and futuristic fairy tales. Dozens of her short stories have appeared at publications including *Tor.com*, *Escape Pod*, and *Odyssey Magazine*. She lives in Minneapolis, where she wrangles her children, pets, and the mad scientist she keeps in the attic. When not writing or wrangling, she collects folk tales and photographs whatever stands still long enough to allow it. Discover more of her fiction at her website, http://www.aswiebe.com.

Staum, Andrea L.
Andrea L. Staum is the author of the Dragonchild Lore series, Scattered Dreams short story collection, The Attic's Secrets novella, and contributed to several best-selling anthologies. She's a trained motorcycle technician, is an amateur home renovator, and somehow manages to find time to write. She lives in south central Wisconsin with her husband and their four overlords...err...cats.

Slav, Irina
Irina writes about the energy industry for a living and has been doing it with no small amount of pleasure for well over a decade. Since writing is the only thing she knows how to do (sort of), she does it pretty much all the time. For some reason, the stories she produces always turn out scary or weird, or plain unpleasant and upsetting but she enjoys writing them anyway.

Stella, Nicholas

Nicholas Stella can often be seen scribbling away on scraps of paper at the oddest of hours and in the most random of locations as inspiration has no respect for time or place. He lives in Sydney with his wife and two little monsters.

Vanian, Wondra

Wondra is an American who lives in the United Kingdom with her husband and an army of fur babies. A writer first, Wondra Vanian is also an avid gamer, photographer, cinephile, and blogger. She was a multiple Top-Ten finisher in the 2017 Preditors and Editors Reader's Poll, including in the Best Author category.

Wellstone, B.B.

Belinda Stoner lives in Cincinnati. Her work has previously appeared on "Flash Fiction Press" and in FATE Magazine, Alfred Hitchcock's Mystery Magazine, and Reader's Digest. "Karma Books" is based on true events: she did accompany her friend to a flea market, and she did purchase a book while there.

Welsh, Thomas

Thomas Welsh is an award-winning fantasy and short story author based in Scotland. He was the winner of the Elbow Room fiction prize for 'And Then I was Floating' and has also been published in *The 404 Ink F Word Collection* and *Leicester Writes*. His fantasy trilogy *Metiks Fade* debuted in March 2018 with book one, *Anna Undreaming* published by Owl Hollow Press. He also writes for games, and is a narrative designer on two major unannounced cyberpunk titles coming in 2019.

Westfield, Morven

Morven Westfield writes supernatural and horror fiction. Her short stories have appeared in multiple anthologies and she regularly contributes articles on folklore and the supernatural to *The Witches Almanac*. Her two novels, *Darksome Thirst* and *The Old Power Returns*, feature vampires who battle modern witches.

She is a member of Broad Universe, the Horror Writers Association, New England Horror Writers, and New England Speculative Writers.

Morven lives in Central Massachusetts with her husband. Like many writers, she keeps a messy office and drinks way too much coffee.

For more information, visit her web site at www.morvenwestfield.com or follow her Facebook page at www.facebook.com/MorvenWestfieldAuthor.

Winton, Melissa A.

Melissa A. Winton is a serial entrepreneur, having owned and operated two charity home-based haunted attractions, a scenic design production company for haunted attractions and escape rooms, co-owning a merchandise and apparel printing service for the Haunted Attractions Industry, and published author within the psychological horror short story genre under the pseudonym, Ann K. Boyer.

With a substantial art background in scenic design for the Halloween and Haunted Attractions Industries, combined with extended education in psychology, specifically the causes of fear, Melissa has earned the moniker, Hauntzilla, for "creating the worlds that the monsters live in." It is this experience that has contributed to Melissa's publications in such anthologies as CHIRAL MAD 2, alongside Jack Ketchum, David Morrell, and Gary McMahon, and the online eZine, HORROR D'OEUVRES, by DarkFuse Magazine.

Zibach, Lindsay

Lindsay Zibach has written for Disney XD, *The Hollywood Reporter*, and *Fast Company*, and is a former producer for *The Ellen DeGeneres Show* and Nat Geo WILD. She won the Grand Prize for the 2016 *Zoetrope: All-Story* Short Fiction Contest and has an M.F.A. in Writing from Spalding University.

JOIN THE TRANSMUNDANE COMMUNITY

- Find your next favorite read.

- Meet new authors to love.

- Win free books and prizes.

- Play games and join the community contests.

- Watch the latest videos.

- Share the infographics, memes, quizzes, and more!

www.transmundanepress.com
transmundanepress@gmail.com

Made in the USA
Middletown, DE
23 January 2019